THE ODD WOMEN

THE ODD WOMEN

by George Gissing

edited by Arlene Young

broadview literary texts

Canadian Cataloguing in Publication Data

Gissing, George, 1857–1903
 The odd women

(Broadview literary texts)
Includes bibliographical references.
ISBN 1-55111-111-X

I. Young, Arlene, 1948-   . II. Title. III. Series.

PR4716.O32 1998   823′.8   C97-932742-3

Broadview Press
Post Office Box 1243, Peterborough, Ontario, Canada K9J 7H5

in the United States of America:
3576 California Road, Orchard Park, NY 14127

in the United Kingdom:
B.R.A.D. Book Representation & Distribution Ltd., 244A, London
Road, Hadleigh, Essex SS7 2DE

Broadview Press is grateful to Professor Eugene Benson for advice on
editorial matters for the Broadview Literary Texts series.

Broadview Press gratefully acknowledges the support of the Canada
Council, the Ontario Arts Council, and the Ministry of Canadian Heritage.

Typesetting and assembly: True to Type Inc., Mississauga, Canada.

The interior of this book is printed on 100% recycled paper.

PRINTED IN CANADA

George Gissing (circa 1895). By permission of the British Library, HEV 13234.

Contents

Introduction

The Odd Women is arguably the most important novel published in Britain in the 1890s. It was not the most popular (an 1895 pot-boiler titled *The Woman Who Did* by Grant Allen would take that questionable honour); it is not the most artistically accomplished, nor the most philosophically profound. It was and is, however, the novel most fundamentally attuned to late Victorian culture and to the social issues defining that culture — gender and class politics, individual experience in an increasingly impersonal urban environment, working conditions in the white-collar sector, the role of marriage in modern society, and the experience of middle-class women in the urban working environment. George Gissing brings to these issues the unique perspective of a writer born into the Victorian era, but living in a proto-modern world. His novel thus reflects the attitudes of an era that is coming to an end, while at the same time anticipating those of the twentieth century. For all his notorious pessimism, Gissing is not, like Matthew Arnold, trapped between one world that is dying and one that is powerless to be born; he is, rather, caught in the emotional upheaval of the birth pangs of the modern world, and nowhere is this more evident than in *The Odd Women.* This novel thus becomes important to the student of literature and culture for two reasons — first, because of its astonishingly detailed evocation of everyday life in London a century ago, and secondly because of the continuing relevance of the issues dramatized in the novel, especially the issues of the rights and wrongs of women.

From its first appearance, *The Odd Women* has been a novel that generated interest and respect because of its intelligent treatment of the plight of single middle-class women in a social system that defined women as daughters, wives, and mothers and that designated women's place as exclusively domestic. The social mores of Victorian Britain dictated that middle-class women should not enter the work force; they were to remain dependent on their fathers and husbands. For the unfortunate minority who did not marry and who had no male relative to support them, there was always recourse to the acceptably genteel and domestic positions of governess or lady's companion. As the century progressed, however, there was a growing imbalance in the ratio of women to men, which produced the problem of what was popularly referred to as "odd," "superfluous," or "redundant" women, i.e. women destined to live their lives singly — "odd" rather then paired—because there weren't enough husbands to go round. The natural imbalance in the birth rate was aggravated by other factors, including the emigration of young men to the United States and the colonies. To these demographic factors were added economic ones; there was a growing tendency for men in the middle and lower middle classes to postpone marriage until they were sufficiently affluent not only to support a family in relative comfort, but also to guard against the kind of misfortune that befalls the Madden family in *The Odd Women* — the unexpected death of the bread-winner. The growing numbers of "odd women" forced to support themselves produced a glut of aspirants for the limited number of genteel positions as governess or companion open to them — another problem faced by the hapless Madden sisters. All of these problems formed a part of the constellation of issues that constitute what the Victorians referred to as "the Woman Question," and that also constitute the ideological framework of *The Odd Women*.

That Gissing should write a novel that so perceptively dramatizes the problems of women is somewhat surprising. His portrayals of women in his other novels are not always especially sympathetic, and his relations with women in his private life were definitely problematic. What Gissing was particularly attuned to, however, was not gender, but social marginality. He was never part of the mainstream, socially or intellectually, and he was never, despite his brilliance and productivity, particularly successful as an author.

Gissing's background is typically — almost stereotypically — lower-middle-class. He was born in Wakefield, a small industrial city and agricultural centre (its population was approximately 40,000 at the end of the nineteenth century) in the north of England, on 22 November 1857, the eldest of five children. His father, Thomas Waller Gissing, was a pharmacist, and the family lived above the shop. Not unlike many other members of his class, the elder Gissing was a man of intellectual pretensions, and was indeed an autodidact of considerable aptitude. Like his son after him, Thomas Gissing considered himself superior to his station, and did not allow his family to fraternise with the families of other shopkeepers. He inspired in his son, along with a large measure of intellectual snobbery, a profound love and respect for learning and for literature, and young George was an intense and brilliant scholar.

After Thomas Gissing's death in 1870, his friends raised the money to send his sons to Lindow Grove School, a Quaker boarding school at Alderley Edge, south of Manchester. George's academic career was stellar. He excelled at school, winning prizes and ultimately a scholarship to Owens College, now part of the University of Manchester. He continued to distinguish himself at college, capturing both local and national academic prizes. That Gissing would one day secure a university professorship seemed assured. But Gissing was still just eighteen, and like many young people of that age, he was also naïve, idealistic, and impetuous — and was prepared to risk his future for love. He became infatuated with Marianne Helen (Nell) Harrison, a young prostitute, and was determined to save her from degradation. In order to keep her off the streets, he gave her money; he also came up with the rather quixotic idea of buying her a sewing machine so that she could earn her living respectably. Gissing's efforts to rehabilitate Nell, however, did not result in her salvation, but led instead to his own degradation. He had no ready source of funds and was reduced to stealing from the college cloakroom to obtain money for her. He was caught by a private detective and was subsequently convicted of theft. On 6 June 1876, he was sentenced to one month's hard labour. Owens College handed down a far more devastating penalty: Gissing was stripped of his prizes and scholarships and expelled, which prevented him from ever writing his final examinations and obtaining the degree for which he had worked so indefatigably.

◀After his release from prison, Gissing sailed for America, where he spent a restless year trying to launch a literary career. He wrote stories for newspapers in Boston and Chicago and taught languages in a high school in New England for two months. In October of 1877, he returned to England and moved to London where Nell joined him. Determined to become an author, Gissing continued to write, while earning a meagre living working as a tutor and as a clerk. He abandoned at least one novel manuscript after it was rejected for publication, and he was forced to finance the publication of *Workers in the Dawn* himself with the money from a small legacy from his father's aunt. This first novel was neither a great literary nor commercial success, but in time Gissing's skill and reputation as a novelist grew, and while he never gained the prominence or affluence of more popular writers like Dickens, he was gradually able to give up tutoring and live comfortably on his literary earnings.

Gissing's private life, however, remained unsettled. He married Nell in 1879, despite the fact that their relationship was troubled. Not only was Nell ill and alcoholic, but she and Gissing were clearly incompatible, especially in that area that mattered most to him — intellectually. Her physical and emotional condition and their relationship deteriorated steadily. They separated in 1883, and Nell died in February 1888. Although Gissing yearned for the companionship of a woman whom he could consider his social and intellectual equal, he entered into a second unsuitable union in 1891, with his marriage to Edith Underwood, an uneducated working-class woman. By the time their second son was born in 1896, they were already hopelessly estranged. They separated in 1897, and Edith was later committed to a mental institution.

While Gissing's private life thus faltered, his intellectual and social life flourished. He developed friendships with the literati of the period, as well as with Clara Collet and Eliza Orme, leading figures in the feminist movement. Collet and Orme, whom he met shortly after publishing *The Odd Women*, were especially helpful during the stormy breakup of Gissing's second marriage. Gissing finally found a measure of happiness in his personal life after meeting Gabrielle Fleury in 1898; Fleury was an educated and refined woman who appreciated his intellectual gifts. Although their relationship was complicated by the demands placed on Fleury by her ailing mother, they were able to live together in her native France for the last few years of Gissing's life. He died in France on 28 December 1903 of chronic lung disease.

Given Gissing's unhappy and unsettled domestic life, it is not surprising that marriage takes some hard knocks in *The Odd Women* (as it does in many of his other novels). Marriages in this novel are generally failures, and they generally fail because the men, like Gissing himself, make poor choices in wives. Everard Barfoot's brother Tom and his friends Poppleton and Orchard marry fools and suffer the consequences. These unhappy unions are only mentioned in passing, providing a rather grim context for the development of the doomed relationships between Monica Madden and Edmund Widdowson, and between Everard Barfoot and Rhoda Nunn. The problems in these two relationships cannot be so easily summed up; none of these characters can be dismissed as a fool, and while each of them makes mistakes, none proceeds thoughtlessly into romantic involvement. They are indeed the most complex characters in the novel, and their actions, emotions, and motives are thoroughly fleshed out. In his careful exploration of these relationships, Gissing exposes the major flaws in marriage as it was understood and practised in late Victorian Britain; he also explores the ways in which the problems created because of these flaws relate to the issues of the "Woman Question."

The central character within the marriage plot is Monica Madden, who more than any other figure in *The Odd Women* is trapped by the clash of values between the Victorian and the modern worlds. Her older sisters have been raised and educated to be ladies, and so can at least eke out a living in the traditional genteel employments of governess or lady's companion. Monica, however, has not had the same level of education and so, as Rhoda tartly observes, has ended up "half a lady and half a shop-girl" (pp. 126–27). The only role she is fit for, as everyone she knows agrees, is that of a wife, but her circumstances do not allow her to meet suitable men. As an impoverished shop assistant, she has no opportunity to meet young men other than those she works with, and she is too genteel to find the Mr. Bullivants of the world attractive. Her experience as a working woman in turn makes her unfit for the role of the traditional Victorian "angel in the house" that Widdowson is determined to have her fulfil. She has been independent and, even more distressing to her husband, has learned to think for herself during her brief sojourn at Miss Barfoot's secretarial school. Widdowson responds with anger and eventually with violence to her entirely reasonable desire to maintain her individuality within marriage.

That Monica is unfit for marriage is not a criticism of her; it is, rather, an indictment of the institution of marriage itself — or at least of the Victorian version of it. The financial security that it brings is no compensation for the psychological tortures that Monica endures. She eventually finds the marriage she had entered as a means of escape from the servitude of the shop and the "philosophic severities of Great Portland Street" (p. 139) an even more oppressive form of bondage. Within a year of her wedding, she thinks "with envy of the shop-girls in Walworth Road" and wishes herself "back there" (p. 212).

Although Widdowson is a less sympathetic character than Monica, Gissing does not turn him into a mere brute and a villain. Like Monica, he is a victim of the society that produced him. His rigidity and obsession with routine are the very qualities that made him a serviceable clerk, before he was able to retire on the income from an inheritance. His attitudes on women and marriage, which seem restrictive to us more than one hundred years later, were the standard ones of his day, espoused by writers like John Ruskin, whose opinions on the subject Widdowson wants Monica to read (see Appendix B). Widdowson becomes a destructive force within the novel not because he is in any way malevolent, but because he is so completely conventional. He is, indeed, convention gone mad, so devoted to its internal logic that he exists only for it, and is unable to access his own humanity or to touch the humanity of others. His passions are routine, punctuality, and organization, and he has no patience or understanding for those who do not similarly order their lives.

The relationship between Rhoda Nunn and Everard Barfoot would seem to be the complete antithesis of that between Monica and Widdowson. They deplore conventionality and the moralism of Victorian social codes, especially with regard to marriage and to women. They have both turned away from the roles expected of them. Everard, in rebellion against his father, trained as an engineer (then a form of technical rather than university education) instead of attending Oxford; Rhoda, instead of adopting the feminine role of governess or teacher, has also chosen technical training in typing and shorthand, and has entered into a business partnership with Miss Barfoot. Everard, in other words, has refused to play the conventional role of educated gentleman, and Rhoda has refused to be a conventional "womanly woman."

Both Rhoda and Barfoot, moreover, claim not to be interested in marriage. But characters in a novel, like people within a society, are shaped by the conventions of their world. Despite their protestations to the contrary, Rhoda and Barfoot are in fact passionately interested in marriage, and their evaluations of it and responses to it are, like Widdowson's, determined by Victorian sexual mores. Rhoda regards it as a veritable duty to the reserve of "odd women" in society to remain single and to "revolt against sexual instinct" (p. 84). When she finds herself responding to Barfoot's advances, however, she can find no yardstick but conventional sexual mores by which to measure either her own or Barfoot's passion and commitment. Neither can Barfoot, and so begins the manipulative cat and mouse game of their courtship. They talk about the evils of marriage and the moral superiority of spinsterhood for women (in Rhoda's opinion) and free unions (in Barfoot's). As their passion for each other mounts, each then makes demands that bring principles and conventions into conflict. Barfoot wants to bring Rhoda to the point of agreeing to a free union as a test of her convictions and love. Rhoda wants Barfoot to agree to legal marriage as a test of his devotion. Finally it is not their manipulative skills in the courtship game but their genuine love that brings them to the brink of a free union. But convention rears its perfidious head once more when Barfoot produces a wedding ring, which Rhoda responds to as a "perilous symbol." "Take it back," she insists. "Custom is too strong for us. We should only play at defying it" (p. 271).

The only marriage in *The Odd Women* that would seem to provide a paradigm for domestic felicity is that of the Micklethwaites. But Micklethwaite and his faithful Fanny in fact further impugn Victorian marriage. Fixed notions of the level of income and the kind of domestic arrangements that are acceptable for a respectable household prevent them from marrying until they are middle-aged. That their union will therefore undoubtedly be barren suggests that they are a dying breed; indeed their charming eccentricity makes them more Dickensian than Gissingesque, characters suited to another era and a less emphatic brand of realism. The Micklethwaites' marriage cannot be a model for the future.

Virtually all women in fin-de-siècle British society, the novel suggests, are "odd." The promise of fulfilment through traditional marriage is a sham, resulting not in harmonious pairing but in agonizing mismatches. Hope for the future then lies not in educating all young women to the role of wife and mother, but in educating them to be intellectually and financially independent, and consequently to have self-respect, which is the mission of Mary Barfoot and Rhoda Nunn. "When *all* women, high and low alike, are trained to self-respect," avers Miss Barfoot, "then men will regard them in a different light, and marriage may be honourable to both" (p. 120).

Inflecting all the complex gender issues within the novel are issues of class. Many of the class indicators that occur in the text are not readily apparent to modern readers, especially those outside Britain, but these indicators are a fundamental part of the context of the novel and of the characterization of all players within it. The concept of the odd woman is in itself class specific, referring mainly to women in the middle class who were single and had to work to support themselves. One of the contentious issues in the woman question was the extent to which respectable women would be degraded by joining the workforce in the public sphere. Single women in the upper-middle and upper classes were unlikely to have to work; those in the lower or working classes were by definition workers, and were beyond the pale of gentility. It was single women in the middle class with no male relative to provide for them who were the focus of the woman question — women like Rhoda Nunn and the Madden sisters.

The position of odd women was a precarious one financially because there were few employment opportunities open to women, and the traditional fields, such as teaching and governessing, were overstocked and poorly paid. The class position of odd women was also precarious. They either worked in someone else's home, like Alice and Virginia, and so existed in a form of domestic limbo — quasi family member and quasi household servant[1] — or they worked in low-paying jobs in the public sector, moving themselves into that greyest of areas within the British class system, the lower middle class, the class inhabited by figures like Widdowson, Newdick, and Bullivant.

The lower middle class was one of the largest and most despised groups in late Victorian society. The class comprised white-collar workers such as office clerks, shop assistants, and small shopkeepers. Both those above them and those below them on the social scale regarded members of the class with contempt and considered them to be dull, insignificant, and small-minded. At the time they were also perceived to be pretentious, to be aping their social superiors in dress, speech, and bearing. Lower-middle-class figures in Victorian fiction are usually comic and slightly pathetic, like Bob Cratchit in Charles Dickens's *A Christmas Carol*, or like H. G. Wells's Kipps (see excerpt in Appendix E). Gissing is drawing on Victorian social and cultural biases and on existing conventions in representing the lower middle class in his characterizations of Mr. Bullivant, Edmund Widdowson and his friend Mr. Newdick.[2] Each of these men betrays personal limitations supposedly typical of his class, limitations in intellect, accomplishments, and general understanding. The notion of lower-middle-class insignificance and ineffectiveness was indeed so entrenched in Victorian culture that mentioning what they did or, in the case of Widdowson, had previously done for a living would have immediately categorized these characters for the late nineteenth-century reader as men of small means, small achievements, and small promise.

Women who entered the white-collar work force tended to be regarded in an entirely different light from their male counterparts. They were aligned less with the idea of the dull and musty office clerk, and more with the cultural concept of the New Woman. The New Woman was the prototype of the modern feminist; she was independent, assertive, and self-assured. She figured prominently in the public debate over the Woman Question during the 1880s and 1890s and was regarded with suspicion and distaste by many contemporary observers (see excerpts in Appendix C). Rhoda Nunn is obviously an exemplary New Woman, and she is regarded by other characters in *The Odd Women* in a variety of ways. Widdowson, the embodiment of conventional responses, clearly regards her with suspicion and distaste, while others' responses manifest curiosity and even bewilderment. Virginia Madden tells Monica that Rhoda is a

---

1 For an excellent discussion of the problematic position of the governess in the Victorian household, see Mary Poovey, "The Anathematized Race: The Governess and *Jane Eyre*," in *Uneven Developments: The Ideological Work of Gender in Mid-Victorian England* (Chicago: University of Chicago Press, 1988) 126–163.

2 For a more detailed discussion of the lower middle class in Victorian culture and fiction, see my "Virtue Domesticated: Dickens and the Lower Middle Class," *Victorian Studies* 39:4 (Summer 1996): 483–511.

"most wonderful person ... [,] quite like a *man* in energy and resources" (p. 57); she excites Everard Barfoot's "curiosity in no common degree" as a novel "example of her sex" (p. 121); and the narrator assesses her as "something like an unfamiliar sexual type" (p. 48). Even contemporary reviewers of the book struggled to define her. One reviewer described her as "the strong, self-reliant, revolted woman, with the old womanly woman still restless underneath as she fights against the recognition of it" (*Pall Mall Gazette* — see Appendix A). She is, as Everard notes, "[m]ore decidedly one of the new women" than his cousin Mary (p. 106), but she is more than just that. Rhoda is so decidedly "new" that she does not fit neatly into the conventional categories of her day.

Rhoda, like many real women of her time, experienced the move from the nursery and the schoolroom into the office setting as a form of liberation.[1] Such an interpretation of what is essentially secretarial work may seem incongruous to the modern reader, for whom the typing pool represents yet another female ghetto. For Rhoda and her real-life counterparts, however, office work marked their movement from the private into the public sphere, and their rejection of employment choices that simply reinscribed traditional feminine roles as the only ones available to women. As Mary Barfoot acknowledges, traditionally feminine work may be valuable, but it is detrimental to women's emancipation: "An excellent governess, a perfect hospital nurse, do work which is invaluable; but for our cause of emancipation they are no good — nay, they are harmful. Men point to them, and say: Imitate these, keep to your proper world" (p. 152). Work in shops is another matter, however, for while it may allow women to move into the public arena, it also moves them down the class scale into a kind of work that lacks the aura of respectability attached to office work. Shops are, indeed, a little too public. Moreover, shop assistants were so egregiously exploited that, as the text of *The Odd Women* repeatedly emphasizes, working in a shop can only be constructed as a form of bondage.

The interplay of these social and cultural themes alone makes *The Odd Women* an important text, both as literature and as a historical document. The text is further enriched, however, by the detailed specificity of its realism, especially in the setting and in the delineation of the minutiae of everyday life. London indeed becomes more than just a setting; it is part of the fabric of the story and of the lives of its characters. London's streets, its parks, its art galleries, its railway lines and stations constitute

---

1 For more information on women working in clerical jobs at the end of the century see Meta Zimmeck, "Jobs for the Girls: The Expansion of Clerical Work for Women, 1850-1914," in *Unequal Opportunities: Women's Employment in England 1800–1918*, ed. Angela V. John (Oxford: Blackwell, 1986) 153–177.

an almost palpable world in which the characters move and act. The routes the characters take as they move about London are traced precisely, often demarcated with specific landmarks. Battersea Park, Chelsea Bridge, Victoria Station and Charing Cross Station, for example, delineate Virginia's weary five mile walk to the booksellers to buy a birthday gift for Monica.

Locations, moreover, become part of the class dynamics within the story. Widdowson's discomfort with Monica's familiarity with public transport systems and his concern over the necessity of her sometimes walking home at night alone, for example, are more an issue of class and respectability than of safety. Their meeting in a public park rather than in the home or in the company of a mutual friend is, as the text makes clear, a circumstance that severely compromises their ability to reveal their relationship to their families. The areas where people work and live also have class significance. Everard and the Bevises live in Bayswater, Mary Barfoot and Rhoda in Chelsea; both these areas were affluent residential sections in the fashionable West End of London, although some portions of Chelsea were considered Bohemian. Virginia's rooming house is in Lavender Hill in southwest London, which was respectable upper working-class; the area around Walworth Road in south London, where Monica lives and works as a shop assistant, was poor. Great Portland Street, where Miss Barfoot's school is located, was in the commercial district in central London. Widdowson's house is in Herne Hill, an affluent suburb south of London. These and other specific names of landmarks, streets, and areas of the city would have reverberated with significance for Victorian readers, just as references to Manhattan, Central Park, and Harlem would to present day readers of a novel set in New York City. Today's reader of *The Odd Women*, rather than immediately recognizing the implications of, say, Virginia trying to find lodgings in Lavender Hill, can learn from the text about the kind of people and the style of life that were typical of that area in the late nineteenth century.

Locations and access to locations outside London, both in the rest of England and on the Continent, also figure prominently in *The Odd Women*, and also resonate with class implications. The characters who inhabit the middle and upper middle classes — Mrs. Luke Widdowson, members of the Barfoot family and their circle of acquaintances — are at ease travelling to or even living in Europe for extended periods. The range of references that they make to European resorts and the casual way in which they do so indicate their level of education, experience, sophistication, and income. Everard has worked in Japan, and has travelled back to England at a leisurely pace through Egypt and Turkey; he later holidays in France and Italy, stopping in Marseilles and Parma respectively. His brother Tom and his wife visit the Portuguese island of Madeira for their health. Mrs. Luke vacations in Trouville, a fashionable seaside resort in the north of France. Rhoda Nunn's travelling is limited by her income, and so she holidays locally, in Somerset, a county in the south of England,

and in the Lake District, a scenic mountain region in the northwest. Widdowson's travels, by contrast, are limited not by his income, which is ample, but by his intellect. He has no experience of travel and has neither the insight to imagine its gratifications nor the self-confidence to risk revealing his lack of sophistication, especially to his wife. When his equally unworldly friend Newdick warns him about the scandalous goings-on in sensational popular novels set on the Continent, Widdowson alters his plans to travel abroad with Monica, as he had promised to do. He decides instead on the less disturbingly "foreign" destination of the Channel island of Guernsey.

The Odd Women also abounds with details about everyday life at different income levels within the middle class, from the "genteel poverty" of Alice and Virginia to the affluence of the Barfoots. We read of the cramped living conditions endured by the Madden sisters and learn the details of their meagre diet. There are fewer explicit details about the conditions of life for the more affluent characters, but there is nonetheless at least as much information. The pattern and rhythm of their lives are part of the pattern and rhythm of the book — the cycle of the London season[1] and of travel, the social forms of entertaining and visiting, of dining with friends, of letter writing, and of courtship. The reader observes the everyday lives of the Madden sisters, but is drawn into the everyday experiences of Barfoot, Rhoda, Monica, and Widdowson, and so must draw back a little in order to see the pattern of middle-class life.

Another area of experience that is closely observed in *The Odd Women* is the life of the shop assistant. Monica's experiences at Messrs. Scotcher and Co. is indeed a minor but damning exposé of the exploitative employment practices in the drapery (i.e. retail textile) business — the long hours, the insalubrious living conditions, the poor food and poor pay. The idea of having shop employees live in will strike the modern reader as strange, but this was in fact standard in the trade at the time, especially with so-called apprentices. Young and inexperienced workers would pay a fee to be taken on as apprentices for a number of years, during which time they were supposed to learn all the finer points of the drapery business, while being paid very little. H. G. Wells relates his experiences as a draper's apprentice in his autobiography, and there and in many of his novels describes the injustices and often blatant corruption within the system (see Appendix E). Gissing's account of Monica's experiences is in complete accord with these,and other accounts of the drapery business in the 1890s, as well as with Clara Collet's report to the Royal Commission on Labour, "The Employment of Women" (see Appendix D).

One of the many problems for those caught in this system of exploita-

---

1 The London "season" was the period between Easter and the end of July, when social activity was at its height.

tion is the one to which Monica draws Mr. Bullivant's attention when he shows a romantic interest in her — the impossibility of considering marriage on the income even of those who rise to higher positions. But of course those in the drapery trade are not the only people at the lower end of the lower middle class who face this problem, as the experience of Fanny and Micklethwaite illustrates. Income levels and what they mean in practical terms — such as whether or not one could marry or, as with Virginia, whether or not one could subsist above bare starvation — are indeed a recurrent theme in *The Odd Women*. Once again, Gissing is highly specific, giving the precise incomes of most of the main characters. Virginia has earned £12 per year as a companion, and Alice £16 as a nursery-governess (governesses and companions would also be provided with room and board). After losing their positions, they are prepared to live meagrely for six months on their pooled resources of seventeen pounds.[1] Alice is offered a position in a family for room and board with no pay, which she refuses, but takes one offering twelve pounds a year. Scotcher's pays its young women fifteen pounds a year plus room and board (although no board is provided on days off). Bullivant hopes to command a salary of three pounds a week, or £150 a year (which would not include room and board) should he be promoted to shop walker (i.e. overseer of one or more departments in the store). As a school teacher, Micklethwaite has earned between thirty and thirty-five pounds a year, plus room. As a lecturer at a London college, he will earn £150 pounds, and will be able to supplement his income with private tutoring and royalties from his book on trilinear co-ordinates. Barfoot's income is £450 a year, and rises to £1500 with the inheritance from his brother. Widdowson's inheritance gives him £600 a year; his sister-in-law gets the princely sum of £4000 a year.

The figures alone do not tell us much about what incomes mean in the 1890s, but the figures in conjunction with information about how the characters live and how they view their level of poverty or of security tell us a great deal. The incomes of Monica and her sisters and of Micklethwaite before getting the position at the London college are clearly too low to allow these characters to have the modest luxury of planning a future; they can live only from day to day, and must focus all their attention on merely getting by financially. For Micklethwaite, as for Bullivant, £150 represents the annual income that will allow him to consider marriage, although Micklethwaite feels that he really needs between two and three hundred, especially since he must also support Fanny's unmarried sister. Earnings in this range would require the wife to be a full-time home-

---

1 Virginia and Alice's agonies over small amounts of money also convey some sense of how far a shilling would go in the 1890s. In the old British monetary system, there were 12 pence (d.) in a shilling (s.), and twenty shillings in a pound (£). Britain converted to a decimal system for its currency in the 1970s.

maker but would allow for the expense of employing some domestic help, ranging from a part-time char woman to a live-in maid-of-all-work.[1]

These arrangements would clearly mark a family as lower-middle-class, and those, such as Everard Barfoot, who see themselves as part of the socially dominant middle to upper middle class would not be satisfied with such modest household arrangements, and would accordingly require more money — hence Barfoot's comment to Micklethwaite that he considers £450 a year "grinding poverty" for a married couple (p. 117). Barfoot is being playful, but his comment reflects the reality that any future Mrs. Barfoot would be expected to supervise servants, not to take care of household duties herself; she would not, like Fanny, be the cook in her own home. Even an income of £600, which Widdowson finds "all-sufficing" (p. 167), would not seem ample to Barfoot because of his class-based assumptions about what constitutes an appropriate style of life for a gentleman and his family; although Monica's contribution to meal preparation never goes beyond ringing the dining-room bell and giving orders, the Widdowsons do not travel, entertain, or socialize as widely or in a manner that would suit a man of Barfoot's style and breeding. The rise in his income that comes with the inheritance from his brother's estate provides Barfoot with the level of affluence that he requires, although obviously not with the considerable wealth enjoyed by the two grasping widows in *The Odd Women*, Mrs. Luke Widdowson and Mrs. Thomas Barfoot. Since Everard must receive about £1000 a year from his inheritance (his income rises from £450 to just under £1500), which is one quarter of the estate, the remainder of which goes to the widow, Mrs. Thomas will presumably have an annual income of £3000; Mrs. Luke has £4000. They alone, of all the characters in *The Odd Women*, are undeniably wealthy, but even £4000 is not sufficient for the extravagant style in which Mrs. Luke aspires to live.

For the alert reader, there is an abundance of further details about everyday life in the late Victorian urban middle classes. There are innumerable unheralded references like the one to Monica ringing the bell and giving orders for dinner (p. 166) that make *The Odd Women* an invaluable text for the student of social and cultural history. We are told, for instance, that Virginia will walk five miles and more, rather than use a train or bus, in order to save money. There are numerous references to servants, usually anonymous and otherwise invisible, answering doors or serving tea. We are informed that Mrs. Luke has her own carriage, a mark

---

1 These concerns within the middle and lower middle classes about the income required to marry were a recurring theme in the second half of the nineteenth century. In 1868, a public debate about incomes and marriage was conducted in the editorial pages of the London newspaper, the *Daily Telegraph*. For a detailed discussion of this debate and of its social and cultural relevance see John Robson, *Marriage or Celibacy? The "Daily Telegraph" on a Victorian Dilemma* (Toronto, Buffalo, London: University of Toronto Press, 1995).

of her elevated social position and wealth. We learn details about how rooms are furnished and how individuals are dressed. We also learn about middle-class vices that are seldom explored in Victorian novels — Virginia's alcoholism, Widdowson's tendency to violence, Barfoot's and Rhoda's tolerance of the physical abuse of women. None of these details is superfluous; each one tells us something about the characters' social and financial positions and about the culture in which they live. We even get an indirect lesson on how to decipher cultural cues in a character's appearance: when Monica first meets Widdowson, she carefully assesses everything about his appearance and manners — what he wears, whether or not his hands betray signs of manual labour, whether or not his speech and bearing are refined. What Monica is doing is trying to determine his social position by reading external signs, a technique that everyone in her society would need to know. *The Odd Women* accordingly not only constitutes a rich tapestry of late Victorian urban culture, but also teaches us how to interpret it.

The Odd Women is more than just another fascinating Victorian novel, although it is that, too. It is a literary, cultural, and historical document of outstanding importance. Its rich detailing of everyday settings and experience draws the reader into the life of ordinary people in the London of the 1890s. Moreover, Gissing's intelligent treatment of the controversial issues that constituted the Woman Question, his relentlessly realistic treatment of gender and class relations, and his psychologically subtle representation of the breakdown of intimate relationships provide the modern reader with an invaluable entrée into a time and a culture that may have long since disappeared, but that nevertheless have left their mark on the collective consciousness of modern Western culture and society.

* * * *

In the appendices that follow the text of *The Odd Women*, I have reconstructed, as far as space would permit, the major social and cultural debates that are part of the context of the novel. I have tried to provide a range of perspectives on each issue. Note the patterns of images that recur throughout these debates, as well as in the text of the novel — the themes of how women should be educated, of the supposedly pernicious influence of novel reading, and of what the "natural" place and function of a woman should be; the debates are also replete with the themes and imagery of slavery and bondage used — as they are in *The Odd Women* — to characterize the plight of women and of white-collar workers.

Acknowledgements

I wish to thank the many friends, colleagues, and students whose advice and comments were of invaluable assistance in preparing this edition. In particular, I appreciated the responses of a number of students at the University of Manitoba — Goldie Weatherhead, Sheila Simonson, and the members of English 4.762, Victorian Fiction, especially Brian Swail, Karl Wunderlich, and Karen Clavelle. Thanks also to Pierre Coustillas, Connie Harsh, Karen Ogden, Monique Callahan, Natalie Johnson, and Nicole Coffey. A very special thanks to my "research assistant," my daughter Jennifer O'Kell. Last but never least, thanks to my husband, Robert O'Kell, whose unstinting support and encouragement make everything possible.

A Note on the Text

This edition of *The Odd Women* is based on the only edition published in Gissing's lifetime. The original edition was published in three volumes. The volume divisions are noted in the table of contents and in the text. In both the text of the novel and in the background materials, I have made occasional minor alterations to correct obvious typographical errors or to eliminate awkwardly archaic spellings.

Cover Photograph: While telephones and telephone operators are not mentioned in *The Odd Women*, the women pictured in the cover photograph are engaged in the kind of white-collar, public sector work that Rhoda Nunn and Mary Barfoot see as the salvation of middle-class single women in the 1890s.

George Gissing: A Brief Chronology

1857 George Robert Gissing born 22 November in Wakefield, Yorkshire, first child of Thomas Waller Gissing and Margaret Bedford Gissing.

1870 Father dies.

1871 George, along with brothers William and Algernon, sent to Lindow Grove School, Alderley Edge, Cheshire.

1872 Enters Owens College, Manchester.

1876 Begins relationship with Marianne Helen (Nell) Harrison. On 31 May, caught stealing money in Owens College cloakroom. Sentenced on 6 June to one month hard labour. Expelled from college 7 June. Sails for America in September.

1877 Teaches high school in Massachusetts briefly. Moves to Chicago; publishes short stories in Chicago newspapers. Returns to New England in summer. Sails for England in September. Arrives 3 October; moves to London.

1879 Marries Nell 27 October. Earns subsistence living working as tutor and clerk.

1880 *Workers in the Dawn* published, financed by a small inheritance from his father. Brother William dies.

1883 Separates from Nell.

1884 *The Unclassed* published.

1886 *Demos* and *Isabel Clarendon* published.

1887 *Thyrza* published.

1888 Nell dies 29 February. *A Life's Morning* published.

1889 *The Nether World* published.

1890 *The Emancipated* published. Meets Edith Underwood.

1891 Moves to Exeter. Marries Edith 25 February. *New Grub Street* published. Son Walter Leonard Gissing born 10 December.

1892 *Denzil Quarrier* and *Born in Exile* published.

1893 *The Odd Women* published. Moves to Brixton.

1894 Moves to Clevedon, then Dorking, and finally Epsom. *In the Year of the Jubilee* published.

1895   *Eve's Ransom, Sleeping Fires,* and *The Paying Guest* published.

1896   Alfred Charles Gissing born 20 January.

1897   Separates from Edith.

1898   *Human Odds and Ends, Charles Dickens: A Critical Study,* and *The Town Traveller* published. Moves to Dorking after a six-month stay in Italy. Meets Gabrielle Fleury 6 July. Sees Edith and son Alfred for the last time 7 September.

1899   Moves to France to live with Gabrielle Fleury. *The Crown of Life* published.

1901   *Our Friend the Charlatan* and *By the Ionian Sea* published. Moves to south of France for milder climate because of chronic lung disease.

1902   Edith committed to an asylum.

1903   *The Private Papers of Henry Ryecroft* published. Dies 28 December in France.

1904   *Veranilda* published.

1905   *Will Warburton* published.

Facsimile title page

THE ODD WOMEN

BY

GEORGE GISSING

Author of "New Grub Street," "Demos," &c.

IN THREE VOLUMES.

VOL. I.

LONDON
LAWRENCE & BULLEN
16 HENRIETTA STREET, COVENT GARDEN, W.C.
1893

Contents

THE ODD WOMEN

CHAPTER I.

THE FOLD AND THE SHEPHERD.

"So to-morrow, Alice," said Dr. Madden, as he walked with his eldest daughter on the coast-downs by Clevedon, "I shall take steps for insuring my life for a thousand pounds."

It was the outcome of a long and intimate conversation. Alice Madden, aged nineteen, a plain, shy, gentle-mannered girl, short of stature, and in movement something less than graceful, wore a pleased look as she glanced at her father's face and then turned her eyes across the blue channel to the Welsh hills. She was flattered by the confidence reposed in her, for Dr. Madden, reticent by nature, had never been known to speak in the domestic circle about his pecuniary affairs. He seemed to be the kind of man who would inspire his children with affection: grave but benign, amiably diffident, with a hint of lurking mirthfulness about his eyes and lips. And to-day he was in the best of humours; professional prospects, as he had just explained to Alice, were more encouraging than hitherto; for twenty years he had practised medicine at Clevedon, but with such trifling emolument that the needs of his large family left him scarce a margin over expenditure; now, at the age of forty-nine — it was 1872 — he looked forward with a larger hope. Might he not reasonably count on ten or fifteen more years of activity? Clevedon was growing in repute as a seaside resort; new houses were rising; assuredly his practice would continue to extend.

"I don't think girls ought to be troubled about this kind of thing," he added apologetically. "Let men grapple with the world; for, as the old hymn says, ''tis their nature to.'[1] I should grieve indeed if I thought my girls would ever have to distress themselves about money matters. But I find I have got into the habit, Alice, of talking to you very much as I should talk with your dear mother, if she were with us."

Mrs. Madden, having given birth to six daughters, had fulfilled her function in this wonderful world; for two years she had been resting in the old churchyard that looks upon the Severn sea. Father and daughter sighed as they recalled her memory. A sweet, calm, unpretending woman; admirable in the domesticities; in speech and thought distinguished by a native refinement, which in the most fastidious eyes would have established her claim to the title of lady. She had known but little repose, and

---

1 The "old hymn" is "Against Quarrelling and Fighting," Song 16 of the *Divine Songs for Children* by Isaac Watts (1674–1748).

secret anxieties told upon her countenance long before the final collapse of health.

"And yet," pursued the doctor — Doctor only by courtesy[1] — when he had stooped to pluck and examine a flower, "I made a point of never discussing these matters with her. As no doubt you guess, life has been rather an up-hill journey with us. But the home must be guarded against sordid cares to the last possible moment; nothing upsets me more than the sight of those poor homes where wife and children are obliged to talk from morning to night of how the sorry earnings shall be laid out. — No, no; women, old or young, should never have to think about money."

The magnificent summer sunshine, and the western breeze that tasted of ocean, heightened his natural cheeriness. Dr. Madden fell into a familiar strain of prescience.

"There will come a day, Alice, when neither man nor woman is troubled with such sordid care. Not yet awhile; no, no; but the day will come. Human beings are not destined to struggle for ever like beasts of prey. Give them time; let civilization grow. You know what our poet says: 'There the common sense of most shall hold a fretful realm in awe'" —[2]

He quoted the couplet with a subdued fervour which characterized the man and explained his worldly lot. Elkanah Madden should never have entered the medical profession; mere humanitarianism had prompted the choice in his dreamy youth; he became an empiric, nothing more. "Our poet," said the doctor; Clevedon was chiefly interesting to him for its literary associations. Tennyson he worshipped; he never passed Coleridge's cottage without bowing in spirit.[3] From the contact of coarse actualities his nature shrank.

When he and Alice returned from their walk it was the hour of family tea.[4] A guest was present this afternoon; the eight persons who sat down to table were as many as the little parlour could comfortably contain. Of the sisters, next in age to Alice came Virginia, a pretty but delicate girl of seventeen. Gertrude, Martha, and Isabel, ranging from fourteen to ten,

---

1 Dr. Madden is apparently not one of the elite members of the medical profession of his time — i.e., he is not a physician but a surgeon or apothecary-surgeon, whose training would have required an apprenticeship rather than university education. Physicians were the only medical practitioners customarily called "doctor."

2 Alfred Lord Tennyson (1809–92), "Locksley Hall," l. 129. Tennyson was the poet laureate from 1850 until his death.

3 Arthur Henry Hallam, the young friend whose death Tennyson mourns in his poem *In Memoriam*, was buried at Clevedon. The poet Samuel Taylor Coleridge (1772–1834) lived in Clevedon for several months during the fall and winter of 1795-96.

4 Tea, in this context, refers to a light meal, served in the late afternoon or early evening, with tea as the usual drink.

had no physical charm but that of youthfulness; Isabel surpassed her eldest sister in downright plainness of feature. The youngest, Monica, was a bonny little maiden only just five years old, dark and bright-eyed.

The parents had omitted no care in shepherding their fold. Partly at home, and partly in local schools, the young ladies had received instruction suitable to their breeding, and the elder ones were disposed to better this education by private study. The atmosphere of the house was intellectual; books, especially the poets, lay in every room. But it never occurred to Dr. Madden that his daughters would do well to study with a professional object. In hours of melancholy he had of course dreaded the risks of life, and resolved, always with postponement, to make some practical provision for his family; in educating them as well as circumstances allowed, he conceived that he was doing the next best thing to saving money, for, if a fatality befell, teaching would always be their resource. The thought, however, of his girls having to work for money was so utterly repulsive to him that he could never seriously dwell upon it. A vague piety supported his courage. Providence would not deal harshly with him and his dear ones. He enjoyed excellent health; his practice decidedly improved. The one duty clearly before him was to set an example of righteous life, and to develop the girls' minds — in every proper direction. For, as to training them for any path save those trodden by English ladies of the familiar type, he could not have dreamt of any such thing. Dr. Madden's hopes for the race were inseparable from a maintenance of morals and conventions such as the average man assumes in his estimate of woman.

The guest at table was a young girl named Rhoda Nunn. Tall, thin, eager-looking, but with promise of bodily vigour, she was singled at a glance as no member of the Madden family. Her immaturity (but fifteen, she looked two years older) appeared in nervous restlessness, and in her manner of speaking, childish at times in the hustling of inconsequent thoughts, yet striving to imitate the talk of her seniors. She had a good head, in both senses of the phrase; might or might not develop a certain beauty, but would assuredly put forth the fruits of intellect. Her mother, an invalid, was spending the summer months at Clevedon, with Dr. Madden for medical adviser, and in this way the girl became friendly with the Madden household. Its younger members she treated rather condescendingly; childish things she had long ago put away, and her sole pleasure was in intellectual talk. With a frankness peculiar to her, indicative of pride, Miss Nunn let it be known that she would have to earn her living, probably as a school-teacher; study for examinations occupied most of her day, and her hours of leisure were frequently spent either at the Maddens or with a family named Smithson, people, these latter, for whom she had a profound and somewhat mysterious admiration. Mr. Smithson, a widower with a consumptive daughter, was a harsh-featured, rough-voiced man of about five-and-thirty, secretly much disliked by Dr. Madden because of his aggressive radicalism; if woman's observation could be trusted, Rhoda

Nunn had simply fallen in love with him, had made him, perhaps unconsciously, the object of her earliest passion. Alice and Virginia commented on the fact in their private colloquy with a shame-faced amusement; they feared that it spoke ill for the young lady's breeding. None the less they thought Rhoda a remarkable person, and listened to her utterances respectfully.

"And what is your latest paradox, Miss Nunn?" inquired the doctor, with grave facetiousness, when he had looked round the young faces at his board.

"Really, I forget, doctor. — Oh, but I wanted to ask you: do you think women ought to sit in Parliament?"

"Why, no," was the response, as if after due consideration. "If they are there at all they ought to stand."

"Oh, I can't get you to talk seriously," rejoined Rhoda, with an air of vexation, whilst the others were good-naturedly laughing. "Mr. Smithson thinks there ought to be female members of Parliament."

"Does he? — Have the girls told you that there's a nightingale in Mr. Williams's orchard?"

It was always thus. Dr. Madden did not care to discuss even playfully the radical notions which Rhoda got from her objectionable friend. His daughters would not have ventured to express an opinion on such topics when he was present; apart with Miss Nunn, they betrayed a timid interest in whatever proposition she advanced, but no gleam of originality distinguished their arguments.

After tea the little company fell into groups, some out of doors beneath the apple-trees, others near the piano at which Virginia was playing Mendelssohn.[1] Monica ran about among them with her five-year-old prattle, ever watched by her father, who lounged in a canvas chair against the sunny ivied wall, pipe in mouth. Dr. Madden was thinking how happy they made him, these kind, gentle girls; how his love for them seemed to ripen with every summer; what a delightful old-age his would be, when some were married and had children of their own, and the others tended him, they whom he had tended. Virginia would probably be sought in marriage; she had good looks, a graceful demeanour, a bright understanding. Gertrude also, perhaps. And little Monica — ah, little Monica! she would be the beauty of the family. When Monica had grown up it would be time for him to retire from practice; by then he would doubtless have saved money.

He must find more society for them; they had always been too much alone, whence their shyness among strangers. If their mother had but lived!

---

1 Felix Mendelssohn (1809–47), German composer and concert pianist whose works include many lyrical piano pieces.

"Rhoda wishes you to read us something, father," said his eldest girl, who had approached whilst he was lost in dream.

He often read aloud to them, from the poets; Coleridge and Tennyson by preference. Little persuasion was needed; Alice brought the volume, and he selected "The Lotos-Eaters." The girls grouped themselves about him, delighted to listen. Many an hour of summer evening had they thus spent, none more peaceful than the present. The reader's cadenced voice blended with the song of a thrush.

> "'Let us alone. Time driveth onward fast,
> And in a little while our lips are dumb.
> Let us alone. What is it that will last?
> All things are taken from us —'"

There came an interruption, hurried, peremptory. A farmer over at Kingston Seymour had been seized with alarming illness; the doctor must come at once.

"Very sorry, girls. — Tell James to put the horse in, sharp as he can."

In ten minutes Dr. Madden was driving at full speed, alone in his dog-cart,[1] towards the scene of duty.

About seven o'clock Rhoda Nunn took leave, remarking with her usual directness, that before going home she would walk along the sea-front in the hope of a meeting with Mr. Smithson and his daughter. Mrs. Nunn was not well enough to leave the house to-day; but, said Rhoda, the invalid preferred being left alone at such times.

"Are you sure she prefers it?" Alice ventured to ask.

The girl gave her a look of surprise.

"Why should mother say what she doesn't mean?"

It was uttered with an ingenuousness which threw some light on Rhoda's character.

By nine o'clock the younger trio of sisters had gone to bed; Alice, Virginia, and Gertrude sat in the parlour, occupied with books, from time to time exchanging a quiet remark. A tap at the door scarcely drew their attention, for they supposed it was the maid-servant coming to lay supper. But when the door opened there was a mysterious silence; Alice looked up and saw the expected face, wearing, however, so strange an expression that she rose with sudden fear.

"Can I speak to you, please, Miss?"

The dialogue out in the passage was brief. A messenger had just arrived with the tidings that Dr. Madden, driving back from Kingston Seymour, had been thrown from his vehicle, and lay insensible at a road-side cottage. .....

---

1 Small two-wheeled horse-drawn open carriage, originally with a compartment under the seat for dogs.

* * * * *

For some time the doctor had been intending to buy a new horse; his faithful old roadster[1] was very weak in the knees. As in other matters, so in this, postponement became fatality; the horse stumbled and fell, and its driver was flung head forward into the road. Some hours later they brought him to his home, and for a day or two there were hopes that he might rally. But the sufferer's respite only permitted him to dictate and sign a brief will; this duty performed, Dr. Madden closed his lips for ever.

---

1 A horse used for riding or driving on roads.

CHAPTER II.

ADRIFT.

Just before Christmas of 1887, a lady past her twenties and with a look of discouraged weariness on her thin face, knocked at a house-door in a little street by Lavender Hill. A card in the window gave notice that a bed-room was here to let. When the door opened and a clean, grave, elderly woman presented herself, the visitor, regarding her anxiously, made known that she was in search of a lodging.

"It may be for a few weeks only, or it may be for a longer period," she said in a low, tired voice, with an accent of good breeding. "I have a difficulty in finding precisely what I want. One room would be sufficient, and I ask for very little attendance."

She had but one room to let, replied the other. It might be inspected.

They went upstairs. The room was at the back of the house, small, but neatly furnished. Its appearance seemed to gratify the visitor, for she smiled timidly.

"What rent should you ask?"

"That would depend, mum, on what attendance was required."

"Yes — of course. I think — will you permit me to sit down? I am really very tired. Thank you. — I require very little attendance indeed. My ways are very simple. I should make the bed myself, and — and, do the other little things that are necessary from day to day. Perhaps I might ask you to sweep the room out — once a week or so."

The landlady grew meditative. Possibly she had had experience of lodgers who were anxious to give as little trouble as possible. She glanced furtively at the stranger.

"And what," was her question at length, "would you be thinking of paying?"

"Perhaps I had better explain my position. For several years I have been companion to a lady in Hampshire. Her death has thrown me on my own resources — I hope only for a short time. I have come to London because a younger sister of mine is employed here in a house of business; she recommended me to seek for lodgings in this part; I might as well be near her whilst I am endeavouring to find another post; perhaps I may be fortunate enough to find one in London. Quietness and economy are necessary to me. A house like yours would suit me very well — very well indeed. Could we not agree upon terms within my — within my power?"

Again the landlady pondered.

"Would you be willing to pay five and sixpence?"

"Yes, I would pay five and sixpence — if you are quite sure that you could let me live in my own way with satisfaction to yourself. I — in fact, I am a vegetarian, and as the meals I take are so very simple, I feel that I might just as well prepare them myself. Would you object to my doing so in this room? A kettle and a saucepan are really all — absolutely all — that I should need to use. As I shall be much at home, it will be of course necessary for me to have a fire."

In the course of half an hour an agreement had been devised which seemed fairly satisfactory to both parties.

"I'm not one of the graspin' ones," remarked the landlady. "I think I may say that of myself. If I make five or six shillings a week out of my spare room, I don't grumble. But the party as takes it must do their duty on *their* side. You haven't told me your name yet, mum."

"Miss Madden. — My luggage is at the railway station; it shall be brought here this evening. And, as I am quite unknown to you, I should be glad to pay my rent in advance."

"Well, I don't ask for that; but it's just as you like."

"Then I will pay you five and sixpence at once. Be so kind as to let me have a receipt."

So Miss Madden established herself at Lavender Hill, and dwelt there alone for three months.

She received letters frequently, but only one person called upon her. This was her sister Monica, now serving at a draper's in Walworth Road. The young lady came every Sunday, and in bad weather spent the whole day up in the little bed-room. Lodger and landlady were on remarkably good terms; the one paid her dues with exactness, and the other did many a little kindness not bargained for in the original contract.

Time went on to the spring of '88. Then, one afternoon, Miss Madden descended to the kitchen and tapped in her usual timid way at the door.

"Are you at leisure, Mrs. Conisbee? Could I have a little conversation with you?"

The landlady was alone, and with no more engrossing occupation than the ironing of some linen she had recently washed.

"I have mentioned my elder sister now and then — I am sorry to say she is leaving her post with the family at Hereford. The children are going to school, so that her services are no longer needed."

"Indeed, mum?"

"Yes. For a shorter or longer time she will be in need of a home. Now it has occurred to me, Mrs. Conisbee, that — that I would ask you whether you would have any objection to her sharing my room with me? — Of course there must be an extra payment. The room is small for two persons, but then the arrangement would only be temporary. My sister is a good and experienced teacher, and I am sure she will have no difficulty in obtaining another engagement.

Mrs. Conisbee reflected, but without a shade of discontent. By this time she knew that her lodger was thoroughly to be trusted.

"Well, it's if *you* can manage, mum," she replied. "I don't see as I could have any fault to find, if you thought you could both live in that little room. And as for the rent, I should be quite satisfied if we said seven shillings instead of five and six."

"Thank you, Mrs. Conisbee, thank you very much indeed. I will write to my sister at once; the news will be a great relief to her. We shall have quite an enjoyable little holiday together."

A week later, the eldest of the three Miss Maddens arrived. As it was quite impossible to find space for her boxes in the bed-room, Mrs. Conisbee allowed them to be deposited in the room occupied by her daughter, which was on the same floor. In a day or two the sisters had begun a life of orderly tenor. When weather permitted they were out either in the morning or afternoon. Alice Madden was in London for the first time; she desired to see the sights, but suffered the restrictions of poverty and ill-health. After nightfall, neither she nor Virginia ever left home.

There was not much personal likeness between them.

The elder (now five-and-thirty) tended to corpulence, the result of sedentary life; she had round shoulders and very short legs. Her face would not have been disagreeable but for its spoilt complexion; the homely features, if health had but rounded and coloured them, would have expressed pleasantly enough the gentleness and sincerity of her character. Her cheeks were loose, puffy, and permanently of the hue which is produced by cold; her forehead generally had a few pimples; her shapeless chin lost itself in two or three fleshy fissures. Scarcely less shy than in girlhood, she walked with a quick, ungainly movement as if seeking to escape from some one, her head bent forward.

Virginia (about thirty-three) had also an unhealthy look, but the poverty, or vitiation, of her blood manifested itself in less unsightly forms. One saw that she had been comely, and from certain points of view her countenance still had a grace, a sweetness, all the more noticeable because of its threatened extinction. For she was rapidly ageing; her lax lips grew laxer, with emphasis of a characteristic one would rather not have perceived there; her eyes sank into deeper hollows; wrinkles extended their net-work; the flesh of her neck wore away. Her tall meagre body did not seem strong enough to hold itself upright.

Alice had brown hair, but very little of it. Virginia's was inclined to be ruddy; it surmounted her small head in coils and plaits not without beauty. The voice of the elder sister had contracted an unpleasant hoarseness; but she spoke with good enunciation; a slight stiffness and pedantry of phrase came, no doubt, of her scholastic habits. Virginia was much more natural in manner and fluent in speech; even as she moved far more gracefully.

It was now sixteen years since the death of Dr. Madden, of Clevedon. The story of his daughters' lives in the interval may be told with brevity suitable to so unexciting a narrative.

When the doctor's affairs were set in order, it was found that the patrimony of his six girls amounted, as nearly as possible, to eight hundred pounds.

Eight hundred pounds is, to be sure, a sum of money, but how, in these circumstances, was it to be applied?

There came over from Cheltenham a bachelor uncle, aged about sixty. This gentleman lived on an annuity of seventy pounds, which would terminate when *he* did. It might be reckoned to him for righteousness that he spent the railway fare between Cheltenham and Clevedon to attend his brother's funeral, and to speak a kind word to his nieces. Influence he had none; initiative, very little. There was no reckoning upon him for aid of any kind.

From Richmond in Yorkshire, in reply to a letter from Alice, wrote an old, old aunt of the late Mrs. Madden, who had occasionally sent the girls presents. Her communication was barely legible; it seemed to contain fortifying texts of Scripture, but nothing in the way of worldly counsel. This old lady had no possessions to bequeath. And, as far as the girls knew, she was their mother's only surviving relative.

The executor of the will was a Clevedon tradesman, a kind and capable friend of the family for many years, a man of parts and attainments superior to his station. In council with certain other well-disposed persons, who regarded the Maddens' circumstances with friendly anxiety, Mr. Hungerford (testamentary instruction allowing him much freedom of action) decided that the three elder girls must forthwith become self-supporting, and that the three younger should live together in the care of a lady of small means, who offered to house and keep them for the bare outlay necessitated. A prudent investment of the eight hundred pounds might, by this arrangement, feed, clothe, and in some sort educate Martha, Isabel, and Monica. To see thus far ahead sufficed for the present; fresh circumstances could be dealt with as they arose.

Alice obtained a situation as nursery-governess, at sixteen pounds a year. Virginia was fortunate enough to be accepted as companion by a gentlewoman at Weston-super-Mare; her payment, twelve pounds. Gertrude, fourteen years old, also went to Weston, where she was offered employment in a fancy-goods shop, — her payment nothing at all, but lodging, board and dress assured to her.

Ten years went by, and saw many changes.

Gertrude and Martha were dead; the former of consumption, the other drowned by the over-turning of a pleasure boat. Mr. Hungerford also was dead, and a new guardian administered the fund which was still a common property of the four surviving daughters. Alice plied her domestic teaching; Virginia remained a "companion." Isabel, now aged twenty, taught in a Board School[1] at Bridgwater, and Monica, just fifteen, was on the point of being apprenticed to a draper at Weston, where Virginia abode. To serve behind a counter would not have been Monica's choice if any more liberal employment had seemed within her reach. She had no

---

1 A state funded school administered by a board. Board schools were established after the passing of the Education Act of 1870, which guaranteed free primary education for all British children.

aptitude whatever for giving instruction; indeed, had no aptitude for anything but being a pretty, cheerful, engaging girl, much dependent on the love and gentleness of those about her. In speech and bearing Monica greatly resembled her mother; that is to say, she had native elegance. Certainly it might be deemed a pity that such a girl could not be introduced to one of the higher walks of life; but the time had come when she must "do something," and the people to whose guidance she looked had but narrow experience of life. Alice and Virginia sighed over the contrast with by-gone hopes, but their own careers made it seem probable that Monica would be better off "in business" than in a more strictly genteel position. And there was every likelihood that, at such a place as Weston, with her sister for occasional chaperon, she would ere long find herself relieved of the necessity of working for a livelihood.

To the others, no wooer had yet presented himself. Alice, if she had ever dreamt of marriage, must by now have resigned herself to spinsterhood. Virginia could scarce hope that her faded prettiness, her health damaged by attendance upon an exacting invalid and in profitless study when she ought to have been sleeping, would attract any man in search of a wife. Poor Isabel was so extremely plain. Monica, if her promise were fulfilled, would be by far the best looking, as well as the sprightliest, of the family. She must marry; of course she must marry! Her sisters gladdened in the thought.

Isabel was soon worked into illness. Brain trouble came on, resulting in melancholia. A charitable institution ultimately received her, and there, at two-and-twenty, the poor hard-featured girl drowned herself in a bath.

Their numbers had thus been reduced by half. Up to now, the income of their eight hundred pounds had served, impartially, the ends now of this, now of that one, doing a little good to all, saving them from many an hour of bitterness which must else have been added to their lot. By a new arrangement, the capital was at length made over to Alice and Virginia jointly, the youngest sister having a claim upon them to the extent of an annual nine pounds. A trifle, but it would buy her clothing, — and then Monica was sure to marry. Thank heaven, she was sure to marry!

Without notable event, matrimonial or other, time went on to this present year of 1888.

Late in June, Monica would complete her twenty-first year; the elders, full of affection for the sister, who so notably surpassed them in beauty of person, talked much about her as the time approached, devising how to procure her a little pleasure on her birthday. Virginia thought a suitable present would be a copy of "The Christian Year."[1]

"She has really no time for continuous reading. A verse of Keble —

---

1 *The Christian Year* (1827), by John Keble (1792–1866), is a small volume of brief devotional poems, one for each Sunday and holiday in the year. Keble was a theologian and poet.

just one verse at bed-time and in the morning might be strength to the poor girl."

Alice assented.

"We must join to buy it, dear," she added, with anxious look. "It wouldn't be justifiable to spend more than two or three shillings."

"I fear not."

They were preparing their midday meal, the substantial repast of the day. In a little saucepan on an oil cooking-stove was some plain rice, bubbling as Alice stirred it. Virginia fetched from downstairs (Mrs. Conisbee had assigned to them a shelf in her larder) bread, butter, cheese, a pot of preserve, and arranged the table (three feet by one and a half) at which they were accustomed to eat. The rice being ready, it was turned out in two portions; made savoury with a little butter, pepper, and salt, it invited them to sit down.

As they had been out in the morning, the afternoon would be spent in domestic occupations. The low cane-chair Virginia had appropriated to her sister, because of the latter's headaches and back-aches, and other disorders; she herself sat on an ordinary chair of the bedside species, to which by this time she had become used. Their sewing, when they did any, was strictly indispensable; if nothing demanded the needle, both preferred a book. Alice, who had never been a student in the proper sense of the word, read for the twentieth time a few volumes in her possession, — poetry, popular history, and half-a-dozen novels such as the average mother of children would have approved in the governess's hands. With Virginia the case was somewhat different. Up to about her twenty-fourth year she had pursued one subject with a zeal limited only by her opportunities; study absolutely disinterested, seeing that she had never supposed it would increase her value as a "companion," or enable her to take any better position. Her one intellectual desire was to know as much as possible about ecclesiastical history. Not in a spirit of fanaticism; she was devout, but in moderation, and never spoke bitterly on religious topics. The growth of the Christian church, old sects and schisms, the Councils, affairs of Papal policy — these things had a very genuine interest for her; circumstances favouring, she might have become an erudite woman. But the conditions were so far from favourable that all she succeeded in doing was to undermine her health. Upon a sudden breakdown there followed mental lassitude from which she never recovered. It being subsequently her duty to read novels aloud for the lady whom she "companioned," new novels at the rate of a volume a day, she lost all power of giving her mind to anything but the feebler fiction. Nowadays she procured such works from a lending library, on a subscription of a shilling a month. Ashamed at first to indulge this taste before Alice, she tried more solid literature, but this either sent her to sleep or induced headache. The feeble novels reappeared, and as Alice made no adverse comment, they soon came and went with the old regularity.

This afternoon, the sisters were disposed for conversation. The same grave thought pre-occupied both of them, and they soon made it their subject.

"Surely," Alice began by murmuring, half-absently, "I shall soon hear of something."

"I am dreadfully uneasy on my own account," her sister replied.

"You think the person at Southend won't write again?"

"I'm afraid not. — And she seemed so *very* unsatisfactory. Positively illiterate; — oh, I couldn't bear that." Virginia gave a shudder as she spoke.

"I almost wish," said Alice, "that I had accepted the place at Plymouth."

"Oh, my dear! Five children and not a penny of salary. It was a shameless proposal."

"It was, indeed," sighed the poor governess. "But there is so little choice for people like myself. Certificates, and even degrees, are asked for on every hand. With nothing but references to past employers, what can one expect? I know it will end in my taking a place without salary."

"People seem to have still less need of *me*," lamented the Companion. "I wish now that I had gone to Norwich as lady-help."

"Dear, your health would *never* have supported it."

"I don't know. Possible the more active life might do me good. It *might* you know, Alice."

The other admitted this possibility with a deep sigh.

"Let us review our position," she then exclaimed.

It was a phrase frequently on her lips, and always made her more cheerful. Virginia also seemed to welcome it as an encouragement.

"Mine," said the Companion, "is almost as serious as it could be. I have only one pound left, with the exception of the dividend."

"I have rather more than four pounds still. — Now, let us think," Alice paused. "Supposing we neither of us obtained employment before the end of this year. We have to live, in that case, more than six months — you on seven pounds, and I on ten."

"It's impossible," said Virginia.

"Let us see. Put it in another form. We have both to live together on seventeen pounds. That is —" she made a computation on a piece of paper —"that is two pounds, sixteen shillings and eightpence a month — let us suppose this month at an end. That represents fourteen shillings and twopence a week. — Yes, we *can* do it!"

She laid down her pencil with an air of triumph. Her dull eyes brightened as though she had discovered a new source of income.

"We cannot, dear," urged Virginia, in a subdued voice. "Seven shillings rent; that leaves only seven and twopence a week for everything — everything."

"We *could* do it, dear," persisted the other. "If it came to the very worst, our food need not cost more than sixpence a day — three and six-

pence a week. I do really believe, Virgie, we could support life on less —
say, on fourpence. Yes, we could dear!"

They looked fixedly at each other, like people about to stake everything on their courage.

"Is such a life worthy of the name?" asked Virginia, in tones of awe.

"We shan't be driven to that. Oh, we certainly shall not. But it helps
one to know that, strictly speaking, we are *independent* for another six
months."

That word gave Virginia an obvious thrill.

"Independent! Oh, Alice, what a blessed thing is independence! —
Do you know, my dear, I am afraid I have not exerted myself as I might
have done to find a new place. These comfortable lodgings, and the pleasure of seeing Monica once a week, have tempted me into idleness. It
isn't really my wish to be idle; I know the harm it does me; but oh, if one
could work in a home of one's own!"

Alice had a startled, apprehensive look, as if her sister were touching
on a subject hardly proper for discussion, or at least dangerous.

"I'm afraid it's no use thinking of that, dear," she answered awkwardly.

"No use; no use whatever. I am wrong to indulge such thoughts."

"Whatever happens, my dear," said Alice presently, with all the
impressiveness of tone she could command, "we must never intrench
upon our capital — never — never!"

"Oh, never! — If we grow old and useless —"

"If no one will give us even board and lodging for our services —"

"If we haven't a friend to look to," Alice threw in, as though they were
answering each other in a doleful litany, "then indeed we shall be glad
that nothing tempted us to intrench on our capital! It would just keep us"
— her voice sank — "from the workhouse."[1]

After this, each took up a volume, and until tea-time they read quietly.

From six to nine in the evening they again talked and read, alternately. Their conversation was now retrospective; each revived memories of
what she had endured in one or the other house of bondage. Never had it
been their lot to serve "really nice" people; — this phrase of theirs was
anything but meaningless. They had lived with more or less well-to-do
families in the lower middle class, people who could not have inherited
refinement, and had not acquired any, neither proletarians nor gentlefolk,
consumed with a disease of vulgar pretentiousness, inflated with the
miasma of democracy. It would have been but a natural result of such a

---

1 Workhouses were prison-like institutions in which the destitute were confined
and forced to work at menial jobs to earn their keep. The workhouse was feared
and resented by the lower classes in Victorian Britain, and savagely criticized by
social reformers.

life if the sisters had commented upon it in a spirit somewhat akin to that of their employers; but they spoke without rancour, without scandal-mongering. They knew themselves superior to the women who had grudgingly paid them, and often smiled at recollections which would have moved the servile mind to venomous abuse.

At nine o'clock they took a cup of cocoa and a biscuit, and half an hour later they went to bed. Lamp-oil was costly; and indeed they felt glad to say as early as possible that another day had gone by.

Their hour of rising was eight. Mrs. Conisbee provided hot water for their breakfast. On descending to fetch it, Virginia found that the postman had left a letter for her. The writing on the envelope seemed to be a stranger's. She ran upstairs again in excitement.

"Who can this be from, Alice?"

The elder sister had one of her headaches this morning; she was clay-colour, and tottered in moving about. The close atmosphere of the bedroom would alone have accounted for such a malady. But an unexpected letter made her for the moment oblivious of suffering.

"Posted in London," she said, examining the envelope eagerly. "Some one you have been in correspondence with?"

"It's months since I wrote to any one in London."

For full five minutes they debated the mystery, afraid of dashing their hopes by breaking the envelope. At length Virginia summoned courage. Standing at a distance from the other, she took out the sheet of paper with tremulous hand, and glanced fearfully at the signature.

"What *do* you think? It's Miss Nunn!"

"Miss Nunn? Never! How could she have got the address?"

Again the difficulty was discussed, whilst its ready solution lay neglected.

"Do read it!" said Alice at length, her throbbing head, made worse by the agitation, obliging her to sink down into the chair.

The letter ran thus: —

"DEAR MISS MADDEN,

"This morning I chanced to meet with Mrs. Darby, who was passing through London on her way home from the sea-side. We had only five minutes' talk (it was at a railway station), but she mentioned that you were at present in London, and gave me your address. After all these years, how glad I should be to see you! The struggle of life has made me selfish; I have neglected my old friends. And yet I am bound to add that some of *them* have neglected *me*. Would you rather that I came to your lodgings or you to mine? Which you like. I hear that your elder sister is with you, and that Monica is also in London somewhere. Do let us all see each other once more. Write as soon as you can. My kindest regards to all of you.

"Sincerely yours,
"RHODA NUNN."

"How like her," exclaimed Virginia, when she had read this aloud, "to remember that perhaps we may not care to receive visitors! She was always so thoughtful. — And it is true that I *ought* to have written to her."

"We shall go to her, of course?"

"Oh yes, as she gives us the choice. How delightful! I wonder what she is doing? She writes cheerfully; I am sure she must be in a good position. — What is the address? Queen's Road, Chelsea. Oh, I'm so glad it's not very far. We can walk there and back easily."

For several years they had lost sight of Rhoda Nunn. She left Clevedon shortly after the Maddens were scattered, and they heard she had become a teacher. About the date of Monica's apprenticeship at Weston, Miss Nunn had a chance meeting with Virginia and the younger girl; she was still teaching, but spoke of her work with extreme discontent, and hinted at vague projects. Whether she succeeded in releasing herself the Maddens never heard.

It was a morning of doubtful fairness. Before going to bed last night they had decided to walk out together this morning and purchase the present for Monica's birthday, which was next Sunday. But Alice felt too unwell to leave the house. Virginia should write a reply to Miss Nunn's letter, and then go to the bookseller's alone.

She set forth at half-past nine. With extreme care, she had preserved an out-of-doors dress into the third summer; it did not look shabby. Her mantle was in its second year only; the original fawn colour had gone to an indeterminate grey. Her hat of brown straw was a possession for ever; it underwent new trimming, at an outlay of a few pence, when that became unavoidable. Yet Virginia could not have been judged anything but a lady. She wore her garments as only a lady can (the position and movement of the arms has much to do with this), and had the step never to be acquired by a person of vulgar instincts.

A very long walk was before her. She wished to get as far as the Strand bookshops, not only for the sake of choice, but because this region pleased her and gave her a sense of holiday. Past Battersea Park, over Chelsea Bridge, then the weary stretch to Victoria Station, and the upward labour to Charing Cross. Five miles, at least, measured by pavement. But Virginia walked quickly; at half-past eleven she was within sight of her goal.

A presentable copy of Keble's work cost less than she had imagined. This rejoiced her. But, after leaving the shop, she had a singular expression on her face — something more than weariness, something less than anxiety, something other than calculation. In front of Charing Cross Station she stopped, looking vaguely about her. Perhaps she had it in her mind to return home by omnibus, and was dreading the expense. Yet of a sudden she turned and went up the approach to the railway.

At the entrance again she stopped. Her features were now working in the strangest way, as though a difficulty of breathing had assailed her. In her eyes was an eager, yet frightened look; her lips stood apart.

Another quick movement, and she entered the station. She went straight to the door of the refreshment room, and looked in through the glass. Two or three people were standing inside. She drew back, a tremor passing through her.

A lady came out. Then again Virginia approached the door. Two men only were within, talking together. With a hurried, nervous movement, she pushed the door open and went up to a part of the counter as far as possible from the two customers. Bending forward, she said to the barmaid in a voice just above a whisper:

"Kindly give me a little brandy."

Beads of perspiration were on her face, which had turned to a ghastly pallor. The barmaid, concluding that she was ill, served her promptly and with a sympathetic look.

Virginia added to the spirit twice its quantity of water, standing, as she did so, half turned from the bar. Then she sipped hurriedly, two or three times, and at length took a draught. Colour flowed to her cheeks; her eyes lost their frightened glare. Another draught finished the stimulant. She hastily wiped her lips, and walked away with firm step.

In the meantime a threatening cloud had passed from the sun; warm rays fell upon the street and its clamorous life. Virginia felt tired in body, but a delightful animation, rarest of boons, gave her new strength. She walked into Trafalgar Square and viewed it like a person who stands there for the first time, smiling, interested. A quarter of an hour passed whilst she merely enjoyed the air, the sunshine, and the scene about her. Such a quarter of an hour — so calm, contented, unconsciously hopeful — as she had not known since Alice's coming to London.

She reached the house by half-past one, bringing in a paper bag something which was to serve for dinner. Alice had a wretched appearance; her head ached worse than ever.

"Virgie," she moaned, "we never took account of illness, you know."

"Oh, we must keep that off," replied the other, sitting down with a look of exhaustion. She smiled, but no longer as in the sunlight of Trafalgar Square.

"Yes, I must struggle against it. We will have dinner as soon as possible. I feel faint."

If both of them had avowed their faintness as often as they felt it, the complaint would have been perpetual. But they generally made a point of deceiving each other, and tried to delude themselves; professing that no diet could be better for their particular needs than this which poverty imposed.

"Ah! it's a good sign to be hungry," exclaimed Virginia. "You'll be better this afternoon, dear."

Alice turned over "The Christian Year," and endeavoured to console herself out of it, whilst her sister prepared the meal.

CHAPTER III.

AN INDEPENDENT WOMAN.

Virginia's reply to Miss Nunn's letter brought another note next morning — Saturday. It was to request a call from the sisters that same afternoon. Alice, unfortunately, would not be able to leave home. Her disorder had become a feverish cold, caught, doubtless, between open window and door whilst the bedroom was being aired for breakfast. She lay in bed, and her sister administered remedies of the chemist's advising.

But she insisted on Virginia's leaving her in the afternoon. Miss Nunn might have something of importance to tell or to suggest. Mrs. Conisbee, sympathetic in her crude way, would see that the invalid wanted for nothing.

So, after a dinner of mashed potatoes and milk ("The Irish peasantry live almost entirely on that," croaked Alice, "and they are physically a fine race"), the younger sister started on her walk to Chelsea. Her destination was a plain, low, roomy old house in Queen's Road, over against the Hospital Gardens.[1] On asking for Miss Nunn, she was led to a back room on the ground floor, and there waited for a few moments. Several large book-cases, a well-equipped writing-table, and kindred objects, indicated that the occupant of the house was studious; the numerous bunches of cut flowers, which agreeably scented the air, seemed to prove the student a woman.

Miss Nunn entered. Younger only by a year or two than Virginia, she was yet far from presenting any sorrowful image of a person on the way to old-maidenhood. She had a clear, though pale skin, a vigorous frame, a brisk movement — all the signs of fairly good health. Whether or not she could be called a comely woman, might have furnished matter for male discussion; the prevailing voice of her own sex would have denied her charm of feature. At first view the countenance seemed masculine, its expression somewhat aggressive, — eyes shrewdly observant and lips consciously impregnable. But the connoisseur delayed his verdict. It was a face that invited, that compelled, study. Self-confidence, intellectual keenness, a bright humour, frank courage, were traits legible enough; and when the lips parted to show their warmth, their fulness, when the eyelids drooped a little in meditation, one became aware of a suggestiveness directed not solely to the intellect, of something like an unfamiliar sexual type, remote indeed from the voluptuous, but hinting a possibility of subtle feminine forces that might be released by circumstance. She wore

---

1 Rhoda Nunn lives adjacent to the Chelsea Royal Hospital for old or disabled soldiers, founded in 1694. The extensive hospital grounds include public gardens.

a black serge gown, with white collar and cuffs; her thick hair rippled low upon each side of the forehead, and behind was gathered into two loose vertical coils; in shadow the hue seemed black, but when illumined it was seen to be the darkest, warmest brown.

Offering a strong, shapely hand, she looked at her visitor with a smile which betrayed some mixture of pain in the hearty welcome.

"And how long have you been in London?"

It was the tone of a busy, practical person. Her voice had not much softness of timbre, and perhaps on that account she kept it carefully subdued.

"So long as that? How I wish I had known you were so near! I have been in London myself about two years. And your sisters?"

Virginia explained Alice's absence, adding:

"As for poor Monica, she has only Sunday free — except one evening a month. She is at business till half-past nine, and on Saturday till half-past eleven or twelve."

"Oh, dear, dear, dear!" exclaimed the other rapidly, making a motion with her hand as if to brush away something disagreeable. "That will never do. You must put a stop to that."

"I am sure we ought to."

Virginia's thin, timid voice and weak manner were thrown into painful contrast by Miss Nunn's personality.

"Yes, yes; we will talk about it presently. Poor little Monica! — But do tell me about yourself and Miss Madden. It is so long since I heard about you."

"Indeed I ought to have written. I remember that at the end of our correspondence I remained in your debt. But it was a troublesome and depressing time with me. I had nothing but groans and moans to send."

"You didn't stay long, I trust, with that trying Mrs. Carr?"

"Three years!" sighed Virginia.

"Oh, your patience!"

"I wished to leave again and again. But at the end she always begged me not to desert her — that was how she put it. After all, I never had the heart to go."

"Very kind of you, but — those questions are so difficult to decide. Self-sacrifice may be quite wrong, I'm afraid."

"Do you think so?" asked Virginia anxiously.

"Yes, I am sure it is often wrong — all the more so, because people proclaim it a virtue without any reference to circumstances. — Then how did you get away at last?"

"The poor woman died. — Then I had a place scarcely less disagreeable. — Now I have none at all; but I really must find one very soon."

She laughed at this allusion to her poverty, and made nervous motions.

"Let me tell you what my own course has been," said Miss Nunn, after a short reflection. "When my mother died, I determined to have done with teaching — you know that. I disliked it too much, and partly, of course, because I was incapable. Half my teaching was a sham — a pretence of knowing what I neither knew nor cared to know. I had gone into it like most girls, as a dreary matter of course."

"Like poor Alice, I'm afraid."

"Oh, it's a distressing subject. — When my mother left me that little sum of money, I took a bold step. I went to Bristol to learn everything I could that would help me out of school-life. Shorthand, book-keeping, commercial correspondence — I had lessons in them all, and worked desperately for a year. It did me good; at the end of the year I was vastly improved in health, and felt myself worth something in the world. I got a place as cashier in a large shop. That soon tired me, and by dint of advertising I found a place in an office at Bath. It was a move towards London, and I couldn't rest till I had come the whole way. My first engagement here was as shorthand writer to the secretary of a company. But he soon wanted some one who could use a type-writer. That was a suggestion. I went to learn type-writing, and the lady who taught me asked me in the end to stay with her as an assistant. This is her house, and here I live with her."

"How energetic you have been!"

"How fortunate, perhaps. — I must tell you about this lady, — Miss Barfoot. She has private means, — not large, but sufficient to allow of her combining benevolence with business. She makes it her object to train young girls for work in offices, teaching them the things that I learnt in Bristol, and type-writing as well. Some pay for their lessons, and some get them for nothing. Our workrooms are in Great Portland Street, over a picture-cleaner's shop. One or two girls have evening lessons, but our pupils, for the most part, are able to come in the day. Miss Barfoot hasn't much interest in the lower classes; she wishes to be of use to the daughters of educated people. And she is of use. She is doing admirable work."

"Oh, I am sure she must be! — What a wonderful person!"

"It occurs to me that she might help Monica."

"Oh, do you think she would?" exclaimed Virginia, with eager attention. "How grateful we should be!"

"Where is Monica employed?"

"At a draper's in Walworth Road. She is worked to death. Every week I see a difference in her, poor child. We hoped to persuade her to go back to the shop at Weston, but if this you speak of were possible — how *much* better! We have never reconciled ourselves to her being in that position — never."

"I see no harm in the position itself," replied Miss Nunn, in her rather blunt tone, "but I see a great deal in those outrageous hours. She won't easily do better in London, without special qualifications; and probably she is reluctant to go back to the country."

"Yes, she is; very reluctant."

"I understand it," said the other, with a nod. "Will you ask her to come and see me?"

A servant entered with tea. Miss Nunn caught the expression in her visitor's eyes, and said cheerfully:

"I had no mid-day meal to-day, and really I feel the omission. Mary, please to put tea in the dining-room, and bring up some meat. — Miss Barfoot," she added, in explanation to Virginia, "is out of town, and I am a shockingly irregular person about meals. I am sure you will sit down with me?"

Virginia sported with the subject. Months of miserable eating and drinking in her stuffy bedroom made an invitation such as this a veritable delight to her. Seated in the dining-room, she at first refused the offer of meat, alleging her vegetarianism; but Miss Nunn, convinced that the poor woman was starving, succeeded in persuading her. A slice of good beef had much the same effect upon Virginia as her more dangerous indulgence at Charing Cross Station. She brightened wonderfully.

"Now let us go back to the library," said Miss Nunn, when their meal was over. "We shall soon see each other again, I hope, but we might as well talk of serious things whilst we have the opportunity. — Will you allow me to be very frank with you?"

The other looked startled.

"What could you possibly say that would offend me?"

"In the old days you told me all about your circumstances. Are they still the same?"

"Precisely the same. Most happily, we have never needed to intrench upon our capital. Whatever happens, we must avoid that — whatever happens!"

"I quite understand you. But wouldn't it be possible to make a better use of that money? It is eight hundred pounds, I think? — Have you never thought of employing it in some practical enterprise?"

Virginia at first shrank in alarm, then trembled deliciously at her friend's bold views.

"Would it be possible? — Really? — You think —"

"I can only suggest, of course. One mustn't argue about others from one's own habit of thought. Heaven forbid" — this sounded rather profane to the listener — "that I should urge you to do anything you would think rash. But how much better if you could somehow secure independence."

"Ah, if we could! The very thing we were saying the other day! — But how? I have no idea how."

Miss Nunn seemed to hesitate.

"I don't advise. You mustn't give any weight to what I say, except in so far as your own judgment approves it. But couldn't one open a preparatory school, for instance? At Weston, suppose, where already you know a good many people. Or even at Clevedon."

Virginia drew in her breath, and it was easy for Miss Nunn to perceive that the proposal went altogether beyond her friend's scope. Impossible, perhaps, to inspire these worn and discouraged women with a particle of

her own enterprise. Perchance they altogether lacked ability to manage a
school for even the youngest children. She did not press the subject; it
might come up on another occasion. Virginia begged for time to think it
over; then, remembering her invalid sister, felt that she must not prolong
the visit.

"Do take some of these flowers," said Miss Nunn, collecting a rich
nosegay from the vases. "Let them be my message to your sister. And I
should be so glad to see Monica. Sunday is a good time; I am always at
home in the afternoon."

With a fluttering heart, Virginia made what haste she could homewards. The interview had filled her with a turmoil of strange new
thoughts, which she was impatient to pour forth for Alice's wondering
comment. It was the first time in her life that she had spoken with a
woman daring enough to think and act for herself.

CHAPTER IV.

MONICA'S MAJORITY.

In the drapery establishment where Monica Madden worked and lived it was not (as is sometimes the case) positively forbidden to the resident employees to remain at home on Sunday; but they were strongly recommended to make the utmost possible use of that weekly vacation. Herein, no doubt, appeared a laudable regard for their health. Young people, especially young women, who are laboriously engaged in a shop for thirteen hours and a half every week day, and on Saturday for an average of sixteen, may be supposed to need a Sabbath of open air. Messrs. Scotcher & Co. acted like conscientious men in driving them forth immediately after breakfast and enjoining upon them not to return until bedtime. By way of well-meaning constraint, it was directed that only the very scantiest meals (plain bread and cheese, in fact) should be supplied to those who did not take advantage of the holiday.

Messrs. Scotcher & Co. were large-minded men. Not only did they insist that the Sunday ought to be used for bodily recreation, but they had no objection whatever to their young friends taking a stroll after closing-time each evening. Nay, so generous and confiding were they, that to each young person they allowed a latch-key. The air of Walworth Road is pure and invigorating about midnight; why should the reposeful ramble be hurried by consideration for weary domestics?

Monica always felt too tired to walk after ten o'clock; moreover, the usual conversation in the dormitory which she shared with five other young women was so little to her taste that she wished to be asleep when the talkers came up to bed. But on Sunday she gladly followed the counsel of her employers. If the weather were bad, the little room at Lavender Hill offered her a retreat; when the sun shone, she liked to spend a part of the day in free wandering about London, which even yet had not quite disillusioned her.

And to-day it shone brightly. This was her birthday, the completion of her one-and-twentieth year. Alice and Virginia of course expected her early in the morning, and of course they were all to dine together — at the table measuring three feet by one and a half; but the afternoon and evening she must have to herself. The afternoon, because a few hours of her sisters' talk invariably depressed her; and the evening, because she had an appointment to keep. As she left the big ugly "establishment," her heart beat cheerfully, and a smile fluttered about her lips. She did not feel very well, but that was a matter of course; the ride in an omnibus[1] would perhaps make her head clearer.

---

1 I.e., a bus. "Omnibus," from which the word "bus" derives, is the dative plural of the Latin word "omnes," meaning "all." The omnibus is accordingly a form of transportation "for all." The late nineteenth-century omnibus was horse-drawn.

Monica's face was of a recognized type of prettiness; a pure oval; from the smooth forehead to the dimpled little chin all its lines were soft and graceful. Her lack of colour, by heightening the effect of black eyebrows and darkly lustrous eyes, gave her at present a more spiritual cast than her character justified; but a thoughtful firmness was native to her lips, and no possibility of smirk or simper lurked in the attractive features. The slim figure was well-fitted in a costume of pale blue, cheap but becoming; a modest little hat rested on her black hair; her gloves and her sunshade completed the dainty picture.

An omnibus would be met in Kennington Park Road. On her way thither, in a quiet cross-street, she was overtaken by a young man who had left the house of business a moment after her, and had followed at a short distance, timidly. A young man of unhealthy countenance, with a red pimple on the side of his nose, but not otherwise ill-looking. He was clad with propriety, — stove-pipe hat, diagonal frock-coat, pink tie, grey trousers, and he walked with a springy gait.

"Miss Madden —"

He had ventured, with perturbation in his face, to overtake Monica. She stopped.

"What is it Mr. Bullivant?"

Her tone was far from encouraging, but the young man smiled upon her with timorous tenderness.

"What a beautiful morning! Are you going far?"

He had the Cockney accent, but not in an offensive degree; his manners were not flagrantly of the shop.

"Yes; some distance." Monica walked slowly on.

"Will you allow me to walk a little way with you?" he pleaded, bending towards her.

"I shall take the omnibus at the end of this street."

They went forward together. Monica no longer smiled, but neither did she look angry. Her expression was one of trouble.

"Where shall *you* spend the day, Mr. Bullivant?" she asked at length, with an effort to seem unconcerned.

"I really don't know."

"I should think it would be very nice up the river." — And she added, diffidently, "Miss Eade is going to Richmond."

"Is she?" he replied vaguely.

"At least, she wished to go, — if she could find a companion."

"I hope she will enjoy herself," said Mr. Bullivant, with careful civility.

"But of course she won't enjoy it very much if she has to go alone. — As you have no particular engagement, Mr. Bullivant, wouldn't it be kind to —?"

The suggestion was incomplete, but intelligible.

"I couldn't ask Miss Eade to let me accompany her," said the young man gravely.

"Oh, I think you could. — She would like it."

Monica looked rather frightened at her boldness, and quickly added: "Now I must say good-bye. There comes the 'bus."

Bullivant turned desperately in that direction. He saw there was as yet no inside passenger.

"Do allow me to go a short way with you?" burst from his lips. "I positively don't know how I shall spend the morning."

Monica had signalled to the driver, and was hurrying forward. Bullivant followed, reckless of consequences. In a minute, both were seated within.

"You will forgive me?" pleaded the young fellow, remarking a look of serious irritation on his companion's face. "I *must* be with you a few minutes longer."

"I think when I have begged you not to —"

"I know how bad my behaviour must seem. But, Miss Madden, may I not be on terms of friendship with you?"

"Of course you may, — but you are not content with that."

"Yes — indeed—I *will* be content —"

"It's foolish to say so. Haven't you broken the understanding three or four times?"

The 'bus stopped for a passenger, a man who mounted to the top.

"I am so sorry," murmured Bullivant, as the starting horses jolted them together. "I try not to worry you. Think of my position. You have told me that there is no one else who — whose rights I ought to respect. Feeling as I do, it isn't in human nature to give up hope!"

"Then will you let me ask you a rude question?"

"Ask me *any* question, Miss Madden."

"How would it be possible for you to support a wife?"

She flushed and smiled. Bullivant, dreadfully discomposed, did not move his eyes from her.

"It wouldn't be possible, for some time," he answered, in a thick voice. "I have nothing but my wretched salary. But every one hopes."

"What reasonable hope have you?" Monica urged, forcing herself to be cruel, because it seemed the only way of putting an end to this situation.

"Oh, there are so many opportunities in our business. I could point to half-a-dozen successful men who were at the counter a few years ago. I may become a walker, and get at least three pounds a week. If I were lucky enough to be taken on as a buyer, I might make — why, some make many hundreds a year — many hundreds."

"And you would ask me to wait on and on for one of these wonderful chances?"

"If I could move your feelings, Miss Madden," he began, with a certain dolorous dignity; but there his voice broke. He saw too plainly that the girl had neither faith in him nor liking for him.

"Mr. Bullivant, I think you ought to wait until you really have prospects. — If you were encouraged by some person, it would be a different thing. — And indeed you haven't to look far. — But where there has never been the slightest encouragement, you are really wrong to act in this way. A long engagement, where everything remains doubtful for years, is so wretched that — oh, if I were a man, I would *never* try to persuade a girl into that! I think it wrong and cruel."

The stroke was effectual. Bullivant averted his face, naturally woebegone, and sat for some minutes without speaking. The 'bus again drew up; four or five people were about to ascend.

"I will say good-morning, Miss Madden," he whispered hurriedly.

She gave her hand, glanced at him with embarrassment, and so let him depart.

Ten minutes restored the mood in which she had set out. Once more she smiled to herself. Indeed, her head was better for the fresh air, and the movement. If only the sisters would allow her to get away soon after dinner!

It was Virginia who opened the door to her, and embraced and kissed her with wonted fondness.

"You are nice and early! Poor Alice has been in bed since the day before yesterday; a dreadful cold and one of her very worst headaches. But I think she is a little better this morning."

Alice — a sad spectacle — was propped up on pillows.

"Don't kiss me, darling," she said, in a voice barely audible. "You mustn't risk getting a sore throat. How well you look!"

"I'm afraid she doesn't look *well*," corrected Virginia, "but perhaps she has a little more colour than of late. — Monica dear, as Alice can hardly use her voice, I will speak for both of us, and wish you many, many happy returns of the day. And we ask you to accept this little book from us. It may be a comfort to you from time to time."

"You are good, kind dears!" replied Monica, kissing the one on the lips and the other on her thinly-tressed head. "It's no use saying you oughtn't to have spent money on me; you *will* always do it. What a nice 'Christian Year'! I'll do my best to read some of it now and then."

With a half-guilty air, Virginia then brought from some corner of the room a very small but delicate currant cake. Monica must eat a mouthful of this; she always had such a wretched breakfast, and the journey from Walworth Road was enough to give an appetite.

"But you are ruining yourselves, foolish people!"

The others exchanged a look, and smiled with such a strange air that Monica could not but notice it.

"I know!" she cried. "There's good news. You have found something, and better than usual, Virgie."

"Perhaps so. Who knows? Eat your slice of cake like a good child, and then I shall have something to tell you."

Obviously the two were excited. Virginia moved about with the recovered step of girlhood, held herself upright, and could not steady her hands.

"You would never guess whom I have seen," she began, when Monica was quite ready to listen. "We had a letter the other morning which did puzzle us so — I mean the writing before we opened it. And it was from — Miss Nunn!" .

This name did not greatly stir Monica.

"You had quite lost sight of her, hadn't you?" she remarked.

"Quite. I didn't suppose we should ever hear of her again. But nothing more fortunate could have happened. My dear, she is wonderful!"

At considerable length Virginia detailed all she had learnt of Miss Nunn's career, and described her present position.

"She will be the most valuable friend to us. Oh, her strength, her resolution! The way in which she discovers the right thing to do! — You are to call upon her as soon as possible. This very afternoon you had better go. She will relieve you from all your troubles, darling. Her friend Miss Barfoot will teach you type-writing, and put you in the way of earning an easy and pleasant livelihood. She will, indeed!"

"But how long does it take?" asked the astonished girl.

"Oh, quite a short time, I should think. We didn't speak of details; they were postponed. You will hear everything yourself. — And she suggested all sorts of ways," pursued Virginia, with quite unintentional exaggeration, "in which we could make better use of our invested money. She is *full* of practical expedients. The most wonderful person! She is quite like a *man* in energy and resources. I never imagined that one of our sex could resolve and plan and act as she does!"

Monica inquired anxiously what the projects for improving their income might be.

"Nothing is decided yet," was the reply, given with a confident smile. "Let us first of all put *you* in comfort and security; that is the immediate need."

The listener was interested, but did not show any eagerness for the change proposed. Presently she stood at the window and lost herself in thought. Alice gave signs of an inclination to doze; she had had a sleepless night, in spite of soporifics. Though no sun entered the room, it was very hot, and the presence of a third person made the air oppressive.

"Don't you think we might go out for half an hour?" Monica whispered, when Virginia had pointed to the invalid's closed eyes. "I'm sure it's very unhealthy for us all to be in this little place."

"I don't like to leave her," the other whispered back. "But I certainly think it would be better for you to have fresh air. Wouldn't you like to go to church, dear? The bells haven't stopped yet."

The elder sisters were not quite regular in their church-going. When weather or lassitude kept them at home on Sunday morning they read the service aloud. Monica found the duty of listening rather grievous. During the months that she was alone in London she had fallen into neglect of public worship; not from any conscious emancipation, but because her companions at the house of business never dreamt of entering a church, and their example by degrees affected her with carelessness. At present she was glad of the pretext for escaping until dinner-time.

She went forth with the intention of deceiving her sisters, of walking to Clapham Common, and on her return inventing some sermon at a church the others never visited. But before she had gone many yards conscience overcame her. Was she not getting to be a very lax-minded girl? And it was shameful to impose upon the two after their loving-kindness to her. As usual, her little prayer-book was in her pocket. She walked quickly to the familiar church, and reached it just as the doors were being closed.

Of all the congregation she probably was the one who went through the service most mechanically. Not a word reached her understanding. Sitting, standing, or on her knees, she wore the same preoccupied look, with ever and again a slight smile or a movement of the lips, as if she were recalling some conversation of special interest.

Last Sunday she had had an adventure, the first of any real moment that had befallen her in London. She had arranged to go with Miss Eade on a steamboat up the river. They were to meet at the Battersea Park landing-stage at half-past two. But Miss Eade did not keep her appointment, and Monica, unwilling to lose the trip, started alone.

She disembarked at Richmond, and strayed about for an hour or two; then had a cup of tea and a bun. As it was still far too early to return, she went down to the riverside, and seated herself on one of the benches. Many boats were going by, a majority of them containing only two persons — a young man who pulled, and a girl who held the strings of the tiller. Some of these couples Monica disregarded; but occasionally there passed a skiff from which she could not take her eyes. To lie back like that on the cushions, and converse with a companion who had nothing of the *shop* about him!

It seemed hard that she must be alone. Poor Mr. Bullivant would gladly have taken her on the river; but Mr. Bullivant —

She thought of her sisters. Their loneliness was for life, poor things. Already they were old; and they would grow older, sadder, perpetually struggling to supplement that dividend from the precious capital — and merely that they might keep alive. Oh! — her heart ached at the misery of such a prospect. How much better if the poor girls had never been born.

Her own future was more hopeful than theirs had ever been. She knew herself good-looking. Men had followed her in the street and tried to make her acquaintance. Some of the girls with whom she lived regarded her enviously, spitefully. But had she really the least chance of marrying a man whom she could respect — not to say love?

One-and-twenty a week hence. At Weston she had kept tolerable health, but certainly her constitution was not strong, and the slavery of Walworth Road threatened her with premature decay. Her sisters counselled wisely. Coming to London was a mistake. She would have had better chances at Weston, notwithstanding the extreme discretion with which she was obliged to conduct herself.

While she mused thus, a profound discouragement settling on her sweet face, some one took a seat by her — on the same bench, that is to say. Glancing aside, she saw that it was an oldish man, with grizzled whiskers and rather a stern visage. Monica sighed.

Was it possible that he had heard her? He looked this way, and with curiosity. Ashamed of herself, she kept her eyes averted for a long time. Presently, following the movement of a boat, her face turned unconsciously towards the silent companion; again he was looking at her, and he spoke. The gravity of his appearance and manner, the good-natured commonplace that fell from his lips, could not alarm her; a dialogue began, and went on for about half an hour.

How old might he be? After all, he was probably not fifty — perchance not much more than forty. His utterance fell short of perfect refinement, but seemed that of an educated man. And certainly his clothes were such as a gentleman wears. He had thin, hairy hands, unmarked by any effect of labour; the nails could not have been better cared for. Was it a bad sign that he carried neither gloves nor walking-stick?

His talk aimed at nothing but sober friendliness; it was perfectly inoffensive — indeed, respectful. Now and then — not too often — he fixed his eyes upon her for an instant. After the introductory phrases, he mentioned that he had had a long drive, alone; his horse was baiting[1] in preparation for the journey back to London. He often took such drives in the summer, though generally on a week-day; the magnificent sky had tempted him out this morning. He lived at Herne Hill.

At length he ventured a question. Monica affected no reluctance to tell him that she was in a house of business, that she had relatives in London, that only by chance she found herself alone to-day.

"I should be sorry if I never saw you again."

These words he uttered with embarrassment, his eyes on the ground. Monica could only keep silence. Half an hour ago she would not have thought it possible for any remark of this man's seriously to occupy her mind, yet now she waited for the next sentence in discomposure which was quite free from resentment.

"We meet in this casual way, and talk, and then say good-bye. Why mayn't I tell you that you interest me very much, and that I am afraid to trust only to chance for another meeting? If you were a man" — he smiled — "I should give you my card, and ask you to my house. The card I may at all events offer."

Whilst speaking, he drew out a little case, and laid a visiting-card[2] on

---

1 To bait is to stop to rest and/or eat during a journey.
2 A small card, like a business card, indicating the bearer's name and address.

the bench within Monica's reach. Murmuring her "thank you," she took
the bit of pasteboard, but did not look at it.

"You are on my side of the river," he continued, still with scrupulous
modesty of tone. "May I not hope to see you some day, when you are
walking? — All days and times are the same to me; but I am afraid it is
only on Sunday that you are at leisure?"

"Yes, only on a Sunday."

It took a long time and many circumlocutions, but in the end an
appointment was made. Monica would see her acquaintance next Sunday
evening on the river front of Battersea Park; if it rained, then the Sunday
after. She was ashamed and confused. Other girls were constantly doing
this kind of thing — other girls in business; but it seemed to put her on
the level of a servant. And why had she consented? The man could never
be anything to her; he was too old, too hard-featured, too grave. Well, on
that very account there would be no harm in meeting him. In truth, she
had not felt the courage to refuse; in a manner, he had overawed her.

And perhaps she would not keep the engagement. Nothing compelled
her. She had not told him her name, nor the house where she was
employed. There was a week to think it over.

All days and times were the same to him — he said. And he drove
about the country for his pleasure. A man of means. His name, according
to the card, was Edmund Widdowson.

He was upright in his walk, and strongly built. She noticed this as he
moved away from her. Fearful lest he should turn round, her eyes glanced
at his figure from moment to moment. But he did not once look back ...

"And now to God the Father" — The bustle throughout the church
wakened her from reverie so complete that she knew not a syllable of the
sermon. After all she must deceive her sisters by inventing a text, and perhaps a comment.

By an arrangement with Mrs. Conisbee, dinner was down in the parlour to-day. A luxurious meal, moreover; for in her excitement Virginia
had resolved to make a feast of Monica's birthday. There was a tiny piece
of salmon, a dainty cutlet, and a cold black-currant tart. Virginia, at home
a consistent vegetarian, took no share of the fish and meat — which was
only enough for one person. Alice, alone upstairs, made a dinner of gruel.

Monica was to be at Queen's Road, Chelsea, by three o'clock. The sisters hoped she would return to Lavender Hill with her news, but that was
left uncertain — by Monica herself purposely. As an amusement, she had
decided to keep her promise to Mr. Edmund Widdowson. She was curious to see him again, and receive a new impression of his personality. If
he behaved as inoffensively as at Richmond, acquaintance with him
might be continued for the variety it brought into her life. If anything
unpleasant happened, she had only to walk away. The slight, very slight,
tremor of anticipation was reasonably to be prized by a shop-girl at
Messrs. Scotcher's.

Drawing near to Queen's Road, — the wrapped-up Keble in her hand, — she began to wonder whether Miss Nunn would have any serious proposal to offer. Virginia's report and ecstatic forecasts were, she knew, not completely trustworthy; though more than ten years her sister's junior, Monica saw the world with eyes much less disposed to magnify and colour ordinary facts.

Miss Barfoot was still from home; Rhoda Nunn received the visitor in a pleasant, old-fashioned drawing-room, where there was nothing costly, nothing luxurious. Yet to Monica it appeared richly furnished; a sense of strangeness amid such surroundings had more to do with her constrained silence for the first few minutes than the difficulty with which she recognized in this lady before her the Miss Nunn whom she had known years ago.

"I should never have known you," said Rhoda, equally surprised. "For one thing, you look like a fever-patient, just recovering. What can be expected? Your sister gave me a shocking account of how you live."

"The work is very hard."

"Preposterous. Why do you stay at such a place, Monica?"

"I am getting experience."

"To be used in the next world?"

They laughed.

"Miss Madden is better to-day, I hope?"

"Alice? — Not much, I'm sorry to say."

"Will you tell me something more about the 'experience' you are getting? For instance, what time is given you for meals?"

Rhoda Nunn was not the person to manufacture light gossip when a matter of the gravest interest waited for discussion. With a face that expressed thoughtful sympathy, she encouraged the girl to speak and confide in her.

"There's twenty minutes for each meal," Monica explained, "but at dinner and tea one is very likely to be called into the shop before finishing. If you are long away, you find the table cleared."

"Charming arrangement! — No sitting down behind the counter, I suppose?"

"Oh, of course not. We suffer a great deal from that. Some of us get diseases. A girl has just gone to the hospital with varicose veins, and two or three others have the same thing in less troublesome form. Sometimes, on Saturday night, I lose all feeling in my feet; I have to stamp on the floor to be sure it's still under me."

"Ah, that Saturday night!"

"Yes, it's bad enough now; but at Christmas! There was a week or more of Saturday nights — going on to one o'clock in the morning. A girl by me was twice carried out fainting, one night after another. They gave her brandy, and she came back again."

"They compelled her to?"

"Well, no, it was her own wish. Her 'book of takings' wasn't very good, poor thing, and if it didn't come up to a certain figure at the end of the week she would lose her place. She lost it, after all. They told her she was too weak. After Christmas she was lucky enough to get a place as a lady's-maid at twenty-five pounds a year; — at Scotcher's she had fifteen. But we heard that she burst a blood-vessel, and now she's in the Hospital at Brompton."

"Delightful story! — Haven't you an early-closing day?"

"They had before I went there; but only for about three months. Then the agreement broke down."

"Like the assistants. A pity the establishment doesn't follow suit."

"But you wouldn't say so, Miss Nunn, if you knew how terribly hard it is for many girls to find a place, even now."

"I know it perfectly well. And I wish it were harder. I wish girls fell down and died of hunger in the streets, instead of creeping to their garrets and the hospitals. I should like to see their dead bodies collected together in some open place, for the crowd to stare at."

Monica gazed at her with wide eyes.

"You mean, I suppose, that people would try to reform things."

"Who knows? Perhaps they might only congratulate each other that a few of the superfluous females had been struck off. — Do they give you any summer holiday?"

"A week, with salary continued."

"Really? With salary continued? That takes one's breath away. — Are many of the girls ladies?"

"None, at Scotcher's. They nearly all come from the country. Several are daughters of small farmers, and those are dreadfully ignorant. One of them asked me the other day in what country Africa was."

"You don't find them very pleasant company?"

"One or two are nice, quiet girls."

Rhoda drew a deep sigh, and moved with impatience.

"Well, don't you think you've had about enough of it — experience and all?"

"I might go into a country business, it would be easier."

"But you don't care for the thought?"

"I wish now they had brought me up to something different. Alice and Virginia were afraid of having me trained for a school; you remember that one of our sisters who went through it died of overwork. And I'm not clever, Miss Nunn. I never did much at school."

Rhoda regarded her, smiling gently.

"You have no inclination to study now?"

"I'm afraid not," replied the other, looking away. "Certainly I should like to be better educated, but I don't think I could study seriously, to earn my living by it. The time for that has gone by."

"Perhaps so. — But there are things you might manage. No doubt your sister told you how I get my living. There's a good deal of employment for women who learn to use a type-writer. — Did you ever have piano lessons?"

"No."

"No more did I, and I was sorry for it when I went to type-writing. The fingers have to be light and supple and quick. Come with me, and I'll show you one of the machines."

They went to a room downstairs, a bare little room by the library; here were two Remingtons,[1] and Rhoda patiently explained their use.

"One must practise until one can do fifty words a minute, at least. I know one or two people who have reached almost twice that speed. It takes a good six months' work to learn for any profitable use. Miss Barfoot takes pupils."

Monica, at first very attentive, was growing absent. Her eyes wandered about the room. The other observed her closely, and, it seemed, doubtfully.

"Do you feel any impulse to try for it?"

"I should have to live for six months without earning anything."

"That is by no means impossible for you, I think?"

"Not really impossible," Monica replied, with hesitation.

Something like dissatisfaction passed over Miss Nunn's face, though she did not allow Monica to see it. Her lips moved in a way that perhaps signified disdain for such timidity. Tolerance was not one of the virtues expressed in her physiognomy.

"Let us go back to the drawing-room and have some tea."

Monica could not become quite at ease. This energetic woman had little attraction for her. She saw the characteristics which made Virginia enthusiastic, but feared rather than admired them. To put herself in Miss Nunn's hands might possibly result in a worse form of bondage than she suffered at the shop; she would never be able to please such a person, and failure, she imagined, would result in more or less contemptuous dismissal.

Then, of a sudden, as if she had divined these thoughts, Rhoda assumed an air of gaiety, of frank kindness.

"So it is your birthday? — I no longer keep count of mine, and couldn't tell you without a calculation what I am exactly. It doesn't matter, you see. Thirty-one or fifty-one is much the same for a woman who has made up her mind to live alone and work steadily for a definite object. But you are still a young girl, Monica. My best wishes!"

Monica emboldened herself to ask what the object was for which her friend worked.

"How shall I put it?" replied the other, smiling. "To make women hard-hearted."

"Hard-hearted? — I think I understand."

"Do you?"

---

1 A make of typewriter.

"You mean that you like to see them live unmarried."

Rhoda laughed merrily.

"You say that almost with resentment."

"No — indeed — I didn't intend it."

Monica reddened a little.

"Nothing more natural, if you had done. At your age, *I* should have resented it."

"But —" the girl hesitated — "don't you approve of any one marrying?"

"Oh, I'm not so severe! — But do you know that there are half a million more women than men in this happy country of ours?"

"Half a million!" echoed Monica.

Her naïve alarm again excited Rhoda to laughter.

"Something like that, they say. So many *odd* women — no making a pair with them. The pessimists call them useless, lost, futile lives. I, naturally — being one of them myself — take another view. I look upon them as a great reserve. When one woman vanishes in matrimony, the reserve offers a substitute for the world's work. True, they are not all trained yet — far from it. I want to help in that — to train the reserve."

"But married women are not idle," protested Monica earnestly.

"Not all of them. Some cook and rock cradles."

Again Miss Nunn's mood changed. She laughed the subject away, and abruptly began to talk of old days down in Somerset, of rambles about Cheddar Cliffs, or at Glastonbury, or on the Quantocks. Monica, however, could not listen, and with difficulty commanded her face to a pleasant smile.

"Will you come and see Miss Barfoot?" Rhoda asked, when it had become clear to her that the girl would gladly get away. "I am only her subordinate, but I know she will wish to be of all the use to you she can."

Monica expressed her thanks, and promised to act as soon as possible on any invitation that was sent her. She took leave just as the servant announced another caller.

CHAPTER V.

THE CASUAL AQUAINTANCE.

At that corner of Battersea Park which is near Albert Bridge there has lain for more than twenty years a curious collection of architectural fragments, chiefly dismembered columns, spread in order upon the ground, and looking like portions of a razed temple. It is the colonnade of Old Burlington House, conveyed hither from Piccadilly who knows why, and likely to rest here, the sporting ground for adventurous infants, until its origin is lost in the abyss of time.

It was at this spot that Monica had agreed to meet with her casual acquaintance, Edmund Widdowson, and there, from a distance, she saw his lank, upright, well-dressed figure moving backwards and forwards upon the grass. Even at the last moment Monica doubted whether to approach. Emotional interest in him she had none, and the knowledge of life she had gained in London assured her that in thus encouraging a perfect stranger she was doing a very hazardous thing. But the evening must somehow be spent, and if she went off in another direction it would only be to wander about with an adventurous mind; for her conversation with Miss Nunn had had precisely the opposite effect of that which Rhoda doubtless intended; she felt something of the recklessness which formerly excited her wonder when she remarked it in the other shop-girls. She could no longer be without a male companion, and as she had given her promise to this man —

He had seen her, and was coming forward. To-day he carried a walking-stick, and wore gloves; otherwise his appearance was the same as at Richmond. At the distance of a few yards he raised his hat, not very gracefully. Monica did not offer her hand, nor did Widdowson seem to expect it. But he gave proof of an intense pleasure in the meeting; his sallow cheeks grew warm, and in the many wrinkles about his eyes played a singular smile, good-natured but anxious, apprehensive.

"I am so glad you were able to come," he said, in a low voice, bending towards her.

"It has been even finer than last Sunday," was Monica's rather vague reply, as she glanced at some people who were passing.

"Yes, a wonderful day. But I only left home an hour ago. — Shall we walk this way?"

They went along the path by the river. Widdowson exhibited none of the artifices of gallantry practised by men who are in the habit of picking up an acquaintance with shop-girls. His smile did not return; an extreme sobriety characterized his manner and speech; for the most part he kept his eyes on the ground, and when silent he had the look of one who inwardly debates a grave question.

"Have you been into the country?" was one of his first inquiries.

"No. I spent the morning with my sisters, and in the afternoon I had to see a lady in Chelsea."

"Your sisters are older than yourself?"

"Yes, some years older."

"Is it long since you went to live apart from them?"

"We have never had a home of our own since I was quite a child."

And, after a moment's hesitation, she went on to give a brief account of her history. Widdowson listened with the closest attention, his lips twitching now and then, his eyes half closed. — But for cheek-bones that were too prominent and nostrils rather too large, he was not ill featured. No particular force of character declared itself in his countenance, and his mode of speech did not suggest a very active brain. Speculating again about his age, Monica concluded that he must be two or three and forty, in spite of the fact that his grizzled beard argued for a higher figure. He had brown hair untouched by any sign of advanced life, his teeth were white and regular, and something — she could not make clear to her mind exactly what — convinced her that he had a right to judge himself comparatively young.

"I supposed you were not a Londoner," he said, when she came to a pause.

"How?"

"Your speech. — Not," he added quickly, "that you have any provincial accent. And even if you had been a Londoner you would not have shown it in that way."

He seemed to be reproving himself for a blunder, and after a short silence asked in a tone of kindness:

"Do you prefer the town?"

"In some ways — not in all."

"I am glad you have relatives here, and friends. So many young ladies come up from the country who are quite alone."

"Yes, many."

Their progress to familiarity could hardly have been slower. Now and then they spoke with a formal coldness which threatened absolute silence. Monica's brain was so actively at work that she lost consciousness of the people who were moving about them, and at times her companion was scarcely more to her than a voice.

They had walked along the whole front of the park, and were near Chelsea Bridge. Widdowson gazed at the pleasure boats lying below on the strand, and said diffidently:

"Would you care to go on the river?"

The proposal was so unexpected that Monica looked up with a startled air. She had not thought of the man as likely to offer any kind of amusement.

"It would be pleasant, I think," he added. "The tide is still running up. We might go very quietly for a mile or two, and be back as soon as you like."

"Yes, I should like it."

He brightened up, and moved with a livelier step. In a few minutes they had chosen their boat, had pushed off, and were gliding to the middle of the broad water. Widdowson managed the sculls without awkwardness, but by no means like a man well trained in this form of exercise. On sitting down, he had taken off his hat, stowed it away, and put on a little travelling-cap, which he drew from his pocket. Monica thought this became him. After all, he was not a companion to be ashamed of. She looked with pleasure at his white hairy hands with their firm grip; then at his boots — very good boots indeed. He had gold links in his white shirt-cuffs, and a gold watch-guard chosen with a gentleman's taste.

"I am at your service," he said, with an approach to gaiety. "Direct me. Shall we go quickly — some distance, or only just a little quicker than the tide would float us?"

"Which you like. To row much would make you too hot."

"You would like to go some distance — I see."

"No, no. Do exactly what you like. — Of course we must be back in an hour or two."

He drew out his watch.

"It's now ten minutes past six, and there is daylight till nine or after. When do you wish to be home?"

"Not much later than nine," Monica answered, with the insincerity of prudence.

"Then we will just go quietly along. — I wish we could have started early in the afternoon. But that may be for another day, I hope."

On her lap Monica had the little brown-paper parcel which contained her present. She saw that Widdowson glanced at it from time to time, but she could not bring herself to explain what it was.

"I was very much afraid that I should not see you to-day," he said, as they glided softly by Chelsea Embankment.

"But I promised to come if it was fine."

"Yes. I feared something might prevent you. You are very kind to give me your company." He was looking at the tips of her little boots. "I can't say how I thank you."

Much embarrassed, Monica could only gaze at one of the sculls, as it rose and fell, the water dripping from it in bright beads.

"Last year," he pursued, "I went on the river two or three times, but alone. This year I haven't been in a boat till to-day."

"You prefer driving?"

"Oh, it's only chance. I do drive a good deal, however. I wish it were possible to take you through the splendid country I saw a day or two ago — down in Surrey. Perhaps some day you will let me. — I live rather a lonely life, as you see. I have a housekeeper; no relative lives with me. My only relative in London is a sister-in-law, and we very seldom meet."

"But don't you employ yourself in any way?"

"I'm very idle. But that's partly because I have worked very hard and hopelessly all my life — till a year and a half ago. I began to earn my own living when I was fourteen, and now I am forty-four — to-day."

"This is your birthday?" said Monica, with an odd look the other could not understand.

"Yes. — I only remembered it a few hours ago. Strange that such a treat should have been provided for me. — Yes, I am very idle. A year and a half ago my only brother died. He had been very successful in life, and he left me what I regard as a fortune, though it was only a small part of what he had."

The listener's heart throbbed. Without intending it, she pulled the tiller so that the boat began to turn towards land.

"The left hand a little," said Widdowson, smiling correctively. "That's right. — Many days I don't leave home. I am fond of reading, and now I make up for all the time lost in years gone by. — Do you care for books?"

"I never read very much, and I feel very ignorant."

"But that is only for want of opportunity, I'm sure."

He glanced at the brown-paper parcel. Acting on an impulse which perturbed her Monica began to slip off the loosely tied string, and to unfold the paper.

"I thought it was a book!" exclaimed Widdowson merrily, when she had revealed a part of her present.

"When you told me your name," said Monica, "I ought perhaps to have told you mine. It's written here. My sisters gave me this to-day."

She offered the little volume. He took it as though it were something fragile, and — the sculls fixed under his elbows — turned to the fly-leaf.

"What? It is *your* birthday?"

"Yes. I am twenty-one."

"Will you let me shake hands with you?" His pressure of her fingers was the lightest possible. "Now that's rather a strange thing — isn't it? Oh, I remember this book very well, though I haven't seen it or heard of it for twenty years. My mother used to read it on Sundays. — And it is really your birthday? — I am more than twice your age, Miss Madden."

The last remark was uttered anxiously, mournfully. Then, as if to reassure himself by exerting physical strength, he drove the boat along with half-a-dozen vigorous strokes. Monica was rustling over the pages, but without seeing them.

"I don't think," said her companion presently, "you are very well contented with your life in that house of business."

"No, I am not."

"I have heard a good deal of the hardships of such a life. Will you tell me something about yours?"

Readily she gave him a sketch of her existence from Sunday to Sunday, but without indignation, and as if the subject had no great interest for her.

"You must be very strong," was Widdowson's comment.

"The lady I went to see this afternoon told me I looked ill."

"Of course I can see the effects of overwork. My wonder is that you endure it at all. — Is that lady an old acquaintance?"

Monica answered with all necessary detail, and went on to mention the proposal that had been made to her. The hearer reflected, and put further questions. Unwilling to speak of the little capital she possessed, Monica told him that her sisters might perhaps help her to live whilst she was learning a new occupation. But Widdowson had become abstracted; he ceased pulling, crossed his arms on the oars, and watched other boats that were near. Two deep wrinkles, rippling in their course, had formed across his forehead, and his eyes widened in a gaze of complete abstraction at the farther shore.

"Yes," fell from him at length, as though in continuation of something he had been saying, "I began to earn my bread when I was fourteen. — My father was an auctioneer at Brighton. A few years after his marriage he had a bad illness, which left him completely deaf. His partnership with another man was dissolved, and as things went worse and worse with him, my mother started a lodging-house, which somehow supported us for a long time. She was a sensible, good, and brave woman. — I'm afraid my father had a good many faults that made her life hard. He was of a violent temper, and of course the deafness didn't improve it. Well, one day a cab knocked him down in the King's Road, and from that injury, though not till a year after, he died. — There were only two children; I was the elder. My mother couldn't keep me at school very long, so, at fourteen, I was sent into the office of the man who had been my father's partner, to serve him and learn the business. I did serve him for years, and for next to no payment, but he taught me nothing more than he could help. He was one of those heartless, utterly selfish men that one meets too often in the business world. I ought never to have been sent there, for my father had always an ill opinion of him; but he pretended a friendly interest in me — just, I am convinced, to make the use of me that he did."

He was silent, and began rowing again.

"What happened then?" asked Monica.

"I mustn't make out that I was a faultless boy," he continued, with the smile that graved wrinkles about his eyes, "quite the opposite. I had a good deal of my father's temper; I often behaved very badly to my mother; what I needed was some stern but conscientious man to look after me and make me work. In my spare time I lay about on the shore, or got into mischief with other boys. It needed my mother's death to make a more sensible fellow of me, and by that time it was too late. I mean I was too old to be trained into profitable business-habits. Up to nineteen I had been little more than an errand and office boy, and all through the after years I never got a much better position."

"I can't understand that," remarked Monica thoughtfully.

"Why not?"

"You seem to — to be the kind of man that would make your way."

"Do I?" The description pleased him; he laughed cheerfully. "But I never found what my way was to be. I have always hated office-work, and business of every kind; yet I could never see an opening in any other direction. I have been all my life a clerk — like so many thousands of other men. Nowadays, if I happen to be in the City[1] when all the clerks are coming away from business, I feel an inexpressible pity for them. I feel I should like to find two or three of the hardest driven, and just divide my superfluous income between them. A clerk's life — a life of the office without any hope of rising — that is a hideous fate!"

"But your brother got on well. Why didn't he help you?"

"We couldn't agree. We always quarrelled."

"Are you really so ill-tempered?"

It was asked in Monica's most naïve tone, with a serious air of investigation which at first confused Widdowson, then made him laugh.

"Since I was a lad," he replied, "I have never quarrelled with any one except my brother. I think it's only very unreasonable people that irritate me. Some men have told me that I was far too easy-going, too good-natured. Certainly I *desire* to be good-natured. But I don't easily make friends; as a rule I can't talk to strangers. I keep so much to myself that those who know me only a little think me surly and unsociable."

"So your brother always refused to help you?"

"It wasn't easy for him to help me. He got into a stockbroker's, and went on step by step until he had saved a little money; then he speculated in all sorts of ways. He couldn't employ me himself — and if he could have done, we should never have got on together. It was impossible for him to recommend me to any one except as a clerk. — He was a born money-maker. I'll give you an example of how he grew rich. In consequence of some mortgage-business, he came into possession of a field at Clapham. As late as 1875, this field brought him only a rent of forty pounds; it was freehold property, and he refused many offers of purchase. Well, in 1885, the year before he died, the ground-rents from that field — now covered with houses — were seven hundred and ninety pounds a year. That's how men get on who have capital, and know how to use it. If *I* had had capital, it would never have yielded me more than three or four per cent. I was doomed to work for other people who were growing rich. — It doesn't matter much now, except that so many years of life have been lost."

"Had your brother any children?"

"No children. All the same, it astonished me when I heard his will; I had expected nothing. In one day — in one hour — I passed from slavery to freedom, from poverty to more than comfort. — We never *hated* each other; I don't want you to think that."

"But — didn't it bring you friends, as well as comfort?"

---

1 "The City" refers to the business and financial district of London, which is located within its medieval boundaries.

"Oh," he laughed, "I am not so rich as to have people pressing for my acquaintance. I have only about six hundred a year."

Monica drew in her breath, silently; then gazed at the distance.

"No, I haven't made any new friends. The one or two men I care for are not much better off than I used to be, and I always feel ashamed to ask them to come and see me. Perhaps they think I shun them because of their position, and I don't know how to justify myself. Life has always been full of worrying problems for me. I can't take things in the simple way that comes natural to other men."

"Don't you think we ought to be turning back, Mr. Widdowson?"

"Yes, we will. — I am sorry the time goes so quickly."

When a few minutes had passed in silence, he asked:

"Do you feel that I am no longer quite a stranger to you, Miss Madden?"

"Yes — you have told me so much."

"It's very kind of you to listen so patiently. I wish I had more interesting things to tell, but you see what a dull life mine has been." He paused, and let the boat waver on the stream for a moment. "When I dared to speak to you last Sunday I had only the faintest hope that you would grant me your acquaintance. You can't, I am sure, repent of having done me that kindness —?"

"One never knows — I doubted whether I ought to talk with a stranger —"

"Rightly — quite rightly. It was my perseverance — you saw, I hope, that I could never dream of giving you offence. The rule is necessary, but you see there may be exceptional cases." He was giving a lazy stroke now and then, which, as the tide was still, just moved the boat onwards. "I saw something in your face that *compelled* me to speak to you. — And now we may really be friends, I hope?"

"Yes — I can think of you as a friend Mr. Widdowson."

A large boat was passing, with four or five young men and girls, who sang in good time and tune. Only a song of the music-hall or of the nigger minstrels,[1] but it sounded pleasantly with the plash of oars. A fine sunset had begun to glow upon the river; its warmth gave a tone to Monica's thin cheeks.

"And you will let me see you again before long? — Let me drive you to Hampton Court next Sunday — or any other place you would choose."

"Very likely I shall be invited to my friend's in Chelsea."

"Do you seriously think of leaving the shop?"

"I don't know — I must have time to think about it —"

"Yes — yes. But if I write a line to you, say on Friday, would you let me know whether you can come?"

---

1 Music halls were theatres in which popular variety entertainment was performed (called vaudeville in North America). "Nigger minstrels" were performers in blackface who presented comic variety acts comprising songs and skits.

"Please to let me refuse for next Sunday. — The one after, perhaps —"

He bent his head, looked desperately grave, and drove the boat on. Monica was disturbed, but held to her resolution, which Widdowson silently accepted. The rest of the way they exchanged only brief sentences, about the beauty of the sky, the scenes on river or bank, and other impersonal matters. After landing, they walked in silence towards Chelsea Bridge.

"Now I must go quickly home," said Monica.

"But how?"

"By train — from York Road to Walworth Road."

Widdowson cast a curious glance at her. One would have imagined that he found something to disapprove in this ready knowledge of London transit.

"I will go with you to the station, then."

Without a word spoken, they walked the short distance to York Road. Monica took her ticket, and offered a hand for good-bye.

"I may write to you," said Widdowson, his face set in an expression of anxiety, "and make an appointment, if possible, for the Sunday after next?"

"I shall be glad to come — if I can."

"It will be a very long time to me."

With a faint smile, Monica hurried away to the platform. In the train she looked like one whose mind is occupied with grave trouble. Fatigue had suddenly overcome her; she leaned back and closed her eyes.

At a street corner very near to Messrs. Scotcher's establishment she was intercepted by a tall, showily dressed, rather coarse-featured girl, who seemed to have been loitering about. It was Miss Eade.

"I want to speak to you, Miss Madden. Where did you go with Mr. Bullivant this morning?"

The voice could not have been more distinctive of a London shop-girl; its tone signified irritation.

"With Mr. Bullivant? I went nowhere with him."

"But I *saw* you both get into the 'bus in Kennington Park Road."

"Did you?" Monica returned coldly. "I can't help it if Mr. Bullivant happened to be going the same way."

"Oh, very well! I though you was to be trusted. It's nothing to me —"

"You behave very foolishly, Miss Eade," exclaimed the other, whose nerves at this moment would not allow her to use patience with the jealous girl. "I can only tell you that I have never thought again of Mr. Bullivant since he left the 'bus somewhere in Clapham Road. I'm tired of talking about such things."

"Now, see here, don't be cross. Come and walk a bit and tell me —"

"I'm too tired. And there's nothing whatever to tell you."

"Oh, well, if you're going to be narsty!"

Monica walked on, but the girl caught her up.

"Don't be so sharp with me, Miss Madden. I don't say as you wanted him to go in the 'bus with you. But you might tell me what he had to say."

"Nothing at all; except that he wished to know where I was going, which was no business of his. I did what I could for you. I told him that if he asked you to go up the river with him I felt sure you wouldn't refuse."

"Oh, you did!" Miss Eade threw up her head. "I don't think it was a very delicate thing to say."

"You are very unreasonable. I myself don't think it was very delicate, but haven't you worried me to say something of the kind?"

"No, that I'm sure I haven't! Worrited you, indeed!"

"Then please never to speak to me on the subject again. I'm tired of it."

"And what did *he* say, when you'd said that?"

"I can't remember."

"Oh, you *are* narsty to-day! Really you are! If it had been the other way about, I'd never have treated *you* like this, that I wouldn't."

"Good-night!"

They were close to the door by which Messrs. Scotcher's resident employees entered at night. Monica had taken out her latch-key. But Miss Eade could not endure the thought of being left in torturing ignorance.

"*Do* tell me!" she whispered. "I'll do anything for you I can. Don't be unkind, Miss Madden!"

Monica turned back again.

"If I were you, I wouldn't be so silly. I can't do more than assure you and promise you that I shall *never* listen to Mr. Bullivant."

"But what did he say about *me*, dear?"

"Nothing."

Miss Eade kept a mortified silence.

"You had much better not think of him at all. I would have more pride. I wish I could make you see him as *I* do."

"And you did really speak about me? — Oh, I do wish you'd find some one to go out with. Then, perhaps —"

Monica stood still, hesitated, at length said:

"Well — I *have* found some one."

"You have?" The girl all but danced with joy. "You really have?"

"Yes — so now don't trouble me any more."

This time she was allowed to turn back and enter the house.

No one else had yet come in. Monica ate a mouthful of bread and cheese, which was in readiness on the long table down in the basement, and at once went to bed. But no welcome drowsiness fell upon her. At half-past eleven, when two of the other five girls who slept in the room made their appearance, she was still changing uneasily from side to side. They lit the gas (it was not turned off till midnight, after which hour the late arrivals had to use a candle of their own procuring), and began a live-ly conversation on the events of the day. Afraid of being obliged to talk, Monica feigned sleep.

At twelve, just as the gas went out, another pair came to repose. They had been quarrelling, and were very gloomy. After a long and acrimonious discussion in the dark as to which of them should find a candle, — it ended in one of the girls who were in bed impatiently supplying a light, — they began sullenly to throw off their garments.

"Is Miss Madden awake?" said one of them, looking in Monica's direction.

There was no reply.

"She's picked up some feller to-day," continued the speaker, lowering her voice, and glancing round at her companions with a grin. "Or else she's had him all along — I shouldn't wonder."

Heads were put forward eagerly, and inquiries whispered.

"He's oldish, I should say. I caught sight of them just as they was going off in a boat from Battersea Park, but I couldn't see his face very well. He looked rather like Mr. Thomas."

Mr. Thomas was a member of the drapery firm, a man of fifty, ugly and austere. At this description the listeners giggled and uttered exclamations.

"Was he a swell?"[1] asked one.

"Shouldn't wonder if he was. You can trust Miss M. to keep her eyes open. She's one of the sly and quiet 'uns."

"Oh, *is* she!" murmured another enviously. "She's just one of those as gets made a fool of—that's *my* opinion."

The point was argued for some minutes. It led to talk about Miss Eade, who was treated with frank contempt because of her ill-disguised pursuit of a mere counter-man. These other damsels had, at present, more exalted views, for they were all younger than Miss Eade.

Just before one o'clock, when silence had reigned for a quarter of an hour, there entered with much bustle the last occupant of the bed-room. She was a young woman with a morally unenviable reputation, though some of her colleagues certainly envied her. Money came to her with remarkable readiness whenever she had need of it. As usual, she began to talk very loud, at first with innocent vulgarity; exciting a little laughter, she became anecdotic and very scandalous. It took her a long time to disrobe, and when the candle was out she still had her richest story to relate, — of point so Rabelaisian[2] that one or two voices made themselves heard in serious protest. The gifted anecdotist replied with a long laugh, then cried, "Good-night, young ladies!" and sank peacefully to slumber.

As for Monica, she saw the white dawn peep at the window, and closed her tear-stained eyes only when the life of a new week had begun noisily in Walworth Road.

---

1 A swell is a man of means and of good social standing. The term also carries the connotation of dash or flair.

2 I.e., in the style of François Rabelais, the sixteenth-century French humorist and satirist whose works are earthy and bawdy in the extreme.

CHAPTER VI.

A CAMP OF THE RESERVE.

In consequence of letters exchanged during the week, next Sunday brought the three Miss Maddens to Queen's Road, to lunch with Miss Barfoot. Alice had recovered from her cold, but was still ailing, and took rather a gloomy view of the situation she had lately reviewed with such courage. Virginia maintained her enthusiastic faith in Miss Nunn, and was prepared to reverence Miss Barfoot with hardly less fervour. Both of them found it difficult to understand their young sister, who, in her letters, had betrayed distaste for the change of career proposed to her. They were received with the utmost kindness, and all greatly enjoyed their afternoon, for not even Monica's prejudice against a house, which in her own mind she had stigmatized as "an old-maid factory," could resist the charm of the hostess.

Though Miss Barfoot had something less than a woman's average stature, the note of her presence was personal dignity. She was handsome, and her carriage occasionally betrayed a consciousness of the fact. According to circumstances, she bore herself as the lady of aristocratic tastes, as a genial woman of the world, or as the fervid prophetess of female emancipation, and each character was supported with a spontaneity, a good-natured confidence, which inspired liking and respect. A brilliant complexion and eyes that sparkled with habitual cheerfulness gave her the benefit of doubt when her age was in question; her style of dress, gracefully ornate, would have led a stranger to presume her a wedded lady of some distinction. Yet Mary Barfoot had known many troubles, poverty among them. Her experiences and struggles bore a close resemblance to those which Rhoda Nunn had gone through, and the time of trial had lasted longer. Mental and moral stamina would have assured her against such evils of celibacy as appeared in the elder Maddens, but it was to a change of worldly fortune that she owed this revival of youthful spirit and energy in middle life.

"You and I must be friends," she said to Monica, holding the girl's soft little hand. "We are both black but comely."

The compliment to herself seemed the most natural thing in the world. Monica blushed with pleasure, and could not help laughing.

It was all but decided that Monica should become a pupil at the school in Great Portland Street. In a brief private conversation, Miss Barfoot offered to lend her the money that might be needful.

"Nothing but a business transaction, Miss Madden. You can give me security; you shall repay me at your convenience. If, in the end, this occupation doesn't please you, you will at all events have regained health. It is clear to me that you mustn't go on in that dreadful place you described to Miss Nunn."

The visitors took their leave at about five o'clock.

"Poor things! Poor things!" sighed Miss Barfoot, when she was alone with her friend. "What can we possibly do for the older ones?"

"They are excellent creatures," said Rhoda; "kind, innocent women; but useful for nothing except what they have done all their lives. The eldest can't teach seriously, but she can keep young children out of mischief and give them a nice way of speaking. Her health is breaking down, you can see."

"Poor woman! One of the saddest types."

"Decidedly. Virginia isn't quite so depressing — but how childish!"

"They all strike me as childish. Monica is a dear little girl; it seemed a great absurdity to talk to her about business. Of course she must find a husband."

"I suppose so."

Rhoda's tone of slighting concession amused her companion.

"My dear, after all we don't desire the end of the race."

"No, I suppose not," Rhoda admitted with a laugh.

"A word of caution. Your zeal is eating you up. At this rate, you will hinder our purpose. We have no mission to prevent girls from marrying suitably, — only to see that those who can't shall have a means of living with some satisfaction."

"What chance is there that this girl will marry suitably?"

"Oh, who knows? At all events, there will be more likelihood of it if she comes into our sphere."

"Really? Do you know any man that would dream of marrying her?"

"Perhaps not, at present."

It was clear that Miss Barfoot stood in some danger of becoming subordinate to her more vehement friend. Her little body, for all its natural dignity, put her at a disadvantage in the presence of Rhoda, who towered above her with rather imperious stateliness. Her suavity was no match for Rhoda's vigorous abruptness. But the two were very fond of each other, and by this time thought themselves able safely to dispense with the forms at first imposed by their mutual relations.

"If she marry at all," declared Miss Nunn, "she will marry badly. The family is branded. They belong to the class we know so well — with no social position, and unable to win an individual one. I must find a name for that ragged regiment."

Miss Barfoot regarded her friend thoughtfully.

"Rhoda, what comfort have you for the poor in spirit?"

"None whatever, I'm afraid. My mission is not to them."

After a pause, she added:

"They have their religious faith, I suppose. — And it's answerable for a good deal."

"It would be a terrible responsibility to rob them of it," remarked the elder woman gravely.

Rhoda made a gesture of impatience.

"It's a terrible responsibility to do anything at all. But I'm glad" — she laughed scornfully — "that it's not my task to release them."

Mary Barfoot mused, a compassionate shadow on her fine face.

"I don't think we can do without the spirit of that religion," she said at length, "the essential human spirit. These poor women — one ought to be very tender with them. I don't like your 'ragged regiment' phrase. When I grow old and melancholy, I think I shall devote myself to poor hopeless and purposeless women, — try to warm their hearts a little before they go hence."

"Admirable!" murmured Rhoda, smiling. "But in the meantime they cumber us; we have to fight."

She threw forward her arms, as though with spear and buckler. Miss Barfoot was smiling at this Palladian attitude[1] when a servant announced two ladies, Mrs. Smallbrook and Miss Haven. They were aunt and niece; the former a tall, ungainly, sharp-featured widow; the latter a sweet-faced, gentle, sensible-looking girl of five-and-twenty.

"I am so glad you are back again," exclaimed the widow, as she shook hands with Miss Barfoot, speaking in a hard, unsympathetic voice. "I do so want to ask your advice about an interesting girl who has applied to me. I'm afraid her past won't bear looking into, but most certainly she is a reformed character. Winifred is most favourably impressed with her —"

Miss Haven, the Winifred in question, began to talk apart with Rhoda Nunn.

"I do wish my aunt wouldn't exaggerate so," she said in a subdued voice, whilst Mrs. Smallbrook still talked loudly and urgently. "I never said that I was favourably impressed. The girl protests far too much; she has played on aunt's weaknesses, I fear."

"But who is she?"

"Oh, some one who lost her character long ago, and lives, I should say, on charitable people. Just because I said that she must once have had a very nice face, aunt misrepresents me in this way, — it's too bad."

"Is she an educated person?" Miss Barfoot was heard to ask.

"Not precisely well educated."

"Of the lower classes, then?"

"I don't like that term, you know. Of the *poorer* classes."

"She never was a lady," put in Miss Haven, quietly but decidedly.

"Then I fear I can be of no use," said the hostess, betraying some of her secret satisfaction in being able thus to avoid Mrs. Smallbrook's

---

1 I.e., in the attitude of Pallas Athena, the Greek goddess of wisdom who sprang, fully armed, from the head of Zeus. Athena was also the goddess of arts and skills, including military ones. There are other parallels between Athena and Rhoda Nunn. Unlike most members of the Classical Pantheon, Athena was a virgin; she was formidable in her power, and beautiful in a somewhat austere and masculine way.

request. Winifred, a pupil at Great Portland Street, was much liked by both her teachers, but the aunt, with her ceaseless philanthropy at other people's expense, could only be considered a bore.

"But surely you don't limit your humanity, Miss Barfoot, by the artificial divisions of society."

"I think those divisions are anything but artificial," replied the hostess good-humouredly. "In the uneducated classes I have no interest whatever. You have heard me say so."

"Yes, but I cannot think — isn't that just a little narrow?"

"Perhaps so. I choose my sphere, that's all. Let those work for the lower classes (I must call them lower, for they are, in every sense), let those work for them who have a call to do so. I have none. I must keep to my own class."

"But surely, Miss Nunn," cried the widow, turning to Rhoda, "we work for the abolition of all unjust privilege? To us, is not a woman a woman?"

"I am obliged to agree with Miss Barfoot. I think that as soon as we begin to meddle with uneducated people, all our schemes and views are unsettled. We have to learn a new language, for one thing. But your missionary enterprise is admirable."

"For my part," declared Mrs. Smallbrook, "I aim at the solidarity of woman. You, at all events, agree with me, Winifred?"

"I really don't think, aunt, that there can be any solidarity of ladies with servant girls," responded Miss Haven, encouraged by a look from Rhoda.

"Then I grieve that your charity falls so far below the Christian standard."

Miss Barfoot firmly guided the conversation to a more hopeful subject.

Not many people visited this house. Every Wednesday evening, from half-past eight to eleven, Miss Barfoot was at home to any of her acquaintances, including her pupils, who chose to call upon her; but this was in the nature of an association with recognized objects. Of society in the common sense Miss Barfoot saw very little; she had no time to sacrifice in the pursuit of idle ceremonies. By the successive deaths of two relatives, a widowed sister and an uncle, she had come into possession of a modest fortune; but no thought of a life such as would have suggested itself to most women in her place ever tempted her. Her studies had always been of a very positive nature; her abilities were of a kind uncommon in women, or at all events very rarely developed in one of her sex. She could have managed a large and complicated business, could have filled a place on a board of directors, have taken an active part in municipal government — nay, perchance in national. And this turn of intellect consisted with many traits of character so strongly feminine that people who knew her best thought of her with as much tenderness as admiration. She did not seek to become known as the leader of a "movement," yet her quiet work was probably more effectual than the public career of women who propagandize for female emancipation. Her aim was to draw from the overstocked profession of teaching as many capable young women as she could lay hands on, and to fit them for certain of the pursuits nowadays thrown open to their sex. She held the conviction that whatever man could do, woman could do equally well — those tasks only excepted which demand great physical strength. At her instance, and with help from her purse, two girls were preparing themselves to be pharmaceutical chemists; two others had been aided by her to open a bookseller's shop; and several who had clerkships in view received an admirable training at her school in Great Portland Street.

Thither every week-day morning Miss Barfoot and Rhoda repaired; they arrived at nine o'clock, and with an hour's interval work went on until five.

Entering by the private door of a picture-cleaner's shop, they ascended to the second story, where two rooms had been furnished like comfortable offices; two smaller on the floor above served for dressing-rooms. In one of the offices, type-writing and occasionally other kinds of work that demanded intelligence were carried on by three or four young women regularly employed; to superintend this department was Miss Nunn's chief duty, together with business correspondence under the principal's direction. In the second room, Miss Barfoot instructed her pupils, never more than three being with her at a time. A bookcase full of works on the Woman-question and allied topics served as a circulating library; volumes were lent without charge to the members of this little society. Once a month Miss Barfoot or Miss Nunn, by turns, gave a brief address on some set subject; the hour was four o'clock, and about a dozen hearers generally assembled. Both worked very hard. Miss Barfoot did not look upon her enterprise as a source of pecuniary profit, but she had made the establishment more than self-supporting. Her pupils increased in number, and the working department promised occupation for a larger staff than was at present engaged. The young women, in general, answered their friend's expectations, but of course there were disappointing instances. One of these had caused Miss Barfoot special distress. A young girl whom she had released from a life of much hardship, and who, after a couple of months' trial, bade fair to develop noteworthy ability, of a sudden disappeared. She was without relatives in London, and Miss Barfoot's endeavours to find her proved for several weeks futile. Then came news of her; she was living as the mistress of a married man. Every effort was made to bring her back, but the girl resisted; presently she again passed out of sight, and now more than a year had elapsed since Miss Barfoot's last interview with her.

This Monday morning, among letters delivered at the house, was one from the strayed girl. Miss Barfoot read it in private, and throughout the day remained unusually grave. At five o'clock, when staff and pupils had all departed, she sat for a while in meditation, then spoke to Rhoda, who was glancing over a book by the window.

"Here's a letter I should like you to read."

"Something that has been troubling you since morning, isn't it?"

"Yes."

Rhoda took the sheet and quickly ran through its contents. Her face hardened, and she threw down the letter with a smile of contempt.

"What do you advise?" asked the elder woman, closely observing her.

"An answer in two lines — with a cheque enclosed, if you see fit."

"Does that really meet the case?"

"More than meets it, I should say."

Miss Barfoot pondered.

"I am doubtful. That is a letter of despair, and I can't close my ears to it."

"You had an affection for the girl. Help her, by all means, if you feel compelled to. But you would hardly dream of taking her back again?"

"That's the point. Why shouldn't I?"

"For one thing," replied Rhoda, looking coldly down upon her friend, "you will never do any good with her. For another, she isn't a suitable companion for the girls she would meet here."

"I can't be sure of either objection. She acted with deplorable rashness, with infatuation, but I never discovered any sign of evil in her. Did you?"

"Evil? Well, what does the word mean? I am not a puritan, and I don't judge her as the ordinary woman would. But I think she has put herself altogether beyond our sympathy. She was twenty-two years old, — no child, — and she acted with her eyes open. No deceit was practised with her. She knew the man had a wife, and she was base enough to accept a share of his — attentions. Do you advocate polygamy? That is an intelligible position, I admit. It is one way of meeting the social difficulty. But not mine."

"My dear Rhoda, don't enrage yourself."

"I will try not to."

"But I can't see the temptation to do so. Come and sit down, and talk quietly. — No, I have no fondness for polygamy. I find it very hard to understand how she could act as she did. But a mistake, however wretched, mustn't condemn a woman for life. That's the way of the world, and decidedly it mustn't be ours."

"On this point, I practically agree with the world."

"I see you do, and it astonishes me. You are going through curious changes, in several respects. A year ago you didn't speak of her like this."

"Partly because I didn't know you well enough to speak my mind. Partly — yes, I have changed a good deal, no doubt. But I should never have proposed to take her by the hand and let bygones be bygones. That is an amiable impulse, but anti-social."

"A favourite word on your lips just now, Rhoda. Why is it anti-social?"

"Because one of the supreme social needs of our day is the education of women in self-respect and self-restraint. There are plenty of people — men chiefly, but a few women also of a certain temperament — who cry for a reckless individualism in these matters. They would tell you that she behaved laudably, that she was *living out herself* — and things of that kind. But I didn't think you shared such views."

"I don't, altogether. — 'The education of women in self-respect.' Very well. Here is a poor woman whose self-respect has given way under grievous temptation. Circumstances have taught her that she made a wild mistake. The man gives her up, and bids her live as she can; she is reduced to beggary. Now, in that position a girl is tempted to sink still further. The letter of two lines and an enclosed cheque would as likely as not plunge her into depths from which she could never be rescued. It would assure her that there was no hope. On the other hand, we have it in our power to attempt that very education of which you speak. She has brains, and doesn't belong to the vulgar. It seems to me that you are moved by illogical impulses — and certainly anything but kind ones."

Rhoda only grew more stubborn.

"You say she yielded to a grievous temptation. What temptation? Will it bear putting into words?"

"Oh yes, I think it will," answered Miss Barfoot, with her gentlest smile. "She fell in love with the man."

"Fell in love!" Concentration of scorn was in this echo. "Oh, for what isn't that phrase responsible!"

"Rhoda, let me ask you a question on which I have never ventured. Do you know what it is to be in love?"

Miss Nunn's strong features were moved as if by a suppressed laugh; the colour of her cheeks grew very slightly warm.

"I am a normal human being," she answered, with an impatient gesture. "I understand perfectly well what the phrase signifies."

"That is no answer, my dear. Have you ever been in love with any man."

"Yes. When I was fifteen."

"And not since," rejoined the other, shaking her head and smiling. "No, not since?"

"Thank heaven, no!"

"Then you are not very well able to judge this case. I, on the other hand, can judge it with the very largest understanding. — Don't smile so witheringly, Rhoda. — I shall neglect your advice for once."

"You will bring this girl back, and continue teaching her as before?"

"We have no one here that knows her, and with prudence she need never be talked about by those of our friends who did."

"Oh, weak — weak — weak!"

"For once I must act independently."

"Yes, and at a stroke change the whole character of your work. — You never proposed keeping a reformatory. Your aim is to help chosen girls, who promise to be of some use in the world. This Miss Royston represents the profitless average — no, she is below the average. Are you so blind as to imagine that any good will ever come of such a person? If you wish to save her from the streets, do so by all means. But to put her among your chosen pupils is to threaten your whole undertaking. Let it once become known — and it *would* become known — that a girl of that character came here, and your usefulness is at an end. In a year's time you will have to choose between giving up the school altogether, and making it a refuge for outcasts."

Miss Barfoot was silent. She tapped with her fingers on the table.

"Personal feeling is misleading you," Rhoda pursued. "Miss Royston had a certain cleverness, I grant, but do you think I didn't know that she would never become what you hoped? All her spare time was given to novel-reading. If every novelist could be strangled and thrown into the sea, we should have some chance of reforming women. The girl's nature was corrupted with sentimentality, like that of all but every woman who is intelligent enough to read what is called the best fiction, but not intelligent enough to understand its vice. Love — love — love; a sickening sameness of vulgarity. What is more vulgar than the ideal of novelists? They won't represent the actual world; it would be too dull for their readers. In real life, how many men and women *fall in love*? Not one in every ten thousand, I am convinced. Not one married pair in ten thousand have felt for each other as two or three couples do in every novel. There is the sexual instinct, of course, but that is quite a different thing; the novelists daren't talk about that. The paltry creatures daren't tell the one truth that would be profitable. The result is that women imagine themselves noble and glorious when they are most near the animals. This Miss Royston — when she rushed off to perdition, ten to one she had in mind some idiot heroine of a book. — Oh, I tell you that you are losing sight of your first duty. There are people enough to act the good Samaritan; *you* have quite another task in life. It is your work to train and encourage girls in a path as far as possible from that of the husband-hunter. Let them marry later, if they must; but at all events you will have cleared their views on the subject of marriage, and put them in a position to judge the man who offers himself. You will have taught them that marriage is an alliance of intellects, — not a means of support, or something more ignoble still. But to do this with effect you must show yourself relentless to female imbecility. If a girl gets to know that you have received back such a person as Miss Royston, she will be corrupted by your spirit of charity, — corrupted, at all events, for our purposes. The endeavour to give women a new soul is so difficult that we can't be cumbered by side-tasks, such as fishing foolish people out of the mud they have walked into. Charity for human weakness is all very well in its place, but it is precisely one of the virtues that you must *not* teach. You have to set an example of the sterner qualities — to discourage anything that resembles sentimentalism. And think if you illustrate in your own behaviour a sympathy for the very vice of character we are trying our hardest to extirpate!"

"This is a terrible harangue," said Miss Barfoot, when the passionate voice had been silent for a few ticks of the clock. "I quite enter into your point of view, but I think you go beyond practical zeal. — However, I will help the girl in some other way, if possible."

"I have offended you."

"Impossible to take offence at such obvious sincerity."

"But surely you grant the force of what I say?"

"We differ a good deal, Rhoda, on certain points which as a rule would never come up to interfere with our working in harmony. You have come to dislike the very thought of marriage — and everything of that kind. I think it's a danger you ought to have avoided. True, we wish to prevent girls from marrying just for the sake of being supported, and from degrading themselves as poor Bella Royston has done; but surely between ourselves we can admit that the vast majority of women would lead a wasted life if they did not marry."

"I maintain that the vast majority of women lead a vain and miserable life just because they *do* marry."

"Don't you blame the institution of marriage with what is chargeable to human fate? A vain and miserable life is the lot of nearly all mortals. Most women, whether they marry or not, will suffer and commit endless follies."

"Most women — as life is at present arranged for them. Things are changing, and we try to have our part in hastening a new order."

"Ah, we use words in a different sense. I speak of human nature, not of the effect of institutions."

"Now it is you who are unpractical. Those views lead only to pessimism and paralysis of effort."

Miss Barfoot rose.

"I give in to your objection against bringing the girl back to work here. I will help her in other ways. It's quite true that she isn't to be relied upon."

"Impossible to trust her in any detail of life. The pity is that her degradation can't be used as an object-lesson for our other girls."

"There again we differ. You are quite mistaken in your ideas of how the mind is influenced. The misery of Bella Royston would not in the least affect any other girl's way of thinking about the destiny of her sex. We must avoid exaggeration. If our friends get to think of us as fanatics, all our usefulness is over. The ideal we set up must be human. — Do you think now that we know one single girl who in her heart believes it is better never to love and never to marry?"

"Perhaps not," admitted Rhoda, more cheerful now that she had gained her point. "But we know several who will not dream of marrying unless reason urges them as strongly as inclination."

Miss Barfoot laughed.

"Pray, who ever distinguished in such a case between reason and inclination?"

"You are most unusually sceptical to-day," said Rhoda, with an impatient laugh.

"No, my dear. We happen to be going to the root of things, that's all. Perhaps it's as well to do so, now and then. — Oh, I admire you immensely, Rhoda. You are the ideal adversary of those care-nothing and believe-nothing women who keep the world back. But don't prepare for yourself a woeful disillusion."

"Take the case of Winifred Haven," urged Miss Nunn. "She is a good-looking and charming girl, and some one or other will want to marry her some day, no doubt."

"Forgive my interrupting you. There is great doubt. She has no money but what she can earn, and such girls, unless they are exceptionally beautiful, are very likely indeed to remain unsought."

"Granted. But let us suppose she has an offer. Should you fear for her prudence?"

"Winifred has much good sense," admitted the other. "I think she is in as little danger as any girl we know. But it wouldn't startle me if she made the most lamentable mistake. — Certainly I don't fear it. The girls of our class are not like the uneducated, who, for one reason or another, will marry almost any man rather than remain single. They have at all events personal delicacy. — But what I insist upon is, that Winifred would rather marry than not. And we must carefully bear that fact in mind. A strained ideal is as bad, practically, as no ideal at all. Only the most exceptional girl will believe it her duty to remain single as an example and support to what we call the odd women; — yet *that* is the most human way of urging what you desire. By taking up the proud position that a woman must be altogether independent of sexual things, you damage your cause. Let us be glad if we put a few of them in the way of living single with no more discontent than an unmarried man experiences."

"Surely that's an unfortunate comparison," said Rhoda coldly. "What man lives in celibacy? Consider that unmentionable fact, and then say whether I am wrong in refusing to forgive Miss Royston. Women's battle is not only against themselves. The necessity of the case demands what you call a strained ideal. — I am seriously convinced that before the female sex can be raised from its low level there will have to be a widespread revolt against sexual instinct. Christianity couldn't spread over the world without help of the ascetic ideal, and this great movement for woman's emancipation must also have its ascetics."

"I can't declare that you are wrong in that. Who knows? But it isn't good policy to preach it to our young disciples."

"I shall respect your wish; but —"

Rhoda paused and shook her head.

"My dear," said the elder woman gravely, "believe me that the less we talk or think about such things, the better for the peace of us all. The odious fault of working-class girls, in town and country alike, is that they are absorbed in pre-occupation with their animal nature. We, thanks to our education and the tone of our society, manage to keep that in the background. Don't interfere with this satisfactory state of things. Be content to show our girls that it is their duty to lead a life of effort — to earn their bread and to cultivate their minds. Simply ignore marriage — that's the wisest. Behave as if the thing didn't exist. You will do positive harm by taking the other course — the aggressive course."

"I shall obey you."

"Good, humble creature!" laughed Miss Barfoot. "Come, let us be off to Chelsea. — Did Miss Grey finish that copy for Mr. Houghton?"

"Yes, it has gone to post."

"Look, here's a big manuscript from our friend the antiquary. Two of the girls must get to work on it at once in the morning."

Manuscripts entrusted to them were kept in a fire-proof safe. When this had been locked up, the ladies went to their dressing-room and prepared for departure. The people who lived on the premises were responsible for cleaning the rooms and other care; to them Rhoda delivered the door-keys.

Miss Barfoot was grave and silent on the way home. Rhoda, annoyed at the subject that doubtless occupied her friend's thoughts, gave herself up to reflections of her own.

CHAPTER VII.

A SOCIAL ADVANCE.

A week's notice to her employers would release Monica from the engage-ment in Walworth Road; such notice must be given on Monday, so that, if she could at once make up her mind to accept Miss Barfoot's offer, the coming week would be her last of slavery behind the counter. On the way home from Queen's Road, Alice and Virginia pressed for immediate deci-sion; they were unable to comprehend how Monica could hesitate for another moment. The question of her place of abode had already been discussed; one of Miss Barfoot's young women, who lived at a convenient distance from Great Portland Street, would gladly accept a partner in her lodging, an arrangement to be recommended for its economy. Yet Monica shrank from speaking the final word.

"I don't know whether it's worth while," she said, after a long silence, as they drew near to York Road Station, whence they were to take train for Clapham Junction.

"Not worth while?" exclaimed Virginia. "You don't think it would be an improvement?"

"Yes, I suppose it would. — I shall see how I feel about it to-morrow morning."

She spent the evening at Lavender Hill, but without change in the mood thus indicated. A strange inquietude appeared in her behaviour. It was as though she were being urged to undertake something hard and repugnant.

On her return to Walworth Road, just as she came within sight of the shop, she observed a man's figure, some twenty yards distant, which instantly held her attention. The dim gas-light occasioned some uncer-tainty, but she believed the figure was that of Widdowson. He was walk-ing on the other side of the street, and away from her. When the man was exactly opposite Scotcher's establishment, he gazed in that direction, but without stopping. Monica hastened, fearing to be seen and approached. Already she had reached the door, when Widdowson — yes, he it was — turned abruptly to walk back again. His eye was at once upon her, but whether he recognized her or not Monica could not know; at that moment she opened the door and passed in.

A fit of trembling seized her, as if she had barely escaped some peril. In the passage she stood motionless, listening with the intensity of dread. She could hear footsteps on the pavement; she expected a ring at the door-bell. If he were so thoughtless as to come to the door, she would on no account see him.

But there was no ring, and after a few minutes' waiting she recovered her self-command. She had not made a mistake; even his features had been discernible as he turned towards her. Was this the first time that he had come to look at the place where she lived — possibly to spy upon her? She resented this behaviour, yet the feeling was confused with a certain satisfaction.

From one of the dormitories there was a view of Walworth Road. She ran upstairs, softly opened the door of that room and peeped in. The low burning gas showed her that only one bed had an occupant, who appeared to be asleep. Softly she went to the window, drew the blind aside, and looked down into the street. But Widdowson had disappeared. He might of course be on this side of the way.

"Who's that?" suddenly asked a voice from the occupied bed.

The speaker was Miss Eade. Monica looked at her, and nodded.

"You? What are you doing here?"

"I wanted to see if some one was standing outside."

"You mean *him*?"

The other nodded.

"I've got a beastly headache. I couldn't hold myself up, and I had to come home at eight o'clock. There's such pains all down my back too. — I shan't stay at this beastly place much longer. I don't want to get ill, like Miss Radford. Somebody went to see her at the hospital this afternoon, and she's awfully bad. — Well, have you seen him?"

"He's gone — good-night."

And Monica left the room.

Next day she notified her intention of leaving her employment. No questions were asked; she was of no particular importance; fifty, or, for the matter of that five score, young women equally capable could be found to fill her place.

On Tuesday morning there came a letter from Virginia, a few lines requesting her to meet her sisters, as soon as possible after closing time that evening, in front of the shop. "We have something *very delightful* to tell you. We *do hope* you gave notice to-day, as things are getting so bright in every direction."

At a quarter to ten she was able to run out, and close at hand were the two eagerly awaiting her.

"Mrs. Darby has found a place for Alice," began Virginia. "We heard by the afternoon post yesterday. A lady at Yatton wants a governess for two young children. Isn't it fortunate?"

"So delightfully convenient for what we were thinking of," put in the eldest, with her croaking voice. "Nothing could have been better."

"You mean about the school?" said Monica dreamily.

"Yes, the school," Virginia replied, with trembling earnestness. "Yatton is convenient both for Clevedon and Weston. Alice will be able to run over to both places, and make inquiries, and ascertain where the best opening would be."

Miss Nunn's suggestion, hitherto but timidly discussed, had taken hold upon their minds as soon as Alice received the practical call to her native region. Both were enthusiastic for the undertaking. It afforded them a novel subject of conversation, and inspirited them by seeming to restore their self-respect. After all, they might have a mission, a task in the world. They pictured themselves the heads of a respectable and thriving establishment, with subordinate teachers, with pleasant social relations; they felt young again, and capable of indefinite activity. Why had they not thought of this long ago? and thereupon they reverted to antistrophic laudation of Rhoda Nunn.

"Is it a good place?" their younger sister inquired.

"Oh, pretty good. Only twelve pounds a year, but nice people, Mrs. Darby says. They want me at once, and it is very likely that in a few weeks I shall go with them to the seaside."

"What *could* have been better?" cried Virginia. "Her health will be established, and in half a year, or less, we shall be able to come to a decision about the great step. — Oh, and have you given notice, darling?"

"Yes, I have."

Both clapped their hands like children. It was an odd little scene on the London pavement at ten o'clock at night; so intimately domestic amid surroundings the very antithesis of domesticity. Only a few yards away, a girl to whom the pavement was a place of commerce stood laughing with two men; the sound of her voice hinted to Monica the advisability of walking as they conversed, and they moved towards Walworth Road Station.

"We thought at first," said Virginia, "that when Alice had gone you might like to share my room; but then the distance from Great Portland Street would be a decided objection. I might move, but we doubt whether that would be worth while. It is so comfortable with Mrs. Conisbee, and for the short remaining time — Christmas, I should think, would be a very good time for opening. If it were possible to decide upon dear old Clevedon, of course we should prefer it; but perhaps Weston will offer more scope. Alice will weigh all the arguments on the spot. — Don't you envy her, Monica? Think of being *there* in this summer weather!"

"Why don't you go as well?" Monica asked.

"I? And take lodgings, you mean? We never thought of that. — But we still have to consider expenditure very seriously, you know. If possible, I must find employment for the rest of the year. Remember how very likely it is that Miss Nunn will have something to suggest for me. And then I think it will be of so much practical use for me to see her frequently for a few weeks. Already I have learnt so much from her and from Miss Barfoot. Their conversation is so encouraging. I feel that it is a training of the mind to be in contact with them."

"Yes, I quite share that view," said Alice, with tremulous earnestness. "Virginia can reap much profit from intercourse with them. They have the new ideas in education, and it would be so good if our school began with the advantage of quite a modern system."

Monica became silent. When her sisters had talked in the same strain for a quarter of an hour, she said absently:

"I wrote to Miss Barfoot last night, so I suppose I shall be able to move to those lodgings next Sunday."

It was eleven o'clock before they parted. Having taken leave of her sisters near the station, Monica turned to walk quickly home. She had gone about half the way, when her name was spoken just behind her, in Widdowson's voice. She stopped, and there stood the man, offering his hand.

"Why are you here at this time?" she asked, in an unsteady voice.

"Not by chance. — I had a hope that I might see you."

He was gloomy, and looked at her searchingly.

"I mustn't wait to talk now, Mr. Widdowson. It's very late."

"Very late indeed. — It surprised me to see you."

"Surprised you? Why should it?"

"I mean that it seemed so very unlikely — at this hour."

"Then how could you have hoped to see me?"

Monica walked on, with an air of displeasure, and Widdowson kept beside her, incessantly eyeing her countenance.

"No, I didn't really think of seeing you, Miss Madden. I wished to be near the place where you were, that was all."

"You saw me come out, I dare say."

"No."

"If you had done, you would have known that I came to meet two ladies, my sisters. I walked with them to the station, and now I am going home. You seem to think an explanation necessary —"

"Do forgive me! What right have I to ask anything of the kind? — But I have been very restless since Sunday. I wished so to meet you, if only for a few minutes. — Only an hour or two ago I posted a letter to you."

Monica said nothing.

"It was to ask you to meet me next Sunday, as we arranged. Shall you be able to do so?"

"I'm afraid I can't. At the end of this week I leave my place here, and on Sunday I shall be moving to another part of London."

"You are leaving? You have decided to make the change you spoke of?"

"Yes."

"And will you tell me where you are going to live?"

"In lodgings near Great Portland Street. I must say good night, Mr. Widdowson. I must, indeed."

"Please — do give me one moment!"

"I can't stay — I can't — good night!"

It was impossible for him to detain her. Ungracefully he caught at his hat, made the salute, and moved away with rapid, uneven strides. In less than half an hour he was back again at this spot. He walked past the shop many times, without pausing; his eyes devoured the front of the building, and noted those windows in which there was a glimmer of light. He saw girls enter by the private door, but Monica did not again show herself. Some time after midnight, when the house had long been dark and perfectly quiet, the uneasy man took a last look, and then sought a cab to convey him home.

The letter of which he had spoken reached Monica's hands next morning. It was a very respectful invitation to accompany the writer on a drive in Surrey. Widdowson proposed to meet her at Herne Hill railway station, where his vehicle would be waiting. "In passing, I shall be able to point out to you the house which has been my home for about a year."

As circumstances were, it would be hardly possible to accept this invitation without exciting curiosity in her sisters. The Sunday morning would be occupied, probably, in going to the new lodgings and making the acquaintance of her future companion there; in the afternoon, her sisters were to pay her a visit, as Alice had decided to start for Somerset on the Monday. She must write a refusal, but it was by no means her wish to discourage Widdowson altogether. The note which at length satisfied her ran thus:

"DEAR MR. WIDDOWSON,

"I am very sorry that it will be impossible for me to see you next Sunday. All day I shall be occupied. My eldest sister is leaving London, and Sunday will be my last day with her, perhaps for a long time. Please do not think that I make light of your kindness. When I am settled in my new life, I hope to be able to let you know how it suits me.

"Sincerely yours,
"MONICA MADDEN."

In a postscript she mentioned her new address. It was written in very small characters — perhaps an unpurposed indication of the misgiving with which she allowed herself to pen the words.

Two days went by, and again a letter from Widdowson was delivered.

"DEAR MISS MADDEN,

"My chief purpose in writing again so soon is to apologize sincerely for my behaviour on Tuesday evening. It was quite unjustifiable. The best way of confessing my fault is to own that I had a foolish dislike of your walking in the streets unaccompanied at so late an hour. I believe that any man who had newly made your acquaintance, and had thought as much about you as I have, would have experienced the same feeling. The life which made it impossible for you to see friends at any other time of the day was so evidently unsuited to one of your refinement that I was made angry by the thought of it. Happily it is coming to an end, and I shall be greatly relieved when I know that you have left the house of business.

"You remember that we are to be friends. I should be much less than your friend if I did not desire for you a position very different from that which necessity forced upon you. Thank you very much for the promise to tell me how you like the new employment, and your new friends. Shall you not henceforth be at leisure on other days besides Sunday? As you will now be near Regent's Park, perhaps I may hope to meet you there some evening before long. I would go any distance to see you and speak with you for only a few minutes.

"Do forgive my impertinence, and believe me, dear Miss Madden,

"Ever yours,

"EDMUND WIDDOWSON."

Now this undoubtedly might be considered a love-letter, and it was the first of its kind that Monica had ever received. No man had ever written to her that he was willing to go "any distance" for the reward of looking on her face. She read the composition many times, and with many thoughts. It did not enchant her; presently she felt it to be dull and prosy — anything but the ideal of a love-letter, even at this early stage.

The remarks concerning Widdowson made in the bedroom by the girl who fancied her asleep had greatly disturbed her conception of him. He was old, and looked still older to a casual eye. He had a stiff dry way, and already had begun to show how precise and exacting he could be. A year or two ago the image of such a man would have repelled her. She did not think it possible to regard him with warm feeling; yet, if he asked her to marry him, — and that seemed likely to happen very soon, — almost certainly her answer would be yes. Provided, of course, that all he had told her about himself could be in some satisfactory way confirmed.

Her acquaintance with him was an extraordinary thing. With what amazement and rapture would any one of her shop companions listen to the advances of a man who had six hundred a year! Yet Monica did not doubt his truthfulness and the honesty of his intentions. His life-story sounded credible enough, and the very dryness of his manner inspired confidence. As things went in the marriage war, she might esteem herself a most fortunate young woman. It seemed that he had really fallen in love with her; he might prove a devoted husband. She felt no love in return; but between the prospect of a marriage of esteem and that of no marriage at all there was little room for hesitation. The chances were that she might never again receive an offer from a man whose social standing she could respect.

In the meantime there had come a civil little note from the girl whose rooms she was to share. "Miss Barfoot has spoken of you so favourably, that I did not think it necessary to see you before consenting to what she suggested. Perhaps she has told you that I have my own furniture; it is very plain, but, I think, comfortable. For the two rooms, with attendance, I pay eight and sixpence a week; my landlady will ask eleven shillings when there are two of us, so that your share would be five-and-six. I hope you won't think this too much. I am a quiet and I think a very reasonable person." The signature was "Mildred H. Vesper."

The day of release arrived. As it poured with rain all the morning, Monica the less regretted that she had been obliged to postpone her meeting with Widdowson. At breakfast time she said good-bye to the three or four girls in whom she had any interest. Miss Eade was delighted to see her go; this rival finally out of the way, Mr. Bullivant might perchance turn his attention to the faithful admirer who remained.

She went by train to Great Portland Street, and thence by cab, with her two boxes, to Rutland Street, Hampstead Road — an uphill little street of small houses. When the cab stopped, the door of the house she sought at once opened, and on the threshold appeared a short, prim, plain-featured girl, who smiled a welcome.

"You are Miss Vesper?" Monica said, approaching her.

"Yes, — very pleased to see you, Miss Madden. As London cabmen have a narrow view of their duties, I'll help you to get the boxes in."

Monica liked the girl at once. Jehu[1] condescending to hand down the luggage, they transferred it to the foot of the staircase, then, the fare having been paid, went up to the second floor, which was the top of the house. Miss Vesper's two rooms were very humble, but homely; she looked at Monica to remark the impression produced by them.

"Will it do?"

"Oh, very nicely indeed. After my quarters in Walworth Road! — But I feel ashamed to intrude upon you."

"I have been trying to find some one to share my rent," said the other, with a simple frankness that was very agreeable. "Miss Barfoot was full of your praises — and indeed I think we may suit each other."

"I shall try to be as little disturbance to you as possible."

"And I, to you. — The street is a very quiet one. Up above here is Cumberland Market; a hay and straw market. Quite pleasant odours, country odours, reach us on market day. I am country-bred; that's why I speak of such a trifle."

"So am I," said Monica. "I come from Somerset."

"And I from Hampshire. Do you know, I have a strong suspicion that all the really nice girls in London *are* country girls."

Monica had to look at the speaker to be sure that this was said in pleasantry. Miss Vesper was fond of making dry little jokes in the gravest tone; only a twinkle of her eyes and a movement of her tight little lips betrayed her.

"Shall I ask the landlady to help me up with the luggage?"

"You are rather pale, Miss Madden. Better let me see to that. I have to go down to remind Mrs. Hocking to put salt into the saucepan with the potatoes. She cooks for me only on Sunday, and if I didn't remind her every week she would boil the potatoes without salt. Such a state of mind is curious, but one ends by accepting it as a fact in nature."

---

1 A humorous term for a cabdriver, especially a reckless one. The original Jehu, a king of Israel in the ninth century B.C., drove his chariot "furiously" (II Kings 9:20).

They joined in merry laughter. When Miss Vesper gave way to open mirth, she enjoyed it so thoroughly that it was a delight to look at her.

By the time dinner was over, they were on excellent terms and had exchanged a great deal of personal information. Mildred Vesper seemed to be one of the most contented of young women. She had sisters and brothers, whom she loved, all scattered about England in pursuit of a livelihood; it was rare for any two of them to see each other, but she spoke of this as quite in the order of things. For Miss Barfoot her respect was unbounded.

"She has made more of me than any one else could have done. When I first met her, three years ago, I was a simpleton; I thought myself ill-used because I had to work hard for next to no payment and live in solitude. Now I should be ashamed to complain of what falls to the lot of thousands of girls."

"Do you like Miss Nunn?" asked Monica.

"Not so well as Miss Barfoot, but I think very highly of her. Her zeal makes her exaggerate a little now and then, but then the zeal is so splendid. I haven't it myself — not in that form."

"You mean —?"

"I mean that I feel a shameful delight when I hear of a girl getting married. It's very weak, no doubt; perhaps I shall improve as I grow older. But I have half a suspicion, do you know, that Miss Barfoot is not without the same weakness."

Monica laughed, and spoke of something else. She was in good spirits; already her companion's view of life began to have an effect upon her; she thought of people and things in a more lightsome way, and was less disposed to commiserate herself.

The bedroom which both were to occupy might with advantage have been larger, but they knew that many girls of instinct no less delicate than their own had to endure far worse accommodation in London, — where poverty pays for its sheltered breathing-space at so much a square foot. It was only of late that Miss Vesper had been able to buy furniture (four sovereigns[1] it cost in all), and thus to allow herself the luxury of two rooms at the rent she previously paid for one. Miss Barfoot did not remunerate her workers on a philanthropic scale, but strictly in accordance with market prices; common sense dictated this principle. In talking over their arrangements, Monica decided to expend a few shillings on the purchase of a chair-bedstead for her own use.

"I often have nightmare," she remarked, "and kick a great deal. It wouldn't be nice to give you bruises."

A week passed. Alice had written from Yatton, and in a cheerful tone. Virginia, chronically excited, had made calls at Rutland Street and at Queen's Road; she talked like one who had suddenly received a great

---

1 A sovereign was a gold coin worth £1.

illumination, and her zeal in the cause of independent womanhood rivalled Miss Nunn's. Without enthusiasm, but seemingly contented, Monica worked at the type-writing machine, and had begun certain studies which her friends judged to be useful. She experienced a growth of self-respect. It was much to have risen above the status of shop-girl, and the change of moral atmosphere had a very beneficial effect upon her.

Mildred Vesper was a studious little person, after a fashion of her own. She possessed four volumes of Maunder's "Treasuries,"[1] and to one or other of these she applied herself for at least an hour every evening.

"By nature," she said, when Monica sought an explanation of this study, "my mind is frivolous. What I need is a store of solid information, to reflect upon. No one could possibly have a worse memory, but by persevering I manage to learn one or two facts a day."

Monica glanced at the books now and then, but had no desire to cultivate Maunder's acquaintance. Instead of reading, she meditated the problems of her own life.

Edmund Widdowson of course wrote to her at the new address; in her reply she again postponed their meeting. Whenever she went out in the evening, it was with expectation of seeing him somewhere in the neighbourhood; she felt assured that he had long ago come to look at the house, and more likely than not his eyes had several times been upon her. That did not matter; her life was innocent, and Widdowson might watch her coming and going as much as he would.

At length, about nine o'clock one evening, she came face to face with him. It was in Hampstead Road; she had been buying at a draper's, and carried the little parcel. At the moment of recognition, Widdowson's face so flushed and brightened that Monica could not help a sympathetic feeling of pleasure.

"Why are you so cruel to me?" he said in a low voice, as she gave her hand. "What a time since I saw you!"

"Is that really true?" she replied, with an air more resembling coquetry than any he had yet seen in her.

"Since I spoke to you, then."

"When did you see me?"

"Three evenings ago. You were walking in Tottenham Court Road, with a young lady."

"Miss Vesper, the friend I live with."

"Will you give me a few minutes now?" he asked humbly. "Is it too late?"

For reply, Monica moved slowly on. They turned up one of the ways

---

1 A series of books for the general reader on broad topics (e.g., literature, biography, history, science) first published in the 1830s and 1840s by Samuel Maunder (1785–1849). Many of the volumes were updated and reissued in the 1860s and 1870s.

parallel with Rutland Street, and so came into the quiet district that skirts Regent's Park, Widdowson talking all the way in a strain of all but avowed tenderness, his head bent towards her and his voice so much subdued that occasionally she lost a few words.

"I can't live without seeing you," he said at length. "If you refuse to meet me, I have no choice but to come wandering about the places where you are. Don't, pray don't think I spy upon you. Indeed, it is only just to see your face, or your form as you walk along. When I have had my journey in vain I go back in misery. You are never out of my thoughts — never."

"I am sorry for that, Mr. Widdowson."

"Sorry? — Are you really sorry? Do you think of me with less friendliness than when we had our evening on the river?"

"Oh, not with less friendliness. But if I only make you unhappy" —

"In one way unhappy, but as no one else ever had the power to. If you would let me meet you at certain times, my restlessness would be at an end. The summer is going so quickly. Won't you come for that drive with me next Sunday? I will be waiting for you at any place you like to appoint? — If you could imagine what joy it would give me!"

Presently Monica assented. If it were fine, she would be by the south-east entrance to Regent's Park at two o'clock. He thanked her with words of the most submissive gratitude, and then they parted.

The day proved doubtful, but she kept her appointment. Widdowson was on the spot with horse and trap;[1] these were not, as he presently informed Monica, his own property, but hired from a livery-stable, according to his custom.

"It won't rain," he exclaimed, gazing at the sky. "It *shan't* rain! These few hours are too precious to me."

"It would be very awkward if it *did*," Monica replied, in merry humour, as they drove along.

The sky threatened till sundown, but Widdowson was able to keep declaring that rain would not come. He took a south-westward course, crossed Waterloo Bridge, and thence by the highways made for Herne Hill. Monica observed that he made a short détour to avoid Walworth Road; she asked his reason.

"I hate the road!" Widdowson answered, with vehemence.

"You hate it?"

"Because you slaved and suffered there. If I had the power, I would destroy it — every house. Many a time," he added, in a lower voice, "when you were lying asleep, I walked up and down there, in horrible misery."

"Just because I had to stand at a counter?"

"Not only that. It wasn't fit for you to work in that way, — but the peo-

1 A two-wheeled carriage.

ple about you! I hated every face of man or woman that passed along the street."

"I didn't like the society."

"I should hope not. — Of course, I know you didn't. Why did you ever come to such a place?"

There was severity rather than sympathy in his look.

"I was tired of the dull country life," Monica replied frankly. "And then I didn't know what the shops and the people were like."

"Do you need a life of excitement?" he asked, with a sidelong glance.

"Excitement? — No, but one must have change."

When they reached Herne Hill, Widdowson became silent, and presently he allowed the horse to walk.

"That is my house, Miss Madden, — the right-hand one."

Monica looked, and saw two little villas,[1] built together, with stone facings, porches at the doors, and ornamented gables.

"I only wanted to show it you," he added quickly. "There's nothing pretty or noticeable about it, and it isn't at all grandly furnished. My old housekeeper and one servant manage to keep it in order."

They passed, and Monica did now allow herself to look back.

"I think it's a nice house," she said presently.

"All my life I have wished to have a house of my own, but I didn't dare to hope I ever should. Men in general don't seem to care so long as they have lodgings that suit them, — I mean unmarried men. But I always wanted to live alone — without strangers, that is to say. I told you that I am not very sociable. — When I got my house, I was like a child with a toy; I couldn't sleep for satisfaction. I used to walk all over it, day after day, before it was furnished. There was something that delighted me in the sound of my footsteps on the staircases and the bare floors. Here I shall live and die, I kept saying to myself. Not in solitude, I hoped. Perhaps I might meet some one —"

Monica interrupted him to ask a question about some object in the landscape. He answered her very briefly, and for a long time neither spoke. Then the girl, glancing at him with a smile of apology, said in a gentle tone:

"You were telling me how the house pleased you. Have you still the same pleasure in living there?"

"Yes. But lately I have been hoping — I daren't say more. You will interrupt me again."

"Which way are we going now, Mr. Widdowson?"

"To Streatham, then on to Carshalton. At five o'clock we will use our right as travellers, and get some innkeeper to make tea for us. — Look, the sun is trying to break through; we shall have a fine evening yet. —

---

1 "Villa" refers to a suburban detached or semi-detached house.

May I, without rudeness, say that you look better since you left that abominable place."

"Oh, I feel better."

After keeping his look fixed for a long time on the horse's ears, Widdowson turned gravely to his companion.

"I told you about my sister-in-law. Would you be willing to make her acquaintance?"

"I don't feel able to do that, Mr. Widdowson," Monica answered with decision.

Prepared for this reply, he began a long and urgent persuasion. It was useless; Monica listened quietly, but without sign of yielding. The subject dropped, and they talked of indifferent things.

On the homeward drive, when the dull sky grew dusk about them, and the suburban street-lamps began to show themselves in long glimmering lines, Widdowson returned with shamefaced courage to the subject which for some hours had been in abeyance.

"I can't part from you this evening without a word of hope to remember. You know that I want you to be my wife. Will you tell me if there is anything I can say or do to make your consent possible? — Have you any doubt of me?"

"No doubt whatever of your sincerity."

"In one sense, I am still a stranger to you. Will you give me the opportunity of making things between us more regular? Will you allow me to meet some friend of yours whom you trust?"

"I had rather you didn't yet."

"You wish to know still more of me, personally?"

"Yes — I think I must know you much better before I can consent to any step of that kind."

"But," he urged, "if we became acquaintances in the ordinary way, and knew each other's friends, wouldn't that be most satisfactory to you?"

"It might be. But you forget that so much would have to be explained. I have behaved very strangely. If I told everything to my friends, I should leave myself no choice."

"Oh, why not? You would be absolutely free. I could do no more than try to recommend myself to you. If I am so unhappy as to fail, how would you be anything but quite free?"

"But surely you must understand me. In this position, I must either not speak of you at all, or make it known that I am engaged to you. I can't have it taken for granted that I am engaged to you, when I don't wish to be."

Widdowson's head drooped; he set his lips in a hard, gloomy expression.

"I have behaved very imprudently," continued the girl. "But I don't see — I can't see — what else I could have done. Things are so badly arranged. It wasn't possible for us to be introduced by any one who knew us both, so I had either to break off your acquaintance after that first conversation, or conduct myself as I have been doing. I think it's a very hard position. My sisters would call me an immodest girl, but I don't think it is true. — I may perhaps come to feel for you as a girl ought to when she marries, and how else can I tell unless I meet you and talk with you? — And your position is just the same. I don't blame you for a moment; I think it would be ridiculous to blame you. Yet we have gone against the ordinary rule, and people would make us suffer for it — or me, at all events."

Her voice at the close was uncertain. Widdowson looked at her with eyes of passionate admiration.

"Thank you for saying that — for putting it so well, and so kindly for me. Let us disregard people, then. Let us go on seeing each other. I love you with all my soul" — he choked a little at this first utterance of the solemn word — "and your rules shall be mine. Give me a chance of winning you. Tell me if I offend you in anything — if there's anything you dislike in me."

"Will you cease coming to look for me when I don't know of it?"

"I promise you. I will never come again. — And you will meet me a little oftener?"

"I will see you once every week. But I must still be perfectly free."

"Perfectly! I will only try to win you as any man may who loves a woman."

The tired horse clattered upon the hard highway, and clouds gathered for a night of storm.

CHAPTER VIII.

COUSIN EVERARD.

As Miss Barfoot's eye fell on the letters brought to her at breakfast time, she uttered an exclamation, doubtful in its significance. Rhoda Nunn, who rarely had a letter from any one, looked up inquiringly.

"I am greatly mistaken if that isn't my cousin Everard's writing. — I thought so. — He is in London."

Rhoda made no remark.

"Pray read it," said the other, handing her friend the epistle after she had gone through it.

The handwriting was remarkably bold, but careful. Punctuation was strictly attended to, and in places a word had been obliterated with a circular scrawl which left it still legible.

"DEAR COUSIN MARY,

"I hear that you are still active in an original way, and that civilization is more and more indebted to you. Since my arrival in London a few weeks ago, I have several times been on the point of calling at your house, but scruples withheld me. Our last interview was not quite friendly on your side, you will remember, and perhaps your failure to write to me means continued displeasure; in that case I might be rejected at your door, which I shouldn't like, for I am troubled with a foolish sense of personal dignity. I have taken a flat, and mean to stay in London for at least half a year. Please let me know whether I may see you. Indeed I should like to. Nature meant us for good friends, but prejudice came between us. Just a line, either of welcome or 'get thee behind me!' In spite of your censures, I always was, and still am, affectionately yours,

"EVERARD BARFOOT."

Rhoda perused the sheet very attentively.

"An impudent letter," said Miss Barfoot. "Just like him."

"Where does he appear from?"

"Japan, I suppose. — 'But prejudice came between us.' I like that! Moral conviction is always prejudice in the eyes of these advanced young men. — Of course he must come. I am anxious to see what time has made of him."

"Was it really moral censure that kept you from writing to him?" inquired Rhoda, with a smile.

"Decidedly. I didn't approve of him at all, as I have frequently told you."

"But I gather that he hasn't changed much."

"Not in theories," replied Miss Barfoot. "That isn't to be expected.

He is far too stubborn. But in mode of life he may possibly be more tolerable."

"After two or three years in Japan," rejoined Rhoda, with a slight raising of the eyebrows.

"He is about three-and-thirty, and before he left England I think he showed possibilities of future wisdom. Of course I disapprove of him, and, if necessary, shall let him understand that, quite as plainly as before. But there's no harm in seeing if he has learnt to behave himself."

Everard Barfoot received an invitation to dine. It was promptly accepted, and on the evening of the appointment he arrived at half-past seven. His cousin sat alone in the drawing-room; at his entrance she regarded him with keen but friendly scrutiny.

He had a tall, muscular frame, and a head of striking outline, with large nose, full lips, deep-set eyes, and prominent eyebrows. His hair was the richest tone of chestnut; his moustache and beard — the latter peaking slightly forward — inclined to redness. Excellent health manifested itself in the warm purity of his skin, in his cheerful aspect, and the lightness of his bearing. The lower half of his forehead was wrinkled, and when he did not fix his look on anything in particular, his eyelids drooped, giving him for the moment an air of languor. On sitting down, he at once abandoned himself to a posture of the completest ease, which his admirable proportions made graceful. From his appearance one would have expected him to speak in rather loud and decided tones; but he had a soft voice, and used it with all the discretion of good-breeding, so that at times it seemed to caress the ear. To this mode of utterance corresponded his smile, which was frequent, but restrained to the expression of a delicate, good-natured irony.

"No one had told me of your return," were Miss Barfoot's first words, as she shook hands with him.

"I fancy, because no one knew. You were the first of my kinsfolk to whom I wrote."

"Much honour, Everard. — You look very well."

"I am glad to be able to say the same of you. And yet I hear that you work harder than ever."

"Who is the source of your information about me?"

"I had an account of you from Tom, in a letter that caught me at Constantinople."

"Tom? I thought he had forgotten my existence. Who told him about me, I can't imagine. — So you didn't come straight home from Japan?"

Barfoot was nursing his knee, his head thrown back.

"No; I loitered a little in Egypt and Turkey. — Are you living quite alone?"

He drawled slightly on the last word, its second vowel making quite a musical note, of wonderful expressiveness. The clear decision of his cousin's reply was a sharp contrast.

"A lady lives with me — Miss Nunn. She will join us in a moment."

"Miss Nunn?" He smiled. "A partner in your activity?"

"She gives me valuable help."

"I must hear all about it — if you will kindly tell me some day. It will interest me greatly. You always were the most interesting of our family. Brother Tom promised to be a genius, but marriage has blighted the hope, I fear."

"The marriage was a very absurd one."

"Was it? I feared so; but Tom seems satisfied. I suppose they will stay at Madeira."

"Until his wife is tired of her imaginary phthisis,[1] and amuses herself with imagining some other ailment that requires them to go to Siberia."

"Ah, that kind of person, is she?" He smiled indulgently, and played for a moment with the lobe of his right ear. His ears were small, and of the ideal contour; the hand too, thus displayed, was a fine example of blended strength and elegance.

Rhoda came in, so quietly that she was able to observe the guest before he had detected her presence. The movement of Miss Barfoot's eyes first informed him that another person was in the room. In the quietest possible way the introduction was performed, and all seated themselves.

Dressed, like the hostess, in black, and without ornaments of any kind save a silver buckle at her waist, Rhoda seemed to have endeavoured to liken herself to the suggestion of her name by the excessive plainness with which she had arranged her hair; its tight smoothness was nothing like so becoming as the mode she usually adopted, and it made her look older. Whether by accident or design, she took an upright chair, and sat upon it in a stiff attitude. Finding it difficult to suspect Rhoda of shyness, Miss Barfoot once or twice glanced at her with curiosity. For settled conversation there was no time; a servant announced dinner almost immediately.

"There shall be no forms, cousin Everard," said the hostess. "Please to follow us."

Doing so, Everard examined Miss Nunn's figure, which in its way was strong and shapely as his own. A motion of his lips indicated amused approval, but at once he commanded himself, and entered the dining-room with exemplary gravity. Naturally, he sat opposite Rhoda, and his eyes often skimmed her face; when she spoke, which was very seldom, he gazed at her with close attention.

During the first part of the meal, Miss Barfoot questioned her relative concerning his Oriental experiences; Everard spoke of them in a light, agreeable way, avoiding the tone of instruction, and, in short, giving evidence of good taste. Rhoda listened with a look of civil interest, but asked

---

1 A wasting disease, such as tuberculosis.

no question, and smiled only when it was unavoidable. Presently the talk turned to things of home.

"Have you heard of your friend Mr. Poppleton?" the hostess asked.

"Poppleton? Nothing whatever. I should like to see him."

"I'm sorry to tell you he is in a lunatic asylum."

As Barfoot kept the silence of astonishment, his cousin went on to tell him that the unhappy man seemed to have lost his wits among business troubles.

"Yet I should have suggested another explanation," remarked the young man, in his most discreet tone. "You never met Mrs. Poppleton?"

Seeing that Miss Nunn had looked up with interest, he addressed himself to her.

"My friend Poppleton was one of the most delightful men, — perhaps the best and kindest I ever knew, and so overflowing with natural wit and humour that there was no resisting his cheerful influence. To the amazement of every one who knew him, he married perhaps the dullest woman he could have found. Mrs. Poppleton not only never made a joke, but couldn't understand what joking meant. Only the flattest literalism was intelligible to her; she could follow nothing but the very macadam of conversation — had no palate for anything but the suet-pudding of talk."[1]

Rhoda's eyes twinkled, and Miss Barfoot laughed. Everard was allowing himself a freedom in expression which hitherto he had sedulously avoided.

"Yet," he continued, "she was by birth a lady — which made the infliction harder to bear. Poor old Poppleton! Again and again I have heard him — what do you think? — laboriously *explaining* jests to her. That was a trial, as you may imagine. There we sat, we three, in the unbeautiful little parlour — for they were anything but rich. Poppleton would say something that convulsed me with laughter — in spite of my efforts, for I always dreaded the result so much that I strove my hardest to do no more than smile appreciation. My laugh compelled Mrs. Poppleton to stare at me — oh, her eyes! Thereupon, her husband began his dread performance. The patience, the heroic patience, of that dear, good fellow! I have known him explain, and re-explain, for a quarter of an hour, and invariably without success. It might be a mere pun; Mrs. Poppleton no more understood the nature of a pun than of the binomial theorem.[2] But worse was when the jest involved some allusion. When I heard Poppleton begin to elucidate, to expound, the perspiration already on his forehead, I looked at him with imploring anguish. Why *would* he attempt the

---

1 Macadam is material for a fairly rudimentary type of road-making in which successive layers of broken stones, often mixed with tar, are pressed together with a roller. Suet puddings (e.g., plum pudding) are steamed puddings which include suet (hard, ground-up animal fat) as an ingredient; they were considered very ordinary fare.

2 A mathematical formula attributed to Sir Isaac Newton (1642–1727).

impossible? But the kind fellow couldn't disregard his wife's request. Shall I ever forget her 'Oh — yes — I see'? — when obviously she saw nothing but the wall at which she sat staring."

"I have known her like," said Miss Barfoot merrily.

"I am convinced his madness didn't come from business anxiety. It was the necessity, ever recurring, ever before him, of expounding jokes to his wife. Believe me, it was nothing but that."

"It seems very probable," asserted Rhoda drily.

"Then there's another friend of yours whose marriage has been unfortunate," said the hostess. "They tell me that Mr. Orchard has forsaken his wife, and without intelligible reason."

"There, too, I can offer an explanation," replied Barfoot quietly, "though you may doubt whether it justifies him. I met Orchard a few months ago in Alexandria, met him by chance in the street, and didn't recognize him until he spoke to me. He was worn to skin and bone. I found that he had abandoned all his possessions to Mrs. Orchard, and just kept himself alive on casual work for the magazines, wandering about the shores of the Mediterranean like an uneasy spirit. He showed me the thing he had last written, and I see it is published in this month's *Macmillan*.[1] Do read it. An exquisite description of a night in Alexandria. One of these days he will starve to death. A pity; he might have done fine work."

"But we await your explanation. What business has he to desert his wife and children?"

"Let me give an account of a day I spent with him at Tintern, not long before I left England. He and his wife were having a holiday there, and I called on them. We went to walk about the Abbey. Now, for some two hours, — I will be strictly truthful, — whilst we were in the midst of that lovely scenery, Mrs. Orchard discoursed unceasingly of one subject — the difficulty she had with her domestic servants. Ten or twelve of these handmaidens were marshalled before our imagination; their names, their ages, their antecedents, the wages they received, were carefully specified. We listened to a *catalogue raisonné*[2] of the plates, cups and other utensils that they had broken. We heard of the enormities which in each case led to their dismissal. Orchard tried repeatedly to change the subject, but only with the effect of irritating his wife. What could he or I do but patiently give ear? Our walk was ruined, but there was no help for it. — Now, be good enough to extend this kind of thing over a number of years. Picture Orchard sitting down in his home to literary work, and liable at any moment to an invasion from Mrs. Orchard, who comes to tell him, at great length, that the butcher has charged for a joint they have not consumed — or something of that kind. He assured me that his choice lay between flight and suicide, and I firmly believed him."

---

1 A popular monthly magazine.
2 A descriptive catalogue or list with explanatory notes.

As he concluded, his eyes met those of Miss Nunn, and the latter suddenly spoke.

"Why will men marry fools?"

Barfoot was startled. He looked down into his plate, smiling.

"A most sensible question," said the hostess, with a laugh. "Why, indeed?"

"But a difficult one to answer," remarked Everard, with his most restrained smile. "Possibly, Miss Nunn, narrow social opportunity has something to do with it. They must marry some one, and in the case of most men choice is seriously restricted."

"I should have thought," replied Rhoda, elevating her eyebrows, "that to live alone was the less of two evils."

"Undoubtedly. But men like these two we have been speaking of haven't a very logical mind."

Miss Barfoot changed the topic.

When, not long after, the ladies left him to meditate over his glass of wine, Everard curiously surveyed the room. Then his eyelids drooped, he smiled absently, and a calm sigh seemed to relieve his chest. The claret had no particular quality to recommend it, and in any case he would have drunk very little, for as regards the bottle his nature was abstemious.

"It is as I expected," Miss Barfoot was saying to her friend, in the drawing-room. "He has changed very noticeably."

"Mr. Barfoot isn't quite the man your remarks had suggested to me," Rhoda replied.

"I fancy he is no longer the man I knew. His manners are wonderfully improved. He used to assert himself in rather alarming ways. — His letter, to be sure, had the old tone, or something of it."

"I will go to the library for an hour," said Rhoda, who had not seated herself. "Mr. Barfoot won't leave before ten, I suppose?"

"I don't think there will be any private talk."

"Still, if you will let me —"

So, when Everard appeared, he found his cousin alone.

"What are you going to do?" she asked of him good-naturedly.

"To do? You mean, how do I propose to employ myself? — I have nothing whatever in view, beyond enjoying life."

"At your age?"

"So young? Or so old? Which?"

"So young, of course. You deliberately intend to waste your life?"

"To enjoy it, I said. I am not prompted to any business or profession; that's all over for me; I have learnt all I care to of the active world."

"But what do you understand by enjoyment?" asked Miss Barfoot, with knitted brows.

"Isn't the spectacle of existence quite enough to occupy one through a lifetime? If a man merely travelled, could he possibly exhaust all the beauties and magnificences that are offered to him in every country? For ten years and more I worked as hard as any man; I shall never regret it, for it has given me a feeling of liberty and opportunity such as I should not have known if I had always lived at my ease. It taught me a great deal, too; supplemented my so-called education as nothing else could have done. But to work for ever is to lose half of life. I can't understand those people who reconcile themselves to quitting the world without having seen a millionth part of it."

"I am quite reconciled to that. An infinite picture-gallery isn't my idea of enjoyment."

"Nor mine. But an infinite series of modes of living. A ceaseless exercise of all one's faculties of pleasure. — That sounds shameless to you? I can't understand why it should. Why is the man who toils more meritorious than he who enjoys? What is the sanction for this judgment?"

"Social usefulness, Everard."

"I admit the demand for social usefulness, up to a certain point. But really, I have done my share. The mass of men don't toil with any such ideal, but merely to keep themselves alive, or to get wealth. I think there is a vast amount of unnecessary labour."

"There is an old proverb about Satan and idle hands.[1] — Pardon me; you alluded to that personage in your letter."

"The proverb is a very true one, but, like other proverbs, it applies to the multitude. If I get into mischief, it will not be because I don't perspire for so many hours every day; but simply because it is human to err. I have no intention whatever of getting into mischief."

The speaker stroked his beard, and smiled with a distant look.

"Your purpose is intensely selfish, and all indulged selfishness reacts on the character," replied Miss Barfoot, still in a tone of the friendliest criticism.

"My dear cousin, for anything to be selfish, it must be a deliberate refusal of what one believes to be duty. I don't admit that I am neglecting any duty to others, and the duty to myself seems very clear indeed."

"Of *that*, I have no doubt," exclaimed the other, laughing. "I see that you have refined your arguments."

"Not my arguments only, I hope," said Everard modestly. "My time has been very ill spent if I haven't, in some degree, refined my nature."

"That sounds very well, Everard. But when it comes to degrees of self-indulgence —"

She paused and made a gesture of dissatisfaction.

"It comes to that, surely, with every man. — But we certainly shall not agree on this subject. You stand at the social point of view; I am an indi-

---

1 "For Satan finds some mischief still/ For idle hands to do," from "Against Idleness and Mischief," Song 20 of *Divine Songs for Children* by Isaac Watts (1674–1748).

vidualist. You have the advantage of a tolerably consistent theory; whilst I have no theory at all, and am full of contradictions. The only thing clear to me is that I have a right to make the most of my life."

"No matter at whose expense?"

"You are quite mistaken. My conscience is a tender one. I dread to do any one an injury. — That has always been true of me, in spite of your sceptical look; and the tendency increases as I grow older. Let us have done with so unimportant a matter. Isn't Miss Nunn able to rejoin us?"

"She will come presently, I think."

"How did you make this lady's acquaintance?"

Miss Barfoot explained the circumstances.

"She makes an impression," resumed Everard. "A strong character, of course. More decidedly one of the new women than you yourself — isn't she?"

"Oh, *I* am a very old-fashioned woman. Women have thought as I do at any time in history. Miss Nunn has much more zeal for womanhood militant."

"I should delight to talk with her. Really, you know, I am very strongly on your side."

Miss Barfoot laughed.

"Oh, sophist! — You despise women."

"Why, yes, the great majority of women — the typical woman. All the more reason for my admiring the exceptions, and wishing to see them become more common. You, undoubtedly, despise the average woman."

"I despise no human being, Everard."

"Oh, in a sense! — But Miss Nunn, I feel sure, would agree with me."

"I am very sure Miss Nunn wouldn't. She doesn't admire the feebler female, but that is very far from being at one with *your* point of view, my cousin."

Everard mused with a smile.

"I must get to understand her line of thought. You permit me to call upon you now and then?"

"Oh, whenever you like, in the evening. — Except," Miss Barfoot added, "Wednesday evening. Then we are always engaged."

"Summer holidays are unknown to you, I suppose?"

"Not altogether. I had mine a few weeks ago. Miss Nunn will be going away in a fortnight, I think."

Just before ten o'clock, when Barfoot was talking of some acquaintances he had left in Japan, Rhoda entered the room. She seemed little disposed for conversation, and Everard did not care to assail her taciturnity this evening. He talked on a little longer, observing her as she listened, and presently took an opportunity to rise for departure.

"Wednesday is the forbidden evening is it not?" he said to his cousin.

"Yes, that is devoted to business."

As soon as he was gone, the friends exchanged a look. Each understood the other as referring to this point of Wednesday evening, but neither made a remark. They were silent for some time. When Rhoda at length spoke it was in a tone of half-indifferent curiosity.

"You are sure you haven't exaggerated Mr. Barfoot's failings?"

The reply was delayed for a moment.

"I was a little indiscreet to speak of him at all. — But no, I didn't exaggerate."

"Curious," mused the other, dispassionately, as she stood with one foot on the fender. "He hardly strikes one as that kind of man."

"Oh, he has certainly changed a great deal."

Miss Barfoot went on to speak of her cousin's resolve to pursue no calling.

"His means are very modest. I feel rather guilty before him; his father bequeathed to me much of the money that would in the natural course have been Everard's. But he is quite superior to any feeling of grudge on that score."

"Practically, his father disinherited him?"

"It amounted to that. From quite a child, Everard was at odds with his father. A strange thing, for in so many respects they resembled each other very closely. Physically, Everard is his father walking the earth again. In character, too, I think they must be very much alike. They couldn't talk about the simplest thing without disagreeing. — My uncle had risen from the ranks, but he disliked to be reminded of it. He disliked the commerce by which he made his fortune. His desire was to win social position; if baronetcies could be purchased in our time, he would have given a huge sum to acquire one. But he never distinguished himself, and one of the reasons was, no doubt, that he married too soon. I have heard him speak bitterly, and very indiscreetly, of early marriages; his wife was dead then, but every one knew what he meant. — Rhoda, when one thinks how often a women is a clog upon a man's ambition, no wonder they regard us as they do."

"Of course, women are always retarding one thing or another. But men are intensely stupid not to have remedied that long ago."

"He determined that his boys should be gentlemen. Tom, the elder, followed his wishes exactly; he was remarkably clever, but idleness spoilt him, and now he has made that ridiculous marriage, — the end of poor Tom. Everard went to Eton, and the school had a remarkable effect upon him; it made him a furious Radical.[1] Instead of imitating the young aristocrats, he hated and scorned them. There must have been great force of originality in the boy. Of course I don't know whether any Etonians of his

---

1 Eton was (and still is) one of England's oldest and most elite "public" (i.e., private) secondary schools, where the sons of members of the aristocracy and of the upper middle class were educated. The Radicals comprised a relatively new, leftist political party that championed the rights of ordinary workers and opposed the kind of social and class privilege that Eton stood for.

time preached Radicalism, but it seems unlikely. I think it was sheer vigour of character, and the strange desire to oppose his father in everything. From Eton he was of course to pass to Oxford, but at that stage came practical rebellion. No, said the boy; he wouldn't go to a University, to fill his head with useless learning; he had made up his mind to be an engineer. This was an astonishment to every one; engineering didn't seem at all the thing for him; he had very little ability in mathematics, and his bent had always been to liberal studies. — But nothing could shake his idea. He had got it into his head that only some such work as engineering, — something of a practical kind, that called for strength and craftsmanship, — was worthy of a man with his opinions. He would rank with the classes that keep the world going with their sturdy toil: that was how he spoke. And after a great fight, he had his way. He left Eton to study civil engineering."

Rhoda was listening with an amused smile.

"Then," pursued her friend, "came another display of firmness or obstinacy, whichever you like to call it. He soon found out that he had made a complete mistake. The studies didn't suit him at all, as others had foreseen. But he would have worked himself to death rather than confess his error; none of us knew how he was feeling till long after. Engineering he had chosen, and an engineer he would be, cost him what effort it might. His father shouldn't triumph over him. And from the age of eighteen till nearly thirty he stuck to a profession which I am sure he loathed. By force of resolve, he even got on in it, and reached a good position with the firm he worked for. Of course his father wouldn't assist him with money after he came of age; he had to make his way just like any young man who has no influence."

"All this puts him in quite another light," remarked Rhoda.

"Yes, it would be all very well, if there were no vices to add to the picture. I never experienced such a revulsion of feeling as the day when I learnt shameful things about Everard. You know, I always regarded him as a boy, and very much as if he had been my younger brother; then came the shock — a shock that had a great part in shaping my life thenceforward. Since, I have thought of him as I have spoken of him to you — as an illustration of evils we have to combat. A man of the world would tell you that I grossly magnified trifles; it is very likely that Everard was on a higher moral level than most men. But I shall never forgive him for destroying my faith in his honour and nobility of feeling."

Rhoda had a puzzled look.

"Perhaps even now you are unintentionally misleading me," she said. "I have supposed him an outrageous profligate."

"He was vicious and cowardly — I can't say any more."

"And that was the immediate cause of his father's leaving him poorly provided for?"

"It had much to do with it, I have no doubt."

"I see. — I imagined that he was cast out of all decent society."

"If society were really decent, he would have been. — It's strange how completely his Radicalism has disappeared. I believe he never had a genuine sympathy with the labouring classes. And what's more, I fancy he has a great deal of his father's desire for command and social distinction. If he had seen his way to become a great engineer, a director of vast enterprises, he wouldn't have abandoned his work. An incredible stubbornness has possibly spoilt his whole life. In a congenial pursuit, he might by this time have attained to something noteworthy. It's too late now, I fear."

Rhoda meditated.

"Does he aim at nothing whatever?"

"He won't admit any ambition. — He has no society. His friends are nearly all obscure people, like those you heard him speak of this evening."

"After all, what ambition should he have?" said Rhoda, with a laugh. "There's one advantage in being a woman. A woman with brains and will may hope to distinguish herself in the greatest movement of our time — that of emancipating her sex. But what can a man do, unless he has genius?"

"There's the emancipation of the working classes. That is the great sphere for men; and Everard cares no more for the working classes than I do."

"Isn't it enough to be free oneself?"

"You mean that he has task enough in striving to be an honourable man?"

"Perhaps. — I hardly know what I meant."

Miss Barfoot mused, and her face lighted up with a glad thought.

"You are right. It's better to be a woman, in our day. With us is all the joy of advance, the glory of conquering. Men have only material progress to think about. But we — we are winning souls, propagating a new religion, purifying the earth!"

Rhoda nodded thrice.

"My cousin is a fine specimen of a man, after all, in body and mind. But what a poor, ineffectual creature compared with *you*, Rhoda! I don't flatter you, dear. I tell you bluntly of your faults and extravagances. But I am proud of your magnificent independence, proud of your pride, dear, and of your stainless heart. Thank heaven we are women!"

It was rare indeed for Miss Barfoot to be moved to rhapsody. Again Rhoda nodded, and then they laughed together, with joyous confidence in themselves and in their cause.

CHAPTER IX.

THE SIMPLE FAITH.

Seated in the reading-room of a club to which he had newly procured admission, Everard Barfoot was glancing over the advertisement columns of a literary paper. His eye fell on an announcement that had a personal interest for him, and at once he went to the writing-table to pen a letter.

"DEAR MICKLETHWAITE,

"I am back in England, and ought before this to have written to you. I see you have just published a book with an alarming title, 'A Treatise on Trilinear Co-ordinates.' My hearty congratulations on the completion of such a labour; were you not the most disinterested of mortals, I would add a hope that it may somehow benefit you financially. I presume there *are* people who purchase such works. But of course the main point with you is to have delivered your soul on Trilinear Co-ordinates. Shall I run down to Sheffield to see you, or is there any chance of the holidays bringing you this way? I have found a cheap flat, poorly furnished, in Bayswater; the man who let it me happens to be an engineer, and is absent on Italian railway work for a year or so. My stay in London won't, I think, be for longer than six months, but we must see each other and talk over old times," &c.

This he addressed to a school at Sheffield. The answer, directed to the club, reached him in three days.

"MY DEAR BARFOOT,

"I also am in London; your letter has been forwarded from the school, which I quitted last Easter. Disinterested or not, I am happy to tell you that I have got a vastly better appointment. Let me know when and where to meet you; or, if you like, come to these lodgings of mine. I don't enter upon duties till end of October, and am at present revelling in mathematical freedom. There's a great deal to tell.

"Sincerely yours,
"THOMAS MICKLETHWAITE."

Having no occupation for his morning, Barfoot went at once to the obscure little street by Primrose Hill where his friend was lodging. He reached the house about noon, and, as he had anticipated, found the mathematician deep in study. Micklethwaite was a man of forty, bent in the shoulders, sallow, but not otherwise of unhealthy appearance; he had a merry countenance, a great deal of lank, disorderly hair, and a beard that reached to the middle of his waistcoat. Everard's acquaintance with him dated from ten years ago, when Micklethwaite had acted as his private tutor in mathematics.

The room was a musty little back-parlour on the ground floor.

"Quiet, perfectly quiet," declared its occupant, "and that's all I care for. Two other lodgers in the house; but they go to business every morning at half-past eight, and are in bed by ten at night. Besides, it's only temporary. I have great things in view — portentous changes! I'll tell you all about it presently."

He insisted, first of all, on hearing a full account of Barfoot's history since they both met. They had corresponded about twice a year, but Everard was not fond of letter-writing, and, on each occasion, gave only the briefest account of himself. In listening, Micklethwaite assumed extraordinary positions, the result, presumably, of a need of physical exercise after hours spent over his work. Now he stretched himself at full length on the edge of his chair, his arms extended above him; now he drew up his legs, fixed his feet on the chair and locked his hands round his knees; thus perched, he swayed his body backwards and forwards, till it seemed likely that he would pitch head foremost on to the floor. Barfoot knew these eccentricities of old, and paid no attention to them.

"And what is the appointment you have got?" he asked at length, dismissing his own affairs with impatience.

It was that of mathematical lecturer at a London college.

"I shall have a hundred and fifty a year, and be able to take private pupils. On two hundred, at least, I can count, and there are possibilities I won't venture to speak of, because it doesn't do to be too hopeful. Two hundred a year is a great advance, for me."

"Quite enough, I suppose," said Everard kindly.

"Not — not enough. I must make a little more somehow."

"Hollo! Why this spirit of avarice all at once?"

The mathematician gave a shrill, cackling laugh, and rolled upon his chair.

"I must have more than two hundred. I should be satisfied with *three* hundred, but I'll take as much more as I can get."

"My revered tutor, this is shameless. I came to pay my respects to a philosopher, and I find a sordid worldling. Look at me! I am a man of the largest needs, spiritual and physical, yet I make my pittance of four hundred and fifty suffice, and never grumble. Perhaps you aim at an income equal to my own?"

"I do! What's four hundred and fifty? If you were a man of enterprise you would double or treble it. I put a high value on money. I wish to be *rich*!"

"You are either mad or are going to get married."

Micklethwaite cackled louder than ever.

"I am planning a new algebra, for school use. If I'm not much mistaken, I can turn out something that will supplant all the present books.

Think! If Micklethwaite's Algebra got accepted in all the schools, what would that mean to Mick? Hundreds a year, my boy, hundreds."

"I never knew you so indecent."

"I am renewing my youth. Nay, for the first time I am youthful. I never had time for it before. At the age of sixteen I began to teach in a school, and ever since I have pegged away at it, school and private. Now luck has come to me, and I feel five-and-twenty. When I was really five-and-twenty, I felt forty."

"Well, what has that to do with money-making?"

"After Mick's Algebra would follow naturally Mick's Arithmetic, Mick's Euclid,[1] Mick's Trigonometry. Twenty years hence I should have an income of thousands — thousands! I would then cease to teach (resign my professorship, that is to say, for of course I should be professor), and devote myself to a great work on Probability. Many a man has begun the best of his life at sixty — the most enjoyable part of it, I mean."

Barfoot was perplexed. He knew his friend's turn for humorous exaggeration, but had never once heard him scheme for material advancement, and evidently this present talk meant something more than a jest.

"Am I right or not? You are going to get married?"

Micklethwaite glanced at the door, then said in a tone of caution:

"I don't care to talk about it here. Let us go somewhere and eat together. I invite you to have dinner with me, — or lunch, as I suppose you would call it, in your aristocratic language."

"No, you had better have lunch with me. Come to my club."

"Confound your impudence! Am I not your father in mathematics?"

"Be so good as to put on a decent pair of trousers, and brush your hair. — Ah, here is your Trilinear production. I'll look over it whilst you make yourself presentable."

"There's a bad misprint in the Preface. Let me show you —"

"It's all the same to me, my dear fellow."

But Micklethwaite was not content until he had indicated the error, and had talked for five minutes about the absurdities that it involved.

"How do you suppose I got the thing published?" he then asked. "Old Bennet, the Sheffield head-master, is security for loss if the book doesn't pay for itself in two years' time. Kind of him, wasn't it? He pressed the offer upon me, and I think he's prouder of the book than I am myself. — But it's quite remarkable how kind people are when one is fortunate. I fancy a great deal of nonsense is talked about the world's enviousness. Now as soon as it got known that I was coming to this post in London, people behaved to me with surprising good-nature, all round. Old Bennet talked in quite an affectionate strain. 'Of course,' he said, 'I have long known that you ought to be in a better place than this; your payment is

---

1 I.e., geometry. Euclid (c. 300 B.C.) was the Greek mathematician whose *Elements* formed the basis of geometry.

altogether inadequate; if it had depended upon *me*, I should long ago have increased it. I truly rejoice that you have found a more fitting sphere for your remarkable abilities.' — No; I maintain that the world is always ready to congratulate you with sincerity, if you will only give it a chance."

"Very gracious of you to give it the chance. But, by-the-bye, how did it come about?"

"Yes, I ought to tell you that. Why, about a year ago, I wrote an answer to a communication signed by a Big Gun in one of the scientific papers. It was a question in Probability, — you wouldn't understand it. My answer was printed, and the Big Gun wrote privately to me, — a very flattering letter. That correspondence led to my appointment; the Big Gun exerted himself on my behalf. The fact is, the world is bursting with good-nature."

"Obviously. — And how long did it take you to write this little book?"

"Oh, only about seven years, — the actual composition. I never had much time to myself, you must remember."

"You're a good soul, Thomas. Go and equip yourself for civilized society."

To the club they repaired on foot. Micklethwaite would talk of anything but that which his companion most desired to hear.

"There are solemnities in life," he answered to an impatient question, "things that can't be spoken of in the highway. When we have eaten, let us go to your flat, and there I will tell you everything."

They lunched joyously. The mathematician drank a bottle of excellent hock,[1] and did corresponding justice to the dishes. His eyes gleamed with happiness; again he enlarged upon the benevolence of mankind, and the admirable ordering of the world. From the club they drove to Bayswater, and made themselves comfortable in Barfoot's flat, which was very plainly, but sufficiently, furnished. Micklethwaite, cigar in mouth, threw his legs over the side of the easy chair in which he was sitting.

"Now," he began gravely, "I don't mind telling you that your conjecture was right. I *am* going to be married."

"Well," said the other, "you have reached the age of discretion. I must suppose that you know what you are about."

"Yes, I think I do. The story is unexciting. I am not a romantic person, nor is my future wife. Now, you must know that when I was about twenty-three years old, I fell in love. You never suspected me of that, I dare say?"

"Why not?"

"Well, I did fall in love. The lady was a clergyman's daughter at Hereford, where I had a place in a school; she taught the infants in an elementary school connected with ours; her age was exactly the same as my own. Now, the remarkable thing was that she took a liking for me, and

---

1 A German white wine.

when I was scoundrel enough to tell her of my feeling, she didn't reject me."

"Scoundrel enough? Why scoundrel?"

"Why? — But I hadn't a penny in the world. I lived at the school, and received a salary of thirty pounds, half of which had to go towards the support of my mother. What could possibly have been more villainous? What earthly prospect was there of my being able to marry?"

"Well, grant the monstrosity of it."

"This lady — a very little lower than the angels — declared that she was content to wait an indefinite time. She believed in me, and hoped for my future. Her father — the mother was dead — sanctioned our engagement. She had three sisters, one of them a governess, another keeping house, and the third a blind girl. Excellent people, all of them. I was at their house as often as possible, and they made much of me. It was a pity, you know, for in those few leisure hours I ought to have been working like a nigger."

"Plainly you ought."

"Fortunately, I left Hereford, and went to a school at Gloucester, where I had thirty-five pounds. How we gloried over that extra five pounds! — But it's no use going on with the story in this way; it would take me till to-morrow morning. Seven years went by; we were thirty years old, and no prospect whatever of our engagement coming to anything. I had worked pretty hard; I had taken my London degree; but not a penny had I saved, and all I could spare was still needful to my mother. It struck me all at once that I had no right to continue the engagement. On my thirtieth birthday I wrote a letter to Fanny, — that is her name, — and begged her to be free. — Now, would you have done the same, or not?"

"Really, I am not imaginative enough to put myself in such a position. It would need a stupendous effort, at all events."

"But was there anything gross in the proceeding?"

"The lady took it ill?"

"Not in the sense of being offended. But she said it had caused her much suffering. She begged me to consider *myself* free. She would remain faithful, and if, in time to come, I cared to write to her again — After all these years, I can't speak of it without huskiness. It seemed to me that I have behaved more like a scoundrel than ever. I thought I had better kill myself, and even planned ways of doing it — I did indeed. But after all we decided that our engagement should continue."

"Of course."

"You think it natural? — Well, the engagement has continued till this day. A month ago I was forty, so that we have waited for seventeen years."

Micklethwaite paused on a note of awe.

"Two of Fanny's sisters are dead; they never married. The blind one, Fanny has long supported, and she will come to live with us. — Long, long ago we had both of us given up thought of marriage. I have never spoken to any one of the engagement; it was something too absurd, and also too sacred."

The smile died from Everard's face, and he sat in thought.

"Now, when are *you* going to marry?" cried Micklethwaite, with a revival of his cheerfulness.

"Probably never."

"Then I think you will neglect a grave duty. Yes. It is the duty of every man, who has sufficient means, to maintain a wife. The life of unmarried women is a wretched one; every man who is able ought to save one of them from that fate."

"I should like my cousin Mary and her female friends to hear you talk in that way. They would overwhelm you with scorn."

"Not sincere scorn, in my belief. Of course I have heard of that kind of woman. Tell me something about them."

Barfoot was led on to a broad expression of his views.

"I admire your old-fashioned sentiment, Micklethwaite. It sits well on you, and you're a fine fellow. But I have much more sympathy with the new idea that women should think of marriage only as men do; — I mean, not to grow up in the thought that they must marry or be blighted creatures. My own views are rather extreme, perhaps; strictly, I don't believe in marriage at all. And I haven't anything like the respect for women, as women, that you have. You belong to the Ruskin school[1]; and I — well, perhaps my experience has been unusual, though I don't think so. You know, by-the-bye, that my relatives consider me a blackguard?"

"That affair you told be about, some years ago?"

"Chiefly that. — I have a good mind to tell you the true story; I didn't care to at the time. I accepted the charge of blackguardism; it didn't matter much. — My cousin will never forgive me, though she has an air of friendliness once more. And I suspect she had told her friend Miss Nunn all about me. Perhaps to put Miss Nunn on her guard — heaven knows!"

He laughed merrily.

"Miss Nunn, I dare say, needs no protection against you."

"I had an odd thought whilst I was there." Everard leaned his head back, and half closed his eyes. "Miss Nunn, I warrant, considers herself proof against any kind of wooing. She is one of the grandly severe women; a terror, I imagine, to any young girl at their place who betrays weak thoughts of matrimony. Now, it's rather a temptation to a man of my kind. There would be something piquant in making vigorous love to Miss Nunn, just to prove her sincerity."

Micklethwaite shook his head.

"Unworthy of you, Barfoot. Of course you couldn't really do such a thing."

---

1 Ruskin's notions of womanhood were highly idealized and also highly constricting. See the extract from "Of Queens' Gardens" in Appendix B.

"But such women really challenge one. If she were rich, I think I could do it without scruple."

"You seem to be taking it for granted," said the mathematician, smiling, "that this lady would — would respond to your love-making."

"I confess to you that women have spoilt me. And I am rather resentful when any one cries out against me for lack of respect to womanhood. I have been the victim of this groundless veneration for females. — Now, you shall hear the story; and bear in mind that you are the only person to whom I have ever told it. I never tried to defend myself when I was vilified on all hands. Probably the attempt would have been useless; and then, it would certainly have increased the odium in which I stood. I think I'll tell cousin Mary the truth some day; it would be good for her."

The listener looked uneasy, but curious.

"Well now, I was staying, in the summer, with some friends of ours at a little place called Upchurch, on a branch line from Oxford. The people were well-to-do, — Goodall their name, — and went in for philanthropy. Mrs. Goodall always had a lot of Upchurch girls about her, educated and not; her idea was to civilize one class by means of the other, and to give a new spirit to both. My cousin Mary was staying at the house whilst I was there. She had more reasonable views than Mrs. Goodall, but took a great interest in what was going on.

"Now one of the girls in process of spiritualization was called Amy Drake. In the ordinary course of things I shouldn't have met her, but she served in a shop where I went two or three times to get a newspaper; we talked a little, — with absolute propriety on my part, I assure you, — and she knew that I was a friend of the Goodalls. The girl had no parents, and she was on the point of going to London to live with a married sister.

"It happened that by the very train which took me back to London, when my visit was over, this girl also travelled, and alone. I saw her at Upchurch Station, but we didn't speak, and I got into a smoking-carriage. We had to change at Oxford, and there, as I walked about the platform, Amy put herself in my way, so that I was obliged to begin talking with her. This behaviour rather surprised me; I wondered what Mrs. Goodall would think of it. But perhaps it was a sign of innocent freedom in the intercourse of men and women. At all events, Amy managed to get me into the same carriage with herself, and on the way to London we were alone. You foresee the end of it. At Paddington Station the girl and I went off together, and she didn't get to her sister's till the evening.

"Of course I take it for granted that you believe my account of the matter. Miss Drake was by no means the spiritual young person that Mrs. Goodall thought her, or hoped to make her; plainly, she was a reprobate of experience. This, you will say, doesn't alter the fact that I also behaved like a reprobate. No; from the moralist's point of view I was to blame. But I had no moral pretensions, and it was too much to expect that I should rebuke the young woman and preach her a sermon. You admit that, I dare say?"

The mathematician, frowning uncomfortably, gave a nod of assent.

"Amy was not only a reprobate, but a rascal. She betrayed me to the people at Upchurch, and, I am quite sure, meant from the first to do so. Imagine the outcry. I had committed a monstrous crime, — had led astray an innocent maiden, had outraged hospitality, — and so on. In Amy's case there were awkward results. Of course I must marry the girl forthwith. But of course I was determined to do no such thing. For the reasons I have explained, I let the storm break upon me. I had been a fool, to be sure, and couldn't help myself. No one would have believed my plea, — no one would have allowed that the truth was an excuse. I was abused on all hands. And when, shortly after, my father made his will and died, doubtless he cut me off with my small annuity on this very account. My cousin Mary got a good deal of the money that would otherwise have been mine. The old man had been on rather better terms with me just before that; in a will that he destroyed I believe he had treated me handsomely."

"Well, well," said Micklethwaite, "every one knows there are detestable women to be found. But you oughtn't to let this affect your view of women in general. — What became of the girl?"

"I made her a small allowance for a year and a half. Then her child died, and the allowance ceased. I know nothing more of her. Probably she has inveigled some one into marriage."

"Well, Barfoot," said the other, rolling about in his chair, "my opinion remains the same. You are in debt to some worthy woman to the extent of half your income. Be quick and find her. It will be better for you."

"And do you suppose," asked Everard, with a smile of indulgence, "that I could marry on four hundred and fifty a year?"

"Heavens! Why not?"

"Quite impossible. A wife *might* be acceptable to me; but marriage with poverty — I know myself and the world too well for that."

"Poverty!" screamed the mathematician. "Four hundred and fifty pounds!"

"Grinding poverty — for married people."

Micklethwaite burst into indignant eloquence, and Everard sat listening with the restrained smile on his lips.

CHAPTER X.

FIRST PRINCIPLES.

Having allowed exactly a week to go by, Everard Barfoot made use of his cousin's permission, and called upon her at nine in the evening. Miss Barfoot's dinner-hour was seven o'clock; she and Rhoda, when alone, rarely sat for more than half an hour at table, and in this summer season they often went out together at sunset to enjoy a walk along the river. This evening they had returned only a few minutes before Everard's ring sounded at the door. Miss Barfoot (they were just entering the library) looked at her friend and smiled.

"I shouldn't wonder if that is the young man. Very flattering if he has come again so soon."

The visitor was in mirthful humour, and met with a reception of corresponding tone. He remarked at once that Miss Nunn had a much pleasanter aspect than a week ago; her smile was ready and agreeable; she sat in a sociable attitude and answered a jesting triviality with indulgence.

"One of my reasons for coming to-day," said Everard, "was to tell you a remarkable story. It connects" — he addressed his cousin — "with our talk about the matrimonial disasters of those two friends of mine. Do you remember the name of Micklethwaite — a man who used to cram me with mathematics? — I thought you would. He is on the point of marrying, and his engagement has lasted just seventeen years."

"The wisest of your friends, I should say."

"An excellent fellow. He is forty, and the lady the same. An astonishing case of constancy."

"And how is it likely to turn out?"

"I can't predict, as the lady is unknown to me. But," he added with facetious gravity, "I think it likely that they are tolerably well acquainted with each other. Nothing but sheer poverty has kept them apart. Pathetic, don't you think? I have a theory that when an engagement has lasted ten years, with constancy on both sides, and poverty still prevents marriage, the State ought to make provision for a man in some way, according to his social standing. When one thinks of it, a whole socialistic system lies in that suggestion."

"If," remarked Rhoda, "it were first provided that no marriage should take place until *after* a ten years' engagement."

"Yes," Barfoot assented, in his smoothest and most graceful tone. "That completes the system. — Unless you like to add that no engagement is permitted except between people who have passed a certain examination; equivalent, let us say, to that which confers a University degree."

"Admirable. And no marriage, except where both, for the whole decennium, have earned their living by work that the State recognizes."

"How would that affect Mr. Micklethwaite's betrothed?" asked Miss Barfoot.

"I believe she has supported herself, all along, by teaching."

"Of course!" exclaimed the other impatiently. "And more likely that not, with loathing of her occupation. The usual kind of drudgery, was it?"

"After all, there must be some one to teach children to read and write."

"Yes; but people who are thoroughly well trained for the task, and who take a pleasure in it. This lady may be an exception; but I picture her as having spent a lifetime of uncongenial toil, longing miserably for the day when poor Mr. Micklethwaite was able to offer her a home. That's the ordinary teacher-woman, and we must abolish her altogether."

"How are you to do that?" inquired Everard suavely. "The average man labours that he may be able to marry, and the average woman certainly has the same end in view. Are female teachers to be vowed to celibacy?"

"Nothing of the kind. But girls are to be brought up to a calling in life, just as men are. It's because they have no such calling that, when need comes, they all offer themselves as teachers. They undertake one of the most difficult and arduous pursuits as if it were as simple as washing up dishes. We can't earn money in any other way, but we can teach children! A man only becomes a schoolmaster or tutor when he has gone through laborious preparation, — anything but wise or adequate, of course, but still conscious preparation; and only a very few men, comparatively, choose that line of work. Women must have just as wide a choice."

"That's plausible, cousin Mary. But remember that when a man chooses his calling, he chooses it for life. A girl cannot but remember that, if she marries, her calling at once changes. The old business is thrown aside — henceforth profitless."

"No. Not henceforth profitless! There's the very point I insist upon. So far is it from profitless, that it has made her a wholly different woman from what she would otherwise have been. Instead of a moping, mawkish creature, with — in most instances — a very unhealthy mind, she is a complete human being. She stands on an equality with the man. He can't despise her as he now does."

"Very good," assented Everard, observing Miss Nunn's satisfied smile. "I like that view very much. But what about the great number of girls who are claimed by domestic duties? Do you abandon them, with a helpless sigh, to be moping, and mawkish, and unhealthy?"

"In the first place, there needn't be a great number of unmarried women claimed by such duties. Most of those you are thinking of are not fulfilling a duty at all; they are only pottering about the house, because they have nothing better to do. And when the whole course of female education is altered; when girls are trained as a matter of course to some definite pursuit; then those who really are obliged to remain at home will do their duty there in quite a different spirit. Home-work will be their serious business, instead of a disagreeable drudgery, or a way of getting through the time till marriage offers. — I would have no girl, however wealthy her parents, grow up without a profession. There should be no such thing as a class of females vulgarized by the necessity of finding daily amusement."

"Nor of males, either, of course," put in Everard, stroking his beard.

"Nor of males either, cousin Everard."

"You thoroughly approve all this, Miss Nunn?"

"Oh yes. But I go further. I would have girls taught that marriage is a thing to be avoided rather than hoped for. I would teach them that for the majority of women marriage means disgrace."

"Ah! Now do let me understand you. Why does it mean disgrace?"

"Because the majority of men are without sense of honour. To be bound to them in wedlock is shame and misery."

Everard's eyelids drooped, and he did not speak for a moment.

"And you seriously think, Miss Nunn, that by persuading as many women as possible to abstain from marriage, you will improve the character of men?"

"I have no hope of sudden results, Mr. Barfoot. I should like to save as many as possible of the women now living from a life of dishonour; but the spirit of our work looks to the future. When *all* women, high and low alike, are trained to self-respect, then men will regard them in a different light, and marriage may be honourable to both."

Again Everard was silent, and seemingly impressed.

"We'll go on with this discussion another time," said Miss Barfoot, with cheerful interruption. "Everard, do you know Somerset at all?"

"Never was in that part of England."

"Miss Nunn is going to take her holiday at Cheddar, and we have been looking over some photographs of that district, taken by her brother."

From the table she reached a scrap-book, and Everard turned it over with interest. The views were evidently made by an amateur, but in general had no serious faults. Cheddar cliffs were represented in several aspects.

"I had no idea the scenery was so fine. Cheddar cheese has quite over-shadowed the hills in my imagination. This might be a bit of Cumberland, or of the Highlands."

"It was my play-ground when I was a child," said Rhoda.

"You were born at Cheddar?"

"No; at Axbridge, a little place not far off. But I had an uncle at Cheddar, a farmer, and very often stayed with him. My brother is farming there now."

"Axbridge? Here is a view of the market-place. What a delightful old town!"

"One of the sleepiest spots in England, I should say. The railway goes through it now, but hasn't made the slightest difference. Nobody pulls down or builds; nobody opens a new shop; nobody thinks of extending his trade. A delicious place!"

"But surely you find no pleasure in that kind of thing, Miss Nunn?"

"Oh yes — at holiday time. I shall doze there for a fortnight, and forget all about the 'so-called nineteenth century.'"

"I can hardly believe it. — There will be a disgraceful marriage at this beautiful old church, and the sight of it will exasperate you."

Rhoda laughed gaily.

"Oh, it will be a marriage of the golden age! Perhaps I shall remember the bride when she was a little girl; and I shall give her a kiss, and pat her on the rosy cheek, and wish her joy. And the bridegroom will be such a good-hearted simpleton, unable to pronounce *f* and *s*. I don't mind that sort of marriage a bit!"

The listeners were both regarding her, Miss Barfoot with an affectionate smile, Everard with a puzzled, searching look, ending in amusement.

"I must run down into that country some day," said the latter.

He did not stay much longer, but left only because he feared to burden the ladies with too much of his company.

Again a week passed, and the same evening found Barfoot approaching the house in Queen's Road. To his great annoyance he learnt that Miss Barfoot was not at home; she had dined, but afterwards had gone out. He did not venture to ask for Miss Nunn, and was moving disappointedly away, when Rhoda herself, returning from a walk, came up to the door. She offered her hand gravely, but with friendliness.

"Miss Barfoot, I am sorry to say, has gone to visit one of our girls, who is ill. — But I think she will very soon be back. Will you come in?"

"Gladly. I had so counted on an hour's talk."

Rhoda led him to the drawing-room, excused herself for a few moments, and came back in her ordinary evening dress. Barfoot noticed that her hair was much more becomingly arranged than when he first saw her; so it had been on the last occasion, but for some reason its appearance attracted his eyes this evening. He scrutinized her, at discreet intervals, from head to foot. To Everard, nothing female was alien; woman, merely as woman, interested him profoundly. And this example of her sex had excited his curiosity in no common degree. His concern with her was purely intellectual; she had no sensual attraction for him, but he longed to see further into her mind, to probe the sincerity of the motives she professed, to understand her mechanism, her process of growth. Hitherto he had enjoyed no opportunity of studying this type. For his cousin was a very different person; by habit he regarded her as old, whereas Miss Nunn, in spite of her thirty years, could not possibly be considered past youth.

He enjoyed her air of equality; she sat down with him as a male acquaintance might have done, and he felt sure that her behaviour would be the same under any circumstances. He delighted in the frankness of her speech; it was doubtful whether she regarded any subject as improper for discussion between mature and serious people. Part cause of this, perhaps, was her calm consciousness that she had not a beautiful face. No, it was not beautiful; yet even at the first meeting it did not repel him. Studying her features, he saw how fine was their expression. The prominent forehead, with its little unevennesses that meant brains;[1] the straight eyebrows, strongly marked, with deep vertical furrows generally drawn between them; the chestnut-brown eyes, with long lashes; the high-bridged nose, thin and delicate; the intellectual lips, a protrusion of the lower one, though very slight, marking itself when he caught her profile; the big, strong chin; the shapely neck; — why, after all, it was a kind of beauty. The head might have been sculptured with fine effect. And she had a well-built frame. He observed her strong wrists, with exquisite vein-tracings on the pure white. Probably her constitution was very sound; she had good teeth, and a healthy brownish complexion.

With reference to the sick girl whom Miss Barfoot was visiting, Everard began what was practically a resumption of their last talk.

"Have you a formal society, with rules and so on?"

"Oh no; nothing of the kind."

"But you of course select the girls whom you instruct or employ?"

"Very carefully."

"How I should like to see them all! — I mean," he added, with a laugh, "it would be so very interesting. The truth is, my sympathies are strongly with you in much of what you said the other day about women and marriage. We regard the matter from different points of view, but our ends are the same."

Rhoda moved her eyebrows, and asked calmly:

"Are you serious?"

"Perfectly. You are absorbed in your present work, that of strengthening women's minds and character; for the final issue of this you can't care much. But to me that is the practical interest. In my mind, you are working for the happiness of men."

"Indeed?" escaped Rhoda's lips, which had curled in irony.

"Don't misunderstand me. I am not speaking cynically or trivially. The gain of women is also the gain of men. You are bitter against the average man for his low morality, but that fault, on the whole, is directly traceable to the ignobleness of women. Think, and you will grant me this."

"I see what you mean. — Men have themselves to thank for it."

"Assuredly they have. I say that I am on your side. Our civilization, in this point, has always been absurdly defective. Men have kept women at a barbarous stage of development, and then complain that they are barbarous. In the same way, society does its best to create a criminal class, and then rages against the criminals. — But, you see, I am one of the men, and an impatient one, too. The mass of women I see about me are so con-

---

1 Everard's appraisal of Rhoda is influenced by phrenology, a pseudo-science based on a system of analyzing character and aptitudes according to the shape, size, and configuration of the head.

temptible that, in my haste, I use unjust language. — Put yourself in the man's place. Say that there are a million or so of us very intelligent and highly educated. Well, the women of corresponding mind number perhaps a few thousands. The vast majority of men must make a marriage that is doomed to be a dismal failure. We fall in love, it is true, but do we really deceive ourselves about the future? A very young man may; why, we know of very young men who are so frantic as to marry girls of the working class — mere lumps of human flesh. But most of us know that our marriage is a *pis aller*.[1] At first we are sad about it; then we grow cynical, and snap our fingers at moral obligation."

"Making a bad case very much worse, instead of bravely bettering it."

"Yes, but human nature is human nature. I am only urging to you the case of average intelligent men. As likely as not — so preposterous are our conventions — you have never heard it put honestly. I tell you the simple truth when I say that more than half these men regard their wives with active disgust. They will do anything to be relieved of the sight of them for as many hours as possible at a time. If circumstances allowed, wives would be abandoned very often indeed."

Rhoda laughed.

"You regret that it isn't done?"

"I prefer to say that I approve it when it is done without disregard of common humanity. There's my friend Orchard. With him, it was suicide or freedom from his hateful wife. Most happily, he was able to make provision for her and the children, and had strength to break his bonds. If he had left them to starve, I should have *understood* it, but couldn't have approved it. There are men who might follow his example, but prefer to put up with a life of torture. Well, they *do* prefer it, you see. I may think that they are foolishly weak, but I can only recognize that they make a choice between two forms of suffering. They have tender consciences; the thought of desertion is too painful to them. And in a great number of cases, mere considerations of money and the like keep a man bound. But conscience and habit — detestable habit — and fear of public opinion generally hold him."

"All this is very interesting," said Rhoda, with grave irony. "By the bye, under the head of detestable habit you would put love of children?"

Barfoot hesitated.

"That's a motive I oughtn't to have left out. Yet I believe, for most men, it is represented by conscience. The love of children would not generally, in itself, be strong enough to outweigh matrimonial wretchedness. Many an intelligent and kind-hearted man has been driven from his wife notwithstanding thought for his children. He provides for them as well as he can, — but, and even for their sakes, he must save himself."

The expression of Rhoda's countenance suddenly changed. An

---

1 A last resort.

extreme mobility of facial muscles was one of the things in her that held Everard's attention.

"There's something in your way of putting it that I don't like," she said, with much frankness, "but of course I agree with you in the facts. I am convinced that most marriages are hateful, from every point of view. — But there will be no improvement until women have revolted against marriage, from a reasonable conviction of its hatefulness."

"I wish you all success — most sincerely I do."

He paused, looked about the room, and stroked his ear. Then, in a grave tone:

"My own ideal of marriage involves perfect freedom on both sides. Of course it could only be realized where conditions are favourable; poverty and other wretched things force us so often to sin against our best beliefs. But there are plenty of people who might marry on these ideal terms. Perfect freedom, sanctioned by the sense of intelligent society, would abolish most of the evils we have in mind. — But women must first be civilized; you are quite right in that."

The door opened, and Miss Barfoot came in. She glanced from one to the other, and without speaking gave her hand to Everard.

"How is your patient?" he asked.

"A little better, I think. It is nothing dangerous. — Here's a letter from your brother Tom. Perhaps I had better read it at once; there may be news you would like to hear."

She sat down and broke the envelope; whilst she was reading the letter to herself, Rhoda quietly left the room.

"Yes, there is news," said Miss Barfoot presently, "and of a disagreeable kind. A few weeks ago, — before writing, that is, — he was thrown off a horse and had a rib fractured."

"Oh? How is he going on?"

"Getting right again, he says. — And they are coming back to England; his wife's consumptive symptoms have disappeared, of course, and she is very impatient to leave Madeira. — It is to be hoped she will allow poor Tom time to get his rib set. Probably that consideration doesn't weigh much with her. — He says that he is writing to you by the same mail."

"Poor old fellow!" said Everard, with feeling. "Does he complain about his wife?"

"He never has done till now, but there's a sentence here that reads doubtfully. 'Muriel,' he says, 'has been terribly upset about my accident. I can't persuade her that I didn't get thrown on purpose; yet I assure you I didn't.'"

Everard laughed.

"If old Tom becomes ironical, he must be hard driven. I have no great longing to meet Mrs. Thomas."

"She's a silly and a vulgar woman. But I told him that in plain terms, before he married. It says much for his good nature that he remains so friendly with me. — Read the letter, Everard."

He did so.

"H'm — very kind things about me. Good old Tom! — Why don't I marry? Well now, one would have thought that his own experience —"

Miss Barfoot began to talk about something else. Before very long, Rhoda came back, and in the conversation that followed it was mentioned that she would leave for her holiday in two days.

"I have been reading about Cheddar," exclaimed Everard, with animation.

"There's a flower grows among the rocks called the Cheddar pink. Do you know it?"

"Oh, very well," Rhoda answered. "I'll bring you some specimens."

"Will you? That's very kind."

"Bring *me* a genuine pound or two of the cheese, Rhoda," requested Miss Barfoot gaily.

"I will. — What they sell in the shops there is all sham, Mr. Barfoot, — like so much else in this world."

"I care nothing about the cheese. That's all very well for a matter-of-fact person like cousin Mary, but I have a strong vein of poetry; you must have noticed it?"

When they shook hands:

"You will really bring me the flowers?" Everard said, in a voice sensibly softened.

"I will make a note of it," was the reassuring answer.

[END OF VOLUME I.]

CHAPTER XI.

AT NATURE'S BIDDING.

The sick girl whom Miss Barfoot had been to see was Monica Madden.

With strange suddenness, after several weeks of steady application to her work, in a cheerful spirit which at times rose to gaiety, Monica became dull, remiss, unhappy; then violent headaches attacked her, and one morning she declared herself unable to rise. Mildred Vesper went to Great Portland Street at the usual hour, and informed Miss Barfoot of her companion's illness. A doctor was summoned; to him it seemed probable that the girl was suffering from consequences of overstrain at her old employment; there was nervous collapse, hysteria, general disorder of the system. Had the patient any mental disquietude? Was trouble of any kind (the doctor smiled) weighing upon her? Miss Barfoot, unable to answer these questions, held private colloquy with Mildred; but the latter, though she pondered a good deal with corrugated brows, could furnish no information.

In a day or two Monica was removed to her sister's lodgings at Lavender Hill. Mrs. Conisbee managed to put a room at her disposal, and Virginia tended her. Thither Miss Barfoot went on the evening when Everard found her away; she and Virginia, talking together after being with the invalid for a quarter of an hour, agreed that there was considerable improvement, but felt a like uneasiness regarding Monica's state of mind.

"Do you think," asked the visitor, "that she regrets the step I persuaded her to take?"

"Oh, I *can't* think that! She has been so delighted with her progress each time I have seen her. No, I feel sure it's only the results of what she suffered at Walworth Road. In a very short time we shall have her at work again, and brighter than ever."

Miss Barfoot was not convinced. After Everard's departure that evening, she talked of the matter with Rhoda.

"I'm afraid," said Miss Nunn, "that Monica is rather a silly girl. She doesn't know her own mind. If this kind of thing is repeated, we had better send her back to the country."

"To shop work again?"

"It might be better."

"Oh, I don't like the thought of that."

Rhoda had one of her fits of wrathful eloquence.

"Now could one have a better instance than this Madden family of the crime that middle-class parents commit, when they allow their girls to go without rational training? — Of course I know that Monica was only a little child when they were left orphans; but her sisters had already grown up into uselessness, and their example has been harmful to her all along. Her guardians dealt with her absurdly; they made her half a lady and half a shop-girl. I don't think she'll ever be good for much. And the elder ones will go on just keeping themselves alive; you can see that. They'll never start the school that there's so much talk of. That poor, helpless, foolish Virginia, alone there in her miserable lodging! How can we hope that any one will take her as a companion? — And yet they are capitalists; eight hundred pounds between them. Think what capable women might do with eight hundred pounds."

"I am really afraid to urge them to meddle with the investments."

"Of course; so am I. One is afraid to do or propose anything. Virginia is starving, *must* be starving. Poor creature! I can never forget how her eyes shone when I put that joint of meat before her."

"I do, do wish," sighed Miss Barfoot, with a pained smile, "that I knew some honest man who would be likely to fall in love with little Monica! In spite of you, my dear, I would devote myself to making the match. But there's no one."

"Oh, I would help," laughed Rhoda, not unkindly. "She's fit for nothing else, I'm afraid. We mustn't look for any kind of heroism in Monica."

Less than half an hour after Miss Barfoot had left the house at Lavender Hill, Mildred Vesper made a call there. It was about half-past nine; the invalid, after sitting up since midday, had gone to bed, but could not sleep. Summoned to the house-door, Virginia acquainted Miss Vesper with the state of affairs.

"I think you might see her for a few minutes."

"I should like to, if you please, Miss Madden," replied Mildred, who had a rather uneasy look.

She went upstairs and entered the bedroom, where a lamp was burning. At the sight of her friend Monica showed much satisfaction; they kissed each other affectionately.

"Good old girl! I had made up my mind to come back to-morrow, or at all events the day after. It's so frightfully dull here. — Oh, and I wanted to know if anything — any letter — had come for me."

"That's just why I came to see you to-night."

Mildred took a letter from her pocket, and half averted her face as she handed it.

"It's nothing particular," said Monica, putting it away under her pillow. "Thank you, dear."

But her cheeks had become hot, and she trembled.

"Monica —"

"Well?"

"You wouldn't care to tell me about — anything? You don't think it would make your mind easier?"

For a minute Monica lay back, gazing at the wall, then she looked round quickly, with a shamefaced laugh.

"It's very silly of me not to have told you long before this. But you're so sensible; I was afraid. I'll tell you everything. Not now, but as soon as I get to Rutland Street. I shall come to-morrow."

"Do you think you can? You look dreadfully bad still."

"I shan't get any better here," replied the invalid, in a whisper. "Poor Virgie does depress me so. She doesn't understand that I can't bear to hear her repeating the kind of things she has heard from Miss Barfoot and Miss Nunn. She tries so hard to look forward hopefully, — but I *know* she is miserable, and it makes me more miserable still. I oughtn't to have left you; I should have been all right in a day or two, with you to help me. You don't make-believe, Milly; it's all real and natural good spirits. It has done me good only to see your dear old face."

"Oh, you're a flatterer. — And you do really feel better?"

"Very much better. I shall go to sleep very soon."

The visitor took her leave. When, a few minutes after, Monica had bidden good-night to her sister (requesting that the lamp might be left), she read what Mildred had brought.

"My DEAREST MONICA," — the missive began — "Why have you not written before this? I have been dreadfully uneasy ever since receiving your last letter. Your headache soon went away, I hope? Why haven't you made another appointment? It is all I can do to keep from breaking my promise and coming to ask about you. Write at once, I implore you, my dearest. It's no use telling me that I must not use these words of affection; they come to my lips and to my pen irresistibly. You know so well that I love you with all my heart and soul; I can't address you like I did when we first corresponded. My darling! My dear, sweet beautiful little girl —"

Four close pages of this, with scarce room at the end for "E.W." When she had gone through it, Monica turned her face upon the pillow and lay so for a long time. A clock in the house struck eleven; this roused her, and she slipped out of bed to hide the letter in her dress-pocket. Not long after, she was asleep.

The next day, on returning from her work and opening the sitting-room door, Mildred Vesper was greeted with a merry laugh. Monica had been here since three o'clock, and had made tea in readiness for her friend's arrival. She looked very white, but her eyes gleamed with pleasure, and she moved about the room as actively as before.

"Virgie came with me, but she wouldn't stay. She says she has a most important letter to write to Alice — about the school, of course. Oh, that school! I do wish they could make up their minds. I've told them they may have all my money, if they like."

"Have you? I should like the sensation of offering hundreds of pounds to some one. It must give a strange feeling of dignity and importance."

"Oh, only *two* hundred! A wretched little sum."

"You are a person of large ideas, as I have often told you. Where did you get them, I wonder?"

"Don't put on that face! It's the one I like least, of all your many faces. It's suspicious."

Mildred went to take off her things, and was quickly at the tea-table.

She had a somewhat graver look than usual, and chose rather to listen than talk.

Not long after tea, when there had been a long and unnatural silence, Mildred making pretence of absorption in a "Treasury," and her companion standing at the window, whence she threw back furtive glances, the thunder of a postman's knock downstairs caused both of them to start, and look at each other in a conscience-stricken way.

"That may be for me," said Monica, stepping to the door. "I'll go and look."

Her conjecture was right. Another letter from Widdowson, still more alarmed and vehement than the last. She read it rapidly on the staircase, and entered the room with sheet and envelope squeezed together in her hand.

"I'm going to tell you all about this, Milly."

The other nodded, and assumed an attitude of sober attention. In relating her story, Monica moved hither and thither; now playing with objects on the mantelpiece, now standing in the middle of the floor, hands locked nervously behind her. Throughout, her manner was that of defence; she seemed doubtful of herself, and anxious to represent the case as favourably as possible; not for a moment had her voice the ring of courageous passion, nor the softness of tender feeling. The narrative hung together but awkwardly, and in truth gave a very indistinct notion of how she had comported herself at the various stages of the irregular courtship. Her behaviour had been marked by far more delicacy and scruple than she succeeded in representing. Painfully conscious of this, she exclaimed at length:

"I see your opinion of me has suffered. You don't like this story. You wonder how I could do such things."

"Well, dear, I certainly wonder how you could begin," Mildred made answer, with her natural directness, but gently. "Afterwards, of course it was different. When you had once got to be sure that he was a gentleman —"

"I was sure of that so soon," exclaimed Monica, her cheeks still red. "You will understand it much better when you have seen him."

"You wish me to?"

"I am going to write now, and say that I will marry him."

They looked long at each other.

"You are — really?"

"Yes. I made up my mind last night."

"But, Monica, — you mustn't mind my speaking plainly, — I don't think you love him."

"Yes, I love him well enough to feel that I am doing right in marrying him." She sat down by the table, and propped her head on her hand. "He loves me; I can't doubt that. If you could read his letters, you would see how strong his feeling is."

She shook with the cold induced by excitement; her voice was at moments all but choked.

"But, putting love aside," went on the other, very gravely, "what do you really know of Mr. Widdowson? Nothing whatever but what he has told you himself. Of course you will let your friends make inquiries for you?"

"Yes. I shall tell my sisters, and no doubt they will go to Miss Nunn at once. I don't want to do anything rash. But it will be all right; — I mean, he has told me the truth about everything. You would be sure of that if you knew him."

Mildred, with hands before her on the table, made the tips of her fingers meet. Her lips were drawn in; her eyes seemed looking for something minute on the cloth.

"You know," she said at length, "I suspected what was going on. I couldn't help."

"Of course you couldn't."

"Naturally I thought it was some one whose acquaintance you had made at the shop."

"How *could* I think of marrying any one of that kind?"

"I should have been grieved."

"You may believe me, Milly; Mr. Widdowson is a man you will respect and like as soon as you know him. He couldn't have behaved to me with more delicacy. Not a word from him, spoken or written, has ever pained me, — except that he tells me he suffers so dreadfully, and of course I can't hear that without pain."

"To respect, and even to like, a man isn't at all the same as loving him."

"I said *you* would respect and like him," exclaimed Monica, with humorous impatience. "I don't want *you* to love him."

Mildred laughed, with constraint.

"I never loved any one yet, dear, and it's very unlikely I ever shall. But I think I know the signs of the feeling."

Monica came behind her, and leaned upon her shoulder.

"He loves me so much that he has made me think I *must* marry him. And I am glad of it. I'm not like you, Milly; I can't be contented with this life. Miss Barfoot and Miss Nunn are very sensible and good people, and I admire them very much; but I *can't* go their way. — It seems to me that it would be dreadful, dreadful, to live all one's life alone. — Don't turn round and snap at me; I want to tell you the truth whilst you can't see me. Whenever I think of Alice and Virginia, I am frightened; I had rather, oh far rather, kill myself than live such a life at their age. You can't imagine how miserable they are, really. And I have the same nature as theirs, you know. Compared with you and Miss Haven, I'm very weak and childish."

After drumming on the table for a moment, with wrinkled brows, Mildred made grave response.

"You must let *me* tell the truth as well. I think you're going to marry with altogether wrong ideas. I think you'll do an injustice to Mr. Widdowson. You will marry him for a comfortable home — that's what it amounts to. And you'll repent it bitterly some day — you'll repent."

Monica raised herself and stood apart.

"For one thing," pursued Mildred, with nervous earnestness, "he's too old. Your habits and his won't suit."

"He has assured me that I shall live exactly the kind of life I please. And that will be what *he* pleases. I feel his kindness to me very much, and I shall do my utmost to repay him."

"That's a very nice spirit; but I believe married life is no easy thing even when the people are well matched. I have heard the most dreadful stories of quarrelling and all sorts of unhappiness between people I thought safe from any such dangers. — You *may* be fortunate; I only say that the chances are very much against it, marrying from such motives as you confess."

Monica drew herself up.

"I haven't confessed any motive to be ashamed of, Milly."

"You say you have decided to marry now because you are afraid of never having another chance."

"No; that's turning it very unkindly. I only said that *after* I had told you that I did love him. And I do love him. He has made me love him."

"Then I have no right to say any more. I can only wish you happiness."

Mildred heaved a sigh, and pretended to give her attention to Maunder.

After waiting irresolutely for some minutes, Monica looked for note-paper, and took it, together with her inkstand, into the bedroom. She was absent half an hour. On her return, there was a stamped letter in her hand.

"It is going, Milly."

"Very well, dear. I have nothing more to say."

"You give me up for lost. We shall see."

It was spoken light-heartedly. Again she left the room, put on her out-of-door things, and went to post the letter. By this time she began to feel the results of exertion and excitement; headache and tremulous failing of her strength obliged her to go to bed almost as soon as she returned. Mildred waited upon her with undiminished kindness.

"It's all right," Monica murmured, as her head sank on the pillow. "I feel so relieved and so glad — so happy — now I have done it!"

"Good-night, dear," replied the other, with a kiss, and went back to her semblance of reading.

Two days later, Monica called unexpectedly at Mrs. Conisbee's. Being told by that worthy woman that Miss Madden was at home, she ran upstairs and tapped at the door. Virginia's voice inquired hurriedly who was there, and on Monica's announcing herself there followed a startled exclamation.

"Just a minute, my love! — Only a minute."

When the door opened Monica was surprised by a disorder in her sister's appearance. Virginia had flushed cheeks, curiously vague eyes, and hair ruffled as if she had just risen from a nap. She began to talk in a hurried, disconnected way, trying to explain that she had not been quite well, and was not yet properly dressed.

"What a strange smell!" Monica exclaimed, looking about the room. "It's like brandy."

"You notice it? — I have — I was obliged to get — to ask Mrs. Conisbee for — I don't want to alarm you, dear, but I felt rather faint. — Indeed, I thought I should have a fainting fit. — I was obliged to call Mrs. Conisbee — But don't think anything about it. It's all over. — The weather is very trying —"

She laughed nervously, and began to pat Monica's hand. The girl was not quite satisfied, and pressed many questions, but in the end she accepted Virginia's assurances that nothing serious had happened. Then her own business occupied her; she sat down, and said with a smile:

"I have brought you astonishing news. If you didn't faint before, you'll be very likely to do so now."

Her sister exhibited fresh agitation, and begged not to be kept in suspense.

"My nerves are in a shocking state to-day. It *must* be the weather. What *can* you have to tell me, Monica?"

"I think I shan't need to go on with type-writing."

"Why? What are you going to do, child?" the other asked sharply.

"Virgie, — I am going to be married."

The shock was a severe one. Virginia's hands fell, her eyes started, her mouth opened; she became the colour of clay, even her lips losing for the moment all their colour.

"Married?" she at length gasped. "Who — who is it?"

"Some one you have never heard of. His name is Mr. Edmund Widdowson. He is very well off, and has a house at Herne Hill."

"A private gentleman?"

"Yes. He used to be in business, but is retired. — Now, I am not going to tell you much more about him until you have made his acquaintance. Don't ask a lot of questions. You are to come with me this afternoon to his house. He lives alone, but a relative of his, his sister-in-law, is going to be with him to meet us."

"Oh, but it's so sudden! I can't go to pay a call like that at a moment's notice. Impossible, darling! — What *does* it all mean? — You are going to be married, Monica? I can't understand it. I can't realize it. — Who is this gentleman? How long —"

"No; you won't get me to tell you more than I have done, till you have seen him."

"But what *have* you told me? I couldn't grasp it. I am quite confused. Mr. — what was the name?"

It took half an hour to familiarize Virginia with the simple fact. When she was convinced of its truth, a paroxysm of delight appeared in her. She laughed, uttered cries of joy, even clapped her hands.

"Monica to be married! — A private gentleman — a large fortune! — My darling, how shall I ever believe it? Yet I felt so sure that the day would come. — What *will* Alice say? — And Rhoda Nunn? Have you — have you ventured to tell her?"

"No, that I haven't. I want you to do that. You shall go and see them to-morrow, as it's Sunday."

"Oh, the delight! Alice won't be able to contain herself. We always said the day would come."

"You won't have any more anxieties, Virgie. You can take the school or not, as you like. Mr. Widdowson —"

"Oh, my dear," interposed Virginia, with sudden dignity, "we shall certainly open the school. We have made up our minds; that is to be our life's work. It is far, far more than a mere means of subsistence. But perhaps we shall not need to hurry. Everything can be matured at our leisure. — If you would only just tell me, darling, when you were first introduced?"

Monica laughed gaily, and refused to explain. It was time for Virginia to make herself ready, and here arose a new perturbation; what had she suitable for wear under such circumstances? Monica had decked herself a little, and helped the other to make the best of her narrow resources. At four o'clock they set out.

CHAPTER XII.

WEDDINGS.

When they reached the house at Herne Hill, the sisters were both in a state of nervous tremor. Monica had only the vaguest idea of the kind of person Mrs. Luke Widdowson would prove to be, and Virginia seemed to herself to be walking in a dream.

"Have you been here often?" whispered the latter, as soon as they came in view of the place. Its aspect delighted her, but the conflict of her emotions was so disturbing that she had to pause and seek the support of her sister's arm.

"I've never been inside," Monica answered indistinctly. "Come; we shall be unpunctual."

"I do wish you would tell me, dear" —

"I can't talk, Virgie. Try and keep quiet, and behave as if it were all quite natural."

This was altogether beyond Virginia's power. It happened most luckily, though greatly to Widdowson's annoyance, that the sister-in-law, Mrs. Luke Widdowson, arrived nearly half an hour later than the time she had appointed. Led by the servant into a comfortable drawing-room, the visitors were received by the master of the house alone; with a grim smile, the result of his embarrassment, with profuse apologies and a courtesy altogether excessive, Widdowson did his best to put them at their ease, of course with small result. The sisters side by side on a settee at one end of the room, and the host seated far away from them, they talked with scarcely any understanding of what was said on either side, — the weather and the vastness of London serving as topics, — until of a sudden the door was thrown open, and there appeared a person of such imposing presence that Virginia gave a start and Monica gazed in painful fascination. Mrs. Luke was a tall and portly woman in the prime of life, with rather a high colour; her features were handsome, but without much refinement, their expression a condescending good-humour. Her mourning garb, if mourning it could be called, represented an extreme of the prevailing fashion; its glint and rustle inspired awe in the female observer. A moment ago the drawing-room had seemed empty; Mrs. Luke, in her sole person, filled and illumined it.

Widdowson addressed this resplendent personage by her Christian name, his familiarity exciting in Monica an irrational surprise. He presented the sisters to her, and Mrs. Luke, bowing grandly at a distance, drew from her bosom a gold-rimmed *pince-nez*,[1] through which she scruti-

---

1 Eyeglasses with a spring to grip the bridge of the nose.

nized Monica. The smile which followed might have been interpreted in several senses; Widdowson, alone capable of remarking it, answered with a look of severe dignity.

Mrs. Luke had no thought of apologizing for the lateness of her arrival, and it was evident that she did not intend to stay long. Her purpose seemed to be to make the occasion as informal as possible.

"Do you, by chance, know the Hodgson Bulls?" she asked of her relative, interrupting him in the nervous commonplaces with which he was endeavouring to smooth the way to a general conversation. She had the accent of cultivation, but spoke rather imperiously.

"I never heard of them," was the cold reply.

"No? — They live somewhere about here. I have to make a call on them. I suppose my coachman will find the place."

There was an awkward silence. Widdowson was about to say something to Monica, when Mrs. Luke, who had again closely observed the girl through her glasses, interposed in a gentle tone.

"Do you like this neighbourhood, Miss Madden?"

Monica gave the expected answer, her voice sounding very weak and timid by comparison. And so, for some ten minutes, an appearance of dialogue was sustained. Mrs. Luke, though still condescending, evinced a desire to be agreeable; she smiled and nodded in reply to the girl's remarks, and occasionally addressed Virginia with careful civility, conveying the impression, perhaps involuntarily, that she commiserated the shy and shabbily dressed person. Tea was brought in, and after pretending to take a cup, she rose for departure.

"Perhaps you will come and see me some day, Miss Madden," fell from her with unanticipated graciousness, as she stepped forward to the girl and offered her hand. "Edmund must bring you — at some quiet time when we can talk. Very glad to have met you — very glad indeed."

And the personage was gone; they heard her carriage roll away from beneath the window. All three drew a breath of relief, and Widdowson, suddenly quite another man, took a place near to Virginia, with whom in a few minutes he was conversing in the friendliest way. Virginia, experiencing a like relief, also became herself; she found courage to ask needful questions, which in every case were satisfactorily met. Of Mrs. Luke there was no word, but when they had taken their leave, — the visit lasted altogether some two hours, — Monica and her sister discussed that great lady with the utmost freedom. They agreed that she was personally detestable.

"But very rich, my dear," said Virginia, in a murmuring voice. "You can see that. I have met such people before; they have a manner — oh! Of course Mr. Widdowson will take you to call upon her."

"When nobody else is likely to be there; that's what she meant," remarked Monica coldly.

"Never mind, my love. You don't wish for grand society. — I am very glad to tell you that Edmund impresses me very favourably. He is reserved, but that is no fault. — Oh, we must write to Alice at once! Her surprise! Her delight!"

When, on the next day, Monica met her betrothed in Regent's Park, — she still lived with Mildred Vesper, but no longer went to Great Portland Street, — their talk was naturally of Mrs. Luke. Widdowson speedily led to the topic.

"I had told you," he said, with careful accent, "that I see very little of her. I can't say that I like her, but she is a very difficult person to understand, and I fancy she often gives offence when she doesn't at all mean it. Still, I hope you were not — displeased?"

Monica avoided a direct answer.

"Shall you take me to see her?" were her words.

"If you will go, dear. — And I have no doubt she will be present at our wedding. Unfortunately, she's my only relative; or the only one I know anything about. After our marriage I don't think we shall see much of her" —

"No, I dare say not," was Monica's remark. And thereupon they turned to pleasanter themes.

That morning, Widdowson had received from his sister-in-law a scribbled post-card, asking him to call upon Mrs. Luke early the day that followed. Of course this meant that the lady was desirous of further talk concerning Miss Madden. Unwillingly, but as a matter of duty, he kept the appointment. It was at eleven in the morning, and, when admitted to the flat in Victoria Street which was his relative's abode, he had to wait a quarter of an hour for the lady's appearance.

Luxurious fashion, as might have been expected, distinguished Mrs. Luke's drawing-room. Costly and beautiful things superabounded; perfume soothed the air. Only since her bereavement had Mrs. Widdowson been able to indulge this taste for modern exuberance in domestic adornment. The deceased Luke was a plain man of business, who clung to the fashions which had been familiar to him in his youth; his second wife found a suburban house already furnished, and her influence with him could not prevail to banish the horrors amid which he chose to live: chairs in maroon rep, Brussels carpets of red roses on a green ground, horse-hair sofas of the most uncomfortable shape ever designed, antimacassars everywhere, chimney ornaments of cut glass trembling in sympathy with the kindred chandeliers.[1] She belonged to an obscure branch of a house that culminated in an obscure Baronetcy; penniless and ambitious, she had to thank her

---

1 I.e., Luke Widdowson's tastes favoured the serviceable rather than the fashionable, and his furnishings were stodgy. "Rep" is a fabric woven with a ribbed effect; Brussels carpets are wool pile with coloured patterns; horse-hair is a stiff fabric made from the mane and tail of horses; antimacassars are small coverings placed over the backs and arms of upholstered furniture to prevent soiling (named after macassar hair oil).

imposing physique for rescue at a perilous age, and though despising Mr. Luke Widdowson for his plebeian tastes, she shrewdly retained the good-will of a husband who seemed no candidate for length of years. The money-maker died much sooner than she could reasonably have hoped, and left her an income of four thousand pounds. Thereupon began for Mrs. Luke a life of feverish aspiration. The Baronetcy to which she was akin had inspired her, even from childhood, with an aristocratic ideal; a handsome widow of only eight-and-thirty, she resolved that her wealth should pave the way for her to a titled alliance. Her acquaintance lay among City people, but with the opportunities of freedom it was soon extended to the sphere of what is known as smart society; her flat in Victoria Street attracted a heterogeneous cluster of pleasure-seekers and fortune-hunters, among them one or two vagrant members of the younger aristocracy. She lived at the utmost pace compatible with technical virtue. When, as shortly happened, it became evident that her income was not large enough for her serious purpose, she took counsel with an old friend great in finance, and thenceforth the excitement of the gambler gave a new zest to her turbid existence. Like most of her female associates, she had free recourse to the bottle; but for such stimulus the life of a smart woman would be physically impossible. And Mrs. Luke enjoyed life, enjoyed it vastly. The goal of her ambition, if all went well in the City, was quite within reasonable hope. She foretasted the day when a vulgar prefix would no longer attach to her name, and when the journals of Society would reflect her rising effulgence.

Widdowson was growing impatient, when his relative at length appeared. She threw herself into a deep chair, crossed her legs, and gazed at him mockingly.

"Well, it isn't quite so bad as I feared, Edmund."

"What do you mean?"

"Oh, she's a decent enough little girl, I can see. But you're a silly fellow, for all that. You couldn't have deceived me, you know. If there'd been anything — you understand? — I should have spotted it at once."

"I don't relish this kind of talk," observed Widdowson acidly. "In plain English, you supposed I was going to marry some one about whom I couldn't confess the truth."

"Of course I did. Now come; tell me how you got to know her."

The man moved uneasily, but in the end related the whole story. Mrs. Luke kept nodding, with an amused air.

"Yes, yes; she managed it capitally. Clever little witch. Fetching eyes, she has."

"If you sent for me to make insulting remarks" —

"Bosh! — I'll come to the wedding, gladly. But you're a silly fellow. Now why didn't you come and ask me to find you a wife? Why, I know two or three girls of really good family who would have jumped, simply jumped, at a man with your money. Pretty girls, too. But you always were so horribly unpractical. Don't you know, my dear boy, that there are heaps of ladies, real ladies, waiting to marry the first decent man who offers them five or six hundred a year? Why haven't you used the opportunities that you knew I could put in your way?"

Widdowson rose from his seat, and stood stiffly.

"I see you don't understand me in the least. I am going to marry because, for the first time in my life, I have met the woman whom I can respect and love."

"That's very nice and very proper. But why shouldn't you respect and love a girl who belongs to good society?"

"Miss Madden is a lady," he replied indignantly.

"Oh — yes — to be sure," hummed the other, letting her head loll back. "Well, bring her here some day when we can lunch quietly together. — I see it's no use. You're not a sharp man, Edmund."

"Do you seriously tell me," asked Widdowson, with grave curiosity, "that there are ladies in good society who would have married me just because I have a few hundreds a year?"

"My dear boy, I would get together a round dozen in two or three days. Girls who would make good, faithful wives, in mere gratitude to the man who saved them from — horrors."

"Excuse me if I say that I don't believe it."

Mrs. Luke laughed merrily, and the conversation went on in this strain for another ten minutes. At the end, Mrs. Luke made herself very agreeable, praised Monica for her sweet face and gentle manners, and so dismissed the solemn man with a renewed promise to countenance the marriage by her gracious presence.

When Rhoda Nunn returned from her holiday, it wanted but a week to Monica's wedding, so speedily had everything been determined and arranged. Miss Barfoot, having learnt from Virginia all that was to be known concerning Mr. Widdowson, felt able to hope for the best; a grave husband, of mature years, and with means more than sufficient, seemed, to the eye of experience, no unsuitable match for a girl such as Monica. This view of the situation caused Rhoda to smile with contemptuous tolerance.

"And yet," she remarked, "I have heard you speak severely of such marriages."

"It isn't the ideal wedlock," replied Miss Barfoot. "But so much in life is compromise. — After all, she may regard him more affectionately than we imagine."

"No doubt she has weighed advantages. If the prospects you offered her had proved more to her taste, she would have dismissed this elderly admirer. His fate has been decided during the last few weeks. It's probably that the invitation to your Wednesday evenings gave her a hope of meeting young men."

"I see no harm if it did," said Miss Barfoot, smiling. "But Miss Vesper would very soon undeceive her on that point."

"I hardly thought of her as a girl likely to make chance friendships with men in highways and by-ways."

"No more did I. And that makes me all the more content with what has come about. She ran a terrible risk, poor child. — You see, Rhoda, nature is too strong for us."

Rhoda threw her head back.

"And the delight of her sister! It is really pathetic. The mere fact that Monica is to be married blinds the poor woman to every possibility of misfortune."

In the course of the same conversation, Rhoda remarked thoughtfully:

"It strikes me that Mr. Widdowson must be of a confiding nature. I don't think men in general, at all events those with money, care to propose marriage to girls they encounter by the way."

"I suppose he saw that the case was exceptional."

"How was he to see that?"

"You are severe. — Her shop training accounts for much. The elder sisters could never have found a husband in this way. The revelation must have shocked them at first."

Rhoda dismissed the subject, lightly, and henceforth showed only the faintest interest in Monica's concerns.

Monica meanwhile rejoiced in her liberation from the work and philosophic severities of Great Portland Street. She saw Widdowson somewhere or other every day, and heard him discourse on the life that was before them, herself for the most part keeping silence. Together they called upon Mrs. Luke, and had luncheon with her; Monica was not displeased with her reception, and began secretly to hope that more than a glimpse of that gorgeous world might some day be vouchsafed to her.

Apart from her future husband, Monica was in a sportive mood, with occasional fits of exhilaration which seemed rather unnatural. She had declared to Mildred her intention of inviting Miss Nunn to the wedding, and her mind was evidently set on carrying out this joke, as she regarded it. When the desire was intimated by letter, Rhoda replied with a civil refusal: she would be altogether out of place at such a ceremony, but hoped that Monica would accept her heartiest good wishes. Virginia was then despatched to Queen's Road, and appealed so movingly that the prophetess at length yielded. On hearing this, Monica danced with delight, and her companion in Rutland Street could not help sharing her merriment.

The ceremony was performed at a church at Herne Hill. By an odd arrangement, — like everything else in the story of this pair, a result of social and personal embarrassments, — Monica's belongings, including her apparel for the day, were previously despatched to the bridegroom's house, whither, in company with Virginia, the bride went early in the morning. It was one of the quietest of weddings, but all ordinary formalities were complied with, Widdowson having no independent views on the subject. Present were Virginia, (to give away the bride,) Miss Vesper, (who looked decidedly odd in a pretty dress given her by Monica,) Rhoda Nunn, (who appeared to advantage in a costume of quite unexpected appropriateness,) Mrs. Widdowson, (an imposing figure, evidently feeling that she had got into strange society,) and, as friend of the bridegroom, one Mr. Newdick, a musty and nervous City clerk. Depression was manifest on every countenance, not excepting Widdowson's; the man had such a stern, gloomy look, and held himself with so much awkwardness, that he might have been imagined to stand here on compulsion. For an hour before going to the church, Monica cried and seemed unutterably doleful; she had not slept for two nights; her face was ghastly. Virginia's gladness gave way just before the company assembled, and she too shed many tears.

There was a breakfast, more dismal fooling than even this species of fooling is wont to be. Mr. Newdick, trembling and bloodless, proposed Monica's health; Widdowson, stern and dark as ever, gloomily responded; and then, *that* was happily over. By one o'clock the gathering began to disperse. Monica drew Rhoda Nunn aside.

"It was very kind of you to come," she whispered, with half a sob. "It all seems very silly, and I'm sure you have wished yourself away a hundred times. I am really, seriously, grateful to you."

Rhoda put a hand on each side of the girl's face, and kissed her, but without saying a word; and thereupon left the house. Mildred Vesper, after changing her dress in the room used by Monica, as she had done on arriving, went off by train to her duties in Great Portland Street. Virginia alone remained to see the married couple start for their honeymoon. They were going into Cornwall, and on the return journey would manage to see Miss Madden at her Somerset retreat. For the present, Virginia was to live on at Mrs. Conisbee's, but not in the old way; henceforth she would have proper attendance, and modify her vegetarian diet, — at the express bidding of the doctor, as she explained to her landlady.

Though that very evening Everard Barfoot made a call upon his friends in Chelsea, the first since Rhoda's return from Cheddar, he heard nothing of the event that marked the day. But Miss Nunn appeared to him unlike herself; she was absent, had little to say, and looked, what he had never yet known her, oppressed by low spirits. For some reason or other, Miss Barfoot left the room.

"You are thinking with regret of your old home," Everard remarked, taking a seat nearer to Miss Nunn.

"No. Why should you fancy that?"

"Only because you seem rather sad."

"One is, sometimes."

"I like to see you with that look. — May I remind you that you promised me some flowers from Cheddar?"

"Oh, so I did," exclaimed the other, in a tone of natural recollection. "I have brought them, scientifically pressed between blotting-paper. I'll fetch them."

When she returned, it was together with Miss Barfoot, and the conversation became livelier.

A day or two after this, Everard left town, and was away for three weeks, part of the time in Ireland.

"I left London for a while," he wrote from Killarney to his cousin, "partly because I was afraid I had begun to bore you and Miss Nunn. Don't you regret giving me permission to call upon you? The fact is, I can't live without intelligent female society; talking with women, as I talk with you two, is one of my chief enjoyments. I hope you won't get tired of my visits; in fact, they are all but a necessity to me, as I have discovered since coming away. But it was fair that you should have a rest."

"Don't be afraid," Miss Barfoot replied to this part of his letter. "We are not at all weary of your conversation. The truth is, I like it much better than in the old days. You seem to me to have a healthier mind, and I am quite sure that the society of intelligent women, (we affect no foolish self-depreciation, Miss Nunn and I,) is a good thing for you. Come back to us as soon as you like; I shall welcome you."

It happened that his return to England was almost simultaneous with the arrival from Madeira of Mr. and Mrs. Thomas Barfoot. Everard at once went to see his brother, who for the present was staying at Torquay. Ill health dictated this choice of residence; Thomas was still suffering from the results of his accident; his wife had left him at an hotel, and was visiting relatives in different parts of England. The brothers exhibited much affectionate feeling after their long separation; they spent a week together, and planned for another meeting when Mrs. Thomas should have returned to her husband.

An engagement called Everard back to town. He was to be present at the wedding of his friend Micklethwaite, now actually on the point of taking place. The mathematician had found a suitable house, very small and of very low rental, out at South Tottenham, and thither was transferred the furniture which had been in his bride's possession since the death of her parents; Micklethwaite bought only a few new things. By discreet inquiry, Barfoot had discovered that "Fanny" though musically inclined, would not possess a piano, her old instrument being quite worn out and not worth the cost of conveyance; thus it came to pass that, a day or two before the wedding, Micklethwaite was astonished by the arrival of an instrument of the Cottage species,[1] mysteriously addressed to a person not yet in existence, Mrs. Micklethwaite.

"You scoundrel!" he cried, when, on the next day, Barfoot presented himself at the house. "This is *your* doing. What the deuce do you mean? A man who complains of poverty! — Well, it's the greatest kindness I ever received, that's all. Fanny will be devoted to you. With music in the house, our blind sister will lead quite a different life. Confound it! I want to begin crying. Why, man, I'm not accustomed to receive presents, even as a proxy; I haven't had one since I was a schoolboy."

---

1 A small upright piano.

"That's an audacious statement. When you told me that Miss Wheatley never allowed your birthday to pass without sending something."

"Oh, Fanny! But I have never thought of Fanny as a separate person. Upon my word, now I think of it, I never have. Fanny and I have been one for ages."

That evening the sisters arrived from their country home. Micklethwaite gave up the house to them, and went to a lodging.

It was with no little curiosity that, on the appointed morning, Barfoot repaired to South Tottenham. He had seen a photograph of Miss Wheatley, but it dated from seventeen years ago. Standing in her presence, he was moved with compassion, and with another feeling more rarely excited in him by a woman's face, that of reverential tenderness. Impossible to recognize in this countenance the features known to him from the portrait. At three-and-twenty she had possessed a sweet simple comeliness on which any man's eye would have rested with pleasure; at forty she was wrinkled, hollow-cheeked, sallow, indelible weariness stamped upon her brows and lips. She looked much older than Mary Barfoot, though they were just of an age. And all this for want of a little money. The life of a pure, gentle, tender-hearted woman worn away in hopeless longing and in hard struggle for daily bread. As she took his hand and thanked him with an exquisite modesty for the present she had received, Everard felt a lump rise in his throat. He was ashamed to notice that the years had dealt so unkindly with her; fixing his look upon her eyes, he gladdened at the gladness which shone in them, at the soft light which they could still shed forth.

Micklethwaite was probably unconscious of the poor woman's faded appearance. He had seen her from time to time, and always with the love which idealizes. In his own pathetic phrase, she was simply a part of himself; he no more thought of criticizing her features than of standing before the glass to mark and comment upon his own. It was enough to glance at him as he took his place beside her, the proudest and happiest of men. A miracle had been wrought for him; kind fate, in giving her to his arms, had blotted out those long years of sorrow, and to-day Fanny was the betrothed of his youth, beautiful in his sight as when first he looked upon her.

Her sister, younger by five years, had more regular lineaments, but she too was worn with suffering, and her sightless eyes made it more distressing to contemplate her. She spoke cheerfully, however, and laughed with joy in Fanny's happiness. Barfoot pressed both her hands with the friendliest warmth.

One vehicle conveyed them all to the church, and in half an hour the lady to whom the piano was addressed had come into being. The simplest of transformations; no bridal gown, no veil, no wreath; only the gold ring for symbol of union. And it might have happened nigh a score of years ago; nigh a score of years lost from the span of human life — all for want of a little money.

"I will say good-bye to you here," muttered Everard to his friend at the church door.

The married man gripped him by the arm.

"You will do nothing of the kind. Fanny, he wants to be off at once! — You won't go until you have heard my wife play something on that blessed instrument."

So all entered the cab again, and drove back to the house. A servant who had come with Fanny from the country, a girl of fifteen, opened the door to them, smiling and curtseying. And all sat together in happy talk, the blind woman gayest among them; she wished to have the clergyman described to her, and the appearance of the church. Then Mrs. Micklethwaite placed herself at the piano, and played simple, old-fashioned music, neither well nor badly, but to the infinite delight of two of her hearers.

"Mr. Barfoot," said the sister at length, "I have known your name for a long time, but I little thought to meet you on such a day as this, and to owe you such endless thanks. So long as I can have music, I forget that I can't see."

"Barfoot is the finest fellow on earth," exclaimed Micklethwaite. "At least, he would be if he understood Trilinear Co-ordinates."

"Are *you* strong in mathematics, Mrs. Micklethwaite?" asked Everard.

"I? Oh dear, no! I never got much past the Rule of Three.[1] But Tom has forgiven me that long ago."

"I don't despair of getting you into plane trigonometry, Fanny. We will gossip about sines and co-sines before we die."

It was said half-seriously, and Everard could not but burst into laughter.

He sat down with them to their plain mid-day meal, and early in the afternoon took his leave. He had no inclination to go home, if the empty flat could be dignified with such a name. After reading the papers at his club, he walked aimlessly about the streets until it was time to return to the same place for dinner. Then he sat with a cigar, dreaming, and at half-past eight went to the Royal Oak Station, and journeyed to Chelsea.

---

1 An elementary algebraic formula for finding the fourth term of a proposition when only three are given (the product of the means equals the product of the extremes). Trigonometry, which Micklethwaite humorously suggests he hopes to gossip about with Fanny one day, is a more advanced branch of mathematics that deals with the study of sides and angles of triangles. "Sine" and "co-sine" are trigonometric terms expressing the ratios of angles and sides.

CHAPTER XIII.

DISCORD OF LEADERS.

A disappointment awaited him. Miss Barfoot was not well enough to see any one. Had she been suffering long? — he inquired. No; it was only this evening; she had not dined, and was gone to her room. Miss Nunn could not receive him.

He went home, and wrote to his cousin.

The next morning he came upon a passage in the newspaper which seemed to suggest a cause for Miss Barfoot's indisposition. It was the report of an inquest. A girl name Bella Royston had poisoned herself. She was living alone, without occupation, and received visits only from one lady. This lady, her name Miss Barfoot, had been supplying her with money, and had just found her a situation in a house of business; but the girl appeared to have gone through troubles which had so disturbed her mind that she could not make the effort required of her. She left a few lines addressed to her benefactress, just saying that she chose death rather than the struggle to recover her position.

It was Saturday. He decided to call in the afternoon and see whether Mary had recovered.

Again a disappointment. Miss Barfoot was better, and had been away since breakfast; Miss Nunn was also absent.

Everard sauntered about the neighbourhood, and presently found himself in the gardens of Chelsea Hospital.[1] It was a warm afternoon, and so still that he heard the fall of yellow leaves as he walked hither and thither along the alleys. His failure to obtain an interview with Miss Nunn annoyed him; but for her presence in the house he would not have got into this habit of going there. As far as ever from harbouring any serious thoughts concerning Rhoda, he felt himself impelled along the way which he had jokingly indicated in talk with Micklethwaite; he was tempted to make love to her as an interesting pastime, to observe how so strong-minded a woman would conduct herself under such circumstances. Had she, or not, a vein of sentiment in her character? Was it impossible to move her as other women are moved? — Meditating thus he looked up, and saw the subject of his thoughts. She was seated a few yards away, and seemingly had not yet become aware of him, for her eyes were on the ground, and troubled reverie appeared in her countenance.

"I have just called at the house, Miss Nunn. How is my cousin to-day?"

She had looked up only a moment before he spoke, and seemed vexed at being thus discovered.

---

1 Chelsea Royal Hospital for old or disabled soldiers, founded in 1694, has extensive grounds that include public gardens.

"I believe Miss Barfoot is quite well," she answered coldly, as they shook hands.

"But yesterday she was not so."

"A headache, or something of the kind."

He was astonished. Rhoda spoke with a cold indifference. She had risen, and showed her wish to move from the spot.

"She had to attend an inquest yesterday. Perhaps it rather upset her?"

"Yes, I think it did."

Unable to adapt himself at once to this singular mood of Rhoda's, but resolved not to let her go before he had tried to learn the cause of it, he walked along by her side. In this part of the Gardens there were only a few nursemaids with children; it would have been a capital place and time for improving his intimacy with the remarkable woman. But possibly she was determined to be rid of him. A contest between his will and hers would be an amusement decidedly to his taste.

"You also have been disturbed by it, Miss Nunn."

"By the inquest?" she returned, with barely veiled scorn. "Indeed I have not."

"Did you know that poor girl?"

"Some time ago."

"Then it is only natural that her miserable fate should sadden you."

He spoke as if with respectful sympathy, ignoring what she had said.

"It has no effect whatever upon me," Rhoda answered, glancing at him with surprise and displeasure.

"Forgive me if I say that I find it difficult to believe that. Perhaps you"

—

She interrupted him.

"I don't easily forgive any one who charges me with falsehood, Mr. Barfoot."

"Oh, you take it too seriously. I beg your pardon a thousand times. — I was going to say that perhaps you won't allow yourself to acknowledge any feeling of compassion in such a case."

"I don't acknowledge what I don't feel. — I will bid you good afternoon."

He smiled at her with all the softness and persuasiveness of which he was capable. She had offered her hand, with cold dignity, and instead of taking it merely for good-bye he retained it.

"You must, you shall forgive me! I shall be too miserable if you dismiss me in this way. — I see that I was altogether wrong. You know all the particulars of the case, and I have only read a brief newspaper account. I am sure the girl didn't deserve your pity."

She was trying to draw her hand away. Everard felt the strength of her muscles, and the sensation was somehow so pleasant that he could not at once release her.

"You do pardon me, Miss Nunn?"

"Please don't be foolish. I will thank you to let my hand go."

Was it possible? Her cheek had coloured, ever so slightly. But with indignation, no doubt, for her eyes flashed sternly at him. Very unwilling, Everard had no choice but to obey the command.

"Will you have the kindness to tell me," he said more gravely, "whether my cousin was suffering only from that cause?"

"I can't say," she added after a pause. "I haven't spoken with Miss Barfoot for two or three days."

He looked at her with genuine astonishment.

"You haven't seen each other?"

"Miss Barfoot is angry with me. I think we shall be obliged to part."

"To part? What can possibly have happened? Miss Barfoot angry with *you*?"

"If I *must* satisfy your curiosity, Mr. Barfoot, I had better tell you at once that the subject of our difference is the girl you mentioned. Not very long ago she tried to persuade your cousin to receive her again, — to give her lessons at the place in Great Portland Street, as before she disgraced herself. Miss Barfoot, with too ready good-nature, was willing to do this, but I resisted. It seemed to me that it would be a very weak and wrong thing to do. At the time, she ended by agreeing with me. Now that the girl has killed herself, she throws the blame upon my interference. We had a painful conversation, and I don't think we can continue to live together."

Barfoot listened with gratification. It was much to have compelled Rhoda to explain herself, and on such a subject.

"Nor even to work together?" he asked.

"It is doubtful."

Rhoda still moved forward, but very slowly, and without impatience.

"You will somehow get over this difficulty, I am sure. Such friends as you and Mary don't quarrel like ordinary unreasonable women. Won't you let me be of use?"

"How?" asked Rhoda, with surprise.

"I shall make my cousin see that she is wrong."

"How do you know that she is wrong?"

"Because I am convinced that *you* must be right. I respect Mary's judgment, but I respect yours still more."

Rhoda raised her head and smiled.

"That compliment," she said, "pleases me less than the one you have uttered without intending it."

"You must explain."

"You said that by making Miss Barfoot see she was wrong you could alter her mind towards me. The world's opinion would hardly support you in that, even in the case of men."

Everard laughed.

"Now this is better. Now we are talking in the old way. — Surely you know that the world's opinion has no validity for me."

She kept silence.

"But, after all, *is* Mary wrong? I'm not afraid to ask the question now that your face has cleared a little. How angry you were with me! But surely I didn't deserve it. You would have been much more forbearing if you had known what delight I felt when I saw you sitting over there. It is nearly a month since we met, and I couldn't keep away any longer."

Rhoda swept the distance with indifferent eyes.

"Mary was fond of this girl?" he inquired, watching her.

"Yes, she was."

"Then her distress, and even anger, are natural enough. We won't discuss the girl's history; probably I know all that I need to. But whatever her misdoing, you certainly didn't wish to drive her to suicide."

Rhoda deigned no reply.

"All the same," he continued, in his gentlest tone, "it turns out that you have practically done so. If Mary had taken the girl back, that despair would most likely never have come upon her. Isn't it natural that Mary should repent of having been guided by you, and perhaps say rather severe things?"

"Natural, no doubt. But it is just as natural for me to resent blame where I have done nothing blameworthy."

"You are absolutely sure that that is the case?"

"I thought you expressed a conviction that I was in the right?"

There was no smile, but Everard believed that he detected its possibility on the closed lips.

"I have got into the way of always thinking you so, — in questions of this kind. But perhaps you tend to err on the side of severity. Perhaps you make too little allowance for human weakness."

"Human weakness is a plea that has been much abused, and generally in an interested spirit."

This was something like a personal rebuke. Whether she so meant it, Barfoot could not determine. He hoped she did, for the more personal their talk became, the better he would be pleased.

"I, for one," he said, "very seldom urge that plea, whether in my own defence or another's. But it answers to a spirit we can't altogether dispense with. Don't you feel ever so little regret that your severe logic prevailed?"

"Not the slightest regret."

Everard thought this answer magnificent. He had anticipated some evasion. However inappropriately, he was constrained to smile.

"How I admire your consistency! We others are poor halting creatures in comparison."

"Mr. Barfoot," said Rhoda suddenly, "I have had enough of this. If your approval is sincere, I don't ask for it. If you are practising your powers of irony, I had rather you chose some other person. I will go my way, if you please."

She just bent her head, and left him.

Enough for the present. Having raised his hat and turned on his heels,

Barfoot strolled away in a mood of peculiar satisfaction. He laughed to himself. She was certainly a fine creature; — yes, physically as well. Her out-of-door appearance on the whole pleased him; she could dress very plainly without disguising the advantages of figure she possessed. He pictured her rambling about the hills, and longed to be her companion on such an expedition; there would be no consulting with feebleness, as when one sets forth to walk with the every-day woman. What daring topics might come up in the course of a twenty-mile stretch across country! No Grundyism[1] in Rhoda Nunn; no simpering, no mincing of phrases. Why, a man might do worse than secure her for his comrade through the whole journey of life.

Suppose he pushed his joke to the very point of asking her to marry him? Undoubtedly she would refuse; but how enjoyable to watch the proud vigour of her freedom asserting itself! — Yet would not an offer of marriage be too commonplace? Rather propose to her to share his life in a free union, without sanction of forms which neither for her nor him were sanction at all. Was it too bold a thought?

Not if he really meant it. Uttered insincerely, such words would be insult; she would see through his pretence of earnestness, and then farewell to her for ever. But if his intellectual sympathy became tinged with passion — and did he discern no possibility of that? An odd thing were he to fall in love with Rhoda Nunn. Hitherto his ideal had been a widely different type of woman; he had demanded rare beauty of face, and the charm of a refined voluptuousness. To be sure, it was but an ideal; no woman that approached it had ever come within his sphere. The dream exercised less power over him than a few years ago; perhaps because his youth was behind him. Rhoda might well represent the desire of a mature man, strengthened by modern culture and with his senses fairly subordinate to reason. Heaven forbid that he should ever tie himself to the tame domestic female; and just as little could he seek for a mate among the women of society, the creatures all surface, with empty pates and vitiated blood. No marriage for him, in the common understanding of the word. He wanted neither offspring nor a "home." Rhoda Nunn, if she thought of such things at all, probably desired a union which would permit her to remain an intellectual being; the kitchen, the cradle, and the work-basket had no power over her imagination. As likely as not, however, she was perfectly content with single life — even regarded it as essential to her purposes. In her face he read chastity; her eye avoided no scrutiny; her palm was cold.

One does not break the heart of such a woman. Heart-break is a very old-fashioned disorder, associated with poverty of brain. If Rhoda were

---

1 Devotion to social propriety and conventional moralism. The source of the term is Mrs. Grundy, the rigid moralist whose censure is feared by her neighbours in *Speed the Plow* (1798), a play by Thomas Morton (1764?–1838).

what he thought her, she enjoyed this opportunity of studying a modern male, and cared not how far he proceeded in his own investigations, sure that at any moment she could bid him fall back. The amusement was only just beginning. And if for him it became earnest, why, what did he seek but strong experiences?

Rhoda, in the meantime, had gone home. She shut herself in her bed-room, and remained there until the bell rang for dinner.

Miss Barfoot entered the dining-room just before her; they sat down in silence, and through the meal exchanged but a few sentences, relative to a topic of the hour which interested neither of them.

The elder woman had a very unhappy countenance; she looked worn out; her eyes never lifted themselves from the table.

Dinner over, Miss Barfoot went to the drawing-room alone. She had sat there about half an hour, brooding, unoccupied, when Rhoda came in and stood before her.

"I have been thinking it over. It isn't right for me to remain here. Such an arrangement was only possible whilst we were on terms of perfect understanding."

"You must do what you think best, Rhoda," the other replied gravely, but with no accent of displeasure.

"Yes, I had better take a lodging somewhere. What I wish to know is, whether you can still employ me with any satisfaction?"

"I don't employ you. That is not the word to describe your relations with me. If we must use business language, you are simply my partner."

"Only your kindness put me into that position. When you no longer regard me as a friend, I am only in your employment."

"I haven't ceased to regard you as a friend. The estrangement between us is entirely of your making."

Seeing that Rhoda would not sit down, Miss Barfoot rose and stood by the fireplace.

"I can't bear reproaches," said the former, "least of all when they are irrational and undeserved."

"If I reproached you, it was in a tone which should never have given you offence.

One would think that I had rated you like a disobedient servant."

"If *that* had been possible," answered Rhoda, with a faint smile, "I should never have been here. You said that you bitterly repented having given way to me on a certain occasion. That was unreasonable; in giving way, you declared yourself convinced. And the reproach I certainly didn't deserve, for I had behaved conscientiously."

"Isn't it allowed me to disapprove of what your conscience dictates?"

"Not when you have taken the same view, and acted upon it. — I don't lay claim to many virtues, and I haven't that of meekness. I could never endure anger; my nature resents it."

"I did wrong to speak angrily, but indeed I hardly knew what I was saying. I had suffered a terrible shock. I loved that poor girl; I loved her all the more for what I had seen of her since she came to implore my help. Your utter coldness — it seemed to me inhuman — I shrank from you. If your face had shown ever so little compassion —"

"I *felt* no compassion."

"No. You have hardened your heart with theory. Guard yourself, Rhoda! To work for women one must keep one's womanhood. You are becoming — you are wandering as far from the true way — Oh, much further than Bella did!"

"I can't answer you. When we argued about our differences in a friendly spirit, all was permissible; now if I spoke my thought, it would be mere harshness and cause of embitterment. I fear all is at an end between us. I should perpetually remind you of this sorrow."

There was a silence of some length. Rhoda turned away, and stood in reflection.

"Let us do nothing hastily," said Miss Barfoot. "We have more to think of than our own feelings."

"I have said that I am quite willing to go on with my work, but it must be on a different footing. The relation between us can no longer be that of equals. I am content to follow your directions. — But your dislike of me will make this impossible."

"Dislike? You misunderstand me wretchedly. I think rather it is you who dislike me, as a weak woman with no command of her emotions."

Again they ceased from speech. Presently Miss Barfoot stepped forward.

"Rhoda, I shall be away all to-morrow; I may not return to London until Monday morning. Will you think quietly over it all? — Believe me, I am not angry with you, and as for disliking you — what nonsense are we talking! But I can't regret that I let you see how painfully your behaviour impressed me. That hardness is not natural to you. You have encouraged yourself in it, and you are warping a very noble character."

"I wish only to be honest. Where you felt compassion, I felt indignation."

"Yes; we have gone through all that. The indignation was a forced, exaggerated sentiment. You can't see it in that light, perhaps. But try to imagine for a moment that Bella had been your sister —"

"That is confusing the point at issue," Rhoda exclaimed irritably. "Have I ever denied the force of such feelings? My grief would have blinded me to all larger considerations, of course. But she was happily *not* my sister, and I remained free to speak the simple truth about her case. It isn't personal feeling that directs a great movement in civilization. If you were right, I also was right. You should have recognized the inevitable discord of our opinions at that moment."

"It didn't seem to me inevitable."

"I should have despised myself if I could have affected sympathy."

"Affected — yes."

"Or have really felt it. That would have meant that I did not know myself. I should never again have dared to speak on any grave subject."

Miss Barfoot smiled sadly.

"How young you are! Oh, there is far more than ten years between our ages, Rhoda! In spirit you are a young girl, and I an old woman. — No, no; we *will not* quarrel. Your companionship is far too precious to me, and I dare to think that mine is not without value for you. Wait till my grief has had its course; then I shall be more reasonable, and do you more justice."

Rhoda turned towards the door, lingered but without looking back, and so left the room.

Miss Barfoot was absent as she had announced, returning only in time for her duties in Great Portland Street on Monday morning. She and Rhoda then shook hands, but without a word of personal reference. They went through the day's work as usual.

This was the day of the month on which Miss Barfoot would deliver her four o'clock address. The subject had been announced a week ago: "Woman as an invader." An hour earlier than usual, work was put aside, and seats were rapidly arranged for the small audience; it numbered only thirteen, the girls already on the premises and a few who came specially. All were aware of the tragedy in which Miss Barfoot had recently been concerned; her air of sadness, so great a contrast to that with which she was wont to address them, they naturally attributed to this cause.

As always, she began in the simplest conversational tone. Not long since, she had received an anonymous letter, written by some clerk out of employment, abusing her roundly for her encouragement of female competition in the clerkly world. The taste of this epistle was as bad as its grammar, but they should hear it; she read it all through. Now, whoever the writer might be, it seemed pretty clear that he was not the kind of person with whom one could profitably argue; no use in replying to *him*, even had he given the opportunity. For all that, his uncivil attack had a meaning, and there were plenty of people ready to urge his argument in more respectable terms. "They will tell you that, in entering the commercial world, you not only unsex yourselves, but do a grievous wrong to the numberless men struggling hard for bare sustenance. You reduce salaries, you press into an already over-crowded field, you injure even your own sex by making it impossible for men to marry, who, if they earned enough, would be supporting a wife." To-day, continued Miss Barfoot, it was not her purpose to debate the economic aspects of the question. She would consider it from another point of view, repeating, perhaps, much that she had already said to them on other occasions, but doing so because these thoughts had just now very strong possession of her mind.

This abusive correspondent, who declared that he was supplanted by a young woman who did his work for smaller payment, doubtless had a grievance. But, in the miserable disorder of our social state, one grievance had to be weighed against another, and Miss Barfoot held, that there was much more to be urged on behalf of women who invaded what had been exclusively the men's sphere, than on behalf of the men who began to complain of this invasion.

"They point to half-a-dozen occupations which are deemed strictly suitable for women. Why don't we confine ourselves to this ground? Why don't I encourage girls to become governesses, hospital nurses, and so on? You think I ought to reply that already there are too many applicants for such places. It would be true, but I don't care to make use of the argument, which at once involves us in a debate with the out-crowded clerk. No; to put the truth in a few words, I am not chiefly anxious that you should *earn money*, but that women in general shall become *rational and responsible human beings*.

"Follow me carefully. A governess, a nurse, may be the most admirable of women. I will dissuade no one from following those careers who is distinctly fitted for them. But these are only a few out of the vast number of girls who must, if they are not to be despicable persons, somehow find serious work. Because I myself have had an education in clerkship, and have most capacity for such employment, I look about for girls of like mind, and do my best to prepare them for work in offices. And (here I must become emphatic once more) I am *glad* to have entered on this course. I am *glad* that I can show girls the way to a career which my opponents call unwomanly.

"Now see why. Womanly and womanish are two very different words, but the latter, as the world uses it, has become practically synonymous with the former. A womanly occupation means, practically, an occupation that a man disdains. And here is the root of the matter. I repeat that I am not first of all anxious to keep you supplied with daily bread. I am a troublesome, aggressive, revolutionary person. I want to do away with that common confusion of the words womanly and womanish, and I see very clearly that this can only be effected by an armed movement, an invasion by women of the spheres which men have always forbidden us to enter. I am strenuously opposed to that view of us set forth in such charming language by Mr. Ruskin,[1] — for it tells on the side of those men who think and speak of us in a way the reverse of charming. Were we living in an ideal world, I think women would not go to sit all day in offices. But the fact is that we live in a world as far from ideal as can be conceived. We live in a time of warfare, of revolt. If woman is no longer to be womanish, but a human being of powers and responsibilities, she must become militant, defiant. She must push her claims to the extremity.

"An excellent governess, a perfect hospital nurse, do work which is invaluable; but for our cause of emancipation they are no good; nay, they are harmful. Men point to them, and say: Imitate these, keep to your proper world. — Our proper world is the world of intelligence, of honest effort, of moral strength. The old types of womanly perfection are no

---

1 In "Of Queens' Gardens"; see Appendix B.

longer helpful to us. Like the Church Service, which to all but one person in a thousand has become meaningless gabble by dint of repetition, these types have lost their effect. They are no longer educational. We have to ask ourselves: What course of training will wake women up, make them conscious of their souls, startle them into healthy activity?

"It must be something new, something free from the reproach of womanliness. I don't care whether we crowd out the men or not. I don't care *what* results, if only women are made strong and self-reliant and nobly independent! The world must look to its concerns. Most likely we shall have a revolution in the social order greater than any that yet seems possible. Let it come, and let *us* help its coming. When I think of the contemptible wretchedness of women enslaved by custom, by their weakness, by their desires, I am ready to cry: Let the world perish in tumult rather than things go on in this way!"

For a moment her voice failed. There were tears in her eyes. The hearers, most of them, understood what made her so passionate; they exchanged grave looks.

"Our abusive correspondent shall do as best he can. He suffers for the folly of men in all ages. We can't help it. It is very far from our wish to cause hardship to any one, but we ourselves are escaping from a hardship that has become intolerable. We are educating ourselves. There must be a new type of woman, active in every sphere of life: a new worker out in the world, a new ruler of the home. Of the old ideal virtues we can retain many, but we have to add to them those which have been thought appropriate only in men. Let a woman be gentle, but at the same time let her be strong; let her be pure of heart, but none the less wise and instructed. Because we have to set an example to the sleepy of our sex, we must carry on an active warfare, must be invaders. Whether woman is the equal of man, I neither know nor care. We are not his equal in size, in weight, in muscle, and, for all I can say, we may have less power of brain. That has nothing to do with it. Enough for us to know that our natural growth has been stunted. The mass of women have always been paltry creatures, and their paltriness has proved a curse to men. — So, if you like to put it in this way, we are working for the advantage of men as well as for our own. Let the responsibility for disorder rest on those who have made us despise our old selves. At any cost — at any cost — we will free ourselves from the heritage of weakness and contempt!"

The assembly was longer than usual in dispersing. When all were gone, Miss Barfoot listened for a footstep in the other room. As she could detect no sound, she went to see if Rhoda was there or not.

Yes; Rhoda was sitting in a thoughtful attitude. She looked up, smiled, and came a few paces forward.

"It was very good."

"I thought it would please you."

Miss Barfoot drew nearer, and added:

"It was addressed to you. It seemed to me that you had forgotten how

I really thought about these things."

"I have been ill-tempered," Rhoda replied. "Obstinacy is one of my faults."

"It is."

Their eyes met.

"I believe," continued Rhoda, "that I ought to ask your pardon. Right or wrong, I behaved in an unmannerly way."

"Yes, I think you did."

Rhoda smiled, bending her head to the rebuke.

"And there's the last of it," added Miss Barfoot. "Let us kiss and be friends."

CHAPTER XIV.

MOTIVES MEETING.

When Barfoot made his next evening call, Rhoda did not appear. He sat for some time in pleasant talk with his cousin, no reference whatever being made to Miss Nunn; then at length, beginning to fear that he would not see her, he inquired after her health. Miss Nunn was very well, answered the hostess, smiling.

"Not at home this evening?"

"Busy with some kind of study, I think."

Plainly, the difference between these women had come to a happy end, as Barfoot foresaw that it would. He thought it better to make no mention of his meeting with Rhoda in the Gardens.

"That was a very unpleasant affair that I saw your name connected with last week," he said presently.

"It made me very miserable, — ill indeed for a day or two."

"That was why you couldn't see me?"

"Yes."

"But in your reply to my note you made no mention of the circumstances."

Miss Barfoot kept silence; frowning slightly, she looked at the fire near which they were both sitting, for the weather had become very cold.

"No doubt," pursued Everard, glancing at her, "you refrained out of delicacy — on my account, I mean."

"Need we talk of it?"

"For a moment, please. — You are very friendly with me nowadays, but I suppose your estimate of my character remains very much the same as years ago?"

"What is the use of such questions?"

"I ask for a distinct purpose. You can't regard me with any respect?"

"To tell you the truth, Everard, I know nothing about you. I have no wish to revive disagreeable memories, and I think it quite possible that you may be worthy of respect."

"So far, so good. Now, in justice, please answer me another question. How have you spoken of me to Miss Nunn?"

"How can it matter?"

"It matters a good deal. Have you told her any scandal about me?"

"Yes, I have."

Everard looked at her with surprise.

"I spoke to Miss Nunn about you," she continued, "before I thought of your ever coming here. Frankly, I used you as an illustration of the evils I abominate."

"You are a courageous and plain-spoken woman, cousin Mary," said

Everard, laughing a little. "Couldn't you have found some other example?"

There was no reply.

"So," he proceeded, "Miss Nunn regards me as a proved scoundrel?"

"I never told her the story. I made known the general grounds of my dissatisfaction with you, that was all."

"Come, that's something. I'm glad you didn't amuse her with that unedifying bit of fiction."

"Fiction?"

"Yes, fiction," said Everard bluntly. "I am not going into details; the thing's over and done with, and I chose my course at the time. But it's as well to let you know that my behaviour was grossly misrepresented. In using me to point a moral, you were grievously astray. I shall say no more. If you can believe me, do; if you can't, dismiss the matter from your mind."

There followed a silence of some moments. Then, with a perfectly calm manner, Miss Barfoot began to speak of a new subject. Everard followed her lead. He did not stay much longer, and, on leaving, asked to be remembered to Miss Nunn.

A week later, he again found his cousin alone. He now felt sure that Miss Nunn was keeping out of his way. Her parting from him in the Gardens had been decidedly abrupt, and possibly it signified more serious offence than at the time he attributed to her. It was so difficult to be sure of anything in regard to Miss Nunn. If another woman had acted thus, he would have judged it coquetry. But perhaps Rhoda was quite incapable of anything of that kind. Perhaps she took herself so very seriously that the mere suspicion of banter in his talk had moved her to grave resentment. Or again, she might be half ashamed to meet him after confessing her disagreement with Miss Barfoot; on recovery from ill temper, (unmistakable ill temper it was,) she had seen her behaviour in an embarrassing light. Between these various conjectures he wavered, whilst talking with Mary. But he did not so much as mention Miss Nunn's name.

Some ten days went by, and he paid a call at the hour sanctioned by society, five in the afternoon; it being Saturday. One of his reasons for coming at this time was the hope that he might meet other callers, for he felt curious to see what sort of people visited the house. And this wish was gratified. On entering the drawing-room, whither he was led by the servant straightway, after the manner of the world, he found not only his cousin and her friend, but two strangers, ladies. A glance informed him that both of these were young and good-looking, one being a type that particularly pleased him, dark, pale, with very bright eyes.

Miss Barfoot received him as any hostess would have done. She was her cheerful self once more, and in a moment introduced him to the lady with whom she had been talking, the dark one, by name Mrs. Widdowson. Rhoda Nunn, sitting apart with the second lady, gave him her hand, but at once resumed her conversation.

With Mrs. Widdowson he was soon chatting in his easy and graceful way, Miss Barfoot putting in a word now and then. He saw that she had not long been married; a pleasant diffidence, and the maidenly glance of her bright eyes, indicated this. She was dressed very prettily, and seemed aware of it.

"We went to hear the new opera at the Savoy last night," she said to Miss Barfoot, with a smile of remembered enjoyment.

"Did you? Miss Nunn and I were there."

Everard gazed at his cousin with humorous incredulity.

"Is it possible?" he exclaimed. "You were at the Savoy?"[1]

"Where is the impossibility? Why shouldn't Miss Nunn and I go to the theatre?"

"I appeal to Mrs. Widdowson. She also was astonished."

"Yes, indeed I was, Miss Barfoot!" exclaimed the younger lady, with a merry little laugh. "I hesitated before speaking of such a frivolous entertainment."

Lowering her voice, and casting a smile in Rhoda's direction, Miss Barfoot replied:

"I have to make a concession occasionally, on Miss Nunn's account. It would be unkind never to allow her a little recreation."

The two at a distance were talking earnestly, with grave countenances. In a few moments they rose, and the visitor came towards Miss Barfoot to take her leave. Thereupon Everard crossed to Miss Nunn.

"Is there anything very good in the new Gilbert and Sullivan opera?" he asked.

"Many good things. You really haven't been yet?"

"No — I'm ashamed to say."

"Do go this very evening, if you can get a seat. Which part of the theatre do you prefer?"

His eye rested on hers, but he could detect no irony.

"I'm a poor man, you know. I have to be content with the cheap places. — Which do you like best, the Savoy operas or the burlesques at the Gaiety?"[2]

A few more such questions and answers, of laboured commonplace or strained flippancy, and Everard, after searching his companion's face, broke off with a laugh.

"There now," he said, "we have talked in the approved five o'clock way. Precisely the dialogue I heard in a drawing-room yesterday. It goes on day after day, year after year, through the whole of people's lives."

---

1 A fashionable London theatre, renown as the venue for Gilbert and Sullivan's comic operas. Gilbert and Sullivan's productions were social satire of the frothiest kind, and Everard and Monica are accordingly surprised that so intensely serious a person as Rhoda Nunn would enjoy them.

2 The Gaiety was a theatre specializing in musical comedies (referred to as burlesques in the 1890s).

"You are on friendly terms with such people?"

"I am on friendly terms with people of every kind." He added, in an undertone, "I hope I may include you, Miss Nunn?"

But to this she paid no attention. She was looking at Monica and Miss Barfoot, who had just risen from their seats. They approached, and presently Barfoot found himself alone with the familiar pair.

"Another cup of tea, Everard?" asked his cousin.

"Thank you. — Who was the young lady you didn't introduce me to?"

"Miss Haven, — one of our pupils."

"Does she think of going into business?"

"She has just got a place in the publishing department of a weekly paper."

"But really — from the few words of her talk that fell upon my ear I should have thought her a highly educated girl."

"So she is," replied Miss Barfoot. "What is your objection?"

"Why doesn't she aim at some better position?"

Miss Barfoot and Rhoda exchanged smiles.

"But nothing could be better for her. Some day she hopes to start a paper of her own, and to learn all the details of such business is just what she wants. — Oh, you are still very conventional, Everard. You meant she ought to take up something graceful and pretty — something ladylike."

"No, no. It's all right. I thoroughly approve. And when Miss Haven starts her paper, Miss Nunn will write for it."

"I hope so," assented his cousin.

"You make me feel that I am in touch with the great movements of our time. It's delightful to know you. But come now, isn't there any way in which I could help?"

Mary laughed.

"None whatever, I'm afraid."

"Well, — 'They also serve who only stand and wait.'"[1]

If Everard had pleased himself, he would have visited the house in Queen's Road every other day. As this might not be, he spent a good deal of his time in other society, not caring to read much or otherwise occupy his solitude. Starting with one or two acquaintances in London, people of means and position, he easily extended his social sphere. Had he cared to marry, he might, notwithstanding his poverty, have wooed with fair chance in a certain wealthy family, where two daughters, the sole children, plain but well-instructed girls, waited for the men of brains who should appreciate them. So rare in society, these men of brains, and alas! so frequently deserted by their wisdom when it comes to choosing a wife. It being his principle to reflect on every possibility, Barfoot of course asked himself whether it would not be reasonable to approach one or other of these young women, the Miss Brissendens. He needed a larger

---

1 John Milton (1608–74), "When I Consider How My Light Is Spent," l. 14 (1673).

income; he wanted to travel in a more satisfactory way than during his late absence. Agnes Brissenden struck him as a very calm and sensible girl; not at all likely to marry any one but the man who would be a suitable companion for her, and probably disposed to look on marriage as a permanent friendship, which must not be endangered by feminine follies. She had no beauty, but mental powers above the average, — superior, certainly, to her sister's.

It was worth thinking about, but in the meantime he wanted to see much more of Rhoda Nunn. Rhoda he was beginning to class with women who are attractive both physically and mentally. Strange how her face had altered to his perception since the first meeting. He smiled now when he beheld it, smiled as a man does when his senses are pleasantly affected. He was getting to know it so well, to be prepared for its constant changes, to watch for certain movements of brows or lips when he had said certain things. That forcible holding of her hand had marked a stage in progressive appreciation; since then he felt a desire to repeat the experiment.

> "Or if thy mistress some rich anger shows,
> Imprison her soft hand, and let her rave —"[1]

The lines occurred to his memory, and he understood them better than heretofore. It would delight him to enrage Rhoda, and then to detain her by strength, to overcome her senses, to watch her long lashes droop over the eloquent eyes. But this was something very like being in love, and he by no means wished to be seriously in love with Miss Nunn.

It was another three weeks before he had an opportunity of private talk with her. Trying a Sunday afternoon, about four, he found Rhoda alone in the drawing-room; Miss Barfoot was out of town. Rhoda's greeting had a frank friendliness which she had not bestowed upon him for a long time; not, indeed, since they met on her return from Cheddar. She looked very well, readily laughed, and seemed altogether in a coming-on disposition. Barfoot noticed that the piano was open.

"Do you play?" he inquired. "Strange that I should still have to ask the question."

"Oh, only a hymn on Sunday," she answered, off-hand.

"A hymn?"

"Why not? I like some of the old tunes very much. They remind me of the golden age."

"In your own life, you mean."

She nodded.

"You have once or twice spoken of that time as if you were not quite happy in the present."

---

1 John Keats (1795–1821), "Ode on Melancholy," ll. 18–19 (1819).

"Of course I am not quite happy. What woman is? I mean, what woman above the level of a petted pussy-cat?"

Everard was leaning towards her on the head of the couch where he sat. He gazed into her face fixedly.

"I wish it were in my power to remove some of your discontents. I would, more gladly than I can tell you."

"You abound in good nature, Mr. Barfoot," she replied, laughing. "But unfortunately you can't change the world."

"Not the world at large. But might I not change your views of it — in some respects?"

"Indeed I don't see how you could. I think I had rather have my own view than any you might wish to substitute for it."

In this humour she seemed more than ever a challenge to his manhood. She was armed at all points. She feared nothing that he might say. No flush of apprehension; no nervous tremor; no weak self-consciousness. Yet he saw her as a woman, and desirable.

"My views are not ignoble," he murmured.

"I hope not. But they are the views of a man."

"Man and woman ought to see life with much the same eyes."

"Ought they? Perhaps so. I am not sure. But they never will in our time."

"Individuals may. The man and woman who have thrown away prejudice and superstition. You and I, for instance."

"Oh, those words have such different meanings. In your judgment, I should seem full of idle prejudice."

She liked this conversation; he read pleasure in her face, saw in her eyes a glint of merry defiance. And his pulses throbbed the quicker for it.

"You have a prejudice against *me*, for instance."

"Pray, did you go to the Savoy?" inquired Rhoda absently.

"I have no intention of talking about the Savoy, Miss Nunn. It is tea-cup time, but as yet we have the room to ourselves."

Rhoda went and rang the bell.

"The tea-cups shall come at once."

He laughed slightly, and looked at her from beneath drooping lids. Rhoda went on with talk of trifles, until the tea was brought and she had given a cup. Having emptied it at two draughts, he resumed his former leaning position.

"Well, you were saying that you had a prejudice against me. Of course my cousin Mary is accountable for that. Mary has used me rather ill. Before ever you saw me, I represented to your mind something very disagreeable indeed. That was too bad of my cousin."

Rhoda, sipping her tea, had a cold, uninterested expression.

"I didn't know of this," he proceeded, "when we met that day in the Gardens, and when I made you so angry."

"I wasn't disposed to jest about what had happened."

"But neither was I. You quite misunderstood me. — Will you tell me how that unpleasantness came to an end?"

"Oh yes. I admitted that I had been ill-mannered and obstinate."

"How delightful! — Obstinate? I have a great deal of that in my character. All the active part of my life was one long fit of obstinacy. As a lad, I determined on a certain career, and I stuck to it in spite of conscious unfitness, in spite of a great deal of suffering, out of sheer obstinacy. I wonder whether Mary ever told you that."

"She mentioned something of the kind, once."

"You could hardly believe it, I dare say? I am a far more reasonable being now. I have changed in so many respects that I hardly know my old self when I look back on it. Above all, in my thoughts about women. If I had married during my twenties, I should have chosen, as the average man does, some simpleton — with unpleasant results. If I marry now, it will be a woman of character and brains. Marry in the legal sense I never shall. My companion must be as independent of forms as I am myself."[1]

Rhoda looked into her tea-cup for a second or two, then said with a smile:

"You also are a reformer?"

"In that direction."

He had a difficulty in suppressing signs of nervousness. The bold declaration had come without forethought, and Rhoda's calm acceptance of it delighted him.

"Questions of marriage," she went on to say, "don't interest me much; but this particular reform doesn't seem very practical. It is trying to bring about an ideal state of things whilst we are yet struggling with elementary obstacles."

"I don't advocate this liberty for all mankind. Only for those who are worthy of it."

"And what" — she laughed a little — "are the sure signs of worthiness? I think it would be very needful to know them."

Everard kept a grave face.

"True. But a free union presupposes equality of position. No honest man would propose it, for instance, to a woman incapable of understanding all it involved, or incapable of resuming her separate life if that became desirable. I admit all the difficulties. One must consider those of feeling, as well as the material. If my wife should declare that she must be released, I might suffer grievously, but being a man of some intelligence I should admit that the suffering couldn't be helped; the brutality of enforced marriage doesn't seem to me an alternative worth considering. It wouldn't seem so to any woman of the kind I mean."

Would she have the courage to urge one grave difficulty that he left

---

1 Everard is referring to a "free union," which was advocated by several social radicals of the period. See, for example, the excerpts from Grant Allen's "Plain Words on the Woman Question" and Mona Caird's "Marriage" in Appendix B. The idea was considered scandalous by most people.

aside? — No. He fancied her about to speak, but she ended by offering him another cup of tea.

"After all, that is *not* your ideal?" he said.

"I haven't to do with the subject at all," Rhoda answered, with perhaps a trace of impatience. "My work and thought are for the women who do not marry — the 'odd women' I call them. They alone interest me. One mustn't undertake too much."

"And you resolutely class yourself with them?"

"Of course I do."

"And therefore you have certain views of life which I should like to change. You are doing good work, but I had rather see any other woman in the world devote her life to it. I am selfish enough to wish —"

The door opened, and the servant announced:

"Mr. and Mrs. Widdowson."

With perfect self-command, Miss Nunn rose and stepped forward. Barfoot, rising more slowly, looked with curiosity at the husband of the pretty, black-browed woman whom he had already met. Widdowson surprised and amused him. How had this stiff, stern fellow with the grizzled beard won such a wife? Not that Mrs. Widdowson seemed a remarkable person, but certainly it was an ill-assorted union.

She came and shook hands. As he spoke a few natural words, Everard chanced to notice that the husband's eye was upon him, and with what a look! If ever a man declared in his countenance the worst species of jealous temper, Mr. Widdowson did so. His fixed smile became sardonic.

Presently, Barfoot and he were introduced. They had nothing to say to each other, but Everard maintained a brief conversation just to observe the man. Turning at length, he began to talk with Mrs. Widdowson, and, because he was conscious of the jealous eye, assumed an especial sprightliness, an air of familiar pleasantry, to which the lady responded, but with a nervous hesitation.

The arrival of these people was an intense annoyance to him. Another quarter of an hour, and things would have come to an exciting pass between Rhoda and himself; he would have heard how she received a declaration of love. Rhoda's self-possession notwithstanding, he believed that he was not without power over her. She liked to talk with him, enjoyed the freedom he allowed himself in choice of subject. Perhaps no man before had ever shown an appreciation of her qualities as woman. But she would not yield, was in no real danger from his love-making. Nay, the danger was to his own peace. He felt that resistance would intensify the ardour of his wooing, and possibly end by making him a victim of genuine passion. Well, let her enjoy that triumph, if she were capable of winning it.

He had made up his mind to outstay the Widdowsons, who clearly would not make a long call. But the fates were against him. Another visitor arrived, a lady named Cosgrove, who settled herself as if for at least an hour. Worse than that, he heard her say to Rhoda:

"Oh, then do come and dine with us. Do, I beg!"

"I will, with pleasure," was Miss Nunn's reply. "Can you wait and take me with you?"

Useless to stay longer. As soon as the Widdowsons had departed he went up to Rhoda and silently offered his hand. She scarcely looked at him, and did not in the least return his pressure.

Rhoda dined at Mrs. Cosgrove's, and was home again at eleven o'clock. When the house was locked up, and the servants had gone to bed, she sat in the library, turning over a book that she had brought from her friend's house. It was a volume of essays, one of which dealt with the relations between the sexes in a very modern spirit, treating the subject as a perfectly open one, and arriving at unorthodox conclusions. Mrs. Cosgrove had spoken of this dissertation with lively interest. Rhoda perused it very carefully, pausing now and then to reflect.

In his reading of her mind, Barfoot came near the truth.

No man had ever made love to her; no man, to her knowledge, had ever been tempted to do so. In certain moods she derived satisfaction from this thought, using it to strengthen her life's purpose; having passed her thirtieth year, she might take it as a settled thing that she would never be sought in marriage, and so could shut the doors on every instinct tending to trouble her intellectual decisions. But these instincts sometimes refused to be thus treated. As Miss Barfoot told her, she was very young for her years, young in physique, young in emotion. As a girl she had dreamt passionately, and the fires of her nature, though hidden beneath aggregations of moral and mental attainment, were not yet smothered. An hour of lassitude filled her with despondency, none the less real because she was ashamed of it. If only she had once been loved, like other women — if she had listened to an offer of devotion, and rejected it — her heart would be more securely at peace. So she thought. Secretly she deemed it a hard thing never to have known that common triumph of her sex. And, moreover, it took away from the merit of her position as a leader and encourager of women living independently. There might be some who said, or thought, that she made a virtue of necessity.

Everard Barfoot's advances surprised her not a little. Judging him as a man wholly without principle, she supposed at first that this was merely his way with all women, and resented it as impertinence. But even then she did not dislike the show of homage; what her mind regarded with disdain, her heart was all but willing to feed upon, after its long hunger. Barfoot interested her, and not the less because of his evil reputation. Here was one of the men for whom women — doubtless more than one — had sacrificed themselves; she could not but regard him with sexual curiosity. And her interest grew, her curiosity was more haunting, as their acquaintance became a sort of friendship; she found that her moral disapprobation wavered, or was altogether forgotten. Perhaps it was to compensate for this that she went the length of outraging Miss Barfoot's feelings on the death of Bella Royston.

Certainly she thought with much frequency of Barfoot, and looked forward to his coming. Never had she wished so much to see him again as after their encounter in Chelsea Gardens, and on that account she forced herself to hold aloof when he came. It was not love, nor the beginning of love; she judged it something less possible to avow. The man's presence affected her with a perturbation which she had no difficulty in concealing at the time, though afterwards it distressed and shamed her. She took refuge in the undeniable fact that the quality of his mind made an impression upon her, that his talk was sympathetic. Miss Barfoot submitted to this influence; she confessed that her cousin's talk had always had a charm for her.

Could it be that this man reciprocated, and more than reciprocated, her complex feeling? To-day, only accident had prevented him from making an avowal of love — unless she strangely mistook him. All the evening she had dwelt on this thought; it grew more and more astonishing. Was he worse than she had imagined? Under cover of independent thought, of serious moral theories, did he conceal mere profligacy and heartlessness? It was an extraordinary thing to have to ask such questions in relation to herself. It made her feel as if she had to learn herself anew, to form a fresh conception of her personality. She the object of a man's passion!

And the thought was exultant. Even thus late, then, the satisfaction of vanity had been granted her — nay, not of vanity alone.

He must be sincere. What motive could he possibly have for playing a part? Might it not be true that he was a changed man in certain respects, and that a genuine emotion at length had control of him? If so, she had only to wait for his next speech with her in private; she could not misjudge a lover's pleading.

The interest would only be that of comedy. She did not love Everard Barfoot, and saw no likelihood of ever doing so; on the whole, a subject for thankfulness. Nor could he seriously anticipate an assent to his proposal for a free union; in declaring that legal marriage was out of the question for him, he had removed his love-making to the region of mere ideal sentiment. But if he loved her, these theories would sooner or later be swept aside; he would plead with her to become his legal wife.

To that point she desired to bring him. Offer what he might, she would not accept it; but the secret chagrin that was upon her would be removed. Love would no longer be the privilege of other women. To reject a lover in so many respects desirable, whom so many women might envy her, would fortify her self-esteem, and enable her to go forward in the chosen path with firmer tread.

It was one o'clock; the fire had died out and she began to shiver with cold. But a trembling of joy at the same time went through her limbs; again she had the sense of exultation, of triumph. — She would not dismiss him peremptorily. He should prove the quality of his love, if love it were. Coming so late, the experience must yield her all it had to yield of delight and contentment.

CHAPTER XV.

THE JOYS OF HOME.

Monica and her husband, on leaving the house in Queen's Road, walked slowly in the eastward direction. Though night had fallen, the air was not unpleasant; they had no object before them, and for five minutes they occupied themselves with their thoughts. Then Widdowson stopped.

"Shall we go home again?" he asked, just glancing at Monica, then letting his eyes stray vaguely in the gloom.

"I should like to see Milly, but I'm afraid I can hardly take you there to call with me."

"Why not?"

"It's a very poor little sitting-room, you know, and she might have some friend. — Isn't there anywhere you could go, and meet me afterwards?"

Frowning, Widdowson looked at his watch.

"Nearly six o'clock. There isn't much time."

"Edmund, — suppose you go home, and let me come back by myself? You wouldn't mind, for once? I should like so much to have a talk with Milly. If I got back about nine or half-past, I could have a little supper, and that's all I should want."

He answered abruptly.

"Oh, but I can't have you going about alone at night."

"Why not?" answered Monica, with a just perceptible note of irritation. "Are you afraid I shall be robbed or murdered?"

"Nonsense. But you mustn't be alone."

"Didn't I always use to be alone?"

He made an angry gesture.

"I have begged you not to speak of that. Why do you say what you know is disagreeable to me? You used to do all sorts of things that you never ought to have been obliged to do, and it's very painful to remember it."

Monica, seeing that people were approaching, walked on, and neither spoke until they had nearly reached the end of the road.

"I think we had better go home," Widdowson at length remarked.

"If you wish it, — but I really don't see why I shouldn't call on Milly, now that we are here."

"Why didn't you speak of it before we left home? You ought to be more methodical, Monica. Each morning I always plan how my day is to be spent, and it would be much better if you would do the same. Then you wouldn't be so restless and uncertain."

"If I go to Rutland Street," said Monica, without heeding this admonition, "couldn't you leave me there for an hour?"

"What in the world am I to do?"

"I should have thought you might walk about. — It's a pity you don't know more people, Edmund. It would make things so much pleasanter for you."

In the end, he consented to see her safely as far as Rutland Street, occupy himself for an hour, and come back for her. They went by cab, which was dismissed in Hampstead Road. Widdowson did not turn away until he had ocular proof of his wife's admittance to the house where Miss Vesper lived, and even then he walked no farther than the neighbouring streets, returning about every ten minutes to watch the house from a short distance, as though he feared Monica might have some project of escape. His look was very bilious; trudging mechanically hither and thither where fewest people were to be met, he kept his eyes on the ground, and clumped to a dismal rhythm with the end of his walking-stick. In the three or four months since his marriage, he seemed to have grown older; he no longer held himself so upright.

At the very moment agreed upon, he was waiting close by the house. Five minutes passed; twice he had looked at his watch, and he grew excessively impatient, stamping as if it were necessary to keep himself warm. Another five minutes, and he uttered a nervous ejaculation. He had all but made up his mind to go and knock at the door, when Monica came forth.

"You haven't been waiting here long, I hope?" she said cheerfully.

"Ten minutes. But it doesn't matter."

"I'm very sorry. We were talking on —"

"Yes, but one must always be punctual. I wish I could impress that upon you. Life without punctuality is quite impossible."

"I'm very sorry, Edmund. I will be more careful. Please don't lecture me, dear. — How shall we go home?"

"We had better take a cab to Victoria. No knowing how long we may have to wait for a train when we get there."

"Now don't be so grumpy. Where have you been all the time?"

"Oh, walking about. What else was I to do?"

On the drive they held no conversation. At Victoria they were delayed about half an hour before a train started for Herne Hill; Monica sat in a waiting-room, and her husband trudged about the platform, still clumping rhythmically with his stick.

Their Sunday custom was to dine at one o'clock, and at six to have tea.[1] Widdowson hated the slightest interference with domestic routine, and he had reluctantly indulged Monica's desire to go to Chelsea this afternoon. Hunger was now added to his causes of discontent.

"Let us have something to eat at once," he said on entering the house. "This disorder really won't do: we must manage better somehow."

Without replying, Monica rang the dining-room bell, and gave orders.

---

1 Tea, in this context, refers to a light meal, served in the late afternoon or early evening, with tea as the usual drink.

Little change had been made in the interior of the house since its master's marriage. The dressing-room adjoining the principal bed-chamber was adapted to Monica's use, and a few ornaments were added to the drawing-room. Unlike his deceased brother, Widdowson had the elements of artistic taste; in furnishing his abode, he took counsel with approved decorators, and at moderate cost had made himself a home which presented no original features, but gave no offence to a cultivated eye. The first sight of the rooms pleased Monica greatly. She declared that all was perfect, nothing need be altered. In those days, if she had bidden him spend a hundred pounds on reconstruction, the lover would have obeyed, delighted to hear her express a wish.

Though competence had come to him only after a lifetime of narrow means, Widdowson felt no temptation to parsimony. Secure in his all-sufficing income, he grudged no expenditure that could bring himself or his wife satisfaction. On the wedding tour in Cornwall, Devon, and Somerset, — it lasted about seven weeks, — Monica learnt, among other things less agreeable, that her husband was generous with money.

He was anxious she should dress well, though only, as Monica soon discovered, for his own gratification. Soon after they had settled down at home, she equipped herself for the cold season, and Widdowson cared little about the price so long as the effect of her new costumes was pleasing to him.

"You are making a butterfly of me," said Monica merrily, when he expressed strong approval of a bright morning dress that had just come home.

"A beautiful woman," he replied, with the nervous gravity which still possessed him when complimenting her, or saying tender things, "a beautiful woman ought to be beautifully clad."

At the same time, he endeavoured to impress her with the gravest sense of a married woman's obligations. His raptures, genuine enough, were sometimes interrupted in the oddest way if Monica chanced to utter a careless remark of which he could not strictly approve, and such interruptions frequently became the opportunity for a long and solemn review of the wifely status. Without much trouble he had brought her into a daily routine which satisfied him. During the whole of the morning, she was to be absorbed in household cares. In the afternoon he would take her to walk or drive, and the evening he wished her to spend either in drawing-room or library, occupied with a book. Monica soon found that his idea of wedded happiness was that they should always be together. Most reluctantly he consented to her going any distance alone, for whatever purpose. Public entertainments he regarded with no great favour, but when he saw how Monica enjoyed herself at concert or theatre, he made no objection to indulging her at intervals of a fortnight or so; his own fondness for music made this compliance easier. He was jealous of her forming new acquaintances; indifferent to society himself, he thought his wife should be satisfied with her present friends, and could not understand why she wished to see them so often.

The girl was docile, and for a time he imagined that there would never be conflict between his will and hers. Whilst enjoying their holiday they naturally went everywhere together, and were scarce an hour out of each other's presence, day or night. In quiet spots by the sea-shore, when they sat in solitude, Widdowson's tongue was loosened, and he poured forth his philosophy of life with the happy assurance that Monica would listen passively. His devotion to her proved itself in a thousand ways; week after week he grew, if anything, more kind, more tender; yet in his view of their relations he was unconsciously the most complete despot, a monument of male autocracy. Never had it occurred to Widdowson that a wife remains an individual, with rights and obligations independent of her wifely condition. Everything he said presupposed his own supremacy; he took for granted that it was his to direct, hers to be guided. A display of energy, purpose, ambition, on Monica's part, which had no reference to domestic pursuits, would have gravely troubled him; at once he would have set himself to subdue, with all gentleness, impulses so inimical to his idea of the married state. It rejoiced him that she spoke with so little sympathy of the principles supported by Miss Barfoot and Miss Nunn; these persons seemed to him well-meaning, but grievously mistaken; Miss Nunn he judged "unwomanly," and hoped in secret that Monica would not long remain on terms of friendship with her. Of course his wife's former pursuits were an abomination to him; he could not bear to hear them referred to.

"Woman's sphere is the home, Monica. Unfortunately, girls are often obliged to go out and earn their living, but this is unnatural, a necessity which advanced civilization will altogether abolish. You shall read John Ruskin;[1] every word he says about women is good and precious. If a woman can neither have a home of her own, nor find occupation in anyone else's, she is deeply to be pitied; her life is bound to be unhappy. I sincerely believe that an educated woman had better become a domestic servant than try to imitate the life of a man."

Monica seemed to listen attentively, but before long she accustomed herself to wear this look whilst in truth she was thinking her own thoughts. And as often as not they were of a nature little suspected by her prosing companion.

He believed himself the happiest of men. He had taken a daring step, but fortune smiled upon him. Monica was all he had imagined in his love-fever; knowledge of her had as yet brought to light no single untruth, no trait of character that he could condemn. That she returned his love he would not and could not doubt. And something she said to him one day, early in their honeymoon, filled up the measure of his bliss.

---

1 See excerpt from "Of Queens' Gardens" in Appendix B for Ruskin's views on women.

"What a change you have made in my life, Edmund! How much I have to thank you for!"

That was what he had hoped to hear. He had thought it, himself; had wondered whether Monica saw her position in this light. And when the words actually fell from her lips, he glowed with joy. This, to his mind, was the perfect relation of wife to husband. She must look up to him as her benefactor, her providence. It would have pleased him still better if she had not possessed a penny of her own, but happily Monica seemed never to give a thought to the sum at her disposal.

Surely he was the easiest of men to live with. When he first became aware that Monica suffered an occasional discontent, it caused him troublous surprise. As soon as he understood that she desired more freedom of movement, he became anxious, suspicious, irritable. Nothing like a quarrel had yet taken place between them, but Widdowson began to perceive that he must exert authority in a way he had imagined would never be necessary. All his fears, after all, were not groundless. Monica's undomestic life, and perhaps the association with those Chelsea people, had left results upon her mind. By way of mild discipline, he first of all suggested a closer attention to the affairs of the house. Would it not be well if she spent an hour a day in sewing or fancy work? Monica so far obeyed as to provide herself with some plain needlework, but Widdowson, watching with keen eye, soon remarked that her use of the needle was only a feint. He lay awake o' nights, pondering darkly.

On the present evening he was more decidedly out of temper than ever hitherto. He satisfied his hunger hurriedly and in silence. Then, observing that Monica ate only a few morsels, he took offence at this.

"I'm afraid you are not well, dear. You have had no appetite for several days."

"As much as usual, I think," she replied absently.

They went into the library, commonly their resort of an evening. Widdowson possessed several hundred volumes of English literature, most of them the works which are supposed to be indispensable to a well-informed man, though very few men even make a pretence of reading them. Self-educated, Widdowson deemed it his duty to make acquaintance with the great, the solid authors. Nor was his study of them affectation. For the poets he had little taste; the novelists he considered only profitable in intervals of graver reading; but history, political economy, even metaphysics, genuinely appealed to him. He had always two or three solid books on hand, each with its marker; he studied them at stated hours, and always sitting at a table, a note-book open beside him. A little work once well-known, Todd's "Student's Manual," had formed his method and inspired him with zeal.[1]

---

1 One of several books on education and self-improvement published in the 1830s and 1840s by Rev. John Todd.

To-night, it being Sunday, he took down a volume of Barrow's Sermons.[1] Though not strictly orthodox in religious faith, he conformed to the practices of the Church of England, and since his marriage had been more scrupulous on this point than before; he abhorred unorthodoxy in a woman, and would not on any account have suffered Monica to surmise that he had his doubts concerning any article of the Christian faith. Like most men of his kind, he viewed religion as a precious and powerful instrument for directing the female conscience. Frequently he read aloud to his wife, but this evening he showed no intention of doing so. Monica, however, sat unoccupied. After glancing at her once or twice, he said reprovingly:

"Have you finished your Sunday book?"

"Not quite. But I don't care to read just now."

The silence that followed was broken by Monica herself.

"Have you accepted Mrs. Luke's invitation to dinner?" she asked.

"I have declined it," was the reply, carelessly given.

Monica bit her lip.

"But why?"

"Surely we needn't discuss that over again, Monica."

His eyes were still on the book, and he stirred impatiently.

"But," urged his wife, "do you mean to break with her altogether? If so, I think it's very unwise, Edmund. What an opinion you must have of me, if you think I can't see people's faults! I know it's very true, all you say about her. But she wishes to be kind to us, I'm sure, — and I like to see something of a life so different from our own."

Widdowson drummed on the floor with his foot. In a few moments, ignoring Monica's remarks, he stroked his beard, and asked, with a show of casual interest:

"How was it you knew that Mr. Barfoot?"

"I had met him before, — when I went there on the Saturday."

Widdowson's eyes fell; his brow was wrinkled.

"He's often there, then?"

"I don't know. Perhaps he is. He's Miss Barfoot's cousin, you know."

"You haven't met him more than once before?"

"No. Why do you ask?"

"Oh, it was only that he seemed to speak as if you were old acquaintances."

"That's his way, I suppose."

Monica had already learnt that the jealousy which Widdowson so often betrayed before their marriage still lurked in his mind. Perceiving why he

---

1 Probably *Familiar Sermons* (1818–21) by William Barrow (1754–1836). Barrow published several volumes of sermons and other expositions on theology and morality intended for lay readers.

put these questions, she could not look entirely unconcerned, and the sense of his eye being upon her caused her some annoyance.

"You talked to him, didn't you?" she said, changing her position in the deep chair.

"Oh, the kind of talk that is possible with a perfect stranger. I suppose he is in some profession?"

"I really don't know. — Why, Edmund? Does he interest you?"

"Only that one likes to know something about the people that are introduced to one's wife," Widdowson answered rather acridly.

Their bedtime was half-past ten. Precisely at that moment, Widdowson closed his book, — glad to be relieved from the pretence of reading, — and walked over the lower part of the house to see that all was right. He had a passion for routine; every night, before going upstairs, he did a number of little things in unvarying sequence: changed the calendar for next day, made perfect order on his writing-table, wound up his watch, and so on. That Monica could not direct her habits with like exactitude was frequently a distress to him; if she chanced to forget any most trivial detail of daily custom, he looked very solemn, and begged her to be more vigilant.

Next morning, after breakfast, as Monica stood by the dining-room window and looked rather cheerlessly at a leaden sky, her husband came towards her as if he had something to say. She turned, and saw that his face no longer wore the austere expression which had made her miserable last night, and even during the meal this morning.

"Are we friends?" he said, with the attempt at playfulness which always made him look particularly awkward.

"Of course we are," Monica answered, smiling, but not regarding him.

"Didn't he behave gruffly last night to his little girl?"

"Just a little."

"And what can the old bear do to show that he's sorry?"

"Never be gruff again."

"The old bear is sometimes an old goose as well, and torments himself in the silliest way. Tell him so, if ever he begins to behave badly. — Isn't it account-book morning?"

"Yes. I'll come to you at eleven."

"And if we have a nice, quiet, comfortable week, I'll take you to the Crystal Palace concert next Saturday."[1]

Monica nodded cheerfully, and went off to look after her housekeeping.

---

1 The Crystal Palace was a large iron and glass building constructed to house the Great Exhibition in 1851. It was originally located in Hyde Park, in west-central London, and was later moved to Sydenham, southeast of London, where it was used for exhibitions and various forms of entertainment. The Crystal Palace was destroyed by fire in 1936.

The week was in all respects what Widdowson desired. Not a soul came to the house; Monica went to see no one. Save on two days it rained, sleeted, drizzled, fogged; on those two afternoons, they had an hour's walk. Saturday brought no improvement of the atmosphere, but Widdowson was in his happiest mood; he cheerfully kept his promise about the concert. As they sat together at night, his contentment overflowed in tenderness like that of the first days of marriage.

"Now why can't we always live like this? What have we to do with other people? Let us be everything to each other, and forget that any one else exists."

"I can't help thinking that's a mistake," Monica ventured to reply. "For one thing, if we saw more people, we should have so much more to talk about when we are alone."

"It's better to talk about ourselves. I shouldn't care if I never again saw any living creature but you. — You see, the old bear loves his little girl better than she loves him."

Monica was silent.

"Isn't it true? You don't feel that my company would be enough for you?"

"Would it be right if I ceased to care for every one else? There are my sisters. I ought to have asked Virginia to come to-morrow; I'm sure she thinks I neglect her, and it must be dreadful living all alone like she does."

"Haven't they made up their mind yet about the school? I'm sure it's the right thing for them to do. If the venture were to fail, and they lost money, we would see that they never came to want."

"They're so timid about it. And it wouldn't be nice, you know, to feel they were going to be dependent upon us for the rest of our lives. — I had better go and see Virgie to-morrow morning, and bring her back for dinner."

"If you like," Widdowson assented slowly. "But why not send a message, and ask her to come here?"

"I had rather go. It makes a change for me."

This was a word Widdowson detested. Change, on Monica's lips, always seemed to mean a release from his society. But he swallowed his dissatisfaction, and finally consented to the arrangement.

Virginia came to dinner, and stayed until nightfall. Thanks to her sister's kindness, she was better clad than in former days, but her face signified no improvement of health. The enthusiasm with which Rhoda Nunn had inspired her appeared only in fitful affectations of interest when Monica pressed her concerning the projected undertaking down in Somerset. In general she had a dreamy reticent look, and became uncomfortable when any one gazed at her inquiringly. Her talk was of the most insignificant things; this afternoon she spent nearly half an hour in describing a kitten which Mrs. Conisbee had given her; care of the little animal appeared to have absorbed her whole attention for many days past.

Another visitor to-day was Mr. Newdick, the City[1] clerk who had been present at Monica's wedding. He and Mrs. Luke Widdowson were the sole friends of her husband that Monica had seen. Mr. Newdick enjoyed coming to Herne Hill; always lugubrious to begin with, he gradually cheered up, and by the time for departure was loquacious. But he had the oddest ideas of talk suitable to a drawing-room; had he been permitted, he would have held forth to Monica by the hour on the history of the business firm which he had served for a quarter of a century. This subject alone could animate him. His anecdotes were as often as not quite unintelligible, save to people of City experience. For all that, Monica did not dislike the man; he was a good, simple, unselfish fellow, and to her he behaved with exaggeration of respect.

A few days later, Monica had a sudden fit of illness. Her marriage, and the long open-air holiday, had given her a much healthier appearance than when she was at the shop; but this present disorder resembled the attack she had suffered in Rutland Street. Widdowson hoped that it signified a condition for which he was anxiously waiting; that, however, did not seem to be the case. The medical man who was called in asked questions about the patient's mode of life. Did she take enough exercise? Had she wholesome variety of occupation? At these inquiries Widdowson inwardly raged. He was tormented with a suspicion that they resulted from something Monica had said to the doctor.

She kept her bed for three or four days, and on rising could only sit by the fireside, silent, melancholy. Widdowson indulged his hope, though Monica herself laughed it aside, and even showed annoyance if he returned to the subject. Her temper was strangely uncertain; some chance word in a conversation would irritate her beyond endurance, and after an outburst of petulant displeasure she became obstinately mute. At other times she behaved with such exquisite docility and sweetness that Widdowson was beside himself with rapture.

After a week of convalescence, she said one morning:

"Couldn't we go away somewhere? I don't think I shall ever be quite well, staying here."

"It's wretched weather," replied her husband.

"Oh, but there are places where it wouldn't be like this. — You don't mind the expense, do you, Edmund?"

"Expense? Not I, indeed! But — were you thinking of abroad?"

She looked at him with eyes that had suddenly brightened.

"Oh! would it be possible? — People do go out of England in the winter."

Widdowson plucked at his grizzled beard, and fingered his watch-chain. It was a temptation. Why not take her away to some place where

---

1 "City" refers to the business and financial district of London, which is located within its medieval boundaries.

only foreigners and strangers would be about them? Yet the enterprise alarmed him.

"I have never been out of England," he said, with misgiving.

"All the more reason why we should go. I think Miss Barfoot could advise us about it. She has been abroad, I know, and she has so many friends."

"I don't see any need to consult Miss Barfoot," he replied stiffly. "I am not such a helpless man, Monica."

Yet a feeling of inability to grapple with such an undertaking as this grew on him the more he thought of it. Naturally, his mind busied itself with such vague knowledge as he had gathered of those places in the South of France, where rich English people go to escape their own climate: Nice, Cannes. He could not imagine himself setting forth to these regions. Doubtless it was possible to travel thither, and live there when one arrived, without a knowledge of French; but he pictured all sorts of humiliating situations resulting from his ignorance. Above everything he dreaded humiliation in Monica's sight; it would be intolerable to have her comparing him with men who spoke foreign languages, and were at home on the Continent.

Nevertheless, he wrote to his friend Newdick, and invited him to dine, solely for the purpose of talking over this question with him in private. After dinner he broached the subject. To his surprise, Newdick had ideas concerning Nice and Cannes and such places. He had heard about them from the junior partner of his firm, a young gentleman who talked largely of his experiences abroad.

"An immoral lot there," he said, smiling and shaking his head. "Queer goings on."

"Oh, but that's among the foreigners, isn't it?"

Thereupon Mr. Newdick revealed his acquaintance with English literature.

"Did you ever read any of Ouida's novels?"[1]

"No, I never did."

"I advise you to, before you think of taking your wife over there. She writes a great deal about those parts. People get mixed up so, it seems. You couldn't live by yourself. You have to eat at public tables, and you'd have all sorts of people trying to make acquaintance with Mrs. Widdowson. They're a queer lot, I believe."

He abandoned the thought, at once and utterly. When Monica learnt this, — he gave only vague and unsatisfactory reasons, — she fell back

---

1 "Ouida" was the pseudonym of Marie Louise de la Ramée (1839–1908), author of numerous popular novels of British high life, often set on the Continent. Her stories were highly romanticized adventures, often depicting scandalous excesses, but were not a faithful representation of the conduct of Britons abroad. Ouida's works were extremely popular in the 1870s and 1880s, but were passé by the 1890s.

into her despondent mood. For a whole day she scarcely uttered a word.

On the next day, in the dreary afternoon, they were surprised by a call from Mrs. Luke. The widow — less than ever a widow in externals — came in with a burst of exuberant spirits, and began to scold the moping couple like an affectionate parent.

"When are you silly young people coming to an end of your honeymoon? Do you sit here day after day, and call each other pretty names? Really it's very charming in its way. I never knew such an obstinate case. — Monica, my black-eyed beauty, change your frock, and come with me to look up the Hodgson Bulls. They're quite too awful; I can't face them alone; but I'm bound to keep in with them. — Be off, and let me pitch into your young man for daring to refuse my dinner. Don't you know, sir, that my invitations are like those of Royalty — polite commands?"

Widdowson kept silence, waiting to see what his wife would do. He could not with decency object to her accompanying Mrs. Luke, yet hated the thought of such a step. A grim smile on his face, he sat stiffly, staring at the wall. To his inexpressible delight, Monica, after a short hesitation, excused herself; she was not well; she did not feel able —

"Oh!" laughed the visitor. "I see, I see! Do just as you like, of course. But if Edmund has any *nous*" — this phrase she had learnt from a young gentleman, late of Oxford, now of Tattersall's and elsewhere[1] — "he won't let you sit here in the dumps. You *are* in the dumps, I can see."

The vivacious lady did not stay long. When she had rustled forth again to her carriage, Widdowson broke into a paean of amorous gratitude. What could he do to show how he appreciated Monica's self-denial on his behalf? For a day or two he was absent rather mysteriously, and in the meantime made up his mind, after consultation with Newdick, to take his wife for a holiday in Guernsey.

Monica, when she heard of this project, was at first moderately grateful, but in a day or two showed by reviving strength and spirits that she looked forward eagerly to the departure. Her husband advertised for lodgings in St. Peter Port; he would not face the disagreeable chances of an hotel. In a fortnight's time all their preparations were made. During their absence, which might extend over a month, Virginia was to live at Herne Hill, in supervision of the two servants.

On the last Sunday, Monica went to see her friends in Queen's Road. Widdowson was ashamed to offer an objection; he much disliked her

---

1 The young man, having left Oxford University, is apparently continuing his "education" at Tattersall's, which was London's horse auction mart (founded in 1766) and a rendez-vous for sporting and betting men. He is, in other words, a member of the frivolous and fashionable world that Widdowson finds distasteful and threatening.

going there alone, but disliked almost equally the thought of accompanying her, for at Miss Barfoot's he could not pretend to sit, stand, or converse with ease.

It happened that Mrs. Cosgrove was again calling. On the first occasion of meeting with Monica, this lady paid her no particular attention; to-day she addressed her in a friendly manner, and their conversation led to the discovery that both of them were about to spend the ensuing month in the same place. Mrs. Cosgrove hoped they might occasionally see each other.

Of this coincidence Monica thought better to say nothing on her return home. She could not be sure that her husband might not, at the last moment, decide to stay at Herne Hill rather than incur the risk of her meeting an acquaintance in Guernsey. On this point he could not be trusted to exercise common sense. For the first time, Monica had a secret she desired to keep from him, and the necessity was one which could not but have an unfavourable effect on her manner of regarding Widdowson. They were to start on Monday evening; through the day her mind was divided between joy in the thought of seeing a new part of the world and a sense of weary dislike for her home; she had not understood till now how terrible would be the prospect of living here for a long time with no companionship but her husband's. On the return that prospect would lie before her. But no; their way of life must somehow be modified; on that she was resolved.

CHAPTER XVI.

HEALTH FROM THE SEA.

From Herne Hill to St. Peter Port was a change which made of Monica a new creature. The weather could not have been more propitious; day after day of still air and magnificent sky, with temperature which made a brisk walk at any hour thoroughly enjoyable, yet allowed one to sit at ease in the midday sunshine. Their lodgings were in the best part of the town, high up, looking forth over blue sea to the cliffs of Sark. Widdowson congratulated himself on having taken this step; it was like a revival of his honeymoon; never since their settling down at home had Monica been so grateful, so affectionate. Why, his wife was what he had thought her from the first, perfect in every wifely attribute. How lovely she looked as she sat down to the breakfast table, after breathing sea air at the open windows, in her charming dress, her black hair arranged in some new fashion just to please him! Or when she walked with him about the quays, obviously admired by men who passed them. Or when she seated herself in the open carriage for a drive which would warm her cheeks and make her lips redder and sweeter.

"Edmund," she said to him one evening, as they talked by the fireside, "don't you think you take life rather too gravely?"

He laughed.

"Gravely? Don't I seem to enjoy myself?"

"Oh yes; just now. But — still in a rather serious way. One would think you always had cares on your mind, and were struggling to get rid of them."

"I haven't a care in the world. I am the most blessed of mortals."

"So you ought to think yourself. But when we get back again, how will it be? You won't be angry with me? I really don't think I can live again as we were doing."

"Not live as" —

His brow darkened; he looked at her in astonishment.

"We ought to have more enjoyment," she pursued courageously. "Think of the numbers of people who live a dull, monotonous life just because they can't help it; how they would envy us, with so much money to spend, and free to do just what we like! Doesn't it seem a pity to sit there day after day alone" —

"Don't, my darling!" he implored. "Don't! That makes me think you don't really love me."

"Nonsense! I want you to see what I mean. I am not one of the silly people who care for nothing but amusement, but I do think we might enjoy our lives more when we are in London. We shan't live for ever, you know; is it right to spend day after day sitting there in the house" —

"But come, come; we have our occupations. Surely it ought to be a pleasure to you to see that the house is kept in order. There are duties" —

"Yes, I know. But these duties I could perform in a hour or two."

"Not thoroughly."

"Quite thoroughly enough."

"In my opinion, Monica, a woman ought never to be so happy as when she is looking after her home."

It was the old pedantic tone. His figure, in sympathy with it, abandoned an easy attitude and became awkward. But Monica would not allow herself to be alarmed. During the past week she had conducted herself so as to smooth the way for this very discussion. Unsuspecting husband!

"I wish to do my duty," she said, in a firm tone, "but I don't think it's right to make dull work for oneself, when one might be living. I don't think it *is* living to go on week after week like that. If we were poor, and I had a lot of children to look after as well as all the housework to do, I believe I shouldn't grumble — at least, I hope I shouldn't. I should know that I ought to do what there was no one else to do, and make the best of it. But" —

"Make the best of it!" he interrupted indignantly. "What an expression to use! It would not only be your duty, dear, but your privilege!"

"Wait a moment, Edmund. If you were a shopman earning fifteen shillings a week, and working from early morning to late at night, should you think it not only your duty but your privilege?"

He made a wrathful gesture.

"What comparison is there? I should be earning a hard livelihood by slaving for other people. But a married woman who works in her own home, for her husband and children" —

"Work is work, and when a woman is overburdened with it, she must find it difficult not to weary of home and husband and children all together. — But of course I don't mean to say that my work is too hard. All I mean is, that I don't see why any one should *make* work, and why life shouldn't be as full of enjoyment as possible."

"Monica, you have got these ideas from those people at Chelsea. That is exactly why I don't care for you to see much of them. I utterly disapprove of" —

"But you are mistaken. Miss Barfoot and Miss Nunn are all for work. They take life as seriously as you do."

"Work? What kind of work? They want to make women unwomanly, to make them unfit for the only duties women ought to perform. You know very well my opinions about that kind of thing."

He was trembling with the endeavour to control himself, to speak indulgently.

"I don't think, Edmund, there's much real difference between men and women. That is, there wouldn't be, if women had fair treatment."

"Not much difference? Oh, come; you are talking nonsense. There's as much difference between their minds as between their bodies. They are made for entirely different duties."

Monica sighed.

"Oh, that word Duty!"

Pained unutterably, Widdowson bent forward and took her hand. He spoke in a tone of the gravest but softest rebuke. She was giving entertainment to thoughts that would lead her who knew whither, that would undermine her happiness, would end by making both of them miserable. He besought her to put all such monstrous speculations out of her mind.

"Dear, good little wife! Do be guided by your husband. He is older than you, darling, and has seen so much more of the world."

"I haven't said anything very dreadful, dear. My thoughts don't come from other people; they rise naturally in my own head."

"Now what do you really want? You say you can't live as we were doing. What change would you make?"

"I should like to make more friends, and to see them often. I want to hear people talk, and know what is going on round about me. And to read a different kind of books; books that would really amuse me, and give me something I could think about with pleasure. Life will be a burden to me before long, if I don't have more freedom."

"Freedom?"

"Yes, I don't think there's any harm in saying that."

"Freedom?" He glared at her. "I shall begin to think that you wish you had never married me."

"I should only wish that, if I were made to feel that you shut me up in a house and couldn't trust me to go where I chose. Suppose the thought took you that you would go and walk about the City some afternoon, and you wished to go alone, just to be more at ease, should I have a right to forbid you, or grumble at you? And yet you are very dissatisfied if I wish to go anywhere alone."

"But here's the old confusion. I am a man; you are a woman."

"I can't see that that makes any difference. A woman ought to go about just as freely as a man. I don't think it's just. When I have done my work at home, I think I ought to be every bit as free as you are — every bit as free. And I'm very sure, Edmund, that love needs freedom if it is to remain love in truth."

He looked at her keenly.

"That's a dreadful thing for you to say. So, if I disapprove of your becoming the kind of woman that acknowledges no law, you will cease to love me?"

"What law do you mean?"

"Why, the natural law that points out a woman's place, and" — he added, with shaken voice — "commands her to follow her husband's guidance."

"Now you are angry. We mustn't talk about it any more, just now."

She rose and poured out a glass of water. Her hand trembled as she drank. Widdowson fell into gloomy abstraction. Later, as they lay side by side, he wished to renew the theme, but Monica would not talk; she declared herself too sleepy, turned her back to him, and soon slept indeed.

That night the weather became stormy; a roaring wind swept the Channel, and when day broke nothing could be seen but cloud and rain. Widdowson, who had rested little, was in a heavy, taciturn mood; Monica, on the other hand, talked gaily, seeming not to observe her companion's irresponsiveness. She was glad of the wild sky; now they would see another aspect of island life, the fierce and perilous surges beating about these granite shores.

They had brought with them a few books, and Widdowson, after breakfast, sat down by the fire to read. Monica first of all wrote a letter to her sister; then, as it was still impossible to go out, she took up one of the volumes that lay on a side-table in their sitting-room, novels left by former lodgers. Her choice was something or other with yellow back.[1] Widdowson, watching all her movements furtively, became aware of the pictured cover.

"I don't think you'll get much good out of that," he remarked, after one or two efforts to speak.

"No harm, at all events," she replied good-humouredly.

"I'm not so sure. Why should you waste your time? Take 'Guy Mannering,' if you want a novel."

"I'll see how I like this first."

He felt himself powerless, and suffered acutely from the thought that Monica was in rebellion against him. He could not understand what had brought about this sudden change. Fear of losing his wife's love restrained him from practical despotism, yet he was very near to uttering a definite command.

In the afternoon it no longer rained, and the wind had less violence. They went out to look at the sea. Many people were gathered about the harbour, whence was a fine view of the great waves that broke into leaping foam and spray against the crags of Sark. As they stood thus occupied, Monica heard her name spoken in a friendly voice, — that of Mrs. Cosgrove.

---

1 From about the mid-nineteenth century, cheap editions of popular novels were published by Chapman and Hall to be sold in railway stations as light fare for travellers. They were referred to as "yellowbacks" because of their yellow covers. French novels, considered by many English readers as likely to be scandalous, also had yellow covers. Monica's choice of reading material thus suggests everything that Widdowson would disapprove of — it is either frivolous or improper. *Guy Mannering* (1815), which Widdowson tries to persuade Monica to read instead, is one of many historical novels written by Sir Walter Scott (1771–1832).

"I have been expecting to see you," said the lady. "We arrived three days ago."

Widdowson, starting with surprise, turned to examine the speaker. He saw a woman of something less than middle age, unfashionably attired, good-looking, with an air of high spirits; only when she offered her hand to him did he remember having met her at Miss Barfoot's. To be graceful in a high wind is difficult for any man; the ungainliness with which he returned Mrs. Cosgrove's greeting could not have been surpassed, and probably would have been much the same even had he not, of necessity, stood clutching at his felt hat.

The three talked for a few minutes. With Mrs. Cosgrove were two persons, a younger woman and a man of about thirty, — the latter a comely and vivacious fellow, with rather long hair of the orange-tawny hue. These looked at Monica, but Mrs. Cosgrove made no introduction.

"Come and see me, will you?" she said, mentioning her address. "One can't get out much in the evenings; I shall be nearly always at home after dinner, and we have music — of a kind."

Monica boldly accepted the invitation, said she would be glad to come. Then Mrs. Cosgrove took leave of them, and walked landwards with her companions.

Widdowson stood gazing at the sea. There was no misreading his countenance; when Monica had remarked it, she pressed her lips together, and waited for what he would say or do. He said nothing, but presently turned his back upon the waves and began to walk on. Neither spoke until they were in the shelter of the streets; then Widdowson asked suddenly:

"Who *is* that person?"

"I only know her name, and that she goes to Miss Barfoot's."

"It's a most extraordinary thing," he exclaimed, in high irritation. "There's no getting out of the way of those people."

Monica also was angry; her cheeks, reddened by the wind, grew hotter.

"It's still more extraordinary that you should object so to them."

"Whether or no — I *do* object, and I had rather you didn't go to see that woman."

"You are unreasonable," Monica answered sharply. "Certainly I shall go and see her."

"I forbid you to do so! If you go, it will be in defiance of my wish."

"Then I am obliged to defy your wish. I shall certainly go."

His face was frightfully distorted. Had they been in a lonely spot, Monica would have felt afraid of him. She moved hurriedly away in the direction of their lodgings, and for a few paces he followed; then he checked himself, turned round about, took an opposite way.

With strides of rage he went along by the quay, past the hotels and the smaller houses that follow, on to St. Sampson. The wind, again preparing for a tempestuous night, beat and shook and at moments all but stopped him; he set his teeth like a madman, and raged on. Past the granite quarries at Bordeaux Harbour, then towards the wild north extremity of the island, the sandy waste of L'Ancresse. When darkness began to fall, no human being was in his range of sight. He stood on one spot for nearly a quarter of an hour, watching, or appearing to watch, the black, low-flying scud.

Their time for dining was seven. Shortly before this, Widdowson entered the house, and went to the sitting-room; Monica was not there. He found her in the bed-chamber, before the looking-glass. At the sight of his reflected face, she turned instantly.

"Monica!" He put his hands on her shoulders, whispering hoarsely, "Monica! don't you love me?"

She looked away, not replying.

"Monica!"

And of a sudden he fell on his knees before her, clasped her about the waist, burst into choking sobs.

"Have you no love for me? — My darling! My dear, beautiful wife! — Have you begun to hate me?"

Tears came to her eyes. She implored him to rise and command himself.

"I was so violent, so brutal with you. I spoke without thinking" —

"But *why* should you speak like that? Why are you so unreasonable? If you forbid me to do simple things, with not the least harm in them, you can't expect me to take it like a child. I shall resist; I can't help it."

He had risen and was crushing her in his arms, his hot breath on her neck, when he began to whisper:

"I want to keep you all to myself. I don't like these people — they think so differently — they put such hateful ideas into your mind — they are not the right kinds of friends for you" —

"You misunderstand them, and you don't in the least understand me. — Oh, you hurt me, Edmund!"

He released her body, and took her head between his hands.

"I had rather you were dead than that you should cease to love me! You shall go to see her; I won't say a word against it. But, Monica, be faithful, be faithful to me!"

"Faithful to you?" she echoed, in astonishment. "What *have* I said or done to put you in such a state? Because I wish to make a few friends as all women do" —

"It's because I have lived so much alone. I have never had more than one or two friends, and I am absurdly jealous when you want to get away from me and amuse yourself with strangers. I can't talk to such people. I am not suited for society. If I hadn't met you in that strange way, by miracle, I should never have been able to marry. — If I allow you to have these friends" —

"I don't like to hear that word. Why should you say *allow*? Do you think of me as your servant, Edmund?"

"You know how I think of you. It is I who am your servant, your slave."

"Oh, I can't believe that!" She pressed her handkerchief to her cheeks, and laughed unnaturally. "Such words don't mean anything. It is you who forbid, and allow, and command, and" —

"I will never again use such words. Only convince me that you love me as much as ever."

"It is so miserable to begin quarrelling" —

"Never again! — Say you love me! Put your arms round my neck — press closer to me" —

She kissed his cheek, but did not utter a word.

"You can't say that you love me?"

"I think I am always showing it. Do get ready for dinner now; it's past seven. — Oh, how foolish you have been!"

Of course their talk lasted half through the night. Monica held with remarkable firmness to the position she had taken; a much older woman might have envied her steadfast yet quite rational assertion of the right to live a life of her own apart from that imposed upon her by the duties of wedlock. A great deal of this spirit and the utterance it found was traceable to her association with the women whom Widdowson so deeply suspected; prior to her sojourn in Rutland Street she could not even have made clear to herself the demands which she now very clearly formulated. Believing that she had learnt nothing from them, and till of late instinctively opposing the doctrines held by Miss Barfoot and Rhoda Nunn, Monica in truth owed the sole bit of real education she had ever received to those few weeks of attendance in Great Portland Street. Circumstances were now proving how apt a pupil she had been, even against her will. Marriage, as is always the case with women capable of development, made for her a new heaven and a new earth; perhaps on no single subject did she now think as on the morning of her wedding-day.

"You must either trust me completely," she said, "or not at all. If you can't and won't trust me, how can I possibly love you?"

"Am I never to advise?" asked her husband, baffled, and even awed, by this extraordinary revelation of a woman he had supposed himself to know thoroughly.

"Oh, that's a very different thing from forbidding and commanding!" she laughed. "There was that novel this morning. Of course I know as well as you do that 'Guy Mannering' is better; but that doesn't say I am not to form my opinion of other books. You mustn't be afraid to leave me the same freedom you have yourself."

The result of it all was that Widdowson felt his passionate love glow with new fire. For a moment he thought himself capable of accepting this change in their relations. The marvellous thought of equality between man and wife, that gospel which in far-off days will re-fashion the world, for an instant smote his imagination and exalted him above his native level.

Monica paid for the energy she had put forth by a day of suffering. Her head ached intolerably; she had feverish symptoms, and could hardly raise herself from the bed. It passed, and she was once more eager to go forth under the blue sky that followed the tempest.

"Will you go with me to Mrs. Cosgrove's this evening?" she asked of her husband.

He consented, and after dinner they sought the hotel where their acquaintance was staying. Widdowson was in extreme discomfort, partly due to the fact that he had no dress clothes to put on; for far from anticipating or desiring any such intercourse in Guernsey, he had never thought of packing an evening suit. Had he known Mrs. Cosgrove, this uneasiness would have been spared him. That lady was in revolt against far graver institutions than the swallow-tail;[1] she cared not a button in what garb her visitors came to her. On their arrival, they found, to Widdowson's horror, a room full of women. With the hostess was that younger lady they had seen on the quay, Mrs. Cosgrove's unmarried sister; Miss Knott's health had demanded this retreat from the London winter. The guests were four, a Mrs. Bevis and her three daughters, all invalidish persons, the mother somewhat lackadaisical, the girls with a look of unwilling spinsterhood.

Monica, noteworthy among the gathering for her sweet, bright prettiness, and the finish of her dress, soon made herself at home; she chatted gaily with the girls, — wondering indeed at her own air of maturity, which came to her for the first time. Mrs. Cosgrove, an easy woman of the world when circumstances required it, did her best to get something out of Widdowson, who presently thawed a little.

Then Miss Knott sat down to the piano, and played more than tolerably well; and the youngest Miss Bevis sang a song of Schubert,[2] with passable voice but in very distressing German — the sole person distressed by it being the hostess.

Meanwhile Monica had been captured by Mrs. Bevis, who discoursed to her on a subject painfully familiar to all the old lady's friends.

"Do you know my son, Mrs. Widdowson? — Oh, I thought you had perhaps met him. You will do so this evening I hope. He is over here on a fortnight's holiday."

"Do you live in Guernsey?" Monica inquired.

"*I*, practically, live here, and one of my daughters is always with me. The other two live with their brother, in a flat in Bayswater. — Do you care for flats, Mrs. Widdowson?"

Monica could only say that she had no experience of that institution.

"I do think them such a boon," pursued Mrs. Bevis. "They are expensive, but the advantages and comforts are so many. My son wouldn't on

---

1 I.e. Mrs. Cosgrove is in revolt against more than social formalities like dress codes. "Swallow-tail" refers to men's formal wear, distinguished by the tailcoat.

2 Franz Schubert (1797–1828) was an Austrian composer renowned for his songs, of which he wrote approximately 600 during his short life.

any consideration give up his flat. As I was saying, he always has two of his sisters to keep house for him. He is quite a young man, not yet thirty, but — would you believe it? — we are all dependent upon him! My son has supported the *whole* of the family for the last six or seven years, and that by his own work. It sounds incredible, doesn't it? But for him, we should be quite unable to live. The dear girls have very delicate health; simply impossible for them to exert themselves in any way. My son has made extraordinary sacrifices on our account. His desire was to be a professional musician, and every one thinks he would have become eminent; myself, I am convinced of it — perhaps that is only natural. But when our circumstances began to grow very doubtful, and we really didn't know what was before us, my son consented to follow a business career — that of wine-merchant, with which his father was connected. And he exerted himself so nobly, and gave proof of such ability, that very soon all our fears were at an end; and now, before he is thirty, his position is quite assured. We have no longer a care. I live here very economically — really sweet lodgings on the road to St. Martin's; I *do* hope you will come and see me. And the girls go backwards and forwards. You see we are *all* here at present. When my son returns to London, he will take the eldest and the youngest with him. The middle girl, dear Grace — she is thought very clever in water-colours, and I am quite sure, if it were necessary, she could pursue the arts in a professional spirit."

Mr. Bevis entered the room, and Monica recognized the sprightly young man whom she had seen on the quay. The hostess presented him to her new friends, and he got into talk with Widdowson. Requested to make music for the company, he sang a gay little piece, which, to Monica at all events, seemed one of the most delightful things she had ever heard.

"His own composition," whispered Miss Grace Bevis, then sitting by Mrs. Widdowson.

That increased her delight. Foolish as Mrs. Bevis undoubtedly was, she perchance had not praised her son beyond his merits. He looked the best of good fellows; so kind and merry and spirited; such a capable man, too. It struck Monica as a very hard fate that he should have this family on his hands. What they must cost him! Probably he could not think of marrying, just on their account.

Mr. Bevis came and took a place by her side.

"Thank you so very much," she said, "for that charming song. Is it published?"

"Oh dear no!" He laughed and shook his thick hair about. "It's one of two or three that I somehow struck out when I was studying in Germany, ages ago. — You play, I hope?"

Monica gave a sad negative.

"Oh, what does it matter? There are hosts of people who will always be overjoyed to play when you ask them. — It would be a capital thing if only those children were allowed to learn an instrument who showed genuine talent for music."

"In that case," said Monica, "there certainly wouldn't be hosts of people ready to play for me."

"No." His merry laugh was repeated. "You mustn't mind when I contradict myself; it's one of my habits. — Are you here for the whole winter?"

"Only a few weeks, unfortunately."

"And do you dread the voyage back?"

"To tell the truth, I do. I had a very unpleasant time, coming."

"As for myself, how I ever undertake the thing, I really don't know. One of these times, I shall die; there's not a shadow of doubt of that. The girls always have to carry me ashore, one holding me by the hair and one by the boots. Happily, I am so emaciated that my weight doesn't distress them. I pick up flesh in a day or two, and then my health is stupendous. As at present. You see how marvellously *fit* I look."

"Yes, you look very well," replied Monica, glancing at the fair, comely face.

"It's deceptive. All our family have wretched constitutions. If I go to work regularly for a couple of months without a holiday, I sink into absolute decrepitude. An office chair has been specially made for me, to hold me up at the desk. — I beg your pardon for this clowning, Mrs. Widdowson," he suddenly added in another voice. "The air puts me in such spirits. What air it is! Speaking quite seriously, my mother was saved by coming to live here. We believed her to be dying, and now I have hopes that she will live ever so many years longer."

He spoke of his mother with evident affection, glancing kindly towards her with his blue eyes.

Only once or twice had Monica ventured to exchange a glance with her husband. It satisfied her that he managed to converse; what his mood really was could not be determined until afterwards. When they were about to leave, she saw him, to her surprise, speaking quite pleasantly with Mr. Bevis. A carriage was procured to convey them home, and as soon as they had started, Monica asked her husband, with a merry look, how he had enjoyed himself.

"There is not much harm in it," he replied drily.

"Harm? How like you, Edmund, to put it in that way! Now confess you will be glad to go again."

"I shall go if you wish."

"Unsatisfactory man! You can't bring yourself to admit that it was pleasant to be among new people. I believe, in your very heart, you think all enjoyment is wrong. The music was nice, wasn't it?"

"I didn't think much of the girl's singing, but that fellow Bevis wasn't bad."

Monica examined him as he spoke, and seemed to suppress a laugh.

"No, he wasn't at all bad. I saw you talking with Mrs. Bevis. Did she tell you anything about her wonderful son?"

"Nothing particular."

"Oh, then I must tell you the whole story."

And she did so, in a tone half of jest, half of serious approval.

"I don't see that he has done anything more than his duty," remarked Widdowson, at the end. "But he isn't a bad fellow."

For private reasons, Monica contrasted this attitude towards Bevis with the disfavour her husband had shown to Mr. Barfoot, and was secretly much amused.

Two or three days after, they went to spend the morning at Petit Bot Bay, and there encountered with Bevis and his three sisters. The result was an invitation to go back and have lunch at Mrs. Bevis's lodgings; they accepted it, and remained with their acquaintances till dusk. The young man's holiday was at an end; next morning he would face the voyage which he had depicted so grotesquely.

"And alone!" he lamented to Monica. "Only think of it. The girls are all rather below par just now; they had better stay here for the present."

"And in London you will be alone, too?"

"Yes. It's very sad. I must bear up under it. The worst of it is, I am naturally subject to depression. In solitude, I sink, sink. — But the subject is too painful. Don't let us darken the last hours with such reflections."

Widdowson retained his indulgent opinion of the facetious young wine-merchant. He even laughed now and then in recalling some phrase or other that Bevis had used to him.

Subsequently, Monica had several long conversations with the old lady. Impelled to gossipy frankness about all her affairs, Mrs. Bevis allowed it to be understood that the chief reason for two of the girls always being with their brother was the possibility thus afforded of their "meeting people," — that is to say, of their having a chance of marriage. Mrs. Cosgrove, and one or two other ladies, did them social service.

"They never *will* marry!" said Monica to her husband, rather thoughtfully than with commiseration.

"Why not? They are nice enough girls."

"Yes, but they have no money; and" — she smiled — "people see that they want to find husbands."

"I don't see that the first matters; and the second is only natural."

Monica attempted no rejoinder, but said presently:

"Now they are just the kind of women who ought to find something to do."

"Something to do? Why, they attend to their mother and their brother. What could be more proper?"

"Very proper, perhaps. But they are miserable, and always will be."

"Then they have no *right* to be miserable. They are doing their duty, and that ought to keep them cheerful."

Monica could have said many things, but she overcame the desire, and laughed the subject aside.

CHAPTER XVII.

THE TRIUMPH.

Not till mid-winter did Barfoot again see his friends the Micklethwaites. By invitation he went to South Tottenham on New Year's Eve, and dined with them at seven o'clock. He was the first guest that had entered the house since their marriage.

From the very door-step Everard became conscious of a domestic atmosphere that told soothingly upon his nerves. The little servant who opened to him exhibited a gentle, noiseless demeanour which was no doubt the result of careful discipline. Micklethwaite himself, who at once came out into the passage, gave proof of a like influence; his hearty greeting was spoken in soft tones; a placid happiness beamed from his face. In the sitting-room (Micklethwaite's study, used for reception because the other had to serve as dining-room), tempered lamplight and the glow of a hospitable fire showed the hostess and her blind sister standing in expectation; to Everard's eyes both of them looked far better in health than a few months ago. Mrs. Micklethwaite was no longer so distressingly old; an expression that resembled girlish pleasure lit up her countenance as she stepped forward; nay, if he mistook not, there came a gentle warmth to her cheek, and the momentary downward glance was as graceful and modest as in a youthful bride. Never had Barfoot approached a woman with more finished courtesy, the sincere expression of his feeling. The blind sister he regarded in like spirit; his voice touched its softest note as he held her hand for a moment and replied to her pleasant words.

No undue indication of poverty disturbed him. He saw that the house had been improved in many ways since Mrs. Micklethwaite had taken possession of it; pictures, ornaments, pieces of furniture were added, all in simple taste, but serving to heighten the effect of refined comfort. Where the average woman would have displayed pretentious emptiness, Mrs. Micklethwaite had made a home which in its way was beautiful. The dinner, which she herself had cooked, and which she assisted in serving, aimed at being no more than a simple, decorous meal, but the guest unfeignedly enjoyed it; even the vegetables and the bread seemed to him to have a daintier flavour than at many a rich table. He could not help noticing and admiring the skill with which Miss Wheatley ate without seeing what was before her; had he not known her misfortune, he would hardly have become aware of it by any peculiarity as she sat opposite to him.

The mathematician had learnt to sit upon a chair like ordinary mortals. For the first week or two it must have cost him severe restraint; now he betrayed no temptation to roll and jerk and twist himself. When the ladies retired, he reached from the sideboard a box which Barfoot viewed with uneasiness.

"Do you smoke here — in this room?"

"Oh, why not?"

Everard glanced at the pretty curtains before the windows.

"No, my boy, you do *not* smoke here. And, in fact, I like your claret; I won't spoil the flavour of it."

"As you please; but I think Fanny will be distressed."

"You shall say that I have abandoned the weed."

Emotions were at conflict in Micklethwaite's mind, but finally he beamed with gratitude.

"Barfoot," — he bent forward and touched his friend's arm, — "there are angels walking the earth in this our day. Science hasn't abolished them, my dear fellow, and I don't think it ever will."

"It falls to the lot of but few men to encounter them, and of fewer still to entertain them permanently in a cottage at South Tottenham."

"You are right." Micklethwaite laughed in a new way, with scarcely any sound; a change Everard had already noticed. "These two sisters — but I had better not speak about them. In my old age I have become a worshipper, a mystic, a man of dream and vision."

"How about worship in a parochial sense?" inquired Barfoot, smiling. "Any difficulty on that point?"

"I conform, in moderation. Nothing would be asked of me. There is no fanaticism, no intolerance. It would be brutal if I declined to go to church on a Sunday morning. You see, my strictly scientific attitude helps in avoiding offence. Fanny can't understand it, but my lack of dogmatism vastly relieves her. I have been trying to explain to her that the scientific mind can have nothing to do with materialism. The new order of ideas is of course very difficult for her to grasp; but in time, in time."

"For heaven's sake, don't attempt conversion!"

"On no account whatever. But I *should* like her to see what is meant by perception and conception, by the relativity of time and space, — and a few simple things of that kind."

Barfoot laughed heartily.

"By-the-bye," he said, shifting to safer ground, "my brother Tom is in London, and in wretched health. *His* angel is from the wrong quarter, from the nethermost pit. I seriously believe that she has a plan for killing her husband. You remember my mentioning in a letter his horse-accident? He has never recovered from that, and as likely as not never will. His wife brought him away from Madeira just when he ought to have stopped there to get well. He settled himself at Torquay, whilst that woman ran about to pay visits. It was understood that she should go back to him at Torquay, but this she at length refused to do. The place was too dull; it didn't suit her extremely delicate health; she must live in London, her pure, native air. If Tom had taken my advice, he would have let her live just where she pleased, thanking heaven that she was at a distance from him. But the poor fellow can't be away from her. He has come up, and here, I feel convinced, he will die. It's a very monstrous thing, but uncommonly like women in general who have got a man into their power."

Micklethwaite shook his head.

"You are too hard upon them. You have been unlucky. — You know my view of your duty."

"I begin to think that marriage isn't impossible for me," said Barfoot, with a grave smile.

"Ha! Capital!"

"But as likely as not it will be marriage without forms, — simply a free union."

The mathematician was downcast.

"I'm sorry to hear that. It won't do. We must conform. Besides, in that case the person decidedly isn't suitable to you. You, of all men, must marry a lady."

"I should never think of any one that wasn't a lady."

"Is emancipation getting as far as that? Do ladies enter into that kind of union?"

"I don't know of any example. That's just why the idea tempts me." Barfoot would go no further in explanation.

"How about your new algebra?"

"Alas! — My dear boy, the temptation is so frightful — when I get back home. Remember that I have never known what it was to sit and talk through the evening with ordinary friends, let alone — It's too much for me just yet. And, you know, I don't venture to work on Sundays. That will come; all in good time. I must grant myself half a year of luxury after such a life as mine has been."

"Of course you must. Let algebra wait."

"I think it over, of course, at odd moments. Church on Sunday morning is a good opportunity."

Barfoot could not stay to see the old year out, but good wishes were none the less heartily exchanged before he went. Micklethwaite walked with him to the railway station; at a few paces' distance from his house, he stood and pointed back to it.

"That little place, Barfoot, is one of the sacred spots of the earth. Strange to think that the house has been waiting for me there through all the years of my hopelessness. I feel that a mysterious light ought to shine about it. It oughtn't to look just like common houses."

On his way home, Everard thought over what he had seen and heard, smiling good-naturedly. Well, that was one ideal of marriage. Not *his* ideal; but very beautiful amid the vulgarities and vileness of ordinary experience. It was the old fashion in its purest presentment; the consecrated form of domestic happiness, removed beyond reach of satire, only to be touched, if touched at all, with the very gentlest irony.

A life by no means for him. If he tried it, even with a woman so perfect, he would perish of *ennui*. For him, marriage must not mean repose, inevitably tending to drowsiness; but the mutual incitement of vigorous minds. Passion — yes, there must be passion, at all events to begin with; passion not impossible of revival in days subsequent to its first indulgence. Beauty in the academic sense he no longer demanded; enough that the face spoke eloquently, that the limbs were vigorous. Let beauty perish, if it cannot ally itself with mind; be a woman what else she may, let her have brains and the power of using them! In that demand the maturity of his manhood expressed itself. For casual amour the odalisque could still prevail with him; but for the life of wedlock, the durable companionship of man and woman, intellect was his first requirement.

A woman with man's capability of understanding and reasoning; free from superstition, religious or social; far above the ignoble weaknesses which men have been base enough to idealize in her sex. A woman who would scorn the vulgarism of jealousy, and yet know what it is to love. This was asking much of nature and civilization; did he grossly deceive himself in thinking he had found the paragon?

For thus far had he advanced in his thoughts of Rhoda Nunn. If the phrase had any meaning, he was in love with her; yet, strange complex of emotions, he was still only half serious in his desire to take her for a wife, wishing, rather, to amuse and flatter himself by merely inspiring her with passion. Therefore he refused to entertain a thought of formal marriage. To obtain her consent to marriage would mean nothing at all; it would afford him no satisfaction. But so to play upon her emotions that the proud, intellectual, earnest woman was willing to defy society for his sake — ah! that would be an end worth achieving.

Ever since the dialogue in which he frankly explained his position, and all but declared love, he had not once seen Rhoda in private. She shunned him purposely beyond a doubt, and did not that denote a fear of him justified by her inclination? The postponement of what must necessarily come to pass between them began to try his patience, as assuredly it inflamed his ardour. If no other resource offered, he would be obliged to make his cousin an accomplice by requesting her, beforehand, to leave him alone with Rhoda some evening when he had called upon them.

But it was time that chance favoured him, and his interview with Miss Nunn came about in a way he could not have foreseen.

At the end of the first week of January he was invited to dine at Miss Barfoot's. The afternoon had been foggy, and when he set forth there seemed to be some likelihood of a plague of choking darkness such as would obstruct traffic. As usual he went by train to Sloane Square, purposing (for it was dry under foot, and he could not disregard small economies) to walk the short distance from there to Queen's Road. On coming out from the station, he found the fog so dense that it was doubtful whether he could reach his journey's end. Cabs were not to be had; he must either explore the gloom, with risk of getting nowhere at all, or give it up and take a train back. But he longed too ardently for the sight of Rhoda to abandon his evening without an effort. Having with difficulty made his way into King's Road, he found progress easier on account of the shop illuminations; the fog, however, was growing every moment more fearsome, and when he had to turn out of the highway, his case appeared desperate. Literally he groped along, feeling the fronts of the houses. As under ordinary circumstances he would have had only just time enough to reach his cousin's punctually, he must be very late: perhaps they would conclude that he had not ventured out on such a night, and were already dining without him. No matter; as well go one way as another, now. After abandoning hope several times, and all but asphyxiated, he found by inquiry of a man with whom he collided that he was actually within a few doors of his destination. Another effort, and he rang a joyous peal at the bell.

A mistake. It was the wrong house, and he had to go two doors farther on.

This time he procured admittance to the familiar little hall. The servant smiled at him, but said nothing. He was led to the drawing-room, and there found Rhoda Nunn alone. This fact did not so much surprise him as Rhoda's appearance. For the first time since he had known her, her dress was not uniform black; she wore a red silk blouse with a black skirt, and so admirable was the effect of this costume that he scarcely refrained from a delighted exclamation.

Some concern was visible in her face.

"I am sorry to say," were her first words, "that Miss Barfoot will not be here in time for dinner. She went to Faversham this morning, and ought to have been back about half-past seven. But a telegram came some time ago. A thick fog caused her to miss the train, and the next doesn't reach Victoria till ten minutes past ten."

It was now half-past eight; dinner had been appointed for the hour. Barfoot explained his lateness in arriving.

"Is it so bad as that? I didn't know."

The situation embarrassed both of them. Barfoot suspected a hope on Miss Nunn's part that he would relieve her of his company, but, even had there been no external hindrance, he could not have relinquished the happy occasion. To use frankness was best.

"Out of the question for me to leave the house," he said, meeting her eyes and smiling. "You won't be hard upon a starving man?"

At once Rhoda made a pretence of having felt no hesitation.

"Oh, of course we will dine immediately." She rang the bell. "Miss Barfoot took it for granted that I would represent her. — Look, the fog is penetrating even to our fireside."

"Cheerful, very. What is Mary doing at Faversham?"

"Some one she has been corresponding with for some time begged her to go down and give an address to a number of ladies on — a certain subject."

"Ah! Mary is on the way to become a celebrity."

"Quite against her will, as you know."

They went to dinner, and Barfoot, thoroughly enjoying the abnormal state of things, continued to talk of his cousin.

"It seems to me that she can't logically refuse to put herself forward. Work of her kind can't be done in a corner. It isn't a case of 'Oh teach the orphan girl to sew.'"[1]

"I have used the same argument to her," said Rhoda.

Her place at the head of the table had its full effect upon Everard's imagination. Why should he hold by a resolve of which he did not absolutely approve the motive? Why not ask her simply to be his wife, and so remove one element of difficulty from his pursuit? True, he was wretchedly poor. Marrying on such an income, he would at once find his freedom restricted in every direction. — But then, more likely than not Rhoda had determined against marriage, and of him, especially, never thought for a moment as a possible husband. Well, that was what he wanted to ascertain.

They conversed naturally enough, till the meal was over. Then their embarrassment revived, but this time it was Rhoda who took the initiative.

"Shall I leave you to your meditations?" she asked, moving a few inches from the table.

"I should much prefer your society, if you will grant it me for a little longer."

Without speaking, she rose and led the way to the drawing-room. There, sitting at a formal distance from each other, they talked — of the fog. Would Miss Barfoot be able to get back at all?

"A propos," said Everard, "did you ever read 'The City of Dreadful Night'?"[2]

"Yes, I have read it."

"Without sympathy, of course?"

"Why 'of course'? Do I seem to you a shallow optimist?"

"No. A vigorous and rational optimist — such as I myself aim at being."

"Do you? But optimism of that kind must be proved by some effort on behalf of society."

"Precisely the effort I am making. If a man works at developing and fortifying the best things in his own character, he is surely doing society a service."

She smiled sceptically.

---

1 Tennyson, "Lady Clara Vere de Vere," l. 70 (1842). The speaker in this poem deplores the haughty Lady Clara's pride and coldness and exhorts her to do good works: "teach the orphan-boy to read" and "the orphan-girl to sew." The more familiar lines from this poem are "Kind hearts are more than coronets, /And simple faith than Norman blood," (ll. 55–56).

2 A long poem by James Thomson (1834–82), first published in 1874. This pessimistic poem anticipates the angst of the nineteenth-century *fin de siècle*. Thomson develops a grotesque cityscape through which the speaker wanders despairingly.

"Yes, no doubt. But how do you develop and fortify yourself?"

She was meeting him half way, thought Everard. Foreseeing the inevitable, she wished to have it over and done with. Or else —

"I live very quietly," was his reply, "thinking of grave problems most of my time. You know, I am a great deal alone."

"Naturally."

"No; anything but naturally."

Rhoda said nothing. He waited a moment, then moved to a seat much nearer hers. Her face hardened, and he saw her fingers lock together.

"Where a man is in love, solitude seems to him the most unnatural of conditions."

"Please don't make me your confidante, Mr. Barfoot," Rhoda replied, with well-assumed pleasantry. "I have no taste for that kind of thing."

"But I can't help doing so. It is you that I am in love with."

"I am very sorry to hear it. Happily, the sentiment will not long trouble you."

He read in her eyes and on her lips a profound agitation. She glanced about the room, and, before he could again speak, had risen to ring the bell.

"You always take coffee, I think?"

Without troubling to give any assent, he moved apart and turned over some books on the table. For full five minutes there was silence. The coffee was brought; he tasted it and put his cup down. Seeing that Rhoda had, as it were, intrenched herself behind the beverage, and would continue to sip at it as long as might be necessary, he went and stood in front of her.

"Miss Nunn, I am more serious than you will give me credit for being. The sentiment, as you call it, has troubled me for some time, and will last."

Her refuge failed her. The cup she was holding began to shake a little.

"Please let me put it aside for you."

Rhoda allowed him to do so, and then locked her fingers.

"I am so much in love with you that I can't keep away from this house more than a few days at a time. Of course you have known it; I haven't tried to disguise why I came here so often. It's so seldom that I see you alone, and now that fortune is kind to me I must speak as best I can. I won't make myself ridiculous in your eyes — if I can help it. You despise the love-making of ball-rooms and garden parties; so do I, most heartily. Let me speak like a man who has few illusions to overcome. I want you for the companion of my life; I don't see very well how I am to do without you. You know, I think, that I have only a moderate competence; it's enough to live upon without miseries, that's all one can say. Probably I shall never be richer, for I can't promise to exert myself to earn money; I wish to live for other things. You can picture the kind of life I want you to share. You know me well enough to understand that my wife — if we use the old word — would be as free to live in her own way as I to live in mine. All the same, it is love that I am asking for. Think how you may about man and woman, you know that there *is* such a thing as love between them, and that the love of a man and a woman who can think intelligently may be the best thing life has to offer them."

He could not see her eyes, but she was smiling in a forced way, with her lips close set.

"As you insisted on speaking," she said at length, "I had no choice but to listen. It is usual, I think, — if one may trust the novels, — for a woman to return thanks when an offer of this kind has been made to her. So — thank you very much, Mr. Barfoot."

Everard seized a little chair that was close by, planted it beside Rhoda's, there seated himself and took possession of one of her hands. It was done so rapidly and vehemently, that Rhoda started back, her expression changing from sportive mockery to all but alarm.

"I will have no such thanks," he uttered in a low voice, much moved, a smile making him look strangely stern. "You shall understand what it means when a man says that he loves you. — I have come to think your face so beautiful that I am in torment with the desire to press my lips upon yours. Don't be afraid that I shall be brutal enough to do it without your consent; my respect for you is stronger even than my passion. When I first saw you, I thought you interesting because of your evident intelligence — nothing more; indeed you were not a woman to me. Now you are the one woman in the world; no other can draw my eyes from you. Touch me with your fingers, and I shall tremble, — that is what my love means."

She was colourless; her lips, just parted, quivered as the breath panted between them. She did not try to withdraw her hand.

"Can you love me in return?" Everard went on, his face still nearer. "Am I anything like this to *you*? Have the courage you boast of. Speak to me as one human being to another, plain, honest words."

"I don't love you in the least. And if I did, I would never share your life."

The voice was very unlike her familiar tones. It seemed to hurt her to speak.

"The reason. — Because you have no faith in me?"

"I can't say whether I have or not. I know absolutely nothing of your life. But I have my work, and no one shall ever persuade me to abandon it."

"Your work? — How do you understand it? What is its importance for you?"

"Oh, and you pretend to know me so well that you wish me to be your companion at every moment!"

She laughed mockingly, and tried to draw away her hand, for it was burnt by the heat of his. Barfoot held her firmly.

"What *is* your work? Copying with a type-machine, and teaching others to do the same — isn't that it?"

"The work by which I earn money, yes. But if it were no more than that" —

"Explain, then."

Passion was overmastering him as he watched the fine scorn in her eyes. He raised her hand to his lips.

"No!" Rhoda exclaimed, with sudden wrath. "Your respect — Oh, I appreciate your respect!"

She wrenched herself from his grasp, and went apart. Barfoot rose, gazing at her with admiration.

"It is better I should be at a distance from you," he said. "I want to know your mind, and not to be made insensate."

"Wouldn't it be better still if you left me?" Rhoda suggested, mistress of herself again.

"If you really wish it." He remembered the circumstances, and spoke submissively. "Yet the fog gives me such a good excuse for begging your indulgence. The chances are I should only lose myself in an inferno."

"Doesn't it strike you that you take an advantage of me, as you did once before? I make no pretence of equalling you in muscular strength, yet you try to hold me by force."

He divined in her a pleasure akin to his own, the delight of conflict. Otherwise, she would never have spoken thus.

"Yes, it is true. Love revives the barbarian; — it wouldn't mean much, if it didn't. In this one respect, I suppose no man, however civilized, would wish the woman he loves to be his equal. Marriage by capture can't quite be done away with. You say you have not the least love for me; if you had, should I like you to confess it instantly? A man must plead and woo; but there are different ways. I can't kneel before you and exclaim about my miserable unworthiness — for I am not unworthy of you. I shall never call you queen and goddess — unless in delirium, and I think I should soon weary of the woman who put her head under my foot. Just because I am stronger than you, and have stronger passions, I take that advantage, — try to overcome, as I may, the womanly resistance which is one of your charms."

"How useless, then, for us to talk. If you are determined to remind me again and again that your strength puts me at your mercy" —

"Oh, not that! I will come no nearer to you. Sit down, and tell me what I asked."

Rhoda hesitated, but at length took the chair by which she was standing.

"You are resolved never to marry?"

"I never shall," Rhoda replied firmly.

"But suppose marriage in no way interfered with your work?"

"It would interfere hopelessly with the best part of my life. I thought you understood this. What would become of the encouragement I am able to offer our girls?"

"Encouragement to refuse marriage?"

"To scorn the old idea that a woman's life is wasted if she does not marry. My work is to help those women who, by sheer necessity, must live alone, — women whom vulgar opinion ridicules. How can I help them so effectually as by living among them, one of them, and showing that my life is anything but weariness and lamentation? I am fitted for this. It gives me a sense of power and usefulness which I enjoy. Your cousin is doing the same work, admirably. If I deserted, I should despise myself."

"Magnificent! If I could bear the thought of living without you, I should bid you persevere and be great."

"I need no such bidding to persevere."

"And for that very reason, because you are capable of such high things, I love you only the more."

There was triumph in her look, though she endeavoured to disguise it.

"Then, for your own peace," she said, "I must hope that you will avoid me. It is so easily done. We have nothing in common, Mr. Barfoot."

"I can't agree with that. For one thing, there are perhaps not half-a-dozen women living with whom I could talk as I have talked with you. It isn't likely that I shall ever meet one. Am I to make my bow, and abandon in resignation the one chance of perfecting my life?"

"You don't know me. We differ profoundly on a thousand essential points."

"You think so because you have a very wrong idea of me."

Rhoda glanced at the clock on the mantelpiece.

"Mr. Barfoot," she said, in a changed voice, "you will forgive me if I remind you that it is past ten o'clock."

He sighed and rose.

"The fog certainly cannot be so thick now. Shall I ask them to try and get you a cab?"

"I shall walk to the station."

"Only one more word." She assumed a quiet dignity which he could not disregard. "We have spoken in this way for the last time. You will not oblige me to take all sorts of trouble merely to avoid useless and painful conversations?"

"I love you, and I can't abandon hope."

"Then I *must* take that trouble." Her face darkened, and she stood in expectation of his departure.

"I mustn't offer to shake hands," said Everard, drawing a step nearer.

"I hope you can remember that I had no choice but to be your hostess."

The face and tone affected him with a brief shame. Bending his head, he approached her, and held her offered hand, without pressure, only for an instant. Then he left the room.

There was a little improvement in the night; he could make his way along the pavement without actual groping, and no unpleasant adventure checked him before he reached the station. Rhoda's face and figure went before him. He was not downcast; for all that she had said, this woman, soon or late, would yield herself; he had a strange, unreasoning assurance of it. Perhaps the obstinacy of his temper supplied him with that confident expectation. He no longer cared on what terms he obtained her; legal marriage or free union — it was indifferent to him. But her life should be linked with his, if fierce energy of will meant anything.

Miss Barfoot arrived at half-past eleven, after many delays on her journey. She was pierced with cold, choked with the poisonous air, and had derived very little satisfaction from her visit to Faversham.

"What happened?" was her first question, as Rhoda came out into the hall with sympathy and solitude. "Did the fog keep our guest away?"

"No; he dined here."

"It was just as well. You haven't been lonely."

They spoke no more on the subject until Miss Barfoot recovered from her discomfort, and was enjoying a much needed supper.

"Did he offer to go away?"

"It was really impossible. It took him more than half an hour to get here from Sloane Square."

"Foolish fellow! Why didn't he take a train back at once?"

There was a peculiar brightness in Rhoda's countenance, and Miss Barfoot had observed it from the first.

"Did you quarrel much?"

"Not more than was to be expected."

"He didn't think of staying for my return?"

"He left about ten o'clock."

"Of course. Quite late enough, under the circumstances. — It was very unfortunate, but I don't suppose Everard cared much. He would enjoy the opportunity of teasing you."

A glance told her that Everard was not alone in his enjoyment of the evening. Rhoda led the talk into other channels, but Miss Barfoot continued to reflect on what she had perceived.

A few evenings after, when Miss Barfoot had been sitting alone for an hour or two, Rhoda came to the library and took a place near her. The elder woman glanced up from her book, and saw that her friend had something special to say.

"What is it, dear?"

"I am going to tax your good-nature, to ask you about unpleasant things."

Miss Barfoot knew immediately what this meant. She professed readiness to answer, but had an uneasy look.

"Will you tell me, in plain terms, what it was that your cousin did, when he disgraced himself?"

"Must you really know?"

"I wish to know."

There was a pause. Miss Barfoot kept her eyes on the page open before her.

"Then I shall take the liberty of an old friend, Rhoda. Why do you wish to know?"

"Mr. Barfoot," answered the other drily, "has been good enough to say that he is in love with me."

Their eyes met.

"I suspected it. I felt sure it was coming. — He asked you to marry him?"

"No, he didn't," replied Rhoda in purposely ambiguous phrase.

"You wouldn't allow him to?"

"At all events, it didn't come to that. — I should be glad if you would let me know what I asked."

Miss Barfoot deliberated, but finally told the story of Amy Drake. Her hands supporting one knee, her head bent, Rhoda listened without comment, and, to judge from her features, without any emotion of any kind.

"That," said her friend at the close, "is the story as it was understood at the time, — disgraceful to him in every particular. He knew what was said of him, and offered not a word of contradiction. But not very long ago, he asked me one evening if you had been informed of this scandal. I told him that you knew he had done something which I thought very base. Everard was hurt, and thereupon he declared that neither I nor any other of his acquaintances knew the truth — that he had been maligned. He refused to say more, and what am I to believe?"

Rhoda was listening with livelier attention.

"He declared that he wasn't to blame?"

"I suppose he meant that. But it is difficult to see" —

"Of course the truth can never be known," said Rhoda, with sudden indifference. "And it doesn't matter. Thank you for satisfying my curiosity."

Miss Barfoot waited a moment, then laughed.

"Some day, Rhoda, you shall satisfy mine."

"Yes — if we live long enough."

What degree of blame might have attached to Barfoot, Rhoda did not care to ask herself; she thought no more of the story. Of course there must have been other such incidents in his career; morally he was neither better nor worse than men in general. She viewed with contempt the women who furnished such opportunities; in her judgment of the male offenders she was more lenient, more philosophical, than formerly.

She had gained her wish, had enjoyed her triumph. A raising of the finger, and Everard Barfoot would marry her. Assured of that, she felt a new contentment in life; at times when she was occupied with things as far as possible from this experience, a rush of joy would suddenly fill her heart, and make her cheek glow. She moved among people with a conscious dignity quite unlike that which had only satisfied her need of distinction. She spoke more softly, exercised more patience, smiled where she had been wont to scoff. Miss Nunn was altogether a more amiable person.

Yet, she convinced herself, essentially quite unchanged. She pursued the aim of her life with less bitterness, in a larger spirit, that was all. But pursued it, and without fear of being diverted from the generous path.

CHAPTER XVIII.

A REINFORCEMENT.

Throughout January, Barfoot was endeavouring to persuade his brother Tom to leave London, where the invalid's health perceptibly grew worse. Doctors were urgent to the same end, but ineffectually; for Mrs. Thomas, though she professed to be amazed at her husband's folly in remaining where he could not hope for recovery, herself refused to accompany him any whither. This pair had no children. The lady always spoke of herself as a sad sufferer from mysterious infirmities, and had, in fact, a tendency to hysteria, which confused itself inextricably with the results of evil nurture and the impulses of a disposition originally base; nevertheless she made a figure in a certain sphere of vulgar wealth, and even gave opportunity to scandalous tongues. Her husband, whatever his secret thought, would hear nothing against her; his temper, like Everard's, was marked with stubbornness, and after a good deal of wrangling he forbade his brother to address him again on the subject of their disagreement.

"Tom is dying," wrote Everard, early in February, to his cousin in Queen's Road. "Dr. Swain assures me that, unless he be removed, he cannot last more than a month or two. This morning I saw the woman," — it was thus he always referred to his sister-in-law, — "and talked to her in what was probably the plainest language she ever had the privilege of hearing. It was a tremendous scene, brought to a close only by her flinging herself on the sofa with shrieks which terrified the whole household. My idea is that we must carry the poor fellow away by force. His infatuation makes me rage and curse, but I am bent on trying to save his life. Will you come and give your help?"

A week later, they succeeded in carrying the invalid back to Torquay. Mrs. Barfoot had abandoned him to his doctors, nurses, and angry relatives; she declared herself driven out of the house, and went to live at a fashionable hotel. Everard remained in Devon for more than a month, devoting himself with affection, which the trial of his temper seemed only to increase, to his brother's welfare. Thomas improved a little; once more there was hope. Then, on a sudden frantic impulse, after writing fifty letters which elicited no reply, he travelled in pursuit of his wife; and three days after his arrival in London he was dead.

By a will executed at Torquay, he bequeathed to Everard about a quarter of his wealth. All the rest went to Mrs. Barfoot, who had declared herself too ill to attend the funeral, but in a fortnight was sufficiently recovered to visit one of her friends in the country.

Everard could now count upon an income of not much less than fifteen hundred a year. That his brother's death would enrich him he had always foreseen, but no man could have exerted himself with more ardent energy to postpone that advantage. The widow charged him, wherever she happened to be, with deliberate fratricide; she vilified his reputation, by word of mouth or by letter, to all who knew him, and protested that his furious wrath at not having profited more largely by the will put her in fear of her life. This last remarkable statement was made in a long and violent epistle to Miss Barfoot, which the recipient showed to her cousin on the first opportunity. Everard had called one Sunday morning, — it was the end of March, — to say good-bye on his departure for a few weeks' travel. Having read the letter, he laughed with a peculiar fierceness.

"This kind of thing," said Miss Barfoot, "may necessitate your prosecuting her. There is a limit, you know, even to a woman's licence."

"I am far more likely," he replied, "to purchase a very nice little cane, and give her an exemplary thrashing."

"Oh! oh!"

"Upon my word, I see no reason against it! That's how I should deal with a man who talked about me in this way, and none the less if he were a puny creature quite unable to protect himself. In that furious scene before we got Tom away, I felt most terribly tempted to beat her. There's a great deal to be said for woman-beating. I am quite sure that many a labouring man who pommels his wife is doing exactly the right thing; no other measure would have the least result. You see what comes of impunity. If this woman saw the possibility that I should give her a public caning, she would be far more careful how she behaved herself. — Let us ask Miss Nunn's opinion."

Rhoda had that moment entered the room. She offered her hand frankly, and asked what the subject was.

"Glance over this letter," said Barfoot. "Oh, you have seen it. I propose to get a light, supple, dandyish cane, and to give Mrs. Thomas Barfoot half-a-dozen smart cuts across the back in her own drawing-room, some afternoon when people are present. What have you to say to it?"

He spoke with such show of angry seriousness that Rhoda paused before replying.

"I sympathize with you," she said at length, "but I don't think I would go to that extremity."

Everard repeated the argument he had used to his cousin.

"You are quite right," Rhoda assented. "I think many women deserve to be beaten, and ought to be beaten. But public opinion would be so much against you."

"What do I care? So is public opinion against *you*."

"Very well. Do as you like. Miss Barfoot and I will come to the police court and give strong evidence in your favour."

"Now there's a woman!" exclaimed Everard, not all in jest, for Rhoda's appearance had made his nerves thrill and his pulse beat. "Look at her, Mary. Do you wonder that I would walk the diameter of the globe to win her love?"

Rhoda flushed scarlet, and Miss Barfoot was much embarrassed. Neither could have anticipated such an utterance as this. "That's the simple truth," went on Everard recklessly, "and she knows it, and yet won't listen to me. Well, good-bye to you both! Now that I have so grossly misbehaved myself, she has a good excuse for refusing even to enter the room when I am here. But do speak a word for me whilst I am away, Mary."

He shook hands with them, scarcely looking at their faces, and abruptly departed.

The women stood for a few moments at a distance from each other. Then Miss Barfoot glanced at her friend and laughed.

"Really my poor cousin is not very discreet."

"Anything but," Rhoda answered, resting on the back of a chair, her eyes cast down. "Do you think he will really cane his sister-in-law?"

"How can you ask such a question?"

"It would be amusing. — I should think better of him for it."

"Well, make it a condition. We know the story of the lady and her glove.[1] I can see you sympathize with her."

Rhoda laughed, and went away, leaving Miss Barfoot with the impression that she had revealed a genuine impulse. It seemed not impossible that Rhoda might wish to say to her lover: "Face this monstrous scandal, and I am yours."

A week passed, and there arrived a letter, with a foreign stamp, addressed to Miss Nunn. Happening to receive it before Miss Barfoot had come down to breakfast, she put it away in a drawer till evening leisure, and made no mention of its arrival. Exhilaration appeared in her behaviour through the day. After dinner she disappeared, shutting herself up to read the letter.

"DEAR MISS NUNN, — I am sitting at a little marble table outside a café on the Cannebière. Does that name convey anything to you? The Cannebière is the principal street of Marseilles, a street of gorgeous cafés and restaurants, just now blazing with electric light. You, no doubt, are shivering by the fireside; here it is like an evening of summer. I have dined luxuriously, and I am taking my coffee whilst I write. At a table near to me sit two girls, engaged in the liveliest possible conversation, of which

---

1 Refers to a tale in which a lady in the court of Francis I of France (sixteenth century) throws her glove into a cage of lions to test the devotion of her lover. Her lover retrieves the glove and throws it in her face. The story was familiar to Victorian readers through two poetic treatments, "The Glove and the lions" by Leigh Hunt (1784-1859) and "The Glove" by Robert Browning (1812-1889). Hunt's treatment reflects badly on the lady and her vanity; Browning's version is more sympathetic to the lady and more psychologically sophisticated, suggesting complex and justifiable motives for her actions. I am grateful to David Latane for drawing my attention to the poems by Hunt and Browning.

I catch a few words now and then, pretty French phrases that caress the ear. One of them is so strikingly beautiful that I cannot take my eyes from her when they have been tempted to that quarter. She speaks with indescribable grace and animation, has the sweetest eyes and lips —

"And all the time I am thinking of some one else. Ah, if you were here! How we would enjoy ourselves among these southern scenes! Alone, it is delightful; but with you for a companion, with you to talk about everything in your splendidly frank way! This French girl's talk is of course only silly chatter; it makes me long to hear a few words from your lips, — strong, brave, intelligent.

"I dream of the ideal possibility. Suppose I were to look up, and see you standing just in front of me, there on the pavement. You have come in a few hours straight from London. Your eyes glow with delight. To-morrow we shall travel on to Genoa, you and I, more than friends, and infinitely more than the common husband and wife! We have bidden the world go round for *our* amusement; henceforth it is our occupation to observe and discuss and make merry.

"Is it all in vain? Rhoda, if you never love me, my life will be poor to what it might have been; and you, you also, will lose something. In imagination, I kiss your hands and your lips.

"EVERARD BARFOOT."

There was an address at the head of this letter, but certainly Barfoot expected no reply, and Rhoda had no thought of sending one. Every night, however, she unfolded the sheet of thin foreign paper, and read, more than once, what was written upon it. Read it with external calm, with a brow of meditation, and afterwards sat for some time in absent mood.

Would he write again? — Her daily question was answered in rather more than a fortnight. This time the letter came from Italy; it was lying on the hall table when Rhoda returned from Great Portland Street, and Miss Barfoot was the first to read the address. They exchanged no remark. On breaking the envelope, — she did so at once, — Rhoda found a little bunch of violets, crushed but fragrant.

"These in return for your Cheddar pinks," began the informal note accompanying the flowers. "I had them an hour ago from a very pretty girl in the streets of Parma. I didn't care to buy, and walked on, but the pretty girl ran by me, and with gentle force fixed the flowers in my buttonhole, so that I had no choice but to stroke her velvety cheek and give her a lira. — How hungry I am for a sight of your face! Think of me sometimes, dear friend."

She laughed, and laid the letter, and its violets, away with the other.

"I must depend on you, it seems, for news of Everard," said Miss Barfoot, after dinner.

"I can only tell you," Rhoda answered lightly, "that he has travelled from the south of France to the north of Italy, with much observation of female countenances."

"He informs you of that?"

"Very naturally. It is his chief interest. One likes people to tell the truth."

Barfoot was away until the end of April, but after that note from Parma he did not write. One bright afternoon in May, a Saturday, he presented himself at his cousin's house, and found two or three callers in the drawing-room, ladies as usual; one of them was Miss Winifred Haven, another was Mrs. Widdowson. Mary received him without effusiveness, and after a few minutes' talk with her he took a place by Mrs. Widdowson, who, it struck him, looked by no means in such good spirits as during the early days of her marriage. As soon as she began to converse, his impression of a change in her was confirmed; the girlishness so pleasantly noticeable when first he knew her had disappeared, and the gravity substituted for it was suggestive of disillusion, of trouble.

She asked him if he knew some people named Bevis, who occupied a flat just above his own.

"Bevis? — I have seen the name on the index at the foot of the stairs; but I don't know them personally."

"That was how I came to know that *you* lived there," said Monica. "My husband took me to call upon the Bevises, and there we saw your name. At least, we supposed it was you, and Miss Barfoot tells me we were right."

"Oh yes; I live there all alone, a gloomy bachelor. How delightful if you knocked at my door some day, when you and Mr. Widdowson are again calling on your friends."

Monica smiled, and her eyes wandered restlessly.

"You have been away — out of England?" she next said.

"Yes; in Italy."

"I envy you."

"You have never been there?"

"No — not yet."

He talked a little of the agreeables and disagreeables of life in that country. But Mrs. Widdowson had become irresponsive; he doubted at length whether she was listening to him, so, as Miss Haven stepped this way, he took an opportunity of a word aside with his cousin.

"Miss Nunn not at home?"

"No. Won't be till dinner-time."

"Quite well?"

"Never was better. — Would you care to come back and dine with us, at half-past seven?"

"Of course I should."

With this pleasant prospect, he took his leave. The afternoon being sunny, instead of walking straight to the station, to return home, he went out on to the Embankment, and sauntered round by Chelsea Bridge Road. As he entered Sloane Square, he saw Mrs. Widdowson, who was coming towards the railway; she walked rather wearily, with her eyes on the ground, and did not become aware of him until he addressed her.

"Are we travelling the same way?" he asked. "Westward?"

"Yes. I am going all the way round to Portland Road."

They entered the station, Barfoot chatting humorously. And so intent was he on the expression of his companion's downcast face, that he allowed an acquaintance to pass close by him unobserved. It was Rhoda Nunn, returning sooner than Miss Barfoot had expected. She saw the pair, regarded them with a moment's keen attentiveness, and went on, out into the street.

In the first class carriage which they entered there was no other passenger as far as Barfoot's station. He could not resist the temptation to use rather an intimate tone, though one that was quite conventional, in the hope that he might discover something of Mrs. Widdowson's mind. He began by asking whether she thought it a good Academy this year.[1] She had not yet visited it, but hoped to do so on Monday. Did she herself do any kind of artistic work? Oh, nothing whatever; she was a very useless and idle person. He believed she had been a pupil of Miss Barfoot's at one time? Yes, for a very short time indeed, just before her marriage. Was she not an intimate friend of Miss Nunn? Hardly intimate. They knew each other a few years ago, but Miss Nunn did not care much about her now.

"Probably because I married," she added, with a smile.

"Is Miss Nunn really such a determined enemy of marriage?"

"She thinks it pardonable in very weak people. — In my case she was indulgent enough to come to the wedding."

This piece of news surprised Barfoot.

"She came to your wedding? And wore a wedding-garment?"

"Oh yes. And looked very nice."

"Do describe it to me. Can you remember?"

Seeing that no woman ever forgot the details of another's dress, on however trivial an occasion, and at whatever distance of time, Monica was of course able to satisfy the inquirer. Her curiosity excited, she ventured, in turn, upon one or two insidious questions.

"You couldn't imagine Miss Nunn in such a costume?"

"I should very much like to have seen her."

"She has a very striking face — don't you think so?"

"Indeed I do. A wonderful face."

Their eyes met. Barfoot bent forward from his place opposite Monica. "To me the most interesting of all faces," he said softly.

His companion blushed with surprise and pleasure.

---

1 I.e. the Royal Academy of Arts, founded in 1768, which held, and still holds, annual exhibitions of works by both old masters and new artists.

"Does it seem strange to you, Mrs. Widdowson?"

"Oh — why? — Not at all."

All at once she had brightened astonishingly. This subject was not pursued, but for the rest of the time they talked with a new appearance of mutual confidence and interest, Monica retaining her pretty, half-bashful smile. And when Barfoot alighted at Bayswater, they shook hands with an especial friendliness, both seeming to suggest a wish that they might soon meet again.

They did so, no later than the following Monday. Remembering what Mrs. Widdowson had said of her intention to visit Burlington House,[2] Barfoot went there in the afternoon. If he chanced to encounter the pretty little woman, it would not be disagreeable. Perhaps her husband might be with her, and in that case he could judge of the terms on which they stood. A surly fellow, Widdowson; very likely to play the tyrant, he thought. If he were not mistaken, she had wearied of him and regretted her bondage — the old story. Thinking thus, and strolling through the rooms with casual glances at a picture, he discovered his acquaintance, catalogue in hand, alone for the present. Her pensive face again answered to his smile. They drew back from the pictures, and sat down.

"I dined with our friends at Chelsea on Saturday evening," said Barfoot.

"On Saturday? You didn't tell me you were going back again."

"I wasn't thinking of it just at the time."

Monica hinted an amused surprise.

"You see," he went on, "I expected nothing, and happy for me that it was so. Miss Nunn was in her severest mood; I think she didn't smile once through the evening. — I will confess to you that I wrote her a letter whilst I was abroad, and it offended her, I suppose."

"I don't think you can always judge of her thoughts by her face."

"Perhaps not. But I have studied her face so often and so closely. — For all that, she is more a mystery to me than any woman I have ever known. That, of course, is partly the reason of her power over me. I feel that if ever — if ever she should disclose herself to me, it would be the strangest revelation. Every woman wears a mask, except to one man; but Rhoda's — Miss Nunn's — is, I fancy, a far completer disguise than I ever tried to pierce."

Monica had a sense of something perilous in this conversation. It arose from a secret trouble in her own heart, which she might, involuntarily, be led to betray. She had never talked thus confidentially with any man; not, in truth, with her husband. There was no fear whatever of her conceiving

---

2 The building in which the Royal Academy of Arts is housed and in which the exhibitions are held.

an undue interest in Barfoot; certain reasons assured her of that; but talk that was at all sentimental gravely threatened her peace — what little remained to her. It would have been better to discourage this man's confidences; yet they flattered her so pleasantly, and afforded such a fruitful subject for speculation, that she could not obey the prompting of prudence.

"Do you mean," she said, "that Miss Nunn seems to disguise her feelings?"

"It is supposed to be wrong — isn't it? — for a man to ask one woman her opinion of another."

"I can't be treacherous, if I wished," Monica replied. "I don't feel that I understand her."

Barfoot wondered how much intelligence he might attribute to Mrs. Widdowson. Obviously her level was much below that of Rhoda. Yet she seemed to possess delicate sensibilities, and a refinement of thought not often met with in women of her position. Seriously desiring her aid, he looked at her with a grave smile, and asked:

"Do you believe her capable of falling in love?"

Monica showed a painful confusion. She overcame it, however, and soon answered.

"She would perhaps try not — not to acknowledge it to herself."

"When, in fact, it had happened?"

"She thinks it so much nobler to disregard such feelings."

"I know. She is to be an inspiring example to the women who cannot hope to marry." He laughed silently. "And I suppose it is quite possible that mere shame would withhold her from taking the opposite course."

"I think she is very strong. But" —

"But?"

He looked eagerly into her face.

"I can't tell. I don't really know her. — A woman may be as much a mystery to another woman as she is to a man."

"On the whole, I am glad to hear you say that. I believe it. It is only the vulgar that hold a different opinion."

"Shall we look at the pictures, Mr. Barfoot?"

"Oh, I am so sorry. I have been wasting your time" —

Nervously disclaiming any such thought, Monica rose and drew near to the canvases. They walked on together for some ten minutes, until Barfoot, who had turned to look at a passing figure, said in his ordinary voice:

"I think that is Mr. Widdowson on the other side of the room."

Monica looked quickly round, and saw her husband, as if occupied with the pictures, glancing in her direction.

CHAPTER XIX.

THE CLANK OF THE CHAINS.

Since Saturday evening, Monica and her husband had not been on speaking terms. A visit she paid to Mildred Vesper, after her call at Miss Barfoot's, prolonged itself so that she did not reach home until the dinner-hour was long past. On arriving, she was met with an outburst of tremendous wrath, to which she opposed a resolute and haughty silence; and since then, the two had kept as much apart as possible.

Widdowson knew that Monica was going to the Academy. He allowed her to set forth alone, and even tried to persuade himself that he was indifferent as to the hour of her return; but she had not been long gone before he followed. Insufferable misery possessed him. His married life threatened to terminate in utter wreck, and he had the anguish of recognizing that to a great extent this catastrophe would be his own fault. Resolve as he might, he found it impossible to repress the impulses of jealousy which, as soon as peace had been declared between them, brought about a new misunderstanding. Terrible thoughts smouldered in his mind; he felt himself to be one of those men who are driven by passion into crime. Deliberately he had brooded over a tragic close to the wretchedness of his existence; he would kill himself, and Monica should perish with him. But an hour of contentment sufficed to banish such visions, as sheer frenzy. He saw once more how harmless, how natural, were Monica's demands, and how peacefully he might live with her but for the curse of suspicion from which he could not free himself. Any other man would deem her a model of wifely virtue. Her care of the house was all that reason could desire. In her behaviour he had never detected the slightest impropriety. He believed her chaste as any woman living. She asked only to be trusted, and that, in spite of all, was beyond his power.

In no woman on earth could he have put perfect confidence. He regarded them as born to perpetual pupilage. Not that their inclinations were necessarily wanton; they were simply incapable of attaining maturity, remained throughout their life imperfect beings, at the mercy of craft, ever liable to be misled by childish misconceptions. Of course he was right; he himself represented the guardian male, the wife-proprietor, who from the dawn of civilization has taken abundant care that woman shall not outgrow her nonage. The bitterness of his situation lay in the fact that he had wedded a woman who irresistibly proved to him her claims as a human being. Reason and tradition contended in him, to his ceaseless torment.

And again, he feared that Monica did not love him. Had she ever loved him? There was too much ground for suspecting that she had only yielded to the persistence of his entreaties, with just liking enough to permit a semblance of tenderness, and glad to exchange her prospect of distasteful work for a comfortable married life. Her liking he might have fostered; during those first happy weeks, assuredly he had done so, for no woman could be insensible to the passionate worship manifest in his every look, his every word. Later, he took the wrong path, seeking to oppose her instincts, to reform her mind, eventually to become her lord and master. Could he not even now retrace his steps? Supposing her incapable of bowing before him, of kissing his feet, could he not be content to make of her a loyal friend, a delightful companion?

In that mood he hastened towards Burlington House. Seeking Monica through the galleries, he saw her at length — sitting side by side with that man Barfoot. They were in closest colloquy. Barfoot bent towards her as if speaking in an undertone, a smile on his face. Monica looked at once pleased and troubled.

The blood boiled in his veins. His first impulse was to walk straight up to Monica and bid her follow him. But the ecstasy of jealous suffering kept him an observer. He watched the pair until he was descried.

There was no help for it. Though his brain whirled, and his flesh was stabbed, he had no choice but to take the hand Barfoot offered him. Smile he could not, nor speak a word.

"So you have come after all?" Monica was saying to him.

He nodded. On her countenance there was obvious embarrassment, but this needed no explanation save the history of the last day or two. Looking into her eyes, he knew not whether consciousness of wrong might be read there. How to get at the secrets of this woman's heart?

Barfoot was talking, pointing at this picture and that, doing his best to smooth what he saw was an awkward situation. The gloomy husband, more like a tyrant than ever, muttered incoherent phrases. In a minute or two, Everard freed himself, and moved out of sight.

Monica turned from her husband, and affected interest in the pictures. They reached the end of the room before Widdowson spoke.

"How long do you want to stay here?"

"I will go whenever you like," she answered, without looking at him.

"I have no wish to spoil your pleasure."

"Really, I have very little pleasure in anything. — Did you come only to keep me in sight?"

"I think we will go home now, and you can come another day."

Monica assented by closing her catalogue and walking on.

Without a word, they made the journey back to Herne Hill. Widdowson shut himself in the library, and did not appear till dinner-time. The meal was a pretence for both of them, and as soon as they could rise from the table, they again parted.

About ten o'clock Monica was joined by her husband in the drawing-room.

"I have almost made up my mind," he said, standing near her, "to take a serious step. As you have always spoken with pleasure of your old home, Clevedon, suppose we give up this house, and go and live there?"

"It is for you to decide."

"I want to know whether you would have any objection."

"I shall do just as you wish."

"No, that isn't enough. — The plan I have in mind is this. I should take a good large house, — no doubt rents are low in the neighbourhood, — and ask your sisters to come and live with us. I think it would be a good thing both for them and for you."

"You can't be sure that they would agree to it. You see that Virginia prefers her lodgings to living here."

Oddly enough, this was the case. On their return from Guernsey they had invited Virginia to make a permanent home with them, and she refused. Her reasons Monica could not understand; those which she alleged — vague arguments as to its being better for a wife's relatives not to burden the husband — hardly seemed genuine. It was possible that Virginia had a distaste for Widdowson's society.

"I think they both would be glad to live at Clevedon," he urged, "judging from your sisters' talk. It's plain that they have quite given up the idea of the school, and Alice, you tell me, is getting dissatisfied with her work at Yatton. — But I must know whether you will enter seriously into this scheme."

Monica kept silence.

"Please answer me."

"Why have you thought of it?"

"I don't think I need explain. We have had too many unpleasant conversations, and I wish to act for the best without saying things you would misunderstand."

"There is no fear of my misunderstanding. You have no confidence in me, and you want to get me away into a quiet country place where I shall be under your eyes every moment. It's much better to say that plainly."

"That means, you would consider it going to prison."

"How could I help? What other motive have you?"

He was prompted to make brutal declaration of authority, and so cut the knot. Monica's unanswerable argument merely angered him. But he made an effort over himself.

"Don't you think it best that we should take some step before our happiness is irretrievably ruined?"

"I see no need for its ruin. As I have told you before, in talking like that you degrade yourself and insult me."

"I have my faults; I know them only too well. One of them is that I cannot bear you to make friends with people who are not of my kind. I shall never be able to endure that."

"Of course you are speaking of Mr. Barfoot."

"Yes," he avowed sullenly. "It was a very unfortunate thing that I happened to come up just as he was in your company."

"You are so very unreasonable," exclaimed Monica tartly. "What possible harm is there in Mr. Barfoot, when he meets me by chance in a public place, having a conversation with me? I wish I knew twenty such men. Such conversation gives me a new interest in life. I have every reason to think well of Mr. Barfoot."

Widdowson was in anguish.

"And I," he replied, in a voice shaken with angry feeling, "feel that I have every reason to dislike and suspect him. He is not an honest man; his face tells me that. I know his life wouldn't bear inspection. You can't possibly be as good a judge as I am in such a case. — Contrast him with Bevis. Now Bevis is a man one can trust; one talk with him produces a lasting favourable impression."

Monica, silent for a brief space, looked fixedly before her, her features all but expressionless.

"Yet even with Mr. Bevis," she said at length, "you don't make friends. That is the fault in you which causes all this trouble. You haven't a sociable spirit. Your dislike of Mr. Barfoot only means that you don't know him, and don't wish to. And you are completely wrong in your judgment of him. I have every reason for being sure that you are wrong."

"Of course you think so. In your ignorance of the world" —

"Which you think very proper in a woman," she interposed caustically.

"Yes, I do! That kind of knowledge is harmful to a woman."

"Then, please, how is she to judge her acquaintances?"

"A married woman must accept her husband's opinion, at all events about men." He plunged on into the ancient quagmire. "A man may know with impunity what is injurious if it enters a woman's mind."

"I don't believe that. I can't and won't believe it."

He made a gesture of despair.

"We differ hopelessly. It was all very well to discuss these things when you could do so in a friendly spirit. Now you say whatever you know will irritate me, and you say it on purpose to irritate me."

"No; indeed I do not. But you are quite right that I find it hard to be friendly with you. Most earnestly I wish to be your friend — your true and faithful friend. But you won't let me."

"Friend!" he cried scornfully. "The woman who has become my wife ought to be something more than a friend, I should think. You have lost all love for me — there's the misery."

Monica could not reply. That word "love" had grown a weariness to her upon his lips. She did not love him; could not pretend to love him. Every day the distance between them widened, and when he took her in his arms she had to struggle with a sense of shrinking, of disgust. Their union was unnatural; she felt herself constrained by a hateful force when he called upon her for the show of wifely tenderness. Yet how was she to utter this? The moment such a truth had passed her lips, she must leave him. To declare that no trace of love remained in her heart, and still to live with him — that was impossible! The dark foresight of a necessity of parting from him corresponded in her to those lurid visions which at times shook Widdowson with a horrible temptation.

"You don't love me," he continued, in harsh, choking tones. "You wish to be my *friend*. That's how you try to compensate me for the loss of your love."

He laughed with bitterness.

"When you say that," Monica answered, "do you ever ask yourself whether you try to make me love you? Scenes like this are ruining my health. I have come to dread your talk. I have almost forgotten the sound of your voice when it isn't either angry or complaining."

Widdowson walked about the room, and a deep moan escaped him.

"That is why I have asked you to go away from here, Monica. We must have a new home if our life is to begin anew."

"I have no faith in mere change of place. You would be the same man. If you cannot command your senseless jealousy here, you never would anywhere else."

He made an effort to say something; seemed to abandon it; again tried, and spoke in a thick, unnatural voice.

"Can you honestly repeat to me what Barfoot was saying to-day, when you were on the seat together?"

Monica's eyes flashed.

"I could; every word. But I shall not try to do so."

"Not if I beseech you to, Monica? To put my mind at rest" —

"No. When I tell you that you might have heard every syllable, I have said all that I shall."

It mortified him profoundly that he should have been driven to make so humiliating a request. He threw himself into a chair, and hid his face, sitting thus for a long time in the hope that Monica would be moved to compassion. But when she rose it was only to retire for the night. And with wretchedness in her heart, because she must needs go to the same chamber in which her husband would sleep. She wished so to be alone. The poorest bed in a servant's garret would have been thrice welcome to her; liberty to lie awake, to think without a disturbing presence, to shed tears if need be — that seemed to her a precious boon. She thought with envy of the shop-girls in Walworth Road; wished herself back there. What unspeakable folly she had committed! And how true was everything she had heard from Rhoda Nunn on the subject of marriage!

The next day, Widdowson resorted to an expedient which he had once before tried in like circumstances. He wrote his wife a long letter, eight close pages, reviewing the cause of their troubles, confessing his own errors, insisting gently on those chargeable to her, and finally imploring her to co-operate with him in a sincere endeavour to restore their happiness. This he laid on the table after lunch, and then left Monica alone that she might read it. Knowing beforehand all that the letter contained, Monica glanced over it carelessly. An answer was expected, and she wrote one as briefly as possible.

"Your behaviour seems to me very weak, very unmanly. You make us both miserable, and quite without cause. I can only say as I have said before, that things will never be better until you come to think of me as your free companion, not as your bondwoman. If you can't do this, you will make me wish that I had never met you, and in the end I am sure it won't be possible for us to go on living together."

She left this note, in a blank envelope, on the hall table, and went out to walk for an hour.

It was the end of one more acute stage in their progressive discord. By keeping at home for a fortnight, Monica soothed her husband and obtained some repose for her own nerves. But she could no longer affect a cordial reconciliation; caresses left her cold, and Widdowson saw that his company was never so agreeable to her as solitude. When they sat together, both were reading. Monica found more attraction in books as her life grew more unhappy. Though with reluctance, Widdowson had consented to a subscription at Mudie's,[1] and from the new catalogues she either chose for herself, necessarily at random, or by the advice of better-read people, such as she met at Mrs. Cosgrove's. What modern teaching was to be got from these volumes, her mind readily absorbed. She sought for opinions and arguments which were congenial to her mood of discontent, all but of revolt.

Sometimes the perusal of a love-story embittered her lot to the last point of endurance. Before marriage, her love-ideal had been very vague, elusive; it found scarcely more than negative expression, as a shrinking from the vulgar or gross desires of her companions in the shop. Now that she had a clearer understanding of her own nature, the type of man correspondent to her natural sympathies also became clear. In every particular he was unlike her husband. She found a suggestion of him in books; and in actual life, already, perhaps something more than a suggestion. Widdowson's jealousy, in so far as it directed itself against her longing for freedom, was fully justified; this consciousness often made her sullen when she desired to express a nobler indignation; but his special prejudice led him altogether astray, and in free resistance on this point she found the relief which enabled her to bear a secret self-reproach. Her refusal to repeat the substance of Barfoot's conversation was, in some degree, prompted by a wish for the continuance of his groundless fears. By persevering in suspicion of Barfoot, he afforded her a firm foothold in their ever renewed quarrels.

A husband's misdirected jealousy excites in the wife derision and a sense of superiority; more often than not, it fosters an unsuspected attachment, prompts to a perverse pleasure in misleading. Monica became aware of this; in her hours of misery she now and then gave a harsh laugh, the result of thoughts not seriously entertained, but tempting the fancy to

---

1 I.e., Mudie's Circulating Library. An annual fee entitled subscribers to borrow books. The library's founder, Charles Mudie, restricted acquisitions to books that would not offend middle-class morality.

recklessness. What, she asked herself again, would be the end of it all? Ten years hence, would she have subdued her soul to a life of weary insignificance, if not of dishonour? For it was dishonour to live with a man she could not love, whether her heart cherished another image or was merely vacant. A dishonour to which innumerable women submitted, a dishonour glorified by social precept, enforced under dread penalties.

But she was so young, and life abounds in unexpected changes.

CHAPTER XX.

THE FIRST LIE.

Mrs. Cosgrove was a childless widow, with sufficient means and a very mixed multitude of acquaintances. In the general belief her marriage had been a happy one; when she spoke of her deceased husband, it was with respect, and not seldom with affection. Yet her views on the matrimonial relation were known to be of singular audacity. She revealed them only to a small circle of intimates; most of the people who frequented her house had no startling theories to maintain, and regarded their hostess as a good-natured, rather eccentric woman, who loved society and understood how to amuse her guests.

Wealth and position were rarely represented in her drawing-room; nor, on the other hand, was Bohemianism. Mrs. Cosgrove belonged by birth and marriage to the staid middle class, and it seemed as if she made it her object to provide with social entertainment the kind of persons who, in an ordinary way, would enjoy very little of it. Lonely and impecunious girls or women were frequently about her; she tried to keep them in good spirits, tried to marry them if marriage seemed possible, and, it was whispered, used a good deal of her income for the practical benefit of those who needed assistance. A sprinkling of maidens who were neither lonely nor impecunious served to attract young men, generally strugglers in some profession or other, on the look-out for a wife. Intercourse went on with a minimum of formalities. Chaperonage — save for that represented by the hostess herself — was as often as not dispensed with.

"We want to get rid of a lot of sham propriety," — so she urged to her closer friends. "Girls must learn to trust themselves, and look out for dangers. If a girl can only be kept straight by incessant watchfulness, why, let her go where she will, and learn by experience. In fact, I want to see experience substituted for precept."

Between this lady and Miss Barfoot there were considerable divergences of opinion, yet they agreed on a sufficient number of points to like each other very well. Occasionally, one of Mrs. Cosgrove's *protégées* passed into Miss Barfoot's hands, abandoning the thought of matrimony for study in Great Portland Street. Rhoda Nunn, also, had a liking for Mrs. Cosgrove, though she made no secret of her opinion that Mrs. Cosgrove's influence was on the whole decidedly harmful.

"That house," she once said to Miss Barfoot, "is nothing more than a matrimonial agency."

"But so is every house where many people are entertained."

"Not in the same way. Mrs. Cosgrove was speaking to me of some girl who has just accepted an offer of marriage. 'I don't think they'll suit each other,' she said, 'but there's no harm in trying.'"

Miss Barfoot could not restrain a laugh.

"Who knows? Perhaps she is right in that view of things. — After all, you know, it's only putting into plain words what everybody thinks on all but every such occasion."

"The first part of her remark — yes," said Rhoda caustically. "But as for the 'no harm in trying,' well, let us ask the wife's opinion in a year's time."

Midway in the London season,[1] on Sunday afternoon, about a score of visitors were assembled in Mrs. Cosgrove's drawing-rooms, — there were two of them, with a landing between. As usual, some one sat at the piano, but a hum of talk went on as undercurrent to the music. Downstairs, in the library, half-a-dozen people found the quietness they preferred, and among these was Mrs. Widdowson. She had an album of portraits on her lap; whilst turning them over, she listened to a chat going on between the sprightly Mr. Bevis and a young married woman who laughed ceaselessly at his jokes. It was only a few minutes since she had come down from the drawing-room. Presently her eyes encountered a glance from Bevis, and at once he stepped over to a seat beside her.

"Your sisters are not here to-day?" she said.

"No. They have guests of their own. And when are you coming to see them again?"

"Before long, I hope."

Bevis looked away and seemed to reflect.

"Do come next Saturday — could you?"

"I had better not promise."

"Do try, and" — he lowered his voice — "come alone. Forgive me for saying that. The girls are rather afraid of Mr. Widdowson, that's the truth. They would so like a free gossip with you. Let me tell them to expect you about half-past three or four. They will rise up and call me blessed."

Laughing, Monica at length agreed to come if circumstances were favourable. Her talk with Bevis continued for a long time, until people had begun to leave. Some other acquaintance then claimed her, but she was now dull and monosyllabic, as if conversation had exhausted her energies. At six o'clock she stole away unobserved, and went home.

Widdowson had resigned himself, in appearance at all events, to these absences. It was several weeks since he had accompanied his wife to call upon any one; a sluggishness was creeping over him, strengthening his disinclination for society. The futile endeavour to act with decision, to

---

1 The London "season," when social activity reached its height, was the period between Easter and the end of July. Although mainly the creation of the wealthy propertied classes, who retired to country estates for the hunting season in August, the "season," as *The Odd Women* indicates, also influenced the social calendar of the less affluent, partly because many public events, such as the exhibition at the Royal Academy that Everard and Monica attended, were included in the season's schedule.

carry Monica away into Somerset, resulted, as futile efforts of that kind are wont to do, in increased feebleness of the will; he was less capable than ever of exerting the authority which he still believed himself to keep for the last resort. Occasionally, some days went by without his leaving the house. Instead of the one daily newspaper he had been used to take, he now received three; after breakfast he sometimes spent a couple of hours over the *Times*, and the evening papers often occupied him from dinner to bedtime. Monica noticed, with a painful conflict of emotions, that his hair had begun to lose its uniform colour, and to show streaks that matched with his grizzled beard. Was *she* responsible for this?

On the Saturday when she was to visit the Bevises, she feared lest he should propose to go with her. She wished even to avoid the necessity of telling him where she was going. As she rose from luncheon Widdowson glanced at her.

"I've ordered the trap, Monica. Will you come for a drive?"

"I have promised to go into the town. — I'm very sorry."

"It doesn't matter."

This was his latest mode of appealing to her, — with an air of pained resignation.

"For a day or two I haven't felt at all well," he continued gloomily. "I thought a drive might do me good."

"Certainly. I hope it will. When would you like to have dinner?"

"I never care to alter the hours. Of course I shall be back at the usual time. Shall *you* be?"

"Oh, yes — long before dinner."

So she got away without any explanation. At a quarter to four she reached the block of flats in which the Bevises (and Everard Barfoot) resided. With a fluttering of the heart, she went very quietly upstairs, as if anxious that her footsteps should not be heard; her knock at the door was timid.

Bevis in person opened to her.

"Delighted! I thought it *might* be" —

She entered, and walked into the first room, where she had been once before. But to her surprise it was vacant. She looked round and saw Bevis's countenance gleaming with satisfaction.

"My sisters will be here in a few minutes," he said. "A few minutes at most. Will you take this chair, Mrs. Widdowson? How delighted I am that you were able to come!"

So perfectly natural was his manner, that Monica, after the first moment of consternation, tried to forget that there was anything irregular in her presence here under these circumstances. As regards social propriety, a flat differs in many respects from a house. In an ordinary drawing-room, it could scarcely have mattered if Bevis entertained her for a short space until his sisters' arrival; but in this little set of rooms it was doubtfully permissible for her to sit *tête-à-tête* with a young man, under any excuse. And the fact of his opening the front door himself seemed to suggest that not even a servant was in the flat. A tremor grew upon her as she talked, due in part to the consciousness that she was glad to be thus alone with Bevis.

"A place like this must seem to you to be very unhomelike," he was saying, as he lounged on a low chair not very far from her. "The girls didn't like it at all at first. I suppose it's a retrograde step in civilization. Servants are decidedly of that opinion; we have a great difficulty in getting them to stay here. The reason seems to be that they miss the congenial gossip of the area door. At this moment we are without a domestic. I found she compensated herself for disadvantages by stealing my tobacco and cigars. She went to work with such lack of discretion — abstracting half a pound of honeydew[1] at a time — that I couldn't find any sympathy for her. Moreover, when charged with the delinquency, she became abusive, so very abusive that we were obliged to insist upon her immediate departure."

"Do you think she smoked?" asked Monica laughingly.

"We have debated that point with much interest. She was a person of advanced ideas, as you see; practically a communist. But I doubt whether honeydew had any charms for her personally. It seems more probable that some milkman, or baker's assistant, or even metropolitan policeman, benefited by her communism."

Indifferent to the progress of time, Bevis talked on with his usual jocoseness, now and then shaking his tawny hair in a fit of laughter the most contagious.

"But I have something to tell you," he said at length more seriously. "I am going to leave England. They want me to live at Bordeaux for a time, two or three years perhaps. It's a great bore, but I shall have to go. I am not my own master."

"Then you sisters will go to Guernsey?"

"Yes. I dare say I shall leave about the end of July."

He became silent, looking at Monica with humorous sadness.

"Do you think your sisters will soon be here, Mr. Bevis?" Monica asked, with a glance round the room.

"I think so. — Do you know, I did a very silly thing. I wanted your visit (if you came) to be a surprise for them, and so — in fact, I said nothing about it. When I got here from business, a little before three, they were just going out. I asked them if they were sure they would be back in less than an hour. Oh, they were quite sure — not a doubt of it. I do hope they haven't altered their mind, and gone to call somewhere. But, Mrs. Widdowson, I am going to make you a cup of tea, — with my own fair hands, as the novelists say."

Monica begged that he would not trouble. Under the circumstances, she had better not stay. She would come again, very soon.

---

1 Tobacco sweetened with molasses.

"No, I can't, I can't let you go!" Bevis exclaimed, softening his gay tone as he stood before her. "How shall I entreat you? If you know what an unforgettable delight it will be to me to make you a cup of tea! I shall think of it at Bordeaux every Saturday."

She had risen, but exhibited no immutable resolve.

"I really must go, Mr. Bevis" —

"Don't drive me to despair. I am capable of turning my poor sisters out of house and home, — flat and home, I mean, — in anger at their delay. On their account, in pity for their youth, do stay, Mrs. Widdowson! — Besides, I have a new song that I want you to hear, — words and music my own. One little quarter of an hour! And I know the girls will be here directly."

His will, and her inclination, prevailed. Monica sat down again, and Bevis disappeared to make the tea. Water must have been already boiling, for in less than five minutes the young man returned with a tray, on which all the necessaries were neatly arranged. With merry homage, he waited upon his guest. Monica's cheeks were warm. After the vain attempt to release herself from what was now distinctly a compromising situation, she had sat down in an easier attitude than before, as though resolved to enjoy her liberty whilst she might. There was a suspicion in her mind that Bevis had arranged this interview; she doubted the truth of his explanation. And indeed she hoped that his sisters would not return until after her departure; it would be very embarrassing to meet them.

Whilst talking and listening, she silently defended herself against the charge of impropriety. What wrong was she committing? What matter that they were alone? Their talk was precisely what it might have been in other people's presence. And Bevis, such a frank, good-hearted fellow, could not by any possibility fail in respect to her. The objections were all cant, and cant of the worst kind. She would not be a slave of such ignoble prejudices.

"You haven't made Mr. Barfoot's acquaintance yet?" she asked.

"No, I haven't. There seems to have been no opportunity. Did you seriously wish me to know him?"

"Oh, I had no wish in the matter at all."

"You like Mr. Barfoot?"

"I think him very pleasant."

"How delightful to be praised by you, Mrs. Widdowson! Now if any one speaks to you about *me*, when I have left England, will you find some nice word? — Don't think me foolish. I do so desire the good opinion of my friends. To know that you spoke of me as you did of Mr. Barfoot would give me a whole day of happiness."

"How enviable! To be so easily made happy."

"Now let me sing you this song of mine. It isn't very good; I haven't composed for years. But" —

He sat down and rattled over the keys. Monica was expecting a lively air and spirited words, as in the songs she had heard at Guernsey; but this composition told of sadness and longing and the burden of a lonely heart. She thought it very beautiful, very touching. Bevis looked round to see the effect it produced upon her, and she could not meet his eyes.

"Quite a new sort of thing for me, Mrs. Widdowson. Does it strike you as so very bad?"

"No — not at all."

"But you can't honestly praise it?" He sighed, in dejection. "I meant to give you a copy. I made this one specially for you, and — if you will forgive me — I have taken the liberty of dedicating it to you. Song-writers do that, you know. Of course it is altogether unworthy of your acceptance" —

"No — no — indeed I am very grateful to you, Mr. Bevis. Do give it me — as you meant to."

"You will have it?" he cried delightedly. "Now for a triumphal march!"

Whilst he played, with look corresponding to the exultant strain, Monica rose from her chair. She stood with eyes downcast and lips pressed together. When the last chord had sounded:

"Now I must say good-bye, Mr. Bevis. — I am so sorry your sisters haven't come."

"So am I — and yet I am not. I have enjoyed the happiest half hour of my life."

"Will you give me the piece of music?"

"Let me roll it up. — There; it won't be very awkward to carry. — But of course I shall see you again before the end of July? You will come some other afternoon?"

"If Miss Bevis will let me know when she is quite sure" —

"Yes, she shall. Do you know, I don't think I shall say a word about what has happened this afternoon. Will you allow me to keep silence about your call, Mrs. Widdowson? They would be so annoyed — and really it was a silly thing not to tell them —"

Monica made no verbal reply. She looked towards the door. Bevis stepped forward, and held it open.

"Good-bye, then. — You know what I told you about my tendency to low spirits. I'm going to have a terrible turn — down, down, down!"

She laughed, and offered her hand. He held it very lightly, looking at her with his blue eyes, which indeed expressed a profound melancholy.

"Thank you," he murmured. "Thank you for your great kindness."

And thereupon he opened the front door for her. Without another look, Monica went quickly down the stairs; she appreciated his motive for not accompanying her to the exit.

Before entering the house, she had managed to conceal the sheet of music which she was carrying. But, happily, Widdowson was still absent. Half an hour passed — half an hour of brooding and reverie — before she heard his footstep ascending the stairs. On the landing she met him with a pleasant smile.

"Have you enjoyed your drive?"

"Pretty well."

"And do you feel better?"

"Not much, dear. But it isn't worth talking about."

Later, he inquired where she had been.

"I had an appointment with Milly Vesper."

The first falsehood she had ever told him, and yet uttered with such perfect assumption of sincerity as would have deceived the acutest observer. He nodded, discontented as usual, but entertaining no doubt.

And from that moment she hated him. If he had plied her with interrogations, if he had seemed to suspect anything, the burden of untruth would have been more endurable. His simple acceptance of her word was the sternest rebuke she could have received. She despised herself, and hated him for the degradation which resulted from his lordship over her.

CHAPTER XXI.

TOWARDS THE DECISIVE.

Mary Barfoot had never suffered from lack of interest in life. Many a vivid moment dwelt in her memory; joys and sorrows, personal or of larger scope, affected her the more deeply because of that ruling intelligence which enabled her to transmute them into principles. No longer anticipating or desiring any great change in her own environment, in the modes and motives of her activity, she found it a sufficient happiness to watch, and when possible to direct, the tendency of younger lives. So kindly had nature tempered her disposition, that already she had been able to outlive those fervours of instinct which often make the middle life of an unwedded woman one long repining; but her womanly sympathies remained. And at present there was going forward under her own roof, within her daily observation, a comedy, a drama, which had power to excite all her disinterested emotions. It had been in progress for twelve months, and now, unless she was strangely mistaken, the *dénouement* drew very near.

For all her self-study, her unflinching recognition of physical and psychical facts which the average woman blinks over, Mary deceived herself as to the date of that final triumph which permitted her to observe Rhoda Nunn with perfect equanimity. Her outbreak of angry feeling on the occasion of Bella Royston's death meant something more than she would acknowledge before the inquisition of her own mind. It was just then that she had become aware of Rhoda's changing attitude towards Everard Barfoot; trifles such as only a woman would detect had convinced her that Everard's interest in Rhoda was awakening a serious response; and this discovery, though it could not surprise her, caused an obscure pang which she attributed to impersonal regret, to mere natural misgiving. For some days she thought of Rhoda in an ironic, half-mocking spirit. Then came Bella's suicide, and the conversation in which Rhoda exhibited a seeming heartlessness, the result, undoubtedly, of grave emotional disturbance. To her own astonishment, Mary was overcome with an impulse of wrathful hostility, and spoke words which she regretted as soon as they had passed her lips.

Poor Bella had very little to do with this moment of discord between two women who sincerely liked and admired each other. She only offered the occasion for an outburst of secret feeling which probably could not have been avoided. Mary Barfoot had loved her cousin Everard; it began when he was one-and-twenty; she, so much older, had never allowed Everard or any one else to suspect her passion, which made her for two or three years more unhappy than she had ever been, or was ever to be when once her strong reason had prevailed. The scandal of Amy Drake, happening long after, revived her misery, which now took the form of truly feminine intolerance; she tried to believe that Everard was henceforth of less than no account to her, that she detested him for his vices. Amy Drake, however, she detested much more.

When her friendship with Rhoda Nunn had progressed to intimacy, she could not refrain from speaking of her cousin Everard, absent at the ends of the earth, and perchance lost to her sight for ever. Her mention of him was severe, yet of a severity so obviously blended with other feeling, that Rhoda could not but surmise the truth. Sentimental confession never entered Miss Barfoot's mind; she had conquered her desires, and was by no means inclined to make herself ridiculous; Rhoda Nunn, of all women, seemed the least likely to make remarks, or put questions, such as would endanger a betrayal of the buried past. Yet, at a later time, when pressing the inquiry whether Rhoda had ever been in love, Mary did not scruple to suggest that her own knowledge in that direction was complete. She did it in lightness of heart, secure under the protection of her forty years. Rhoda, of course, understood her as referring to Everard.

So the quarrel was one of jealousy. But no sooner had it taken place than Mary Barfoot experienced a shame, a distress, which in truth signified the completion of self-conquest. She thought herself ashamed of being angry where anger was uncalled for; in reality, she chastised herself for the last revival of a conflict practically over and done with so many years ago. And on this very account, precisely because she was deceiving herself as to her state of mind, she prolonged the painful situation. She said to herself that Rhoda had behaved so wrongly that displeasure was justified, that to make up the quarrel at once would be unwise, for Miss Nunn needed a little discipline. This insistence upon the side issue helped her to disregard the main one, and when at length she offered Rhoda the kiss of reconcilement, that also signified something other than was professed. It meant a hope that Rhoda might know the happiness which to her friend had been denied.

Everard's announcement of his passion for Miss Nunn seemed to Mary a well-calculated piece of boldness. If he seriously sought Rhoda for his wife, this frank avowal of the desire before a third person might remove some of the peculiar difficulties of the case. Whether willing or not to be wooed, Rhoda, in mere consistency with her pronounced opinions, must needs maintain a scornful silence on the subject of Everard's love-making; by assailing this proud reserve, this dignity which perchance had begun to burden its supporter, Everard made possible, if not inevitable, a discussion of his suit between the two women. She who talks of her lover will be led to think of him.

Miss Barfoot knew not whether to hope for the marriage of this strange pair. She was distrustful of her cousin, found it hard to imagine him a loyal husband, and could not be sure whether Rhoda's qualities were such as would ultimately retain or repel him. She inclined to think his wooing a mere caprice. But Rhoda gave ear to him, of that there could be little doubt; and since his inheritance of ample means the affair began to have a new aspect. That Everard persevered, though the world of women was now open to him, — for, on a moderate computation, any man with Barfoot's personal advantages, and armed with fifteen hundred a year, may choose among fifty possible maidens, — seemed to argue that he was really in love. But what it would cost Rhoda to appear before her friends in the character of a bride! What a humbling of her glory!

Was she capable of the love which defies all humiliation? Or, loving ardently, would she renounce a desired happiness from dread of female smiles and whispers? Or would it be her sufficient satisfaction to reject a wealthy suitor, and thus pose more grandly than ever before the circle who saw in her an example of woman's independence? Powerful was the incitement to curiosity in a situation which, however it ended, would afford such matter for emotional hypothesis.

They did not talk of Everard. Whether Rhoda replied to his letters from abroad Miss Barfoot had no means of ascertaining. But after his return, he had a very cold reception, — due, perhaps, to some audacity he had allowed himself in his correspondence. Rhoda again avoided meeting with him, and, as Miss Barfoot noticed, threw herself with increased energy into all her old pursuits.

"What about your holiday this year?" Mary asked one evening in June. "Shall you go first, or shall I?"

"Please make whatever arrangements you like."

Miss Barfoot had a reason for wishing to postpone her holiday until late in August. She said so, and proposed that Rhoda should take any three weeks she liked prior to that.

"Miss Vesper," she added, "can manage your room very well. We shall be much more at ease in that respect than last year."

"Yes. Miss Vesper is getting to be very useful and trustworthy."

Rhoda mused when she had made this remark.

"Do you know," she asked presently, "whether she sees much of Mrs. Widdowson?"

"I have no idea."

They decided that Rhoda should go away at the close of July. Where was her holiday to be spent? Miss Barfoot suggested the lake country.

"I was thinking of it myself," said Rhoda. "I should like to have some sea-bathing, though. A week by the shore, and then the rest of the time spent in vagabondage among the mountains, would suit me very well. Mrs. Cosgrove is at home in Cumberland; I must ask her advice."

This was done, and there resulted a scheme which seemed to excite Rhoda with joyous anticipation. On the coast of Cumberland, a few miles south of St. Bees, is a little place called Seascale, unknown to the ordinary tourist, but with a good hotel and a few scattered houses where lodgings can be obtained. Not far away rise the mountain-barriers of lakeland, Wastdale clearly discernible. At Seascale, then, Rhoda would spend her first week, the quiet shore with its fine stretch of sand affording her just the retreat that she desired.

"There are one or two bathing-machines,[1] Mrs. Cosgrove says, but I hope to avoid such abominations. How delicious it was in one's childhood, when one ran into the sea naked! I will enjoy that sensation once more, if I have to get up at three in the morning."

About this time, Barfoot made one of his evening calls. He had no hope of seeing Rhoda, and was agreeably surprised by her presence in the drawing-room. Just as happened a year ago, the subject of Miss Nunn's holiday was brought into the conversation, Barfoot making a direct inquiry. With lively interest, Mary waited for the reply, and was careful not to smile when Rhoda made known her intentions.

"Have you planned a route after your stay at Seascale?" Barfoot asked.

"No. I shall do that when I am there."

Whether or not he intended a contrast to these homely projects, Barfoot presently began to talk of travel on a grander scale. When he next left England, he should go by the Orient Express,[2] right away to Constantinople. His cousin asked questions about the Orient Express, and he supplied her with details very exciting to the imagination of any one who longs to see the kingdoms of the earth — as undoubtedly Rhoda did. The very name, Orient Express, has a certain sublimity, such as attaches, more or less, to all the familiar nomenclature of world-transits. He talked himself into fervour, and kept a watch on Rhoda's countenance. As also did Miss Barfoot. Rhoda tried to appear unaffected, but her coldness betrayed its insincerity.

The next day, when work at Great Portland Street was just finished, she fell into conversation with Mildred Vesper. Miss Barfoot had an engagement to dine out that evening, and Rhoda ended by inviting Milly to come home with her to Chelsea. To Milly this was a great honour; she hesitated because of her very plain dress, but easily allowed herself to be persuaded when she saw that Miss Nunn really desired her company.

Before dinner they had a walk in Battersea Park. Rhoda had never been so frank and friendly; she induced the quiet, unpretending girl to talk of her early days, her schools, her family. Remarkable was Milly's quiet contentedness; not long ago she had received an increase of payment from Miss Barfoot, and one would have judged that scarcely a wish now troubled her, unless it were that she might see her scattered brothers and sisters, all of whom, happily, were doing pretty well in the struggle for existence.

"You must feel rather lonely in your lodgings sometimes?" said Rhoda.

---

1 Small wheeled changing houses that could be drawn into the sea, allowing the bather to enter the water without being exposed.

2 An opulently appointed train that travelled from Paris to Constantinople (now Istanbul) in Turkey. The Orient Express represented the ultimate in luxurious and slightly exotic travel.

"Very rarely. In future, I shall have music in the evening. Our best room has been let to a young man who has a violin, and he plays 'The Blue Bells of Scotland' — not badly."

Rhoda did not miss the humorous intention, veiled, as usual, under a manner of extreme sedateness.

"Does Mrs. Widdowson come to see you?"

"Not often. She came a few days ago."

"You go to her house sometimes?"

"I haven't been there for several months. At first I used to go rather frequently, but — it's a long way."

To this subject Rhoda returned after dinner, when they were cosily settled in the drawing-room.

"Mrs. Widdowson comes here now and then, and we are always very glad to see her. But I can't help thinking she looks rather unhappy."

"I'm afraid she does," assented the other gravely.

"You and I were both at her wedding. It wasn't very cheerful, was it? I had a disagreeable sense of bad omens all the time. — Do you think she is sorry?"

"I'm really afraid she is."

Rhoda observed the look that accompanied this admission. ·

"Foolish girl! Why couldn't she stay with us, and keep her liberty? — She doesn't seem to have made any new friends. Has she spoken to you of any?"

"Only of people she has met here."

Rhoda yielded — or seemed to yield — to an impulse of frankness; bending slightly forward, with an anxious expression, she said in confidential tones:

"Can you help to put my mind at rest about Monica? You saw her a week ago. Did she say anything, or give any sign, that might make one really uneasy on her account?"

There was a struggle in Milly before she answered. Rhoda added:

"Perhaps you had rather not" —

"Yes, I had rather tell you. She said a good many strange things, and I *have* been uneasy about her. I wished I could speak to some one" —

"How strange that I should feel urged to ask you about this," said Rhoda, her eyes, peculiarly bright and keen, fixed on the girl's face. "The poor thing is very miserable, I am sure. Her husband seems to leave her entirely to herself."

Milly looked surprised.

"Monica made quite the opposite complaint to me. She said that she was a prisoner."

"That's very odd. She certainly goes about a good deal, and alone."

"I didn't know that," said Milly. "She has very often talked to me about a woman's right to the same freedom as a man, and I always understood that Mr. Widdowson objected to her going anywhere without him, except just to call here or at my lodgings."

"Do you think she has any acquaintance that he dislikes?"

The direct answer was delayed, but it came at length.

"There is some one. She hasn't told me who it is."

"In plain words, Mr. Widdowson thinks he has cause for jealousy?"

"Yes, I understood Monica to mean that."

Rhoda's face had grown very dark. She moved her hands nervously.

"But — you don't think she could deceive him?"

"Oh, I can't think that!" replied Miss Vesper, with much earnestness. "But what I couldn't help fearing, after I saw her last, was that she might almost be tempted to leave her husband. She spoke so much of freedom — and of a woman's right to release herself if she found her marriage was a mistake."

"I am so grateful to you for telling me all this. We must try to help her. Of course I will make no mention of you, Miss Vesper. — Then you are really under the impression that there's some one she — prefers to her husband?"

"I can't help thinking there is," admitted the other very solemnly. "I was so sorry for her, and felt so powerless. She cried a little. All I could do was to entreat her not to behave rashly. I thought her sister ought to know" —

"Oh, Miss Madden is useless. Monica cannot look to her for advice or support."

After this conversation, Rhoda passed a very unquiet night, and gloom appeared in her countenance for the next few days.

She wished to have a private interview with Monica, but doubted whether it would in any degree serve her purpose, that of discovering whether certain suspicions she entertained had actual ground. Confidence between her and Mrs. Widdowson had never existed, and in the present state of things she could not hope to probe Monica's secret feelings. Whilst she still brooded over the difficulty there came a letter for her from Everard Barfoot. He wrote formally; it had occurred to him that he might be of some slight service, in view of her approaching holiday, if he looked through the guide-books, and jotted down the outline of such a walking-tour as she had in mind. This he had done, and the results were written out on an enclosed sheet of paper. — Rhoda allowed a day to intervene, then sent a reply. She thanked Mr. Barfoot sincerely for the trouble he had so kindly taken. "I see you limit me to ten miles a day. In such scenery of course one doesn't hurry on, but I can't help informing you that twenty miles wouldn't alarm me. I think it very likely that I shall follow your itinerary, after my week of bathing and idling. I leave on Monday week."

Barfoot did not again call. Every evening she sat in expectation of his coming. Twice Miss Barfoot was away until a late hour, and on those occasions, after dinner, Rhoda sat in complete idleness, her face declaring the troubled nature of her thoughts. On the Sunday before her departure, she took a sudden resolve, and went to call upon Monica at Herne Hill.

Mrs. Widdowson, she learnt from the servant, had left home about an hour since.

"Is Mr. Widdowson at home?"

Yes, he was. And Rhoda waited for some time in the drawing-room until he made his appearance. Of late, Widdowson had grown so careless in the matter of toilet, that an unexpected visit obliged him to hurry through a change of apparel before he could present himself. Looking upon him for the first time for several months, Rhoda saw that misery was undermining the man's health. Words could not have declared his trouble more plainly than the haggard features and stiff, depressed, self-conscious manner. He fixed his sunken eyes upon the visitor, and smiled, as was plain, only for civility's sake. Rhoda did her best to seem at ease; she explained (standing, for he forgot to ask her to be seated) that she was going away on the morrow, and had hoped to see Mrs. Widdowson, who, she was told, had not been very well of late.

"No, she is not in very good health," said Widdowson vaguely. "She has gone this afternoon to Mrs. Cosgrove's — I think you know her."

Less encouragement to remain could not have been offered, but Rhoda conceived a hope of hearing something significant if she persevered in conversation. The awkwardness of doing so was indifferent to her.

"Shall you be leaving town shortly, Mr. Widdowson?"

"We are not quite sure — But pray sit down, Miss Nunn. You haven't seen my wife lately?"

He took a chair, and rested his hands upon his knees, gazing at the visitor's skirt.

"Mrs. Widdowson hasn't been to see us for more than a month — if I remember rightly."

His look expressed both surprise and doubt.

"A month? But I thought — I had an idea — that she went only a few days ago."

"In the day time?"

"To Great Portland Street, I mean — to hear a lecture, or something of that kind, by Miss Barfoot."

Rhoda kept silence for a moment. Then she replied hastily:

"Oh yes — very likely — I wasn't there that afternoon."

"I see. That would explain" —

He seemed relieved, but only for the instant; then his eyes glanced hither and thither, with painful restlessness. Rhoda observed him closely. After fidgeting with his feet, he suddenly took a stiff position, and said in a louder voice:

"We are going to leave London altogether. — I have decided to take a house at my wife's native place, Clevedon. Her sisters will come and live with us."

"That is a recent decision, Mr. Widdowson?"

"I have thought about it for some time. London doesn't suit Monica's health; I'm sure it doesn't. She will be much better in the country."

"Yes, I think that very likely."

"As you say that you have noticed her changed looks, I shall lose no time in getting away." He made a great show of determined energy. "A few weeks — We will go down to Clevedon at once, and find a house. Yes, we will go to-morrow, or the day after. Miss Madden, also, is very far from well. I wish I hadn't delayed so long."

"You are doing very wisely, I think. I had meant to suggest something of this kind to Mrs. Widdowson. Perhaps, if I went at once to Mrs. Cosgrove's, I might be fortunate enough to find her still there?"

"You might. — Did I understand you to say that you go away to-morrow? — For three weeks. — Ah, then we may be getting ready to remove when you come back."

The change that had come over him was remarkable. He could not keep his seat, and began to pace the end of the room. Seeing no possibility of prolonging the talk for her own purposes, Rhoda accepted this dismissal, and with the briefest leave-taking went her way to Mrs. Cosgrove's.

She was deeply agitated. Monica had not attended that lecture of Miss Barfoot's, and so, it was evident, had purposely deceived her husband. To what end? Where were those hours spent? Mildred Vesper's report supplied grounds for sombre conjecture, and the incident at Sloane Square Station, the recollection of Monica and Barfoot absorbed in talk, seemed to have a possible significance which fired Rhoda with resentment.

Her arrival at Mrs. Cosgrove's was too late. Monica had been there, said the hostess, but had left nearly half an hour ago.

Rhoda's instant desire was to go on to Bayswater, and somehow keep watch near the flats where Barfoot lived. Monica might be there. Her coming forth from the building might be detected.

But the difficulty of the undertaking, and, still more, a dread of being seen hovering about that quarter, checked her purpose as soon as it was formed. She returned home, and for an hour or two kept in solitude.

"What has happened?" asked Miss Barfoot, when they at length met.

"Happened? Nothing that I know of."

"You look very strange."

"Your imagination. — I have been packing; perhaps it's from stooping over the trunk."

This by no means satisfied Mary, who felt that things mysterious were going on about her. But she could only wait, repeating to herself that the grand *dénouement* decidedly was not far off.

At nine o'clock sounded the visitor's bell. If, as she thought likely, the caller was Everard, Miss Barfoot decided that she would disregard everything but the dramatic pressure of the moment, and leave those two alone together for half an hour. Everard it was; he entered the drawing-room with an unusual air of gaiety.

"I have been in the country all day," were his first words; and he went on to talk of trivial things — the doings of a Cockney excursion party that had come under his notice.

In a few minutes, Mary made an excuse for absenting herself. When she was gone, Rhoda looked steadily at Barfoot, and asked:

"Have you really been out of town?"

"Why should you doubt it?"

"You left this morning, and have only just returned?"

"As I told you."

She averted her look. After examining her curiously, Everard came and stood before her.

"I want to ask your leave to meet you somewhere during these next three weeks. At any point on your route. We could have a day's ramble together, and then — say good-bye."

"The lake country is free to you, Mr. Barfoot."

"But I mustn't miss you. You will leave Seascale to-morrow week?"

"At present I think so. But I can't restrict myself by any agreement. Holiday must be a time of liberty."

They looked at each other, she with a carelessness which was all but defiance, he with a significant smile.

"To-morrow week, then, perhaps we may meet again."

Rhoda made no reply, beyond a movement of her eyebrows, as if to express indifference.

"I won't stay longer this evening. A pleasant journey to you!"

He shook hands, and left the room. In the hall Miss Barfoot came to meet him; they exchanged a few words, unimportant and without reference to what had passed between him and Rhoda. Nor did Rhoda speak of the matter when joined by her friend. She retired early, having settled all the arrangements for her departure by the ten o'clock express from Euston next morning.

Her luggage was to consist of one trunk and a wallet[1] with a strap, which would serve the purposes of a man's knapsack. Save the indispensable umbrella, she carried no impeding trifles. A new costume, suitable for shore and mountain, was packed away in the trunk; Miss Barfoot had judged of its effect, and was of opinion that it became the wearer admirably.

But Rhoda, having adjusted everything that she was going to take with her, still had an occupation which kept her up for several hours. From a locked drawer she brought forth packets of letters, the storage of many years, and out of these selected carefully perhaps a tithe, which she bound together and deposited in a box; the remainder she burnt in the empty fireplace. Moreover, she collected from about the room a number of little objects, ornaments and things of use, which also found a place in the same big box. All her personal property which had any value for her, except books, was finally under lock and key, and in portable repositories. But still she kept moving, as if in search of trifles that might have escaped

---

1 A bag to carry provisions and other necessities.

her notice; silently, in her soft slippers, she strayed hither and thither, till the short summer night had all but given place to dawn; and when at length weariness compelled her to go to bed, she was not able to sleep.

Nor did Mary Barfoot enjoy much sleep that night. She lay thinking, and forecasting strange possibilities.

On Monday evening, returned from Great Portland Street, the first thing she did was to visit Rhoda's chamber. The ashes of burnt paper had been cleared away, but a glance informed her of the needless and unprecedented care with which Miss Nunn had collected and packed most of the things that belonged to her. Again Mary had a troubled night.

[END OF VOLUME II.]

CHAPTER XXII.

HONOUR IN DIFFICULTIES.

At Mrs. Cosgrove's, this Sunday afternoon, Monica had eyes and thoughts for one person only. Her coming at all was practically an appointment to meet Bevis, whom she had seen twice since her visit to the flat. A day or two after that occasion, she received a call from the Bevis girls, who told her of their brother's approaching departure for Bordeaux, and thereupon she invited the trio to dine with her. A fortnight subsequently to the dinner, she had a chance encounter with Bevis in Oxford Street; constraint of business did not allow him to walk beside her for more than a minute or two, but they spoke of Mrs. Cosgrove's on the following Sunday, and there, accordingly, found each other.

Tremor of self-consciousness kept Monica in dread of being watched and suspected. Few people were present to-day, and after exchanging formal words with Bevis, she moved away to talk with the hostess. Not till half an hour had passed did she venture to obey the glances which her all but avowed lover cast towards her, and to take a seat where he could naturally engage her in conversation. He was so much at ease, so like what she had always known him, that Monica asked herself whether she had not mistaken the meaning of his homage. One moment she hoped it might be so; the next, she longed for some sign of passionate devotion, and thought with anguish of the day, now so near, when he would be gone for ever. This, she ardently believed, was the man who should have been her husband. Him she could love with heart and soul, could make his will her absolute law, could live on his smiles, could devote herself to his interests. The independence she had been struggling to assert ever since her marriage meant only freedom to love. If she had understood herself as she now did, her life would never have been thus cast into bondage.

"The girls," Bevis was saying, "leave on Thursday. The rest of the week I shall be alone. On Monday the furniture will be stowed away at the Pantechnicon,[1] and on Tuesday — off I go."

A casual listener could have supposed that the prospect pleased him. Monica, with a fixed smile, looked at the other groups conversing in the room; no one was paying any attention to her. In the same moment, she heard a murmur from her companion's lips; he was speaking still, but in a voice only just audible.

"Come on Friday afternoon, about four o'clock."

Her heart began to throb painfully, and she knew that a treacherous colour had risen to her cheeks.

---

1. Storage warehouse for furniture.

"Do come — once more — for the last time. It shall be just as before — just as before. An hour's talk, and we will say good-bye to each other."

She was powerless to breathe a word. Bevis, noticing that Mrs. Cosgrove had thrown a look in this direction, suddenly laughed as if at some jest between them, and resumed his lively strain of talk. Monica also laughed. An interval of make-believe, and again the soft murmur fell upon her ear.

"I shall expect you. I know you won't refuse me this one last kindness. — Some day," his voice was all but extinguished, "some day — who knows?"

Dreadful hope struck through her. A stranger's eyes turned this way, and again she laughed.

"On Friday, at four. — I shall expect you."

She rose, looked for an instant about the room, then offered him her hand, uttering some commonplace word of leave-taking. Their eyes did not meet. She went up to Mrs. Cosgrove, and as soon as possible left the house.

Widdowson met her as she crossed the threshold of home. His face told her that something extraordinary had happened, and she trembled before him.

"Back already?" he exclaimed, with a grim smile. "Be quick, and take your things off, and come to the library."

If he had discovered anything (the lie, for instance, that she told him a month ago, or that more recent falsehood when she pretended, without serious reason, to have been at Miss Barfoot's lecture), he would not look and speak thus. Hurrying, panting, she made a change of dress, and obeyed his summons.

"Miss Nunn has been here," were his first words.

She turned pale as death. Of course he observed it; she was now prepared for anything.

"She wanted to see you because she is going away on Monday.— What's the matter?"

"Nothing. You spoke so strangely" —

"Did I? And you *look* very strangely. I don't understand you. Miss Nunn says that everybody has noticed how ill you seem. It's time we did something. Tomorrow morning we are going down into Somerset, to Clevedon, to find a house."

"I thought you had given up that idea."

"Whether I had or not doesn't matter." In the determination to appear, and be, energetic, he spoke with a rough obstinacy, a doggedness that now and then became violence. "I am decided on it now. There's a train to Bristol at ten-twenty. You will pack just a few things; we sha'n't be away for more than a day or two."

Tuesday, Wednesday, Thursday — By Friday they might be back. Till now, in an anguish of uncertainty, Monica had made up her mind. She would keep the appointment on Friday, come of it what might. If she could not be back in time, she would write a letter.

"Why are you talking in this tone?" she said coldly.

"What tone? I am telling you what I have decided to do, that's all. — I shall easily find a house down there, no doubt. Knowing the place, you will be able to suggest the likely localities."

She sat down, for strength was failing her.

"It's quite true," Widdowson went on, staring at her with inflamed eyes. "You are beginning to look like a ghost. — Oh, we'll have an end of this!" He cackled in angry laughter. "Not a day's unnecessary delay! Write to both you sisters this evening, and tell them. I wish them both to come and live with us."

"Very well."

"Now, won't you be glad? Won't it be better in every way?"

He came so near that she felt his feverish breath.

"I told you before," she answered, "to do just as you liked."

"And you won't talk about being kept a prisoner?"

Monica laughed.

"Oh no, I won't say anything at all."

She scarcely knew what words fell from her lips. Let him propose, let him do what he liked; to her it was indifferent. She saw something before her — something she durst not, even an hour ago, have steadily contemplated; it drew her with the force of fate.

"You know we couldn't go on living like this — don't you, Monica?"

"No, we couldn't."

"You see!" He almost shouted in triumph, misled by the smile on her face. "All that was needed was resolution on my part. I have been absurdly weak, and weakness in the husband means unhappiness in the wife. From to-day you look to me for guidance. — I am no tyrant, but I shall rule you for your own good."

Still she smiled.

"So there's an end of our misery — isn't it, darling? What misery! Good God, how I have suffered! — Haven't you known it?"

"I have known it too well."

"And now you will make up to me for it, Monica?"

Again prompted by the irresistible force, she answered mechanically:

"I will do the best for both."

He threw himself on the ground beside her, and clasped her in his arms.

"Now, that is my own dear wife once more! Your face has altogether changed. See how right it is that a husband should take the law into his own hands! — Our second year of marriage shall be very different from the first. And yet we *were* happy, weren't we, my beautiful? It's only this cursed London that has come between us. At Clevedon we shall begin our life over again — like we did at Guernsey. All our trouble, I am convinced, has come of your ill-health. This air has never suited you; you have felt miserable, and couldn't be at peace in your home. — Poor little girl! My poor darling!"

Through the evening he was in a state of transport, due partly to the belief that Monica really welcomed his decision, partly to the sense of having behaved at length like a resolute man. His eyes were severely blood-shot, and before bedtime headache racked him intolerably.

Everything was carried out as he had planned it. They journeyed down into Somerset, put up at a Clevedon hotel, and began house-hunting. On Wednesday the suitable abode was discovered, a house of modest pretensions, but roomy and well situated. It could be made ready for occupation in a fortnight. Bent on continuing his exhibition of vigorous promptitude, Widdowson signed a lease that same evening.

"To-morrow we will go straight home, and make our preparations for removal. When all is ready, you shall come down here and live at the hotel until the house is furnished. Go to your sister Virginia, and simply bid her do as you wish. Imitate me!" He laughed fatuously. "Don't listen to any objection. When you have once got her away, she will thank you."

By Thursday afternoon they were back at Herne Hill. Widdowson still kept up the show of extravagant spirits, but he was worn out. He spoke so hoarsely that one would have thought he had contracted a severe sore-throat; it resulted merely from nervous strain. After a pretence of dinner, he seated himself as if to read; glancing at him a few minutes later, Monica found that he was fast asleep.

She could not bear to gaze at him, yet her eyes turned thither again and again. His face was repulsive to her; the deep furrows, the red eye-lids, the mottled skin moved her to loathing. And yet she pitied him. His frantic exultation was the cruellest irony. — What would he do? What would become of him? — She turned away, and presently left the room, for the sound of his uneasy breathing made her suffer too much.

When he woke up, he came in search of her, and laughed over his involuntary nap.

"Well now, you will go and see your sister to-morrow morning."

"In the afternoon, I think."

"Why? Don't let us have any procrastination. The morning, the morning!"

"Please do let me have my way in such a trifle as that," Monica exclaimed nervously. "I have all sorts of things to see to here, before I can go out."

He caressed her.

"You sha'n't say that I am unreasonable. In the afternoon, then. And don't listen to any objections."

"No, no."

It was Friday. All the morning, Widdowson had business with house agents and furniture removers, for he would not let a day go by without some practical step towards release from the life he detested. Monica seemed to be equally active in her own department; she was turning out drawers and wardrobes, and making selection of things — on some principle understood by herself. A flush remained upon her cheeks, in marked contrast to the pallor which for a long time had given her an appearance of wasting away. That and her singularly bright eyes endowed her with beauty suggestive of what she might have gained in happy marriage.

They had luncheon at one o'clock, and at a quarter to two Monica started by train for Clapham Junction. It was her purpose to have a short conversation with Virginia, who knew of the trip to Clevedon, and to speak as though she were quite reconciled to the thought of removal; after that, she would pursue her journey so as to reach Bayswater by four o'clock. But Virginia was not at home. Mrs. Conisbee said she had gone out at eleven in the morning, and with the intention of returning by tea-time. After a brief hesitation, Monica requested the landlady to deliver a message.

"Please ask her not to come to Herne Hill until she hears from me, as I am not likely to be at home for a day or two."

This left more time at her disposal than she knew how to employ. She returned to the railway-station, and travelled on to Victoria; there, in the corner of a waiting-room, she sat, feverishly impatient, until her watch told her that she might take the next train westward.

A possible danger was before her, — though perhaps she need not trouble herself with the thought of such dangers. What if Mr. Barfoot happened to encounter her as she ascended the stairs? But most likely he had no idea that her female friends, who dwelt on the floor above him, were gone away. Did it matter what he might think? In a day or two —

She came to the street, approached the block of flats, involuntarily casting anxious glances about her. And when she was within twenty yards of the door, it opened, and forth came Barfoot. Her first sensation was unreasoning terror; her next, thankfulness that she had not been a few minutes sooner, when the very meeting she had feared, within the building itself, would have come to pass. He walked this way; he saw her; and the pleasantest smile of recognition lit up his face.

"Mrs. Widdowson! — Not a minute ago you were in my thoughts. I wished I could see you."

"I am going — to make a call in this neighbourhood" —

She could not command herself. The shock had left her trembling, and the necessity of feigning calmness was a new trial of her nerves. Barfoot, she felt certain, was reading her face like a printed page; he saw guilt there; his quickly averted eyes, his peculiar smile, seemed to express the facile tolerance of a man of the world.

"Allow me to accompany you to the end of the street."

His words buzzed in her ears. She walked on without conscious effort, like an automaton obedient to a touch.

"You know that Miss Nunn has gone down into Cumberland?" Barfoot was saying, his look bent upon her.

"Yes. I know."

She tried to glance at him with a smile.

"To-morrow," he pursued, "I am going there myself."

"To Cumberland?"

"I shall see her, I hope. — Perhaps she will only be angry with me."

"Perhaps. — But perhaps not."

Her confusion would not be overcome. She felt a burning in her ears, on her neck. It was an agony of shame. The words she spoke sounded imbecile mutterings, which must confirm Barfoot in his worst opinion of her.

"If it is all in vain," he continued, "then I shall say good-bye, and there's an end."

"I hope not — I should think" —

Useless. She set her lips and became mute. If only he would leave her! — And almost immediately he did so, with a few words of kind tone. She felt the pressure of his hand, and saw him walk rapidly away; — doubtless he knew this was what she desired.

Until he had passed out of sight, Monica kept the same direction. Then she turned round, and hurried back, fearful lest the detention might make her late, and Bevis might lose hope of her coming. There could be no one in the building now whom she need fear to meet. She opened the big entrance door, and went up.

Bevis must have been waiting for the sound of her light footstep; his door flew open before she could knock. Without speaking, a silent laugh of joy upon his lips, he drew back to make room for her entrance, and then pressed both her hands.

In the sitting-room were beginnings of disorder. Pictures had been taken down from the walls, and light ornaments removed.

"I sha'n't sleep here after to-night," Bevis began, his agitation scarcely less obvious than Monica's. "To-morrow I shall be packing what is to go with me. — How I hate it all!"

Monica dropped into a chair near the door.

"Oh, not there!" he exclaimed. "Here, where you sat before. We are going to have tea together again."

His utterances were forced, and the laugh that came between them betrayed the quivering of his nerves.

"Tell me what you have been doing. I have thought of you day and night."

He brought a chair close to her, and when he had seated himself he took one of her hands. Monica, scarcely repressing a sob, the result of reaction from her fears and miseries, drew the hand away. But again he took it.

"There's the glove on it," he said, in a shaking voice. "What harm in my holding your glove? — Don't think of it, and talk to me. I love music, but no music is like your voice."

"You go on Monday?"

It was her lips spoke the sentence, not she.

"No, on Tuesday — I think."

"My — Mr. Widdowson is going to take me away from London."

"Away?"

She told him the circumstances. Bevis kept his eyes upon her face, with a look of rapt adoration which turned at length to pain and woeful perplexity.

"You have been married a year," he murmured. "Oh, if I had met you before that! What a cruel fate that we should know each other only when there was no hope!"

The man revealed himself in this dolorous sentimentality. His wonted blitheness and facetiousness, his healthy features, his supple, well-built frame, suggested that when love awoke within him he would express it with virile force. But he trembled and blushed like a young girl, and his accents fell at last into a melodious whining.

He raised the gloved fingers to his lips. Monica bent her face away, deadly pale, with closed eyes.

"Are we to part to-day, and never again see each other?" he went on. "Say that you love me! Only say that you love me!"

"You despise me for coming to you like this."

"Despise you?"

In a sudden rapture he folded his arms about her.

"Say that you love me!"

He kissed away the last syllable of her whispered reply.

"Monica! — what is there before us? How can I leave you?"

Yielding herself for the moment in a faintness that threatened to subdue her, she was yet able, when his caresses grew wild with passion, to put back his arms and move suddenly away. He sprang up, and they stood speechless. Again he drew near.

"Take me away with you!" Monica then cried, clasping her hands together. "I can't live with *him*. Let me go with you to France."

Bevis's blue eyes widened with consternation.

"Dare you — dare you do that?" he stammered.

"Dare I? — What courage is needed? — How *dare* I remain with a man I hate?"

"You must leave him. Of course you must leave him."

"Oh, before another day has passed!" sobbed Monica. "It is wrong even to go back to-day. I love you, and in that there is nothing to be ashamed of; but what bitter shame to be living with *him*, practising hypocrisy. He makes me hate myself as much as I hate *him*."

"Has he behaved brutally to you, dearest?"

"I have nothing to accuse him of, except that he persuaded me to marry him — made me think that I could love him when I didn't know what love meant. And now he wishes to get me away from all the people I know, because he is jealous of every one. And how can I blame him? Hasn't he cause for jealousy? I am deceiving him — I have deceived him for a long time, pretending to be a faithful wife when I have often wished that he might die and release me. It is I who am to blame. I ought to have left him. Every woman who thinks of her husband as I do ought to go away from him. It is base and wicked to stay there — pretending — deceiving" —

Bevis came towards her, and took her in his arms.

"You love me?" she panted, under his hot kisses. "You will take me away with you?"

"Yes, you shall come. — We mustn't travel together, but you shall come — when I am settled there" —

"Why can't I go with you?"

"My own darling, think what it would mean if our secret were discovered" —

"Discovered? But how can we think of that? — How can I go back there, with your kisses on my lips? Oh, I must live somewhere in secret until you go, and then — I have put aside the few things that I want to take. I could never have continued to live with him, even if you hadn't said you love me. I was obliged to pretend that I agreed to everything, but I will beg and starve rather than bear that misery any longer. — Don't you love me enough to face whatever may happen?"

"I love you with all my soul, Monica! — Sit down again, dearest; let us talk about it, and see what we can do."

He half led, half carried, her to a couch, and there, holding her embraced, gave way to such amorous frenzy that again Monica broke from him.

"If you love me," she said, in tones of bitter distress, "you will respect me as much as before I came to you. Help me — I am suffering so dreadfully. Say at once that I shall go away with you, even if we travel as strangers. If you are afraid of it becoming known, I will do everything to prevent it. I will go back and live there until Tuesday, and come away only at the last hour, so that no one will ever suspect where —. I don't care how humbly I live, when we are abroad. I can have lodgings somewhere, in the same town, or near, and you will come" —

His hair disordered, his eyes wild, quivering throughout with excitement, he stood as if pondering possibilities.

"Shall I be a burden to you?" she asked, in a faint voice. "Is the expense more than you" —

"No, no, no! How can you think of such a thing? — But it would be so much better if you could wait here until I — Oh, what a wretched thing to have to seem so cowardly to you! But the difficulties are so great, darling. I shall be a perfect stranger in Bordeaux. I don't even speak the language at all well. When I reach there, I shall be met at the station by one of our people, and — just think, how could we manage? You know, if it were discovered that I had run away with you, it would damage my position terribly. I can't say what might happen. — My darling, we shall have to be very careful. In a few weeks, it might all be managed very easily. I would write to you, to some address, and as soon as ever I had made arrangements" —

Monica broke down. The unmanliness of his tone was so dreadful a disillusion. She had expected something so entirely different, — swift, virile passion, eagerness even to anticipate her desire of flight, a strength, a courage to which she could abandon herself, body and soul. She broke down utterly, and wept with her hands upon her face.

Bevis, in sympathetic distraction, threw himself on his knees before her, clutching at her waist.

"Don't, don't!" he wailed. "I can't bear that! — I will do as you wish, Monica. Tell me some place where I can write to you. — Don't cry, darling — don't" —

She went to the couch again, and rested her face against the back, sobbing. For a time they exchanged mere incoherences. Then passion seized upon both, and they clung together, mute, motionless.

"To-morrow I shall leave him," whispered Monica, when at length their eyes met. "He will be away in the morning, and I can take what I need. Tell me where I shall go to, dear — to wait until you are ready. No one will ever suspect that we have gone together. He knows I am miserable with him; he will believe that I have found some way of supporting myself in London. Where shall I live till Tuesday?"

Bevis scarcely listened to her words. The temptation of the natural man, basely selfish, was strengthening its hold upon him.

"Do you love me? Do you really love me?" he replied to her, with thick, agitated utterance.

"Why should you ask that? How can you doubt it?"

"If you really love me" —

His face and tones frightened her.

"Don't make me doubt *your* love! — If I have not perfect trust in you, what will become of me?"

Yet once more she drew resolutely away from him. He pursued, and held her arms with violence.

"Oh, I am mistaken in you!" Monica cried, in fear and bitterness. "You don't know what love means, as *I* feel it. You won't speak, you won't think, of our future life together" —

"I have promised" —

"Leave loose of me! — It's because I have come here. — You think me a worthless woman, without sense of honour, with no self-respect" —

He protested vehemently. The anguished look in her eyes had its effect upon his senses; by degrees it subjugated him, and made him ashamed of his ignoble impulse.

"Shall I find a lodging for you till Tuesday?" he asked, after moving away and returning.

"Will you?"

"You are sure you can leave home to-morrow — without being suspected?"

"Yes, I am sure I can. He is going to the City[1] in the morning. Appoint some place where I can meet you. I will come in a cab, and then you can take me on to the" —

"But you are forgetting the risks. If you take a cab from Herne Hill, with your luggage, he will be able to find out the driver afterwards, and learn where you went."

"Then I will drive only as far as the station, and come to Victoria, and you shall meet me there."

The necessity of these paltry arrangements filled her soul with shame. On the details of her escape she had hardly reflected. All such considerations were, she deemed, naturally the care of her lover, who would act with promptitude, and so as to spare her a moment's perplexity. She had imagined everything in readiness within a few hours; on *her*, no responsibility save that of breaking the hated bond. Inevitably she returned to the wretched thought that Bevis regarded her as a burden. Yes, he had already his mother and his sisters to support; she ought to have remembered that.

"What time would it be?" he was asking.

Unable to reply, she pursued her reflections. She had money, but how to obtain possession of it? Afterwards, when her flight was accomplished, secrecy, it appeared, would be no less needful than now. That necessity had never occurred to her; declaration of the love that had freed her seemed inevitable — nay, desirable. Her self-respect demanded it; only thus could she justify herself before his sisters, and other people who knew her. *They*, perhaps, would not see it in the light of justification, but that mattered little; her own conscience would approve what she had done. But to steal away, and live henceforth in hiding, like a woman dishonoured even in her own eyes — from that she shrank with repugnance. Rather than that, would it not be preferable to break with her husband, and openly live apart from him, alone?

"Be honest with me," she suddenly exclaimed. "Had you rather I didn't come?"

"No, no! I can't live without you" —

"But, if that is true, why haven't you the courage to let every one know it? In your heart you must think that we are acting wrongly."

"I don't! I believe, as you do, that love is the only true marriage — Very well!" He made a desperate gesture. "Let us defy all consequences. For your sake" —

His exaggerated vehemence could not deceive Monica.

"What is it," she asked, "that you most fear?"

He began to babble protestations, but she would not listen to them.

"Tell me — I have every right to ask — what you most fear?"

"I fear nothing, if *you* are with me. — Let my relatives say and think

---

1 "The City" refers to the business and financial district of London, which is located within its medieval boundaries.

what they like. I have made great sacrifices for them; to give up *you* would be too much."

Yet his distress was evident. It strained the corners of his mouth, wrinkled his forehead.

"The disgrace would be more than you could bear. You would never see your mother and your sisters again."

"If they are so prejudiced, so unreasonable, I can't help it. They must" —

He was interrupted by a loud rat-tat at the outer door. Blanched herself, Monica saw that her lover's face turned to ghastly pallor.

"Who can that be?" he whispered hoarsely. "I expect no one."

"Need you answer?"

"Can it be —? Have you been followed? Does any one suspect—?"

They stared at each other, still half-paralysed, and stood waiting thus until the knock was repeated, impatiently.

"I daren't open," Bevis whispered, coming close to her, as if on the impulse of seeking protection — for to offer it was assuredly not in his mind. "It might be" —

"No! That's impossible."

"I daren't go to the door. The risk is too frightful. He will go away, whoever it is, if no one answers."

Both were shaking in the second stage of terror. Bevis put his arm about Monica, and felt her heart give great throbs against his own. Their passion, for the moment, was effectually quenched.

"Listen! — That's the clink of the letter-box. A card or something has been put in. Then it's all right. I'll wait a moment."

He stepped to the door of the room, opened it without sound, and at once heard footsteps descending the stairs. In the look which he cast back at her, a grin rather than a smile, Monica saw something that gave her a pang of shame on his behalf. On going to the letter-box, he found a card, with a few words scribbled upon it.

"Only one of our partners!" he exclaimed gleefully. "Wants to see me to-night. Of course he took it for granted I was out."

Monica was looking at her watch. Past five o'clock.

"I think I must go," she said timidly.

"But what are our arrangements? — Do you still intend" —

"Intend? Isn't it for you to decide?"

There was a coldness in the words of both, partly the result of the great shock they had undergone, in part due to their impatience with each other.

"Darling — do what I proposed at first. Stay for a few days, until I am settled at Bordeaux."

"Stay with my — my husband?"

She used the word purposely, significantly, to see how it would affect him. The bitterness of her growing disillusion allowed her to think and speak as if no ardent feeling were concerned.

"For both our sakes, dearest, dearest love! A few days longer, until I have written to you, and told you exactly what to do. The journey won't be very difficult for you; and think how much better, dear Monica, if we can escape discovery, and live for each other without any shame or fear to disturb us. — You will be my own dear true wife. I will love and guard you as long as I live."

He embraced her with placid tenderness, laying his cheek against hers, kissing her hands.

"We must see each other again," he continued. "Come on Sunday, will you? And in the meantime find out some place where I could address letters to you. You can always find a stationer's shop where they will receive letters. — Be guided by me, dear little girl. Only a week or two — to save the happiness of our whole lives."

Monica listened, but with half-attention, her look fixed on the floor. Encouraged by her silence, the lover went on in a strain of heightening enthusiasm, depicting the raptures of their retirement from the world in some suburb of Bordeaux. How this retreat was to escape the notice of his business companions, through whom the scandal might get wind, he did not suggest. The truth was, Bevis found himself in an extremely awkward position, with issues he had not contemplated, and all he cared for was to avert the immediate peril of public discovery. The easy-going, kindly fellow had never considered all the responsibility involved in making mild love — timorously selfish from the first — to a married woman who took his advances with desperate seriousness. He had not in him the stuff of vigorous rascality, still less the only other quality which can support a man in such a situation as this — heroism of moral revolt. So he cut a very poor figure, and was dolefully aware of it. He talked, talked; trying to disguise his feebleness in tinsel phrases; and Monica still kept her eyes cast down.

When another half hour had passed, she sighed deeply and rose from her seat. She would write to him, she said, and let him know where a reply would reach her. No, she must not come here again; all he had to tell her could be communicated by letter. The subdued tone, the simple sadness of her words, distressed Bevis, and yet he secretly congratulated himself. He had done nothing for which this woman could justly reproach him; marvellous — so he considered — had been his self-restraint; absolutely, he had behaved "like a gentleman." To be sure, he was miserably in love, and, if circumstances by any means allowed of it, would send for Monica to join him in France. Should the thing prove impossible, he had nothing whatever on his conscience.

He held out his arms to her. Monica shook her head, and looked away.

"Say once more that you love me, darling," he pleaded. "I shall not rest for an hour until I am able to write and say 'Come to me!'"

She permitted him to hold her once more in his soft embrace.

"Kiss me, Monica!"

She put her lips to his cheek, and withdrew them, still shunning his look.

"Oh, not that kind of kiss. Like you kissed me before."

"I can't," she replied, with choking voice, the tears again starting forth.

"But what have I done that you should love me less, dearest?"

He kissed the falling drops, murmuring assurances, encouragements.

"You sha'n't leave me until I have heard you say that your love is unchanged. Whisper it to me, sweetest!"

"When we meet again — not now."

"You frighten me. Monica, we are not saying good-bye for ever?"

"If you send for me, I will come."

"You promise faithfully? You *will* come?"

"If you send for me, I will come."

That was her last word. He opened the door for her, and listened as she departed.

CHAPTER XXIII.

IN AMBUSH.

Hitherto, Widdowson had entertained no grave mistrust of his wife. The principles she had avowed, directly traceable, as it seemed, to her friendship with the militant women in Chelsea, he disliked and feared; but her conduct he fully believed to be above reproach. His jealousy of Barfoot did not glance at Monica's attitude towards the man; merely at the man himself, whom he credited with native scoundreldom. Barfoot represented to his mind a type of licentious bachelor; why, he could not have made perfectly clear to his own understanding. Possibly the ease of Everard's bearing, the something aristocratic in his countenance and his speech, the polish of his manner, especially in formal converse with women, from the first gave offence to Widdowson's essentially middle-class sensibilities. If Monica were in danger at all, it was, he felt convinced, from that quarter. The subject of his wife's intimate dialogue with Barfoot at the Academy still remained a mystery to him. He put faith in her rebellious declaration that every word might have been safely repeated in his hearing, but, be the matter what it might, the manner of Barfoot's talk meant evil. Of that conviction he could not get rid.

He had read somewhere that a persistently jealous husband may, not improbably, end by irritating an innocent wife into affording real ground for jealousy. A man with small knowledge of the world is much impressed by dicta such as these; they get into the crannies of his mind, and thence direct the course of his thinking. Widdowson, before his marriage, had never suspected the difficulty of understanding a woman; had he spoken his serious belief on that subject, it would have been found to represent the most primitive male conception of the feminine being. Women were very like children; it was rather a task to amuse them and to keep them out of mischief. Therefore the blessedness of household toil, in especial the blessedness of child-bearing and all that followed. Intimacy with Monica had greatly affected his views, yet chiefly by disturbing them; no firmer ground offered itself to his treading when he perforce admitted that his former standpoint was every day assailed by some incontestable piece of evidence. Women had individual characters; that discovery, though not a very profound one, impressed him with the force of something arrived at by independent observation. Monica often puzzled him gravely; he could not find the key to her satisfactions and discontents. To regard her simply as a human being was beyond the reach of his intelligence. He cast the blame of his difficulties upon sex, and paid more attention to the hints on such topics afforded him by his reading. He would endeavour to keep his jealousy out of sight, lest the mysterious tendency of the female nature might prompt Monica to deliberate wrong-doing.

To-day, for the first time, there flashed across him the thought that already he might have been deceived. It originated in a peculiarity of Monica's behaviour at luncheon. She ate scarcely anything; she seemed hurried, frequently glancing at the clock; and she lost herself in reverie. Discovering that his eye was upon her, she betrayed uneasiness, and began to talk without considering what she meant to say. All this might mean nothing more than her barely concealed regret at being obliged to leave London; but Widdowson remarked it with a vivacity of feeling perhaps due to the excitement in which he had lived for the past week. Perhaps the activity, the resolution, to which he had urged himself caused a sharpening of his perceptions. And the very thought, never out of his mind, that only a few days had to elapse before he carried off his wife from the scene of peril, tended to make him more vividly conscious of that peril. Certain it was that a moment's clairvoyance assailed his peace, and left behind it all manner of ugly conjectures. Women — so said the books — are adepts at dissimulation. Was it conceivable that Monica had taken advantage of the liberty he had of late allowed her? If a woman could not endure a direct, searching gaze, must it not imply some enormous wickedness? — seeing that nature has armed them for this very trial.

In her setting forth for the railway-station, hurry was again evident, and disinclination to exchange parting words. Why should she be so eager to go and see Virginia? If the eagerness were simple and honest, would she not have accepted his suggestion and have gone in the morning?

For five minutes after her departure, he stood in the hall, staring before him. A new jealousy, a horrible constriction of the heart, had begun to torture him. He went and walked about in the library, but could not dispel his suffering. Vain to keep repeating that Monica was incapable of baseness. Of that he was persuaded, but none the less a hideous image returned upon his mental vision — a horror — a pollution of thought.

One thing he could do to restore his sanity. He would walk over to Lavender Hill, and accompany his wife on her return home. Indeed, the mere difficulty of getting through the afternoon advised this project. He could not employ himself, and knew that his imagination, once inflamed, would leave him not a moment's rest. — Yes, he would walk to Lavender Hill, and ramble about that region until Monica had had reasonable time for talk with her sister.

About three o'clock there fell a heavy shower of rain. Strangely against his habits, Widdowson turned into a quiet public-house, and sat for a quarter of an hour at the bar, drinking a glass of whisky. During the past week he had taken considerably more wine than usual, at meals; he seemed to need the support. Whilst sipping at his glass of spirits, he oddly enough fell into talk with the barmaid, a young woman of some charms, and what appeared to be unaffected modesty. Not for twenty years had Widdowson conversed with a member of this sisterhood. Their dialogue was made up of the most trifling of trivialities — weather, a railway accident, the desirability of holidays at this season. And when at length he rose and put an end to the chat, it was with appreciable reluctance.

"A good, nice sort of girl," he went away, saying to himself. "Pity she should be serving at a bar — hearing doubtful talk, and seeing, very often, vile sights. — A nice, soft-spoken little girl."

And he mused upon her remembered face with a complacency which soothed his feelings.

Of a sudden, he was checked by the conversion of his sentiment into thought. Would he not have been a much happier man if he had married a girl distinctly his inferior in mind and station? Provided she were sweet, lovable, docile, such a wife would have spared him all the misery he had known with Monica. From the first he had understood that Monica was no representative shopgirl, and on that very account he had striven so eagerly to win her. But it was a mistake. He had loved her, still loved her, with all the emotion of which he was capable; how many hours' genuine happiness of soul had that love afforded him? The minutest fraction of the twelve months for which she had been his wife. And of suffering, often amounting to frantic misery, he could count many weeks. Could such a marriage as this be judged a marriage at all, in any true sense of the word?

"Let me ask myself a question. If Monica were absolutely free to choose between continuing to live with me and resuming her perfect liberty, can I persuade myself that she would remain my wife? She would not. Not for a day; not for an hour. Of that I am morally convinced. And I acknowledge the grounds of her dissatisfaction. We are unsuited to each other. We do not understand each other. Our marriage is physical, and nothing more. My love — what is my love? I do not love her mind, her intellectual part. If I did, this frightful jealousy from which I suffer would be impossible. My ideal of the wife perfectly suited to me is far liker that girl at the public-house bar than Monica. Monica's independence of thought is a perpetual irritation to me. I don't know what her thoughts really are, what her intellectual life signifies. — And yet I hold her to me with the sternest grasp. If she endeavoured to release herself, I should feel capable of killing her. Is not this a strange, a brutal thing?"

Widdowson had never before reached this height of speculation. In the moment, by the very fact, of admitting that Monica and he ought not to be living together, he became more worthy of his wife's companionship than ever hitherto.

Well, he would exercise greater forbearance. He would endeavour to win her respect by respecting the freedom she claimed. His recent suspicions of her were monstrous. If she knew them, how her soul would revolt from him! — What if she took an interest in other men, perchance more her equals than he? Why, had he not just been thinking of another woman, reflecting that she, or one like her, would have made him a more suitable wife than Monica? Yet this could not reasonable be called unfaithfulness.

They were bound together for life, and their wisdom lay in mutual toleration, the constant endeavour to understand each other aright — not in fierce restraint of each other's mental liberty. How many marriages were anything more than mutual forbearance? Perhaps there ought not to be such a thing as enforced permanence of marriage. This was daring speculation; he could not have endured to hear it from Monica's lips. But — perhaps, some day, marriage would be dissoluble at the will of either party to it. Perhaps the man who sought to hold a woman when she no longer loved him, would be regarded with contempt and condemnation.

What a simple thing marriage had always seemed to him, and how far from simple he had found it! Why, it led him to musings which overset the order of the world, and flung all ideas of religion and morality into wildest confusion. It would not do to think like this. He was a man wedded to a woman very difficult to manage — there was the practical upshot of the matter. His duty was to manage her. He was responsible for her right conduct. With intentions perfectly harmless, she might run into unknown jeopardy — above all just at this time, when she was taking reluctant leave of her friends. The danger justified him in exceptional vigilance.

So, from his excursion into the realms of reason did he return to the safe sphere of the commonplace. And now he might venture to press on towards Mrs. Conisbee's house, for it was half-past four, and already Monica must have been talking with her sister for a couple of hours.

His knock at the door was answered by the landlady herself. She told of Mrs. Widdowson's arrival and departure. — Ah, then Monica had no doubt gone straight home again. But, as Miss Madden had returned, he would speak with her.

"The poor lady isn't very well, sir," said Mrs. Conisbee, fingering the hem of her apron.

"Not very well? But couldn't I see her for a moment?"

Virginia answered this question by appearing on the staircase.

"Some one for me, Mrs. Conisbee?" she called from above. "Oh, is it *you*, Edmund? — So very glad! — I'm sure Mrs. Conisbee will have the kindness to let you come into her sitting-room. — What a pity I was away when Monica called! I've had — business to see to in town; and I've walked and walked, until I'm really — hardly able" —

She sank upon a chair in the room, and looked fixedly at the visitor with a broad, benevolent smile, her head moving up and down. Widdowson was for a moment in perplexity. If the evidence of his eyes could be trusted, Miss Madden's indisposition pointed to a cause so strange that it seemed incredible. He turned to look for Mrs. Conisbee, but the landlady had hurriedly withdrawn, closing the door behind her.

"It is so foolish of me, Edmund," Virginia rambled on, addressing him with a familiarity she had never yet used. "When I am away from home I forget all about my meals — really forget — and then all at once I find that I am quite exhausted — quite exhausted — as you see. And the worst of it is, I have altogether lost my appetite by the time I get back. I couldn't eat a mouthful of food — not a mouthful — I assure you I couldn't. And it does so distress good Mrs. Conisbee. She is exceedingly kind to me — exceedingly careful about my health. — Oh, and in Battersea Park Road I saw such a shocking sight; a great cart ran over a poor little dog, and it was killed on the spot. It unnerved me dreadfully. I do think, Edmund, those drivers ought to be more careful. I was saying to Mrs. Conisbee only the other day — and that reminds me, I do so want to know all about your visit to Clevedon. Dear, dear Clevedon! And have you really taken a house there, Edmund? Oh, if we could all end our days at Clevedon! You know that our dear father and mother are buried in the old churchyard. You remember Tennyson's lines about the old church at Clevedon?[1] — Oh, and what did Monica decide about — about — really, what *was* I going to ask? It is so foolish of me to forget that dinner-time has come and gone. I get so exhausted, and even my memory fails me."

He could doubt no longer. This poor woman had yielded to one of the temptations that beset a life of idleness and solitude. His pity was mingled with disgust.

"I only wished to tell you," he said gravely, "that we have taken a house at Clevedon" —

"You really *have*!" She clasped her hands together. "Whereabouts?"

"Near Dial Hill."

Virginia began a rhapsody which her brother-in-law had no inclination to hear. He arose abruptly.

"Perhaps you had better come and see us to-morrow."

"But Monica left a message that she wouldn't be at home for the next few days, and that I wasn't to come till I heard from her."

"Not at home —? I think there's a mistake."

"Oh, impossible! We'll ask Mrs. Conisbee."

She went to the door, and called. From the landlady Widdowson learnt exactly what Monica had said. He reflected for a moment.

"She shall write to you, then. Don't come just yet. I mustn't stay any longer now."

And with a mere pretence of shaking hands he abruptly left the house.

Suspicions thickened about him. He would have thought it utterly impossible for Miss Madden to disgrace herself in this vulgar way, and the appalling discovery affected his view of Monica. They were sisters; they had characteristics in common, family traits, weaknesses. If the elder woman could fall into this degradation, might there not be possibilities in Monica's character such as he had refused to contemplate? Was there not terrible reason for mistrusting her? — What did she mean by her message to Virginia?

---

1 *In Memoriam*, LXVII, ll. 1253-1268. Arthur Henry Hallam, whose death Tennyson mourns in the poem, is buried in the church at Clevedon.

Black and haggard, he went home as fast as a hansom[1] could take him. It was half-past five when he reached the house. He wife was not here, and had not been here.

At this moment, Monica was starting by train from Bayswater, after her parting with Bevis. Arrived at Victoria, she crossed to the main station, and went to the ladies' waiting-room, for the purpose of bathing her face. She had red, swollen eyes, and her hair was in slight disorder. This done, she inquired as to the next train for Herne Hill. One had just gone; another would leave in about a quarter of an hour.

A dreadful indecision was harassing her. Ought she, did she dare, to return home at all? Even if her strength sufficed for simulating a natural manner, could she consent to play so base a part?

There was but one possible alternative. She might go to Virginia's lodgings, and there remain, writing to her husband that she had left him. The true cause need not be confessed. She would merely declare that life with him had become intolerable to her, that she demanded a release. Their approaching removal to Clevedon offered the occasion. She would say that her endurance failed before that prospect of solitude, and that, feeling as she did, it was dishonourable to make longer pretence of doing her duty as a wife. — Then, if Bevis wrote to her in such a way as to revive her love; if he seriously told her to come to him; all difficulties could be solved by her disappearance.

Was such revival of disheartened love a likely or a possible thing? At this moment, she felt that to flee in secret, and live with Bevis as he proposed, would be no less dishonour than abiding with the man who had a legal claim upon her companionship. Her lover, as she had thought of him for the past two or three months, was only a figment of her imagination; Bevis had proved himself a complete stranger to her mind; she must re-shape her knowledge of him. His face was all that she could still dwell upon with the old desire; nay, even that had suffered a change.

Insensibly the minutes went by. Whilst she sat in the waiting-room, her train started; and when she had become aware of that, her irresolution grew more tormenting.

Suddenly there came upon her a feeling of illness, of nausea. Perspiration broke out on her forehead; her eyes dazzled; she had to let her head fall back. It passed, but in a minute or two the fit again seized her, and with a moan she lost consciousness.

Two or three women who were in the room rendered assistance. The remarks they exchanged, though expressing uncertainty and discreetly ambiguous, would have been significant to Monica. On her recovery, which took place in a few moments, she at once started up, and with hurried thanks to those about her, listening to nothing that was said and

---

1 A two-wheeled horse-drawn cab.

answering no inquiry, went out on to the platform. There was just time to catch the train now departing for Herne Hill.

She explained her fainting fit by the hours of agitation through which she had passed. There was no room for surprise. She had suffered indescribably, and still suffered. Her wish was to get back into the quietness of home, to rest and to lose herself in sleep.

On entering, she saw nothing of her husband. His hat hung on the hall-tree, and he was perhaps sitting in the library; the more genial temper would account for his not coming forth at once to meet her, as had been his custom when she returned from an absence alone.

She changed her dress, and disguised as far as was possible the traces of suffering on her features. Weakness and tremor urged her to lie down, but she could not venture to do this until she had spoken to her husband. Supporting herself by the banisters, she slowly descended, and opened the library door. Widdowson was reading a newspaper. He did not look round, but said carelessly:

"So you are back?"

"Yes. — I hope you didn't expect me sooner."

"Oh, it's all right." He threw a rapid glance at her over his shoulder. "Had a long talk with Virginia, I suppose?"

"Yes. I couldn't get away before."

Widdowson seemed to be much interested in some paragraph. He put his face closer to the paper, and was silent for two or three seconds. Then he again looked round, this time observing his wife steadily, but with a face that gave no intimation of unusual thoughts.

"Does she consent to go?"

Monica replied that it was still uncertain; she thought, however, that Virginia's objections would be overcome.

"You look very tired," remarked the other.

"I am, very."

And thereupon she withdrew, unable to command her countenance, scarce able to remain standing, for another moment.

CHAPTER XXIV.

TRACKED.

When Widdowson went up to the bedroom that night, Monica was already asleep. He discovered this on turning up the gas; the light fell upon her face, and he was drawn to the bedside to look at her. The features signified nothing but repose; her lips were just apart, her eyelids lay softly with their black fringe of exquisite pencilling, and her hair was arranged as she always prepared it for the pillow. He watched her for full five minutes, and detected not the slightest movement, so profound was her sleep. Then he turned away, muttering savagely under his breath — "Hypocrite! Liar!"

But for a purpose in his thoughts, he would not have lain down beside her. On getting into bed, he kept as far away as possible, and all through the wakeful night his limbs shrank from the touch of hers.

He rose an hour earlier than usual. Monica had long been awake, but she moved so seldom that he could not be sure of this; her face was turned from him. When he came back to the room after his bath, Monica propped herself on her elbow and asked why he was moving so early.

"I want to be in the City at nine," he replied, with a show of cheerfulness. "There's a money affair I must see after."

"Something that's going wrong?"

"I'm afraid so. I must lose no time in looking to it. — What plans have you for to-day?"

"None whatever."

"It's Saturday, you know. I promised to see Newdick this afternoon. Perhaps I may bring him to dinner."

About twelve o'clock he returned from his business. At two he went away again, saying that he should not be back before seven, it might be a little later. In Monica these movements excited no special remark; they were merely a continuance of his restlessness. But no sooner had he departed, after luncheon, than she went to her dressing-room, and began to make slow, uncertain preparations for leaving home herself.

This morning she had tried to write a letter for Bevis, but vainly. She knew not what to say to him, uncertain of her own desires and of what lay before her. Yet, if she were to communicate with him henceforth at all, it was necessary, this very afternoon, to find an address where letters could be received for her, and to let him know of it. To-morrow, Sunday, was useless for the purpose, and on Monday it might be impossible for her to go out alone, — besides that, she could not be sure of the safety of a letter delivered at the flat on Monday night or Tuesday morning.

She dressed at length, and went out. Her wisest course, probably, was to seek for some obliging shopkeeper near Lavender Hill. Then she could call on Virginia, transact the business she had pretended to discharge yesterday, and there pen a note to Bevis.

Her moods alternated with distracting rapidity. A hundred times she had resolved that Bevis could be nothing more to her, and again had thought of him with impulses of yearning, trying to persuade herself that he had acted well and wisely. A hundred times she determined to carry out her idea of yesterday, — to quit her husband, and resist all his efforts to recall her, and again had all but resigned herself to live with him, accepting degradation as so many wives perforce did. Her mind was in confusion, and physically she felt far from well. A heaviness weighed upon her limbs, making it hardship to walk however short a distance.

Arrived at Clapham Junction, she began to search wearily, indifferently, for the kind of shop that might answer her purpose. The receiving of letters which, for one reason or another, must be dispatched to a secret address, is a very ordinary complaisance on the part of small London stationers; hundreds of such letters are sent and called for every week within the metropolitan postal area. It did not take Monica long to find an obliging shopkeeper; the first to whom she applied — a decent woman behind a counter which displayed newspapers, tobacco, and fancy articles — willingly accepted the commission.

She came out of the shop with flushed cheeks. Another step in shameful descent, — yet it had the result of strengthening once more her emotions favourable to Bevis. On his account she had braved this ignominy, and it drew her towards him, instead of producing the effect which would have seemed more natural. Perhaps the reason was that she felt herself more hopelessly an outcast from the world of honourable women, and therefore longed in her desolation for the support of a man's love. Did he not love her? It was *her* fault if she expected him to act with a boldness that did not lie in his nature. Perhaps his discretion, which she had so bitterly condemned as weakness, meant a wise regard for her interests as well as his own. The public scandal of divorce was a hideous thing; if it damaged his prospects, and sundered him from his relatives, how could she hope that his love of her, the cause of it all, would long endure?

The need of love overcame her. She would submit to any conditions rather than lose this lover whose kisses were upon her lips, and whose arms had held her so passionately. She was too young to accept a life of resignation, too ardent. Why had she left him in despondency, in doubt whether he would ever again see her?

She turned back on her way to Virginia's lodgings, re-entered the station, and journeyed townwards. It was an odd incident, by Monica unperceived, that when she was taking her ticket there stood close by her a man, seemingly a mechanic,[1] who had also stood within hearing when she

---

1 A skilled workman.

booked at Herne Hill. This same man, though he had not travelled in the compartment with her, followed her when she changed trains at Victoria, and yet again followed her when she alighted at Bayswater. She did not once observe him.

Instead of writing, she had resolved to see Bevis again — if it were possible. Perhaps he would not be at the flat; yet his wish might suggest the bare hope of her coming to-day. The risk of meeting Barfoot probably need not be considered, for he had told her that he was travelling to-day into Cumberland, and for so long a journey he would be sure to set forth in the morning. At worst she would suffer a disappointment. Indulgence of her fervid feelings had made her as eager to see Bevis as she was yesterday. Words of tenderness rushed to her lips for utterance. When she reached the building, all but delirium possessed her.

She had hurried up to the first landing, when a footstep behind drew her attention. It was a man in mechanic's dress, coming up with head bent, doubtless for some task or other in one of the flats. Perhaps he was going to Bevis's. She went forward more slowly, and on the next landing, allowed the man to pass her. Yes, more likely than not he was engaged in packing her lover's furniture. She stood still. At that moment a door closed above, and another step, lighter and quicker, that of a woman, came downstairs. As far as her ear could judge, this person might have left Bevis's flat. A conflict of emotions excited her to panic. She was afraid either to advance or to retreat, and in equal dread of standing without purpose. She stepped up to the nearest door, and gave a summons with the knocker.

This door was Barfoot's. She knew that; in the first instant of fear occasioned by the workman's approach, she had glanced at the door and reminded herself that here Mr. Barfoot dwelt, immediately beneath Bevis. But for the wild alarm due to her conscience-stricken state, she could not have risked the possibility of the tenant being still at home; and yet it seemed to her that she was doing the only thing possible under the circumstances. For this woman whom she heard just above might perchance be one of Bevis's sisters, returned to London for some purpose or other, and in that case she preferred being seen at Barfoot's door to detection as she made for her lover's.

Uncertainty on this point lasted but a few seconds. Dreading to look at the woman, Monica yet did so, just as she passed, and beheld the face of a perfect stranger. A young and good-looking face, however. Her mind, sufficiently tumultuous, received a new impulse of disturbance. Had this woman come forth from Bevis's flat, or from the one opposite? — for on each floor there were two dwellings.

In the meantime, no one answered her knock. Mr. Barfoot had gone; she breathed thankfully. Now she might venture to ascend to the next floor. But then sounded a knock from above. That, she felt convinced, was at Bevis's door, and if so her conjecture about the workman was correct. She stood waiting for certainty, as if still expecting a reply to her own signal at Mr. Barfoot's door. The mechanic looked down at her over the banisters, but of this she was unaware.

The knock above was repeated. Yes, this time there could be no mistake; it was on this side of the landing; that is to say, at her lover's door. But the door did not open; thus, without going up herself, she received assurance that Bevis was not at home. He might come later. She still had an hour or two to spare. So, as if disappointed in a call at Mr. Barfoot's, she descended the stairs and issued into the street.

Agitation had exhausted her, and a dazzling of her eyes threatened a recurrence of yesterday's faintness. She found a shop where refreshments were sold, and sat for half an hour over a cup of tea, trying to amuse herself with illustrated papers. The mechanic who had knocked at Bevis's door passed once or twice along the pavement, and, as long as she remained here, kept the shop within sight.

At length she asked for writing materials, and penned a few lines. If on her second attempt she failed to see Bevis, she would drop this note into his letter-box. It acquainted him with the address to which he might direct letters, assured him passionately of her love, and implored him to be true to her, to send for her as soon as circumstances made it possible.

Self-torment of every kind was natural to her position. Though the relief of escaping from several distinct dangers had put her mind comparatively at ease for a short time, she had now begun to suffer a fresh uneasiness with reference to the young and handsome woman who came downstairs. The fact that no one answered the workman's knock had seemed to her a sufficient proof that Bevis was not at home, and that the stranger must have come forth from the flat opposite his. But she recollected the incident which had so alarmingly disturbed her and her lover yesterday. Bevis did not then go to the door, and suppose — oh, it was folly! But suppose that woman had been with him; suppose he did not care to open to a visitor whose signal sounded only a minute or two after that person's departure?

Had she not anguish enough to endure, without the addition of frantic jealousy? She would not give another thought to such absurd suggestions. The woman had of course come from the dwelling opposite. — Yet why might she not have been in Bevis's flat when he himself was absent? Suppose her an intimate to whom he had entrusted a latch-key. If any such connection existed, might it not help to explain Bevis's half-heartedness?

To think thus was courting madness. Unable to sit still any longer, Monica left the shop, and strayed for some ten minutes about the neighbouring streets, drawing nearer and nearer to her goal. Finally, she entered the building and went upstairs. On this occasion no one met her, and no one entered in her rear. She knocked at her lover's door, and stood longing, praying, that it might open. But it did not. Tears started to her eyes; she uttered a moan of bitterest disappointment, and slipped the envelope she was carrying into the letter-box.

The mechanic had seen her go in, and he waited outside, a few yards away. Either she would soon reappear, or her not doing so would show that she had obtained admittance somewhere. In the latter case, this workman of much curiosity and leisure had only to lurk about the staircase until she came forth again. But this trial of patience was spared him. He found that he had simply to follow the lady back to Herne Hill. Acting on very suggestive instructions, it never occurred to the worthy man that the lady's second visit was not to the same flat as in the former instance.

Monica was home again long before dinner-time. When that hour arrived, her husband had not yet come; the delay, no doubt, was somehow connected with his visit to Mr. Newdick. But time went on. At nine o'clock Monica still sat alone, hungry, yet scarce conscious of hunger owing to her miseries. Widdowson had never behaved thus. Another quarter of an hour, and she heard the front-door open.

He came to the drawing-room, where she sat waiting.

"How late you are! — Are you alone?"

"Yes, alone."

"You haven't had dinner?"

"No."

He seemed to be in rather a gloomy mood, but Monica noticed nothing that alarmed her. He was drawing nearer, his eyes on the ground.

"Have you had bad news — in the City?"

"Yes, I have."

Still he came nearer, and at length, when a yard or two away, raised his look to her face.

"Have you been out this afternoon?"

She was prompted to a falsehood, but durst not utter it, so keenly was he regarding her.

"Yes. — I went to see Miss Barfoot."

"Liar!"

As the word burst from his lips, he sprang at her, clutched her dress at the throat, and flung her violently upon her knees. A short cry of terror escaped her; then she was stricken dumb, with eyes starting and mouth open. It was well that he held her by the garment, and not by the neck, for his hand closed with murderous convulsion, and the desire of crushing out her life was for an instant all his consciousness.

"Liar!" again burst from him. "Day after day you have lied to me. — Liar! Adulteress!"

"I am not! I am not that!"

She clung upon his arms and strove to raise herself. The bloodless lips, the choked voice, meant dread of him, but the distortion of her features was hatred and the will to resist.

"Not that? What is your word worth? The prostitute in the street is sooner to be believed. She has the honesty to say what she is, but you — Where were you yesterday, when you were *not* at your sister's? Where were you this afternoon?"

She had nearly struggled to her feet; he thrust her down again, crushed her backwards until her head all but touched the floor.

"Where were you? Tell the truth; or you shall never speak again!"

"Oh — help! help! — He will kill me!"

Her cry rang through the room.

"Call them up — let them come and look at you and hear what you are. Soon enough, every one will know. — Where were you this afternoon? — You were watched every step of the way from here to that place where you have made yourself a base, vile, unclean creature" —

"I am not that! Your spies have misled you" —

"Misled? Didn't you go to that man Barfoot's door and knock there? And because you were disappointed, didn't you wait about, and go there a second time?"

"What if I did? It doesn't mean what you think."

"What? You go time after time to the private chambers of an unmarried man — a man such as that, and it means no harm?"

"I have never been there before."

"You expect me to believe you?" Widdowson cried, with savage contumely. He had just loosed his hold of her, and she was upright again before him, her eyes flashing defiance, though every muscle in her frame quivered. "When did your lies begin? Was it when you told me you had been to hear Miss Barfoot's lecture, and never went there at all?"

He aimed the charge at a venture, and her face told him that his suspicion had been grounded.

"For how many weeks, for how many months, have you been dishonouring me and yourself?"

"I am not guilty of what you believe, but I sha'n't try to defend myself. Thank heaven, this is the end of everything between us! Charge me with what you like. I am going away from you, and I hope we may never meet again."

"Yes, you are going — no doubt of that. But not before you have answered my questions. Whether with lies or not, doesn't matter much. You shall give your own account of what you have been doing."

Both panting as if after some supreme effort of their physical force, they stood and looked at each other. Each to the other's eyes was incredibly transformed. Monica could not have imagined such brutal ferocity in her husband's face, and she herself had a wild recklessness in her eyes, a scorn and abhorrence in all the lines of her countenance, which made Widdowson feel as if a stranger were before him.

"I shall answer no question whatever," Monica replied. "All I want is to leave your house, and never see you again."

He regretted what he had done. The result of the first day's espionage being a piece of evidence so incomplete, he had hoped to command himself until more solid proof of his wife's guilt were forthcoming. But jealousy was too strong for such prudence, and the sight of Monica as she uttered her falsehood made a mere madman of him. Predisposed to believe a story of this kind, he could not reason as he might have done if fear of Barfoot had never entered his thoughts. The whole course of dishonour seemed so clear; he traced it from Monica's earliest meetings with Barfoot at Chelsea. Wavering between the impulse to cast off his wife with every circumstance of public shame, and the piteous desire to arrest her on her path of destruction, he rushed into a middle course, compatible with neither of these intentions. If, at this stage, he chose to tell Monica what had come to his knowledge, it should have been done with the sternest calm, with dignity capable of shaming her guilt. As it was, he had spoilt his chances in every direction. Perhaps Monica understood this; he had begun to esteem her a mistress in craft and intrigue.

"You say you were never at that man's rooms before to-day?" he asked, in a lower voice.

"What I have said, you must take the trouble to recollect. I shall answer no question."

Again the impulse assailed him to wring confession from her by terror. He took a step forward, the demon in his face. Monica, in that moment leapt past him, and reached the door of the room before he could stop her.

"Stay where you are!" she cried. "If your hands touch me again, I shall call for help until some one comes up. I won't endure your touch!"

"Do you pretend you are innocent of any crime against me?"

"I am not what you called me. Explain everything as you like. I will explain nothing. I want only to be free from you."

She opened the door, rapidly crossed the landing, and went upstairs. Feeling it was useless to follow, Widdowson allowed the door to remain wide, and waited. Five minutes passed, and Monica came down again, dressed for leaving the house.

"Where are you going?" he asked, stepping out of the room to intercept her.

"It is nothing to you. I am going away."

They subdued their voices, which might else have been audible to the servants below.

"No, that you shall not!"

He stepped forward to block the head of the stairs, but again Monica was too quick for him. She fled down, and across the hall, and to the house-door. Only there, as she was arrested by the difficulty of drawing back the two latches, did Widdowson overtake her.

"Make what scandal you like, you don't leave this house."

His tones were violent rather than resolute. What could he do? If Monica persisted, what means had he of confining her to the house — short of carrying her by main force to an upper room and there locking her in? He knew that his courage would not sustain him through such a task as this.

"For scandal I care nothing," was her reply. — "One way or another I will leave the house."

"Where are you going?"

"To my sister's."

His hand on the door, Widdowson stood as if determined in opposition. But her will was stronger than his. Only by homicide can a man maintain his dignity in a situation of this kind; Widdowson could not kill his wife, and every moment that he stood there made him more ridiculous, more contemptible.

He turned back into the hall, and reached his hat. Whilst he was doing so, Monica opened the door. Heavy rain was falling, but she paid no heed to it. In a moment, Widdowson hastened after her, careless, he too, of the descending floods. Her way was towards the railway-station, but the driver of a cab chancing to attract her notice, she accepted the man's offer, and bade him drive to Lavender Hill.

On the first opportunity, Widdowson took like refuge from the rain, and was driven in the same direction. He alighted not far from Mrs. Conisbee's house. That Monica had come hither he felt no doubt, but he would presently make sure of it. As it still rained, he sought shelter in a public-house, where he quenched a painful thirst, and then satisfied his hunger with such primitive foods as a licensed victualler is disposed to vend. It was nearing eleven o'clock, and he had neither eaten nor drunk since luncheon.

After that, he walked to Mrs. Conisbee's, and knocked at the door. The landlady came.

"Will you please to tell me," he asked, "whether Mrs. Widdowson is here?"

The sly curiosity of the woman's face informed him at once that she saw something unusual in these circumstances.

"Yes, sir. Mrs. Widdowson is with her sister."

"Thank you."

Without another word he departed. But went only a short distance, and until midnight kept Mrs. Conisbee's door in view. The rain fell, the air was raw; shelterless, and often shivering with fever, Widdowson walked the pavement with a constable's regularity. He could not but remember the many nights when he thus kept watch in Walworth Road and in Rutland Street, with jealousy, then too, burning in his heart, but also with amorous ardours, never again to be revived. — A little more than twelve months ago! And he had waited, longed, for marriage through half a lifetime.

CHAPTER XXV.

THE FATE OF THE IDEAL.

Rhoda's week at the seashore was spoilt by uncertain weather. Only two days of abiding sunshine; for the rest, mere fitful gleams across a sky heaped with stormclouds. Over Wastdale hung a black canopy; from Scawfell came mutterings of thunder; and on the last night of the week — when Monica fled from her home in pelting rain — tempest broke upon the mountains and the sea. Wakeful until early morning, and at times watching the sky from her island-looking window, Rhoda saw the rocky heights that frown upon Wastwater illumined by lightning-flare of such intensity and duration that miles of distance were annihilated, and it seemed but a step to those stern crags and precipices.

Sunday began with rain, but also with promise of better things; far over the sea was a broad expanse of blue, and before long the foam of the fallen tide glistened in strong, hopeful rays. Rhoda wandered about the shore, towards St. Bee's head. A broad stream flowing into the sea stopped her progress before she had gone very far; the only way of crossing it was to go up on to the line of railway, which here runs along the edge of the sands. But she had little inclination to walk further. No house, no person within sight, she sat down to gaze at the gulls fishing by the little river-mouth, their screams the only sound that blended with that of the subdued breakers.

On the horizon lay a long, low shape that might have been mistaken for cloud, though it resembled land. It was the Isle of Man. In an hour or two the outline had grown much clearer; the heights and hollows were no longer doubtful. In the north became visible another remote and hilly tract; it was the coast of Scotland beyond Solway Firth.

These distant objects acted as incentives to Rhoda's imagination. She heard Everard Barfoot's voice as he talked of travel, — of the Orient Express. That joy of freedom he had offered her. Perhaps he was now very near her, anxious to repeat his offer. If he carried out the project suggested at their last interview, she would see him to-day, or to-morrow morning, then she must make her choice. To have a day's walk with him among the mountains would be practically deciding. But for what? If she rejected his proposal of a free union, was he prepared to marry her in legal form? — Yes; she had enough power over him for that. But how would it affect his thought of her? Constraining him to legal marriage, would she not lower herself in his estimation, and make the endurance of his love less probable? Barfoot was not a man to accept with genuine satisfaction even the appearance of bondage, and more likely than not his love of her depended upon the belief that in her he had found a woman capable of regarding life from his own point of view, a woman who, when she once loved, would be scornful of the formalities clung to by feeble minds. He would yield to her if she demanded forms, but afterwards — when passion had subsided —

A week had been none too long to ponder these considerations, by themselves; but they were complicated with doubts of a more disturbing nature. Her mind could not free itself from the thought of Monica. That Mrs. Widdowson was not always truthful with her husband, she had absolute proof; whether that supported her fear of an intimacy between Monica and Everard she was unable to determine. The grounds of suspicion seemed to her very grave; so grave, that during her first day or two in Cumberland she had all but renounced the hopes long secretly fostered. She knew herself well enough to understand how jealousy might wreck her life, — even if it were only retrospective. If she married Barfoot (forms or none — that question in no way touched this other), she would demand of him a flawless faith. Her pride revolted against the thought of possessing only a share in his devotion; the moment that any faithlessness came to her knowledge, she would leave him, perforce, inevitably, — and what miseries were then before her!

Was flawless faith possible to Everard Barfoot? His cousin would ridicule the hope of any such thing — or so Rhoda believed. A conventional woman would of course see the completest evidence of his untrustworthiness in his dislike of legal marriage; but Rhoda knew the idleness of this argument. If love did not hold him, assuredly the forms of marriage could be no restraint upon Everard; married ten times over, he would still deem himself absolutely free from any obligation save that of love. Yet how did he think of that obligation? He might hold it perfectly compatible with the indulgence of casual impulse. And this (which she suspected to be the view of every man) Rhoda had no power of tolerating. It must be all or nothing, whole faith or none whatever.

In the afternoon she suffered from impatient expectancy. If Barfoot came to-day, — she imagined him somewhere in the neighbourhood, approaching Seascale as the time of his appointment drew near, — would he call at her lodgings? The address she had not given him, but doubtless he had obtained it from his cousin. Perhaps he would prefer to meet her unexpectedly, not a difficult thing in this little place, with its handful of residents and visitors. Certain it was she desired his arrival. Her heart leapt with joy in the thought that this very evening might bring him. She wished to study him under new conditions, and — possibly — to talk with him even more frankly than ever yet, for there would be opportunity enough.

About six o'clock a train coming from the south stopped at the station, which was visible from Rhoda's sitting-room window. She had been waiting for this moment. She could not go to the station, and did not venture even to wait anywhere in sight of the exit. Whether any passenger had alighted must remain uncertain. If Everard had arrived by this train, doubtless he would go to the hotel, which stood only a few yards from the line. He would take a meal, and presently come forth.

Having allowed half an hour to elapse, she dressed and walked shoreward. Seascale has no street, no shops; only two or three short rows of houses irregularly placed on the rising ground above the beach. To cross the intervening railway, Rhoda could either pass through the little station, in which case she would also pass the hotel and be observable from its chief windows, or descend by a longer road which led under a bridge, and in this way avoid the hotel altogether. She took the former route. On the sands were a few scattered people, and some children subdued to Sunday decorum. The tide was rising; she went down to the nearest tract of hard sand, and stood there for a long time, a soft western breeze playing upon her face.

If Barfoot were here, he would now be coming out to look for her. From a distance he might not recognize her figure, clad as she was in a costume such as he had never seen her wearing. She might venture now to walk up towards the dry, white sand-heaps, where the little convolvulus grew in abundance, and other flowers of which she neither knew nor cared to learn the names. Scarcely had she turned, when she saw Everard approaching, still far off, but unmistakable. He signalled by taking off his hat, and quickly was beside her.

"Did you know me before I happened to look round?" she asked laughingly.

"Of course I did. Up there by the station, I caught sight of you. Who else bears herself as you do — with splendid disdain of common mortals?"

"Please don't make me think that my movements are ridiculous."

"They are superb. — The sea has already touched your cheeks. But I am afraid you have had abominable weather."

"Yes, rather bad; but there's hope to-day. — Where do you come from?"

"By train, only from Carnforth. I left London yesterday morning, and stopped at Morecambe, — some people I know are there. As trains were awkward to-day, I drove from Morecambe to Carnforth. — Did you expect me?"

"I thought you might come, as you spoke of it."

"How I have got through the week, I couldn't tell you. I should have been here days ago, but I was afraid. — Let us go nearer to the sea. — I was afraid of making you angry."

"It's better to keep one's word."

"Of course it is. And I am all the more delighted to be with you for the miserable week of waiting. Have you bathed?"

"Once or twice."

"I had a swim this morning before breakfast, in pouring rain. Now *you* can't swim."

"No, I can't. But why were you sure about it?"

"Only because it's so rare for any girl to learn swimming. A man who can't swim is only half the man he might be, and to a woman I should think it must be of even more benefit. As in everything else, women are trammelled by their clothes; to be able to get rid of them, and to move about with free and brave exertion of all the body, must tend to every kind of health, physical, mental, and moral."

"Yes, I quite believe that," said Rhoda, gazing at the sea.

"I spoke rather exultantly, didn't I? — I like to feel myself superior to you in some things. You have so often pointed out to me what a paltry, ineffectual creature I am."

"I don't remember ever using those words, or implying them."

"How does the day stand with you?" asked Everard, in the tone of perfect comradeship. "Have you still to dine?"

"My dining is a very simple matter; it happens at one o'clock. About nine I shall have supper."

"Let us walk a little, then. And may I smoke?"

"Why not?"

Everard lit a cigar, and, as the tide drove them back, they moved eventually to the higher ground, whence there was a fine view of the mountains, rich in evening colours.

"To-morrow you leave here?"

"Yes," Rhoda answered. "I shall go by railway to Coniston, and walk from there towards Helvellyn, as you suggested."

"I have something else to propose. A man I talked to in the train told me of a fine walk in this neighbourhood. From Ravenglass, just below here, there's a little line runs up Eskdale, to a terminus at the foot of Scawfell, a place called Boot. From Boot one can walk, either over the top of Scawfell, or by a lower track, to Wastdale Head. It's very grand, wild country, especially the last part, the going down to Wastwater, and not many miles in all. — Suppose we have that walk to-morrow? From Wastdale we could drive back to Seascale in the evening, and then the next day — just as you like."

"Are you quite sure about the distances?"

"Quite. I have the ordnance map[1] in my pocket. Let me show you."

He spread the map on the top of a wall, and they stood side by side inspecting it.

"We must take something to eat; I'll provide for that. And at the Wastdale Head hotel we can have dinner — about three or four, probably. It would be enjoyable, wouldn't it?"

"If it doesn't rain."

"We'll hope it won't. As we go back, we can look out the trains at the station. No doubt there's one soon after breakfast."

Their rambling, with talk in a strain of easy friendliness, brought them back to Seascale half an hour after sunset, which was of a kind that seemed to promise well for the morrow.

"Won't you come out again after supper?" Barfoot asked.

---

1 A detailed and accurate map prepared as the result of a government survey.

"Not again to-night."

"For a quarter of an hour," he urged. "Just down to the sea and back."

"I have been walking all day. I shall be glad to rest and read."

"Very well. To-morrow morning."

Having discovered the train which would take them to Ravenglass, and connect with one on the Eskdale line, they agreed to meet at the station. Barfoot was to bring with him such refreshment as would be necessary.

Their hopes for the weather had complete fulfilment. The only fear was lest the sun's heat might be oppressive, but this anxiety could be cheerfully borne. Slung over his shoulders, Barfoot had a small forage-bag[1] which gave him matter for talk on the railway journey; it had been his companion in many parts of the world, and had held strange kinds of food.

The journey up Eskdale, from Ravenglass to Boot, is by a miniature railway, with the oddest little engine and a carriage or two of primitive simplicity. At each station on the upward winding track, stations represented only by a wooden shed like a tool-house, the guard jumps down and acts as booking-clerk, if passengers there be desirous of booking. In a few miles the scenery changes from beauty to grandeur, and at the terminus no further steaming would be possible, for the great flank of Scawfell bars the way.

Everard and his companion began their climb, through the pretty straggling village of Boot. A mountain torrent roared by the wayside, and the course they had marked upon the map showed that they must follow this stream for some miles up to the tarn[2] where it originated. Houses, human beings, and even trodden paths they soon left behind, coming out on to a vast moorland, with hill summits near and far. Scawfell they could not hope to ascend; with the walk that lay before them it was enough to make a way over one of his huge shoulders.

"If your strength fails," said Everard merrily, when for an hour they had been plodding through grey solitudes, "there is no human help. I should have to choose between carrying you back to Boot or on to Wastdale."

"My strength is not likely to fail sooner than yours," was the laughing reply.

"I have chicken sandwiches, and wine that maketh glad the heart of man. Tell me when hunger overcomes you. I should think we had better make our halt at Burmoor Tarn."

That, indeed, proved to be the convenient resting-place. A wild spot, a hollow amid the rolling expanse of moorland, its little lake of black water glistening under the midday-sun. And here stood a shepherd's cottage, the only habitation they had seen since leaving Boot. Somewhat

---

1 A bag for provisions.
2 A tarn is a small mountain lake.

uncertain about the course to be henceforth followed, they made inquiry at this cottage, and a woman who appeared to be quite alone gave them the needful direction. Thus at ease in mind, they crossed the bridge at the foot of the tarn, and just beyond it found a spot suitable for repose. Everard brought forth his sandwiches and his flask of wine, moreover a wine-glass, which was for Rhoda's use. They ate and drank festively.

"Now this is just what I have enjoyed in imagination for a year or more," said Barfoot, when the luncheon was over, and he lay propped upon his elbow, gazing at Rhoda's fine eyes and her sun-warmed cheeks. "An ideal realized, for once in one's life. A perfect moment."

"Don't you like the scent of burning peat from that cottage?"

"Yes. I like everything about us, in heaven and earth, and most of all I like your companionship, Rhoda."

She could not resent this first use of her Christian name; it was so natural, so inevitable; yet she moved her head as if with a slight annoyance.

"Is mine as agreeable to you?" he added, stroking the back of her hand with a spray of heather. "Or do you just tolerate me out of good-nature?"

"I have liked your companionship all the way from Seascale. Don't disturb my enjoyment of it for the rest of the way."

"That would be a misfortune indeed. The whole day shall be perfect. Not a note of discord. But I must have liberty to say what comes into my mind, and when you don't choose to answer, I shall respect your silence."

"Wouldn't you like to smoke a cigar before we start again?"

"Yes. But I like still better not to. The scent of peat is pleasanter to you than that of tobacco."

"Oblige me by lighting the cigar."

"If you command —" He did her bidding. "The whole day shall be perfect. A delightful dinner at the inn, a drive to Seascale, an hour or two of rest, and then one more quiet talk by the sea, at nightfall."

"All but the last. I shall be too tired."

"No. I must have that hour of talk by the sea. You are free to answer me or not, but your presence you must grant me. We are in an ideal world, remember. We care nothing for all the sons and daughters of men. You and I will spend this one day together between cloudless heaven and silent earth — a memory for lifetime. At nightfall you will come out again, and meet me down by the sea, where you stood when I first saw you yesterday."

Rhoda made no reply. She looked away from him, at the black, deep water.

"What an opportunity," he went on, raising his hand to point at the cottage, "for saying the silliest of conceivable things!"

"What *might* that be, I wonder?"

"Why, that to dwell there together, for the rest of our lives, would be supreme felicity. — You know the kind of man that would say that."

"Not personally, thank goodness!"

"A week — a month, even — with weather such as this. Nay, with a storm for variety; clouds from the top of Scawfell falling thick about us; a fierce wind shrieking across the tarn; sheets and torrents and floods of rain beating upon our roof; and you and I by the peat-fire. With a good supply of books, old and new, I can picture it for three months, for half a year!"

"Be on your guard. Remember 'that kind of man.'"

"I am in no danger. There is a vast difference between six months and all one's life. — When the half year was over we would leave England."

"By the Orient Express?"

They laughed together, Rhoda colouring, for the words that had escaped her meant too much for mere jest.

"By the Orient Express. We would have a house by the Bosphorus for the next half year, and contrast our emotions with those we had known by Burmoor Tarn. Think what a rich year of life that would make! How much we should have learnt from nature and from each other!"

"And how dreadfully tired of each other we should be!"

Barfoot looked keenly at her. He could not with certainty read her countenance.

"You mean that?" he asked.

"You know it is true."

"Hush! The day is to be perfect. I won't admit that we could ever tire of each other, with reasonable variety of circumstances. You, to me, are infinitely interesting, and I believe that I might become so to you."

He did not allow himself to vary from this tone of fanciful speculation, suited to the idle hour. Rhoda said very little; her remarks were generally a purposed interruption of Everard's theme. When the cigar was smoked out, they rose and set forward again. This latter half of their walk proved the most interesting, for they were expectant of the view down upon Wastdale. A bold summit came in sight, dark, desolate, which they judged to be Great Gabel; and when they had pressed on eagerly for another mile, the valley opened beneath them with such striking suddenness that they stopped on the instant and glanced at each other in silence. From a noble height they looked down upon Wastwater, sternest and blackest of the lakes, on the fields and copses of the valley-head with its winding stream, and the rugged gorges which lie beyond in mountain shadow.

The descent was by a path which in winter becomes the bed of a torrent, steep and stony, zigzagging through a thick wood. Here, and when they had reached the level road leading into the village, their talk was in the same natural, light-hearted strain as before they rested. So at the inn where they dined, and during their drive homewards, — by the dark lake with its woods and precipices, out into the country of green hills, and thence, through Gosforth, on the long road descending seaward. Since their early departure, scarcely a cloud had passed over the sun, — a perfect day.

They alighted before reaching Seascale. Barfoot discharged his debt to the driver — who went on to bait[1] at the hotel — and walked with Rhoda for the last quarter of a mile. This was his own idea; Rhoda made no remark, but approved his discretion.

"It is six o'clock," said Everard, after a short silence. "You remember our arrangement. At eight, down on the shore."

"I should be much more comfortable in the arm-chair with a book."

"Oh, you have had enough of books. It's time to live."

"It's time to rest."

"Are you so very tired? Poor girl! The day has been rather too much for you."

Rhoda laughed.

"I could walk back again to Wastwater if it were necessary."

"Of course; I knew that. You are magnificent. At eight o'clock, then" —

Nothing more was said on the subject. When in sight of Rhoda's lodgings, they parted without hand-shaking.

Before eight, Everard was straying about the beach, watching the sun go down in splendour. He smiled to himself frequently. The hour had come for his last trial of Rhoda, and he felt some confidence as to the result. If her mettle endured his test, if she declared herself willing not only to abandon her avowed ideal of life, but to defy the world's opinion by becoming his wife without forms of mutual bondage, — she was the woman he had imagined, and by her side he would go cheerfully on his way as a married man. Legally married; the proposal of free union was to be a test only. Loving her as he had never thought to love, there still remained with him so much of the temper in which he first wooed her that he could be satisfied with nothing short of unconditional surrender. Delighting in her independence of mind, he still desired to see her in complete subjugation to him, to inspire her with unreflecting passion. Tame consent to matrimony was an every-day experience. Agnes Brissenden, he felt sure, would marry him whenever he chose to ask her — and would make one of the best wives conceivable. But of Rhoda Nunn he expected and demanded more than this. She must rise far above the level of ordinary intelligent women. She must manifest an absolute confidence in him — that was the true significance of his present motives. The censures and suspicions which she had not scrupled to confess in plain words must linger in no corner of her mind.

His heart throbbed with impatience for her coming. Come she would; it was not in Rhoda's nature to play tricks; if she had not meant to meet him, she would have said so, resolutely, as last night.

At a few minutes past the hour, he looked landward and saw her figure against the golden sky. She came down from the sand-bank very slowly, with careless, loitering step. He moved but a little way to meet her, and

---

1 To stop for food or rest.

then stood still. He had done his part; it was now hers to forego female privileges, to obey the constraint of love. The western afterglow touched her features, heightening the beauty Everard had learnt to see in them. Still she loitered, stooping to pick up a piece of seaweed; but still he kept his place, motionless, and she came nearer.

"Did you see the light of sunset on the mountains?"

"Yes," he replied.

"There has been no such evening since I came."

"And you wanted to sit at home with a book. That was no close for a perfect day."

"I found a letter from your cousin. She was with her friends the Goodalls yesterday."

"The Goodalls — I used to know them."

"Yes."

The word was uttered with significance. Everard understood the allusion, but did not care to show that he did.

"How does Mary get on without you?"

"There's no difficulty."

"Has she any one capable of taking your place?"

"Yes. Miss Vesper can do all that's necessary."

"Even to inspiring the girls with zeal for an independent life?"

"Perhaps even that."

They went along by the waves, in the warm-coloured twilight, until the houses of Seascale were hidden. Then Everard stopped.

"To-morrow we go to Coniston?" he said, smiling as he stood before her.

"You are going?"

"Do you think I can leave you?"

Rhoda's eyes fell. She held the long strip of seaweed with both hands, and tightened it.

"Do you *wish* me to leave you?" he added.

"You mean that we are to go through the lakes together — as we have been to-day?"

"No. I don't mean that."

Rhoda took a few steps onward, so that he remained standing behind. Another moment, and his arms had folded about her, his lips were on hers. She did not resist. His embrace grew stronger, and he pressed kiss after kiss upon her mouth. With exquisite delight he saw the deep crimson flush that transfigured her countenance; saw her look for one instant into his eyes, and was conscious of the triumphant gleam she met there.

"Do you remember my saying in the letter how I hungered to taste your lips? I don't know how I have refrained so long" —

"What is your love worth?" asked Rhoda, speaking with a great effort. She had dropped the seaweed, and one of her hands rested upon his shoulder, with a slight repelling pressure.

"Worth your whole life!" he answered, with a low, glad laugh.

"That is what I doubt. — Convince me of that."

"Convince you? With more kisses? — But what is *your* love worth?"

"Perhaps more than you yet understand. Perhaps more than you *can* understand."

"I will believe that, Rhoda. I know, at all events, that it is something of inestimable price. The knowledge has grown in me for a year and more."

"Let me stand away from you again. There is something more to be said before — No, let me be quite apart from you."

He released her, after one more kiss.

"Will you answer me a question with perfect truthfulness?"

Her voice was not quite steady, but she succeeded in looking at him with unflinching eyes.

"Yes, I will answer you *any* question."

"That is spoken like a man. Tell me, then — is there at this moment any woman living who has a claim upon you, — a moral claim?"

"No such woman exists."

"But — do we speak the same language?"

"Surely," he answered, with great earnestness. "There is no woman to whom I am bound by any kind of obligation."

A long wave rolled up, broke, and retreated, whilst Rhoda stood in silent uncertainty.

"I must put the question in another way. During the past month — the past three months — have you made profession of love — have you even pretended love — to any woman?"

"To no woman whatever," he answered firmly.

"That satisfies me."

"If I knew what is in your mind!" exclaimed Everard, laughing. "What sort of life have you imagined for me? Is this the result of Mary's talk?"

"Not immediately."

"Still, she planted the suspicion. Believe me, you have been altogether mistaken. I never was the kind of man Mary thought me. Some day you shall understand more about it, — in the meantime, my word must be enough. I have no thought of love for any woman but you. — Did I frighten you with those joking confessions in my letters? I wrote them purposely — as you must have seen. The mean, paltry jealousies of women such as one meets every day are so hateful to me. They argue such a lack of brains. If I were so unfortunate as to love a woman who looked sour when I praised a beautiful face, I would snap the bond between us like a bit of thread. But you are not one of those poor creatures."

He looked at her with some gravity.

"Should you think me a poor creature if I resented any kind of unfaithfulness? — whether love, in any noble sense, had part in it or not?"

"No. That is the reasonable understanding between man and wife. If I exact fidelity from you, and certainly I should, I must consider myself under the same obligation."

"You say 'man and wife.' Do you say it with the ordinary meaning?"

"Not as it applies to us. You know what I mean when I ask you to be my wife. If we cannot trust each other without legal bonds, any union between us would be unjustified."

Suppressing the agitation which he felt, he awaited her answer. They could still read each other's faces perfectly in a pale yellow light from across the sea. Rhoda's manifested an intense conflict.

"After all, you doubt of your love for me?" said Barfoot quietly.

That was not her doubt. She loved with passion, allowing herself to indulge the luxurious emotion as never yet. She longed once more to feel his arms about her. But even thus she could consider the vast issues of the step to which she was urged. The temptation to yield was very strong, for it seemed to her an easier and a nobler thing to proclaim her emancipation from social statutes, than to announce before her friends the simple news that she was about to marry. That announcement would excite something more than surprise. Mary Barfoot could not but smile with gentle irony; other women would laugh among themselves; the girls would feel a shock, as at the fall of one who had made heroic pretences. A sure way of averting this ridicule was by furnishing occasion for much graver astonishment. If it became known that she had taken a step such as few women would have dared to take — deliberately setting an example of new liberty — her position in the eyes of all who knew her remained one of proud independence. Rhoda's character was specially exposed to the temptation of such a motive. For months this argument had been in her mind, again and again she decided that the sensational step was preferable to a common-place renunciation of all she had so vehemently preached. And now that the moment of actual choice had come, she felt able to dare everything — as far as the danger concerned herself; but she perceived more strongly than hitherto that not only her own future was involved. How would such practical heresy affect Everard's position?

She uttered this thought.

"Are you willing, for the sake of this idea, to abandon all society but that of the very few people who would approve or tolerate what you have done?"

"I look upon the thing in this way. We are not called upon to declare our principles wherever we go. If we regard each other as married, why, we *are* married. I am no Quixote, hoping to convert the world. It is between you and me — our own sense of what is reasonable and dignified."

"But you would not make it a mere deception?"

"Mary would of course be told, and any one else you like."

She believed him entirely serious. Another woman might have suspected that he was merely trying her courage, either to assure himself of her love, or to gratify his vanity. But Rhoda's idealism enabled her to take him literally. She herself had for years maintained an exaggerated standard of duty and merit; desirous of seeing Everard in a nobler light than hitherto, she endeavoured to regard his scruple against formal wedlock as worthy of all respect.

"I can't answer you at once," she said, half turning away.

"You must. Here and at once."

The one word of assent would have satisfied him. This he obstinately required. He believed that it would confirm his love beyond any other satisfaction she could render him. He must be able to regard her as magnanimous, a woman who had proved herself worth living or dying for. And he must have the joy of subduing her to his will.

"No," said Rhoda firmly. "I can't answer you to-night. I can't decide so suddenly."

This was disingenuous, and she felt humiliated by her subterfuge. Anything but a sudden decision was asked of her. Before leaving Chelsea, she had foreseen this moment, and had made preparations for the possibility of never returning to Miss Barfoot's house, — knowing the nature of the proposal that would be offered to her. But the practical resolve needed a greater effort than she had imagined. Above all, she feared an ignominious failure of purpose after her word was given; *that* would belittle her in Everard's eyes, and so shame her in her own that all hope of happiness in marriage must be at an end.

"You are still doubtful of me, Rhoda."

He took her hand, and again drew her close. But she refused her lips.

"Or are you doubtful of your own love?"

"No. If I understand what love means, I love you."

"Then give me the kiss I am waiting for. You have not kissed me yet."

"I can't — until I am sure of myself — of my readiness" —

Her broken words betrayed the passion with which she was struggling. Everard felt her tremble against his side.

"Give me your hand," he whispered. "The left hand."

Before she could guess his purpose, he had slipped a ring upon her finger, a marriage ring. Rhoda started away from him, and at once drew off the perilous symbol.

"No — that proves to me I can't! What should we gain? You see, you dare not be quite consistent. It's only deceiving the people who don't know us."

"But I have explained to you. — The consistency is in our selves, our own minds" —

"Take it back. Custom is too strong for us. We should only play at defying it. Take this back — or I shall drop it on the sand."

Profoundly mortified, Everard restored the gold circlet to its hiding place, and stood gazing at the dim horizon. Some moments passed, then he heard his name murmured. He did not look round.

"Everard — dearest" —

Was that Rhoda's voice, so low, tender, caressing? It thrilled him, and with a silent laugh of scorn at his own folly, he turned to her, every thought burnt up in passion.

"Will you kiss me?"

For answer she laid her hands on his shoulders and gazed at him. Barfoot understood. He smiled constrainedly, and said in a low voice:

"You wish for that old, idle form —?"

"Not the religious form, which has no meaning for either of us. But" —

"You have been living here seven or eight days. Stay till the fifteenth, then we can get a licence from the registrar of the district. — Does that please you?"

Her eyes made reply.

"Do you love me any the less, Everard?"

"Kiss me."

She did, and consciousness was lost for them as their mouths clung together, and their hearts throbbed like one.

"Isn't it better?" Rhoda asked, as they walked back in the darkness. "Won't it make our life so much simpler and happier?"

"Perhaps."

"You know it will." She laughed joyously, trying to meet his look.

"Perhaps you are right."

"I shall let no one hear of it, until — Then let us go abroad."

"You dare not face Mary?"

"I dare, if you wish it. Of course she will laugh at me. They will all laugh at me."

"Why, you may laugh as well."

"But you have spoilt my life, you know. Such a grand life it might have been. Why did you come and interfere with me? And you have been so terribly obstinate."

"Of course; that's my nature. — But after all I have been weak."

"Yielding in one point that didn't matter to you at all? — It was the only way of making me sure that you loved me."

Barfoot laughed slightingly.

"And what if I needed the other proof that you loved *me*?"

CHAPTER XXVI.

THE UNIDEAL TESTED.

And neither was content.

Barfoot, over his cigar and glass of whisky at the hotel, fell into a mood of chagrin. The woman he loved would be his, and there was matter enough for ardent imagination in the indulgence of that thought; but his temper disturbed him. After all, he had not triumphed. As usual the woman had her way. She played upon his senses, and made him her obedient slave. To prolong the conflict would have availed nothing; Rhoda, doubtless, was in part actuated by the desire to conquer, and she knew her power over him. So it was a mere repetition of the old story — a marriage like any other. And how would it result?

She had great qualities; but was there not much in her that he must subdue, reform, if they were really to spend their lives together? Her energy of domination perhaps excelled his. Such a woman might be unable to concede him the liberty in marriage which theoretically she granted to be just. Perhaps she would torment him with restless jealousies, suspecting on every trivial occasion an infringement of her right. From that point of view, it would have been far wiser to persist in rejecting legal marriage, that her dependence upon him might be more complete. Later, if all went well, the concession could have been made — if, for instance, she became a mother. But then returned the exasperating thought that Rhoda had overcome his will. Was not that a beginning of evil augury?

To be sure, after marriage their relations would be different. He would not then be at the mercy of his senses. But how miserable to anticipate a long, perhaps bitter, struggle for predominance. After all, that could hardly come about. The commencement of any such discord would be the signal for separation. His wealth assured his freedom. He was not like the poor devils who must perforce live with an intolerable woman because they cannot support themselves and their families in different places. Need he entertain that worst of fears — the dread that his independence might fail him, subdued by his wife's will?

Free as he boasted himself from lover's silliness, he had magnified Rhoda's image. She was not the glorious rebel he had pictured. Like any other woman, she mistrusted her love without the sanction of society. — Well, that was something relinquished, lost. Marriage would after all be a compromise. He had not found his ideal — though in these days it assuredly existed.

And Rhoda, sitting late in the little lodging-house parlour, visited her soul with questionings no less troublesome. Everard was not satisfied with her. He had yielded, perhaps more than half contemptuously, to what he thought a feminine weakness. In going with her to the registrar's office, he would feel himself to be acting an ignoble part. Was it not a bad beginning, to rule him against his conscience?

She had triumphed splendidly. In the world's eye, this marriage of hers was far better than any she could reasonably have hoped, and her heart approved it with rapture. At a stage in life when she had sternly reconciled herself never to know a man's love, this love had sought her with passionate persistency of which even a beautiful young girl might feel proud. She had no beauty; she was loved for her mind, her very self. — But must not Everard's conception of her have suffered? In winning her, had he obtained the woman of his desire?

Why was she not more politic? Would it not have been possible to gratify him, and yet to gain his consent to legal marriage? By first of all complying, she would have seemed to confirm all he believed of her; and then, his ardour at height, how simple to point out to him — without entreaty, without show of much concern — that by neglecting formalities they gained absolutely nothing. Artifice of that kind was perhaps demanded by the mere circumstances. Possibly he himself would have welcomed it, — after the grateful sense of inspiring such complete devotion. It is the woman's part to exercise tact; she had proved herself lamentably deficient in that quality.

To-morrow she must study his manner. If she discerned any serious change, any grave indication of disappointment —

What was her life to be? At first, they would travel together; but before long it might be necessary to have a settled home, and what then would be her social position, her duties and pleasures? Housekeeping, mere domesticities, could never occupy her for more than the smallest possible part of each day. Having lost one purpose in life, dignified, absorbing, likely to extend its sphere as time went on, what other could she hope to substitute for it?

Love of husband — perhaps of child. There must be more than that. Rhoda did not deceive herself as to the requirements of her nature. Practical activity in some intellectual undertaking; a share — nay, leadership — in some "movement"; contact with the revolutionary life of her time; — the impulses of her heart once satisfied, these things would again claim her. But how if Everard resisted such tendencies? Was he in truth capable of respecting her individuality? Or would his strong instinct of lordship urge him to direct his wife as a dependant, to impose upon her his own view of things? She doubted whether he had much genuine sympathy with woman's emancipation, as she understood it. Yet in no particular had her convictions changed; nor would they change. She herself was no longer one of the "odd women"; fortune had — or seemed to have — been kind to her; none the less her sense of a mission remained. No longer an example of perfect female independence, and unable therefore to use the same language as before, she might illustrate woman's claim of equality in marriage. — If her experience proved no obstacle.

* * * * *

Next morning, as had been agreed, they met at some distance from Seascale, and spent two or three hours together. There was little danger of observation, unless by a casual peasant; for the most part, their privacy could not have been more secure in a locked chamber. Lest curiosity should be excited by his making inquiries at the hotel, Barfoot proposed to walk over to Gosforth, the nearest town, this afternoon, and learn where the registrar for the locality of Seascale might be found. By neither was allusion made to their difference of last evening, but Rhoda distressed herself by imagining a diminished fervour in her companion; he seemed unusually silent and meditative, and was content to hold her hand now and then.

"Shall you stay here all the week?" she inquired.

"If you wish me to."

"You will find it wearisome."

"Impossible, with you here. But if I run up to London for a day or two, it might be better. There are preparations. — We shall go first of all to my rooms" —

"I would rather not have stayed in London."

"I thought you might wish to make purchases."

"Let us go to some other town, and spend a few days there before leaving England."

"Very well. Manchester, or Birmingham."

"You speak rather impatiently," said Rhoda, looking at him with an uneasy smile. "Let it be London, if you prefer" —

"On no account. It's all indifferent to me, so long as we get safely away together. Every man is impatient of these preliminaries. — Yes, in that case I must of course go up to London. To-morrow, and back on Saturday?"

A shower of rain caused them some discomfort. Through the afternoon it still rained at intervals, whilst Barfoot was discharging his business at Gosforth. He was to see Rhoda again at eight o'clock, and as the time threatened to hang heavily on his hands, he returned by a long détour, reaching the Seascale hotel about half-past six. No sooner had he entered than there was delivered to him a letter, brought by messenger an hour or two ago. It surprised him to recognize Rhoda's writing on the envelope, which seemed to contain at least two sheets of note-paper. What now? Some whimsey? Agitated and annoyed by the anticipation of trouble, he went apart and broke the letter open.

First appeared an enclosure, — a letter in his cousin Mary's writing. He turned to the other sheet, and read these lines:

"I send you something that has come by post this afternoon. Please to bring it with you when you meet me at eight o'clock — if you still care to do so."

His face flushed with anger. What contemptible woman's folly was this? "If you still care to do so" — and written in a hand that shook. If this was to be his experience of matrimonial engagement. — What rubbish had Mary been communicating?

"MY DEAR RHODA, — I have just gone through a very painful scene, and I feel bound to let you know of it without delay, as it *may* concern you. This evening (Monday), when I came home from Great Portland Street, Emma told me that Mr. Widdowson had called, that he wished to see me as soon as possible, and would be here again at six o'clock. He came, and his appearance alarmed me, he was looking so dreadfully ill. Without preface, he said, 'My wife has left me; she has gone to her sister, and refuses to return.' This was astonishing, in itself, and I wondered still more why he should come and tell *me* about it in so strange a way. The explanation followed very promptly, and you may judge how I heard it. Mr. Widdowson said that his wife had been behaving very badly of late; that he had discovered several falsehoods she had told him as to her employment during absences from home, in day time and evening. Having cause for suspecting the worst, he last Saturday engaged a private detective to follow Mrs. Widdowson wherever she went. This man saw her go to the flats in Bayswater where Everard lives, and knock at *his* door. As no one replied, she went away for a time, and returned, but again found no one at home. This being at once reported to Mr. Widdowson, he asked his wife where she had been that afternoon. The answer was false; she said she had been here, with me. Thereupon he lost command of himself, and charged her with infidelity. She refused to offer any kind of explanation, but denied that she was guilty, and at once left the house. Since, she has utterly refused to see him. Her sister can only report that Monica is very ill, and that she charges her husband with accusing her falsely.

"He had come to me, he said, in unspeakable anguish and helplessness, to ask me whether I had seen anything suspicious in the relations between Monica and my cousin, when they met at this house or elsewhere. A nice question! Of course I could only reply that it had never even occurred to me to observe them — that to my knowledge they had met so rarely — and that I should never have dreamt of suspecting Monica. 'Yet you see she *must* be guilty,' he kept on repeating. I said no, that I thought her visit *might* have an innocent significance — though I couldn't suggest why she had told falsehoods. Then he inquired what I knew about Everard's present movements. I answered that I had every reason to think he was out of town, but didn't know when he went, or when he might be expected to return. The poor man was grievously dissatisfied; he looked at me as if I were in a base plot against him. It was an immense relief when he went away, after begging me to respect his confidence.

"I write very hurriedly, as you see. That I *ought* to write, is, I think, clear — though I may be doing lamentable mischief. I cannot credit this charge against Mrs. Widdowson; there must surely be some explanation.

— If you have already left Seascale, no doubt this letter will be forwarded.

"Ever yours, dear Rhoda,
"MARY BARFOOT."

Everard laughed bitterly. The completeness of the case against him in Rhoda's eyes must be so overwhelming, and his absolute innocence made it exasperating to have to defend himself. How, indeed, was he to defend himself?

The story was strange enough. Could he be right in the interpretation which at once suggested itself to his mind — or perhaps to his vanity? He remembered the meeting with Mrs. Widdowson, near his abode, on Friday. He recollected, moreover, the signs of interest in himself which, as he now thought, she had shown on previous occasions. Had the poor little woman — doubtless miserable with her husband — actually let herself fall in love with him? But, even in that case, what a reckless thing to do — to come to his rooms! Why, she must have been driven by a despair that blinded her to all sense of delicacy! Perhaps, had he been at home, she would have made a pretence of wishing to speak about Rhoda Nunn. That was imprudent behaviour of his, making such a person his confidante. But he was tempted by his liking for her.

"By Jove!" he muttered, overcome by the thought. "I'm glad I was not at home!"

But then — he had told her that he was going away on Saturday. How could she expect to find him? The hour of her visit was not stated; probably she hoped to catch him before he left. And was her appearance in the neighbourhood on Friday — her troubled aspect — to be explained as an abortive attempt to have a private interview with him?

The queerest affair — and maddening in its issues! Rhoda was raging with jealousy. Well, he too would rage. And without affectation. It was strange that he felt almost glad of a ground of quarrel with Rhoda. All day he had been in an irritable temper, and so far as he could understand himself it was due to resentment of his last night's defeat. He thought of Rhoda as ardently as ever, but an element that was very like brutality had intruded into his emotions; that was his reason for refraining from caresses this morning; he could not trust himself.

He would endure no absurdities. If Rhoda did not choose to accept his simple assurance — let her take the consequences. Even now, perhaps, he would bring her to her knees before him. Let her wrong him by baseless accusation! Then it would no longer be *he* who sued for favour. He would whistle her down the wind, and await her penitent reappearance. Sooner or later, his pride and hers, the obstinacy in their natures, must battle it out; better that it should be now, before the irrevocable step had been taken.

He ate his dinner with savage appetite, and drank a good deal more wine than of wont. Then he smoked until the last minute of delay that his engagement allowed. — Of course she had sent the letter to the hotel because he might be unable to read it in twilight. Wise precaution. And he was glad to have been able to think the matter over, to work himself into reasonable wrath. If ever man did well to be angry — !

There she was, down by the edge of the waves. She would not turn to see if he were coming; he felt sure of that. Whether she heard his footsteps he could not tell. When quite close to her, he exclaimed:

"Well, Rhoda?"

She must have known of his approach, for she gave no start. She faced slowly to him. No trace of tears on her countenance; no, Rhoda was above that. Gravity of the sternest — that was all.

"Well," he continued, "what have you to say to me?"

"I? — Nothing."

"You mean that it is my business to explain what Mary has told you. — I can't, so there's an end of it."

"What do you mean by that?" she asked, in clear, distant tones.

"Precisely what I say, Rhoda. — And I am obliged to ask what *you* mean by this odd way of speaking to me. What has happened since we parted this morning?"

Rhoda could not suppress her astonishment; she gazed fixedly at him.

"If you can't explain this letter, who can?"

"I suppose Mrs. Widdowson would be able to account for her doings. I certainly am not able to. And it seems to me that you are strangely forgetful of something that passed between us yesterday."

"Of what?" she asked coldly, her face, which was held proudly up, turning towards the sea.

"Evidently you accuse me of concealing something from you. Please to remember a certain plain question you asked me, and the equally plain answer I gave."

He detected the beginning of a smile about her rigid lips.

"I remember," she said.

"And you can still behave to me with indignation? — Surely the indignation should be on my side. You are telling me that I deceived you."

For a moment Rhoda lost her self-control.

"How can I help thinking so?" she exclaimed, with a gesture of misery. "What can this letter mean? Why should she go to your rooms?"

"I simply don't know, Rhoda."

He preserved the show of calmness just because he saw that it provoked her to anger.

"She has never been there before?"

"Never, to my knowledge."

Rhoda watched his face with greedy attention. She seemed to find there a confirmation of her doubts. Indeed, it was impossible for her to credit his denials, after what she had observed in London, and the circumstances which, even before Mary's letter, had made her suspicious.

"When did you last see Mrs. Widdowson?"

"No, I sha'n't consent to be cross-examined," replied Everard, with a disdainful smile. "As soon as you refuse to accept my word, it's folly to ask further questions. You don't believe me. Say it honestly, and let us understand each other."

"I have good reason for thinking that you could explain Mrs. Widdowson's behaviour if you chose."

"Exactly. There's no misunderstanding *that*. And if I get angry, I am an unpardonable brute. — Come now, you can't be offended if I treat you as simply my equal, Rhoda. Let me test your sincerity. Suppose I had seen you talking somewhere with some man who seemed to interest you very much, and then — to-day, let us say — I heard that he had called upon you when you were alone. I turn with a savage face, and accuse you of grossly deceiving me — in the worst sense. What would your answer be?"

"These are idle suppositions," she exclaimed scornfully.

"But the case is possible, you must admit. I want you to realize what I am feeling. — In such a case as that, you could only turn from me with contempt. How else can I behave to *you* — conscious of my innocence, yet in the nature of things unable to prove it?"

"Appearances are very strongly against you."

"That's an accident — to me quite unaccountable. If I charged you with dishonour, you would only have your word to offer in reply. So it is with me. And my word is bluntly rejected. You try me rather severely."

Rhoda kept silence.

"I know what you are thinking. My character was previously none of the best. There is a prejudice against me in such a matter as this. — Well, you shall hear some more plain speech, altogether for your good. My record is not immaculate; nor, I believe, is any man's. I have gone here and there, and have had my adventures, like other men. One of them you have heard about — the story of that girl Amy Drake — the subject of Mrs. Goodall's righteous wrath. — You shall know the truth, and if it offends your ears, I can't help it. The girl simply threw herself into my arms, on a railway journey, when we met by pure chance."

"I don't care to hear that," said Rhoda, turning away.

"But you *shall* hear it. That story has predisposed you to believe the worst things of me. If I hold you by force, you shall hear every word of it. Mary seems to have given you mere dark hints" —

"No; she has told me the details. I know it all."

"From their point of view. Very well; that saves me a lot of narrative. What those good people didn't understand was the girl's character. They thought her a helpless innocent; she was a — I'll spare you the word. She simply planned to get me into her power, — thought I should be forced to marry her. It's the kind of thing that happens far oftener than you would suppose; that's the reason why men so often smile in what you would call a brutal way, when certain stories are told to other men's discredit. You will have to take this into account, Rhoda, before you reach satisfactory results on the questions that have occupied you so much. I was not in the least responsible for Amy Drake's desertion of creditable paths. At the worst, I behaved foolishly; and knowing I had done so, knowing how thankless it was to try and clear myself at her expense, I let people say what they would; it didn't matter. — And you don't believe me; I can see you don't. Sexual pride won't let you believe me. In such a case, the man must necessarily be the villain."

"What you mean by saying you only behaved 'foolishly,' I can't understand."

"Perhaps not, and I can't explain as I once did in telling the story to a man, a friend of mine. But however strict your moral ideas, you will admit that a girl of thoroughly bad character isn't a subject for the outcry that was raised about Miss Amy Drake. By taking a little trouble, I could have brought things to light which would have given worthy Mrs. Goodall, and cousin Mary, a great shock. — Well, that's enough. I have never pretended to sanctity, but on the other hand I have never behaved like a scoundrel. You charge me, deliberately, with being a scoundrel, and I defend myself as best I can. You argue that the man who would mislead an innocent girl and then cast her off is more likely than not to be guilty in a case like this of Mrs. Widdowson, when appearances are decidedly against him. There is only my word in each instance. The question is — will you accept my word?"

For a wonder, their privacy was threatened by the approach of two men who were walking this way from Seascale. Voices in conversation caused Rhoda to look round; Barfoot had already observed the strangers.

"Let us go up on to the higher sand," he said.

Without reply, Rhoda accompanied him, and for several minutes they exchanged no word. The men, talking and laughing loudly, went by; they seemed to be tourists of a kind that do not often trouble this quiet spot on the coast; their cigars glowed in the dusk.

"After all this, what have you to say to me, Rhoda?"

"Will you please to give me your cousin's letter?" she said coldly.

"Here it is. — Now you will go back to your lodgings, and sit with that letter open before you half through the night. You will make yourself unutterably wretched, and all for what?"

He felt himself once more in danger of weakness. Rhoda, in her haughty, resentful mood, was very attractive to him. He was tempted to take her in his arms, and kiss her until she softened, pleaded with him. He wished to see her shed tears. But the voice in which she now spoke to him was far enough from tearfulness.

"You must prove to me that you have been wrongly suspected."

Ah, that was to be her line of conduct. She believed her power over him was absolute. She stood on her dignity, would bring him to supplication, would give him all the trouble she could before she professed herself satisfied.

"How am I to prove it?" he asked bluntly.

"If there was nothing wrong between you and Mrs. Widdowson, there must be some very simple explanation of her coming to your rooms, and being so anxious to see you."

"And it is my business to discover that explanation?"

"Can it be mine?"

"It must either be yours, Rhoda, or no one's. I shall take no single step in the matter."

The battle was declared. Each stood at full height, pertinacious, resolved on victory.

"You are putting yourself wildly in the wrong," Everard continued. "By refusing to take my word, you make it impossible for me to hope that we could live together as we imagined."

The words fell upon her heart like a crushing weight. But she could not yield. Last night she had suffered in his opinion by urging what he thought a weak, womanly scruple; she had condescended to plead tenderly with him, and had won her cause. Now she would prevail in another way. If he were telling the truth, he should acknowledge that natural suspicion made it incumbent upon him to clear so strange a case of its difficulties. If he were guilty of deception, as she still believed, though willing to admit to herself that Monica might be most at fault, that there might have been no actual wrong-doing between them — he should confess with humblest penitence, and beseech pardon. Impossible to take any other attitude. Impossible to marry him with this doubt in her mind — equally out of the question to seek Monica, and humiliate herself by making inquiries on such a subject. Guilty or not, Monica would regard her with secret disdain, with woman's malice. Were she *able* to believe him, that indeed would be a grand consummation of their love, an ideal union of heart and soul. Listening to him, she had tried to put faith in his indignant words. But it was useless. The incredulity she could not help must either part them for ever, or be to her an occasion of new triumph.

"I don't refuse to take your word," she said, with conscious quibbling. "I only say that your name must be cleared from suspicion. Mr. Widdowson is sure to tell his story to other people. Why has his wife left him?"

"I neither know nor care."

"You must prove to me that you are not the cause of it."

"I shall make not the slightest effort to do so."

Rhoda began to move away from him. As he kept silence, she walked on in the Seascale direction. He followed at a distance of a few yards, watching her movements. When they had gone so far that five minutes more must bring them within sight of the hotel, Everard spoke.

"Rhoda!"

She paused and awaited him.

"You remember that I was going to London to-morrow. It seems that I had better go, and not trouble to return."

"That is for you to decide."

"For you, rather."

"I have said all that I *can* say."

"And so have I — But surely you must be unconscious how grossly you are insulting me."

"I want only to understand what purpose Mrs. Widdowson had in going to your rooms."

"Then why not ask her? You are friends. She would doubtless tell you the truth."

"If she comes to me voluntarily, to make an explanation, I will hear it. But I shall not ask her."

"Your view of the fitness of things is that *I* should request her to wait upon you for that purpose?"

"There are others who can act for you."

"Very well. Then we are at a deadlock. It seems to me that we had better shake hands like sensible people, and say good-bye."

"Much better — if it seems so to you."

The time for emotional help was past. In very truth they had nothing more to say to each other, being now hardened in obstinacy. Each suffered from the other's coldness, each felt angry with the other's stubborn refusal to concede a point of dignity. Everard put out his hand.

"When you are ready to say that you have used me very ill, I shall remember only yesterday. Till then — good-bye, Rhoda."

She made a show of taking his hand, but said nothing. And so they parted.

At eight o'clock next morning, Barfoot was seated in the southward train. He rejoiced that his strength of will had thus far asserted itself. Of final farewell to Rhoda he had no thought whatever. Her curiosity would of course compel her to see Monica; one way or another she would learn that he was blameless. His part was to keep aloof from her, and to wait for her inevitable submission.

Violent rain was beating upon the carriage windows; it drove from the mountains, themselves invisible, though dense low clouds marked their position. Poor Rhoda! She would not have a very cheerful day at Seascale. Perhaps she would follow him by a later train. Certain it was that she must be suffering intensely, — and that certainly rejoiced him. The keener her suffering, the sooner her submission. Oh, but the submission should be perfect! He had seen her in many moods, but not yet in the anguish of broken pride. She must shed tears before him, declare her spirit worn and subjugated by torment of jealousy and fear. Then he would raise her, and seat her in the place of honour, and fall down at her feet, and fill her soul with rapture.

Many times, between Seascale and London, he smiled in anticipation of that hour.

CHAPTER XXVII.

THE REASCENT.

Whilst the rain pelted, and it did so until afternoon, Rhoda sat in her little parlour, no whit less miserable than Barfoot imagined. She could not be sure whether Everard had gone to London; at the last moment, reflection or emotion might have detained him. Early in the morning she had sent to post a letter for Miss Barfoot, written last night; a letter which made no revelation of her feelings, but merely expressed a cold curiosity to hear anything that might become known as to the course of Mr. Widdowson's domestic troubles. "You may still write to this address; if I leave, letters shall be forwarded."

When the sky cleared, she went out. In the evening she again rambled about the shore. Evidently Barfoot had gone; if still here, he would have watched and joined her.

Her solitude now grew insufferable, yet she could not decide whither to betake herself. The temptation to return to London was very strong, but pride prevailed against it. Everard might perhaps go to see his cousin, and relate all that had happened at Seascale, justifying himself as he had here done. Whether Miss Barfoot became aware of the story or not, Rhoda could not reconcile it with her self-respect to curtail the stipulated three weeks of holiday. Rather she would strain her nerves to the last point of endurance, — and if she were not suffering, then never did woman suffer.

Another cheerless day helped her to make up her mind. She cared nothing now for lake and mountain; human companionship was her supreme need. By the earliest train next day she started, not for London, but for her brother's home in Somerset, and there she remained until it was time to return to work. Miss Barfoot wrote twice in the interval, saying that she had heard nothing more of Monica. Of Everard she made no mention.

Rhoda got back again to Chelsea on the appointed Saturday afternoon. Miss Barfoot knew when she would arrive, but was not at home to meet her, and did not return till a couple of hours had passed. They met at length as if nothing remarkable had occurred during the three weeks. Mary, if she felt any solicitude, effectually concealed it; Rhoda talked as if very glad to be at home again, explaining her desertion of the lake country by the bad weather that prevailed there. It was not till after dinner that the inevitable subject came up between them.

"Have you seen Everard since you went away?" Miss Barfoot began by asking.

So he had not been here to tell his story and plead his cause — or it seemed not.

"Yes, I saw him at Seascale," Rhoda replied, without sign of emotion.

"Before or after that news came?"

"Both before and after. I showed him your letter, and all he had to say was that he knew nothing of the affair."

"That's all he has to say to me. I haven't seen him. A letter I sent to his address was answered, after a week, from a place I never heard of — Arromanches, in Normandy. The shortest and rudest letter I ever had from him. Practically he told me to mind my own business. — And there things stand."

Rhoda smiled a little, conscious of the extreme curiosity her friend must be feeling, and determined not to gratify it. For by this time, though her sunken cheeks were hard to reconcile with the enjoyment of a summer holiday, she had matured a resolve to betray nothing of what she had gone through. Her state of mind resembled that of the ascetic who has arrived at a morbid delight in self-torture. She regarded the world with an intense bitterness, and persuaded herself not only that the thought of Everard Barfoot was hateful to her soul, but that sexual love had become, and would ever be, to her an impure idea, a vice of blood.

"I suppose," she said carelessly, "Mr. Widdowson will try to divorce his wife."

"I am in dread of that. — But they may have made it up."

"Of course you have no doubt of her guilt?"

Mary tried to understand the hard, austere face, with its touch of cynicism. Conjecture as to its meaning was not difficult, but, in the utter absence of information, certainty there could be none. Under any circumstances, it was to be expected that Rhoda would think and speak of Mrs. Widdowson no less severely than of the errant Bella Royston.

"I have *some* doubt," was Miss Barfoot's answer. "But I should be glad of some one else's favourable opinion to help my charity."

"Miss Madden hasn't been here, you see. She certainly would have come, if she had felt convinced that her sister was wronged."

"Unless a day or two saw the end of the trouble, — when naturally none of them would say any more about it."

This was the possibility which occupied Rhoda's reflections as long as she lay awake that night.

Her feelings on entering the familiar bedroom were very strange. Even before starting for her holiday, she had bidden it good-bye, and at Seascale, that night following upon the "perfect day," she had thought of it as a part of her past life, a place abandoned for ever, already infinitely remote. Her first sensation when she looked upon the white bed was one of disgust; she thought it would be impossible to use this room hence-forth, and that she must ask Miss Barfoot to let her change to another. To-night she did not restore any of the ornaments which were lying packed up. The scent of the room revived so many hours of conflict, of hope, that it caused her a sick faintness. In frenzy of detestation, she cursed the man who had so disturbed and sullied the swift, pure stream of her life.

Arromanches, in Normandy —? On Sunday she sought the name on a map, but it was not marked, being doubtless too insignificant. Improbable that he had gone to such a place alone; he was enjoying himself with friends, careless what became of her. Having allowed all this time to go by, he would never seek her again. He found that her will was the equal of his own, and, as he could not rule her, she was numbered among the women who had afforded him interesting experiences, to be thought of seriously no more.

During the next week she threw herself with energy upon her work, stifling the repugnance with which at first it affected her, and seeming at length to recover the old enthusiasm. This was the only way of salvation. Idleness and absence of purpose would soon degrade her in a sense she had never dreamt of. She made a plan of daily occupation, which by leaving not a vacant moment from early morning to late at night, should give her the sleep of utter weariness. New studies were begun in the hour or two before breakfast. She even restricted her diet, and ate only just enough to support life, rejecting wine and everything that was most agreeable to her palate.

She desired to speak privately with Mildred Vesper, and opportunity might have been made, but, as part of her scheme of self-subdual, this conversation was postponed until the second week. It took place one evening when work was over.

"I have been wanting to ask you," Rhoda began, "whether you have any news of Mrs. Widdowson."

"I wrote to her not long ago, and she answered from a new address. She said she had left her husband, and would never go back to him."

Rhoda nodded gravely.

"Then what I had heard was true. You haven't seen her?"

"She asked me not to come. She is living with her sister."

"Did she give you any reason for the separation from her husband?"

"None," answered Mildred. "But she said it was no secret; that every one knew. That's why I haven't spoken to you about it — as I should have done otherwise, after our last conversation."

"The fact is no secret," said Rhoda coldly. "But why will she offer no explanation?"

Mildred shook her head, signifying inability to make any satisfactory reply, and there the dialogue ended; for Rhoda could not proceed in it without appearing to encourage scandal. The hope of eliciting some suggestive information had failed; but whether Mildred had really disclosed all she knew seemed doubtful.

At the end of the week, Miss Barfoot left home for her own holiday; she was going to Scotland, and would be away for nearly the whole of September. At this time of year the work in Great Portland Street was very light; not much employment offered for the type-writers, and the pupils numbered only about half a dozen. Nevertheless, it pleased Rhoda to have the establishment under her sole direction; she desired authority, and by magnifying the importance of that which now fell into her hands, she endeavoured to sustain herself under the secret misery which, for all her efforts, weighed no less upon her as time went on. It was a dreary make-believe. On the first night of solitude at Chelsea, she shed bitter tears; and not only wept, but agonized in mute frenzy, the passions of her flesh torturing her until she thought of death as a refuge. Now she whispered the name of her lover with every word and phrase of endearment that her heart could suggest; the next moment she cursed him with the fury of deadliest hatred. In the half-delirium of sleeplessness, she revolved wild, impossible schemes for revenging herself, or, as the mood changed, all but resolved to sacrifice everything to her love, to accuse herself of ignoble jealousy, and entreat forgiveness. Of many woeful nights, this was the worst she had yet suffered.

It recalled to her with much vividness a memory of girlhood, or indeed of childhood. She thought of that figure in the dim past, that rugged, harsh-featured man, who had given her the first suggestion of independence; thrice her own age, yet the inspirer of such tumultuous emotion in her ignorant heart; her friend at Clevedon — Mr. Smithson. A question from Mary Barfoot had caused her to glance back at him across the years, but only for an instant, and with self-mockery. What she now endured was the ripe intensity of a woe that fell upon her, at fifteen, when Mr. Smithson passed from her sight and away for ever. Childish folly; but the misery of it, the tossing at night, the blank outlook! How contemptible to revive such sensations, with mature intellect, after so long and stern a discipline!

Dreading the Sunday, so terrible in its depressing effect upon the lonely and unhappy, she breakfasted as soon as possible, and left home — simply to walk, to exert herself physically, that fatigue and sleep might follow. There was a dull sky, but no immediate fear of rain; the weather brightened a little towards noon. Careless of the direction, she walked on and on until the last maddening church-bell had ceased its clangour; she was far out in the western suburbs, and weariness began to check her quick pace. Then she turned back. Without intending it, she passed by Mrs. Cosgrove's house, or rather would have passed, when she saw Mrs. Cosgrove at the dining-room window, making signs to her. In a moment the door opened, and she went in. She was glad of this accident, for the social lady might have something to tell about Mrs. Widdowson, who often visited her.

"In mercy, come and talk to me!" exclaimed Mrs. Cosgrove. "I am quite alone, and feel as if I could hang myself. Are you obliged to go anywhere?"

"No. I was having a walk."

"A walk? What astonishing energy! It never occurs to me to take a walk in London. I came from the country last night, and expected to find my sister here, but she won't arrive till Tuesday. I have been standing at the window for an hour, getting crazy with *ennui*."

They went to the drawing-room. It was not long before Mrs. Cosgrove made an allusion which enabled Rhoda to speak of Mrs. Widdowson. For a month or more Mrs. Cosgrove had seen and heard nothing of her; she had been out of town all the time. Rhoda hesitated, but could not keep silence on the subject that had become a morbid pre-occupation of her mind. She told as much as she knew — excepting the suspicion against Everard Barfoot.

"It doesn't in the least surprise me," said the listener, with interest. "I saw they wouldn't be able to live together very well. Without children, the thing was impossible. Of course she has told you all about it?"

"I haven't seen her since it happened."

"Do you know, I always have a distinct feeling of pleasure when I hear of married people parting. — How horrible that would seem to some of our good friends! But it isn't a malicious pleasure; there's nothing personal in it. As I have told you before, I think, I led a very contented life with my husband. But marriage in general is *such* humbug — you forgive the word."

"Of course it is," assented Rhoda, laughing with forced gaiety.

"I am glad of anything that seems to threaten it as an institution — in its present form. A scandalous divorce-case is a delight to me, — anything that makes it evident how much misery would be spared if we could civilize ourselves in this respect. There are women whose conduct I think personally detestable, and whom yet I can't help thanking for their assault upon social laws. We shall have to go through a stage of anarchy, you know, before reconstruction begins. Yes, in that sense I am an anarchist. — Seriously, I believe if a few men and women in prominent position would contract marriages of the free kind, without priest or lawyer, openly and defiantly, they would do more benefit to their kind than in any other possible way. I don't declare this opinion to every one, but only because I am a coward. Whatever one believes with heart and soul, one ought to make known."

Rhoda wore a look of anxious reflection.

"It needs a great deal of courage," she said. "To take that step, I mean."

"Of course. We need martyrs. — And yet I doubt whether the martyrdom would be very long, or very trying, to intellectual people. A woman of brains who boldly acted upon her conviction would have no lack of congenial society. The best people are getting more liberal than they care to confess to each other. Wait until some one puts the matter to the test, and you will see."

Rhoda became so busy with her tumultuous thoughts, that she spoke only a word now and then, allowing Mrs. Cosgrove to talk at large on this engrossing theme.

"Where is Mrs. Widdowson living?" the revolutionist at length inquired.

"I don't know. But I can get you her address."

"Pray do. I shall go and see her. We are quite friendly enough for me to do so without impertinence."

Having lunched with her acquaintance, Rhoda went in the afternoon to Mildred Vesper's lodgings. Miss Vesper was at home, reading, in her usual placid mood. She gave Rhoda the address that was on Mrs. Widdowson's last brief note, and that evening Rhoda sent it to Mrs. Cosgrove by letter.

In two days she received a reply. Mrs. Cosgrove had called upon Mrs. Widdowson at her lodgings at Clapham. "She is ill, wretched, and unwilling to talk. I could only stay about a quarter of an hour, and to ask questions was impossible. She mentioned your name, and appeared very anxious to hear about you; but when I asked whether she would like you to call she grew timid all at once, and said she hoped you wouldn't unless you really desired to see her. Poor thing! Of course I don't know what it all means, but I came away with maledictions on marriage in my heart — one is always safe in indulging that feeling."

A week or so after this, there arrived for Miss Barfoot a letter from Everard. The postmark was Ostend.

Never before had Rhoda been tempted to commit a breach of confidence such as in any one else she would have scorned beyond measure. She had heard, of course, of people secretly opening letters with the help of steam; whether it could be done with absolute security from detection, she did not feel sure, but her thoughts dwelt on the subject for several hours. It was terrible to hold this letter of Everard's writing, and yet be obliged to send it away without knowledge of the contents, which perhaps gravely concerned her. She could not ask Miss Barfoot to let her know what Everard had written. The information might perhaps be voluntarily granted; but perhaps not.

To steam the back of the envelope — would it not leave marks, a rumpling or discolouration? Even to be suspected of such dishonour would be more bitter to her than death. Could she even think of it? How she was degraded by this hateful passion, which wrought in her like a disease!

With two others which that day had arrived, she put the letter into a large envelope, and so dispatched it. But no satisfaction rewarded her; her heart raged against the world, against every law of life.

When, in a few days, a letter come to her from Miss Barfoot, she tore it open, and there — yes, there was Everard's handwriting. Mary had sent the communication for her to read.

"DEAR COUSIN MARY,

"After all, I was rather too grumpy in my last note to you. But my patience had been desperately tried. I have gone through a good deal; now at last I am recovering sanity, and can admit that you had no choice but to ask those questions. I know and care nothing about Mrs. Widdowson. By her eccentric behaviour she either did me a great injury or a great service, I'm not quite sure which, but I incline to the latter view. Here is a conundrum — not very difficult to solve, I dare say.

"Do you know anything about Arromanches? A very quiet little spot on the Normandy coast; you get to it by an hour's coach from Bayeux. Not infested by English. I went there on an invitation from the Brissendens, who discovered the place last year. Excellent people, these. I like them better the more I know of them. A great deal of quiet liberality — even extreme liberality — in the two girls; they would suit you, I am sure. Well instructed. Agnes, the younger, reads half-a-dozen languages, and shames me by her knowledge of all sorts of things. And yet delightfully feminine.

"As they were going to Ostend, I thought I might as well follow them, and we continue to see each other pretty frequently.

"By-the-bye, I shall have to find new quarters if I come back to London. The engineer, back from Italy after a longer absence than he anticipated, wants his flat, and of course must have it. But then, I may not come back at all, except to gather my traps. I shall not call on you, unless I have heard that you don't doubt the assurance I have now twice given.

"Your profligate relative,
"E.B."

"I think," wrote Mary, "that we may safely believe him. Such a lie would be too bad; he is incapable of it. Remember, I have never charged him with falsehood. I shall write and tell him that I accept his word. Has it, or has it not, occurred to you to see Mrs. Widdowson herself? Or, if there are insuperable objections, why not see Miss Madden? — We talk to each other in a sort of cipher, dear Rhoda. Well, I desire nothing but your good, as I think you know, and you must decide for yourself where that good lies."

Everard's letter put Rhoda beside herself with wrath. In writing it, he knew it would come into her hands; he hoped to sting her with jealousy. So Mrs. Widdowson had done him a service. He was free to devote himself to Agnes Brissenden, with her six languages, her extreme liberality, her feminine charm.

If she could not crush out her love for this man, she would poison herself, — as she had so often decided she would do if ever some hopeless malady, such as cancer, took hold upon her —

And be content to feed his vanity? To give him the lifelong reflection that, for love of him, a woman excelled by few in qualities of brain and heart, had died like a rat?

She walked about the rooms, here and there, upstairs and downstairs, in a fever of unrest. — After all, was he not behaving in the very way she ought to desire? Was he not helping her to hate him? He struck at her with unmanly blows, thinking, no doubt, to quell her pride, and bring her to him in prostrate humility. Never! Even if it were proved in the clearest way that she ought to have believed him, she would make no submission. If he loved her, he must woo once more.

But the suggestion in Mary's letter was not fruitless. When she had thought over it for a day or two, she wrote to Virginia Madden, asking her, as a favour, to come to Queen's Road on Saturday afternoon. Virginia quickly replied with a promise to call, and punctually kept the engagement. Though she was much better dressed than in the days previous to Monica's marriage, she had lost something for which costume could not compensate: her face had no longer that unmistakable refinement which had been wont to make her attire a secondary consideration. A disagreeable redness tinged her eyelids and the lower part of her nose; her mouth was growing coarse and lax, the under lip hanging a little; she smiled with a shrinking, apologetic shyness only seen in people who have done something to be ashamed of, — smiled even when she was endeavouring to look sorrowful; and her glance was furtive. She sat down on the edge of a chair, like an anxious applicant for work or charity, and a moistness of the eyes, which obliged her to use her handkerchief frequently, strengthened this resemblance.

Rhoda could not play at smooth phrases with this poor, dispirited woman, whose change during the last few years, and especially during the last twelve months, had often occupied her thoughts in a very unpleasant way. She came almost at once to the subject of their interview.

"Why have you not been to see me before this?"

"I — I really couldn't. The circumstances — everything is so very painful. You know — of course you know what has happened?"

"Of course I do."

"How," asked Virginia timidly, "did the news first of all reach you?"

"Mr. Widdowson came here, and told Miss Barfoot everything."

"He came? — We didn't know that. Then you have heard the accusation he makes?"

"Everything."

"It is quite unfounded, I do assure you. Monica is not guilty. The poor child has done nothing — it was an indiscretion — nothing more than indiscretion" —

"I am very anxious to believe it. Can you give me certainty? Can you explain Monica's behaviour — not only on that one occasion, but the deceit she practised at other times? Her husband told Miss Barfoot that she had frequently told him untruths — such as saying that she called here when she certainly did not."

"I can't explain that," lamented Virginia. "Monica won't tell me why she concealed her movements."

"Then how can you ask me to believe your assurance that she isn't guilty?"

The sternness of this question caused Virginia to redden and become utterly disconcerted. She dropped her handkerchief, fumbled for it, breathed hard.

"Oh, Miss Nunn! How can you think Monica —? You know her better; I'm sure you do!"

"Any human being may commit a crime," said the other impatiently, exasperated by what seemed to be merely new evidence against Barfoot. "Who knows any one well enough to say that a charge *must* be unfounded?"

Miss Madden began to sob.

"I'm afraid that is true. — But my sister — my dear sister" —

"I didn't wish to distress you. Do command yourself, and let us talk about it calmly."

"Yes — I will — I shall be so glad to talk about it with you. — Oh, if I could persuade her to return to her husband! He is willing to receive her. I meet him very often on Clapham Common, and — We are living at his expense. When Monica had been with me in my old lodgings for about a week. He took these new rooms for us, and Monica consented to remove. But she won't hear of going back to live with him. He has offered to let us have the house to ourselves, but it's no use. He writes to her, but she won't reply. Do you know that he has taken a house at Clevedon — a beautiful house? They were to go to it in a week or two, and Alice and I would have gone to share it with them — then this dreadful thing happened. And Mr. Widdowson doesn't even insist on her telling him what she keeps secret. He is willing to take her back under any circumstances. And she is so ill" —

Virginia broke off, as if there were something more that she did not venture to impart. He cheeks coloured, and she looked distressfully about the room.

"Seriously ill, do you mean?" inquired Rhoda, with difficulty softening her voice.

"She gets up each day, but I'm often afraid that — She has had fainting fits" —

Rhoda gazed at the speaker with pitiless scrutiny.

"What can have caused this? Is it the result of her being falsely accused?"

"Partly that. But" —

Suddenly Virginia rose, stepped to Rhoda's side, and whispered a word or two. Rhoda turned pale; her eyes glared fiercely.

"And *still* you believe her innocent?"

"She has sworn to me that she is innocent. She says that she has a proof of it, which I shall see some day — and her husband also. A presentiment has fixed itself in her mind that she can't live, and before the end she will tell everything."

"Her husband knows of this, of course — of what you have told me?"

"No. She has forbidden me to say anything — and how could I, Miss Nunn? She has made me promise solemnly that he shall not be told. I haven't even told Alice. But she will know very soon. At the end of September she leaves her place, and will come to London, to be with us — for a time at all events. We do so hope that we shall succeed in persuading Monica to go to the house at Clevedon. Mr. Widdowson is keeping it, and will move the furniture from Herne Hill at any moment. — Couldn't you help us, dear Miss Nunn? Monica would listen to you; I am sure she would."

"I'm afraid I can be of no use," Rhoda answered coldly.

"She has been hoping to see you."

"She has said so?"

"Not in so many words — but I am sure she wishes to see you. She has asked about you several times, and when your note came she was very pleased. It would be a great kindness to us" —

"Does she declare that she will never return to her husband?"

"Yes — I am sorry to say she does. But the poor child believes that she has only a short time to live. Nothing will shake her presentiment. 'I shall die, and give no more trouble,' — that's what she always says to me. And a conviction of that kind is so likely to fulfil itself. She never leaves the house, and of course that is very wrong; she ought to go out every day. She won't see a medical man."

"Has Mr. Widdowson given her any cause for disliking him?" Rhoda inquired.

"He was dreadfully violent, when he discovered — I'm afraid it was natural — he thought the worst of her, and he has always been so devoted to Monica. She says he seemed on the point of killing her. He is man of very severe nature, I have always thought. He never could bear that Monica should go anywhere alone. They were very, very unhappy, I'm afraid — so ill-matched in almost every respect. Still, under the circumstances — surely she ought to return to him?"

"I can't say. I don't know."

Rhoda's voice signified a conflict of feeling. Had she been disinterested, her opinion would not have wavered for a moment; she would have declared that the wife's inclination must be the only law in such a case. As it was, she could only regard Monica with profound mistrust and repugnance. The story of decisive evidence kept back seemed to her only a weak woman's falsehood, a fiction due to shame and despair. Undoubtedly it would give some vague relief to her mind if Monica were persuaded to go to Clevedon, but she could not bring herself to think of visiting the suffering woman. Whatever the end might be, she would have no part in bringing it about. Her dignity, her pride, should remain unsullied by such hateful contact.

"I mustn't stay longer," said Virginia, rising after a painful silence. "I am always afraid to be away from her even for an hour; the fear of dreadful things that might happen haunts me day and night. How glad I shall be when Alice comes!"

Rhoda had no words of sympathy. Her commiseration for Virginia was only such as she might have felt for any stranger involved in sordid troubles; all the old friendliness had vanished. Nor would she have been greatly shocked, or astonished, had she followed Miss Madden on the way to the railway station, and seen her, after a glance up and down the street, turn quickly into a public-house, and come forth again holding her handkerchief to her lips. A feeble, purposeless, hopeless woman; type of a whole class; living only to deteriorate —

Will! Purpose! Was *she* not in danger of forgetting these watchwords, which had guided her life out of youth into maturity? That poor creature's unhappiness was doubtless in great measure due to the conviction that in missing love and marriage she had missed everything. So thought the average woman, and in her darkest hours she too had fallen among those poor of spirit, the flesh prevailing. But the soul in her had not finally succumbed. Passion had a new significance; her conception of life was larger, more liberal; she made no vows to crush the natural instincts. But her conscience, her sincerity should not suffer. Wherever destiny might lead, she would still be the same proud and independent woman, responsible only to herself, fulfilling the nobler laws of her existence.

A day or two after this she had guests to dine with her, Mildred Vesper and Winifred Haven. Among the girls whom she had helped to educate, these two seemed by far the most self-reliant, the most courageous and hopeful. In minor details of character they differed widely, and intellectually Miss Haven was far in advance. Rhoda had a strong desire to observe them as they talked about the most various subjects; she knew them well, but hoped to find in them some new suggestion of womanly force, which would be of help to her in her own struggle for redemption.

It was seldom that either of them ailed anything. Mildred still showed traces of her country breeding; she was the more robust, walked with a heavier step, had less polish of manner. Under strain of any kind, Winifred's health would sooner give way, but her natural vivacity promised long resistance to oppressing influences. Mildred had worked harder, and amid privations of which the other girl knew nothing; she would never distinguish herself, but it was difficult indeed to imagine her repining so long as she had her strength and her congenial friends; twenty years hence, in all probability, she would keep the same clear, steady eye, the same honest smile, and the same dry humour in her talk. Winifred was more likely to traverse a latitude of storm. For one thing, her social position brought her in the way of men who might fall in love with her, whereas Mildred lived absolutely apart from the male world; doubtless, too, her passions were stronger. She loved literature, spent as much time as possible in study, and had set her mind upon helping to establish that ideal woman's-paper of which there was often talk at Miss Barfoot's.

In this company, Rhoda felt her old ambitions regaining their power over her. To these girls she was an exemplar; it made her smile to think how little they could dream of what she had experienced during the last few weeks; if ever a moment of discontent assailed them, they must naturally think of her, of the brave, encouraging words she had so often spoken. For a moment she had deserted them, abandoning a course which her reason steadily approved for one that was beset with perils of indignity. It would shame her if they knew the whole truth, — and yet she wished it were possible for them to learn that she had been passionately wooed. A contemptible impulse of vanity; away with it!

There was a chance, it seemed to her, that during Miss Barfoot's absence, Everard might come to the house. Mary had written to him; he would know that she was away. What better opportunity, if he had not dismissed her memory from his thoughts?

Every evening she made herself ready to receive a possible visitor. She took thought for her appearance. But the weeks passed by, Miss Barfoot returned, and Everard had given no sign.

She would set a date, a limit. If before Christmas he neither came nor wrote, all was at an end; after that she would not see him, whatever his plea. And having persuaded herself that this decision was irrevocable, she thought it as well to gratify Miss Barfoot's curiosity, for by now she felt able to relate what had happened in Cumberland with a certain satisfaction, — the feeling she had foreseen when, in the beginning of her acquaintance with Everard, it flattered her to observe his growing interest. Her narrative, to which Mary listened with downcast eyes, presented the outlines of the story veraciously; she told of Everard's wish to dispense with the legal bond, of her own indecision, and of the issue.

"When your letter came, could I very well have acted otherwise than I did? It was not a flat refusal to believe him; all I asked was that things should be cleared up before our marriage. For his own sake, he ought to have willingly agreed to that. He preferred to take my request as an insult. His unreasonable anger made me angry too. — And now I don't think we shall ever meet again, unless as mere acquaintances."

"I think," commented the listener, "that he behaved with extraordinary impudence."

"In the first proposal? — But I myself attach no importance to the marriage ceremony."

"Then why did you insist upon it?" asked Mary, with a smile which might have become sarcastic, but that her eye met Rhoda's.

"Would you have received us?"

"In the one case as readily as in the other."

Rhoda was silent, and darkly thoughtful.

"Perhaps I never felt entire confidence in him."

Mary smiled, and sighed.

CHAPTER XXVIII.

THE BURDEN OF FUTILE SOULS.

"My own dearest love, if I could but describe to you all I have suffered before sitting down to write this letter! Since our last meeting I have not known one hour of quietness. To think that I missed you when you called and left that note — for it was you yourself, was it not? The journey was horrible, and the week that I have spent here — I assure you I have not slept for more than a few minutes at a time, and I am utterly broken down by misery. My darling," — &c. "I regard myself as a criminal; if *you* have suffered a thousandth part of what *I* have, I deserve any punishment that could be devised. For it has all been my fault. Knowing, as I did, that our love could never end in happiness, it was my duty to hide what I felt. I ought never to have contrived that first meeting alone — for it *was* contrived; I sent my sisters away on purpose. I ought never" — &c. "The only reflection that can ever bring me comfort is that our love has been pure. We can always think of each other without shame. And why should this love ever have an end? We are separated, and perhaps shall never see each other again, but may not our hearts remain for ever true? May we not think" — &c. "If I were to bid you leave your home and come to me, I should be once more acting with base selfishness. I should ruin your life, and load my own with endless self-reproach. I find that even mere outward circumstances would not allow of what for a moment we dreamt might be possible, and of that I am *glad*, since it helps me to overcome the terrible temptation. Oh, if you knew how that temptation" — &c. "Time will be a friend to both of us, dearest Monica. Forget each other we never can, we never *will*. But our unsullied love" — &c.

Monica read it through again, the long rigmarole. Since the day that she received it — addressed to "Mrs. Williamson" at the little stationer's by Lavender Hill — the day before she consented to accompany her sister into new lodgings, the letter had lain in its hiding-place. Alone this afternoon, for Virginia was gone to call on Miss Nunn, alone and miserable, every printed page a weariness to her sight, she took out the French-stamped envelope and tried to think that its contents interested her. But not a word had power of attraction or of repulsion. The tender phrases affected her no more than if they had been addressed to a stranger. Love was become a meaningless word. She could not understand how she had ever drifted into such relations with the writer. Fear and anger were the sole passions surviving in her memory from those days which had violently transformed her life, and it was not with Bevis, but her husband, that these emotions were connected. Bevis's image stood in that already distant past like a lay figure, the mere semblance of a man. And with such conception of him his letter corresponded; it was artificial, lifeless, as if extracted from some vapid novel.

But she must not destroy it. Its use was still to come. Letter and envelope must go back again into hiding, and await the day which would give them power over human lives.

Suffering, as always, from headache and lassitude, she sat by the window and watched the people who passed along, her daily occupation. This sitting-room was on the ground floor. In a room above some one was receiving a music-lesson; every now and then the teacher's voice became audible, raised in sharp impatience, and generally accompanied by a clash upon the keys of the piano. At the area-gate of the house opposite, a servant was talking angrily with a tradesman's errand boy, who at length put his thumb to his nose with insulting significance, and scampered off. Then, at the house next to that one, there stopped a cab, from which three busy-looking men alighted. Cabs full of people were always stopping at that door; Monica wondered what it meant, who might live there. She thought of asking the landlady.

Virginia's return aroused her. She went upstairs with her sister into the double-bedded room which they occupied.

"What have you heard?"

"He went there. He told them every thing."

"How did Miss Nunn look? How did she speak?"

"Oh, she was very, very distant," lamented Virginia. "I don't quite know why she sent for me. She said there would be no use in her coming to see you, — and I don't think she ever will. I told her that there was no truth in" —

"But how did she look?" asked Monica impatiently.

"Not at all well, I thought. She has been away for her holiday, but it doesn't seem to have done her much good."

"He went there and told them everything?"

"Yes — just after it happened. But he hasn't seen them since that. I could see they believed him. It was no use, all that I said. She looked so stern and" —

"Did you ask anything about Mr. Barfoot?"

"My dear, I didn't venture to. It was impossible. But I feel quite sure that they must have broken off all intercourse with him. Whatever he may have said, they evidently didn't believe it. Miss Barfoot is away now."

"And what did you tell her about me?"

"Everything that you said I might, dear."

"Nothing else — you are sure?"

Virginia coloured, but made asseveration that nothing else had passed her lips.

"It wouldn't have mattered if you had," said Monica indifferently. "I don't care."

The sister, struggling with shame, was irritated by the needlessness of her falsehood.

"Then why were you so particular to forbid me, Monica?"

"It was better — but I don't care. I don't care for anything. Let them believe and say what they like" —

"Monica, if I find out at last that you have deceived me" —

"Oh, do, do, do be quiet!" cried the other wretchedly. "I shall go somewhere and live alone — or die alone. You worry me — I'm tired of it."

"You are not very grateful, Monica" —

"I can't be grateful! You must expect nothing from me. If you keep talking and questioning, I shall go away. I don't care what becomes of me. The sooner I die the better."

Scenes such as this had been frequent lately. The sisters were a great trial to each other's nerves. Tedium and pain drove Monica to the relief of altercation, and Virginia, through her secret vice, was losing all self-control. They wrangled, wailed, talked of parting, and only became quiet when their emotions had exhausted them. Yet no ill-feeling resulted from these disputes. Virginia had a rooted faith in her sister's innocence; when angry, she only tried to provoke Monica into a full explanation of the mystery, so insoluble by unaided conjecture. And Monica, say what she might, repaid this confidence with profound gratitude. Strangely, she had come to view herself as not only innocent of the specific charge brought against her, but as a woman in every sense maligned. So utterly void of significance, from her present point of view, was all that had passed between her and Bevis. One reason for this lay in the circumstance that, when exchanging declarations with her lover, she was ignorant of a fact which, had she known it, would have made their meetings impossible. Her husband she could never regard but as a cruel enemy; none the less, nature had set a seal upon their marriage against which the revolt of her heart was powerless. If she lived to bear a child, that child would be his. Widdowson, when he heard of her condition, would declare it the final proof of infidelity; and this injustice it was that exclusively occupied her mind. On this account she could think only of the accusation which connected her name with Barfoot's, — all else was triviality. Had there been no slightest ground for imputation upon her conduct, she could not have resented more vigorously her husband's refusal to acquit her of dishonour.

On the following day, after their early dinner, Monica unexpectedly declared that she must go out.

"Come with me. We'll go into the town."

"But you refused to go out this morning, when it was fine," complained Virginia. "And now you can see it will rain."

"Then I shall go alone."

The sister at once started up.

"No, no; I'm quite ready. — Where do you wish —?"

"Anywhere, out of this dead place. We'll go by train, and walk from Victoria — anywhere. To the Abbey, if you like."

"You must be very careful not to catch cold. After all this time that you haven't left the house" —

Monica cut short the admonition, and dressed herself with feverish impatience. As they set forth, drops of rain had begun to fall, but Monica would not hear of waiting. The journey by train made her nervous, but affected her spirits favourably. At Victoria it rained so heavily that they could not go out into the street.

"It doesn't matter. There's plenty to see here. Let us walk about and look at things. We'll buy something at the bookstall to take back."

As they turned again towards the platform, Monica was confronted by a face which she at once recognized, though it had changed noticeably in the eighteen months since she last saw it. The person was Miss Eade, her old acquaintance at the shop. But the girl no longer dressed as in those days; cheap finery of the "loudest" description arrayed her form, and it needed little scrutiny to perceive that her thin cheeks were artificially reddened. The surprise of the meeting was not Monica's only reason for evincing embarrassment; seeing that Miss Eade was uncertain whether to make a sign of acquaintance, she felt it would be wiser to go by. But this was not permitted. As they were passing each other, the girl bent her head and whispered:

"I want to speak to you — just a minute."

Virginia perceived the communication, and looked in surprise at her sister.

"It's one of the girls from Walworth Road," said Monica. "Just walk on; I'll meet you at the bookstall."

"But, my dear, she doesn't look respectable" —

"Go on; I won't be a minute."

Monica motioned to Miss Eade, who followed her towards a more retired spot.

"You have left the shop?"

"Left — I should think so. Nearly a year ago. I told you I shouldn't stand it much longer. — Are you married?"

"Yes."

Monica did not understand why the girl should eye her so suspiciously.

"You are?" said Miss Eade. "Nobody that I know, I suppose?"

"Quite a stranger to you."

The other made an unpleasant click with her tongue, and looked vaguely about her. Then she remarked inconsequently that she was waiting the arrival of her brother by train.

"He's a traveller for a West-end shop; makes five hundred a year. I keep house for him, because of course he's a widower."

The "of course" puzzled Monica for a moment, but she remembered that it was an unmeaning expletive much used by people of Miss Eade's education. However, the story did not win her credence; by this time her disagreeable surmises had too much support.

"Was there anything you wished particularly to speak about?"

"You haven't seen nothing of Mr. Bullivant?"

To what a remote period of her life this name seemed to recall Monica! She glanced quickly at the speaker, and again detected suspicion in her eyes.

"I have neither seen nor heard of him since I left Walworth Road. Isn't he still there?"

"Not he. He went about the same time you did, and nobody knew where he hid himself."

"Hid? Why should he hide?"

"I only mean he got out of sight somewheres. I thought perhaps you might have come acrosst him."

"No, I haven't. — Now I must say good-bye. That lady is waiting for me."

Miss Eade nodded, but immediately altered her mind and checked Monica as she was turning away.

"You wouldn't mind telling me what you married name may be?"

"That really doesn't concern you, Miss Eade," replied the other stiffly. "I must go" —

"If you don't tell me, I'll follow you till I find out, and chance it!"

The change from tolerable civility to coarse insolence was so sudden that Monica stood in astonishment. There was unconcealed malignity in the gaze fixed upon her.

"What do you mean? What interest have you in learning my name?"

The girl brought her face near, and snarled in the true voice of the pavement:

"Is it a name as you're ashamed to let out?"

Monica walked away to the bookstall. When she had joined her sister, she became aware that Miss Eade was keeping her in sight.

"Let us buy a book," she said, "and go home again. The rain won't stop."

They selected a cheap volume, and, having their return tickets, moved towards the departure platform. Before she could reach the gates, Monica heard Miss Eade's voice just behind her; it had changed again, and the appealing note reminded her of many conversations in Walworth Road.

"Do tell me! — I beg your pardon for bein' rude. — Don't go without telling me."

The meaning of this importunity had already flashed upon Monica, and now she felt a slight pity for the tawdry, abandoned creature, in whom there seemed to survive that hopeless passion of old days.

"My name," she said abruptly, "is Mrs. Widdowson."

"Are you telling me the truth?"

"I have told you what you wish to know. I can't talk" —

"And you don't really know nothing about *him*?"

"Nothing whatever."

Miss Eade moved sullenly away, not more than half convinced. Long after Monica's disappearance, she strayed about the platform, and the approaches to the station. Her brother was slow in arriving. Once or twice she held casual colloquy with men who also stood waiting — perchance for their sisters; and ultimately one of these was kind enough to offer her refreshment, which she graciously accepted. — Rhoda Nunn would have classed her and mused about her: a not unimportant type of the odd woman.

After this, Monica frequently went out, always accompanied by her sister. It happened more than once that they saw Widdowson, who walked past the house at least every other day; he didn't approach them, and, had he done so, Monica would have kept an obstinate silence.

For more than a fortnight he had not written to her. At length there came a letter, merely a repetition of his former appeals.

"I hear," he wrote, "that your elder sister is coming to London. Why should she live here in lodgings, when a comfortable house is at the disposal of you all? Let me again entreat you to go to Clevedon. The furniture shall be moved any moment you wish. I solemnly promise not to molest you in any way, not even by writing. It shall be understood that business makes it necessary for me to live in London. For your sister's sake, do accept this offer. If I could see you in private, I should be able to give you a very good reason why your sister Virginia would benefit by the change; perhaps you yourself know of it. Do answer me, Monica. Never again will I refer by word or look to what has passed. I am anxious only to put an end to the wretched life that you are leading. Do go to the house at Clevedon, I implore you."

It was not the first time he had hinted darkly at a benefit that might accrue to Virginia if she left London. Monica had no inkling of what he meant. She showed her sister this communication, and asked if she could understand the passage which concerned her.

"I haven't the least idea," Virginia replied, her hand trembling as she held the paper. "I can only suppose that he thinks I am not looking well."

The letter was burnt, as all the others had been, no answer vouchsafed. Virginia's mind seemed to waver with regard to the proposed settlement at Clevedon. Occasionally she had urged Monica, with extreme persistence, to accept what was offered; at other times, as now for instance, she said nothing. Yet Alice had written beseeching her to use all means for Monica's persuasion. Miss Madden infinitely preferred the thought of dwelling at Clevedon — however humble the circumstances had been — to that of coming back into London lodgings whilst she sought for a new engagement. The situation she was about to quit had proved more laborious than any in her experience. At first merely a governess, she had gradually become children's nurse as well, and for the past three months had been expected to add the tendence of a chronic invalid to her other duties. Not a day's holiday since she came. She was broken down and utterly woebegone.

But Monica could not be moved. She refused to go again under her husband's roof until he had stated that his charge against her was absolutely unfounded. This concession went beyond Widdowson's power; he would forgive, but still declined to stultify himself by a statement that could have no meaning. To what extent his wife had deceived him might be uncertain, but the deception was a proved fact. Of course it never occurred to him that Monica's demand had a significance which emphasized the name of Barfoot. Had he said, "I am convinced that your relations with Barfoot were innocent," he would have seemed to himself to be acquitting her of all criminality; whereas Monica, from her point of view, illogically supposed that he might credit her on this one issue without overthrowing all the evidence that declared her untrustworthy. In short, she expected him to read a riddle which there was scarcely a possibility of his understanding.

Alice was in correspondence with the gloomy husband. She promised him to use every effort to gain Monica's confidence. Perhaps as the eldest sister she might succeed where Virginia had failed. Her faith in Monica's protestations had been much shaken by the item of intelligence which Virginia secretly communicated; she thought it too likely that her unhappy sister saw no refuge from disgrace but in stubborn denial of guilt. And in the undertaking that was before her, she had no hope save through the influence of religion — with her a much stronger force than with either of the others.

Her arrival was expected on the last day of September. The evening before, Monica went to bed soon after eight o'clock; for a day or two she had suffered greatly, and at length had allowed a doctor to be called. Whenever her sister retired very early, Virginia also went to her own bedroom, saying that she preferred to sit there.

The room much surpassed in comfort that which she had occupied at Mrs. Conisbee's; it was spacious, and provided with a couple of very soft arm-chairs. Having locked her door, Virginia made certain preparations which had nothing to do with natural repose. From the cupboard she brought out a little spirit-kettle, and put water to boil. Then from a more private repository were produced a bottle of gin and a sugar-basin, which, together with a tumbler and spoon, found a place on a little table drawn up within reach of the chair where she was going to sit. On the same table lay a novel procured this afternoon from the library. Whilst the water was boiling, Virginia made a slight change of dress, conducive to bodily ease. Finally, having mixed a glass of gin and water — one-third only of the diluent — she sat down with one of her frequent sighs, and began to enjoy the evening.

The last, the very last, of such enjoyment; so she assured herself. Alice's presence in the house would render impossible what she had hitherto succeeded in disguising from Monica. Her conscience welcomed the restraint, which was coming none too soon, for her will could no longer be depended upon. If she abstained from strong liquors for three or four days it was now a great triumph; yet worthless, for even in abstaining she knew that the hour of indulgence had only been postponed. A fit of unendurable depression soon drove her to the only resource which had immediate efficacy. The relief, she knew, was another downward step; but presently she would find courage to climb back again, up to the sure ground. Save for her trouble on Monica's account, the temptation would already have been conquered. And now Alice's arrival made courage a mere necessity.

Her bottle was all but empty; she would finish it to-night, and in the morning, as her custom was, take it back to the grocer's in her little handbag. How convenient that this kind of thing could be purchased at the grocer's! In the beginning she had chiefly made use of railway refreshment-rooms. Only on rare occasions did she enter a public-house, and always with the bitterest sense of degradation. To sit comfortably at home, the bottle beside her and a novel on her lap, was an avoidance of the worst shame attaching to this vice; she went to bed, and in the morning — ah, the morning brought its punishment, but she incurred no risk of being detected.

Brandy had first of all been her drink, as is generally the case with women of the educated classes. There are so many plausible excuses for taking a drop of brandy. But it cost too much. Whisky she had tried, and did not like. Finally she had recourse to gin, which was palatable and very cheap. The name, debased by such foul associations, still confused her when she uttered it;[1] as a rule, she wrote it down in a list of groceries which she handed over the counter.

To-night she drank her first glass quickly; a consuming thirst was upon her. By half-past eight, the second was gently steaming at her elbow. At nine she had mixed the third; it must last a long time, for the bottle was now empty.

The novel entertained her, but she often let her thoughts stray from it. She reflected with exultation that to-night's indulgence was her very last. On the morrow she would be a new woman. Alice and she would devote themselves to their poor sister, and never rest till they had restored her to a life of dignity. This was a worthy, a noble, task; success in it must needs minister to her own peace. Before long, they would all be living at Clevedon — a life of ideal contentment. It was no longer necessary to think of the school, but she would exert herself for the moral instruction of young women — on the principles inculcated by Rhoda Nunn.

The page before her was no longer legible; the book dropped from her lap. Why this excited her laughter, she could not understand; but she laughed for a long time, until her eyes were dim with tears. It might be better to go to bed. What was the hour? She tried vainly to read her watch, and again laughed at such absurd incapacity. Then —

---

1 In the nineteenth century, gin was the drink of the lower classes and was associated with poverty and drunkenness. The switch from brandy to gin is an indication of Virginia's degeneration.

Surely that was a knock at her door? Yes; it was repeated, with a distinct calling of her name. She endeavoured to stand up.

"Miss Madden!" — It was the landlady's voice. — "Miss Madden! Are you in bed yet?"

Virginia succeeded in reaching the door.

"What is it?"

Another voice spoke.

"It is I, Virginia. I have come this evening instead of to-morrow. Please let me in."

"Alice? — You can't — I'll come — wait downstairs."

She was still able to understand the situation, and able, she thought, to speak coherently, to disguise her condition. The things on the table must be put out of sight. In trying to do this, she upset her glass and knocked the empty bottle on to the floor. But in a few minutes bottle, glass, and spirit-kettle were hidden away. The sugar-basin she lost sight of; it still remained in its former place.

Then she opened the door, and with uncertain step went out into the passage.

"Alice!" she called aloud.

At once both her sisters appeared, coming out of Monica's chamber. Monica had partly dressed herself.

"Why have you come to-night?" Virginia exclaimed, in a voice which seemed to her own ears perfectly natural.

She tottered, and was obliged to support herself against the wall. The light from her room fell full upon her, and Alice, who had stepped forward to give her a kiss, not only saw, but smelt, that something very strange was the matter. The odour proceeding from the bedroom, and that of Virginia's breath, left small doubt as to the cause of delay in giving admittance.

Whilst Alice stood bewildered, Monica received an illumination which instantly made clear to her many things in Virginia's daily life. At the same moment, she understood those mysterious hints concerning her sister in Widdowson's letters.

"Come into the room," she said abruptly. "Come, Virgie."

"I don't understand — why has Alice come to-night? — what's the time?"

Monica took hold of the tottering woman's arm, and drew her out of the passage. The cold air had produced its natural effect upon Virginia, who now with difficulty supported herself.

"Oh, Virgie!" cried the eldest sister, when the door was closed. "What is the matter? What does it mean?"

Already she had been shedding tears at the meeting with Monica, and now distress overcame her; she sobbed and lamented.

"What have you been doing, Virgie?" asked Monica, with severity.

"Doing? — I feel a little faint — surprise — didn't expect" —

"Sit down, at once. You are disgusting! — Look, Alice." She pointed to the sugar-basin on the table; then, after a rapid glance round the room, she went to the cupboard and threw the door open. "I thought so. Look, Alice. — And to think I never suspected this! It has been going on a long time — oh, a long time. She was doing it at Mrs. Conisbee's, before I was married. I remembered smelling spirits" —

Virginia was making efforts to rise.

"What are you talking about?" she exclaimed, in a thick voice, and with a countenance which was changing from dazed astonishment to anger. "It's only when I feel faint. — Do you suppose I drink? — Where's Alice? Wasn't Alice here?"

"Oh, Virgie! What *does* it mean? How *could* you?"

"Go to bed at once, Virginia," said Monica. "We're ashamed of you. — Go back into my room, Alice, and I'll get her to bed."

Ultimately this was done. With no slight trouble, Monica persuaded her sister to undress, and got her into a recumbent position, Virginia all the time protesting that she had perfect command of her faculties, that she needed no help whatever, and was utterly at a loss to comprehend the insults directed against her.

"Lie quiet, and go to sleep," was Monica's last word, uttered contemptuously.

She extinguished the lamp, and returned to her own room, where Alice was still weeping. The unexpected arrival had already been explained to Monica. Sudden necessity for housing a visitor had led to the proposition that Miss Madden, for her last night, should occupy a servant's bedroom; glad to get away, Alice chose the alternative of leaving the house at once. It had been arranged that she should share Virginia's room, but to-night this did not seem advisable.

"To-morrow," said Monica, "we must talk to her very seriously. I believe she has been drinking like that night after night. It explains the look she always has the first thing in the morning. Could you have imagined anything so disgraceful?"

But Alice had softened towards the erring woman.

"You must remember what her life has been, dear. I'm afraid loneliness is very often a cause" —

"She needn't have been lonely. She refused to come and live at Herne Hill, and now of course I understand why. Mrs. Conisbee must have known about it, and it was her duty to tell me. Mr. Widdowson had found out, somehow, I feel sure."

She explained the reason of this belief.

"You know what it all points to," said Miss Madden, drying her sallow, pimpled cheeks. "You must do as your husband wishes, dearest. We must go to Clevedon. There the poor girl will be out of temptation."

"You and Virgie may go."

"You too, Monica. — My dear sister, it is your duty."

"Don't use that word to me!" exclaimed the other angrily. "It is *not* my duty. It can be no woman's duty to live with a man she hates — or even to make a pretence of living with him."

"But, dearest" —

"You mustn't begin this to-night, Alice. I have been ill all day, and now my head is aching terribly. Go downstairs, and eat the supper they have laid for you."

"I couldn't touch a morsel," sobbed Miss Madden. "Oh, everything is too dreadful! Life is too hard!"

Monica had returned to bed, and lay there with her face half hidden against the pillow.

"If you don't want any supper," she said, in a moment, "please go and tell them, so that they needn't sit up for you."

Alice obeyed. When she came up again, her sister either was, or pretended to be, asleep; even the noise made by bringing luggage into the room did not cause her to move. Having sat in despondency for a while, Miss Madden opened one of her boxes, and sought in it for the Bible which it was her custom to make use of every night. She read in the book for about half an hour, then covered her face with her hands and prayed silently. This was *her* refuge from the barrenness and bitterness of life.

CHAPTER XXIX.

CONFESSION AND COUNSEL.

The sisters did not exchange a word until morning, but both of them lay long awake. Monica was the first to lose consciousness; she slept for about an hour, then the pains of a horrid dream disturbed her, and again she took up the burden of thought. Such waking after brief, broken sleep, when mind and body are beset by weariness, yet cannot rest, when night with its awful hush and its mysterious movements makes a strange, dread habitation for the spirit — such waking is a grim trial of human fortitude. The blood flows sluggishly, yet subject to sudden tremors that chill the veins, and for an instant choke the heart. Purpose is idle, the will impure; over the past hangs a shadow of remorse, and life that must yet be lived shows lurid, a steep pathway to the hopeless grave. Of this cup Monica drank deeply.

A fear of death compassed her about. Night after night it had thus haunted her. In the daytime she could think of death with resignation, as a refuge from miseries of which she saw no other end; but this hour of silent darkness shook her with terrors. Reason availed nothing; its exercise seemed criminal. The old faiths, never abandoned, though modified by the breath of intellectual freedom that had just touched her, reasserted all their power. She saw herself as a wicked woman, in the eye of truth not less wicked than her husband declared her. A sinner stubborn in impenitence, defending herself by a paltry ambiguity that had all the evil of a direct lie. Her soul trembled in its nakedness.

What redemption could there be for her? What path of spiritual health was discoverable? She could not command herself to love the father of her child; the repugnance with which she regarded him seemed to her a sin against nature, yet how was she responsible for it? Would it profit her to make confession and be humbled before him? The confession must some day be made, if only for her child's sake; but she foresaw in it no relief of mind. Of all human beings her husband was the one least fitted to console and strengthen her. She cared nothing for his pardon; from his love she shrank. But if there were some one to whom she could utter her thoughts with the certainty of being understood —

Her sisters had not the sympathetic intelligence necessary for aiding her; Virginia was weaker than she herself, and Alice dealt only in sorrowful commonplaces, profitable perhaps to her own heart, but powerless over the trouble of another's. Among the few people she had called her friends, there was one strong woman — strong of brain, and capable, it might be, of speaking the words that go from soul to soul; this woman she had deeply offended, yet owing to mere mischance. Whether or no Rhoda Nunn had lent ear to Barfoot's wooing, she must be gravely offended; she had given proof of it in the interview reported by Virginia. The scandal spread abroad by Widdowson might even have been fatal to a happiness of which she had dreamt. — To Rhoda Nunn some form of reparation was owing, and might not an avowal of the whole truth elicit from her counsel of gratitude — some solace, some guidance?

Amid the tremors of night Monica felt able to take this step, for the mere chance of comfort that it offered. But when day came, the resolution had vanished; shame and pride again compelled her to silence.

And this morning she had new troubles to think about. Virginia was keeping her room; would admit no one; answered every whisper of appeal with brief, vague words that signified anything or nothing. The others breakfasted in gloom that harmonized only too well with the heavy, dripping sky visible from their windows. Only at mid-day did Alice succeed in obtaining speech with her remorseful sister. They were closeted together for more than an hour, and the elder woman came forth at last with red, tear-swollen eyes.

"We must leave her alone to-day," she said to Monica. "She won't take any meal. Oh, the wretched state she is in! If only I could have known of this before!"

"Has it been going on for very long?"

"It began soon after she went to live at Mrs. Conisbee's. She has told me all about it — poor girl, poor thing! Whether she can ever break herself of it, who knows? She says that she will take the pledge of total abstinence, and I encouraged her to do so; it may be some use, don't you think?"

"Perhaps — I don't know" —

"But I have no faith in her reforming unless she goes away from London. She thinks herself that only a new life in a new place will give her the strength. — My dear, at Mrs. Conisbee's she starved herself to have money to buy spirits; she went without any food but dry bread day after day."

"Of course that made it worse. She must have craved for support."

"Of course. — And your husband knows about it. He came once when she was in that state — when you were away" —

Monica nodded sullenly, her eyes averted.

"Her life has been so dreadfully unhealthy. She seems to have become weak-minded. All her old interests have gone; she reads nothing but novels, day after day."

"I have noticed that."

"How can we help her, Monica? Won't you make a sacrifice for the poor girl's sake? Cannot I persuade you, dear? Your position has a bad influence on her; I can see it has. She worries so about you, and then tries to forget the trouble — you know how."

Not that day, nor the next, could Monica listen to these entreaties. But her sister at length prevailed. It was late in the evening; Virginia had gone to bed, and the others sat silently, without occupation. Miss Madden, after several vain efforts to speak, bent forward and said in a low, grave voice:

"Monica — you are deceiving us all. You are guilty."

"Why do you say that?"

"I know it. I have watched you. You betray yourself when you are thinking."

The other sat with brows knitted, with hard, defiant lips.

"All your natural affection is dead, and only guilt could have caused that. You don't care what becomes of your sister. Only the fear, or the evil pride, that comes of guilt could make you refuse what we ask of you. You are afraid to let your husband know of your condition."

Alice could not have spoken thus had she not believed what she said. The conviction had become irresistible to her mind. Her voice quivered with intensity of painful emotion.

"That last is true," said her sister, when there had been silence for a minute.

"You confess it? Oh, Monica" —

"I don't confess what you think," went on the younger, with more calmness than she had yet commanded in these discussions. "Of that I am *not* guilty. — I am afraid of his knowing, because he will never believe me. I have a proof which would convince any one else; but, even if I produced it, it would be no use. I don't think it is possible to persuade him — when once he knows" —

"If you were innocent, you would disregard that."

"Listen to me, Alice. If I were guilty, I should not be living here at his expense. I only consented to do that when I knew what my condition was. But for this thing, I should have refused to accept another penny from him. I should have drawn upon my own money until I was able to earn my living again. — If you won't believe this, it shows you know nothing of me. Your reading of my face is all foolishness."

"I would to God I were sure of what you say!" moaned Miss Madden, with vehemence which seemed extraordinary in such a feeble, flabby person.

"You know that I told my husband lies," exclaimed Monica, "so you think I am never to be trusted. I did tell him lies; I can't deny it, and I am ashamed of it. But I am not a deceitful woman — I can say that boldly. I love the truth better than falsehood. If it weren't for that, I should never have left home. A deceitful woman, in my circumstances — you don't understand them — would have cheated her husband into forgiving her — such a husband as mine. She would have calculated the most profitable course. I left my husband because it was hateful to me to be with a man for whom I had lost every trace of affection. In keeping away from him I am acting honestly. — But I have told you that I am also afraid of his making a discovery. I want him to believe — when the time comes" —

She broke off.

"Then, Monica, you ought to make known to him what you have been concealing. If you are telling the truth, that confession can't be anything very dreadful."

"Alice, I am willing to make an agreement. — If my husband will promise never to come near Clevedon until I send for him, I will go and live there, with you and Virgie."

"He has promised that, darling," cried Miss Madden delightedly.

"Not to me. He has only said that he will make his home in London for a time. That means he would come whenever he wished, if it were only to speak to you and Virgie. But he must undertake never to come near until I give him permission. If he will promise this, and keep his word, I pledge myself to let him know the whole truth in less than a year. Whether I live or die, he shall be told the truth in less than a year."

Before going to bed, Alice wrote and dispatched a few lines to Widdowson, requesting an interview with him as soon as possible. She would come to his house at any hour he liked to appoint. The next afternoon brought a reply, and that same evening Miss Madden went to Herne Hill. As a result of what passed there, a day or two saw the beginning of the long-contemplated removal to Clevedon. Widdowson found a lodging in the neighbourhood of his old home; he had engaged never to cross the bounds of Somerset until he received his wife's permission.

As soon as this compact was established, Monica wrote to Miss Nunn. A short submissive letter. "I am about to leave London, and before I go I very much wish to see you. Will you allow me to call at some hour when I could speak with you in private? There is something I must make known to you, and I cannot write it." — After a day's interval came the reply, which was still briefer. Miss Nunn would be at home at half-past eight this or the next evening.

Monica's announcement that she must go out alone after nightfall alarmed her sisters. When told that her visit was to Rhoda Nunn they were somewhat relieved, but Alice begged to be permitted to accompany her.

"It will be lost trouble," Monica declared. "More likely than not, there is a spy waiting to follow me wherever I go. Your assurance that I really went to Miss Barfoot's won't be needed."

When the others still opposed her purpose she passed from irony to anger.

"Have you undertaken to save him the expense of private detectives? Have you promised never to let me go out of your sight?"

"Certainly I have not," said Alice.

"Nor I, dear," protested Virginia. "He has never asked anything of the kind."

"Then you may be sure that the spies are still watching me. Let them have something to do, poor creatures. I shall go alone, so you needn't say any more."

She took the train to York Road station, and thence, as the night was fine, walked to Chelsea. This semblance of freedom, together with the sense of having taken a courageous resolve, raised her spirits. She hoped that a detective might be tracking her; the futility of such measures afforded her a contemptuous satisfaction. Not to arrive before the appointed hour, she loitered on Chelsea Embankment, and it gave her pleasure to reflect that in doing this she was outraging the proprieties. Her mind was in a strange tumult of rebellious and distrustful thought. She had determined on making a confession to Rhoda; but would she benefit by it? Was Rhoda generous enough to appreciate her motives? It did not matter much. She would have discharged a duty at the expense of much shame, and this fact alone might strengthen her to face the miseries beyond.

As she stood at Miss Barfoot's door, her heart quailed. To the servant who opened she could only speak Miss Nunn's name; fortunately, instructions had been given, and she was straightway led to the library. Here she waited for nearly five minutes. Was Rhoda doing this on purpose? Her face, when at length she entered, made it seem probable; a cold dignity, only not offensive haughtiness, appeared in her bearing. She did not offer to shake hands, and used no form of civility beyond requesting her visitor to be seated.

"I am going away," Monica began, when silence compelled her to speak.

"Yes, so you told me."

"I see that you can't understand why I have come" —

"Your note only said that you wished to see me."

Their eyes met, and Monica knew, in the moment that succeeded, that she was being examined from head to foot. It seemed to her that she had undertaken something beyond her strength; her impulse was to invent a subject of brief conversation, and escape into the darkness. But Miss Nunn spoke again.

"Is it possible that I can be of any service to you?"

"Yes. You might be. But — I find it is very difficult to say what I" —

Rhoda waited, offering no help whatever, not even that of a look expressing interest.

"Will you tell me, Miss Nunn, why you behave so coldly to me?"

"Surely that doesn't need any explanation, Mrs. Widdowson?"

"You mean that you believe everything Mr. Widdowson has said?"

"Mr. Widdowson has said nothing to me. But I have seen your sister, and there seemed no reason to doubt what she told me."

"She couldn't tell you the truth, because she doesn't know it."

"I presume she at least told no untruth."

"What did Virginia say? — I think I have a right to ask that."

Rhoda appeared to doubt it. She turned her eyes to the nearest bookcase, and for a moment reflected.

"Your affairs really don't concern me, Mrs. Widdowson," she said at length. "They have been forced upon my attention, and perhaps I regard them from a wrong point of view. Unless you have come to defend yourself against a false accusation, is there any profit in our talking of these things?"

"I *have* come for that."

"Then I am not so unjust as to refuse to hear you."

"My name has been spoken of together with Mr. Barfoot's. This is wrong. It began from a mistake."

Monica could not shape her phrases. Hastening to utter the statement that would relieve her from Miss Nunn's personal displeasure, she used the first simple words that rose to her lips.

"When I went to Bayswater that day, I had no thought of seeing Mr. Barfoot. I wished to see some one else."

The listener manifested more attention. She could not mistake the signs of sincerity in Monica's look and speech.

"Some one," she asked coldly, "who was living with Mr. Barfoot?"

"No. Some one in the same building; in another flat. When I knocked at Mr. Barfoot's door, I knew — or I felt sure — no one would answer. I knew Mr. Barfoot was going away that day — going into Cumberland."

Rhoda's look was fixed on the speaker's countenance.

"You knew he was going to Cumberland?" she asked, in a slow, careful voice.

"He told me so. I met him, quite by chance, the day before."

"Where did you meet him?"

"Near the flats," Monica answered, colouring. "He had just come out — I saw him come out. I had an appointment there that afternoon, and I walked a short way with him, so that he shouldn't" —

Her voice failed. She saw that Rhoda had begun to mistrust her, to think that she was elaborating falsehoods. The burdensome silence was broken by Miss Nunn's saying repellently:

"I haven't asked for your confidence, remember."

"No — and if you try to imagine what it means for me to be speaking like this — I am not shameless. I have suffered a great deal before I could bring myself to come here and tell you. — If you were more human — if you tried to believe" —

The agitation which found utterance in these words had its effect upon Rhoda. In spite of herself, she was touched by the note of womanly distress.

"Why have you come? Why do you tell me this?"

"Because it isn't only I that have been falsely accused. I felt I must tell you that Mr. Barfoot had never — that there was nothing between us. What has he said? How did he meet the charge Mr. Widdowson made against him?"

"Simply by denying it."

"Hasn't he wished to appeal to *me*?"

"I don't know. I haven't heard of his expressing such a wish. — I can't see that you are called upon to take any trouble about Mr. Barfoot. He ought to be able to protect his own reputation."

"Has he done so?" Monica asked eagerly. "Did you believe him when he denied —?"

"But what does it matter whether I believed him or not?"

"He would think it mattered a great deal."

"Mr. Barfoot would think so? — Why?"

"He told me how much he wished to have your good opinion. — That is what we used to talk about. I don't know why he took me into his confidence. It happened first of all when we were going by train — the same train, by chance — after we had both been calling here. He asked me many questions about you, and at last said — that he loved you — or something that meant the same."

Rhoda's eyes had fallen.

"After that," pursued Monica, "we several times spoke of you. We did so when we happened to meet near his rooms — as I have told you. He told me he was going to Cumberland with the hope of seeing you; and I understood him to mean that he wished to ask you" —

The sudden and great change in Miss Nunn's expression checked the speaker. Scornful austerity had given place to a smile, stern indeed, but exultant. There was warmth upon her face; her lips moved and relaxed; she altered her position in the chair as if inclined for more intimate colloquy.

"There was never more than that between us," pursued Monica, with earnestness. "My interest in Mr. Barfoot was only on your account. I hoped he might be successful. — And I have come to you because I feared you would believe my husband — as I see you have done."

Rhoda, though she thought it very unlikely that all this should be admirable acting, showed that the explanation had by no means fully satisfied her. Unwilling to put the crucial question, she waited, with gravity which had none of the former harshness, for what else Mrs. Widdowson might choose to say. A look of suffering appeal obliged her to break the silence.

"I am very sorry you have laid this task upon yourself" —

Still Monica looked at her, and at length murmured:

"If only I could know that I had done any good" —

"But," said Rhoda, with a searching glance, "you don't wish me to repeat what you have said?"

"It was only for you. I thought — if you felt able to let Mr. Barfoot know that you had no longer any" —

A flash of stern intelligence shot from the listener's eyes.

"You have seen him, then?" she asked, with abrupt directness.

"Not since."

"He has written to you?" — still in the same voice.

"Indeed he has not. Mr. Barfoot never wrote to me. I know nothing whatever about him. No one asked me to come to you — don't think that. No one knows of what I have been telling you."

Again Rhoda was oppressed by the difficulty of determining how much credit was due to such assertions. Monica understood her look.

"As I have said so much, I must tell you all. It would be dreadful, after this, to go away uncertain whether you believed me or not."

Human feeling prompted the listener to declare that she had no doubts left. Yet she could not give utterance to the words. She knew they would sound forced, insincere. Shame at inflicting shame caused her to bend her head. Already she had been silent too long.

"I will tell you everything," Monica was saying, in low, tremulous tones. "If no one else believes me, you at all events shall. I have not done what" —

"No — I can't hear this," Rhoda broke in, the speaker's voice affecting her too powerfully. "I will believe you without this."

Monica broke into sobbing. The strain of this last effort had overtaxed her strength.

"We won't talk any more of it," said Rhoda, with an endeavour to speak kindly. "You have done all that could be asked of you. I am grateful to you for coming on my account."

The other controlled herself.

"Will you hear what I have to say, Miss Nunn? — Will you hear it as a friend? — I want to put myself right in your thoughts. I have told no one else; I shall be easier in mind if you will hear me. My husband will know everything before very long — but perhaps I shall not be alive" —

Something in Miss Nunn's face suggested to Monica that her meaning was understood. Perhaps, notwithstanding her denial, Virginia had told more, when she was here, than she had permission to make known.

"Why should you wish to tell *me*?" asked Rhoda uneasily.

"Because you are so strong. You will say something that will help me. — I know you think that I have committed a sin which it is a shame to speak of. That isn't true. If it were true, I should never consent to go and live in my husband's house."

"You are returning to him?"

"I forgot that I haven't told you."

And Monica related the agreement that had been arrived at. When she spoke of the time that must elapse before she would make a confession to her husband, it again seemed to her that Miss Nunn understood.

"There is a reason why I consent to be supported by him," she continued. "If it were true that I had sinned as he suspects, I would rather kill myself than pretend still to be his wife. — The day before he had me watched, I thought I had left him for ever. I thought that if I went back to the house again, it would only be to get the few things that I needed. — It was some one who lived in the same building as Mr. Barfoot. You have met him" —

She raised her eyes for an instant, and they encountered the listener's. Rhoda was at no loss to supply the omitted name, she saw at once how plain things were becoming.

"He has left England," pursued Monica, in a hurried but clear voice. "I thought then that I should go away with him. But — it was impossible. I loved him — or thought I loved him, but I was guiltless of anything more than consenting to leave my husband. — Will you believe me?"

"Yes, Monica, I do believe you."

"If you have any doubt, I can show you a letter he wrote to me from abroad, which will prove" —

"I believe you, absolutely."

"But let me tell you more. I must explain how the misunderstanding" —

Rapidly she recounted the incidents of that fatal Saturday afternoon. At the conclusion, her self-command was again overcome; she shed tears, and murmured broken entreaties for kindness.

"What shall I do, Miss Nunn? — How can I live until —? I know it's only for a short time. My wretched life will soon be at an end" —

"Monica — there is one thing you must remember."

The voice was so gentle, though firm; so unlike what she had expected to hear; that the sufferer looked up with grateful attention.

"Tell me — give me what help you can."

"Life seems so bitter to you that you are in despair. Yet isn't it your duty to live as though some hope were before you?"

Monica gazed in uncertainty.

"You mean —?" she faltered.

"I think you will understand. — I am not speaking of your husband. Whether you have duties to him nor not, I can't say; that is for your own mind and heart to determine. — But isn't it true that your health has a graver importance than if you yourself only were concerned?"

"Yes — you have understood me" —

"Isn't it your duty to remember at every moment that your thoughts, your actions, may affect another life — that by heedlessness, by abandoning yourself to despair, you may be the cause of suffering it was in your power to avert?"

Herself strongly moved, Rhoda had never spoken so impressively, had never given counsel of such earnest significance. She felt her power in quite a new way, without touch of vanity, without posing or any trivial self-consciousness. When she least expected it, an opportunity had come for exerting the moral influence on which she prided herself, and which she hoped to make the ennobling element of her life. All the better that the case was one calling for courage, for contempt of vulgar reticences; the combative soul in her became stronger when faced by such conditions. Seeing that her words were not vain, she came nearer to Monica and spoke yet more kindly.

"Why do you encourage that fear of your life coming to an end?"

"It's more a hope than a fear — at most times. I can see nothing before me. I don't wish to live."

"That's morbid. It isn't yourself that speaks, but your trouble. You are young and strong, and in a year's time very much of this unhappiness will have passed."

"I have felt it like a certainty — as if it had been foretold to me — ever since I knew" —

"I think it very likely that young wives have often the same dread. It is physical, Monica, and in your case there is so little relief from dark brooding. But again you must think of your responsibility. You will live, because the poor little life will need your care."

Monica turned her head away and moaned.

"I shall not love my child."

"Yes, you will. And that love, that duty, is the life to which you must look forward. You have suffered a great deal, but after such sorrow as yours there comes quietness and resignation. Nature will help you."

"Oh, if you could give me some of *your* strength! I have never been able to look at life as you do. I should never have married him if I hadn't been tempted by the thought of living easily — and I feared so — that I might always be alone — My sisters are so miserable; it terrified me to think of struggling on through life as they do" —

"Your mistake was in looking only at the weak women. You had other examples before you — girls like Miss Vesper and Miss Haven, who live bravely and work hard and are proud of their place in the world. — But it's idle to talk of the past, and just as foolish to speak as if you were sorrowing without hope. How old are you, Monica?"

"Two-and-twenty."

"Well, I am two-and-thirty — and I don't call myself old. When you have reached my age, I prophesy you will smile at your despair of ten years ago. At your age, one talks so readily of 'wrecked life' and 'hopeless future,' and all that kind of thing. My dear girl, you may live to be one of the most contented and most useful women in England. Your life isn't wrecked at all — nonsense! You have gone through a storm, that's true, but more likely than not you will be all the better for it. Don't talk or think about *sins*; simply make up your mind that you won't be beaten by trials and hardships. There cannot — can there? — be the least doubt as to how you ought to live through these coming months. Your duty is perfectly clear. Strengthen yourself in body and mind. You *have* a mind, which is more than can be said of a great many women. Think bravely and nobly of yourself! Say to yourself: This and that it is in me to do, and I will do it!"

Monica bent suddenly forward, and took one of her friend's hands, and clung to it.

"I knew you could say something that would help me. You have a way of speaking. — But it isn't only now. I shall be so far away, and so lonely, all through the dark winter. Will you write to me?"

"Gladly. And tell you all we are doing."

Rhoda's voice sank for a moment; her eyes wandered; but she recovered the air of confidence.

"We seemed to have lost you; but before long you will be one of us again. I mean, you will be one of the women who are fighting in woman's cause. You will prove by your life that we can be responsible human beings — trustworthy, conscious of purpose."

"Tell me — do you think it right for me to live with my husband when I can't even regard him as a friend?"

"In that, I dare not counsel you. — If you *can* think of him as a friend, in time to come, surely it will be better. But here you must guide yourself. You seem to have made a very sensible arrangement, and before long you will see many things more clearly. Try to recover health — health; that is what you need. Drink in the air of the Severn Sea; it will be a cordial to you after this stifling London. Next summer I shall — I hope I shall be at Cheddar, and then I shall come over to Clevedon — and we shall laugh and talk as if we had never known a care."

"Ah, if that time were come! — But you have done me good. I shall try" —

She rose.

"I mustn't forget," said Rhoda, without looking at her, "that I owe you thanks. You have done what you felt was right, in spite of all it cost you; and you have very greatly relieved my mind. Of course it is all a secret between us. If I make it understood that a doubt is no longer troubling me, I shall never say how it was removed."

"How I wish I had come before."

"For your own sake, if I have really helped you, I wish you had. But as for anything else — it is much better as it is."

And Rhoda stood with erect head, smiling her smile of liberty. Monica did not dare to ask any question. She moved up to her friend, holding out both hands timidly.

"Good-bye!"

"Till next summer."

They embraced, and kissed each other, Monica, when she had withdrawn her hot lips, again murmuring words of gratitude. Then in silence they went together to the house-door, and in silence parted.

CHAPTER XXX.

RETREAT WITH HONOUR.

Alighting, on his return to London, at the Savoy Hotel, Barfoot insensibly prolonged his stay there. For the present he had no need of a more private dwelling; he could not see more than a few days ahead; his next decisive step was as uncertain as it had been during the first few months after his coming back from the East.

Meantime, he led a sufficiently agreeable life. The Brissendens were not in town, but his growing intimacy with that family had extended his social outlook, and in a direction correspondent with the change in his own circumstances. He was making friends in the world with which he had a natural affinity; that of wealthy and cultured people who seek no prominence, who shrink from contact with the circles known as "smart," who possess their souls in quiet freedom. It is a small class, especially distinguished by the charm of its women. Everard had not adapted himself without difficulty to this new atmosphere; from the first he recognized its soothing and bracing quality, but his experiences had accustomed him to an air more rudely vigorous; it was only after those weeks spent abroad in frequent intercourse with the Brissendens that he came to understand the full extent of his sympathy with the social principles these men and women represented.

In the houses where his welcome was now assured, he met some three or four women among whom it would have been difficult to assign the precedence for grace of manner and of mind. These persons were not in declared revolt against the order of things, religious, ethical, or social; that is to say, they did not think it worth while to identify themselves with any "movement"; they were content with the unopposed right of liberal criticism. They lived placidly; refraining from much that the larger world enjoined, but never aggressive. Everard admired them with increasing fervour. With one exception they were married, and suitably married; that member of the charming group who kept her maiden freedom was Agnes Brissenden, and it seemed to Barfoot that if preference were at all justified, Agnes should receive the palm. His view of her had greatly changed since the early days of their acquaintance; in fact, he perceived that till of late he had not known her at all. His quick assumption that Agnes was at his disposal if he chose to woo her had been mere fatuity; he misread her perfect simplicity of demeanour, the unconstraint of her intellectual sympathies. What might now be her personal attitude to him, he felt altogether uncertain, and the result was a genuine humility such as he had never known. Nor was it Agnes only that subdued his masculine self-assertiveness; her sisters in grace had scarcely less dominion over him; and at times, as he sat conversing in one of these drawing-rooms, he broke off to marvel at himself, to appreciate the perfection of his own suavity, the vast advance he had been making in polished human-ism.

Towards the end of November, he learnt that the Brissendens were at their town house, and a week later he received an invitation to dine with them.

Over his luncheon at the hotel, Everard reflected with some gravity, for, if he were not mistaken, the hour had come when he must make up his mind on a point too long in suspense. What was Rhoda Nunn doing? He had heard nothing whatever of her. His cousin Mary wrote to him, whilst he was at Ostend, in a kind and friendly tone, informing him that his simple assurance with regard to a certain disagreeable matter was all she had desired, and hoping that he would come and see her as usual when he found himself in London. But he had kept away from the house in Queen's Road, and it was probable that Mary did not even know his address. As the result of meditation, he went to his sitting-room, and with an air of reluctance sat down to write a letter. It was a request that Mary would let him see her somewhere or other — not at her house. Couldn't they have a talk at the place in Great Portland Street, when no one else was there?

Miss Barfoot answered with brief assent. If he liked to come to Great Portland Street at three o'clock on Saturday, she would be awaiting him.

On arriving, he inspected the rooms with curiosity.

"I have often wished to come here, Mary. Show me over the premises, will you?"

"That was your purpose —?"

"No, not altogether. But you know how your work interests me."

Mary complied, and freely answered his various questions. Then they sat down on hard chairs by the fire, and Everard, leaning forward as if to warm his hands, lost no more time in coming to the point.

"I want to hear about Miss Nunn."

"To hear about her? Pray, what do you wish to hear?"

"Is she well?"

"Very well indeed."

"I'm very glad of that. — Does she ever speak of me?"

"Let me see — I don't think she has referred to you lately."

Everard looked up.

"Don't let us play a comedy, Mary. I want to talk very seriously. Shall I tell you what happened when I went to Seascale?"

"Ah, you went to Seascale, did you?"

"Didn't you know that?" he asked, unable to decide the question from his cousin's face, which was quite friendly but inscrutable.

"You went when Miss Nunn was there?"

"Of course. You must have known I was going, when I asked you for her Seascale address."

"And what did happen? I shall be glad to hear — if you feel at liberty to tell me."

After a pause, Everard began the narrative. But he did not see fit to give it with all the detail which Mary had learnt from her friend. He spoke of the excursion to Wastwater, and of the subsequent meeting on the shore.

"The end of it was that Miss Nunn consented to marry me."

"She consented?"

"That comes as a surprise?"

"Please go on."

"Well, we arranged everything. Rhoda was to stay till the fifteen days were over, and the marriage would have been there. But then arrived your letter, and we quarrelled about it. I wasn't disposed to beg and pray for justice. I told Rhoda that her wish for evidence was an insult, that I would take no step to understand Mrs. Widdowson's behaviour. Rhoda was illogical, I think. She did not refuse to take my word, but she wouldn't marry me until the thing was cleared up. I told her that she must investigate it for herself, and so we parted, in no very good temper."

Miss Barfoot smiled and mused. Her duty, she now felt convinced, was to abstain from any sort of meddling. These two people must settle their affairs as they chose. To interfere was to incur an enormous responsibility. For what she had already done in that way Mary reproved herself.

"Now I want to ask you a plain question," Everard resumed. "That letter you wrote to me at Ostend — did it represent Rhoda's mind as well as your own?"

"It's quite impossible for me to say. I didn't know Rhoda's mind."

"Well, perhaps that is a satisfactory answer. It implies, no doubt, that she was still resolved not to concede the point on which I insisted. But since then? Has she come to a decision?"

It was necessary to prevaricate. Mary knew of the interview between Miss Nunn and Mrs. Widdowson, knew its result; but she would not hint at this.

"I have no means of judging how she regards you, Everard."

"It is possible she even thinks me a liar?"

"I understood you to say that she never refused to believe you."

He made a movement of impatience.

"Plainly — you will tell me nothing?"

"I have nothing to tell."

"Then I suppose I must see Rhoda. Perhaps she will refuse to admit me?"

"I can't say. But if she does, her meaning would be unmistakable."

"Cousin Mary," — he looked at her and laughed, — "I think you will be very glad if she *does* refuse."

She seemed about to reply with some pleasantry, but checked herself, and spoke in a serious voice.

"No. I have no such feeling. Whatever you both agree upon will satisfy me. So come by all means, if you wish. I can have nothing to do with it. You had better write and ask her if she will see you, I should think."

Barfoot rose from his seat, and Mary was glad to be released so quickly from a disagreeable situation. For her own part, she had no need to put indiscreet questions; Everard's manner acquainted her quite sufficiently with what was going on in his thoughts. However, he had still something to say.

"You think I have behaved rather badly — let us say, harshly?"

"I am not so foolish as to form any judgment in such a case, cousin Everard."

"Speaking as a woman, should you say that Rhoda had reason on her side — in the first instance?"

"I think," Mary replied, with reluctance, but deliberately, "that she was not unreasonable in wishing to postpone her marriage until she knew what was to be the result of Mrs. Widdowson's indiscreet behaviour."

"Well, perhaps she was not," Everard admitted thoughtfully. "And what *has* been the result?"

"I only know that Mrs. Widdowson has left London, and gone to live at a house her husband has taken somewhere in the country."

"I'm relieved to hear that. — By-the-bye, the little lady's 'indiscreet behaviour' is as much a mystery to me as ever."

"And to me," Mary replied, with an air of indifference.

"Well, then, let us take it for granted that I was rather harsh with Rhoda. But suppose she still meets me with the remark that things are just as they were — that nothing has been explained?"

"I can't discuss your relations with Miss Nunn."

"However, you defend her original action. Be so good as to admit that I can't go to Mrs. Widdowson, and request her to publish a statement that I have never —"

"I shall admit nothing," interrupted Miss Barfoot rather tartly. "I have advised you to see Miss Nunn — if she is willing. And there's nothing more to be said."

"Good. I will write to her."

He did so, in the fewest possible words, and received an answer of equal brevity. In accordance with permission granted, on the Monday evening he found himself once more in his cousin's drawing-room, sitting alone, waiting Miss Nunn's appearance. He wondered how she would present herself, in what costume. Her garb proved to be a plain dress of blue serge, certainly not calculated for effect; but his eye at once distinguished the fact that she had arranged her hair as she wore it when he first knew her, a fashion subsequently abandoned for one that he thought more becoming.

They shook hands. Externally, Barfoot was the more agitated, and his embarrassment appeared in the awkward words with which he began.

"I had made up my mind never to come until you let me know that I was tried and acquitted. But, after all, it is better to have reason on one's side."

"Much better," replied Rhoda, with a smile which emphasized her ambiguity.

She sat down, and he followed her example. Their relative positions called to mind many a conversation they had held in this room. Barfoot — he wore evening-dress — settled in the comfortable chair as though he were an ordinary guest.

"I suppose you would never have written to me?"

"Never," she answered quietly.

"Because you are too proud, or because the mystery is still a mystery?"

"There is no longer any mystery."

Everard made a movement of surprise.

"Indeed? You have discovered what it all meant?"

"Yes, I know what it all meant."

"Can you gratify my not unnatural curiosity?"

"I can say nothing about it, except that I know how the misunderstanding arose."

Rhoda was betraying the effort it had cost her to seem so self-possessed when she entered. Her colour had deepened, and she spoke hurriedly, unevenly.

"And it didn't occur to you that it would be a kindness, not inconsistent with your dignity, to make me in some way acquainted with this fact?"

"I feel no uneasiness on your account."

Everard laughed.

"Splendidly frank, as of old. You really didn't care in the least how much I suffered?"

"You misunderstand me. I felt sure that you didn't suffer at all."

"Ah, I see. You imagined me calm in the assurance that I should some day be justified."

"I had every reason for imagining it," rejoined Rhoda. "Otherwise, you would have given some sign."

Of course he had deeply offended her by his persistent silence. He had intended to do so, first of all; and afterwards — had thought it might be as well. Now that he had got over the difficulty of the meeting, he enjoyed his sense of security. How the interview would end, he knew not; but on his side there should be nothing hasty, unconsidered, merely emotional. Had Rhoda any new revelation of personality within her resources? — that was the question. If so, he would be pleased to observe it. If not — why, it was only the end to which he had long ago looked forward.

"It was not for me to give any sign," he remarked.

"Yet you have said that it is well to have reason on one's side."

Perhaps a softer note allowed itself to be detected in these words. In any case, they were not plainly ironical.

"Admit, then, that an approach was due from me. I have made it. I am here."

Rhoda said nothing. Yet she had not an air of expectancy. Her eye was grave, rather sad, as though for the moment she had forgotten what was at issue, and had lost herself in remoter thought. Regarding her, Everard felt a nobility in her countenance which amply justified all he had ever felt and said. But was there anything more — any new power?

"So we go back," he pursued, "to our day at Wastwater. The perfect day — wasn't it?"

"I shall never wish to forget it," said Rhoda reflectively.

"And we stand as when we quitted each other that night — do we?" She glanced at him.

"I think not."

"Then what is the difference?"

He waited some seconds, and repeated the question before Rhoda answered.

"You are conscious of no difference?" she said.

"Months have elapsed. We are different because we are older. — But you speak as if you were conscious of some greater change."

"Yes, you are changed noticeably. I thought I knew you; perhaps I did. Now I should have to learn you all over again. — It is difficult, you see, for me to keep pace with you. Your opportunities are so much wider."

This was puzzling. Did it signify mere jealousy, or a profounder view of things? Her voice had something even of pathos, as though she uttered a simple thought, without caustic intention.

"I try not to waste my life," he answered seriously. "I have made new acquaintances."

"Will you tell me about them?"

"Tell me first about yourself. — You say you would never have written to me. That means, I think, that you never loved me. When you found that I had been wrongly suspected — and you suspected me yourself, say what you will — if you had loved me, you would have asked forgiveness."

"I have a like reason for doubting *your* love. If you had loved me, you could never have waited so long without trying to remove the obstacle that was between us."

"It was you who put the obstacle there," said Everard, smiling.

"No. An unlucky chance did that. — Or a lucky one. Who knows?"

He began to think: If this woman had enjoyed the social advantages to which Agnes Brissenden and those others were doubtless indebted for so much of their charm, would she not have been their equal, or more? For the first time he compassionated Rhoda. She was brave, and circumstances had not been kind to her. At this moment, was she not contending with herself? Was not her honesty, her dignity, struggling against the impulses of her heart? Rhoda's love had been worth more than his, and it would be her one love in life. A fatuous reflection, perhaps; yet every moment's observation seemed to confirm it.

"Well now," he said, "there's the question which we must decide. If you incline to think that the chance was fortunate" —

She would not speak.

"We must know each other's mind."

"Ah, that is so difficult!" Rhoda murmured, just raising her hand and letting it fall.

"Yes, unless we give each other help. — Let us imagine ourselves back at Seascale, down by the waves. (How cold and grim it must be there, to-night!) I repeat what I said then: Rhoda, will you marry me?"

She looked fixedly at him.

"You didn't say that then."

"What do the words matter?"

"That was not what you said."

He watched the agitation of her features, until his gaze seemed to compel her to move. She stepped towards the fireplace, and moved a little screen that stood too near the fender.

"Why do you want me to repeat exactly what I said?" Everard asked, rising and following her.

"You speak of the 'perfect day.' Didn't the day's perfection end before there was any word of marriage?"

He looked at her with surprise. She had spoken without turning her face towards him; it was visible, now, only by the glow of the fire. Yes, what she said was true, but a truth which he had neither expected, nor desired, to hear. Had the new revelation prepared itself?

"Who first used the word, Rhoda?"

"Yes; I did."

There was silence. Rhoda stood unmoving, the fire's glow upon her face, and Barfoot watched her.

"Perhaps," he said at length, "I was not quite serious when I" —

She turned sharply upon him, a flash of indignation in her eyes.

"Not quite serious? — Yes, I have thought that. — And were you quite serious in *anything* you said?"

"I loved you," he answered curtly, answering her steady look.

"Yet wanted to see whether" —

She could not finish the sentence; her throat quivered.

"I loved you, that's all. — And I believe I still love you."

Rhoda turned to the fire again.

"Will you marry me?" he asked, moving a step nearer.

"I think you are 'not quite serious.'"

I have asked you twice. I ask for the third time."

"I won't marry you with the forms of marriage," Rhoda answered, in an abrupt, harsh tone.

"Now it is you who play with a serious matter."

"You said we had both changed. I see now that our 'perfect day' was marred by my weakness at the end. If you wish to go back in imagination to that summer night, restore everything, only let *me* be what I now am."

Everard shook his head.

"Impossible. It must be then or now, for both of us."

"Legal marriage," she said, glancing at him, "has acquired some new sanction for you, since then?"

"On the whole, perhaps it has."

"Naturally. — But I shall never marry, so we will speak no more of it."

As if finally dismissing the subject, she walked to the opposite side of the hearth, and there turned towards her companion with a cold smile.

"In other words, then, you have ceased to love me?"

"Yes, I no longer love you."

"Yet, if I had been willing to revive that fantastic idealism — as you thought it" —

She interrupted him sternly.

"What *was* it?"

"Oh, a kind of idealism, undoubtedly. I was so bent on making sure that you loved me."

She laughed.

"After all, the perfection of our day was half make-believe. You never loved me with entire sincerity. And you will never love any woman — even as well as you loved me."

"Upon my soul, I believe it, Rhoda. And even now" —

"And even now it is just possible for us to say good-bye with something like friendliness. But not if you talk longer. Don't let us spoil it; things are so straight — and clear" —

A threatened sob made her break off, but she recovered herself, and offered him her hand.

He walked all the way back to his hotel, and the cold, clammy night restored his equanimity. A fortnight later, sending a Christmas present, with greetings, to Mr. and Mrs. Micklethwaite, he wrote thus:

"I am about to do my duty — as you put it — that is, to marry. The name of my future wife is Miss Agnes Brissenden. It will be in March, I think. But I shall see you before then, and give you a fuller account of myself."

CHAPTER XXXI.

A NEW BEGINNING.

Widdowson tried two or three lodgings; he settled at length in a small house at Hampstead; occupying two plain rooms. Here, at long intervals, his friend Newdick came to see him; but no one else. He had brought with him a selection of solid books from his library, and over these the greater part of each day was spent. Not that he studied with any zeal; reading, and of a kind that demanded close attention, was his only resource against melancholia; he knew not how else to occupy himself. Adam Smith's classical work, perused with laborious thoroughness, gave him employment for a couple of months; subsequently he plodded through all the volumes of Hallam.[1]

His landlady, and the neighbours who were at leisure to observe him when he went out for his two hours' walk in the afternoon, took him for an old gentleman of sixty-five or so. He no longer held himself upright, and when out of doors seldom raised his eyes from the ground; grey streaks had begun to brindle his hair; his face grew yellower and more deeply furrowed. Of his personal appearance, even of cleanliness, he became neglectful, and occasionally it happened that he lay in bed all through the morning, reading, dozing, or in a state of mental vacuity.

It was long since he had seen his relative, the sprightly widow; but he had heard from her. On the point of leaving England for her summer holiday, Mrs. Luke sent him a few lines, urging him, in the language of her world, to live more sensibly and let his wife "have her head" now and then; it would be better for both of them. Then followed the time of woe, and for many weeks he gave no thought to Mrs. Luke. But close upon the end of the year, he received one day a certain Society Journal, addressed in a hand he knew to the house at Herne Hill. In it was discoverable, marked with a red pencil, the following paragraph:

"Among the English who this year elected to take their repose and recreation at Trouville, there was no more brilliant figure than Mrs. Luke Widdowson. This lady is well known in the *monde*[2] where one never *s'ennuie*;[3] where smart people are gathered together, there is the charming widow sure to be seen. We are able to announce that, before leaving Trouville, Mrs. Widdowson had consented to a private engagement with Capt. William Horrocks, — no other, indeed, than 'Captain Bill,' the universal

---

1 Adam Smith's (1723-1790) classic work is *The Wealth of Nations* (1776), which lays the foundation of laissez-faire economics. Henry Hallam (1777-1859) was a historian (and the father of Tennyson's friend Arthur Hallam).
2 The (fashionable) world.
3 Weary, bored.

favourite, so beloved by hostesses as a sure dancing-man. By the lamented death of his father, this best of good fellows has now become Sir William, and we understand that his marriage will be celebrated after the proper delays. Our congratulations!"

Subsequently arrived a newspaper, with an account of the marriage. Mrs. Luke was now Lady Horrocks, she had the title desired of her heart.

Another two months went by, and there came a letter — re-addressed, like the other communications, at the Post Office — in which the baronet's wife declared herself anxious to hear of her friends. She found they had left Herne Hill; if this letter reached him, would not Edmund come and see her at her house in Wimpole Street?

Misery of solitude, desire for a woman's sympathy and counsel, impelled him to use this opportunity, little as it seemed to promise. He went to Wimpole Street, and had a very long private talk with Lady Horrocks, who, in some way he could not understand, had changed from her old self. She began frivolously, but in rather a dull, make-believe way; and when she heard that Widdowson had parted from his wife, when a few vague, miserable words had suggested the domestic drama so familiar to her observation, she at once grew quiet, sober, sympathetic, as if really glad to have something serious to talk about.

"Now look here, Edmund. Tell the whole story, from the first. You're the sort of man to make awful blunders in such a case as this. Just tell me all about it. I'm not a bad sort, you know, and I have troubles of my own — I don't mind telling you so much. Women make fools of themselves — well, never mind. Just tell me about the little girl, and see if we can't square things somehow."

He had a struggle with himself, but at length narrated everything, often interrupted by shrewd questions.

"No one writes to you?" the listener finally inquired.

"I am expecting to hear from them," was Widdowson's answer, as he sat in the usual position, head hanging forward and hands clasped between his knees.

"To hear what?"

"I think I shall be sent for."

"Sent for? To make it up?"

"She is going to give birth to a child."

Lady Horrocks nodded twice, thoughtfully, and with a faint smile.

"How did you find this out?"

"I have know it long enough. Her sister Virginia told me before they went away. I had a suspicion all at once, and I forced her to tell me."

"And if you are sent for, shall you go?"

Widdowson seemed to mutter an affirmative, and added:

"I shall hear what she has to tell me, as she promised."

"Is it — is it possible —?"

The lady's question remained incomplete. Widdowson, though he understood it, vouchsafed no direct answer. Intense suffering was manifest in his face, and at length he spoke vehemently.

"Whatever she tells me — how can I believe it? When once a woman has lied, how can she ever again be believed? I can't be sure of anything."

"All that fibbing," remarked Lady Horrocks, "has an unpleasant look. No denying it. She got entangled somehow. But I think you had better believe that she pulled up just in time."

"I have no love for her left," he went on, in a despairing voice. "It all perished in those frightful days. I tried hard to think that I still loved her. I kept writing letters — but they meant nothing — or they only meant that I was driven half crazy by wretchedness. — I had rather we lived on as we have been doing. It's miserable enough for me, God knows; but it would be worse to try and behave to her as if I could forget everything. I know her explanation won't satisfy me. Whatever it is, I shall still suspect her. — I don't know that the child is mine. It may be. Perhaps as it grows up there will be a likeness, to help me to make sure. But what a life! Every paltry trifle will make me uneasy, and if I discovered any fresh deceit, I should do something terrible. — You don't know how near I was" —

He shuddered, and hid his face.

"The Othello business[1] won't do," said Lady Horrocks not unkindly. "You couldn't have gone on together, of course; you had to part for a time. Well, that's all over; take it as something that couldn't be helped. You were behaving absurdly, you know; I told you plainly; I guessed there'd be trouble. You oughtn't to have married at all, that's the fact; it would be better for most of us if we kept out of it. Some marry for a good reason, some for a bad, and mostly it all comes to the same in the end. But there, never mind. Pull yourself together, dear boy. It's all nonsense about not caring for her. Of course you're eating your heart out for want of her. And I'll tell you what I think: it's very likely Monica was pulled up just in time by discovering — you understand? — that she was more your wife than any one else's. Something tells me that's how it was. Just try to look at it in that way. If the child lives, she'll be different. She has sowed her wild oats — why shouldn't a woman as well as a man? Go down to Clevedon, and forgive her. You're an honest man, and it isn't every woman — but never mind. I could tell you stories about people — but you wouldn't care to hear them. Just take things with a laugh — we *all* have to. Life's as you take it: all gloom or moderately shiny."

---

1 In Shakespeare's *Othello* (1604), the eponymous protagonist, like Widdowson, agonizes over his suspicions that his wife, Desdemona, has a lover. Othello finally strangles Desdemona in jealous despair and then kills himself when he learns that she is innocent.

With much more to the same solacing effect. For the time, Widdowson was perchance a trifle comforted; at all events, he went away with a sense of gratitude to Lady Horrocks. And when he had left the house, he remembered that not even a civil formality with regard to Sir William had fallen from his lips. But Sir William's wife, for whatever reason, had also not once mentioned the baronet's name.

Only a few days passed before Widdowson received the summons he was expecting. It came in the form of a telegram, bidding him hasten to his wife; not a word of news added. At the time of its arrival, he was taking his afternoon walk; this delay made it doubtful whether he could get to Paddington by six-twenty, the last train which would enable him to reach Clevedon that night. He managed it, with only two or three minutes to spare.

Not till he was seated in the railway carriage could he fix his thoughts on the end of the journey. An inexpressible repugnance then affected him; he would have welcomed any disaster to the train, any injury which might prevent his going to Monica at such a time. Often, in anticipation, the event which was now come to pass had confused and darkened his mind; he loathed the thought of it. If the child, perhaps already born, were in truth his, it must be very long before he could regard it with a shadow of paternal interest; uncertainty, to which he was condemned, would in all likelihood make it an object of aversion to him as long as he lived.

He was at Bristol by a quarter-past nine, and had to change for a slow train, which by ten o'clock brought him to Yatton, the little junction for Clevedon. It was a fine, starry night, but extremely cold. For the few minutes of detention he walked restlessly about the platform. His chief emotion was now a fear lest all might not go well with Monica. Whether he could believe what she had to tell him or not, it would be worse if she were to die before he could hear her exculpation. The anguish of remorse would seize upon him.

Alone in his compartment, he did not sit down, but stamped backwards and forwards on the floor, and before the train stopped he jumped out. No cab was procurable; he left his bag at the station, and hastened with all speed in the direction that he remembered. But very soon the cross-ways had confused him. As he met no one whom he could ask to direct him, he had to knock at a door. Streaming with perspiration, he came at length within sight of his own house. A church clock was striking eleven.

Alice and Virginia were both standing in the hall when the door was opened; they beckoned him into a room.

"Is it over?" he asked, staring from one to the other with his dazzled eyes.

"At four this afternoon," answered Alice, scarce able to articulate. "A little girl."

"She had to have chloroform," said Virginia, who looked a miserable, lifeless object, and shook like one in an ague.[1]

"And all's well?"

"We think so — we hope so," they stammered together.

Alice added that the doctor was to make another call to-night. They had a good nurse. The infant seemed healthy, but was a very, very little mite, and had only made its voice heard for a few minutes.

"She knows you sent for me?"

"Yes. — And we have something to give you. You were to have this as soon as you arrived."

Miss Madden handed him a sealed envelope; then both the sisters drew away, as if fearing the result of what they had done. Widdowson just glanced at the unaddressed missive, and put it into his pocket.

"I must have something to eat," he said, wiping his forehead. "When the doctor comes, I'll see him."

This visit took place while he was engaged on his supper. On coming down from the patient, the doctor gave him an assurance that things were progressing "fairly well"; the morning, probably, would enable him to speak with yet more confidence. Widdowson had another brief conversation with the sisters, then bade them good-night, and went to the room that had been prepared for him. As he closed the door, he heard a thin, faint wail, and stood listening until it ceased; it came from a room on the floor below.

Having brought himself with an effort to open the envelope he had received, he found several sheets of note-paper, one of them, remarked immediately, in a man's writing. At this he first glanced, and the beginning showed him that it was a love-letter, written to Monica. He threw it aside and took up the other sheets, which contained a long communication from his wife; it was dated two months ago. In it Monica recounted to him, with scrupulous truthfulness, the whole story of her relations with Bevis.

"I only make this confession" — so she concluded — "for the sake of the poor child that will soon be born. The child is yours, and ought not to suffer because of what I did. The enclosed letter will prove this to you, if anything can. For myself I ask nothing. I don't think I shall live. If I do, I will consent to anything you propose. I only ask you to behave without any pretence; if you cannot forgive me, do not make a show of it. Say what your will is, and that shall be enough."

He did not go to bed that night. There was a fire in the room, and he kept it alight until daybreak, when he descended softly to the hall, and let himself out of the house.

In a fierce wind that swept from the northwest down the foaming channel, he walked for an hour or two, careless whither the roads direct-

---

1 A paroxysm of fever and shivering associated with malaria.

ed him. All he desired was to be at a distance from that house, with its hideous silence and the faint cry that could scarcely be called a sound. The necessity of returning, of spending days there, was an oppression which held him like a nightmare.

Monica's statement he neither believed nor disbelieved; he simply could not make up his mind about it. She had lied to him so resolutely before; was she not capable of elaborate falsehood to save her reputation and protect her child? The letter from Bevis might have been a result of conspiracy between them.

That Bevis was the man against whom his jealousy should have been directed, at first astounded him. By now he had come to a full perception of his stupidity in never entertaining such a thought. The revelation was equivalent to a second offence just discovered; for he found it impossible to ignore his long-cherished suspicion of Barfoot, and he even surmised the possibility of Monica's having listened to love-making from that quarter previously to her intimacy with Bevis. He loathed the memory of his life since marriage; and as for pardoning his wife, he could as soon pardon and smile upon the author of that accursed letter from Bordeaux.

But go back to the house he must. By obeying his impulse and straightway returning to London, he might be the cause of a fatal turn in Monica's illness. Constraint of bare humanity would keep him here until his wife was out of danger. But he could not see her, and as soon as possible he must escape from such unendurable circumstances.

Re-entering at half-past eight, he was met by Alice, who seemed to have slept as little as he himself had done. They went into the dining-room.

"She has been inquiring about you," began Miss Madden timorously.

"How is she?"

"Not worse, I believe. But so very weak. — She wishes me to ask you" —

"What?"

His manner did not encourage the poor woman.

"I shall be obliged to tell her something. If I have nothing to say, she will fret herself into a dangerous state. She wants to know if you have read her letter, and if — if you will see the child."

Widdowson turned away, and stood irresolute. He felt Miss Madden's hand upon his arm.

"Oh, don't refuse! Let me give her some comfort."

"It's the child she's anxious about?"

Alice admitted it, looking into her brother-in-law's face with woeful appeal.

"Say I will see it," he answered, "and have it brought into some room, — then say I *have* seen it."

"Mayn't I take her a word of forgiveness?"

"Yes, say I forgive her. — She doesn't wish me to go to her?"

Alice shook her head.

"Then say I forgive her."

As he directed, so it was done; and in the course of the morning Miss Madden brought word to him that her sister had experienced great relief. She was sleeping.

But the doctor thought it necessary to make two visits before nightfall, and late in the evening he came again. He explained to Widdowson that there were complications, not unlikely to be dangerous, and finally he suggested that, if the morrow brought no decided improvement, a second medical man should be called in to consult. This consultation was held. In the afternoon, Virginia came weeping to her brother-in-law, and told him that Monica was delirious. That night the whole household watched. Another day was passed in the gravest anxiety, and at dusk the medical attendant no longer disguised his opinion that Mrs. Widdowson was sinking. She became unconscious soon after, and in the early morning breathed her last.

Widdowson was in the room, and at the end sat by the bedside for an hour. But he did not look upon his wife's face. When it was told him that she had ceased to breathe, he rose and went into his own chamber, death-pale but tearless.

On the day after the funeral — Monica was buried in the cemetery, which is hard by the Old Church — Widdowson and the elder sister had a long conversation in private. It related, first of all, to the motherless baby. Widdowson's desire was that Miss Madden should undertake the care of the child. She and Virginia might live wherever they preferred; their needs would be provided for. Alice had hardly dared to hope for such a proposal — as it concerned the child, that is to say. Gladly she accepted it.

"But there's something I must tell you," she said, with embarrassed appeal in her wet eyes. "Poor Virginia wishes to go into an Institution."

Widdowson looked at her, not understanding; whereupon she broke into tears, and made known that her sister was such a slave to strong drink that they both despaired of reformation unless by help of the measure she had indicated. There were people, she had heard, who undertook the care of inebriates.

"You know that we are by no means penniless," sobbed Alice. "We can very well bear the expense. But will you assist us to find a suitable place?"

He promised to proceed at once in the matter.

"And when she is cured," said Miss Madden, "she shall come and live with me. And when baby is about two years old, we will do what we have been purposing for a long time. We will open a school for young children, either here or at Weston. That will afford my poor sister occupation. Indeed, we shall both be better for the exertion of such an undertaking — don't you think so?"

"It would be a wise thing, I have no doubt whatever."

The large house was to be abandoned, and as much of the furniture as seemed needful transported to a smaller dwelling in another part of Clevedon. For Alice resolved to stay here, in spite of painful associations. She loved the place, and looked forward with quiet joy to the life that was prepared for her. Widdowson's books would go back to London; not to the Hampstead lodgings, however. Fearful of solitude, he proposed to his friend Newdick that they should live together, he, as a man of substance, bearing the larger share of the expense. And this plan also came into execution.

Three months went by, and on a day of summer, when the wooded hills and green lanes and rich meadows of Clevedon looked their best, when the Channel was still and blue, and the Welsh mountains loomed through a sunny haze, Rhoda Nunn came over from the Mendips to see Miss Madden. It could not be a gladsome meeting, but Rhoda was bright and natural and her talk as inspiriting as ever. She took the baby in her arms, and walked about with it for a long time in the garden, often murmuring, "Poor little child! Dear little child!" There had been doubt whether it would live, but the summer seemed to be fortifying its health. Alice, it was plain, had found her vocation; she looked better than at any time since Rhoda had known her. Her complexion was losing its muddiness and spottiness; her step had become light and brisk.

"And where is your sister?" inquired Miss Nunn.

"Staying with friends at present. She will be back before long, I hope. And as soon as baby can walk, we are going to think very seriously about the school. You remember?"

"The school? You will really make the attempt?"

"It will be so good for us both. Why, look," she added laughingly, "here is one pupil growing for us!"

"Make a brave woman of her," said Rhoda kindly.

"We will try, — ah, we will try! — And is your work as successful as ever?"

"More!" replied Rhoda. "We flourish like the green bay-tree. We shall have to take larger premises. By-the-bye, you must read the paper we are going to publish; the first number will be out in a month, though the name isn't quite decided upon yet. Miss Barfoot was never in such health and spirits — nor I myself. The world is moving!"

Whilst Miss Madden went into the house to prepare hospitalities, Rhoda, still nursing, sat down on a garden bench. She gazed intently at those diminutive features, which were quite placid and relaxing in soft drowsiness. The dark, bright eye was Monica's. And as the baby sank into sleep, Rhoda's vision grew dim; a sigh made her lips quiver, and once more she murmured, "Poor little child!"

THE END.

Appendix A: Contemporary Reviews of The Odd Women

1. *Glasgow Herald* (20 April 1893) 9.

Mr. Gissing is a very prolific writer, for it cannot be six weeks since we reviewed his "Born in Exile," but one cannot grumble at a novelist for writing too often who gives us such excellent work as the book under notice. It distinctly marks a great advance in his art, showing him among the "arriving" novelists of the day, if, indeed, he may not now be said already to have "arrived." There is always thought in Mr. Gissing's books; sometimes more thought than action, but he has arrived at a happy and artistic combination in the work under review. It is altogether a story of odd women, women who suffer in the dreadful whirl of English daily life, because the brutal truth is there are too many women to be married, and most of them are quite unfitted to realise for themselves that to be successful, to burst the bonds which encompass their narrow, sordid lives, they must be "odd." It is Rhoda Nunn's mission, and that of her friend Miss Barfoot (Mr. Gissing's characters have invariably the strangest names and the ugliest), to work with and for the helpless women; the women who do not belong to the working classes, but are ten times weaker than the women of that class, and pitiably helpless. They help them to find occupations which the age readily admits women can adequately fill. And across Rhoda's almost stern life, so full is it of duty, comes a romance. She, like other women, has at last a proposal, and even though she determines to refuse it, yet the fact makes her stronger and happier in a way Mr. Gissing has very delicately and beautifully shown. The other men and women of the story present various aspects of the marriage question, ingeniously contrasted and unsparedly outlined. We only wish that in the end Mr. Gissing would occasionally make his men and women happy, or some of them. We always feel at the opening pages of his books inclined to say of his characters "Heedless of their doom, the little victims play,"[1] for the author luxuriates as he closes in a holocaust of the affections — death, madness, or misery. Still it is all very human, and "The Odd Women" is a genuine work of art, remarkable among the novels of the day.

2. *Saturday Review* 75 (29 April 1893) 459–60.

Many of us — perhaps even most of us — disagree with Mr. Gissing in his views of life and his plans for improving it; but the mere fact that he has

---

1   Thomas Gray (1716–71), "Ode on a Distant Prospect of Eton College," ll. 51–52 (written 1742, published 1747). Original reads "regardless of their doom."

any views at all gives him a claim to our interest and to our careful consideration. The "Odd Women" who form the subject of his latest work have nothing in common with lunatics, but are simply the million or so of surplus females who have to struggle through their span somehow, independently of men. To emphasize his point the better Mr. Gissing has drawn a sharp contrast. On the one hand there is a shiftless family of doctor's daughters who have been taught nothing that is useful at home; on the other there is a friend of these girls who sets to work to remedy her own helplessness, and ends by making a comfortable livelihood in the type-writing line. Of course the story is not as bald as this. The types of character are each distinct, and are not exaggerated either for moral or artistic purposes. The well-meaning, ill-educated, unhealthy, conventional Alice Madden; her equally well-meaning, ill-educated, unhealthy sister Virginia, who out of sheer poverty and weariness takes to drink; their younger, prettier, and more practical sister Monica, who wrecks her life by an unsuitable marriage out of a pardonable desire to escape from the shop in the Walworth Road where she is an assistant — these women are in no way single specimens of their kind, nor are they meant to be. No more is the harder, more successful Rhoda Nunn, above alluded to. Curious to state, Mr. Gissing's women are far truer to nature than his men. Their conduct is intelligible from their varied points of view, but the personality and the behaviour of Mr. Everard Barfoot, for instance, would baffle the understanding of most people. He is meant to be a charming and aristocratic (though rather wild) person: in reality he is a very pronounced cad. It is not very easy to see how far the doctrines of terminable marriages, and "marriage in the sight of God" (which always means no marriage in the sight of men) are really Mr. Gissing's own, and how far they are merely attributed to his characters. Mr. Barfoot decides, when he declares his affection to that advocate of celibacy Rhoda Nunn, that if she consents to forego the ceremony he will make her his legal wife; but that if in the first instance she insists on even the Registrar, she will lower herself for ever in his eyes. This, at least, is what we have understood; but Mr. Gissing has not expressed himself very clearly. The best chapters in the book are those which describe the loving and zealous tyranny of the middle-aged Widdowson, who having become the husband of the young and pretty Monica Madden, wishes to shut her up exclusively with himself, and drives her into telling lies and offering to elope with a gentleman, who looks on her proposition as manifesting "*trop de zèle*," and there the matter ends. Humour is never the "crowning glory" of Mr. Gissing's novels; but he shows some when he allows us to see that he thinks that boredom is an excellent reason for rending marriage; only in a book that sets forth the perfect equality of women it is rather strange that the acts of boring cited should all be on the one side. And, in spite of her somewhat blatant self-assertion, it is at once sad and comic and true to notice that all her dislike to matrimony does not prevent Miss Rhoda Nunn from rising in her own esteem when, at the age of thirty-three, she has an offer. This is the attitude many persons assume towards life in general. They do not care to *have*, but they wish to be able to *reject*.

3. *Athenaeum* no. 3422 (27 May 1893) 667.

As might be expected, Mr. Gissing's new novel 'The Odd Women' is intensely modern, actual in theme as well as in treatment. Amidst the vexed social questions that surround us on all sides, and seem to defy solution, he has chosen one of real interest, and has turned it to clever and original purpose. The problem of the odd woman and what is to be done with her presents, in truth, a grim enough aspect. As treated by Mr. Gissing the interest is of almost too painful a character; yet it is full of suggestion and significance. Those who know him best recognize that his manner and method are generally vivid and, to some extent, individual, though by no means enchanting. Here, as in former novels, we have pages of something more resembling the reporter's than the artist's touch. The story is anything but crude or unsympathetic, yet in the telling it is often a little inadequate. Journalese is conspicuous, not by its absence. In spite of this the book is better than merely readable, it is absorbing. One feels that the author is more than master of his subject; that he has turned it about and around, and thoroughly knows its capabilities. As a novel it is decidedly "uncheering"; the outlook is, in some ways, even more depressing than in 'New Grub Street.' Yet latent in it all is an element of hope, a something that encourages the idea that with time and effort the baffling problem of the odd women may be successfully solved. Many of the characters and episodes are extremely well drawn; the dialogue is of the right sort — natural and to the purpose. Mr. Gissing has not, perhaps, on the whole, written anything stronger or more striking.

4. *Pall Mall Gazette* (29 May 1893) 4.

It would have been a real calamity if Mr. Gissing had tried to palm off upon us under the guise of a novel, a treatise, or even a dialogue, on the Woman question. To an active mind like his, profoundly interested in the phenomena of the civilization round him, the danger must have been great. None the less, he has kept his story very free from sociological dialectic. To make a novel pivot on a sociological rather than what unquestioning fetish-worship calls a "purely human" motive, is not at all the same thing as to write a narrative tract, after the manner of Mrs. Humphrey Ward or Sarah Grand.[1] As the threads of society are compli-

---

1 Popular novelists of the period. Grand (1854–1943) wrote "New Woman" novels, while Ward (1851-1920) developed social and religious themes in her fiction.

cated more and more it is difficult to avoid this, and Zola and Ibsen[1] have shown us that the widest and loosest ideas can be treated in a purely artistic way. Mr. Gissing succeeds in doing this, though obviously not without a certain effort. His book represents the Woman question made flesh; his people live it instead of talking it. His method is to take types that represent the question, or rather the fact, in all its divagations — the old love marriage, the marriage of convenience, the womanly old-maid, the emancipated woman, and all the rest; then to make them in a purely natural way develop that side of themselves that bears on the position of women in the society of to-day. Obviously the danger of the method lies in the difficulty of keeping the story together. On this count Mr. Gissing has not been blameless in the past, and it is a palpable fault in "The Odd Women" that it tends to part into two divergent channels. That is the danger of taking too large an idea; it is too lax to bind all its modifications into an organic whole. But in our judgment Mr. Gissing has succeeded as far as was possible in suggesting the general idea that puts all his characters on the same plane, and yet has not obtruded it so much as to make them counters in the game of sociology instead of living human beings.

Certainly his people live. You might brush against any of them in the Strand[2] from morning till morning again. And, better, they live transfigured by the artist, who shows you the exact significance of each life. "The Odd Women" is a great vindication of realism from the charge of dulness. At afternoon tea his women, odd and even, would be totally uninteresting to any but the most sympathetic; in the book you follow them breathless. Moreover Mr. Gissing steers clear of another danger that besets the psychological treatment of motive and character. His work is, in the main, presentative; many pages of wiredrawn analysis are replaced by one of living conversation. That parts off good from bad realism. Mr. Gissing's power of unravelling the tangled influences that draw one hither and thither is admirably shown in the figure of Rhoda Nunn, the strong, self-reliant, revolted woman, with the old womanly woman still restless underneath as she fights against the recognition of it. Monica, the girl who marries in haste, Virginia, the lady's companion who drinks gin while she is waiting for her next engagement, are drawn with masterly insight and pathos. In fine "The Odd Women" falls short of genius only through its author's characteristic limitations — the complete lack of dash, the strange occasional flatness of the writing, the curious blindness (effective too, in its way, and especially in this book) that refuses to see any colour in the world but grey. But to a modern mind it is, for all that, the most interesting novel of the year.

---

1 Émile Zola (1840–1902) was a French naturalist writer. Henrik Ibsen (1828–1906) was a Norwegian dramatist often associated with the New Woman and women's rights because of the influence of his play, *A Doll's House* (1879).
2 A major thoroughfare in central London.

5. *Nation* [New York] (13 July 1893) 30–31.

One of the most encouraging signs of the times is the recognition of the virtues of the "old maid." Unless she is rich, she is not yet accorded any particular social status, but she is no longer an object for contumely and derision, and it is generally conceded that she is not necessarily either an old cat or an old fool. When she gets a novel written in her praise and honor (euphemistically called 'The Odd Women'), she may be said to have cast off the last shred of disability. If half that Mr. Gissing affirms and predicts about them is true, the hope of the future certainly lies in our old maids. Through the intemperance of partisanship he has perhaps put a scourge in the hands of the enemies of that class which he wishes to exalt, the self-supporting unmarried women. His examples of marriage go to show that that institution is a failure, and the drift of his conclusions on sexual relations is in favor of the *union libre.* "We told you so," cry the conservators of morals; "freedom for women means license and the sacred hearth gone to the dogs!" Far be it from them to read patiently and to learn that Mr. Gissing points to the voluntary relation between men and women only as the far-off ideal consummation of human striving towards self-knowledge, self-reverence and self-control. But the time is not yet, and we go so far with the adorers of home and humdrum as to fail to see that its coming is in the line of social progress. The great thing is for society to give the odd women a fighting chance, and to consider with charity those who fall in the fray.

The story in which the 'Odd Women' are thus ably championed is excellent both for construction and for characterization. The novel with a good purpose is too apt to be a very bad novel, and it is a pleasure to testify that Mr. Gissing's is, in spite of and on account of its intensity of purpose, an uncommonly good one.

6. Clementina Black, *Illustrated London News* (5 August 1893) 155.
[Clementina Black (1855–1923) was a novelist, journalist, and activist for the rights of working women.]

The "odd women" — the half million or so for whom there is "no making a pair" — these are the theme of Mr. Gissing's latest novel, a novel which is in many ways a distinct advance upon anything which he has done yet. Like most persons who contemplate the problem of the unmarried and untrained woman, he is inclined to think the problem due to a far greater extent than is really the case to mere difference in the numbers of the sexes. It is not so much because, as one of Miss Mary Wilkins's[1] personages says, there are not husbands "enough to go round,"

---

1 Mary E. Wilkins Freeman (1852–1930) was an American writer of novels and short stories. The "personages" are probably from *A New England Nun and Other Stories* (1891). The "New England nun" was a confirmed spinster.

as because of various social and economic conditions that women (and men, too) remain unmarried. The apparent surplus of women is largely due to the fact that they live longer. If a hundred men and a hundred women were to be born ever year, and if all the men lived to fifty, while all the women lived to fifty-one, there would be a permanent surplus of a hundred women, and yet every one of these might have been married to one of the hundred men born in the same year as herself. Still, it remains true for practical purposes that a large group of women, especially in the poorer middle class, has no opportunity of suitable marriage. That these women should be trained to callings by which they can live — partly, among many other reasons, in the interests of the dignity of marriage — is the moral of Mr. Gissing's book, and he develops it out of a variety of different situations, all of which rise in natural connection. He gives us a shop-girl of gentle breeding who accepts marriage as a mere escape from slavery, and finds that she has but forged herself a heavier chain; an out-of-work "companion" led gradually, by semi-starvation and lack of mental interests, to drink; a well-meaning young man debarred from marriage by the necessity of supporting his unmarried sisters, and consoling himself by a disastrous flirtation with another man's wife; and glimpses of several varieties of married life, mostly unhappy. Finally, he shows us a little group of active, intelligent women, working for themselves and for their sisters, and regarding the world with a courage and a resolution that make the bright spot in a gloomy picture. In the conversations of these women is contained the argumentative kernel of the book; and Mr. Gissing has succeeded in the feat, so often attempted in the modern novel, but so seldom achieved, of giving to discussions of social problems the twofold interest attaching to them in real life — an interest, namely, in the thing said, for its own sake, and an interest in it as a display of character on the part of the person saying it. This double interest is especially well marked when the speakers are Rhoda Nunn and Everard Barfoot. The growth of intimacy and regard between the enlightened independent spinster and the rather dilettante wandering bachelor is singularly well told, but it leads up to the weak point of the story. We feel, as we read, that between two persons so clear-sighted, so outspoken, and so fully aware of the pitfalls of married life, the natural end would be a real marriage — that is to say, an equal union, in which each would respect the freedom and individuality of the other, and in which each would find the completest development. Surely such a man and woman — both, be it remembered, over thirty years old — are not likely to spoil their own and each other's lives by a display of sheer perverse stubbornness. As long as they hover on the edge of a decisive avowal their conduct is natural and reasonable enough; but when they come to the crisis they show themselves as touchy, as unreasonable, and as eager "not to give in" as a pair of lovers still in their teens. The conduct of Rhoda, in particular, is gravely out of character. On one day she receives from Everard the most solemn, deliberate, and repeated assurances that no woman has any moral claim upon him, and that he has not "during the past three months made professions of love or even pretended love to any woman." On the next, a story reaches her which seems at first sight seriously compromising to him. Of course, such a story told of the man to whom she has just engaged herself would distress any woman; and a quite young girl, inexperienced in pain, might not improbably visit hers on her lover, as a child beats the table against which it has knocked its head. But surely a mature woman of unusually sincere, just, and open-minded character would not, while those words of assurance were still ringing in her ears, take up an attitude of cold estrangement. And if by any chance, in any sudden gust of unreasonable jealousy, she had taken up such a position, is it credible that later, when a complete explanation reached her, which not only exonerated Everard, but showed him ignorant of the very facts, she should still have kept up her offended attitude, experiencing no remorse and making no sign? Surely to such a woman as Rhoda the perception that she had acted unjustly and ungenerously would involve immediate confession of her error. But, no; *she* will not take the first step and *he* will not take the first step — which really, under the circumstances, is more pardonable; and when, after all, he does make the first advance, she neither acknowledges nor apologises for the grave wrong she did him, but refuses — still with the manner of an injured person — to make up the quarrel, which was so clearly no fault of his. This is the conduct of an ungenerous, a selfish, and especially an undisciplined woman, and is out of keeping with all the previous history of Rhoda Nunn. It would almost seem as if hatred of the conventional "happy ending" had led Mr. Gissing to that same sacrifice of truthful portraiture into which so many of his predecessors have been betrayed by their love of it.

Happily, in a good novel it is the impression of the best part which remains, while the weaker pages fade away. Who remembers the loves of Madeline Bray (if, indeed, that was her name) and Nicholas Nickleby? but who forgets Mrs. Nickleby or the Crummles family?[1] The parts that remain of "The Odd Women" are the picture of the three sisters Madden, and that of Rhoda and Miss Barfoot, comrades in work, hope, and friendship. These parts of the book are better, truer, and, it may be fairly added, better written than anything which Mr. Gissing had previously published; and to say that is not to say little.

---

1 In *Nicholas Nickleby* (1838–39), by Charles Dickens (1812–70), Madeline Bray is Nicholas's rather colourless first love. Mrs. Nickleby and the Crummles are some of the many engaging comic characters in the novel.

Appendix B: Attitudes towards Women and Marriage in Victorian Culture

1. **Sarah Ellis, extract from** *The Daughters of England. Their Position in Society, Character, and Responsibilities* **(1842).**
[Sarah Ellis (1812–72) was the author of numerous didactic novels and treatises. She was especially interested in women's education. Her *Women of England, Their Social Duties and Domestic Habits* (1839) and *The Daughters of England*, from which the following extract is taken, were popular and influential conduct manuals for women in the Victorian period.]

I have already stated, that women, in their position in life, must be content to be inferior to men; but as their inferiority consists chiefly in their want of power, this deficiency is abundantly made up to them by their capability of exercising influence; it is made up to them also in other ways, incalculable in their number and extent, but in none so effectually as by that order of Divine Providence which places them, in a moral and religious point of view, on the same level with man; nor can it be a subject of regret to any right-minded woman, that they are not only exempt from the most laborious occupations both of mind and body, but also from the necessity of engaging in those eager pecuniary speculations, and in that fierce conflict of worldly interests, by which men are so deeply occupied as to be in a manner compelled to stifle their best feelings, until they become in reality the characters they at first only assumed. Can it be a subject of regret to any kind and feeling woman, that her sphere of action is one adapted to the exercise of the affections, where she may love, and trust, and hope, and serve, to the utmost of her wishes? Can it be a subject of regret that she is not called upon, so much as man, to calculate, to compete, to struggle, but rather to occupy a sphere in which the elements of discord cannot with propriety be admitted — in which beauty and order are expected to denote her presence, and where the exercise of benevolence is the duty she is most frequently called upon to perform.

Women almost universally consider themselves, and wish to be considered by others, as extremely affectionate; scarcely can a more severe libel be pronounced upon a woman than to say that she is not so. Now the whole law of woman's life is a law of love. I propose, therefore, to treat the subject in this light — to try whether the neglect of their peculiar duties does not imply an absence of love, and whether the principle of love, thoroughly carried out, would not so influence their conduct and feelings as to render them all which their best friends could desire.

Let us, however, clearly understand each other at the outset. To love, is a very different thing from a desire to be beloved. To love, is woman's nature — to be beloved is the consequence of her having properly exercised and controlled that nature. To love, is woman's duty — to be beloved, is her reward.

Does the subject, when considered in this point of view, appear less attractive? "No," you reply, "it constitutes the happiness of every generous soul, to love; and if that be the secret of our duty, the whole life of woman must be a pleasant journey on a path of flowers."

* * * *

I have been compelled, during the course of these remarks, to use an expression which requires some explanation. I have said, that a young woman may with propriety learn even the dead languages, provided she has nothing better to do; by which, I would be understood to mean, provided she does not consequently leave undone what would render her more useful or amiable as a woman. The settlement of this question must depend entirely upon the degree of her talent, and the nature of her position in life. If she has no other talent likely to make her so useful as that which is employed in learning Greek, Latin, and Hebrew, this settles the point at once, or if she has no duties so important to her as to ascertain the derivation of words, or to study the peculiarities of heathen writers, then by all means let her be a learned lady, for every study, every occupation of mind, provided it does not include what is evil, must be preferable to absolute idleness.

But may we not turn to the consideration of science as opening a wide field of interesting study, which does more to enlarge the mind, and give right views of common things, than the mere acquisition of language?

"Science! — what have we to do with science?" exclaim half a dozen soft voices at once. Certainly not to give public lectures, nor always to attend them, unless you go, with your understanding prepared by some previous reading, or acquaintance with the subjects, which in the lecture-room are necessarily rather illustrated, than fully explained. Neither is it necessary that you should sacrifice any portion of your feminine delicacy by diving too deep, or approaching too near the professor's chair. A slight knowledge of science in general is all which is here recommended, so far as it may serve to obviate some of those groundless and irrational fears, which arise out of mistaken apprehensions of the phenomena of nature and art; but, above all, to enlarge our views of the great and glorious attributes of the Creator, as exhibited in the most sublime, as well as the most insignificant, works of his creation.

Perhaps one of the lowest advantages, and I am far from thinking it a low one either, which is derived by women from a general knowledge of science, is, that it renders them more companionable to men. If they are solicitous to charm the nobler sex by their appearance, dress, and manners, surely it is of more importance to interest them by their conversation. By the former they may please; by the latter they may influence, and that to the end of their lives. Yet, how is it possible to interest by their conversation, without some understanding of the subjects which chiefly occupy the minds of men? Most kindly, however, has it been accorded by man to his feeble sister, that it should not be necessary for her to *talk much*, even on his favourite topics, in order to obtain his favour. An attentive listener is generally all that he requires; but in order to listen attentively, and with real interest, it is highly important that we should have considerable understanding of the subject discussed; for the interruption of a single foolish or irrelevant question, the evidence of a wandering thought, the constrained attitude of attention, or the rapid response which conveys no proof of having received an idea, are each sufficient to break the charm, and destroy the satisfaction which most men feel in conversing with really intelligent women.

* * * *

It is the taste of the present times to invest the material with an immeasurable extent of importance beyond the ideal. It is the tendency of modern education to instil into the youthful mind the necessity of knowing, rather than the advantage of feeling. And, to a certain extent, "knowledge is power;" but neither is knowledge all that we live for, nor power all that we enjoy. There are deep mysteries in the book of nature which all can feel, but none will ever understand, until the veil of mortality shall be withdrawn. There are stirrings in the heart of man which constitute the very essence of his being, and which power can neither satisfy nor subdue. Yet this mystery reveals more truly than the clearest proofs, or mightiest deductions of science, that a master-hand has been for ages, and is still at work, above, beneath, and around us; and this moving principle is for ever reminding us, that, in our nature, we inherit the germs of a future existence, over which time has no influence, and the grave no victory.[1]

If, then, for man it be absolutely necessary that he should sacrifice the poetry of his nature for the realities of material and animal existence, for woman there is no excuse — for woman, whose whole life, from the cradle to the grave, is one of feeling, rather than of action; whose highest duty is so often to suffer, and be still; whose deepest enjoyments are all relative; who has nothing, and is nothing, of herself; whose experience, if unparticipated, is a total blank; yet, whose world of interest is wide as the realm of humanity, boundless as the ocean of life, and enduring as eternity! For woman, who, in her inexhaustible sympathies, can live only in the existence of another, and whose very smiles and tears are not exclusively her own — for woman to cast away the love of poetry, is to pervert from their natural course the sweetest and loveliest tendencies of a truly femi-

---

1 Author's note: "The Poetry of Life" [a work published by Ellis in 1835 in which she outlines her ideas about the true nature of the poetic. Ed.]

nine mind, to destroy the brightest charm which can adorn her intellectual character, to blight the fairest rose in her wreath of youthful beauty.

* * * *

I have said, that women, above all created beings, have cause for gratitude. Deprived of the benefits of the Christian dispensation, woman has ever been, and will be ever the most abject, and the most degraded of creatures, oppressed in proportion to her weakness, and miserable in proportion to her capability of suffering. Yet, under the Christian dispensation, she who was the first in sin, is raised to an equality with man, and made his fellow-heir in the blessings of eternal life. Nor is this all. A dispensation which had permitted her merely to creep, and grovel through this life, so as to purchase by her patient sufferings a title to the next, would have been unworthy of that law of love by which pardon was offered to a guilty world. In accordance with the ineffable beneficence of this law, woman was therefore raised to a moral, as well as a spiritual equality with man; and from being first his tempter, and then his slave, she has become his helpmate, his counsellor, his friend, the object of his most affectionate solicitude, the sharer of his dignity, and the partaker in his highest enjoyments.

2. Alfred Lord Tennyson, extract from *The Princess* (1847).

[Tennyson (1809–92), the most prominent poet of the Victorian period, was England's poet laureate from 1850 until his death. He frequently addressed philosophical and social issues in his poetry, as he does in *The Princess*. The Princess of the title founds a women's university, and is determined to eschew marriage and devote herself to furthering women's rights. In the following passage near the end of the poem, the Prince, to whom the Princess has been betrothed since childhood, successfully woos her away from her radical position to a more moderate one which they will promote together.]

From Section VII

The woman's cause is man's: they rise or sink
Together, dwarf'd or godlike, bond or free:
For she that out of Lethe[1] scales with man   245
The shining steps of Nature, shares with man
His nights, his days, moves with him to one goal,
Stays all the fair young planet in her hands —
If she be small, slight-natured, miserable,
How shall men grow? but work no more alone!   250
Our place is much: as far as in us lies

---

1 In classical mythology, the river of forgetfulness.

We two[1] will serve them both in aiding her —
Will clear away the parasitic forms
That seem to keep her up but drag her down —
Will leave her space to burgeon out of all   255
Within her — let her make herself her own
To give or keep, to live and learn and be
All that not harms distinctive womanhood.
For woman is not undevelopt man,
But diverse: could we make her as the man,   260
Sweet Love were slain: his dearest bond is this,
Not like to like, but like in difference.
Yet in the long years liker must they grow;
The man be more of woman, she of man;
He gain in sweetness and in moral height,   265
Nor lose the wrestling thews that throw the world;
She mental breadth, nor fail in childward care,
Nor lose the childlike in the larger mind;
Till at the last she set herself to man,
Like perfect music unto noble words;   270
And so these twain, upon the skirts of Time,
Sit side by side, full-summ'd in all their powers,
Dispensing harvest, sowing the To-be,
Self-reverent each and reverencing each,
Distinct in individualities,   275
But like each other ev'n as those who love.
Then comes the statelier Eden back to men:
Then reign the world's great bridals, chaste and calm:
Then springs the crowning race of humankind.

3. Coventry Patmore, extract from *The Angel in the House* (1854).
[Patmore (1823–96) was a popular, if undistinguished, Victorian poet. His
lengthy cycle of poems, *The Angel in the House*, celebrates an idealized version of marriage and especially of Victorian womanhood. The title, more
than anything in the poems themselves, was highly influential in the Victorian period, becoming the ultimate catch-phrase for the ideal of feminine domesticity.]

The Rose of the World

Lo, when the Lord made North and South
    And sun and moon ordainèd, He,
Forthbringing each by word of mouth
    In order of its dignity,

---

1 I.e., the Prince and Princess.

Did man from the crude clay express   5
   By sequence, and, all else decreed,
He formed the woman; nor might less
   Than Sabbath such a work succeed.
And still with favour singled out,
   Marred less than man by mortal fall,   10
Her disposition is devout,
   Her countenance angelical;
The best things that the best believe
   Are in her face so kindly writ
The faithless, seeing her, conceive   15
   Not only heaven, but hope of it;
No idle thought her instinct shrouds,
   But fancy chequers settled sense,
Like alteration of the clouds
   On noonday's azure permanence;   20
Pure dignity, composure, ease
   Declare affections nobly fix'd,
And impulse sprung from due degrees
   Of sense and spirit sweetly mix'd.
Her modesty, her chiefest grace,   25
   The cestus clasping Venus' side,[1]
How potent to deject the face
   Of him who would affront its pride!
Wrong dares not in her presence speak,
   Nor spotted thought its taint disclose   30
Under the protest of a cheek
   Outbragging Nature's boast the rose.
In mind and manners how discreet;
   How artless in her very art;
How candid in discourse; how sweet   35
   The concord of her lips and heart;
How simple and how circumspect;
   How subtle and how fancy-free;
Though sacred to her love, how deck'd
   With unexclusive courtesy;   40
How quick in talk to see from far
   The way to vanquish or evade;
How able her persuasions are
   To prove, her reasons to persuade;
How (not to call true instinct's bent   45
   And woman's very nature, harm),

---

1 In classical mythology, Venus's cestus — i.e., belt or girdle — endowed whoever
   wore it with the power to excite love.

How amiable and innocent
   Her pleasure in her power to charm;
How humbly careful to attract
   Though crown'd with all the soul desires,   50
Connubial aptitude exact,
   Diversity that never tires.

4. Thomas Henry Huxley, extract from "Emancipation — Black and White," *Reader*, 20 May 1865.

[Huxley (1825–95) was an eminent biologist, lecturer, essayist, and popularizer of science. In his essays and lectures, he addressed a variety of current issues, especially those concerning science, education, philosophy, and religion.]

The doctrine of equal natural rights may be an illogical delusion; emancipation may convert the slave from a well fed animal into a pauperised man; mankind may even have to do without cotton shirts; but all these evils must be faced, if the moral law, that no human being can arbitrarily dominate over another without grievous damage to his own nature, be, as many think, as readily demonstrable by experiment as any physical truth. If this be true, no slavery can be abolished without a double emancipation, and the master will benefit by freedom more than the freed-man.

The like considerations apply to all the other questions of emancipation which are at present stirring the world — the multifarious demands that classes of mankind shall be relieved from restrictions imposed by the artifice of man, and not by the necessities of Nature. One of the most important, if not the most important, of all these, is that which daily threatens to become the "irrepressible" woman question. What social and political rights have women? What ought they to be allowed, or not allowed to do, be, and suffer? And, as involved in, and underlying all these questions, how ought they to be educated?

There are philogynists as fanatical as any "misogynists" who, reversing our antiquated notions, bid the man look upon the woman as the higher type of humanity; who ask us to regard the female intellect as the clearer and the quicker, if not the stronger; who desire us to look up to feminine moral sense as the purer and the nobler; and bid man abdicate his usurped sovereignty over Nature in favour of the female line. On the other hand, there are persons not to be outdone in all loyalty and just respect for woman-kind, but by nature hard of head and haters of delusion, however charming, who not only repudiate the new woman-worship which so many sentimentalists and some philosophers are desirous of setting up, but, carrying their audacity further, deny even the natural equality of the sexes. They assert, on the contrary, that in every excellent character, whether mental or physical, the average woman is inferior to the average man, in the sense of having that character less in quantity, and lower in quality. [...]

Supposing, however, that all these arguments [against the equality of women with men] have a certain foundation; [...] are they of any value as against woman-emancipation? Do they afford us the smallest ground for refusing to educate women as well as men — to give women the same civil and political rights as men? No mistake is so commonly made by clever people as that of assuming a cause to be bad because the arguments of its supporters are, to a great extent, nonsensical. And we conceive that those who may laugh at the arguments of the extreme philogynists, may yet feel bound to work heart and soul towards the attainment of their practical ends.

As regards education, for example. Granting the alleged defects of women, is it not somewhat absurd to sanction and maintain a system of education which would seem to have been specially contrived to exaggerate all these defects?

Naturally not so firmly strung, nor so well balanced, as boys, girls are in great measure debarred from the sports and physical exercises which are justly thought absolutely necessary for the full development of the vigour of the more favoured sex. Women are, by nature, more excitable than men — prone to be swept by tides of emotion, proceeding from hidden and inward, as well as from obvious and external causes; and female education does its best to weaken every physical counterpoise to this nervous mobility — tends in all ways to stimulate the emotional part of the mind and stunt the rest. We find girls naturally timid, inclined to dependence, born conservatives and we teach them that independence is unladylike; that blind faith is the right frame of mind; and that whatever we may be permitted, and indeed encouraged, to do to our brother, our sister is to be left to the tyranny of authority and tradition. With few insignificant exceptions, girls have been educated either to be drudges, or toys, beneath man; or a sort of angels above him; the highest ideal aimed at oscillating between Clärchen and Beatrice.[1] The possibility that the ideal of womanhood lies neither in the fair saint, nor in the fair sinner; that the female type of character is neither better nor worse than the male, but only weaker; that women are meant neither to be men's guides nor their playthings, but their comrades, their fellows and their equals, so far as Nature puts no bar to that equality, does not seem to have entered into the minds of those who have had the conduct of the education of girls.

If the present system of female education stands self-condemned, as inherently absurd; and if that which we have just indicated is the true position of woman, what is the first step towards a better state of things? We reply, emancipate girls. Recognise the fact that they share the senses,

---

1 Clärchen is the heroine of *Egmont* (1788), a historical drama by Johann Wolfgang von Goethe (1749-1832). She is the embodiment of constancy and devotion. Beatrice is immortalized in the poetry of Dante (1265–1321), including *The Divine Comedy*, and is the emblem of perfect and unattainable womanhood.

perceptions, feelings, reasoning powers, emotions, of boys, and that the mind of the average girl is less different from that of the average boy, than the mind of one boy is from that of another; so that whatever argument justifies a given education for all boys, justifies its application to girls as well. So far from imposing artificial restrictions upon the acquirement of knowledge by women, throw every facility in their way. [...]

And the result? For our parts, though loth to prophesy, we believe it will be that of other emancipations. Women will find their place, and it will neither be that in which they have been held, nor that to which some of them aspire. Nature's old salique law[1] will not be repealed, and no change of dynasty will be effected. The big chests, the massive brains, the vigorous muscles and stout frames, of the best men will carry the day, whenever it is worth their while to contest the prizes of life with the best women. And the hardship of it is, that the very improvement of the women will lessen their chances. Better mothers will bring forth better sons, and the impetus gained by the one sex will be transmitted, in the next generation, to the other. The most Darwinian of theorists will not venture to propound the doctrine, that the physical disabilities under which women have hitherto laboured, in the struggle for existence with men, are likely to be removed by even the most skilfully conducted process of educational selection.[2]

5. John Ruskin, extract from "Of Queens' Gardens," in *Sesame and Lilies* (1865).

[Ruskin (1819–1900) was a prolific and outspoken critic of art and of society. "Of Queens' Gardens" was originally part of a lecture series, later published as *Sesame and Lilies*, in which he delineates the duties and suitable educational preparation for boys ("Of Kings' Treasuries") and for girls ("Of Queens' Gardens"). His discussion in the latter of women's education and social role, partially reproduced below, was especially influential.]

We are foolish, and without excuse foolish, in speaking of the "superiority" of one sex to the other, as if they could be compared in similar things. Each has what the other has not: each completes the other, and is completed by the other: they are in nothing alike, and the happiness and perfection of both depends on each asking and receiving from the other what the other only can give.

---

1 Code of law of the Salic Franks, an old Germanic tribe, that excluded women from dynastic succession and from inheriting land.

2 Huxley is making an elaborate pun on Charles Darwin's theory of evolution, which was based on the process of natural selection. Huxley's implication is that natural selection will continue to assert the superiority of men. Huxley was a friend of Darwin (1809–82) and a supporter of his theories in the heated public debates that ensued after the publication of *On the Origin of Species* (1859).

Now their separate characters are briefly these. The man's power is active, progressive, defensive. He is eminently the doer, the creator, the discoverer, the defender. His intellect is for speculation and invention; his energy for adventure, for war, and for conquest, wherever war is just, wherever conquest necessary. But the woman's power is for rule, not for battle, — and her intellect is not for invention or creation, but for sweet ordering, arrangement, and decision. She sees the qualities of things, their claims, and their places. Her great function is Praise; she enters into no contest, but infallibly adjudges the crown of contest. By her office, and place, she is protected from all danger and temptation. The man, in his rough work in open world, must encounter all peril and trial; — to him, therefore, must be the failure, the offence, the inevitable error: often he must be wounded, or subdued; often misled; and *always* hardened. But he guards the woman from all this; within his house, as ruled by her, unless she herself has sought it, need enter no danger, no temptation, no cause of error or offence. This is the true nature of home — it is the place of Peace; the shelter, not only from all injury, but from all terror, doubt, and division. [...]

And wherever a true wife comes, this home is always round her. The stars only may be over her head; the glowworm in the night-cold grass may be the only fire at her foot; but home is yet wherever she is; and for a noble woman it stretches far round her, better than ceiled with cedar, or painted with vermilion, shedding its quiet light far, for those who else were homeless.

This, then, I believe to be, — will you not admit it to be? — the woman's true place and power. But do not you see that, to fulfil this, she must — as far as one can use such terms of a human creature — be incapable of error? So far as she rules, all must be right, or nothing is. She must be enduringly, incorruptibly good; instinctively, infallibly wise — wise, not for self-development, but for self-renunciation: wise, not that she may set herself above her husband, but that she may never fail from his side: wise, not with the narrowness of insolent and loveless pride, but with the passionate gentleness of an infinitely variable, because infinitely applicable, modesty of service — the true changefulness of woman.

* * * *

The perfect loveliness of a woman's countenance can only consist in that majestic peace, which is founded in the memory of happy and useful years, — full of sweet records; and from the joining of this with that yet more majestic childishness, which is still full of change and promise; — opening always — modest at once, and bright, with hope of better things to be won, and to be bestowed. There is no old age where there is still that promise — it is eternal youth.

Thus, then, you have first to mould her physical frame, and then, as the strength she gains will permit you, to fill and temper her mind with all knowledge and thoughts which tend to confirm its natural instincts of justice, and refine its natural tact of love.

All such knowledge should be given her as may enable her to understand, and even to aid, the work of men: and yet it should be given, not as knowledge, — not as if it were, or could be, for her an object to know; but only to feel, and to judge. It is of no moment, as a matter of pride or perfectness in herself, whether she knows many languages or one; but it is of the utmost, that she should be able to show kindness to a stranger, and to understand the sweetness of a stranger's tongue. It is of no moment to her own worth or dignity that she should be acquainted with this science or that; but it is of the highest that she should be trained in habits of accurate thought; that she should understand the meaning, the inevitableness, and the loveliness of natural laws; and follow at least some one path of scientific attainment.

* * * *

I believe, then, with this exception [the study of theology], that a girl's education should be nearly, in its course and material of study, the same as a boy's; but quite differently directed. A woman, in any rank of life, ought to know whatever her husband is likely to know, but to know it in a different way. His command of it should be foundational and progressive; hers, general and accomplished for daily and helpful use. Not but that it would often be wiser in men to learn things in a womanly sort of way, for present use, and to seek for the discipline and training of their mental powers in such branches of study as will be afterwards fittest for social service; but, speaking broadly, a man ought to know any language or science he learns, thoroughly — while a woman ought to know the same language, or science, only so far as may enable her to sympathise in her husband's pleasures, and in those of his best friends.

Yet, observe, with exquisite accuracy as far as she reaches. There is a wide difference between elementary knowledge and superficial knowledge — between a firm beginning, and a feeble smattering. A woman may always help her husband by what she knows, however little; by what she half-knows, or mis-knows, she will only tease him.

And indeed, if there were to be any difference between a girl's education and a boy's, I should say that of the two the girl should be earlier led, as her intellect ripens faster, into deep and serious subjects: and that her range of literature should be, not more, but less frivolous; calculated to add the qualities of patience and seriousness to her natural poignancy of thought and quickness of wit; and also to keep her in a lofty and pure element of thought. I enter not now into any question of choice of books; only let us be sure that her books are not heaped up in her lap as they fall out of the package of the circulating library, wet with the last and lightest spray of the fountain of folly.

Or even of the fountain of wit; for with respect to the sore temptation of novel reading, it is not the badness of a novel that we should dread, so much as its over-wrought interest. The weakest romance is not so stupefying as the lower forms of religious exciting literature, and the worst romance is not so corrupting as false history, false philosophy, or false political essays. But the best romance becomes dangerous, if, by its excitement, it renders the ordinary course of life uninteresting, and increases the morbid thirst for useless acquaintance with scenes in which we shall never be called upon to act.

* * * *

Generally, we are under an impression that a man's duties are public, and a woman's private. But this is not altogether so. A man has a personal work or duty, relating to his own home, and a public work or duty, which is the expansion of the other, relating to the state. So a woman has a personal work or duty, relating to her own home, and a public work or duty, which is also the expansion of that.

[...] [W]hat the women is to be within her gates, as the centre of order, the balm of distress, and the mirror of beauty: that is she also to be without her gates, where order is more difficult, distress more imminent, loveliness more rare.

And as within the human heart there is always set an instinct for all its real duties, — an instinct which you cannot quench, but only warp and corrupt if you withdraw it from its true purpose: — as there is the intense instinct of love, which, rightly disciplined, maintains all the sanctities of life, and, misdirected, undermines them; and *must* do either the one or the other; — so there is in the human heart an inextinguishable instinct, the love of power, which, rightly directed, maintains all the majesty of law and life, and, misdirected, wrecks them.

Deep rooted in the innermost life of the heart of man, and of the heart of woman, God set it there, and God keeps it there. — Vainly, as falsely, you blame or rebuke the desire of power! — For Heaven's sake, and for Man's sake, desire it all you can. But *what* power? That is all the question. Power to destroy? the lion's limb, and the dragon's breath? Not so. Power to heal, to redeem, to guide, and to guard. Power of the sceptre and shield; the power of the royal hand that heals in touching, — that binds the fiend, and looses the captive; the throne that is founded on the rock of Justice, and descended from only by steps of Mercy. Will you not covet such power as this, and seek such throne as this, and be no more housewives, but queens?

* * * *

Have you ever considered what a deep undermeaning there lies, or at least may be read, if we choose, in our custom of strewing flowers before those whom we think most happy? Do you suppose it is merely to deceive them into the hope that happiness is always to fall thus in showers at their feet? — that wherever they pass they will tread on herbs of sweet scent, and that the rough ground will be made smooth for them by depths of roses? So surely as they believe that, they will have, instead, to walk on bitter herbs and thorns; and the only softness to their feet will be of snow. But it is not thus intended they should believe; there is a better meaning in that old custom. The path of a good woman is indeed strewn with flowers; but they rise behind her steps, not before them. "Her feet have touched the meadows, and left the daisies rosy."[1]

You think that only a lover's fancy; — false and vain! How if it could be true? You think this also, perhaps, only a poet's fancy —

> "Even the light harebell raised its head
> Elastic from her airy tread."[2]

But it is little to say of a woman, that she only does not destroy where she passes. She should revive; the harebells should bloom, not stoop, as she passes. You think I am rushing into wild hyperbole! Pardon me, not a whit — I mean what I say in calm English, spoken in resolute truth.

6. John Stuart Mill, extract from *The Subjection of Women* (1869).

[Mill (1806–73) was a highly influential political philosopher and economist. He published extensively on classical liberal themes, his most famous work being *On Liberty* (1859). Mill credited his long-time companion Harriet Taylor (later his wife) with much of the insight in *The Subjection of Women*, and indeed some scholars now attribute the work jointly. *The Subjection of Women* was received with considerable hostility when it first appeared, and by the end of the century, social and literary critic Frederic Harrison (1831–1923) still assessed it as promoting "rank moral and social anarchy."[3]]

From Chapter I

The object of this Essay is to explain, as clearly as I am able, the grounds of an opinion which I have held from the very earliest period when I had formed any opinions at all on social or political matters, and which, instead of being weakened or modified, has been constantly growing stronger by the progress of reflection and the experience of life: That the principle which regulates the existing social relations between the two

---

1 Tennyson, *Maud*, Part I, ll. 434–5.
2 Sir Walter Scott, *The Lady of the Lake*, Canto I, ll. 356–7. "Light" is "slight" in the original.
3 *Tennyson, Ruskin, Mill and Other Literary Estimates* (London and New York: Macmillan, 1899), p. 310.

sexes — the legal subordination of one sex to the other — is wrong in itself, and now one of the chief hindrances to human improvement; and that it ought to be replaced by a principle of perfect equality, admitting no power or privilege on the one side, nor disability on the other.

The very words necessary to express the task I have undertaken, show how arduous it is. But it would be a mistake to suppose that the difficulty of the case must lie in the insufficiency or obscurity of the grounds of reason on which my conviction rests. The difficulty is that which exists in all cases in which there is a mass of feeling to be contended against. So long as an opinion is strongly rooted in the feelings, it gains rather than loses in stability by having a preponderating weight of argument against it. For if it were accepted as a result of argument, the refutation of the argument might shake the solidity of the conviction; but when it rests solely on feeling, the worse it fares in argumentative contest, the more persuaded its adherents are that their feeling must have some deeper ground, which the arguments do not reach; and while the feeling remains, it is always throwing up fresh entrenchments of argument to repair any breach made in the old. And there are so many causes tending to make the feelings connected with this subject the most intense and most deeply-rooted of all those which gather round and protect old institutions and customs, that we need not wonder to find them as yet less undermined and loosened than any of the rest by the progress of the great modern spiritual and social transition; nor suppose that the barbarisms to which men cling longest must be less barbarisms than those which they earlier shake off.

[Mill goes on to develop an exhaustively detailed argument illustrating the parallels between the supposedly "natural" subjection of women and other forms of unjust domination of one group over another that had been practised in earlier and less enlightened periods of history.]

* * * *

Some will object, that a comparison cannot fairly be made between the government of the male sex and the forms of unjust power which I have adduced in illustration of it, since these are arbitrary, and the effect of mere usurpation, while it on the contrary is natural. But was there ever any domination which did not appear natural to those who possessed it? There was a time when the division of mankind into two classes, a small one of masters and a numerous one of slaves, appeared, even to the most cultivated minds, to be a natural, and the only natural, condition of the human race. No less an intellect, and one which contributed no less to the progress of human thought, than Aristotle, held this opinion without doubt or misgiving; and rested it on the same premisses on which the same assertion in regard to the dominion of men over women is usually based, namely that there are different natures among mankind, free natures, and slave natures; that the Greeks were of a free nature, the barbarian races of Thracians and Asiatics of a slave nature. But why need I go back to Aristotle? Did not the slave-owners of the Southern United States maintain the same doctrine, with all the fanaticism with which men cling to the theories that justify their passions and legitimate their personal interests? Did they not call heaven and earth to witness that the dominion of the white man over the black is natural, that the black race is by nature incapable of freedom, and marked out for slavery? — some even going so far as to say that the freedom of manual labourers is an unnatural order of things anywhere. Again, the theorists of absolute monarchy have always affirmed it to be the only natural form of government; issuing from the patriarchal, which was the primitive and spontaneous form of society, framed on the model of the paternal, which is anterior to society itself, and, as they contend, the most natural authority of all. Nay, for that matter, the law of force itself, to those who could not plead any other, has always seemed the most natural of all grounds for the exercise of authority. Conquering races hold it to be Nature's own dictate that the conquered should obey the conquerors, or, as they euphoniously paraphrase it, that the feebler and more unwarlike races should submit to the braver and manlier. The smallest acquaintance with human life in the Middle Ages shows how supremely natural the dominion of the feudal nobility over men of low condition appeared to the nobility themselves, and how unnatural the conception seemed, of a person of the inferior class claiming equality with them, or exercising authority over them. It hardly seemed less so to the class held in subjection. The emancipated serfs and burgesses, even in their most vigorous struggles, never made any pretension to a share of authority; they only demanded more or less of limitation to the power of tyrannizing over them. So true is it that unnatural generally means only uncustomary, and that everything which is usual appears natural. The subjection of women to men being a universal custom, any departure from it quite naturally appears unnatural.

* * * *

All causes, social and natural, combine to make it unlikely that women should be collectively rebellious to the power of men. They are so far in a position different from all other subject classes, that their masters require something more from them than actual service. Men do not want solely the obedience of women, they want their sentiments. All men, except the most brutish, desire to have, in the woman most nearly connected with them, not a forced slave but a willing one; not a slave merely, but a favourite. They have therefore put everything in practice to enslave their minds. The masters of all other slaves rely, for maintaining obedience, on fear; either fear of themselves, or religious fears. The masters of women wanted more than simple obedience, and they turned the whole force of education to effect their purpose. All women are brought up from the very earliest years in the belief that their ideal of character is the very opposite to that of men; not self-will, and government by self-control, but submission, and yielding to the control of others. All the moralities tell them that it is the duty of women, and all the current sentimentalities that it is their nature, to live for others; to make complete abnegation of themselves, and to have no life but in their affections. And by their affections are meant the only ones they are allowed to have — those to the men with whom they are connected, or to the children who constitute an additional and indefeasible tie between them and a man. When we put together three things — first, the natural attraction between opposite sexes; secondly, the wife's entire dependence on the husband, every privilege or pleasure she has being either his gift, or depending entirely on his will; and lastly, that the principal object of human pursuit, consideration, and all objects of social ambition, can in general be sought or obtained by her only through him — it would be a miracle if the object of being attractive to men had not become the polar star of feminine education and formation of character. And, this great means of influence over the minds of women having been acquired, an instinct of selfishness made men avail themselves of it to the utmost as a means of holding women in subjection, by representing to them meekness, submissiveness, and resignation of all individual will into the hands of a man, as an essential part of sexual attractiveness.

* * * *

The general opinion of men is supposed to be, that the natural vocation of a woman is that of a wife and mother. I say, is supposed to be, because, judging from acts — from the whole of the present constitution of society — one might infer that their opinion was the direct contrary. They might be supposed to think that the alleged natural vocation of women was of all things the most repugnant to their nature; insomuch that if they are free to do anything else — if any other means of living, or occupation of their time and faculties, is open, which has any chance of appearing desirable to them — there will not be enough of them who will be willing to accept the condition said to be natural to them. If this is the real opinion of men in general, it would be well that it should be spoken out. I should like to hear somebody openly enunciating the doctrine (it is already implied in much that is written on the subject) — "It is necessary to society that women should marry and produce children. They will not do so unless they are compelled. Therefore it is necessary to compel them." The merits of the case would then be clearly defined. It would be exactly that of the slaveholders of South Carolina and Louisiana. "It is necessary that cotton and sugar should be grown. White men cannot produce them. Negroes will not, for any wages which we choose to give. *Ergo* they must be compelled." An illustration still closer to the point is that of impressment. Sailors must absolutely be had to defend the country. It often happens that they will not voluntarily enlist. Therefore there must be the power of forcing them. How often has this logic been used! and, but for one flaw in it, without doubt it would have been successful up to this day. But it is open to the retort — First pay the sailors the honest value of their labour. When you have made it as well worth their while to serve you, as to work for other employers, you will have no more difficulty than others have in obtaining their services. To this there is no logical answer except "I will not": and as people are now not only ashamed, but are not desirous, to rob the labourer of his hire, impressment is no longer advocated. Those who attempt to force women into marriage by closing all other doors against them, lay themselves open to a similar retort. If they mean what they say, their opinion must evidently be, that men do not render the married condition so desirable to women, as to induce them to accept it for its own recommendations. It is not a sign of one's thinking the boon one offers very attractive, when one allows only Hobson's choice, "that or none." And here, I believe, is the clue to the feelings of those men, who have a real antipathy to the equal freedom of women. I believe they are afraid, not lest women should be unwilling to marry, for I do not think that any one in reality has that apprehension; but lest they should insist that marriage should be on equal conditions; lest all women of spirit and capacity should prefer doing almost anything else, not in their own eyes degrading, rather than marry, when marrying is giving themselves a master, and a master too of all their earthly possessions. And truly, if this consequence were necessarily incident to marriage, I think that the apprehension would be very well founded. I agree in thinking it probable that few women, capable of anything else, would, unless under an irresistible *entrainement*,[1] rendering them for the time insensible to anything but itself, choose such a lot, when any other means were open to them of filling a conventionally honourable place in life: and if men are determined that the law of marriage shall be a law of despotism, they are quite right, in point of mere policy, in leaving to women only Hobson's choice. But, in that case, all that has been done in the modern world to relax the chain on the minds of women, has been a mistake. They never should have been allowed to receive a literary education. Women who read, much more women who write, are, in the existing constitution of things, a contradiction and a disturbing element: and it was wrong to bring women up with any acquirements but those of an odalisque, or of a domestic servant.

From Chapter IV

It will be said, perhaps, that the greater nervous susceptibility of women is a disqualification for practice, in anything but domestic life, by render-

---

1 Urge or impulse.

ing them mobile, changeable, too vehemently under the influence of the moment, incapable of dogged perseverance, unequal and uncertain in the power of using their faculties. I think that these phrases sum up the greater part of the objections commonly made to the fitness of women for the higher class of serious business. Much of all this is the mere overflow of nervous energy run to waste, and would cease when the energy was directed to a definite end. Much is also the result of conscious or unconscious cultivation; as we see by the almost total disappearance of "hysterics" and fainting fits, since they have gone out of fashion. Moreover, when people are brought up, like many women of the higher classes (though less so in our country than in any other), a kind of hot-house plants, shielded from the wholesome vicissitudes of air and temperature, and untrained in any of the occupations and exercises which give stimulus and development to the circulatory and muscular system, while their nervous system, especially in its emotional department, is kept in unnaturally active play; it is no wonder if those of them who do not die of consumption, grow up with constitutions liable to derangement from slight causes, both internal and external, and without stamina to support any task, physical or mental, requiring continuity of effort. But women brought up to work for their livelihood show none of these morbid characteristics, unless indeed they are chained to an excess of sedentary work in confined and unhealthy rooms. Women who in their early years have shared in the healthful physical education and bodily freedom of their brothers, and who obtain a sufficiency of pure air and exercise in after-life, very rarely have any excessive susceptibility of nerves which can disqualify them for active pursuits.

* * * *

What marriage may be in the case of two persons of cultivated faculties, identical in opinions and purposes, between whom there exists that best kind of equality, similarity of powers and capacities with reciprocal superiority in them — so that each can enjoy the luxury of looking up to the other, and can have alternately the pleasure of leading and of being led in the path of development — I will not attempt to describe. To those who can conceive it, there is no need; to those who cannot, it would appear the dream of an enthusiast. But I maintain, with the profoundest conviction, that this, and this only, is the ideal of marriage; and that all opinions, customs, and institutions which favour any other notion of it, or turn the conceptions and aspirations connected with it into any other direction, by whatever pretences they may be coloured, are relics of primitive barbarism. The moral regeneration of mankind will only really commence, when the most fundamental of the social relations is placed under the rule of equal justice, and when human beings learn to cultivate their strongest sympathy with an equal in rights and in cultivation.

What, in unenlightened societies, colour, race, religion, or in the case of a conquered country, nationality, are to some men, sex is to all women; a peremptory exclusion from almost all honourable occupations, but either such as cannot be filled by others, or such as those others do not think worthy of their acceptance. Sufferings arising from causes of this nature usually meet with so little sympathy, that few persons are aware of the great amount of unhappiness even now produced by the feeling of a wasted life. The case will be even more frequent, as increased cultivation creates a greater and greater disproportion between the ideas and faculties of women, and the scope which society allows to their activity.

When we consider the positive evil caused to the disqualified half of the human race by their disqualification — first in the loss of the most inspiriting and elevating kind of personal enjoyment, and next in the weariness, disappointment, and profound dissatisfaction with life, which are so often the substitute for it; one feels that among all the lessons which men require for carrying on the struggle against the inevitable imperfections of their lot on earth, there is no lesson which they more need, than not to add to the evils which nature inflicts, by their jealous and prejudiced restrictions on one another. Their vain fears only substitute other and worse evils for those which they are idly apprehensive of: while every restraint on the freedom of conduct of any of their human fellow creatures (otherwise than by making them responsible for any evil actually caused by it), dries up *pro tanto*[1] the principal fountain of human happiness, and leaves the species less rich, to an inappreciable degree, in all that makes life valuable to the individual human being.

7. Mona Caird, extract from "Marriage," *Westminster Review* 130 (August 1888).

[Caird (1854–1932) was a "New Woman" novelist whose works were highly critical of marriage. Even more controversial than novels like *The Daughters of Danaus* (1894), however, was the article from which the following extract is taken. This highly provocative piece sparked a lengthy popular debate in the editorial pages of The Daily Telegraph on "Is Marriage a Failure?"]

[...] In Mongolia there are large cages in the market-place wherein condemned prisoners are kept and starved to death. The people collect in front of these cages to taunt and insult the victims as they die slowly day by day before their eyes. In reading the history of the past, and even the literature of our own day, it is difficult to avoid seeing in that Mongolian market-place a symbol of our own society, with its iron cage, wherein

---

1 To that extent.

women are held in bondage, suffering moral starvation, while the thoughtless gather round to taunt and to insult their lingering misery. Let any one who thinks this exaggerated and unjust, note the manner in which our own novelists, for instance, past and present, treat all subjects connected with women, marriage, and motherhood, and then ask himself if he does not recognize at once its ludicrous inconsistency and its cruel insults to womanhood, open and implied. The very respect, so called, of man for woman, being granted solely on condition of her observing certain restrictions of thought and action dictated by him, conceals a subtle sort of insolence. It is really the pleased approval of a lawgiver at the sight of obedient subjects. The pitiful cry of Elsie in *The Golden Legend*[1] has had many a repetition in the hearts of women age after age —

> "Why should I live? Do I not know
> The life of woman is full of woe!
> Toiling on, and on, and on,
> With breaking heart, and tearful eyes,
> And silent lips, and in the soul
> The secret longings that arise
> Which this world never satisfies!"

So much for the past and its relation to the present. Now we come to the problem of to-day. This is extremely complex. We have a society ruled by Luther's[2] views on marriage; we have girls brought up to regard it as their destiny; and we have, at the same time, such a large majority of women that they cannot all marry, even (as I think Miss Clapperton[3] puts it) if they had the fascinations of Helen of Troy and Cleopatra rolled into one. We find, therefore, a number of women thrown on the world to earn their own living in the face of every sort of discouragement. Competition runs high for all, and even were there no prejudice to encounter, the struggle would be a hard one; as it is, life for poor and single women becomes a mere treadmill. It is folly to inveigh against mercenary marriages, however degrading they may be, for a glance at the position of affairs shows that there is no reasonable alternative. We cannot ask every woman to be a heroine and choose a hard and thorny path when a comparatively smooth one, (as it seems), offers itself, and when the pressure of public opinion urges strongly in that direction. A few higher natures

---

1 *The Golden Legend* (1851) is a dramatic poem by the American poet Henry Wadsworth Longfellow (1807–1882). Elsie is the self-sacrificing heroine.
2 Martin Luther (1483-1546) was the German leader of the Protestant Reformation. Caird argues at the beginning of "Marriage" that the Reformation, and especially Luther, had a demoralizing effect on the institution of marriage, making it subject to the pernicious influence of "Respectability" (i.e., slavish conformity to conventional and outward forms of propriety).
3 *Scientific Meliorism*. By Jane Hume Clapperton. [Author's note.]

will resist and swell the crowds of worn-out, underpaid workers, but the majority will take the voice of society for the voice of God, or at any rate of wisdom, and our common respectable marriage — upon which the safety of all social existence is supposed to rest — will remain, as it is now, the worst, because the most hypocritical, form of woman-purchase. Thus we have on the one side a more or less degrading marriage, and on the other side a number of women who cannot command an entry into that profession, but who must give up health and enjoyment of life in a losing battle with the world.

* * * *

Mrs. Augusta Webster[1] amusingly points out the inconsistencies of popular notions on this subject. She says: — "People think women who do not want to marry unfeminine; people think women who do want to marry immodest; people combine both opinions by regarding it as unfeminine for women not to look forward longingly to wifehood as the hope and purpose of their lives, and ridiculing and contemning any individual woman of their acquaintance whom they suspect of entertaining such a longing. They must wish and not wish; they must by no means give, and they must certainly not withhold, encouragement — and so it goes on, each precept cancelling the last, and most of them negative." There are, doubtless, equally absurd social prejudices which hamper a man's freedom, by teaching girls and their friends to look for proposals, instead of regarding signs of interest and liking in a more wholesome spirit. We shall never have a world really worth living in until men and women can show interest in one another, without being driven either to marry or to forego altogether the pleasure and profit of frequent meeting. Nor will the world be really a pleasant world while it continues to make friendship between persons of opposite sexes well-nigh impossible by insisting that they *are* so, and thereby in a thousand direct and indirect ways bringing about the fulfilment of its own prophecy. All this false sentiment and shallow shrewdness, with the restrictions they imply, make the ideal marriage — that is, a union prompted by love, by affinity or attraction of nature and by friendship — almost beyond the reach of this generation.

* * * *

Amongst other absurdities, we have well-meaning husbands and wives harassing one another to death for no reason in the world but the desire of conforming to current notions regarding the proper conduct of married people. These victims are expected to go about perpetually together, as if they were a pair of carriage-horses; to be forever holding claims over one

---

1 Augusta Webster (1837–1894) was a poet, playwright, and contributor to the periodical press on issues of women's rights.

another, exacting or making useless sacrifices, and generally getting in one another's way. The man who marries finds that his liberty has gone, and the woman exchanges one set of restrictions for another. She thinks herself neglected if her husband does not always return to her in the evenings, and the husband and society think her undutiful, frivolous, and so forth if she does not stay at home alone, trying to sigh him back again. The luckless man finds his wife so *very* dutiful and domesticated, and so *very* much confined to her "proper sphere," that she is, perchance, more exemplary than entertaining. Still, she may look injured and resigned, but she must not seek society and occupation on her own account, adding to the common mental store, bringing new interest and knowledge into the joint existence, and becoming thus a contented, cultivated, and agreeable being. No wonder that while all this is forbidden we have so many unhappy wives and bored husbands. The more admirable the wives the more profoundly bored the husbands!

Of course there are bright exceptions to this picture of married life, but we are not dealing with exceptions. In most cases, the chain of marriage chafes the flesh, if it does not make a serious wound; and where there is happiness the happiness is dearly bought and is not on a very high plane. For husband and wife are then apt to forget everything in the absorbing but narrow interests of their home, to depend entirely upon one another, to steep themselves in the same ideas, till they become mere echoes, half creatures, useless to the world, because they have run into a groove and have let individuality die. There are few things more stolidly irritating than a very "united" couple. The likeness that may often be remarked between married people is a melancholy index of this united degeneration.

We come then to the conclusion that the present form of marriage — exactly in proportion to its conformity with orthodox ideas — is a vexatious failure. If certain people have made it a success by ignoring those orthodox ideas, such instances afford no argument in favour of the institution as it stands. We are also led to conclude that modern "Respectability" draws its life-blood from the degradation of womanhood in marriage and in prostitution. But what is to be done to remedy these manifold evils? how is marriage to be rescued from a mercenary society, torn from the arms of "Respectability," and established on a footing which will make it no longer an insult to human dignity?

First of all we must set up an ideal, undismayed by what will seem its Utopian impossibility. Every good thing that we enjoy to-day was once the dream of a "crazy enthusiast" mad enough to believe in the power of ideas and in the power of man to have things as he wills. The ideal marriage then, despite all dangers and difficulties, should *free*. So long as love and trust and friendship remain, no bonds are necessary to bind two people together; life apart will be empty and colourless; but whenever these cease the tie becomes false and iniquitous, and no one ought to have power to enforce it. The matter is one in which any interposition, whether of law or of society, is an impertinence. Even the idea of "duty" ought to be excluded from the most perfect marriage, because the intense attraction of one being for another, the intense desire for one another's happiness, would make interchanges of whatever kind the outcome of a feeling far more passionate than that of duty. It need scarcely be said that there must be a full understanding and acknowledgment of the obvious right of the woman to *possess herself* body and soul, to give or withhold herself body and soul exactly as she wills. The moral right here is so palpable, and its denial implies ideas so low and offensive to human dignity, that no fear of consequences ought to deter us from making this liberty an element of our ideal, in fact its fundamental principle. Without it, no ideal could hold up its head. Moreover, "consequences" in the long run are never beneficent, where obvious moral rights are disregarded. The idea of a perfectly free marriage would imply the possibility of any form of contract being entered into between the two persons, the State and society standing aside, and recognizing the entirely private character of the transaction.

The economical independence of woman is the first condition of free marriage. She ought not to be tempted to marry, or to remain married, for the sake of bread and butter. But the condition is a very hard one to secure. Our present competitive system, with the daily increasing ferocity of the struggle for existence, is fast reducing itself to an absurdity, woman's labour helping to make the struggle only the fiercer. The problem now offered to the mind and conscience of humanity is to readjust its industrial organization in such a way as to gradually reduce this absurd and useless competition within reasonable limits, and to bring about in its place some form of cooperation, in which no man's interest will depend on the misfortune of his neighbour, but rather on his neighbour's happiness and welfare. It is idle to say that this cannot be done; the state of society shows quite clearly that it *must* be done sooner or later; otherwise some violent catastrophe will put an end to a condition of things which is hurrying towards impossibility. Under improved economical conditions the difficult problem of securing the real independence of women, and thence of the readjustment of their position in relation to men and to society would find easy solution.

Appendix C: Debate Over the "Woman Question"

1. **Grant Allen, extract from "Plain Words on the Woman Question,"** *Fortnightly Review* 46 n.s. (October 1889).
[Allen (1848–1899) was a prolific novelist and contributor to the periodical press, especially in the areas of popular science and topical social issues. His best fiction was comic, but his most successful novel by far, in terms of sales, was the unrelentingly awful *The Woman Who Did* (1895), which created a scandal because of its endorsement of "free unions" (i.e., common-law marriages). Allen alludes to free unions near the end of the following extract when he refers to women's role as wives "in the broadest sense."]

[...] [W]hat is the ideal that most of these modern women agitators set before them? Is it not clearly the ideal of an unsexed woman? Are they not always talking to us as though it were not the fact that most women must be wives and mothers? Do they not treat any reference to that fact as something ungenerous, ungentlemanly, and almost brutal? Do they not talk about our "casting their sex in their teeth"? — as though any man ever resented the imputation of manliness. Nay, have we not even, many times lately, heard those women who insist upon the essential womanliness of women described as "traitors to the cause of their sex"? Now, we men are (rightly) very jealous of our virility. We hold it a slight not to be borne that anyone should impugn our essential manhood. And we do well to be angry: for virility is the keynote to all that is best and most forcible in the masculine character. Women ought equally to glory in their femininity. A woman ought to be ashamed to say she has no desire to become a wife and mother. Many such women there are no doubt — it is to be feared, with our existing training, far too many: but instead of boasting of their sexlessness as a matter of pride, they ought to keep it dark, and to be ashamed of it — as ashamed as a man in a like predicament would be of his impotence. They ought to feel they have fallen short of the healthy instincts of their kind, instead of posing as in some sense the cream of the universe, on the strength of what is really a functional aberration.

Unfortunately, however, just at the present moment, a considerable number of the ablest women have been misled into taking this unfeminine side, and becoming real "traitors to their sex" in so far as they endeavour to assimilate women to men in everything, and to put upon their shoulders, as a glory and privilege, the burden of their own support. Unfortunately, too, they have erected into an ideal what is really an unhappy necessity of the passing phase. They have set before them as an aim what ought to be regarded as a *pis-aller*.[1] And the reasons why they

---

1 A last resort

have done so are abundantly evident to anybody who takes a wide and extended view of the present crisis — for a crisis it undoubtedly is — in the position of women.

In the first place, the movement for the Higher Education of Women, in itself an excellent and most praiseworthy movement, has at first, almost of necessity, taken a wrong direction, which has entailed in the end much of the present uneasiness. Of course, nothing could well be worse than the so-called education of women forty or fifty years ago. Of course, nothing could be narrower than the view of their sex then prevalent as eternally predestined to suckle fools and chronicle small beer.[1] But when the need for some change was first felt, instead of reform taking a rational direction — instead of women being educated to suckle strong and intelligent children, and to order well a wholesome, beautiful, reasonable household, — the mistake was made of educating them like men — giving a like training for totally unlike functions. The result was that many women became unsexed in the process, and many others acquired a distaste, an unnatural distaste, for the functions which nature intended them to perform. At the present moment, a great majority of the ablest women are wholly dissatisfied with their own position as women, and with the position imposed by the facts of the case upon women generally: and this as the direct result of their false education. They have no real plan to propose for the future of women as a sex: but in a vague and formless way they protest inarticulately against the whole feminine function in women, often even going the length of talking as though the world could get along permanently without wives and mothers.

* * * *

[I]t has unfortunately happened that a period of great upheaval in the female mind has coincided with a period when the number of unmarried women in the cultivated classes was abnormally large. The upheaval would undoubtedly have taken place in our time, even without the co-operation of this last exacerbating cause. The position of women was not a position which could bear the test of nineteenth-century scrutiny. Their education was inadequate; their social status was humiliating; their political power was *nil*; their practical and personal grievances were innumerable: above all, their relations to the family — to their husbands, their children, their friends, their property — was simply insupportable. A real Woman Question there was, and is, and must be. The pity of it is that the coincidence of its recognition with the dearth of marriageable men in the middle and upper classes has largely deflected the consequent movement into wrong and essentially impracticable channels.

---

1 Trivialities.

For the result has been that instead of subordinating the claims of the unmarried women to the claims of the wives and mothers, the movement has subordinated the claims of the wives and mothers to the claims of the unmarried women. Almost all the Woman's Rights women have constantly spoken, thought, and written as though it were possible and desirable for the mass of women to support themselves, and to remain unmarried for ever. The point of view they all tacitly take is the point of view of the self-supporting spinster. Now, the self-supporting spinster is undoubtedly a fact — a deplorable accident of the passing moment. Probably, however, even the most rabid of the Woman's Rights people would admit, if hard pressed, that in the best-ordered community almost every woman should marry at twenty or thereabouts. We ought, of course, frankly to recognise the existence of the deplorable accident; we ought for the moment to make things as easy and smooth as possible for her; we ought to remove all professional barriers, to break down the absurd jealousies and prejudices of men, to give her fair play, and if possible a little more than fair play, in the struggle for existence. So much our very chivalry ought to make obligatory upon us. That we should try to handicap her heavily in the race for life is a shame to our manhood. But we ought at the same time fully to realise that she is an abnormality, not the woman of the future. We ought not to erect into an ideal what is in reality a painful necessity of the present transitional age. We ought always clearly to bear in mind — men and women alike — that to all time the vast majority of women must be wives and mothers; that on those women who become wives and mothers depends the future of the race; and that if either class must be sacrificed to the other, it is the spinsters whose type perishes with them that should be sacrificed to the matrons who carry on the life and qualities of the species.

For this reason a scheme of female education ought to be mainly a scheme for the education of wives and mothers. And if women realised how noble and important a task it is that falls upon mothers, they would ask no other. If they realised how magnificent a nation might be moulded by mothers who devoted themselves faithfully and earnestly to their great privilege, they would be proud to carry out the duties of their maternity. Instead of that, the scheme of female education now in vogue is a scheme for the production of literary women, schoolmistresses, hospital nurses, and lecturers on cookery. All these things are good in themselves, to be sure — I have not a word to say against them; but they are not of the centre. They are side-lines off the main stream of feminine life, which must always consist of the maternal element. "But we can't know beforehand," say the advocates of the mannish training, "which women are going to be married, and which to be spinsters." Exactly so; and therefore you sacrifice the many to the few, the potential wives to the possible lady-lecturers. You sacrifice the race to a handful of barren experimenters. What is thus true of the blind groping after female education is true throughout of almost all the Woman Movement. It gives precedence to the wrong element in the problem. What is essential and eternal it neglects in favour of what is accidental and temporary. What is feminine in women it neglects in favour of what is masculine. It attempts to override the natural distinction of the sexes, and to make women men — in all but virility.

* * * *

There is, and ought to be, a genuine Woman Question and a genuine Woman Movement. But that movement, if it is ever to do any good, must not ignore — nay, on the contrary, must frankly and unreservedly accept and embrace the fact that the vast majority of adult women are and will always be wives and mothers (and when I say "wives," I say so only in the broadest sense, subject to all possible expansions or modifications of the nature of wifehood). It must also recognise the other fact that in an ideal community the greatest possible number of women should be devoted to the duties of maternity, in order that the average family may be kept small, that is to say, healthy and educable. It must assume as its goal, not general celibacy and the independence of women, but general marriage and the ample support of women by the men of the community. While allowing that exceptional circumstances call for exceptional tenderness towards those women who are now compelled by untoward conditions to earn their own livelihood, it will avoid creating that accident into a positive goal, and it will endeavour to lessen the necessity for the existence of such exceptions in the future. In short, it will recognise maternity as the central function of the mass of women, and will do everything in its power to make that maternity as healthy, as noble, and as little burdensome as possible.

2. **Bernard Shaw, extract from "The Womanly Woman," in** *The Quintessence of Ibsenism* **(1891).**
[(George) Bernard Shaw (1856–1950) was a celebrated playwright and outspoken social critic. His plays often feature strong, independent-minded women — e.g., *Major Barbara* (1905). He was influenced by the Norwegian dramatist, Henrik Ibsen (1828–1906), whose work he appraises in the collection from which the following extract is taken. This extract is reprinted with the permission of The Society of Authors on behalf of the Bernard Shaw Estate.]

The domestic career is no more natural to all women than the military career is natural to all men; and although in a population emergency it might become necessary for every ablebodied woman to risk her life in childbed just as it might become necessary in a military emergency for every man to risk his life in the battlefield, yet even then it would by no means follow that the child-bearing would endow the mother with domestic aptitudes and capacities as it would endow her with milk. It is of course quite true that the majority of women are kind to children and prefer their own to other people's. But exactly the same thing is true of the majority of men, who nevertheless do not consider that their proper sphere is the nursery. The case may be illustrated more grotesquely by the fact that the majority of women who have dogs are kind to them, and prefer their own dogs to other people's; yet it is not proposed that women should restrict their activities to the rearing of puppies. If we have come to think that the nursery and the kitchen are the natural sphere of a woman, we have done so exactly as English children come to think that a cage is the natural sphere of a parrot: because they have never seen one anywhere else. No doubt there are Philistine parrots who agree with their owners that it is better to be in a cage than out, so long as there is plenty of hempseed and Indian corn[1] there. There may even be idealist parrots who persuade themselves that the mission of a parrot is to minister to the happiness of a private family by whistling and saying Pretty Polly, and that it is in the sacrifice of its liberty to this altruistic pursuit that a true parrot finds the supreme satisfaction of its soul. I will not go so far as to affirm that there are theological parrots who are convinced that imprisonment is the will of God because it is unpleasant; but I am confident that there are rationalist parrots who can demonstrate that it would be a cruel kindness to let a parrot out to fall a prey to cats, or at least to forget its accomplishments and coarsen its naturally delicate fibres in an unprotected struggle for existence. Still, the only parrot a free-souled person can sympathize with is the one that insists on being let out as the first condition of making itself agreeable. A selfish bird, you may say: one that puts its own gratification before that of the family which is so fond of it — before even the greatest happiness of the greatest number: one that, in aping the independent spirit of a man, has unparroted itself and become a creature that has neither the home-loving nature of a bird nor the strength and enterprise of a mastiff. All the same, you respect that parrot in spite of your conclusive reasoning; and if it persists, you will have either to let it out or kill it.

The sum of the matter is that unless Woman repudiates her womanliness, her duty to her husband, to her children, to society, to the law, and to everyone but herself, she cannot emancipate herself. But her duty to herself is no duty at all, since a debt is cancelled when the debtor and creditor are the same person. Its payment is simply a fulfilment of the individual will, upon which all duty is a restriction, founded on the conception of the will as naturally malign and devilish. Therefore Woman has to repudiate duty altogether. In that repudiation lies her freedom; for it is false to say that Woman is now directly the slave of Man: she is the immediate slave of duty; and as man's path to freedom is strewn with the wreckage of the duties and ideals he has trampled on, so must hers be. She may indeed mask her iconoclasm by proving in rationalist fashion, as

---

1 Maize, referred to in North America simply as "corn." In Britain, "corn" refers to grain crops in general.

Man has often done for the sake of a quiet life, that all these discarded idealist conceptions will be fortified instead of shattered by her emancipation. To a person with a turn for logic, such proofs are as easy as playing the piano is to Paderewski.[1] But it will not be true. A whole basketful of ideals of the most sacred quality will be smashed by the achievement of equality for women and men. Those who shrink from such a clatter and breakage may comfort themselves with the reflection that the replacement of the broken goods will be prompt and certain. It is always a case of "The ideal is dead: long live the ideal!" And the advantage of the work of destruction is that every new ideal is less of an illusion than the one it has supplanted; so that the destroyer of ideals, though denounced as an enemy of society, is in fact sweeping the world clear of lies.

3a. Eliza Lynn Linton, extract from "The Wild Women: As Politicians," *Nineteenth Century* 30 (July 1891).

[Mrs. Linton (1822–1898) was a highly successful novelist and journalist. She was an outspoken and indefatigable critic of the nineteenth-century women's movement.]

All women are not always lovely, and the wild women never are. As political firebrands and moral insurgents they are specially distasteful, warring as they do against the best traditions, the holiest functions and the sweetest qualities of their sex. Like certain "sports" which develop hybrid characteristics, these insurgent wild women are in a sense unnatural. They have not "bred true" — not according to the general lines on which the normal woman is constructed. There is in them a curious inversion of sex, which does not necessarily appear in the body, but is evident enough in the mind. Quite as disagreeable as the bearded chin, the bass voice, flat chest, and lean hips of a woman who has physically failed in her rightful development, the unfeminine ways and works of the wild women of politics and morals are even worse for the world in which they live. Their disdain is for the duties and limitations imposed on them by nature, their desire as impossible as that of the moth for the star. Marriage, in its old-fashioned aspect as the union of two lives, they repudiate as a one-sided tyranny; and maternity, for which, after all, women primarily exist, they regard as degradation. Their idea of freedom is their own preponderance, so that they shall do all they wish to do without let or hindrance from outside regulations or the restraints of self-discipline; their idea of morality, that men shall do nothing they choose to disallow. Their grand aim is to directly influence imperial politics, while they, and those men who uphold them, desire to shake off their own peculiar responsibilities.

Such as they are, they attract more attention than perhaps they

---

1 Ignace Jan Paderewski (1860–1941) was a Polish composer and virtuoso pianist. He was later prime minister of Poland (1919).

deserve, for we believe that the great bulk of Englishwomen are absolutely sound at heart, and in no wise tainted with this pernicious craze. Yet, as
young people are apt to be caught by declamation, and as false principles
know how to present themselves in specious paraphrases, it is not waste
of time to treat the preposterous claims put forth by the wild women as if
they were really serious — as if this little knot of noisy Maenads[1] did really threaten the stability of society and the well-being of the race.

Be it pleasant or unpleasant, it is none the less an absolute truth — the
raison d'être of a woman is maternity. For this and this alone nature has dif-
ferentiated her from man, and built her up cell by cell and organ by organ.
The continuance of the race in healthy reproduction, together with the fit
nourishment and care of the young after birth, is the ultimate end of
woman as such; and whatever tells against these functions, and reduces
either her power or her perfectness, is an offence against nature and a
wrong done to society. If she chooses to decline her natural office altogether, and to dedicate to other services a life which has no sympathy with
the sex of humanity, that comes into her lawful list of preferences and dis-
cords. But neither then nor while she is one with the rest, a wife and
mother like others, is she free to blaspheme her assigned functions; nor to
teach the young to blaspheme them; nor yet to set afoot such undertak-
ings as shall militate against the healthy performance of her first great natural duty and her first great social obligation.

3b. Eliza Lynn Linton, extract from "The Wild Women: As Social Insurgents," *Nineteenth Century* 30 (October 1891).

We must change our ideals. The Desdemonas and Dorotheas, the Enids
and Imogens, are all wrong. Milton's Eve is an anachronism; so is the
Lady; so is Una; so are Christabel and Genevieve.[2] Such women as

---

1 Female participants in Bacchanalian celebrations; hence, unrestrained, noisy, or
   carousing women.
2 "The Desdemonas, Dorotheas," etc. refers to characters from works of English
   literature who are representative of feminine virtue. Desdemona (heroine of
   Shakespeare's Othello [c. 1602–4]), Dorothea (heroine of George Eliot's *Middle-
   march* [1871–2]), Enid (heroine of one segment of Tennyson's *The Idylls of the
   King* [1859–1885], and Imogen (heroine of Shakespeare's *Cymbeline* [c. 1609–10])
   are all virtuous women who are unjustly suspected of inconstancy by their husbands, and who nevertheless remain loyal and forbearing. Eve, the Lady, and
   Una are more allegorical figures than characters, and also represent aspects of the
   feminine ideal. In John Milton's *Paradise Lost* (1667), Eve is inferior to Adam in
   all things, and, with the exception of the episode of the actual fall, subservient;
   the Lady in Milton's *Comus* (1637) is the type of unassailable chastity and Una,
   the heroine of the first book of Herbert Spencer's *The Faerie Queene* (1590–96),
   embodies absolute truth or true religion. Christabel and Genevieve are the vir-
   ginal heroines of two poems by Samuel Taylor Coleridge, the fragment *Christabel*
   (1816) and *Love* (1799).

Panthea and Alcestis, Cornelia and Lucretia,[1] are as much out of date as the chiton and the peplum,[2] the bride's hair parted with a spear, or the worth of a woman reckoned by the flax she spun and the thread she wove, by the number of citizens she gave to the State, and the honour that reflected on her through the heroism of her sons. All this is past and done with — effete, rococo, dead. For the "*tacens et placens uxor*"[3] of old-time dreams we must acknowledge now as our Lady of Desire the masterful *domina*[4] of real life — that loud and dictatorial person, insurgent and something more, who suffers no-one's opinion to influence her mind, no venerable law hallowed by time, nor custom consecrated by experience, to control her actions. Mistress of herself, the Wild Woman as a social insurgent preaches the "lesson of liberty" broadened into lawlessness and licence. Unconsciously she exemplifies how beauty can degenerate into ugliness, and shows how the once fragrant flower, run to seed, is good for neither food nor ornament.

Her ideal of life for herself is absolute personal independence coupled with supreme power over men. She repudiates the doctrine of individual conformity for the sake of the general good; holding the self-restraint involved as an act of slavishness of which no woman worth her salt would be guilty. She makes between the sexes no distinctions, moral or aesthetic, nor even personal; but holds that what is lawful to the one is permissible to the other. Why should the world have parcelled out qualities or habits into two different sections, leaving only a few common to both alike? Why, for instance, should men have the fee-simple of courage, and women that of modesty? to men be given the right of the initiative — to women only that of selection? to men the freer indulgence of the senses — to women the chaster discipline of self-denial? The Wild Woman of modern life asks why; and she answers the question in her own way.

"Rien n'est sacre pour un sapeur."[5] Nothing is forbidden to the Wild Woman as a social insurgent; for the one word that she cannot spell is, Fitness. Devoid of this sense of fitness, she does all manner of things which

---

1 Virtuous women from classical legends and history. When her husband is slain in battle, Panthea kills herself and falls on his corpse. Alcestis gives up her life to save that of her husband, and is returned from Hades by Hercules. Cornelia was a Roman matron and mother of two respected statesmen and reformers, Tiberius and Caius Gracchus; she was greatly revered by the Romans. Lucretia, after apprising her husband and father that she has been raped, stabbed herself rather than live with dishonour.
2 A Chiton is the loose tunic worn by ancient Greeks. A peplum is the outer garment worn by women in ancient Greece.
3 Quiet and agreeable wife.
4 Latin feminine of *dominum*, lord, implying a woman who leads or dominates.
5 Literally, "Nothing is sacred to the sapper," which could be roughly translated as "Nothing is forbidden to the insurgent." A sapper is a soldier who prepares for an attack on an enemy position by undermining fortifications.

she thinks bestow on her the power, together with the privileges, of a man; not thinking that in obliterating the finer distinctions of sex she is obliterating the finer traits of civilisation, and that every step made towards identity of habits is a step downwards in refinement and delicacy — wherein lies the essential core of civilisation. She smokes after dinner with the men; in railway carriages; in public rooms — when she is allowed. She thinks she is thereby vindicating her independence and honouring her emancipated womanhood.

* * * *

The Wild Women, in their character of social insurgents, are bound by none of the conventions which once regulated society. In them we see the odd social phenomenon of the voluntary descent of the higher to the lower forms of ways and works. "Unladylike" is a term that has ceased to be significant. Where "unwomanly" has died out we could scarcely expect this other to survive.

4. **Mona Caird, extract from "A Defence of the So-Called 'Wild Women,'"** *Nineteenth Century* **31 (May 1892).**
[Caird (1854–1932) was a "new woman" novelist, whose works were highly critical of the institution of marriage. Even more controversial than novels like *The Daughters of Danaus* (1894), however, was an article she wrote for the Westminster Review in 1888 titled "Marriage," (see Appendix B, #7 above) which sparked a lengthy popular debate in the editorial pages of The *Daily Telegraph* on "Is Marriage a Failure?"]

It would be interesting to make a collection from the writings of Mrs. Lynn Linton of all the terrific charges she has brought against her sex, adding them up in two columns, and placing side by side the numerous couples that contradict each other. At the end of this sad list one might place the simple sentence of defence, "No, we aren't!" and although this would certainly lack the eloquence and literary quality of Mrs. Lynn Linton's arguments, I deny that it would yield to them in cogency.

There is nothing that is mean, paltry, ungenerous, tasteless, or ridiculous of which the woman who repudiates the ancient doctrines is not capable, according to this lady, unless, indeed, they are such abject fools that they have not the energy to be knaves. The logic is stern: either a women is a "modest violet, blooming unseen," unquestioning, uncomplaining, a patient producer of children regardless of all costs to herself; suffering "everyone's opinion to influence her mind," and "all venerable laws hallowed by time ... to control her actions" — either this, or a rude masculine creature, stamping over moors with a gun that she may ape the less noble propensities of man; an adventuress who exposes herself to the dangers of travel simply that she may advertise herself in a book on her return; a virago who desires nothing better than to destroy in others the liberty that she so loudly demands for herself.[1] There is, according to Mrs. Lynn Linton, no medium between Griselda[2] and a sublimated Frankenstein's monster, which we have all so often heard of and seldom seen. Mrs. Lynn Linton's experience in this respect appears to have been ghastly. This is greatly to be regretted, for it has induced her to divide women roughly into two great classes: the good, beautiful, submissive, charming, noble, and wise on the one hand, and on the other, the bad, ugly, rebellious, ill-mannered, ungenerous, and foolish. The "wild women" are like the plain and wicked elder sisters in a fairy tale, baleful creatures who go about the world doing bad deeds and oppressing innocence as it sits rocking the cradle by the fireside. It seems hard for the poor elder sisters to be told off to play this dreadful rôle, amid the hisses of the gallery, and they deserve some sympathy after all, for truly the world offers temptations to evil courses, and innocence at the cradle can be desperately exasperating at times! It has a meek, placid, sneaky, virtuous way of getting what it wants, and making it hot and uncomfortable for unpopular elder sisters. After all, in spite of Mrs. Lynn Linton, there is no more finished tyrant in the world than the meek sweet creature who cares nothing for her "rights," because she knows she can get all she wants by artifice; who makes a weapon of her womanhood, a sword of strength of her weakness, and does not disdain to tyrannise over men to her heart's content by an ungenerous appeal to their chivalry. She is a woman — poor, weak, helpless, and her husband may not call his soul his own! Tears are a stock-in-trade, and nerves a rock of defence. She claims no rights — she can't understand what all this absurd talk is about — she is quite satisfied with things as they are. Personal dignity she has none; it would sadly interfere with her successful methods of insinuating herself through life, in serpentine fashion; she gets what she can as best she may, living by her wits; a mere adventuress, after all, in spite of her unblemished character; appealing to men's passions, frailties, chivalry; often differing from a class of women whose very name she would scarcely mention, in the nature of her surroundings and her supreme sense of respectability, rather than in the essential nature of her position.

But far be it from me to affirm, in simple opposition to Mrs. Lynn Linton, that all women of the old school are of this kind. My object is not merely to bring a counter-charge, but to point to the type which power on the one side and subordination on the other tend to produce. There are thousands, however, of the time-honoured school who never dream of attempting this unconscious retaliation. Many of them neither demand rights nor win their way by artifice. They accept their lot, just as it is, in a

---

1 These are examples that Linton constructs and presents as plausible in "The Wild Women as Social Insurgents."

2 Heroine of the *Clerk's Tale* in Geoffrey Chaucer's *Canterbury Tales* (written sometime between 1388–95). She is the model of patience and constancy.

literal spirit, being just enough developed to see the meanness of trading upon the chivalry of men, and not enough so to resent being placed in a position which makes them dependent, utterly and hopelessly, upon their favour. These women — the most pathetic class of all — have been so well drilled to accept their position without question, that they launch their complaints only at Fate and Nature, if ever they are moved to complain at all. Their conscience and their generosity forbid them to make use of the usual weapons of a dependent race, artifice and flattery; so that they are denied even this redress, which less sensitive women enjoy without stint. These half-developed women respond loyally to the stern demands made upon them by public sentiment; they are martyrs to "duty" in its narrowest sense; they turn a meek ear to society when it addresses homilies to them, inculcating the highest principles, and showering upon them the heaviest responsibilities, without dreaming of bestowing corresponding rights.

In short, the women of the old order and the women of the new have faults and virtues each after their own kind, and it is idle to make general affirmation about either class.

* * * *

It will be a happy day for humanity when a woman can stay in her own home without sacrificing her freedom. Shortsighted is the policy which would keep the wife and mother helpless in the hands of the man whose home she sustains and holds together, which would give her but a meagre share of right to the children which have cost her so much to bear and tend, while burdening her with the fullest responsibility regarding them. To this point I would especially call the attention of that large portion of the community who are convinced of the importance of the fireside and the home, who believe that in every other locality the woman is out of her sphere. Would they not use their influence most wisely, from their own point of view, in seeking to remove some of the heavy penalties that are attached to the enjoyment of home and fireside, and to make them deserve a little better all the sentiment that has been lavished upon them?

It is easy indeed to see the frightful peril to the well-being of the race that lies in the labour of women outside the home; that peril can scarcely be exaggerated; but if women demand the natural human right to take their share of the opportunities, such as they are, which the world has to offer — if they desire the privilege of independence (a privilege denied them, work as they will, within the home), by what right does society refuse their demand? Men are living lives and committing actions day by day which imperil and destroy the well-being of the race; on what principle are women only to be restrained? Why this one-sided sacrifice, this artificial selection of victims for the good of society? The old legends of maidens who were chosen every year and chained to a rock by the shore to propitiate gods or sea-monsters seem not in the least out of date. Sacrifices were performed more frankly in those days, and nobody tried to persuade the victims that it was enjoyable and blessed to be devoured; they did not talk about "woman's sphere" to a maiden chained to the rock within sight of the monster, nor did they tell her that the "true woman" desired no other destiny. They were brutal, but they did not add sickly sentiment to their crime against the individual; they carried out the hideous old doctrine of vicarious sacrifice, which is haunting us like an evil spirit to this day, in all good faith and frankness, and there was no attempt to represent the monster as an engaging beast when you got to know him.

Society has no right to exact these sacrifices; every member of it must stand equal in its sight, if it would claim the name of a free state. On the soil of such a state there must be no arbitrary selection of victims for the general good made from a certain class, or, still worse, from a certain sex. One can imagine the heaven-assaulting howl that would go up were it proposed to deal in this way with a certain body of men; if it were decreed that they should be restricted from seeking their fortunes as might seem good to them, restrained only by the laws that all the rest of the community were called upon to obey. No argument about the welfare of the race would reconcile a nation of free-born men to such a proposal. Yet this is the argument that free-born men do not hesitate to use regarding women.

The attempt to force upon these any sacrifice on the sole ground of their sex, to demand of them a special act of renunciation on that account, gives us an exact analogue of the old tribute to its gods of a nation which chose its victims not by fair hazard from the entire population, but from a class set apart for the cruel purpose. Such actions are subversive of all social life, for the existence of a community depends finally upon its respect for individual rights. Upon these rights society is built; without them, nothing is possible but an aggregation of tyrants and slaves, which does not deserve the name of a society, since it is bound together by force, and the union between its members is accidental, not organic. On what rests finally my safety and freedom as a citizen, but on the understanding that if I leave your rights intact you will also respect mine?

But, further, the argument which takes its stand upon the danger to society of the freedom of women, besides being unfair (since it would select a whole sex for the propitiatory victims), is, on its own ground, unsound. True, indeed, is it that if all women were to rush into the labour market and begin to compete with men and with one another, the result would be evil; but it is *not* true that if they were to be placed on an equality with men in the eye of the law, if in marriage they were free from legal or pecuniary disadvantage, if in society they had no special prejudices to contend with — it is not true in that case that the consequences of this change in their position would be detrimental to the real interests of society. On the contrary, its influence would be for good, and for more good than perhaps any one now dares to believe. And among the many causes of this beneficent result we may number this, that women would be able to choose the work for which they were best suited. We should have fewer governesses who loathed teaching, fewer wives who could do most things better than look after a house, and fewer mothers to whom the training of children was an impossible task. Moreover, society would rejoice in more of that healthy variety among her members which constitutes one of the elements of vitality. There is room for all kinds of women, did we but realise it, and there is certainly no reason why the present movement should sweep away all those of the ancient type in whom Mrs. Lynn Linton takes delight. They have their charm, but it must be acknowledged that, for all their meekness, nothing would please them better than tyrannically to dictate their own mode of life to their sisters. By what charter or authority does the domestic woman (like the person in the train who wants the window up) attempt to restrict within her own limits women who entirely disagree with her in opinion and in temperament?

5. **Extract from "Character Note: The New Woman," (anon.)** *Cornhill Magazine*, **23 n.s. (October 1894).**
[This is one of a series of satiric "Character Notes" published in *Cornhill* in the 1890s.]

"L'esprit de la plupart des femmes sert plus a fortifier leur folie que leur raison." [1]

She is young, of course. She looks older than she really is. And she calls herself a woman. Her mother is content to be called a lady, and is naturally of small account. Novissima's [2] chief characteristic is her unbounded self-satisfaction.

She is dark; and one feels that if she were fair she would be quite a different person. For fairness usually goes with an interest in children, and other gentle weaknesses of which Novissima is conspicuously innocent.

She dresses simply in close-fitting garments, technically known as tailor-made. She wears her elbows well away from her side. It has been hinted that this habit serves to diminish the apparent size of the waist. This may be so. Men do not always understand such things. It certainly adds to a somewhat aggressive air of independence which finds its birth in the length of her stride. Novissima strides in (from the hip) where men and angels fear to tread.

In the evening simplicity again marks her dress. Always close-fitting — always manly and wholly simple. Very little jewellery, and

---

1 "For the majority of women, the mind serves more to strengthen their madness rather than their reason."
2 *Novissima* is Latin for "very new" or "the latest." It also implies something extreme.

close-fitting hair. Which description is perhaps not technical. Her hands are steady and somewhat *en evidence*. Her attitudes are strong and independent, indicative of a self-reliant spirit.

With mild young men she is apt to be crushing. She directs her conversation and her glance above their heads. She has a way of throwing scraps of talk to them in return for their mild platitudes — crumbs from a well-stored intellectual table.

"Pictures — no, I do not care about pictures," she says. "They are all so pretty nowadays."

She has a way of talking of noted men by their surnames *tout court*[1] indicative of a familiarity with them not enjoyed by her hearer. She has a certain number of celebrities whom she marks out for special distinction — obscurity being usually one of their merits.

Prettiness is one of her pet aversions. Novissima is, by the way, not pretty herself. She is white. Pink girls call her sallow. She has a long face, with a discontented mouth, and a nose indicative of intelligence, and too large for feminine beauty as understood by men. Her equanimity, like her complexion, is unassailable. One cannot make her blush. It is the other way round.

In conversation she criticises men and books freely. The military man is the object of her deepest scorn. His intellect, she tells one, is terribly restricted. He never reads — Reads, that is, with a capital. For curates she has a sneaking fondness — a feminine weakness too deeply engrained to be stamped out in one generation of advancement.

Literary men she tolerates. They have probably read some of the books selected out of the ruck for her approval. But even to these she talks with an air suggestive of the fact that she could tell them a thing or two if she took the trouble. Which no doubt she could.

6. Nat Arling, extract from "What is the Rôle of the 'New Woman?'" *Westminster Review* 150 (November 1898).

The "new woman" has no desire to imitate the bad points of the other sex: she sees no shame in womanliness; but, unfortunately, neither men nor women exactly agree in their definitions of womanliness. Men, and the women who follow their lead, think it exists in timidity, self-depreciation and effacement, and deference to the views and opinions covered by a coat and trousers, and doubtless because of the last, they load with opprobrium and regard jealously the unfortunate individuals who seek safety and health in some scheme of rational dress which will suit active healthy human beings who have ceased to shun exercise and mud as did

---

1 Without addition of title — i.e., she refers to men by their surnames only (e.g., "Smith" or "Derby" rather than "Mr. Smith" or "Lord Derby"), which in the nineteenth century denoted familiarity.

their grandmothers. This definition applies to what we call artificially developed womanliness: it is not natural to human nature; womanliness should no more include these things than manliness should. Timidity is not a virtue at all, it is a misfortune; self-effacement is a law of Christianity, and should be equally binding on both sexes; self-depreciation is false, and likely to lead to harm; deference to the opinions of others is sometimes a virtue; but if exhibited to those from whom we differ, is deceit, and too common in the handicapped sex.

Manliness is too often confounded with mere brute strength, brute courage (which is not the highest), self-assertion, independence of character (too often another word for selfishness), and lack of consideration for the feelings and ways of others. The Christian type of man is what the world might often style a woman, and the unlicked cub, a muff — one that does not revenge himself but suffers wrong, denies himself, treats others as he would wish to be treated, places himself last, not first, ministers and serves, not making himself the intermediary between others, be they men or women, and God.

A womanly woman, to our thinking, should have courage; in fact, courage is an integral part of woman's condition; without it she could not face her life; she should have self-respect, humility — equally with men — deference to the opinions of those older or wiser, men or women, modesty in setting out her own, but independence enough to have them, and truth enough not to hide them. Manliness, we hold, should be the same. Where, then, does the difference come in? We think it arises from, and exists in, a man's estimate of his physical strength gloried in through centuries, and which has become so much an instinct that feeble men imagine they are stronger, and, by a false conclusion, more capable, than women, and exercise the rôle of protection and guidance however unfitted for it; while a woman imagines that a man only can act as her defender, for, never having used her own strength, she is unaware of its possession. We hold, however, that, as long as women are the mothers of humanity, this difference will remain.

* * * *

We regret that women should ever cast a slur on their name by affecting the rougher ways and methods of the other sex, and that men should deny them equality because they are in some ways dissimilar to themselves, but it is really the argument of the latter that drives women to the mimicry they satirise. "You're only a girl"; "You're only a woman" have so long been the stock phrases of males, young and old, to express their sense of superiority, that the despised sex may well be pardoned for believing its only chance is to say, "We will be women no longer."

Why, though every human being is born into the world with a distinct individuality, is it to be crushed out in the larger half of the race? Why must women be treated as a conglomerate, or rather, a homogeneous mass? By the laws of nature, vitality and activity must produce segregation. The movement has commenced, and women must and will continue to assert their right to freedom of thought and conduct, and they may be trusted not to overstep the bounds of womanliness, which means, in our view, they will do nothing that will ruin their motherliness, which is the great civilising motive of the race. We hold that war and hard manual and agricultural labour would do this, and militate against the tenderness of women's nature, which is needful as a palliative. But we see no reason why women should only have, as practically they had, two courses open to them — that of mothers or nurses; as a matter of fact, women have, by men's leave or without, played every rôle, and often, missing one of their own, made or marred that of men.

* * * *

[W]omen used to be the doctors, weavers, brewers, and bakers of the community, till machinery drove them out of their professions. Thousands work in manufactories and shops, sacrificing health and life that others may live in comfort, hundreds teach in our schools and homes, and if they have been prevented by men in their selfishness from entering higher walks of life, or reaping the rewards for duty done they do themselves, that is women's misfortune, not their fault. As far as manual work goes, we have yet to learn why a sempstress, a laundress, a factory hand, and last, not least, a teacher, is inferior to or less necessary than a mason, a ploughman, a stonebreaker, or a schoolmaster. The motherliness that is in women has made them good rulers, where men too often thought only of selfish gratification or lust of conquest; and good administrators of money and property, where men have squandered their patrimony in riotous living. Does this make men more ready to admit them to the same level? Alas, no; laws of primogeniture are laid aside in their case for disqualification of sex; men leave thousands to their sons and hundreds to their daughters; women are allowed to have only wants where men are encouraged to have tastes, and equipped accordingly; and still men add insult to injury by telling women they must not vote, because they do not do the work of men.

* * * *

[W]omen must take life more seriously, and not look to a gilded cage for sustenance. They must resist being handicapped and underpaid, by combination, walk on their own feet, learn their part without needing a prompter, respect their own opinions, their own powers, and not seek aid and advice only from men; but that they must enter the ranks of the army and navy, build houses, make railways, mine, plough, sow and reap, we do not admit. This would not be good for themselves, because not good for the race; what coarsens them must tell against their work of civilising.

The errand of woman is one of love and mercy; to become callous to suffering, or to inflict it, should not be the rôle of the feminine half of creation; and happy, indeed, is it in not having to do so on its dearest without thought or consideration, as is too often the case with men.

If we believed that political power, or the practice of professions, would have a debasing effect on women, we should be doubtful of claiming either for them, but we do not.

The elevation of responsibility is what women need to check the impulsiveness that produces results grievous to the world at large, and the superficiality of ignorance that equally ends in disaster. Experience shows us that women will have power and exercise influence, and it were wiser that they used both more advisedly. They are the best women who take up professions and claim loudest the vote; they are not the women who lead aimless lives of selfish indulgence, exist to pose as leaders of fashion, neglect homes and children for the sake of amusement, bring disgrace on themselves and families or ruin on their husbands. They are not the fast women who copy men's failings, live for sport, or swagger about in imitation of the worst types of the male species. They form the real basis of the "new woman," ennobling their smallest duties with understanding, calling nothing small, indeed, that can benefit in the slightest degree the individual or the race.

* * * *

When women, untrammelled by unjust laws, with their intellects cultivated, their views enlarged by civic and political responsibility, are treated with respect *as women*, with their work, whatever it be, held in like esteem as that of men; when they are enfranchised, because either unmarried or as mothers, they, equally with men, support the State, or imperil their lives for its well-being, and because, though equally concerned in its prosperity, and affected by its laws, they hold views tinctured by their own woman's nature, which are valuable and necessary of consideration, as long as humanity is made up of male and female, then we shall hear no more of women wishing to be men, or holding marriage and motherhood, as they are accused of doing, in contempt or abhorrence.

The typing class at the Woolwich Polytechnic, from the "Calendar of Classes" prospectus for the Woolwich Polytechnic, 1906–7

Appendix D: Women and Paid Employment: The Limitations of Aspirations and the Actualities

1. Charlotte Brontë, extract from *Shirley* (1849).

[Charlotte Brontë (1816–55) was and is one of the best-loved and esteemed women novelists of the Victorian period. She is best known for her novel *Jane Eyre* (1847). Although *Shirley* is named for the character Shirley Keeldar, a spirited and unconventional young heiress, the real heroine of the novel is the gentle and unassuming Caroline Helstone. Despite her apparently conventional femininity, Caroline has strong feelings about the culturally enforced dependency of women. Shirley asks her at one point if she wouldn't like to have a profession or a trade, to which Caroline responds with passion: "I wish it fifty times a day. As it is, I often wonder what I came into the world for. I long to have something absorbing and compulsory to fill my head and hands, and to occupy my thoughts." In the following extract, Caroline is musing to herself about the hopeless position of single women. Throughout the second half of the nineteenth century social activists in the women's movement — including Clara Collet whose report on the employment of women is partially reprinted below — found Caroline's vision of middle-class women's situation vivid and convincing and they frequently quoted from this passage in essays and public addresses.]

"Nobody, ... nobody in particular is to blame, that I can see, for the state in which things are; and I cannot tell, however much I puzzle over it, how they are to be altered for the better; but I feel there is something wrong somewhere. I believe single women should have more to do — better chances of interesting and profitable occupation than they possess now. And when I speak thus, I have no impression that I displease God by my words; that I am either impious or impatient, irreligious or sacrilegious. My consolation is, indeed, that God hears many a groan, and compassionates much grief which man stops his ears against, or frowns on with impotent contempt. I say *impotent*, for I observe that to such grievances as society cannot readily cure, it usually forbids utterance, on pain of its scorn: this scorn being only a sort of tinselled cloak to its deformed weakness. People hate to be reminded of ills they are unable or unwilling to remedy: such reminder, in forcing on them a sense of their own incapacity, or a more painful sense of an obligation to make some unpleasant effort, troubles their ease and shakes their self-complacency. Old maids, like the houseless and unemployed poor, should not ask for a place and an occupation in the world: the demand disturbs the happy and rich: it disturbs parents. [...] Men of England! look at your poor girls, many of them fading around you, dropping off in consumption or decline; or, what is worse, degenerating to sour old maids, — envious, backbiting, wretched, because life is a desert to them; or, what is worst of all, reduced to strive, by scarce modest coquetry and debasing artifice, to gain that position and consideration by marriage, which to celibacy is denied. Fathers! cannot you alter these things? Perhaps not all at once; but consider the matter well when it is brought before you, receive it as a theme worthy of thought: do not dismiss it with an idle jest or an unmanly insult. You would wish to be proud of your daughters and not to blush for them — then seek for them an interest and an occupation which shall raise them above the flirt, the manoeuvrer, the mischief-making tale-bearer. Keep your girls' minds narrow and fettered — they will still be a plague and a care, sometimes a disgrace to you: cultivate them — give them scope and work — they will be your gayest companions in health; your tenderest nurses in sickness; your most faithful prop in age."

2. Extract from "The Disputed Question," (anon.) *English Woman's Journal* 1 (August 1858).

[The *English Woman's Journal* was the organ of the Society for Promoting the Employment of Women, which may have been the model for Miss Barfoot's organization in *The Odd Women*.]

With an increasing majority of above half a million of the one sex over the other, and many thousands of the single and widowed unemployed, it is still a disputed question whether women should work, either with head or hands, except in domestic life. They are existences of being, rather then doing, of "beauty not use," sing the poets. Social economists rather lament their employment otherwise than in the household as a temporary exigency, than admit it as a practical axiom, while philanthropists are of opinion that our superfluous numbers, to avoid starvation, must emigrate, or become the recipients of charity at home — nothing else being left for them.

* * * *

When we venture to pronounce that as the daughters of Deity, as part of that humanity common to both sexes, women, besides being created for wives and mothers, are also created for themselves and for that Deity, we are sensible that only by great and long continued efforts, can they hope to gain the position of workers in the world's affairs, instead of the idlers they have been hitherto. Nay, that to attain this, they must be prepared to undergo a species of martyrdom, which those most in advance of the rest, and hence of their times, shall receive from their own sex, even more than from the other. The progress of women, so often declared to be an Utopian idea, must change places with the popular idea of their everlasting stationariness, or men will assuredly still cheat themselves about them, and they in turn cheat men.

[...] Time and conditions only are required to show, that *of whatever women are capable, for that they were intended.* Though the present is an age of much progress, yet as this progress partakes largely of the material, it is perhaps scarcely so surprising that the improvement of women should be considered a novel experiment yet to be tried, rather than a truth to be wrought out from any higher principle or wider view. So greatly does feeling instead of understanding enter into the merits of the question, that what is fragmentary and minor in their being is chiefly addressed even by the friends of the cause, and the passing and secondary purposes to which such portions may be applied. Hence it is propounded that if they are to work, it must be work small in its own value, and only indirectly productive to themselves, or indeed to be requited, not in this life, but in the life beyond the tomb.

Statistics show thousands of women burthensome to male relatives, useless to the community — without note of the other thousands *useless to themselves*; — and we are forced here to confine our remarks to the narrower basis, as the likeliest to gain attention. It is asked, why do not these women act instead of speaking about it, why not work instead of writing about working — in short, why not practise instead of theorizing? Well, some attempt all these, but only a few are successful; trained to no real work, educated for no adequate end, making efforts all but obnoxious in the public eye, if they succeed they do so in the face of obstacles such as never confront the other sex, and thus accomplish in the little they effect (comparatively) more than men. In the pecuniary sense, they succeed only by giving the same work at lower remuneration; in working at all, they sink from their former position, and even among the working classes, where labor is a necessity alike for them and for the uses of those above them, they lose the chance of husbands, who invariably make the great mistake of preferring idlers as the better fitted for wives. We are barely, and, apparently unwillingly, beginning to discover that women cannot perform all they have to do in life by untutored instinct, and as in many other states of transition, the trial is a severe one to those undergoing it, and one of shuddering uncertainty to observers.

* * * *

To obtain a firmer footing on the earth's broad surface, to acquire some weight in affairs, to be taken into some real account as the half of humanity, women must work, and so work as they have not done yet. The tricks of attraction — nay, the sobrieties of domestic sympathies, have been tried for centuries, and when has woman's condition been best? Not when she was loved, but when she was esteemed; not when she was idle and indulged, but when she was useful; when physical beauty itself was sideways acknowledged to be enhanced by mental beauty.

* * * *

Exceptional women, in all ages and countries, and in all ranks, have worked; in savage life, and in the humbler classes of civilized life, necessity has made numbers do the same; and in times of urgency, women have been recognised as auxiliaries, for which ordinary circumstances afforded them no opportunity. Assisted and directed, they have overcome work demanding considerable strength, both of body and mind, and often contending against all the obstacles in their way, continued from choice what was undertaken from exigency. We dislike women to work, lest it pervert their sympathies, detract from their charms; we dislike still more their working in public, lest it impair their morals; but our dislike amounts to horror when we consider them as in danger of being, what is called, undomesticated by the change. Yet the change is going on, and the theory of one generation will be the practice of the next. Marriage is every day becoming more difficult, the position of women more troublesome, while, what will weigh perhaps more than these with many persons, husbands suffer from their wives' frivolity, and sons from their mothers' weakness of every kind. While a few women are endeavouring to leaven the lump by showing that the sex are linked to the universe and all it contains, they are advised to be content with the possession of that portion which is at their fingers' ends.

The fractional number of working women in the middle classes are, when they marry, bound over to abandon work, for some cause or none. Men follow occupations for which women are better fitted, and many women labor at special employments, for which, having no real vocation, they are inefficient. And while men are wanted for occupations congenial to their tastes, they refuse the offer on account of their female relatives depending helplessly on their presence, not only for maintenance, but protection. Ignorant, and untrained to work or to think as women are, much cannot be claimed for them, beyond the removal of those conventional obstructions which mar their efforts at advance. To obtain even this, an exhibition of greater moral courage and an effort at some combination among women themselves, are as necessary as an expression of a more liberal opinion on the part of the public. Time and instruction are required to fit woman for work; but during the process, the sense of greater utility in the community would stimulate the sex's reliance, while firmness of nerve, skill and invention, would be increased by practice.

Our character as a people, of more importance than our numbers, would, through the development of the higher energies of women, be unquestionably improved. To argue that they are too weak to work, their minds too flimsy for mental effort, is to insist that the poor shall be ignorant and vicious, the rich idle, vague, and morbid; while in truth it were easier to decide for what efforts the capabilities of our women were unsuited, if exercised, than the reverse. What a few have accomplished, all may in a measure accomplish; the first are not exceptions, so much as tried samples of an untried stock. For success, the support of the other sex being of course required, husbands and fathers should associate the female members of their families in their own pursuits; the educated and opulent should be left to choose their occupations in the various departments of utility and taste; general instruction should be offered to others, and their employment encouraged publicly and privately on as wide a scale as possible.

3. Evelyn March Phillips, extract from "The Working Lady in London," *Fortnightly Review* 52 n.s. (August 1892).

[Phillips (d. 1915) wrote several articles on women and labour for the periodical press.]

"Lady" is a term of wide meaning in these days. It must be taken in this place to signify any woman whose birth or breeding has been such as to make a certain standard of comfort and refinement a necessity of life and who cannot sink to the level of the daughter of the artisan, or even of the small tradesman, without undergoing real hardship and suffering of mind and body. I have tried in vain to get any approximate estimate of the numbers of these ladies — so many are not regularly employed, are partly dependent on private means, or make a living in ways which give little clue to social status. One person thinks their numbers are overstated, another that they are much higher than is generally supposed, but we shall certainly not exceed the mark if we reckon them at least at several thousands. They may be roughly divided into two classes — the trained and the untrained. [...] Trained workers are largely on the increase, as the next issue of the Census will undoubtedly show. Fewer girls sit down with folded hands nowadays, waiting for a possible husband to solve the problem of the future, or resign themselves to the monotony of making one of several gradually aging spinsters in a not always harmonious family interior. An important position is occupied now by these vigorous and well-trained women workers, and it would puzzle one to say what would happen to all the employments which now require women and which were hardly dreamed of fifty years ago, if as many girls were now as then absorbed into the ranks of married women. There was a time, not so long ago, when hardly any paid employment except that of governess or companion was open to a lady, and when those who had the courage to launch out in any new direction were assailed by a storm of ridicule and opposition from their own as well as the opposite sex. That has nearly passed away, and though difficulties are still thrown in the way of women's work it would take too long to enumerate all the channels which are open to them and are constantly increasing in number. [...] There is the large class who have nothing and can do nothing, or, at least, cannot do any one thing well, who work because they must chose between work and dire poverty, if not absolute starvation. They are of all ages; they include the young and insufficiently trained, the old and only moderately capable, who are forced to accept low pay (which, indeed, is usually all that their services are worth), and whose prospects are not encouraging. It is a tragic thing how many men who have lived fairly well-off die, leaving wives and daughters absolutely penniless and very little able to earn their own living. A lady who devotes her life to finding employment for women says she can reckon the applications for work, on an average, at ten a day, those for workers at ten a week; and the majority of these would-be wage-earners have learned nothing, and in many cases never expected to be obliged to work for a living. "They all want to be companions," said another lady, "and there is no demand whatever for companions." She added, "Whenever and wherever you can, preach training."

4. Clara Collet, extract from "The Employment of Women," report to the Royal Commission on Labour (1893).
[Collet (1860–1948) was a social investigator and writer on issues of poverty, working conditions, and education for women. She initiated a correspondence with Gissing in 1893, after delivering a public lecture on his novels. They subsequently became close friends.]

CONDITIONS OF WORK IN LONDON
[...]
Evidence has been obtained from 157 persons who have had personal experience or have been in a position to make definite statements, capable of verification, with regard to the conditions of labour. The evidence of 97 of these witnesses referred to the conditions of employment of shop assistants, milliners, dressmakers, laundresses, and match makers. [...]

II. — SHOP ASSISTANTS.

* * * *

1. Evidence of shop assistants.
Five assistants in shops closing at 2 p.m. on Thursdays gave evidence at the office of the Early Closing Association;[1] two, working short hours in the West End,[2] gave evidence at a girls' club to which they belonged; four girls working in a draper's shop in East London were allowed to leave

---

1 The Early Closing Association had been set up in London in 1842 to promote the limitation of hours of work in the retail trade. Although several Parliamentary bills were proposed and acts passed between then and the end of the century, they were not enforced, and working conditions in shops remained shockingly bad. See Lee Holcombe, *Victorian Ladies at Work* (Hamden, CT: Archon, 1973), pp. 122–32.

2 The West End, which included Oxford St. (referred to below) was the fashionable area of London, where the more exclusive shops were located. These shops tended to provide better working conditions. East London was the poorer quarter of the city, and included Hackney; Woolwich and Forest Gate were working-class suburbs southeast and northeast of London respectively (all referred to below).

their counter and to give me information as to the conditions of employment in other shops where they had worked, the employer allowing me to see each one alone in his office.

* * * *

(a.) Hours of work and salaries.

Of the two assistants working in the West End, one was working 50 1/2 hours a week, receiving 2*l.* a week without board and lodging, and had in a previous situation in Oxford Street, worked 64 1/2 hours a week, receiving 50*l.* a year and board and lodging. The other was working 60 1/2 hours a week in a shop in Oxford Street, receiving by salary and premiums nearly, if not quite, 60*l.* a year in addition to board and lodging. This witness (No. 50) had formerly worked in shops in East London; in one shop in Hackney the hours were from 8.30 to 10 on four days of the week, 8.30 to 11.30 on Saturday, and till 5 on Thursday, making 77 1/2 hours in all. For this she received 45*l.* a year and board and lodging. Notwithstanding these long hours she stated that she had never had a day's illness, and that in these small shops there were many things to compensate for the long hours provided the employers were considerate. She said, however, that several girls, not so strong as herself, suffered severely from the long confinement in a close atmosphere.

Of the five witnesses (all from East London) who gave evidence at the offices of the Early Closing Association, one (No. 15) worked 70 3/4 hours, No. 16 worked 71 hours, No. 17 worked 73 1/4 hours, and Nos. 19 and 20 worked 73 5/6 hours. The maximum salary in addition to board and lodging ever paid to women in the shop working 70 3/4 hours was stated at 35*l.* to 40*l.*; in the other shops 30*l.* was stated as the maximum salary ever given. These girls declared that they had nothing to complain of, except the long hours of work and the short time allowed for meals, which had seriously affected their health. Not one closed earlier than 11 p.m. on Saturdays, 9.30 on Fridays, and 9 on Mondays, Tuesdays, and Wednesdays, beginning in each case at 8.30 a.m.

Of the other four witnesses, No. 123 worked between 74 and 75 hours in Woolwich, receiving 20*l.* a year with board and lodging; No. 124 worked 72 hours in Forest Gate, receiving 25*l.* salary; No. 125 worked 73 5/6 hours nominally, being an apprentice for three years, and afterwards receiving 12*l.* and then 15*l.* salary without residence; No. 126 worked as an apprentice at least 69 3/4 hours the first few months, and then 72 3/4 hours. This last witness lived at home, and was eventually dismissed, owing to absence through headache and illness brought on by long standing.

* * * *

(b.) Meals.

The total of hours given above includes time allowed for dinner and tea, and in some cases for rest. Half an hour is the usual time allowed for dinner, 20 or 30 minutes being the usual time allowed for tea.[1] Shop assistants are liable to interruption during meals, and acquire a habit of "bolting" their food in a remarkably short time; one employer (Witness 122) stated that his assistants nearly all finished their dinner in about 10 minutes, and devoted the remaining 20 minutes to rest or amusement. Another employer (Witness 27) stated that his shop assistants ate very little at meals, but were much addicted to eating sweet stuff and pastry in the morning; this habit of eating sweet stuff was alluded to by the employer already referred to. Indigestion and anaemia are very common amongst the girls, and their hasty meals and short time for rest may fairly be assigned as the cause of their illness and their craving for unwholesome food. A physician with considerable experience amongst West End shop assistants has drawn attention to the fact, confirmed by employers and the few shop assistants I have seen, that according as a business is conducted on a large scale, and the girls are placed under the direction of men instead of women, there is much greater hesitation in applying for leave to take necessary rest during temporary illness, and less willingness to grant it; serious injury to health arises in consequence. In shops where late hours are the custom on Saturday, but little time is allowed for supper, and in some cases the girls do not sit down to supper until nearly midnight.

* * * *

(d.) Arrangements on Sunday

The practice of obliging shop assistants to go out on Sunday for the whole day is much rarer than it used to be some 20 years ago, when, according to employers I have visited, it was very common. One employer (Witness 74) believes that the practice still exists, as applicants for situations frequently ask him whether absence on Sunday is compulsory. In a firm in which he himself formerly served, the employer made it a rule to employ no persons who said they had no relations in London, with the result that those without friends willing to receive them on Sundays concealed the fact. Witness 130 confirmed [...] that assistants in [... his/her] shop were obliged to go out on Sundays, adding that all the assistants had relatives in London. Writing of this firm Witness 73 says: — "I declined to go, as I considered Sunday being the Lord's day should be a day of rest, and that young girls should not be compelled to go out on Sunday, ill or well, after working hard all the week, and then obliged to pay 2s. 6d. or 3s. every Sunday for food and travelling expenses, besides the misery of it. If people have friends they do not want them every Sunday."

---

1 Dinner refers here to a hot meal served at midday. Tea was a light meal served in the late afternoon or early evening.

(e.) Disadvantages in poorer neighbourhoods.

The shop assistants in the poorer neighbourhoods, besides working longer hours and lifting heavy weights usually raised by men in better class shops, are more frequently obliged to work in badly ventilated rooms; the windows are frequently blocked with articles, and so little light admitted from any source, that in some cases gas will be found burning at any time in the day.

(f.) Seats.

Seats were only provided in four of the 33 shops of which information has been obtained.

Of the existence of very real grievances amongst shop assistants there can be no doubt, but of expressed discontent there is very little. On this point Witness 73 writes: — "I must also say the young girls employed in these houses had the patience and endurance of martyrs, but it is not advisable to have too much patience, because then evils could not be checked. The Government would think there was no grievance."

CONDITIONS OF EMPLOYMENT OF SHOP ASSISTANTS [...] IN PROVINCIAL TOWNS

* * * *

The constant supervision of the shop-walker, the patience and politeness to be shown to the most trying customers, the difficulty of telling the truth about the goods without incurring the displeasure of the managers, the long standing, the close atmosphere even in well ventilated shops when crowded with customers, the short time for meals, the care required to keep things in their right places and to make out accounts correctly, the long evenings with gaslight and the liability to dismissal without warning or explained reason all tend to render the occupation of the shop assistants most trying to the nerves and injurious to health.

Of the immediate effects such as headache, backache, and other results of indigestion every witness gave evidence; and also of the absence of provision for the comfort of any girls suffering from temporary illness. Of the more serious consequences which show themselves later on it is impossible to obtain direct evidence because when seriously ill the shop assistants return to their homes, which are in many cases in small country districts. Of the evil effects which are experienced after marriage no statistical record is obtainable, as the previous occupation of the mother is never noted down in the hospital registers, but indirect evidence has been given me of the injury done.

It is a significant fact that whereas large numbers of factory girls cannot be prevailed upon to give up their factory work after marriage, the majority of shop assistants look upon marriage as their one hope of release, and would, as one girl expressed it, "marry anybody to get out of the drapery business."

5. Frances H. Low, extract from "How Poor Ladies Live," *Nineteenth Century* **41 (March 1897).**

[Low (1862–1939) was a miscellaneous writer, whose interests ranged from fairy tales to women and journalism.]

The congested condition of the labour market for educated middle-class women, the competition that prevails therein, and the increasing difficulty for middle-aged ladies to obtain any occupation by which they can maintain themselves, are serious problems which will have ere long to be faced, if the present distress is to be prevented from becoming chronic and incurable and of greater intensity.

That there has ever been a certain proportion of gentlewomen who, from incompetency[1] and sickness and improvidence, have found it difficult to provide themselves with the necessaries of life, no one will of course question, and when the evil exists within reasonable limits it can be met and to a great extent relieved. But when we have a condition of "progress" which, instead of keeping the proportion within tolerable limits, actually tends to increase it, then it begins to be time to consider whether the experiment is in the right direction, and whether the change may not be retrogressive rather than progressive.

The causes of this increasing difficulty in obtaining work are easily recognisable and unmistakable. They are (1) The increasing swarm of women who have entered the labour market during the last twenty years, causing the supply of trained labour to be out of all proportion to the demand; and this, notwithstanding that certain new channels of work have been opened up to women, such as dentistry, certain branches of the Civil Service, medicine, and the like. Fifty years ago a professional man in a good position, making, say, a thousand a year, would have deemed it incumbent upon him to live within his income, and make some provision for his daughters after his death. Daughters of the middle class in those days exacted less of their parents, and were able to see that a professional man cannot provide his daughter with the same expensive amusements as the wealthy leisured aristocrat. To-day the father in precisely the same position sends his daughter to Girton,[2] in order that she may become a High School teacher. If she do not turn her talents to this immediate commercial equivalent, she is regarded as a dull and useless blank upon the map of time. Self-culture in a comfortable home, leisure for intercourse with one's family and society, service for others, which can only be rendered by those removed from immediate and pressing necessity, are, however, such antiquated privileges that one needs to apologise for reminding enlightened progressive women that they once existed and were cherished.

---

1 No means of living — i.e., no secure income.
2 Girton was a Cambridge college for women, incorporated in 1872.

It is clear that, as the increase in the number of Public Schools for Girls is not in the same proportion as the number of teachers turned out every year willing and eager to teach [, ...] there will be an increasing difficulty to get posts; and we have women with University degrees or a training college education willing to take 80*l.* a year for salary. As a fact, this salary of 80*l.* or 90*l.*, or even a 110*l.*, which is about the maximum that a non-resident assistant mistress reaches, compares very disadvantageously with the salaries that accomplished resident governesses commanded in the past, which ranged from 30*l.* to 80*l.*, the average, so far as I can ascertain, being 40*l.* to 50*l.*

Precisely the same process is going on in the lower ranks of "skilled" labour, and the typewriting market is now so overcrowded that, unless a girl be very expert, and in addition be an accomplished shorthand writer and French and German scholar, she can make but the most wretched income.

A second cause is that we have a class of smart, sharp, semi-educated women who, beginning at Board schools,[1] pass by means of one of the numerous scholarships that are now so recklessly and mistakenly offered into the higher grade schools, and ultimately become inferior teachers, authors, journalists, typewriters, clerks, and so forth. Joubert[2] said the object of true education was to make the person as useful and contented as possible in the sphere in which he was born, whereas the whole system of modern lower-middle-class female education is to drag girls out of their sphere into the one that is just above them, and one that is entirely unsuited to their real capacities. The writer of this article not so very long ago went into a large middle-class (not Board) school for girls, many of whom were daughters of professional men, and found the teacher, an extremely able person, delivering her lesson with a cockney pronunciation and a twang that would hardly appear to compensate for the acquisition of valuable mathematical facts. Consequently we have a large and entirely different class of women to-day competing with those of birth and culture for educational functions which were formerly in the hands of the latter only; who, one ventures to think, if less highly trained, were characterised by qualities of deeper importance in an education worthy of the name than those boasted by their successors.

Thirdly, there is to be reckoned as one of the principal causes of the distress and starvation amongst elderly cultured women to-day, the increasing passion for employing very young women. The young girl fresh from the training college is preferred; she is cheaper and more manageable, and against her crudeness, immaturity, and cocksureness we

---

1 State funded schools administered by boards. These schools were established after the passing of the Education Act of 1870, which guaranteed free primary education for all British children.
2 Joseph Joubert (1754–1824), French philosopher and inspector of the *lycées* (secondary schools in France).

have of course to set the valuable qualities of youth and energy. Why very young teachers should be desirable for any but quite young children is not very obvious, unless it be an incontrovertible fact proved by mothers and head-teachers that women cannot sustain their freshness and interest in their work after thirty-five.

* * * *

Furthermore, so far as private governesses are concerned, the present mode of educating girls in Public Schools in herds seems to have permeated all classes; and only recently the papers gave publicity to the democratic action of a wealthy Countess, who (clearly not of Joubert's opinion) sends her little daughter to the High School to sit side by side and share lessons with her local butcher's daughter. So that where numbers of cultured competent women, who were formerly governesses in high-class families, find their places and functions filled to-day by the assistant mistresses of the schools.

These, then, though they are bound up with other issues that have to be regarded and accounted for, appear to be the primary causes of the intensity of the struggle and the sufferings which so many estimable, hard-working, frugal-living ladies are enduring to-day. The suffering is of the kind that does not lend itself to sensation and rhetorical description; it is of the kind that is so sedulously and strenuously concealed from the public eye that you must probe with the tenderest and most skilful of touches before you will get any idea of its existence. You may see, day after day, a neat, pale-faced, aged lady, without suspecting for an instant that she is starving; and yet that is so widespread a misery that any one who begins to make careful investigation will speedily find that the excellent Beneficent Societies, which give away thousands of pounds in small annuities of 20*l*., hardly touch the worst cases, which have neither friends nor money to enable them to get the necessary votes for election.[1]
[The remainder of Low's article is largely anecdotal, based on conversations with poverty-stricken elderly ladies and on brief case histories. The main points of her argument are well summarized in Eliza Orme's "Reply" below.]

6. Eliza Orme, extract from "How Poor Ladies Live: A Reply," *Nineteenth Century* 41 (April 1897).
[Orme (1848–?) was one of the Assistant Commissioners who worked, along with Clara Collet, on the Royal Commission reports on the employment of women. She was the niece of Coventry Patmore's first wife, the original angel in the house. Orme herself was no demure Victorian paragon. She had a professional career as a conveyancer, and Gissing

---

1 I.e., be selected by the directors of the benevolent society to receive an annuity.

reports in his diary that when he first met her, at a dinner with his publishers in 1894, she took a cigar after dinner "as a matter of course." See *London and the Life of Literature in Late Victorian England: The Diary of George Gissing, Novelist*, ed. Pierre Coustillas (Hassocks, Sussex: Harvester, 1978), pp. 584, 353.]

In the March number of this Review Miss Frances H. Low has told us not only how unmarried ladies of advanced age and inadequate income live, but why there is an increasing number of such persons and how the evil can be met. It is with the causes and cures that I desire to deal. The graphic and painful picture of the sufferings of these ladies I accept without question.

In the first place we are told of "the increasing swarm" of female workers during the last twenty years, resulting in a glut of the skilled labour market.

> Fifty years ago a professional man in a good position, making, say, a thousand a year, would have deemed it incumbent upon him to live within his income, and make some provision for his daughters after his death ... . To-day the father in precisely the same position sends his daughter to Girton, in order that she may become a High School teacher.

Miss Low makes it quite clear that this change, in her opinion, is to be regretted, and that there would be fewer "poor ladies" if the daughters of professional men stayed at home to give "service for others," by which is meant voluntary work. But the income of 1,000*l.* was worth more fifty years ago than it is now. House rent, butchers' bills, and other disagreeable necessities did not make such a hole in it. Professional fees have to a great extent remained stationary by convention, whereas the price of many necessaries has enormously increased. How much does it cost to make this very desirable provision for a daughter? Surely the lowest sum to be of any use for the maintenance of an educated woman is 1,000*l.* But for less than a third of that sum a girl can be trained in a ladies' college for a useful breadwinning employment, and for much less than that if she takes prizes or scholarships. Then, again, why assume that the Girton girl[1] must be a teacher? Just as the prejudices of the English father have been destroyed by hard necessity, and he now allows his daughters to work because he cannot afford to leave them independent, so the prejudices of English women have been similarly destroyed as to what constitutes "ladylike" work. If one employment is already overstocked, another must be found, and the question no longer is "Has this work been pronounced fit for ladies?" but "Can I do this work with a chance of earning sufficient money to live upon, and without losing my self-respect?" At this moment

---

1 I.e., a graduate of Girton College, Cambridge, a women's college.

highly educated women, bred in gentle homes, and retaining the affection and approval of their relatives, are working as milliners, dressmakers, clerks, bookkeepers, auditors, overseers in work-rooms, housekeepers, nurses, and in various other capacities in which, fifty years ago, they could not have employed themselves without loss of social status. Miss Low thinks that the salaries of high school teachers compare unfavourably with those which used to be given, in addition to board and lodging, to resident governesses. I think she greatly over-estimates the latter if she is considering the same class in both cases. Resident governesses at high salaries are still employed by wealthy people as a general rule. The countess who sends her girls to a high school is an exception. The poorer people, who now take advantage of the good education given at high schools, used to send their girls to boarding schools of the kind we read of in Miss Austen's *Emma*,[1] or else availed themselves of the services of a relative or dependent at a very low salary. The other instance given of the supposed glut in the labour market, causing low pay, is that of typewriting, and Miss Low says that "unless a girl be very expert, and in addition be an accomplished shorthand writer and French and German scholar, she can make but the most wretched income." This only shows that inefficient work is badly paid. A thoroughly good typewriter, with a tolerable knowledge of shorthand and the ordinary education of a college graduate, has no difficulty in earning an excellent income, often with very interesting surroundings. The truth is that in an over-populated country the struggle to live must become harder every day; but the fewer drones there are, the less hard it will become, and the better the training of the workers, the easier will it be for them to do the necessary amount of work. I think Miss Low might extend the sympathy she feels for impecunious old ladies to the class of overworked professional men who can scarcely make two ends meet when Christmas bills come in, even without investing 1,000*l.* apiece for able-bodied young women.

The second cause for the existence of "poor ladies" is, we are told, "that we have a class of smart, sharp, semi-educated women who, beginning at Board schools, pass by means of one of the numerous scholarships that are now so recklessly and mistakenly offered into the higher grade schools, and ultimately become inferior teachers, authors, journalists, typewriters, clerks, and so forth." Miss Low saw a teacher, "an extremely able person," but with a cockney pronunciation, teaching in a middle-class school. It is possible that the managers of a school may be tempted by exceptional talent to overlook the defect of speech so disagreeable to Miss Low; but surely editors and the public may be trusted to choose their own authors and journalists, and the business man who pays a clerk is the best judge of whether the wages are earned. Who is to decide what is "inferior"? The child of the working-class parents who earns and

---

1 Mrs. Goddard's boarding school in Jane Austen's *Emma* (1816) is notable for its wholesome surroundings, rather than its pedagogical virtues.

profits by a scholarship in spite of the terrible drawbacks of a noisy home, poor food, lack of country holidays, and all the other disadvantages not felt by middle-class children, is generally so much above the average in brain and energy that it would be a loss to the community to suppress her on the remote chance of keeping the labour market open for well-born ladies. And it may be considered on general grounds a good sign when the old boundaries which separate class from class in the matter of work are seen to be breaking down. [...]

The third cause Miss Low gives is a supposed preference of employ- ers for *young* women. I believe this is merely part of the demand for effi- ciency. In some positions young women are useless and a certain age is a necessary qualification. Our headmistresses, the wardrobe keepers and housekeepers in the boarding-houses of our great public schools, matrons in public institutions, not to speak of authoresses and actresses, will open their eyes if they read "that women cannot sustain their freshness and interest in their work after thirty-five." Perhaps Miss Low only applies this very depressing dictum to the profession of teachers; but I do not see any essential difference between teaching and other work to account for such early decrepitude. The fact of young women being sometimes pre- ferred to older ones is only because teachers who have benefited by the enormous strides recently made in the education of women are compara- tively young. [...]

The remedies suggested by Miss Low are such as one would expect after reading what she believes to be the causes of the evil. Her first sug- gestion is the establishment of a bureau for middle-class women's work. Any centre of information is useful, and if such a bureau can be made self- supporting, or be worked by competent volunteers, let us by all means have one. But she further says there should be "an inquiry into the fields of labour ... where a real and not artificial need for women's services exists; and it is for this real demand that girls should be rigidly trained." Now, we have it on the authority of the Prime Minister, recently answer- ing a deputation of Irish landlords, that little good can be obtained from a commission of inquiry when the subject is one that has been hotly con- troverted by the persons who will have to conduct the inquiry. Who are the impartial judges to decide between a real and an artificial need for women's work? Few doctors would admit them to any branch of the med- ical profession, whilst, on the other hand, some very eminent female phil- anthropists would declare that nothing, not even the army and navy or the front bench itself,[1] is complete without them. I remember a hairdresser being asked by a friend of mine what he thought of Miss Jex Blake's cam- paign in Edinburgh.[2] "Ah, sir," he said, "I've always been in favour of the

---

1 The front row of seats in the House of Commons in Parliament, where the most influential cabinet ministers sit.

2 Sophia Jex-Blake was a pioneering woman doctor who founded a medical school for women in Edinburgh in 1886.

ladies learning to be doctors and lawyers too. But they'll never be hair-dressers. It's too difficult. It took *me* a year and more to learn it thorough-ly." Most men share this worthy tradesman's opinion applied to their own particular craft. And supposing, by a miracle, some compromise could be arrived at in such a very controversial matter, by what authority is the "rigid training" to be enforced? If it is to be by the unwritten law of pub-lic opinion there will be a great harvest for those who refuse to obey, since the prohibited openings will be left temptingly free. If it is to be by law, some of Miss Low's impecunious old ladies should apply at once to be appointed inspectors, for it is certain that an army of them would be required.

The second suggestion is to limit the number of workers to those com-pelled to be breadwinners. This fallacy is a well-known old friend. We have met it constantly ever since the movement began in favour of open-ing professions to women. Ladies of independent means who increase their incomes and their enjoyment of life by pursuing any kind of paid work are assailed by the taunt of taking the money out of some poor woman's pocket. But earners of money are spenders of money, and the professional woman will very likely give employment to a dozen of her sex by paying for work which she would otherwise do herself without spe-cial skill or interest. [...] The fallacy of supposing a woman keeps other women in employment by living economically on a small income instead of earning and spending a larger one has been so often exposed that an apology seems needed for repeating the argument. Moreover, when "the labour of intelligent, educated women is badly, nay, urgently, needed," why should it be unpaid? Sometimes, no doubt, special circumstances make voluntary work preferable, at any rate for the time being. In the vast majority of cases such work would be better and more regularly done, and would be more strictly supervised if it were paid for. The erroneous idea still fogging the mind of so many ladies of independent means that work is only "genteel" if it is voluntary does immeasurable mischief in lower-ing the rate of women's wages. Unless a woman can undertake to perform her task so regularly and competently as to deserve payment, she had bet-ter make room for another who can. It is unpaid work, taken up for nov-elty or excitement or the love of admiration, and thrown aside whenever Society makes more pressing claims, that injures the prospect of those who need employment. I do not believe any one is hurt by good work fair-ly paid for, and the freer the market, the better for the workers and for their employers.

After making some suggestions as to teachers' pensions, Miss Low considers the best way of helping the older women already reduced to penury. She advocates increased charity and especially the establishment of small asylums all over the country, to which urgent cases might be admitted without the long delays which now occur. She forgets that, how-ever numerous such asylums were, they would soon be filled to over-flowing and their existence and the easy access to them would augment the very evil she deplores. The pay of incompetent women, incompetent from age or want of training or otherwise, would fall in proportion to the certainty of an asylum being ready for them at the end of their term of work. And the improvidence which is at the root of all the misery Miss Low describes would undoubtedly increase with every new scheme devised to reward it. It is a thankless task to discourage any proposal to relieve want and sorrow, but these proposals have failure and mischief writ large on them.

Having disagreed with Miss Low's exposition, it remains for me to put forward my own explanation of the poverty of middle-class women without private fortunes and too old to work. If the cause can be discovered, the remedy will not be far to seek; but it is quite possible that a remedy may be described which it is impossible to carry out. So I fear it will prove to be in the present case. The principal reason why women are generally so unwilling to insure themselves against future want is that during the years when they might do so they always look forward to the possibility of avoiding pecuniary responsibility by marriage. The young teacher who told Miss Low that in twenty-five years she would either be a head-mistress or starving, and that in either case an annuity of 20*l*. would not be worth having, had the third alternative stowed away in her mind, and very likely it was the most probable of the three. People often say that women do not save because their wages are too low to allow of their saving. Wages would be higher if it were the general opinion of the whole body of skilled women workers that a provision for old age is as necessary as a dinner to-morrow. It is not the general opinion and never will be, because a large proportion of these workers are provided for by marriage, and every one of them thinks that she may be of the number. There are certain kinds of work which can only be satisfactorily performed by women — such, for instance, as the management of girls and infants. Any necessity must be paid for by persons who want such work done. Nurses and governesses must receive enough for food and clothing; and, similarly, if a provision for the future were a necessity, it would be paid for by the employer as a matter of course. Hence when people say women's wages are too low to save out of, it is only another way of saying that it is not thought necessary to save, or, to put it shortly, women as a class are improvident.

Appendix E: Conditions of Work for Men in the White-Collar Sector; Attitudes towards Male White-Collar Workers

1. **James Fitzjames Stephen, extract from "Gentlemen,"** *Cornhill Magazine* **5 (March 1862).**
[Stephen (1829–94) was a barrister and high court judge. He regularly contributed articles on legal, historical, literary, social, and moral issues to the major periodicals of the era.]

It may appear paradoxical, but it is strictly true, that the manners of an English gentleman have much more in common with the manners of a labourer than with the manners of a mercantile clerk or a small shop-keeper. It is true that a gentleman's accent differs from a labourer's; he holds himself differently, and his features express altogether a different class of emotions and recollections, but the manner of the two men has a radical similarity which ought not to be overlooked by any one who wishes to understand English society. The great characteristic of the manners of a gentleman, as we conceive them in England, is plain, downright, frank simplicity. It is meant to be, and to a great extent it is, the outward and visible sign of the two great cognate virtues — truth and courage. It is the manner of men who expect each other to say, in the plainest way, just what they mean, and to stand to what they say, with but little regard either for the opinions or for the approbation of others, though with full respect to their feelings.

This sturdy mixture of frankness when they do speak, with a perfect willingness to hold their tongues when they have nothing to say, is the great distinguishing feature of educated Englishmen, and is the one which always strikes foreigners with surprise. It is their incapacity to appreciate the qualities which it covers, which makes their criticisms on us so wildly remote from the truth as they often are. This manner prevails much more amongst the labouring than amongst the shopkeeping classes. Their language proves it conclusively. A gentleman and a labouring man would tell the same story in nearly the same words, differently pronounced, of course, and arranged in the one case grammatically, and in the other not. In either case the words themselves would be plain, racy, and smacking of the soil from which they grow. The language of the commercial clerk, and the manner in which he brings it out, are both framed on quite a different model. He thinks about himself, and constantly tries to talk fine. He calls a school an academy, speaks of proceeding when he means going, and talks, in short, much in the style in which the members of his own class write police reports and accounts of appalling catastrophes for the newspapers. The manners of a sailor, a non-commissioned officer in the army, a gamekeeper, or of the better kind of labourers — men whose masters trust them, and who are well-conducted and sober (as hundreds of thousands are) — are much better in themselves, and are capable of a far higher polish, than the manners of a bagman[1] or a small shopkeeper.

2. B. G. Orchard, extract from *The Clerks of Liverpool* (1871).

[Orchard was a clerk and had been the secretary of the Liverpool Clerks' Provident and Annuity Association, which apparently collapsed for want of interest among clerks. His writing betrays some resentment of his colleagues' lack of commitment and solidarity.]

[...] [C]lerks, as a class, have singularly overstrained conceptions of the part they perform in the great drama of commercial enterprise, and of their just title to a proportion of the profits resulting therefrom; and if the hard and unsympathetic treatment they often receive has tended to provoke a spirit of envious and revengeful antagonism amongst them, perhaps this treatment was due, in some degree, to their own errors. There is no cordiality between various large sections of Liverpool clerks and their employers. There is scarcely a pretence of friendliness.

[...] [I]ndeed, if many clerks work with the spirit of slaves, it is because they receive slaves' treatment. [...] As a class, clerks are weary-souled and long-suffering. Their countenances are down-cast — they murmur rather than speak. Having no capital with which to invoke the law when oppressed, or to fall back on when suddenly left without employment, if disputes arise between master and servant, the servant finds himself practically a bondsman; and the power to act ungenerously being felt, is too often put in force. Employers treat clerks just as they choose. If with kindness, they know they are not under compulsion, and expect the fact to be recognised. When irritated by family annoyances or business troubles, they take it out of their *employés*. There is no code of equity — implied or expressed — which can be appealed to; no trade union to take up his cause; the complainant's sole resource is to seek another principal, who may be worse, and, in any case, will act with equal impunity. Thus, though on the whole employers may be less arbitrary and selfish than might be expected, there are thousands of clerks whose hearts have been scalded by cruel injustice, whose souls have angrily chafed against their immoveable bonds, and who, remembering this, thenceforward grow hard and selfish, and cease to care for men who, they believe, would see them starve with scarcely a passing sigh.

* * * *

Certainly thoughtful observers say that they [clerks] have little force of character, and that they manifest little *esprit de corps*, are somewhat sup-

---

1 Commercial traveller or travelling salesman.

planting and treacherous, and in various other ways evince that they are serfs. They are declared to imbibe their masters' vices without their virtues; and while illustrating vividly the debasing effects of penury, to do very little to prove the poets' theory that it strengthens and ennobles. There is a concurrence of opinion that, as a class, clerks proper deserve the mingled pity and contempt with which other classes of society appear to regard them.

3. **Charles Edward Parsons, extract from** *Clerks: their Position and Advancement* (1876).

Underpaid, with a great deal of very laborious and monotonous work, in addition to heavy responsibilities and anxieties as his position gradually "improves," his constitution frequently impaired (often ruined) by sedentary duties and confinement in ill-ventilated back offices, without either time or means to enjoy the recreation necessary to everyone so employed, he grows up an unhealthy, dissatisfied man. [...] [He must also face the] fear of losing his precarious situation, and, lastly the anxieties of a home-life often destitute, as he increases in years, of the comforts which render middle-age enjoyable to other classes. He commences life as an ill-paid clerk, his ambitions are never encouraged, all the hopes of his manhood are thwarted, his employer can get numberless others to replace him at even less than he earns; and so he continues at the only calling he is capable of following and with nearly every feeling soured by adversity — he dies: a hard-worked, ill-paid clerk from beginning to end.

4. **Thomas Sutherst, extract from** *Death and Disease Behind the Counter* (1884).

False Notions

I am at a loss to understand why so many persons send their children to be clerks and [shop-]assistants. The world is simply glutted with such persons, and yet still they come. Is it because they do not like to dirty their hands, or double up their sleeves? Is it because they like to assume the appearance of gentlemen? Is it because they despise the anvil, the lathe, the chisel, the vice, or the shuttle? Is it because the desk and the counter are more profitable, or more respectable? If so, no greater mistake was ever made. A scholar can always become a clerk, and a sharp man or woman can always be an assistant. These occupations should be a last resort, and to know a useful handicraft trade should be the first aim of every youth. Parents should abandon false notions of gentility. A black coat[1] in these days frequently hides a sad heart, and clean hands often

---

1 The standard required attire for male clerks and shop-assistants.

mean starvation. A man who can turn his hand to a good trade is always independent, and need be the slave of no one. I sincerely trust that parents will discontinue sending their children to the desk or the counter, and make them useful mechanics, or artizans of some kind; for in the latter case they may become prosperous manufacturers, but in the former they may probably be servilely poor all their lives, and die prematurely into the bargain. We shall soon be an educated nation, and we should above all see that the increased intelligence is rightly directed. The tendencies are unquestionably to avoid producing wealth, and to participate in its distribution. The factories and workshops — the real sources of wealth — are too often regarded as beneath the attention of persons whose parents have prospered therein. I beseech everyone having the custody of children to see that the education they possess is directed to the manipulating and fashioning of the products of the earth for the use and enjoyment of man, and not to the counter and quill-driving. Of course there must always be clerks and assistants, and I have no fear of the supply ever being inadequate to the demand. There are, however, grave reasons why the energies of young persons should be directed into healthier and more profitable channels.

A Glaring Contrast

I have often thought that it must be very aggravating to the shop assistant to know that the majority of the working classes enjoy short hours and a weekly half-holiday whilst he is boxed up behind the counter. The contrast is great. The mechanic or artizan works on an average nine hours a day, and has a full half day to himself every week. He can attend meetings or classes, or do anything he feels inclined to do at a reasonable time, but the shop assistant works from twelve to fifteen hours a day — is deprived of all social and educational advantage, and instead of enjoying a half-holiday has a half a day added to the already long hours. The difference in the two conditions becomes more apparent if the hours are summarised. The mechanic or artizan works, as a rule, fifty-four hours a week, the assistant seventy-five to ninety hours a week. Assistants whose hours are twelve and a half a day on five days of the week, and fourteen on a Saturday, work fifteen weeks in every year more than the majority of the working classes work. Assistants whose hours are thirteen and a half a day on five days of the week, and fifteen and a half on a Saturday, work about twenty-one weeks (of six days a week of nine hours a day) longer than the majority of the working classes work. The majority come under the last category. Shop assistants thus labour seventy-three weeks in every year, whilst the mechanic or artizan works only fifty-two. The system I am endeavouring to expose thus filches from the young men and women behind the counter twenty-one weeks of overwork in every year — without, I believe, any of the overtime being paid for. I merely mention this in passing, because, as previously stated, my object is to protect the health and strength of assistants, and not to fill their purses, but it is only right that the public should know that in the majority of instances there is no compensation whatever for all the bodily weariness and suffering resulting from twenty-one weeks of overwork. If, however, they had a guinea an hour it could not possibly compensate them for the physical deterioration which they suffer. Money is no solace to either employers or assistants for a broken down constitution or an early grave. The knowledge of the marked inequality which I have just indicated should act as an incentive to increased enthusiasm on the part of the employers and assistants in this early closing crusade.[1] What stores of health, knowledge, and happiness might be obtained in the twenty-one weeks of imprisonment thus unnecessarily spent behind the counter! Cheeks would glow with health, sad pale faces would disappear, latent talent would be cultivated, and in fact the world would become bright and cheerful to the shop assistant. We should find the young men enjoying manly sports, attending lectures or improvement societies, and generally becoming useful members of society. The young women would not then despise their lot — they would be happy because healthy — contented because not overworked, and their chances, in consequence, of making suitable matrimonial alliances would be considerably improved. As to the employers, although apparently they might at first experience a slight pecuniary loss, they would gain in the end, because all the extra energy resulting from healthy conditions would be devoted to their interests. A weary body cannot wear a smile without displaying some mark of discontent, nor can a sad heart be eloquent in a service of oppression.

* * * *

A shop assistant sends the following verses: —

A Plea for the Shopman

With faces so pallid and worn,
    And with weary and swollen feet,
And with eyes that longingly turn
    Into the sunlit street.
With hearts that ache with longing   5
    To live like their fellow men,
To go with the crowd a thronging,
    To fly from that heated den.

---

1 The Early Closing Association had been set up in London in 1842 to promote the limitation of hours of work in the retail trade. Although several Parliamentary bills were proposed and acts passed between then and the end of the century, they were not enforced, and working conditions in shops remained shockingly bad. See Lee Holcombe, *Victorian Ladies at Work* (Hamden, CT: Archen, 1973), pp. 122-32.

Ah, Heaven! will no one aid us?
   Will none in their pleasure pause?   10
Alas, though many upbraid us,
   None will espouse our cause.
And we gasp thro' the sultry summer,
   The air of the poisonous shop,
And greet with a smile each comer,   15
   Tho' almost ready to drop.

Why the poorest drudge in the city
   Can fly from the noisome town,
But the shopman gets no pity
   From either the "lord" or clown;   20
And he yearns to leave the shop,
   To breathe in the pure cool air,
On the heath or the green hill's top,
   Or the river so bright and fair.

And those that amass their wealth   25
   By the sweat of the shopman's brow,
O what care they for *his* health,
   While they've gold from this human plough?
O look at his careworn features
   And think of his pleasures small,   30
And then if you're human creatures,
   Down let the shutters fall.

5a. H.G. Wells, extract from *Kipps* (1905).

[Herbert George Wells (1866–1946) is best known for science fiction novels like *The Time Machine* (1895) and *The War of the Worlds* (1898). He also wrote comic novels like *Kipps* (1905), set in the lower-middle-class world of shop assistants and small shop keepers. Whatever the genre, his work was essentially social satire. Wells based his lower-middle-class novels on his own youthful experiences as a member of that class, which he recounts in his *Experiment in Autobiography* (1934). In the extract from *Kipps* below, young Artie Kipps is beginning his apprenticeship as a "draper's assistant" — i.e., a salesclerk in a retail textiles store.]

The indentures that bound Kipps to Mr Shalford were antique and complex; they insisted on the latter gentleman's parental privileges, they forbade Kipps to dice and game, they made him over, body and soul, to Mr Shalford for seven long years, the crucial years of his life. In return there were vague stipulations about teaching the whole art and mystery of the trade to him, but as there was no penalty attached to negligence, Mr Shalford, being a sound, practical, business man, considered this a mere rhetorical flourish, and set himself assiduously to get as much out of Kipps and to put as little into him as he could in the seven years of their inter-course.

What he put into Kipps was chiefly bread and margarine, infusions of chicory and tea-dust, colonial meat by contract at threepence a pound, potatoes by the sack, and watered beer. If, however, Kipps chose to buy any supplementary material for growth, Mr Shalford had the generosity to place his kitchen resources at his disposal free — if the fire chanced to be going. He was also allowed to share a bedroom with eight other young men, and to sleep in a bed which, except in very severe weather, could be made, with the help of his overcoat and private under-linen, not to mention newspapers, quite sufficiently warm for any reasonable soul. In addition, Kipps was taught the list of fines, and how to tie up parcels, to know where goods were kept in Mr Shalford's systematised shop, to hold his hands extended upon the counter, and to repeat such phrases as "What can I have the pleasure —?" "No trouble, I assure you," and the like; to block, fold, and measure materials of all sorts, to lift his hat from his head when he passed Mr Shalford abroad, and to practise a servile obedience to a large number of people. But he was not, of course, taught the "cost" mark of the goods he sold, nor anything of the method of buying such goods. Nor was his attention directed to the unfamiliar social habits and fashions to which his trade ministered. The use of half the goods he saw sold and was presently to assist in selling he did not understand; materials for hangings, cretonnes, chintzes,[1] and the like; serviettes, and all the bright, hard whitewear of a well-ordered house; pleasant dress materials, linings, stiffenings; they were to him from first to last no more than things, heavy and difficult to handle in bulk, that one folded up, unfolded, cut into lengths, and saw dwindle and pass away out into that mysterious, happy world in which the Customer dwells. Kipps hurried from piling linen table-cloths, that were, collectively, as heavy as lead, to eat off oil-cloth in a gas-lit dining-room underground, and he dreamt of combing endless blankets beneath his overcoat, spare undershirt, and three news-papers. So he had at least the chance of learning the beginnings of phi-losophy.

In return for these benefits he worked so that he commonly went to bed exhausted and footsore. His round began at half-past six in the morn-ing, when he would descend, unwashed and shirtless, in old clothes and a scarf, and dust boxes and yawn, and take down wrappers and clean the windows until eight. Then in half and hour he would complete his toilet, and take an austere breakfast of bread and margarine and what only an Imperial Englishman would admit to be coffee, after which refreshment he ascended to the shop for the labours of the day.

* * * *

---

1 Types of printed cotton cloth.

At half-past seven o'clock — except on late nights — a feverish activity of "straightening up" began, and when the last shutter was up outside, Kipps, with the speed of an arrow leaving a bow, would start hanging wrappers over the fixtures and over the piles of wares upon the counters, preparatory to a vigorous scattering of wet sawdust and the sweeping out of the shop.

Sometimes people would stay long after the shop was closed. "They don't mind a bit at Shalford's," these ladies used to say, and while they loitered it was forbidden to touch a wrapper or take any measures to conclude the day until the doors closed behind them.

Mr Kipps would watch these later customers from the shadow of a stack of goods, and death and disfigurement was the least he wished for them. Rarely much later than nine, a supper of bread and cheese and watered beer awaited him downstairs, and, that consumed, the rest of the day was entirely at his disposal for reading, recreation, and the improvement of his mind ... .

The front door was locked at half-past ten, and the gas in the dormitory extinguished at eleven.

On Sundays he was obliged to go to church once, and commonly he went twice, for there was nothing else to do. He sat in the free seats[1] at the back; he was too shy to sing, and not always clever enough to keep his place in the Prayer Book, and he rarely listened to the sermon. But he had developed a sort of idea that going to church had a tendency to alleviate life.

* * * *

At times there came breaks in this routine — sale-times, darkened by extra toil and work past midnight, but brightened by a sprat supper and some shillings in the way of "premiums." And every year — not now and then, but every year — Mr Shalford, with parenthetic admiration of his own generosity and glancing comparisons with the austerer days when *he* was apprenticed, conceded Kipps no less than ten days holiday — ten whole days every year! Many a poor soul at Portland[2] might well envy the fortunate Kipps. Insatiable heart of man! but how those days were grudged and counted as they snatched themselves away from him one after another!

---

1 Church pews were commonly rented by members of the congregation. Those who could not afford to rent a seat sat at the back.
2 Portland is a small and relatively inaccessible peninsula on the southwest coast of England. A naval base and harbour were built there in the mid-nineteenth century. There were famous prisons on Portland, and convict labour was used to build the harbour and breakwaters.

5b. H. G. Wells, extract from Experiment in *Autobiography*, Volume I (1934).

[The experiences described here occurred circa 1880, when Wells was fourteen.]

My mother [...] was within her limits a very determined little woman. Almost as unquestioning as her belief in Our Father and Our Saviour, was her belief in drapers. I know not whether that heartless trifler of her early years was a draper, but she certainly thought that to wear a black coat and tie behind a counter was the best of all possible lots attainable by man — at any rate by man at our social level. She had bound my brother Frank, resisting weakly, to Mr. Crowhurst in the Market Square, Bromley, for five years and she had bound my brother Freddy to Mr. Sparrowhawk of the Pavement for four, to obey those gentlemen as if they were parents and learn the whole art and mystery of drapery from them, and she was now making a very resolute attempt to incarcerate me and determine my future in the same fashion. It did not dawn upon her that my queer gifts of drawing and expression were of any value at all. [...]

I am told that for lots of poor boys, leaving school and going into employment about thirteen or fourteen is a very exhilarating experience. But that is because they get pay, freedom in the evening and on Sundays, and an enhanced dietary. And they are released from the irksomeness of lessons and school tasks. But I had rather liked lessons and school tasks and drapers' apprentices did not get pay. An immense fuss, entirely unjustifiable, was made about the valuable trade apprentices were going to learn, and in the past the parents of the victim, if he "lived in," usually paid a premium of forty or fifty pounds or so for his immolation. I knew that the new start meant a farewell to many childish things. I had seen both my brothers pass into servitude, and I can still remember my brother Freddy having a last game of "marble runs" with toy bricks on the tilted kitchen table, a game of which he was particularly fond, before he submitted to the yoke of Mr. Sparrowhawk and began that ritual of stockkeeping, putting things away, tidying things up, bending over the counter, being attentive and measuring off, that lasted thereafter for forty-odd years of his life. He knew what he was going to, did my brother Fred; and that game was played with sacrificial solemnity. "I enjoyed that game," said Freddy, who has always displayed a certain gentle stoicism. "It's supper time Bert.[1] ... Let's put the things away."

Now it was my turn to put the things away, put the books away, give up drawing and painting and every sort of free delight, stop writing stories and imitations of *Punch*,[2] give up all vain hopes and dreams, and serve an employer.

---

1 Diminutive of Herbert, Wells's first name.
2 Popular satirical periodical.

I hated this place into which I had been put from the outset, but I was far too childish, as yet, to make any real resistance to the closing in of the prison about me. But I would not, I could not, give myself satisfactorily to this strange restricted life. It was just by the luck of that incapacity that the prison rejected me.

I was set down from Uncle Pennicott's dog-cart,[1] with a small portmanteau containing all my earthly goods, at the side door of the establishment of Messrs Rodgers and Denyer, I was taken up a narrow staircase to the men's dormitory, in which were eight or ten beds and four miserable wash-hand stands, and I was shown a dismal little sitting-room with a ground glass window opening on a blank wall, in which the apprentices and assistants might "sit" of an evening, and then I was conducted downstairs to an underground dining-room, lit by naked gas-jets and furnished with two long tables covered with American cloth,[2] where the eating was to be done. Then I was introduced to the shop and particularly to the cash desk, where it had been arranged for the first year of my apprenticeship that I was sit on a tall stool and receive money, give change, enter the amount on a sheet and stamp receipts. I was further instructed in a ritual of dusting and window cleaning. I was to come down at half past seven in the morning, I learnt, without fail, dust, clean windows, eat a bread-and-butter breakfast at half past eight, prepare my cash sheet and so to the routine of the day. I had to add up my cash at the end of the day, count the money in the till, make sheet and cash agree, help to wrapper-up and sweep out the shop, and so escape at half-past seven or eight to drink the delights of freedom until ten, when I had to be in. Lights out at half past ten. And this was to go on day after day — for ever it seemed to me — with an early closing day once a week at five, and Sunday free.

---

1 Small two-wheeled horse-drawn open carriage, originally with a compartment under the seat for dogs.
2 Oil-cloth.

Appendix F: Map of London from 1892
"Baedeker for London"

Select Bibliography

Letters and Diaries

Gissing, George. *London and the Life of Literature in Late Victorian England: The Diary of George Gissing, Novelist.* Ed. Pierre Coustillas. Hassocks, Sussex: Harvester Press; Lewisburg PA: Bucknell University Press, 1978.

Coustillas, Pierre, Paul F. Mattheisen, and Arthur C. Young, eds. *The Collected Letters of George Gissing.* 9 vols. Athens, Ohio: Ohio University Press, 1990–97.

Biographies and Critical Biographies

Collie, Michael. *George Gissing: A Biography.* Folkestone, England: Dawson; Hamden, CT: Archon, 1977.

Donnelly, Mabel Collins. *George Gissing: Grave Comedian.* Cambridge, MA: Harvard University Press, 1954.

Halperin, John. *Gissing: A Life in Books.* Oxford: Oxford University Press, 1982.

Korg, Jacob. *George Gissing: A Critical Biography.* Seattle: University of Washington Press, 1963.

Selig, Robert L. *George Gissing.* Boston: Twayne, 1983.

Tindall, Gillian. *The Born Exile: George Gissing.* London: Temple Smith, 1974.

Criticism

Auerbach, Nina. *Communities of Women: An Idea in Fiction.* Cambridge, MA: Harvard University Press, 1978.

Buckley, William K. "George Gissing's *The Odd Women.*" *Recovering Literature* 6:1 (1977): 27–50.

Chase, Karen. "The Literal Heroine: A Study of Gissing's *The Odd Women.*" *Criticism* 26:3 (Summer 1984): 231-44.

Collie, Michael. *The Alien Art: A Critical Study of George Gissing's Novels.* Folkestone, England: Dawson; Hamden CT: Archon, 1979.

Cotes, Alison. "New Women and Odd Women." *Gissing Newsletter* 14:2 (1978): 1–20.

—. "Gissing, Grant Allen and 'Free Union.'" *Gissing Newsletter* 19:4 (1983): 1–18.

Cronin, M. "The Unclassed in *The Odd Women.*" *Gissing Journal* 31:2 (1995): 1–14.

Cunningham, Gail. *The New Woman and the Victorian Novel.* New York: Barnes & Noble, 1978.

David, Deirdre. "Ideologies of Patriarchy, Feminism, and Fiction in *The Odd Women*." *Feminist Studies* 10:1 (Spring 1984): 117–39.

Evans, Joyce. "Some Notes on *The Odd Women* and the Woman's Movement." *Gissing Newsletter* 2 (1966): 1–4.

Goode, John. *George Gissing: Ideology and Fiction*. New York: Barnes & Noble, 1979.

Kennedy, George E. "Gissing's Narrative of Change: *The Odd Women*." *Gissing Newsletter* 18:2 (1982): 12–27.

Lesser, Wendy. "Even-Handed Oddness: George Gissing's *The Odd Women*." *Hudson Review* 37:2 (1984): 209–20.

Ledger, Sally. *The New Woman: Fiction and Feminism at the* fin de siècle. Manchester and New York: Manchester University Press, 1997.

Linehan, Katherine Bailey. "*The Odd Women*: Gissing's Imaginative Approach to Feminism." *Modern Language Quarterly* 40 (1979): 358–75.

Maglin, Nan B. "Fictional Feminists in *The Bostonians* and *The Odd Women*." *Images of Women in Fiction: Feminist Perspectives*. Ed. Susan K. Cornillon. Bowling Green, Ohio: Bowling Green University Popular Press, 1972. 216–36.

Markow, Alice B. "George Gissing: Advocate or Provocateur of the Women's Movement?" *English Literature in Transition* 1880–1920. 25:2 (1982): 58–73.

Perry, Carolyn J. "A Voice of the Past: Ruskin's Pervasive Presence in Gissing's *The Odd Women*." *Publications of the Missouri Philological Association* 13 (1988): 63–70.

Poole, Adrian. *Gissing in Context*. London & Basingstoke: Macmillan, 1975.

Selig, Robert L. "The Gospel of Work in *The Odd Women*: Gissing's Double Standard." *Supplement* to *Gissing Newsletter* 15 (January 1979): 17–25.

Squires, Michael. "Structure and Theme in Gissing's *The Odd Women*." *Modern British Literature* 3 (1978): 3–18.

Young, Arlene. *Culture, Class and Gender in the Victorian Novel: Gentlemen, Gents and Working Women*. Houndmills: Macmillan; New York: St. Martin's, 1999.

Cultural and Historical Backgrounds

Beckson, Karl. *London in the 1890s: A Cultural History*. New York and London: Norton, 1992.

Calder, Jenni. *Women and Marriage in Victorian Fiction*. London: Thames and Hudson; New York: Oxford University Press, 1976.

Holcombe, Lee. *Victorian Ladies at Work: Middle-Class Working Women in England and Wales 1850–1914*. Hamden CT: Archon, 1973.

Poovey, Mary. *Uneven Developments: The Ideological Work of Gender in Mid-Victorian England*. Chicago: University of Chicago Press, 1988.

Robson, John. *Marriage or Celibacy? The "Daily Telegraph" on a Victorian Dilemma*. Toronto, Buffalo, and London: University of Toronto Press, 1995.

Showalter, Elaine. *Sexual Anarchy: Gender and Culture at the Fin de Siècle.* Harmondsworth: Penguin, 1990.

Walkowitz, Judith R. *City of Dreadful Delight: Narratives of Sexual Danger in the Late Victorian City.* Chicago: University of Chicago Press, 1992.

Young, Arlene. "Virtue Domesticated: Dickens and the Lower Middle Class." *Victorian Studies* 39:4 (Summer 1996): 483–511.

Zimmeck, Meta. "Jobs for the Girls: The Expansion of Clerical Work for Women." *Unequal Opportunities: Women's Employment in England 1800–1918.* Ed. Angela V. John. Oxford: Blackwell, 1986.